EARLY ONE MORNING

Also by Robert Ryan

Underdogs
Nine Mil
Trans Am

EARLY ONE MORNING

Robert Ryan

review

First Published in 2002
by Review

An imprint of Headline Book Publishing

10 9 8 7 6 5 4 3 2 1

British Library Cataloguing in Publication Data

Ryan, Rob
   Early one morning
   1.World War, 1939-1945 – Secret service –
   Great Britain – Fiction 2.World War, 1939-1945 –
   Underground movements – France – Fiction
   3.War stories
   I.Title
   823.9'14[F]

ISBN 0 7472 6872 X (hardback)
ISBN 0 7553 0093 9 (trade paperback)

Typeset by
Letterpart Limited, Reigate, Surrey

Printed and bound in Great Britain by
Mackays of Chatham plc, Chatham, Kent

HEADLINE BOOK PUBLISHING
A division of Hodder Headline
338 Euston Road
LONDON NW1 3BH

www.reviewbooks.co.uk
www.hodderheadline.com

For Jack Cameron Bond

Early One Morning is a novel inspired by the lives of
Robert Benoist, William Grover and Eve Aubicq

'It was simply terrific: 112mph and still accelerating over the crossroads past the Barn – and the road cluttered with the usual Friday-evening traffic. Along the next stretch we did 122mph and I thought, under the circumstances, that was enough, and said so in no uncertain fashion. Thereafter we "cruised" along at a mere 90–95mph, and doing just over 100mph in third gear . . . it was the most alarming experience ever, yet Williams drove superbly, absolutely at ease and complete master of every situation . . .'

– C.W.P. Hamilton describing his test run of an Atlantic in England with Williams at the wheel, 1937, quoted in *Bugatti, The Man and The Marque* by Jonathan Wood

Prologue

DUBLIN, OCTOBER 1926

They took him with embarrassing ease. The young man had left his rooms to attend the meeting at six thirty in the morning, well before the majority of workers would be out and about, and walked through a damp, drizzly Temple Bar deserted but for the odd bundle of slimy rags that marked the street dwellers' stations. He emerged next to the looming edifice of the Bank of Ireland and was about to cross Dame Street, hesitating only to let a cart and a slow-moving Riley pass, when he was aware of a man standing too close behind him. As he turned, he was sandwiched by a second figure who stepped into the gutter. Both were big, stocky men, wearing heavy tweeds and bowlers. The one behind produced a revolver, and quickly they had him in the back of the car down on the floor behind the driver and a coarse blanket, smelling of fresh horse, was thrown across him.

Twisted into a near-foetal position in the grey gloom, a heavy boot resting on his back, his heart flapping in his chest, the young man tried hard to calm himself as they progressed through the city. He was sure that they were following the river, familiar as he

1

was with the distinctive jarring rhythm of the oversized cobble-stones, and he fancied he could smell, even over the heavy equine musk, the yeasty aroma of the brewery, but soon the sounds of motor traffic fell away, and from the bucking of the Riley he guessed that they were on country roads.

By the time they stopped he was biting his lip, trying to contain the agony of the terrible pins and needles that were shooting up his legs. The blanket was pulled back and he was unfolded from the tiny space and allowed to stretch and stamp until circulation slowly, painfully returned. The driver didn't even look his way, and the kidnappers looked bored as he paced up and down the yard, pulling the wet air into his lungs.

He looked around for clues to his whereabouts. They had come down a long track to a cottage, once small, now badly extended with a lean-to at one side. A country drinking establish-ment of some kind he reckoned, where the parlour simply grew an additional space to welcome local farmers. No customers at this time of day, though. Although the road was well rutted and led off to a series of paddocks, there were no other vehicles visible, not so much as a tractor, and high hedges and a line of lime trees prevented him from checking beyond the farm for landmarks. He had no idea where they had brought him. It had been well chosen.

Satisfied his circulation had recovered, the pair pushed him inside the cottage and closed the door, leaving him alone in a gloamy half-light. The sour-smelling room was square, low ceilinged, blackened by cigarette and peat smoke, with a serving hatch crudely carved into the wall at one end, a single table, and a motley assortment of mostly home-made furniture. There was one rather grand armchair, probably the perch of the grandfather or grandmother who would hold court over this shebeen in the evenings, but now a rather dapper man was occupying it. His host was in his mid-thirties, he would guess, with a pencil moustache, immaculate brilliantined hair, well-cut suit and long, manicured fingers gripping the arms of the chair.

The stranger smiled, stood and held out his hand as if they had been introduced at his St James's club. 'Slade,' he said in plummy English. 'How do you do?'

The young man didn't take the proffered hand, but Slade wasn't fazed at all, turning his palm upwards in a please-yourself gesture. 'Sorry about the transport arrangements. Doesn't do to be seen to get into a CID car these days. Not in your line of work. Take a seat.' Slade sat down and produced a pack of cigarettes. 'Smoke? No?'

'What's going on?'

Slade lit his cigarette. 'Oh please. The accent. You don't have to do all that top o' the morning bog-trotter rot for me. You're as English as I am, man.'

It wasn't true. He was half-French and the English part of him had a hefty dose of Irish on his paternal side. It was tracing that branch of the family that had led him to this place. However, Slade was right about the accent, he had deliberately let his vowels soften and slur over the last few months. English voices closed as many doors as they opened these days.

'For goodness' sake, sit down, there's a good fellow. Nothing to be gained by standing there glaring at me. If I had wanted you arrested I could have you shipped north and imprisoned under DORA or for membership of a proscribed organisation.'

Defence of the Realm Act. Slade was British Intelligence. Reluctantly Williams grabbed a chair and lowered himself into it gingerly, as if it might collapse under his weight. 'What is an Englishman doing with Dublin CID men?'

'Just helping our Irish brothers.'

He snorted.

3

'Trying to make sure the Irish Free State has a chance against . . . well, against your new chums. O'Malley, isn't it?' Then slowly, savouring each name, he continued, 'Clarke, Mellows, O'Donovan, Lemass, MacBride, Carroll, O'Higgins, Kenny . . . nine in the flying column. Ten with yourself.'

Informer. The word flashed across his brain, illuminated in flaming letters. How else could a British spy know about all those people?

'Now, we have reason to believe.' Slade stopped and laughed at himself, a metallic, staccato sound, devoid of real humour. 'Sorry, force of habit. We *know* that you drove the getaway vehicles on the night of the Knockadore Garda station attack, the Crumlin Barracks, the Dundalk Post Office and the Ballinakill bank raids. That you stole the cars for these actions. That most of them are probably at the bottom of the Liffey right now.'

He said nothing.

'Let us take a magnanimous view of all that. Let us say that these were legitimate acts of war.' He opened his mouth to speak and Slade raised a hand. 'Please, I am not in the market for rhetoric. I have heard it all before. The Irish can be so poetic when their entrails are hanging out of their arse.'

'Is that a threat?'

Slade sighed with a surprising weariness. 'No. Just an observation. So, police stations for revenge, army barracks for weapons, banks and post offices for funds, driving the odd gun shipment up from Cork. I can see all that. But why the moneylenders?'

'I—' I have nothing to do with that, he had started to say, realising that it would be a confirmation that he knew something about the other matters.

'You what?'

'I don't know what you are talking about.'

'Is it because they are mostly Jews? Is that it?'

4

Although he had heard some anti-semitic remarks, especially from Kenny, he had always assumed the systematic harassment was a political action, not racial. However, he had made it clear to Sean he wanted nothing to do with the savage beatings and intimidations that the column had handed down these past weeks, no matter what the motives, and Sean had respected that.

'It has to stop. I have here a letter for O'Malley, who I believe is your commander.' From his inside pocket Slade produced an envelope and offered it. The young man stayed stock still, as if accepting it was a certain admission of guilt.

'Why would you be worried about moneylenders?' he asked Slade, knowing that the IRA had killed or shot at plenty of soldiers and police in the last twelve months.

'That's our business. What is in here is a . . . peace offering.' He shook the letter. 'Take it.'

Williams hesitated. Even talking with this man could earn him a death sentence from the column. Delivering messages made the bullet to the head almost inevitable.

'I know what you are thinking. You'll be all right. In there is the name of the informer within your flying column.' He felt his jaw drop. 'As an indication of our good faith. With the evidence to back up the accusation.'

Slowly the young man stretched across and took the document, half anticipating it would burn through his fingertips. He slid it into the pocket of his jacket and fancied he could feel the incendiary contents reddening his skin. 'What kind of game is this? The Brits giving up one of their own?'

'No game. I want the moneylenders left alone and I am willing to deal.'

The penny dropped. People desperate enough to use money-lenders were vulnerable, corruptible. It was at the moneylenders that men like Slade did their recruiting for the army of

5

informers that plagued the city.

'My chaps will take you back, drop you off somewhere appropriate. Best you go under the blanket again, though. Just in case.'

Slade stood up and so did the young man. 'I can see you aren't convinced.'

'Why should I be?'

'No reason. No reason at all, Mr Williams.' So they even knew his real name. Everyone else in Dublin knew him only as Grover. 'Except you have my word as a fellow Englishman that I am telling you the truth.' He held out his hand again. 'You must trust me on this.'

After a moment's hesitation the young man took the hand and felt Slade's long white fingers close tightly over his own.

Part One

One

AUSTRIA, OCTOBER 2001

John Deakin glances across at his passenger and wonders when she is going to speak. The old woman is sitting stock still and upright, the bony hands crossed on her lap, staring out at the backdrop of Alpine scenery. For a moment he thinks she must have fallen asleep, but he catches a movement as she blinks, a long slow stroke of a blue-veined eyelid across watery, opaque eyes. The old lady has barely said a word since Salzburg where he picked her up off the plane, other than a thank you when he helped her into the hired Mercedes.

He sees the sign for the lake and makes the right, carefully feeding through the Autobahn traffic heading east towards Linz. Habit makes him check for a tail, but nobody else pulls off and there is nothing ahead on the road snaking up into the high glacial valley where the lake sits. They have the route to themselves. At this time of year, after the summer walkers have gone, the cows brought down from pasture and before the first snows fall, the mountains and lakes get a little peace. Except for Lake Senlitz. It will not have any for a few months yet.

Not for the first time that day he wonders about the old woman next to him. Fly out to Salzburg and await instructions he was told. He'd barely been there a day when the message came from the Consulate that he was to pick up one Dame Rose Miller. Extra–VIP. Deakin hadn't argued. The phone call that followed from Sir Charles, no less, was very clear. She deserves our respect and our thanks and she won't be with us much longer. Indulge her this once.

And, if he was honest, it was nice to be back in the old firm, even if this time it was a UDA. Ten thousand for a week's work. Pretty good money. Better than he got organising security at corporate events. It had been four years since they had said, sorry, Deakin, too many spies, not enough enemies. Not a bad severance package, but he'd been only thirty-eight. Hardly the age he had expected to be put out to grass.

Deakin has asked around, made some discreet calls, trying to get some operational background but the truth about his elderly passenger came from well before even his time. Fifties, possibly sixties, about the time of the real scandals, your Blakes and your Burgesses. Then finally he'd tracked Seagrove on a secure line and he'd admitted he'd heard the old girl was involved in a UDA back in the immediate postwar period. Berlin, Vienna, some-where like that. Unofficial Deniable Actions. Off the meter, as they used to say in his department.

'It's about another twenty kilometres.'

Her thin voice may lack power but it still makes him jump.

'Yes, ma'am.'

She turns and looks at him, fixing him with those cloudy eyes. 'Deakin isn't it?'

'Yes, ma'am.'

'When we get there I should like to stay in the car. Not up to messing about in boats.'

'As you wish, ma'am.'

'Not ma'am, please. Makes me feel dead already. Rose will do, Deakin.'

He nods, knowing he will never be able to bring himself to call this dignified and scary old lady anything of the sort.

She reaches into her handbag and extracts a pair of Zeiss binoculars. 'Just park me so I can keep an eye on things, Deakin, eh?'

'Yes, ma'am.'

'And ring me.'

She hands him a card with a mobile number on it. Not such a relic of the past after all. 'Of course.'

Then, from the bag, Rose takes a Cartier watch, and Deakin gets the impression of great weight, and catches the sparkle of diamonds. She slips it on to her wrist, ludicrously large against the shrunken flesh clinging to the bones. She catches him staring and says, 'Lovely, isn't it? It's coming home, Deakin. At long last.'

Then, after being a silent companion, she turns positively garrulous.

Deakin pulls his coat tighter as he crunches down the gravel path from the makeshift car park to the mirrored waters of Lake Senlitz, its surface glinting like polished obsidian. It may only be autumn, with the hills and mountainsides still dappled with delicate yellow and purple flowers, but Senlitz exists in permanent winter, deep and icy and forbidding, the chill it exudes lowering the temperature in the valley by a couple of degrees. Below him, on the edge of the inky water, he can see Simon Warner, the Chief Archivist of the Imperial War Museum.

Warner looks to Deakin like a slumming Oxford don, a man who would be more at home in tweeds and an egg-stained knitted tie than the blue overalls and green wellingtons he is currently wearing. Behind Warner, out on the lake, are a pair of low, functional dive barges, hoists spouting from each side, with black inflatable Zodiacs zipping around like worker bees feeding the queen. On the very far shore, standing on the low cliffs that ring the southern end of the lake, is a derelict cottage with a dangerously crooked chimney. Around a kilometre from it to the west squats a large steam-powered crane, its jib hanging over the water, a hawser disappearing into the liquid night below.

Deakin reaches Warner who stands, clearly an irritated man, but one whose sense of good manners overrules any other considerations. He holds out his hand and says without much expression, 'Mr Deakin? Simon Warner. Imperial War Museum. Welcome to Lake Senlitz.'

Deakin takes the hand with his firmest grip and says, 'Hello. Thanks for waiting for me.'

'Six days. It's a long time.' Yes, thinks Deakin, he's pissed off. The Department has put a block on his activities for close to a week until they could rustle up him and Rose. He'd warrant Warner would be even more angry before the day was out. They were about to take his baby away from him.

'I know, I know. My people are very grateful.'

'Talking of which . . .' says Warner.

Deakin hesitates, gets his drift and shows some ID, hastily arranged by the Consulate to bring him on-side.

Warner nods. 'So why are you chaps so damn' interested? When we were trying to get funding for this, we were told by the FO and all its many, many departments that this was ancient history.'

'That was before your divers stumbled across some of our property. Shall we go?'

12

'Your—?' he begins, but Deakin is off, striding over to one of the black rubber Zodiacs. Without being asked, he clambers inside, wrinkling his nose at the smell, a combination of fetid water and the synthetic skin that suggests a thousand condoms fused together. Warner starts the engine and they putter out on to the lake, heading for the nearer dive barge.

By way of conversation, Warner asks, 'Do you know what else we are doing here? Other than recovering *your* property?'

'I know it probably isn't Nazi gold.'

Warner smiles for the first time. 'Yes, it's always Reichsgeld, isn't it? At least as far as the newspapers are concerned anyway. What we have got are the plates that the Germans created to flood Britain with forged currency. Do you know that by the end of the war up to a quarter of the five-pound notes in circulation were thought to be fakes? That's why they had to be changed.'

Deakin knows, but he just grunts. Let the man show off.

'Plus there is believed to be a lot of the money itself. More importantly there are also records of several concentration camps. Sachsenhausen among them.'

Deakin is interested now. 'Really?'

'Really,' and he adds pointedly, 'that is why we have some financial help from the Holocaust Center in New York.'

They pull level with the dive barge. A few figures wave, including what looks like a policeman. Warner catches Deakin's puzzled expression.

'Austrian police. It's their lake now, so we have to observe certain protocols. Keep them in the picture, basically.'

A thought occurs to Deakin. 'Won't it all be rotten? The money and the records?'

'Not at all. Very cold, very anaerobic down there. If the containers were properly sealed, no reason why everything shouldn't at least be legible if treated properly. That's why we have that.' Warner points to a large marquee on the shoreline. 'To preserve the material as soon as it comes out of the water, by whatever method is appropriate.'

They are around a hundred metres from the far shore now and Warner heaves to. He takes a mobile phone from inside his overalls, dials, and tells the crane operator he can begin, adding, with a sarcastic sneer, now that their VIP has arrived. Deakin glances back to the car park, the Mercedes a small outline now, but fancies he can see the binoculars trained on them. He can certainly feel Rose Miller's stare, even at this distance.

The crane engine starts a rhythmic thumping and belches black smoke. The hawser twitches, like an angler's line when the bait is taken by something large and unseen, then tensions and finally starts to move. Off to the left a pair of divers surface in a flurry of bubbles to witness their handiwork.

The steel line reels in and in, starting to swing a little as the object gains a little buoyancy, then tightens again as a bubble of long-trapped stale air escapes from the hidden treasure. The main hawser ends in a large ring and sends off four sub-divisions, each cable connected to the corner of the sunken bulk. Finally, like the back of a metal cetacean, a curve of rust appears, then the full roofline of a car.

'It's a Humber, we believe,' says Warner, 'although there was quite a lot of sediment over it. Probably a British staff car.' Deakin says nothing. Of course it was. Dame Rose has told him what to expect.

The remains of the windows have cleared the surface and black water starts to pour from within, receding in a rush, revealing the shattered windscreen and, grinning the strange mocking rictus of the human skull, a de-fleshed head, peering over the driver's side door.

14

★ ★ ★

It takes an agonising two hours to get the Humber across onto a stable platform, for the Austrian police to take their photographs of the body in situ and for a scene-of-crime team to arrive from Salzburg. The SoCs set to work with a desultory air. Old skeletons – old British skeletons judging from the tattered great-coat cloaking the bones – don't seem to push their enthusiasm buttons overmuch.

Deakin walks away from the activity and finally rings the old lady, imagining her digging in the bag for the mobile, the claw-like fingers trying to find the tiny buttons. But instead she is on the line immediately.

'Can you see it, ma'am?'

'Very well, Deakin, very well. Taking their time, aren't they? But I can't read the number. Is it still there?'

From his notebook he reads off the faded, barely legible serial number from the side of the bonnet.

'Yes,' she says, softly, 'that's mine. That's my car.'

'And that's him?'

'Open the trunk.'

'The police are treating it as a crime scene, ma'am.'

'Bugger the police,' she snaps. 'You hear me? Sort it out, Deakin. Remember who you are.'

He rings off, feeling admonished. Bugger the police. Remember who you are. Fine when you're sitting on the other side of the lake playing at being Queen Victoria. We are not amused, get on with it. He takes a deep breath, walks around to the boot of the car and, before anyone can stop him, yanks it open. A thin stream of gritty water sploshes down onto his trousers and he curses. Inside is more silt, wrapped around what was clearly a trunk of some kind. Warner comes round to see what he has found.

'Should you be doing this?' he asks priggishly.

15

Deakin ignores him and uses a finger to scrape away at the top of the trunk, revealing the ghostly imprint of the famed Louis Vuitton pattern, now bubbled and split. Riveted to the front is a brass name plate with a single word in copperplate writing, still clear after all these years.

Williams.

'Well,' says Warner, looking up as the Austrian pathology team slowly lever the bony remains from their resting place behind the wheel, 'at least we know who he was now.'

Two

VERSAILLES, MARCH 1928

Williams was halfway up the stairs to the main salon with the bottle of Margaux when he heard the insistent hiss behind him. He turned to find Eve making a series of strange faces at him, as if trying to settle on a suitable expression.

'Wait. You can't go in there looking like that.'

Williams looked down at himself and studied his dark woollen chauffeur's uniform. It was freshly cleaned and pressed, and the brass buttons shone proudly. True, it was the second-best winter outfit, but smart enough for most formal occasions. 'What's wrong, Miss?'

From the salon above came a peal of laughter, and he recognised the tone. One decanter down already, another on the way. It was going to be a four or five bottler.

Williams checked as surreptitiously as he could that his fly buttons were fastened, then repeated the question. 'What's wrong, Miss?'

Eve advanced two steps and shook her ringlets from her face. Although, as usual, she wore no makeup, she appeared to have rouged her cheeks. Williams looked closer. No, she was blushing, something he had never seen her do in the months he had worked for Sir William. And he had seen her in positions that would make a brothel madam colour up. She nodded at the silver tray and its contents.

'Can I take it in?'

'You?'

A second more piercing laugh. The guest.

'Do you know who that is in there with Bill?' Eve Aubicq always insisted on speaking English to him, even though she knew his own French was word perfect.

'No.'

'You'll never guess.' Williams wasn't even going to try. Sooner or later they all came by, from David, Prince of Wales down-wards, all the great and the not-so-good, seeing if they could get themselves Orpen-ed for posterity. Eve lowered her voice and in a hoarse whisper she finally told him: 'Charlie Chaplin.'

'Chaplin? Here?' Chaplin was a massive star in France and the city had been flattered by his full-length film *Woman of Paris*, possibly the only place where it received unanimous praise. 'Is Chaplin after a portrait, Miss?'

'From what I hear Orps doesn't have a canvas big enough to accommodate his head.'

Williams smiled and handed over the wine, glasses and cork-screw. 'And now is your chance to find out?'

She nodded eagerly. 'I'll let you know.'

Williams wondered where Eve stood on the subject of Lita Grey, the young wife whom Chaplin had married at sixteen and who three years later sued the star for insisting she performed 'abnormal, unnatural, perverted and degenerate' sexual acts. The French avant garde had rallied to the Chaplin cause, with one magazine claiming the act of fellatio was 'general, pure and

18

defendable'. Williams then realised the strange sound in his ears was his breathing and he had best stop thinking too closely about Eve's attitude to such things.

He retraced his steps downstairs to his subterranean rooms next to the wine cellar, changed into coveralls and headed back up for the front drive, where the Rolls stood.

This was the time of year when the big car earned its keep, gliding between Dieppe and Longchamps and the Champs Elysées, ferrying Orpen and Eve from one point on the French social carousel to another, occasionally dipping off into the dark sidestreets of Pigalle and along Raspaill for an invigorating – to Orpen at least – taste of the seamier side of Paris. It was a beautiful car, a six-cylinder Phantom 1, not two years old, but it required plenty of love and attention if it was to perform at its finest.

Williams had reached the top of the stairs when Eve reappeared in the hallway, her face still flushed, but now a darker colour, as if her skin had been bruised.

'Are you all right, Miss?' he enquired cautiously.

She spluttered for a second before blurting, in French this time, 'He asked if I had a younger sister for him. Younger.'

She pursed her lips to show her deep irritation and stomped upstairs, her heels clacking on the polished runners. Williams waited until she was two floors up before he allowed himself to smile.

Sir William Orpen grunted to himself as he traced the line of Eve's breast. Still not right. So hard to capture the complex shape, the muscles and fat and tendons, the way the right one rested on the rumpled sheets, the beautifully delineated curve running from her left armpit, the glorious blush of pink at the tip. He'd done her twenty, twenty-five times, and on each occasion he reached this stage where he was convinced he could no longer capture Eve's beauty. He had to work through it. He always had before. Now she was no longer a teenager, it was getting harder. The unlined, guileless, still-pubescent body has been simple. In her late twenties, she was becoming more complex, more interesting, more of a challenge. More beautiful. He could see it in the new lust in the eyes of his friends, even if not in Mr Chaplin's.

When he had taken Eve as a mistress at nineteen, his circle had just considered it the sad sign of an aging roué, and they treated her as a child. Now, though, they could see what Orpen had been feeding off all along, a luminescence, something ethereal that took your breath away. Now they were jealous. Some, he was sure, wondered how long before she grew bored of a fat, wheezy old man losing his teeth and hair, and moved on to someone else. Like themselves, perhaps.

'Bill.'

He looked up from the canvas, across the squalid clutter of the studio, over empty champagne cases, discarded palettes, abandoned portraits, to the bed where Eve reclined in all her glory.

'Bill.'

'Shush.'

'Bill, I am freezing.'

Orpen made a harrumphing sound. He had his overcoat on, and was sweating, but maybe she had a point. He'd put weight on these past three years, an extra layer of insulation. Perhaps too much. His small frame didn't suit it, and his once chiseled face was beginning to soften and sag around the edges. But there was one noticeable benefit of keeping the studio cool. 'As Orpsie always says – it makes y'nipples stand up.'

'It'll make them drop off unless you put some heating on.'

The phone made its ineffectual rattling sound at him and he

snatched it from the cradle. 'Hoi-hoi? Antoine. Yes. That '25 Margaux you got me. Got any more? What do you mean? I drank it. Don't be ridiculous. Lay it down, my arse. It's for drinking, man, not mollycoddling.' He watched Eve wrap the sheet around her. 'Just get me two more cases, quick as you like. As you were, love.'

'Not without a bit of warmth.'

Orpen considered this for a moment and finally yelled: 'Williams, *Williams*.'

The door opened a fraction and he could see the top of his chauffeur/valet's head. 'Williams. Put some heat on in here, will you, there's a good fellow? Oh, and bring me some more wine. Bit of cheese. You know the drill.'

The door closed again. Orpen heard the whoosh of the boiler and the gurgle of pipes. 'Happy? Come on then, be like a furnace in here before long and your tits'll go all droopy.'

Eve obligingly rearranged herself on the bed, and Orpen made some speedy adjustments to the line of her breasts on the canvas, rationalising that it was deliberation that was causing him to get it wrong. Go with the moment, the impression. Sure enough the fast lines began to capture her perfectly.

There was something slightly off, though. He had run out of the soft rosy red, the blush that Chenil in Chelsea did so well. Must get some more sent over, he thought. Stuff from Barbeux just not the same. He flopped off his stool and stood back to admire the likeness.

As if he had been waiting for the interval, like a patron late for a concert, Williams entered with a tray bearing bread, cheese, olives and red wine. He cleared a space on the paint-encrusted table and proceeded to ease the cork from the bottle, careful not to look at Eve. Orpen caught her playful smile as she spoke.

'I'd like a glass, Williams.'

'Yes, Miss. I brought two glasses.'

'I'll have it over here.'

Williams hesitated. He poured three big glugs into each goblet, glanced at the smirking Orpen, and crossed the minefield of a studio to the bed, keeping eye contact all the time. As he handed her the drink, Eve raised herself on one elbow and opened her legs slightly.

Williams couldn't help it, his eyes flicking down to the blond tangle of hair. He felt himself redden, and heard Orpen guffaw. As he left Orpen shouted: 'Careful, Williams, men have got lost in there,' then ducked as an empty paint can whistled by his ear.

Williams turned around and looked at the ruddy-faced painter. 'Don't worry, sir, I'm like Theseus. Always carry a ball of twine.' As he closed the door he heard an explosion of joy burst forth from his diminutive employer.

The following day Orpen was still wrapped in his dressing gown at midday, coughing and spluttering. Eve had donned a knee-length dress in *velours frappe*, the embossed velvet currently sprouting up across Paris shops, with simple black pointed-toe high heels. As always the face was scrubbed, devoid of any trace of powder or lipstick, and the only jewellery was a simple crucifix. While Williams stood mute in the corner she towered over Orpen, who seemed to be shrinking down into the winged armchair.

'Come on, Bill. I promised Sylvie. She wants to meet a racing driver.'

'Bloody stupid sport,' he rumbled. 'All that noise and smell. Eh, Williams?' He looked over for support. 'Oh, forgot. You like that kind of thing, don't you?'

'I shall take Sylvie myself,' said Eve petulantly.

'Off you go then. I'll finish you off from my imagination.

Should know what you look like naked by now I suppose.'

Eve thumped him on the arm and swept past Williams. Orpen looked balefully after her. 'You'd better go, Williams, or she'll try to drive the damn' Rolls. Then we'll all be in trouble.'

Thanks to Orpen's vacillation, they were a good forty minutes late for the premier race at the Montlhery circuit. The grand-stands of the banked track were full, most of Paris having turned out to see the last race of Robert Benoist, former world champion, before he took up a post as sales manager for Ettore Bugatti.

Williams was forced to park the Rolls in a field some consider-able distance from the entrance, and worried as he felt the wheels of the giant vehicle slip and slide on the mixture of grass and mud that was the legacy of a long, wet winter.

When he finally switched off the engine, happy they were on solid enough ground to give him traction when it was time to leave, Eve opened the door, peered down at the ground and sniffed.

'Williams. What is this?'

'What, Miss?'

'Where is the ... car park? The Tarmacadam? The gravel. This is ... this is mud.'

'And I have white shoes.' Sylvie was a willowy brunette with a high-pitched voice and a rather skittish, nervous manner. If she had been a horse Williams was certain she would have been a bolter.

Williams felt his boots squelch as he stepped down and looked at the flesh-coloured stockings the women were wearing. There was no doubt what contact with the field would do to them. He rolled up his sleeves and held out his arms.

'All right, then. Who would like to go first? Miss?'

23

★ ★ ★

Having seen the two women to the VIP box, Williams had his boots polished by one of the gnarled old men – a 'ruined face' from the war – touting for business around the car parks then took to the tunnel and walked through to the central grassed reserve of the track. Passing through the damp concrete tube he could feel the vibrations from the cars above, and as he emerged the raucous noise assaulted his ears. Now he could smell the fumes, the stink of benzol and the acrid stench of burnt rubber. Twenty cars were out there, Talbots, Alfas, Maseratis and Bugattis, hammering around the oval track, engaged in a mechanical dance, positions swapping with each lap, some passing on the straight, others taking the dangerous 'big lick' around the banking at each end.

Williams shook hands with a few of the other chauffeurs, turned and surveyed the track once more. Down here, the noise was intense, amplified by the giant horns of concrete created by the banking, boxing their ears as the cars screeched and growled their way around the track.

Williams could not make much sense of the race. He sought out and found Robert Benoist, the man who should be out front, but unless he was behind a couple of very fast back markers, he was trailing.

Williams borrowed a pair of binoculars and scanned the crowd. Eventually he found Eve and her friend Sylvie over by the finish line, in the cordoned-off area where champagne and canapés were getting more attention than what was happening out on the track. To the people in the VIP enclosure, motor racing was just another backdrop to the social calendar – it could be horses, shooting, opera, the scenes changing as if it were theatre. The two women were attracting a coterie of admirers, emboldened by the absence of Orpen who, he was under strict instructions not to reveal, was actually suffering from gout, rather than a hangover.

Williams spent a few seconds studying Eve, and switched back to the track and his struggling hero.

Robert Benoist was a great driver but clearly in decline. A former world champion, a World War One fighter ace at the age of twenty, a man with as many mistresses as cars – and he had a lot of cars – he was manfully struggling with his Delage. The company were about to withdraw from racing – like so many other small outfits, the economic situation was forcing them to retrench. So both man and machine were bowing out, but not as gracefully as they would have liked.

Williams removed his cap, pushed back his oiled hair and repositioned the binoculars. As he did so he thought he saw something. Benoist seemed to be on fire.

Robert Benoist was convinced he was on fire. Smoke was drifting up through the cockpit to his nostrils. At the moment it was rubber and canvas, but he could tell from the pains shooting across the soles of his feet that flesh would be next. He tried to lift them away from the glowing metal of the footwell, but the revs dropped alarmingly. He had always complained about the heat from the exhaust that ran along the outside close to his shoulder, but that was nothing compared to this. Someone had come up with the bright idea of lowering the driving position to enable the car to be more streamlined. Now he was virtually driving with his feet on the engine block. As he neared the pit entrance he yanked the wheel to enter.

As he skidded to a halt at his station, mechanics surged forward to begin refuelling and Robert leapt out and signalled to his brother. 'Maurice. Here. Now!'

Maurice was recounting his tales of Verdun, and the heroic story of how he got his limp, to the exquisite Annie Dubrey, and was slightly irritated by this interruption. Then he noticed that Robert's feet were smouldering.

Maurice held up his palm to Annie to show he would continue his heartbreaking exposition shortly and ran down, exaggerating his disability as he went. 'Your hat.' Maurice hesitated. Robert had a perfectly good white racing helmet on. Why should he want his prize felt trilby with the silk petersham band?

Robert snatched it from his head, ran to the water barrel and plunged it in. 'Robert. It's new, damn it,' whined Maurice.

Robert climbed back in and placed the limp hat over the accelerator pedal. 'I'll buy you ten, brother.' He roared away, savouring the temporary sense of cold bleeding through the ruined tread of his racing boots. All he had to do now was keep off the glowing brake pedal.

Williams watched Benoist wiggle out of the pits, lunging with the power full on, giving him a back end dangerously close to breaking away and spinning him. He felt a little prickle at the back of his neck. Maybe he's not such a slow old man after all. For twenty minutes he watched Benoist reel in the rest of the pack, until he swept past the leader in a big arc, right up the banking, his outside wheels threatening to grab nothing but air, before he swooped down and almost removed his opponent's radiator.

Williams looked up at the VIP enclosure, to where Sylvie and Eve were clearly leaving, not even waiting for Benoist to take the flag for the final time. Reluctantly he pulled himself away and headed for the car park.

As the chequered flag flashed by in a blur Robert Benoist felt himself deflate, his bones turn to rubber, and he had to fight to stop himself slumping over the wheel. Finished. Over. Getting out on a high note, that's what he liked. Or at least, that is what he had convinced himself.

He raised an arm in salute as sections of the crowd began to stand and applaud, more for the last decade, he knew, than any performance over the last hour or two. Robert pulled over into the pits, holding out his hands to try to keep the well-wishers back. A few camera bulbs detonated and he tried to remember to smile with his mouth closed – oil-specked dirty teeth looked so unattractive in the newspaper.

He took off his helmet and goggles and searched the faces for his brother. And there he was, behind one of the new hand-held cine cameras, his precious toy, making hand signals, as if he expected Robert to dance.

'Maurice, turn that damned thing off, come over here.'

Maurice limped to his side, the signal for others to press in, thrusting programmes for Robert to sign, photographs, scraps of paper.

'Sorry about your hat.'

Robert reached down and brought up a few crispy strands of felt, stiff like over-cooked bacon. He wondered how his feet had held up, but was frightened to look. They felt as if they had been flayed and then toasted.

'Ettore Bugatti has organised a welcome-to-the-firm dinner for you. But you may want to make your excuses.'

'Why would I want to do that?'

Maurice whispered in his ear. 'Your friend Françoise has come from Nantes. She wants to see you.'

Robert laughed. Maurice knew he would have to take his wife to any dinner, if only for appearance's sake. 'Where is she?'

'At the Hotel Plasse.'

Robert paused to sign a few more souvenirs, desperate for a drink and a bath. 'Can you get a message to her?'

27

'Of course.'

'Tell her to wait up for me. I am sure I shall need an early night after all this exertion.'

Before Maurice could answer a snapper barged his way through. 'Gentlemen, could I get a picture of both of you? For *Paris Life*? The retiring driver and his younger brother.'

'Older brother,' corrected Robert, poking Maurice in the ribs.

'Just a second,' said Maurice. Maurice arranged himself on the side of the car and there was a flash and detonation.

'Now, can I get out?' asked Robert.

Maurice moved out of the way and pushed the crowd back. Robert eased himself out of the cockpit and swung his legs out. As his feet hit the ground a powerful column of pain shot up his limbs, exploding in his cerebrum and expelling all consciousness as he slumped into his brother's arms.

Williams had to repeat the trick of carrying the two women over the muddy field although now they were full of champagne it was rather trickier, as both kept wriggling.

'Keep still. I might drop you, Miss,' he said to Eve, trying not to think about the lithe body – or the rustling silk chemise – under the velvet dress.

'And then Orpsie will sack you for sullying his little Evie. "Gee, honey," he will say, "did Willie boy hurt my little peach?" ' She smiled and Williams wondered about letting her fall into the gloop anyway. The baby talk that Orpen affected was irritating at the best of times, but recently he had begun to sprinkle it with Americanisms. The constant stream of writers, journalists, negro dancers and jazz musicians appearing in Paris had made US slang the affectation of the year. There were rumoured to be fifty thousand Yanks in total, and they appeared to be in the habit of all turning up in the same place at the same time. The attraction was obvious – a devalued franc gave them twenty-five to a dollar, and the very idea of prohibition was anathema to the French.

Eventually both women were installed, more or less stain-free, in the rear of the car and Williams slammed the door on them. He started the engine, set the advance-retard, selected a higher gear than normal and eased the Rolls out of the muddy grooves it had settled into. Eve spoke in a loud voice, making sure it carried through to the driver's compartment.

'I'm sorry you didn't get a man, Sylvie.'

'Oh, don't worry, I'm going off them anyway. Present company excepted.'

They giggled and Williams glanced in the mirror to see if they were talking about him.

'Oh, never with the staff, darling,' insisted Eve, wrinkling her nose.

'Why ever not?'

'Because you never know where they have been.'

Williams had negotiated the worst of the mud and was easing on to the metalled section of the car park, now full of cars being cranked and pushed.

Eve continued in a yet louder voice. 'He turned up six months ago. No references to speak of. Couldn't use a knife and fork properly. Wasn't even a very good driver—'

Williams floored the big beast and the giant engine responded with astonishing liveliness. The Rolls leapt forward, and Williams began to swerve through the crowd streaming out of the stadium, fishtailing as the wheels flicked up a spray of sharp stones. Eve and Sylvie fell together in a heap in the back, squealing with a mixture of fear and delight.

Clear of the people, Williams began to fling the machine harder, and there was another loud exclamation as limbs tangled and dresses rode up, to reveal elasticated silk garters. Williams glanced into the rear-view mirror as often as he dared. He managed to spin a one-eighty-degree turn and head for the exit when, from the corner of his eye, he saw the blur of blue bodywork and stamped on the brakes, rotating the wheel as hard as he could until the Rolls broadsided, two wheels lifting off the ground, leaving several tons of metal perched daintily on two tyres before it flopped back down and buried itself deep into the gravel.

The Citroën with the fold-back roof slowly pulled level. Williams recognised the driver, Maurice Benoist, and felt himself redden when he saw his brother in the passenger seat, two bandaged feet on the dashboard.

It was the latter who leaned across and wagged a finger at Williams. 'Who do you think you are? Robert Benoist?'

The two brothers pulled away in an insulting spray of muck, their laughter caught by the slipstream and thrown back into Williams' face.

Three

PARIS, APRIL 1928

Chauffeuring, Williams had decided soon after joining the Orpen household, wasn't so much about being able to drive as being able to wait. The evening had begun with him waiting for Orpen and Eve to get ready, waiting while they picked up Jessop, the young American writer who was on his way south and had been so for more than a year, then waiting on the Champs Elysées near Fouquet's while the trio had an early supper, then, swollen to a quartet by Raymond Berri, an industrialist who was after having his portrait painted by Orpen for his boardroom, waiting while they had taken in a show at the Bobino. Then they had completed the group by picking up yet another American, this one called George, from the Majestic.

Now Williams was killing time once more while they all drank Aquavit at Select among the crop-headed lesbians in their mannish *le smoking* suits who had struggled to keep their monocles in place as Eve swished by in her asymmetrical gold mesh dress with the deep v-neck line. Even Madame Select, as usual counting the cash in her fingerless gloves while her husband supervised the endless stream of welsh rarebits, had looked up from her arithmetic to see who was causing such a stir.

Orpen had imbibed prodigiously and from where he stood Williams could hear him on the terrace, seated as close as possible to the stove, buttonholing Barley, another young American sent abroad by his parents to gather a few rough edges. Orpen was doing his best to oblige.

'So I was there when they brought her in. Beautiful she was. Eighteen. French. The Belgians were convinced she was a spy. They tried her, sentenced her to death by firing squad.'

'And you saw her shot?' asked Barley, his jaw almost on the table.

Williams could see that several women had joined the party, including Sylvie and a rather imposing woman who towered over her.

'Had to. Official war artist. Orpsie saw some terrible things. Terrible. So she was asked if she had any last requests and the girl says, I would like to die in my mink coat. Okey-dokey, said the Belgian officer and it was delivered to her cell. Another round here. Yes, another set of drinks. So, come the morning, first light, she is led out to the execution wall, in her mink coat. Six Belgian soldiers stand there. The officer says, shoulder arms, take aim, all that, and just as they are about to fire she drops the mink coat off her shoulders.' There was a pause while Orpen knocked back a drink. 'And there she was totally bloody naked as the day she was born.'

'Gosh.'

'Gosh indeed. That's what we all said to ourselves. Gosh. Should've seen those Belgies' rifles shake. End of the barrel going up and down like they had St Vitus's dance.'

'What happened?' asked Barley.

32

'Happened? They shot her. She was a spy.'

Williams allowed himself a smirk. He had heard the story a dozen times, and knew it was pure fiction. Orpen had spun it round one of the first portraits of Eve he had executed of her in her late teens, when he caught her bare shouldered and innocent, with her curly blond hair falling on to that angelic skin. He had made the mistake of repeating the tale to someone at the War Office and a whole inquiry into the ungentlemanly conduct of the Belgians had been launched. Orpen was obliged to admit he created the whole story to up the value of the painting by a few thousand guineas.

Williams instinctively straightened his slouch as he saw the two-man police night patrol approach on cycles. These were the watchdogs of nocturnal Paris – Madame Select was famed for her readiness to summon them in the case of the slightest fracas – and were of a different order to most cops, seeming to consist mostly of rough, resentful Corsicans. Williams instinctively checked he had his identity card with him, but the pair cycled by, one of them even giving him a respectful nod, as if in workers' solidarity.

Ten minutes after the end of the execution story the party were out, with Orpen in the vanguard, weaving as he approached, hanging on to Eve's arm, his bulk forcing her to trace the same sinuous pattern on the pavement as him. 'OK, Williams, we have to squeeze eight in now. Including Hettie there.' He indicated the towering woman with the rice-powdered face at the rear of the group, a Lilly Dache cloche hat pulled down over her ears and a red squirrel fur coat. 'The tallest transvestite in Paris. Off to the Jockey Bar. Apricot cocktails. Then *dancings*. And Barley here wants to try Chez Hibou.'

The group all guffawed and young Barley managed a good-sport grin, even though all had clearly neglected to mention that Chez Hibou, on rue St Apolline, was a leading licensed brothel, one, if the rumours and the portrait above the mantelpiece were to be believed, which once had regular, if anonymous, royal patronage in the form of Edward VII.

One of the party, though, made his excuses. 'Thanks for the drinks and tall stories, Bill, but I gotta go.'

'George,' protested Orpen. 'Come on. Be fun.'

'I've got work to do.'

'Work. Call that bloody awful racket you write work?'

George laughed good naturedly and adjusted his glasses. 'Unless I do something I'll be just like every other American in Paris. A bum.'

'You can write as much of that jazzy stuff as you like, George. You'll always be a bum to me.'

George smiled, waved a hand and disappeared in search of a cab. Orpen looked at Williams. 'He thinks I'm joking. Have you heard his stuff? All right, off to Hibou.'

Williams sighed as he opened the door for Orpen. Heading for the discreet pink light of Chez Hibou meant more waiting, even though Orpen, Eve and the *travesti* would spend the time in the bar, paying for the naked girls to drink a harmless mixture of lemonade and grenadine while they sipped overpriced iced *mousseux* and tried to slip some into the *poules'* drinks whenever the eyes in the back of the fearsome Madame Hibou's head blinked.

Williams looked the fresh-faced American up and down as he climbed in beside Eve, and noticed the slight nervous tremor in his hands, the moist upper lip. A dizzying mixture of more alcohol, dancing with the *tapettes* and *dinges* at Bal des Chiffoniers, then on to choose from the flesh rack at a brothel. Boy was out of his depth. Eve caught Williams' eye and winked. Perhaps the wait wouldn't be too long at Chez Hibou after all.

★ ★ ★

34

Williams had grown used to Orpen's bouts of melancholy. Sometimes late into the evening when Eve was off with her own friends or visiting her father in Lille, Orpen would ring the bell and summon Williams with a bottle of Johnnie Walker or, if he was feeling homesick for Ireland, Jameson, and invite him to sit and chat in the living room in front of the fire.

Two nights after the Chez Hibou episode – when the Barley boy had finally figured out what was going on and fled, leaving the rest of them to go on to Bricktop's and hear the flame-haired negress sing Cole Porter songs – Orpen did just that.

He was in his cardigan, worn as usual over a waistcoat in place of a jacket, shirt with bow tie, spectacles on the end of his nose, swirling the drink in his glass, when he asked a startling question. 'How much d'you think I earned last year, Williams?'

Williams sipped at his own whiskey, eking it out. He was rarely offered a refill. 'I have no idea, Sir William.'

Orpen sniffed. 'Have a guess.'

'I really—'

'Have a guess, man, damn you.'

'Twenty thousand.'

Orpen smiled. 'Forty-six thousand, three hundred and ninety-four pounds.'

Williams raised a cautious eyebrow. 'Very good, sir.'

'Good? Bloody marvellous. And you know what?'

'No?'

'I'd give it all away if I could stop being a portrait painter. I hate bloody portraits. All little Orps gets to do is one pompous fool after another.' He paused and considered this for a moment. 'No, they are not all fools. Chamberlain I liked. Asquith, too. And Berri's not a fool. Except he wants to pose with a falcon. Told him he'll have to get his own. Get it stuffed. Not having a live falcon in here. Against the terms of the lease. No birds of

35

prey in the house. Must say it somewhere.' He winked just to underline the jest.

He handed a piece of paper across. 'Look at this. Chaplin.'

Williams looked down at the drawing, a caricature of the Little Tramp, signed and dated. 'Man comes to my studio . . . *my* studio, greatest portrait painter in Europe, the world. Comes to my studio and does his *own* fucking portrait. Ha.'

Orpen drained his glass and refilled. 'Just three fingers, as the Yanks say. Forty-six thousand. I should be happy shouldn't I? But look, my wife hates me. Mrs St George never writes to Orpsie boy now.' This, Williams knew, was a former mistress, a long-standing affair that had soured some time ago. 'And I hardly see my children. Have you heard Kit play? Bloody good pianist she is. I'll get her to play for you when she comes over.'

Williams steeled himself for a long, slow ramble. Any minute now they were going to hit the how-life-should-have-been section, and this was open ended, a long improvisation on his woes. He snapped out of it, and even refreshed Williams' drink – just the one finger he noticed – and said jauntily, 'Forty-six thousand, eh? How about we go to Dieppe at the weekend and see if we can lose some of it?'

That night Eve lay in bed, listening to the tidal snoring of Orpen, a great nasal gush as air came into his tubes, a softer whistling as it ebbed. He had announced earlier in the evening that he would be heading off for London in a couple of months in time for his daughter Kit's series of concert recitals. There was no mention of Eve accompanying him.

Which is just as well, as she probably wouldn't have gone. The last time had been a disaster, as Orpen spent his time in male-only clubs and she searched in vain for some hint of levity in the grey, drizzly capital, so lifeless and buttoned-up after Paris.

When they did go out together, Orpen's fellow artists treated her as some kind of prize specimen, a lurid professional model and mistress like Kiki de Montparnasse, whose over-cooked memoirs they had all devoured.

It was hard to explain to outsiders why she was with this corpulent, somnambulant man. That ever since he captured her horrendous experiences at the hands of a German soldier at the age of fourteen on canvas, she had been smitten by his intuition, his generosity, the kindness, albeit attributes increasingly buried under hangovers and sore feet, but still alive and well at his core. Perhaps she'd buy a dog while he was away. Or two. She would love a dog, but Orpen hated canines, and would certainly order its destruction upon his return. No, not worth it.

To cap it all, Orpen was slipping away from her as a lover. Too tired, too fat he would complain. Eve could hardly remember the last time. She had to sit astride him now, because his tendency to flop, unannounced, his full weight on her could break a girl's ribs.

Her hand sought out between her legs, trying to conjure up some erotic image to initiate the proceedings, but none came. She heard the muffled slam of a door far downstairs, either Cook or Williams, and she felt a little electric spark. Not her type, but he'd do.

At that moment Orpen made an alarming barking sound and threw a stubby arm across her chest as he rolled over. She suddenly felt herself pinned and constricted, the limb as solid as a fallen tree trunk. She eased her hand away from her groin. Ah well, something else that will have to wait for another day.

Four

FRANCE, MAY 1928

Summer arrived quickly that year, turning Paris warm and golden. The casino at Dieppe was finally completed, and so the twice weekly exodus from Paris began in earnest, Williams motoring Orpen and Eve plus their companions of the week up to Rouen, where they sometimes took lunch at La Toque, partly because it tickled Orpen to be dining overlooking the very spot where the English burned Joan of Arc, and partly because he was slowly reeling in the flamboyantly moustachioed chef as a model for a portrait he wanted to execute.

Then it was an appearance, an entry, no less, in Dieppe, a long slow drive along the Esplanade, as if Orpen were royalty inspecting Dieppe's parade of grand mansions and apartments, then a few hours at Charlie's Bar, before the main business of the evening, a burst of intense gambling. Outside, as always, was Williams.

That day, the entourage consisted of Orpen and Eve with Raymond Berri, the chemist, Nick Jessop, the saturnine American writer, and his rather fey friend Patrick, a professional hanger-on from Philadelphia who had managed to pick up Louisa, one of the half-starved, but fully drunk artists who hung around the Dome hoping to hitch their wagon to a passing patron.

Jessop insisted that he was trying to pull himself away from the crowd that ricocheted from La Coupole to the Dome, Select, Falstaff's and back. He was complaining to whoever would listen that the scene was infected with a fatal lethargy. Except for those licking up what he called the 'literary vomit' at Gertrude Stein's famous gatherings. Rather than worship at the foot of a grim old lesbian in a circus tent, Jessop declaimed, he wanted to write and he needed discipline. He had been in Paris fifty-eight weeks, he protested, and had written only two dozen words. Williams wasn't sure that hooking up, as Jessop would have it, with Orpen was a passport to productivity.

Williams watched them slowly crank up the alcohol levels between Café Pirouette and Charlie's Bar, Orpen and Berri sticking to his habitual whisky and Eve to grenadine, the others moving through increasingly florid cocktails as they switchbacked from Sidecars to Cablegrams to Crystal Bronxes, Silk Ladies to Southsides, Picons to Ping-pongs.

Williams took a light dinner at the Bistro du Pollet – the monkfish livers followed by a sea bream fillet – with a handful of other drivers and sat out a sudden summer shower by indulging in a rare after-dinner brandy. By the time he emerged to stroll back to the car the rain had left the streets of the port shiny and streaming, the last heat of the day making the atmosphere delightfully Turkish bath-thick.

Williams took up his place at the car, lit a Salambo, cursing the useless French matches which were all spark and no flame, and read the latest issue of the *Light Car*, with its appreciation of Robert Benoist, starting with a smattering of war stories (including the time he was put on a charge for wearing a lavish foxfur collar while strolling down the Champs Elysées in full Air Force uniform) and a critique of his driving skills. Sphinx-like the author called him, a man difficult to read until it was too late and he had struck, leaving his opponent breathing in his benzol. A man who, the article concluded, was, above all, loathe to walk away from any challenge. Williams lit another cigarette, his last.

He looked up as he heard a familiar clack of heels on the steps of the casino, heading down from the vast baroque doorway of the wedding-cake building towards him. Eve, hips swaggering, suggesting she'd moved from grenadine to something more potent.

She crossed the street, stretched out her arms and did a little twirl on her gold-barred kid shoes, the scalloped hemline of her skirt lifting as she did so.

'It's so stuffy in there,' she said by way of both greeting and exclamation. He could smell aniseed on her breath, which made it warm and intoxicating.

'I would imagine, Miss.'

'Have you never been in?'

'Casinos, yes. Dieppe casino, no.'

She grabbed his arm. 'Well, come on.'

Williams looked down at his uniform, the summer lightweight wool one, and shook his head. 'Hardly dressed for it, Miss.'

Eve nodded and stepped away. 'Oops. I was forgetting your position.' She let the last word slur. 'May I have a cigarette?'

'It's my last I am afraid, Miss.'

'We'll share.' She took the cigarette from his lips, inhaled deeply, tipped her head back and blew a long stream of smoke up towards where the gulls whirled in the dusk sky.

'How is it inside, Miss?'

'Oh, everybody has eyes for Babette.'

'And how is Babette dressed?'

She smiled. 'Mostly as Vander Clyde.'

For the past few years Babette, with her high wire and trapeze act at the Cirque Nedrano on Boulevard de Rouchechouart, was the only serious rival for Josephine Baker's crown as darling expat American of Paris. Under the blond wig, however, Babette just happened to be a Texan male called Vander Clyde, which he demonstrated by tearing off his hair at the climax of each performance.

'Tell me, Williams, what's a man like you doing here?'

He smiled and sidestepped the question. 'What's a man like me?'

'Ah, that's another question. What is a man like Williams? English but excellent French. None of that ugly, grating accent.'

'French mother,' he explained.

'Good driver, despite what Mr Benoist says.'

He nodded, not sure whether it was a compliment.

'Handsome in a kind of . . . English way.'

'What way is that?'

'Oh, more direct and conventional than the French I think.'

'And?'

'And you are young. You should be ruining your health with absinthe and ogling the dancing girls at Le Palermo. Yet for the last six months you have spent your days and nights waiting on Orpsie's whims. What is your secret, Mr Williams? And don't tell me you haven't got one.'

'Eve.'

The familiar rasping bellow, now slurred and rounded by whisky, carried across the street and bounced around them. 'Get in here. Don't worry about Williams.'

She turned and raised a hand to Orpen, who ducked unsteadily back in. She handed Williams the remains of the cigarette. 'Sorry. Seem to have done more than my fair share.' Eve smiled and

41

turned around, affording him a good look at the oscillation of her hips accentuated by the low sash on the dress.

Three hours later, and Orpen was facing a chilling sobriety as fifty thousand francs crossed the roulette table to the croupier in half as many minutes. Eve tried to coax him away, but he grew more irascible with each spin of the wheel.

Berri was playing *chemin de fer*, and Jessop, Patrick and Louisa, the skin-and-bone Bohemian, had spun off into an argument about Dostoevsky and James Joyce, which was way over Eve's head and, she suspected, theirs as well. She could feel the slow drip of alcohol into her system over the last twelve hours souring her liver and the pall of smoke that rolled around the gilt fittings was beginning to sting her eyes. The atmosphere reeked of sweat and desperation. The night was slowly turning rancid. She had to go. Eve hovered over Berri as he won a couple of hands, then bust on the third and solicited his help.

'Ray, I'm tired and Orps is on one of his losing streaks. We should leave.'

Berri smiled. He knew they were in for a long night, no matter what Eve said. 'I'd get a room if I were you. He'll stay till he's winning again or broke. And broke'd take quite some time.'

Eve pouted at what she took to be a refusal to assist and stalked through the thin smattering of punters to the roulette table where Orpen was cursing the croupier under his breath. 'Y'slippery bastard. I know the owner y'know.' Then louder: 'OK, on the black this time, my friend.'

'Orpsie, come on. Enough.'

He swung his diminutive frame around and snarled. 'Enough? You mean this man here has enough of my money? Only just started, Evie.'

She tried to keep the petulance out of her voice but failed. 'I want to go home.'

'Go home then. Take Williams. I'll get back one way or another or take a room and he can come and get me tomorrow. Come on, come on, spin the damn' thing.'

As the ball clattered into the blurring wheel, Eve turned and walked off, glancing over her shoulder to see if Orpen acknowledged her departure. She was vaguely aware of Jessop rising as she brushed past his table at the perimeter of the gaming area. 'Eve.' She carried on walking.

Outside she sucked in the warm air, still deliciously damp with the last of the evaporated rain and skipped down the steps towards the Rolls. She could see Williams in the front, hat pulled down over his eyes and she let out a shrill whistle using two fingers that almost woke the entire town. Williams calmly pushed up the peak of his cap and pulled at his uniform to correct himself.

'Eve.' She felt the hot brandy-laden breath of Jessop on her neck. 'You're not leaving are you?'

'I'm tired, Mr Jessop—'

'Nick. It's Nick.'

'Don't worry, Orpsie won't leave you high and dry. He never does.'

'No. I wanted a chance to talk to you. Patrick and I are pushing off for Spain in a few days . . .'

She hesitated, trying to decode what this meant. 'It's an interesting country I hear.'

'Patrick has a commission to write a piece for *American Mercury* . . .'

'What about Louisa?'

Jessop hesitated. 'What about her?'

'I thought she was rather sweet. Shame to leave her.'

43

'She's bisexual,' he said dismissively.

'Are they mutually exclusive then?'

'I guess not,' he laughed at himself. 'Rats. I'm not going very well here, am I?'

She laughed at his hitherto unheard admission of fallibility and walked towards the Rolls as Williams slipped out to open the door for her. 'Nick, I would love to sit and talk, but I am very, very tired.'

Jessop's voice quavered as he said: 'Let's go to bed then.'

Eve didn't stop or break stride at this proposition, just made a slight huffing sound, a hiss of displeasure. She stepped into the car and Williams slammed the door. Jessop tapped on the glass and she cracked open the window a few centimetres as the car moved off.

'I can pay you know.'

It only needed a minuscule flick of the wheel and Williams managed to take the full weight of the Rolls over Jessop's foot as he pulled away, crushing several toes. Eve spun round as he shrieked and watched him hopping on one leg, his eyes screwed up in pain, bellowing that he would 'fix that man's clock'.

'Good God, Williams. Will he be all right?'

'Eventually, Miss. A few days. One shouldn't get too close to machinery. It can be dangerous.'

Eve looked back again as Jessop hobbled for the casino steps and began to laugh. 'The poor man.' She could feel the staleness of the casino clinging to her and sniffed at her arm. She shuffled her dress up to her hips and pulled it over her head with a grunt, aware of the driver's eyes flicking into the mirror. 'Williams,' she said firmly, 'I need a swim.'

Eve directed them west, towards St Valery, and down a narrow lane that snaked along the small valley that bisected the coastal cliffs. There was something of a moon, but not enough to aid navigation of a big car along a tiny track, and Williams was grateful for the large saucer-like headlamps of the Rolls. Eventually the track gave out to a small cove, where several boats lay beached and neglected on the crescent of sand.

Williams bumped the big car down the launch ramp on to the soft, gritty surface, hoping it was solid enough to support the weight. Sensing his tentativeness, Eve said, 'It's quite safe, Williams. I've done this before. Take it to the water's edge.'

'Yes, Miss.'

Williams did as he was told and stopped within ten yards of the sea, not wanting to risk the treacherous shoreline where the retreating water had so recently been lapping. He turned off the engine and for a few seconds listened to the faintest of ticks as it cooled down.

'Lights, Williams.'

'I'm sorry?'

'Put on the headlamps, please.'

'I'll have to start the car again to get the dynamo going. Otherwise we risk flattening the electro-chemical cells.'

'Whatever you need to do.'

Williams re-fired the engine, which turned over with the merest mechanical fuss, and stepped out to open the rear door. Eve came naked, her skin ghostly pale in the thin moonlight, already goosebumping. 'Won't it be cold, Miss?' he managed to ask.

'I expect. Get the whisky ready, will you?' With that she ran in, squealing as the water rose above her knees, then arcing into the frothy waves, disappearing for a second, gasping as she surfaced, air exploding from her lungs.

She struck out a few yards from the shore, framed in the yellowy orbs of the lights as if this were some extravagant Folies

Bergère number. 'It's . . .' Her teeth chattered and she had to clench them before she could speak again. 'It's not too bad, once you get used to it.'

She began to propel herself up and down within the illuminated patch of sea, first a crawl, then breaststroke and finally she turned on her back.

Williams positioned himself at the front of the car, rug in one hand, Orpen's emergency hip flask from the glove compartment in the other.

'Come in,' she shouted, her voice drifting away into the surf.

'I can't swim, Miss.'

Eve laughed, a full-throated sound that made his skin prickle with embarrassment, rolled on to her front and produced several long, powerful strokes, which torpedoed her way out of the yellow ellipse of the Rolls' lights. For a few moments he could hear the sound of her limbs breaking the waves and then nothing, just the soft burble of the car engine and the hiss of the ebbing waves.

Williams waited a decent interval before his first tenuous shout. 'Miss?'

His voice sounded tiny and ineffectual against the sea, as insignificant an event as throwing a pebble into the waters.

'Miss?' Louder, harder, trying to keep the panic from his voice. He thought about removing his boots. Should he wade in?

'Eve?'

There was a rope in the boot of the car. He could use that if she was out there with cramp. But first he should use the headlamps to scan the water's surface surely.

'Yvonne.'

That was it, Williams decided, he'd search by the lights of the Rolls and then summon help. He turned to step into the car and felt the slap of her wet skin against him.

'Nobody calls me Yvonne any longer.'

She pushed against his uniform, trying to catch some of his body warmth. He could feel her shaking, a deep, muscular contraction as her body sought to generate enough heat to push up her plunging core temperature. Williams flung the rug around her and began to rub as vigorously as he could. 'Whisky?' she asked with castanet teeth.

'Not yet. Too dangerous. What the hell did you think you were doing?'

'Having fun. Hold me.'

He grasped her to him but continued massaging her back.

'This'll ruin my reputation,' she said.

'And my uniform.'

As warmth and sensation returned she pulled away from him, looking up into his eyes. 'What are you thinking?'

'That the car will overheat soon. We must leave.'

'Ah. The ever-practical Williams. Yes, of course we must go.' But she made no movement. Williams lifted the wet hair plastered across her face, pushed it to one side and they kissed, a soft, unhurried, gentle touch of the mouths, a preliminary skirmish. He pushed his hips back, just in case she could feel the effect she was having.

'Are you hungry?' he whispered.

'Starved.'

'I'll cook you something.'

Sir William Orpen whooped as the tiny ball landed on the number twelve and his losses toppled, at last, over into winnings. For the first time in hours he looked at his watch and realised dawn wasn't too far away. Berri and the others had retreated to the bar, running on his account, no doubt, but what the hell. It wasn't the money that mattered here, it was walking away with your head held high. He just wished Eve had a little more stamina for the long run, that was all. He was meant to be the ancient one, after all.

He tipped the croupier and headed for the bar for one last whisky before gathering up his waif and strays. He was sure they would find a driver somewhere, even at this hour.

When he got there the two Americans were face down on the table, asleep, and Berri and the girl deep in discussion with a chap he had never seen before.

Orpen slammed the chips down on the table. 'Fifteen thousand ahead, Ray. We should settle up and go. One more drink.' He signalled to the barman for his usual Johnnie Walker and waited for the introductions.

Berri said; 'Sir William Orpen, Josef Halken. In the same business as me. Degesch. Chemicals. Makes paints and dyes. Hamburg, isn't it?'

Halken nodded.

'How's business?' asked Orpen more out of politeness than anything else. His animosity towards the German people, stoked by his experiences at the front, had faded in the last decade, but was not extinguished entirely.

'Good, now. We have had a few bad years, as you know. Shameful. And dangerous. But since this new dye process—'

'Excellent,' said Orpen, heading the man off before he gave them a lecture on the finer points of the synthetics industry. 'Ray, see if you can summon up a car and driver. Eve's taken the bloody chauffeur.' Orpen scooped up his chips, ready to head for the cashier. 'Can't wait to see her face.'

Williams brushed the hair from Eve's face yet again, a face flushed from exertion and pleasure and she rolled off him on to the thin strip of bed left to her. 'God,' was all she said.

The first rays of warming sunlight were creeping through the shutters of the room, and Williams listened as a motor car chuffed along the lane outside, followed by the clop of a horse-drawn carriage. Versailles was waking.

Eve slid off the bed and paced, shaking her limbs, stretching, unabashed as he leant up on one elbow to watch her. It was nothing he hadn't seen before, but now it had changed. It was as if all those times in the studio he had kept his feelings, his thoughts and desires shut behind lock gates, barriers that had tumbled some time during the last few hours. Now he could finally acknowledge a connection, that, as the little voice in his head had wished for all these months, she was finally in his bed.

Eve put another *boulet* into the small stove, having kept the place heated all night after her chilling experience in the sea, even though it meant they sweated as if they were in the tropics during the lovemaking and looked around properly for the first time.

The room was simple, a square semi-basement with high windows, a bed, a dresser and a wind-up gramophone with Sidney Bechet on the turntable. She stopped at the little display of his worldly goods on the dresser. Lined up in a row, a small clockwork race car, two silver hairbrushes, a photograph of Williams on a car bonnet, some hair oil, a man's grooming kit and a silver trophy of a winged nude. Two neat stacks of thrillers – Agatha Christie, Marjory Allingham, Leslie Charteris – bookended the collection. After a moment's hesitation Eve picked up the photo.

Williams was perched on the bonnet, one leg on the floor, and around him, holding up a flag as a backdrop, were four badly dressed young men, smiling gap-toothed at the camera. With a shock she realised one of them was cradling a tommy gun.

'What on earth is this?'

'I was young,' Williams said with a yawn.

She looked at the face in the picture and back at Williams. 'Not that young. What were you playing at?'

'I was playing at being Irish,' he said eventually.

The flag was a tricolour. She finally pieced it together. 'A getaway driver?' She laughed. 'How romantic.'

Williams looked across at her standing there, naked, her stomach an erotic protuberance pressing against his furniture. Yes, that was what he had fallen for. The idea of the IRA as a noble cause, a group of Robin Hoods striking the occupiers and speeding away in stolen cars. Then the reality had sunk in. 'Only from the outside.'

'Is this your secret, Mr Williams?' She picked up the trophy. 'Or this? Number one, La Baule, Brittany?'

'A sand race. Borrowed car.'

'So. On the one hand, maybe a man on the run from Irish gangsters. Or the British? Huh? Orpen gives you shelter and a job while you . . . what's the term . . . ?'

'Lie low?'

'Aha. Yes.' She pointed to the pile of books. 'Just like your Agatha Christie. I have the solution. Or maybe . . .' She held up the trophy. 'Maybe you just want to drive. Anything you can get. Be Mr Robert Benoist.'

He snorted. 'Do you know how much a Bugatti costs?'

'So . . .' She put down the photograph and trophy. 'Let's see what else we have.'

Before he could stop her she slid open the drawer and saw the pair of stiff-backed blue passports. She picked them up and opened each in turn, her jaw slack with wonder. 'Mr Grover. And Mr Williams. Which is it?'

'Grover-Williams,' he said, 'Siamese twins. But we were separated at birth.'

She threw a passport at him and he caught it. The Grover one.

50

His given name. The one who shrugged off a stiflingly boring family and went in search of his wild, free-spirited Irish relations and found more than he bargained for. The Grover who had ended up with another man's life in his inside pocket, a letter that meant a bullet in the neck and a body thrown outside the police barracks at midnight. So after meeting Slade that morning Grover had gone back to his room and burnt the missive, unopened, and the reckless young man with a lot of growing up to do had skipped the country.

'I give up,' laughed Eve. 'You are even more of a mystery than when I started. Come on, tell me the answer.'

He put his arms behind his head and smiled, considering how much to tell her. Then a door slam reverberated through the whole house, and they both heard the fall of heavy, tired footsteps on stair treads. Coming down.

'Shit.' Eve dived under the covers just as the door burst open, and Williams managed to arrange himself so that the shapeless form crammed at the bottom of the bed looked like an extension of his own body. If he was eight feet tall. And multi-limbed. He just hoped his employer was too bleary eyed to notice.

'Williams. Ah, you're awake. Good. Did it. Got the money back. And more. Where's Evie?'

Williams couldn't answer. Eve was starting to nuzzle him under the covers, and he knew every word would come out two octaves higher than it should. He shrugged.

'She'll turn up. I'm off to bed. You can take the day off.'

As he turned Orpen heard the squeak from under the covers. He took three paces back into the room and pulled the blankets away in a great flowing crescent, revealing the curled-up Eve, eyes tight shut, as if because she couldn't see Orpen, he would be unable to see her.

51

Five

FRANCE, JULY 1928–JANUARY 1929

Williams sat outside the Floreal café on the corner of Boulevard Bonne Nouvelle, watching the weekend's entertainers arrive as he sipped at a chicory-laced coffee and smoked his last Celtique under the watchful glare of the smoker on the giant hoarding opposite, whose six-foot-long cigarette puffed out a thin stream of smoke advertising the very brand he had between his lips. At night the face glowed a blue-ish neon, bright enough to illuminate the four corners of Williams' tiny – or compact, as the concierge had it – room.

The first of the evening street bands was warming up on the wide pavement, a *baratineur* selling hats was practising his patter, half singing the praises of his cheap Princess Eugenie-style headwear that was currently going out of fashion all over central Paris. Here, though, in the second arrondissement, an area of honest artisans, dentists and furriers and dishonest vice, there might still be a market.

A light breeze occasionally carried the biting ammoniacal smell from the local *vespasienne*, a particularly ornate example of the type, spiral like a snail's shell, which was prone to blockage and overflowing and was, in the small hours, the venue for brief and sordid sexual acts by the lowest of the street girls.

Near by a gypsy guitarist picked a mournful refrain, some paean to his dead horse no doubt, that did little to lift Williams' mood. He dug out his last few sou and tossed them over to the guitarist and asked for some hot jazz. The man smiled, revealing teeth like piss-stained stalagtites and upped the tempo to sluggish. Now it sound like a paean to a dead horse who quite liked Django.

Seeing the transaction, one of the burly flame swallowers headed over, but Williams raised a hand to indicate he wanted no private show. A street band finally started up, playing 'Madame la Marquise'. The guitarist redoubled his efforts against the vulgar brassiness from across the boulevard.

It had been an eventful few weeks since Orpen's discovery of Eve's perfidy, as he denounced it. Williams had, of course, packed and left, which put him at something of a disadvantage. Drivers normally moved with cars – a chauffeur went to whoever bought the vehicle. But now he and the Rolls had been split asunder he really did feel like a recently parted Siamese twin, as if a large section of him was missing. He could still feel the wheel, the clutch, the advance-retard, but they were phantom sensations, coming to taunt him.

He had taken a few stand-in jobs, sitting in one of the *restaurants des chauffeurs* around rue des Favourites in the fifteenth, where news of vacancies, or whichever driver on the circuit was taking a holiday or ill, rapidly circulated over the huge plates of *bouef gros sel*, with mounds of leeks and carrots, the traditional driver's fuel.

He knew the positions would dry up come August, when Paris, and the restaurants, closed and the chauffeured classes moved south or north to the coast. There were other options. He could rejoin his father in the long-distance driving business – if he'd have him after that jaunt in Ireland – or he could get a regular non-driving job. Or he could go and see Constantini or Benoist and tell them that he was the man to move Bugatti and its race cars forward.

The latter fantasy make him smile and he took up a newspaper discarded on the wicker chair next to him and scanned it for a jobs section, but couldn't find one. He looked at the front cover. Gringoire. Some right wing diatribe was spread across the front, lamenting the paralysis, both intellectual and industrial, that gripped the country at the moment. The *années folies* were over, it claimed: France was about to pick up the tab for its decadence and plunge into turmoil.

Williams threw the rag back on to the seat and picked up the new detective paperback he had bought at the bookstore on rue de l'Odeon, opposite the one run by the strange American woman who published unreadable novels. Georges Simenon might be a Belgique, but he knew Paris well – in fact Orpen and the author had dined together at Maisonette Russe and the Château Madrid, the upper end of the social milieu. But in the novel the Belgian had captured the other, grittier end of Paris, not that of slumming, allowance-fed Americans in St Germain, but the cafés along the Canal St Martin, the slaughterhouses at La Villette, the market traders at Les Halles, the marshalling yards beyond the Batignolles and the ateliers of rue St Charles, the seedy nightlife of Pigalle, where the whores flap at tourists like crows, and the *truants* of rue de Lappe – those who, for whatever reason, would prefer not to see the inside of Police Judicaire.

Williams had just immersed himself in the tale of a country girl come to a sticky end when he heard the soft tattoo of elegant heels – glued, not nailed, as was the new style – crossing the paved street. Eve, dressed in a simple navy blue suit and carrying a large valise, which she placed on the floor. She signalled for a coffee as if this were a pre-arranged meeting and smiled broadly at him.

'How did . . . ?'

'Joe the Bum.'

'Ah.' The waiter at the Falstaff, a man with a Brooklyn accent so thick it came out like soup, had long acted as a letter drop for his regulars. 'Then the concierge at that horrible building you inhabit.'

He laughed. 'I can see the Rex and the Baths of Neptune from my balcony.'

'And the whores,' she said sniffily.

It was true. There were some *hotels de passe* – the far end of the sexual scale from the brothels that Orpen sometimes frequented – on the rue de la Lune, just up the steps at his side, where the amiable but low-fee prostitutes bantered with prospective clients and each other.

The waiter delivered her coffee and Eve said, 'And two Aquavits.' She nodded at the discarded paper beside him. 'Looking for a position?'

'Yes. Driver wanted. Must fuck employer's mistress behind his back.'

She laughed. 'Feeling guilty?'

'Aren't you?'

'No, I did it with the entire staff. Every week.' It took a moment before he realised she was joking. 'I particularly like gardeners. All those calluses.' She shuddered with mock pleasure.

'It still felt like betrayal.'

Eve nodded but didn't say anything for a moment. It had happened because it had happened. She felt the hand of inevitability in it. Just as all Orpen's other mistresses had had a natural lifespan, so her tenure had all but run its course.

'Betrayal? We all betray each other.'

Williams leaned forward and whispered: 'If you were mine I'd never betray you.'

Eve tried hard to stop giggling at his seriousness. 'Ha. Am I hearing some happy-ever-after fantasies here?'

He reached over and picked a strand of hair from her face. 'How could I hurt a beautiful woman like you?'

Eve hurled back her Aquavit and pursued her lips. 'Show me a beautiful woman and I'll show you a man who's tired of fucking her.'

Williams let out a roar of laugher, causing the guitarist to falter. 'So why did you do it? Was it me, or could it have been anyone?'

'How can you ask?' she said indignantly. 'I could have done it with Mr Jessop and been paid into the bargain.'

'Because I'm insecure.'

She looked into his eyes and saw it was true. He was like a sixteen year old, nervous, indecisive, daring himself to believe what was happening. She realised she hadn't told him why she had sought him out.

'Orpen is going back to London. Not permanently, but to renew ties with his family and no doubt Mrs St George.' Adding, in case Williams didn't know, 'One of my predecessors.'

'I'm sorry.'

'Don't be. It was amicable.'

'Even after . . .'

She grinned. 'I suspect you didn't get your sense of morality from your French mother. Orpen only raged for a day or two. You would have been forgiven. But you wouldn't wait. Too English by half.'

Williams had mostly been raised in France, but there were still prayers for the home country and God Save The King at the dinner table. Although only a boy when Edward VII died, he still remembered the black-draped portrait and the household that spoke in whispers for weeks and weeks until he was certain they were losing the power of speech and every now and then he would cycle down the road so he could shout at the top of his lungs. After sipping his drink for a while he said: 'I didn't want to be forgiven. I couldn't have gone back to how it was. Not me servant, you mistress. There are times when it is best to move on.'

The guitarist came over, his hand outstretched, but Williams shooed him away, his pockets empty. The gypsy went back to his more plaintive pluckings.

'Bill said,' she lowered her voice into a gruff whisky-soaked Orpen impersonation, 'I expect you are going to live in some cold garrett with that damn' chauffeur and starve.'

Williams smirked at the accuracy. In a way he missed the old soak. 'And are you?'

'Not quite.' She reached down to the valise, unzipped it, and brought out a wad of large denomination notes with a gummed band around it and threw it at Williams. He caught it just before it hit his chest, but he missed the second and the third and the fourth. He tried to catch his Aquavit, but it fell, rolled over and smashed on to the pavement.

'Not quite,' she repeated, standing and upending the valise on the tables, scores of packets, millions of francs cascading over the table, laughing at the way Williams' eyes bulged in his sockets.

Aware of a mournful gaze a few yards down the street, Eve picked up a thin bundle and tossed it to the guitarist who deftly plucked it from the air and burst into rapid fire chords of explosive joy.

'Dinner at Maxim's?' she asked.

'On you?'

'On us.' She leaned across the mound of cash and kissed him.

★ ★ ★

Eve could not sleep. The supposedly furtive noises she heard from outside were as loud as claps of thunder, the detonation of guns, the fireworks on Bastille Day. The men outside had promised to be as silent as ghosts, but they were the clumsiest spirits she had ever encountered. Still Williams slept on. Since the day on the Boulevard Bonne Nouvelle, several months ago now, Eve had pulled together several strands of her life plan. She had bought a converted watermill on the River Vie in the Pays d'Auge, Normandy, complete with kennels for her Scottish terriers, an apartment in Paris and enough money in the bank to see them through for the foreseeable future.

But Williams, she hadn't forgotten Williams in her master plan. He deserved something from all the money that came her way after the split with Orpen, a split she now began to suspect Orpen had somehow engineered. He had certainly picked up a new mistress with indecent, and suspicious, haste. And had showered embarrassing riches on Eve with a guilty fervour, as if it was him that had been found in bed with the chauffeur.

Williams had worked hard. He had fixed the place up, pruned the neglected apple trees in the orchard with the intention of making his own cider and calvados one day, built the kennels, helped choose the dogs – they settled on specialising in black Scottish terriers and white West Highland terriers – with an enthusiasm that surprised her, and ingratiated himself with the local village cafés and bars – scrupulously rotating his custom – and the *marie*, important conquests for newcomers to any rural area. Especially unmarried ones.

Winter's thin dawn chorus had come and gone by the time Williams opened his eyes and rolled over, a sleepy smile on his face. Light headed and exhausted from her long vigil, she kissed him on the cheek, enjoying the rough feel of stubble. 'Happy

58

birthday, darling.' Williams kissed her back. 'I know I should get the breakfast, but would you mind getting the coffee?'

Williams got up, stretched, and wrapped a robe round himself. He threw open the window and looked over the valley floor, to the pastures and orchards of the fertile land, glistening with winter frost, and wondered why the view didn't make his heart sing quite as much as it should. Possibly the thought of the long months to spring, till the scene blossomed and plumped with fresh greenery. But no, he had to admit even now it had an austere, diamond-hard beauty.

Maybe it was another birthday. Thirty was coming over the horizon fast. By which time he wanted to have made his mark at something other than having a rich lover, no matter how beautiful. Maybe Eve had been partly right. Not that he'd grown tired of fucking her, but somehow it wasn't enough, there were still missing pieces to the jigsaw puzzle.

Williams went downstairs, selected two large bowls and placed a sugar cube in the bottom of each. He poured in the thick black coffee and then crushed the cube with a spoon. That would be enough for Eve, but he hadn't quite shaken off the very English need for milk in the morning. He tried the wire-fronted larder, but there was none. Two of the porcelain containers, but empty. Which meant going outside to the cool shed across the courtyard.

Eve paced out his actions in her mind, timing him. Put on coffee, get bowl, fetch sugar, pour coffee, crush cube, discover no milk, go outside, take two paces and . . .

Williams' whoop must have been heard in Caen, a window-rattling scream that conveyed disbelief and delirium all in one rush of air from his lungs. She heard him run back, halt, retrace his steps and then a sound like tearing calico, sweeping to a deeper throb as the engine revved.

Leaving it ticking over, Williams sprinted up the stairs and threw himself across the room into her arms and smothered her with kisses.

'Is it the right one?' she asked disingenuously, as if talking about a hat or a shirt.

'A Thirty-five B? Absolutely gorgeous.' He looked very serious. 'There is only one thing.'

'What?'

He listened to that rasping engine note as if something mechanical was bothering him.

'What?'

He stepped closer. 'The colour. Blue. Bugatti Blue. It'll have to be British Racing Green.' He puffed out his chest with mock pomposity. 'I am, after all, an Englishman.'

Eve reached up and grabbed him and outside the beautiful sleek Bugatti racing car chugged on, alone and neglected, for another twenty minutes until the new owner came down to take it for a spin.

Six

TRIALS DAY, MONACO, APRIL 1929

Robert Benoist sat on the terrace of the Café de Paris and watched the cars come round the Casino Square as they powered through the gap between the casino itself and the Hotel de Paris, checking the braking and handling of each one, paying particular attention to the Bugattis. Trial day, the first time most of the cars had run this new street-racing circuit. Already it was taking its toll – Benoist had seen two cars limping round, their mechanicals or engines unsettled by such a low-revving, convoluted and bumpy course.

Benoist wasn't convinced by this circuit. He liked big sweeping autodromes, like Montlhery and Avus in Germany, where the driver could go flat out. Here, he doubted if any of them could get into top gear, and rattling over cobblestones and tram lines put extreme stress on tyres and chassis. He as much as anyone would concede that Ettore Bugatti was a genius, but mechanical reliability was not his strongest suit when it came to race models. He knew there were other dissenters, too – the *Autocar* magazine had editorialised that such a Grand Prix was 'astonishing' and 'dangerous'.

Behind him his brother Maurice scanned the crowd, the faces at the hotel windows, those on the makeshift grandstand across the way and played his own running commentary.

'Josephine Mannion. You know all about her. I think that is her sister with her. Very different proposition. They say you need a car jack to get her legs apart. Ah, look, Kiki with some ugly artists. I hear Mistinguett is coming tomorrow. See, Noghes has got a few famous faces down here.' Antony Noghes was the cigarette tycoon who had bankrolled this attempt to start the Monte Carlo season early by running what he hoped would become the most fashionable motor race in the world. Maurice lowered the glasses. 'And shouldn't you be in the pits?'

'Ettore banished me. Says I intimidate the drivers.' Maurice laughed. He could just imagine his brother, eyes so piercing you felt as if he could see into your soul, making the young blades feel uneasy, as if they weren't up to the job of filling his shoes. Which, as far as Robert was concerned, they weren't.

A light drizzle had started and Robert watched the big seven-litre Mercedes of Rudi Caracciola roar into the square, pass the Hotel de Paris and slide into the bend, with Rudi having to steer it like a boat. Robert wondered how Rudi was coping with the Station hairpin and the demanding Gasworks bend.

As if to show how it should be done, a Bugatti came into view, power as full on as the driver dared in a fresh fall of rain on cobbles, and nimbly took the bend, straightening and flooring the pedal up the Avenue des Spellugues towards the downhill zig-zag to Monte Carlo station. Perfect. But something wasn't quite right with number 12. Then it struck him. It had been green. Not blue. It was a green Bugatti 35B. How could Ettore allow this?

Robert looked at Maurice. 'Who is that?' But it was gone. 'Number twelve.'

Maurice consulted his *liste de engages*. 'Williams. Englishman.'

'Do we know him?'

'Some talentless peasant.'

Robert brooded until, three minutes later, Williams came by again and he watched the same mix of looseness and precision guide the car through the bends. 'Peasant maybe . . .' he mused.

'Look. Over there. In navy blue.' Maurice's attention, as usual, was elsewhere.

Robert picked up his binoculars and scanned the sparse crowd on the opposite side of the square. 'Where?'

'At the top. Blonde.'

Robert focused on a mass of curly hair framing a face made even more beautiful by its lack of makeup. 'That's his woman.'

'Whose?'

'Williams,' said Maurice in triumph.

'And what do we know about her?'

'Sucks like a nanny goat.'

Robert lowered his binoculars and gave Maurice one of his powerful stares. 'Meaning you have tried and got nowhere?'

Maurice grinned. 'Something like that.' In fact, nothing like that. He'd introduced himself and been greeted with a I've-just-stepped-in-a-dog-turd expression from the woman.

Robert raised the glasses again, but she had gone, off to find another vantage point. Robert watched the Alfas, Maseratis and Bugattis come round one more time, followed by Rudi's Mercedes, now making its way through the field as its talented driver got the measure of the track. 'Where are they holding the draw for the start positions?'

'The Salles Touzet in the casino. Tomorrow night.'

Robert ordered another glass of wine and thought about the blonde. 'Make sure we're there. I'd like a closer look.'

63

Seven

RACE DAY, MONACO, APRIL 1929

One hundred laps. One hundred and ninety-seven miles. Sixteen cars.

Eve positioned herself near the pits, under the trees, just before the Ste Devote bend, right behind where their two ad hoc mechanics, Bernard and Jacques, hired, cajoled and flattered from the village garage and trained in the art of refuelling and tyre changing in the yard at the Normandy house, had set up shop. A large board in front of each station proclaimed the name and number of the driver. She tried not to dwell on all those hours ahead, hours in which her lover would try to drive as quickly as humanly possible through streets designed for horses and trams.

A lap of honour by Prince Louis, Antony Noghes accompanying, beaming. A year of hard work. Lobbying the International Association of Recognised Automobile Clubs, the Automobile Club de Monaco, the drivers and the manufacturers. Now, a happy man.

Robert and Maurice were positioned further along behind the

Dreyfus pit stop, with Ettore and his son Jean Bugatti. Maurice could not fail to notice that, even at the start when the tension mounted as Prince Louis did a lap of honour and the crowd cheered his vision and generosity in allowing the race, Robert's attention wandered along to where Williams was making frantic adjustments to his car, and Eve looked on, concerned and nervous.

Two laps of warm-up and the cars shuffled their way on to the grid under the watchful eye of Charles Faroux, the hard-bitten race organiser. Engines, gentlemen please.

The mechanics cranked the handles, engines fired, each one emitting its distinctive note, the low thrum of the Mercedes, the haughty cough of the Maserati, the piercing scream of the Alfa in the upper register and the strange tearing-fabric sound of the Bugattis. The drivers raised their hands one by one as the cars caught.

Williams watched Faroux move to the starter's podium, his sombre face showing none of the excitement he must feel, at least if he had a human bone in his body, which, to be fair, many doubted. Williams tried not to notice the thousands of pairs of eyes raking the field, to concentrate on the clutch, the accelerator, the brake, the gear lever on his right-hand side, on the co-ordination that would be needed to get this car round the first bend. He started to breathe as Rudi suggested, purging the heart-flapping chemicals from his blood, remembering his words. Calm. Clinical.

At the back of the field, thanks to a terrible draw, with a sea of metal in front of him, mostly Alfa red and Bugatti blue, Rudi also began the process of clearing his mind, reducing his world to the immediate vicinity only, stripping away the background like so much scenery in a music hall, flats to be taken away. Everything shrank to the vibrating microcosm of the cockpit and the next straight, bend, gear change, chicane, tunnel, uphill, downhill, round.

The flag raised.

Williams reached up and swivelled his flat tweed cap so the peak pointed towards the rear and pulled down his goggles.

The flag dropped. Away.

Rudi saw the stalled car just in time, yanked the wheel to the left, felt himself clip the bodywork, corrected. He pressed the accelerator and listened to the noise of the car, straining his ears for a sign, a torn cowling, a shredded tyre, a bent drive shaft. Tell me, tell me. It told him. No damage. Fifteen cars. Fourteen ahead of him into the first sharp bend with its deceptive kink at the far side. Lot of work to do, Rudi, he thought. Lot of work.

Eight laps gone.

It was a sight to make Ettore Bugatti's heart leap. Out of the tunnel towards the chicane they came, four of them, powering majestically down the incline like ships of the line. One, two, three, four. All Bugattis. In the lead, Williams, bringing the pack home, having snatched the vanguard from Lehoux in a daring manoeuvre along the Quai. But even without seeing that distinctive green, Ettore would have known which car it was by the engine note. So he had no trouble pinpointing number twelve, especially as Williams, this unknown Englishman, was adding something to the usual staccato roar of the engine, with gear

66

changes so smooth as to be almost sensual, precise, yet delicate. Even Bugatti had to admit he was making the little car sing.

And then he saw the white shape and the familiar helmet. Rudi. Fifth. Fifth in a car that should have needed first gear and a team of horses to get round the hairpins, and here he was having bullied and pushed and sweated his way through the entire field to be a contender. Ettore watched the white behemoth close on Dreyfus and as they disappeared from view he knew Caracciola wasn't going to let his Bugattis have it all their own way.

Lap 25.

Williams felt him before he saw him. As he entered the mouth of the tunnel the scream of the supercharger became a bouncing banshee, smacking off the multifaceted rock face. Then, almost subsonically, came the deeper whump of Caracciola's Mercedes, the lazy 7.1 litre seeming to fire once every fifty metres, but delivering a magnificent amount of torque.

As number twelve exited the tunnel, the wail receding, Williams could feel the SSK looming behind, could hear the bassy boom of its big bore exhausts boxing his ears. He looked in the dancing mirror, and saw Rudi edge out, starting to probe.

Down the hill they accelerated towards the twitch of the chicane, until Caracciola could almost touch the shapely tail of the Bugatti. Now along the Quai, a glance at the open-mouthed crowds, their cheering unable to penetrate the gruff roar of the engine, instruments blurring as he braked for Tabac, down through the gears for the left hander, then back on the throttle, worrying the feisty little Bugatti all the way to Gasworks. Then he felt the slide, the wheels slither on the road surface, scrabbling for grip, and the back swing wildly. Trouble.

A rattle over the tram lines and up the hill now, and Rudi saw the Bugatti twitch on the oil-slicked surface. Rudi dived to the right, gambling on how the Englishman would correct his line, saw the supercharger of the twelve car vent smoke and flame through the hole in the bonnet, knew he had him, corrected his own back end as a wheel caught the oil slick on the cobbles, and was away powering up towards Ste Devote, in first place.

Lap 35.

Eve covered her eyes as Williams bravely stormed after the German, could feel his despair as the Mercedes rounded the bend first. She hated this, hated it. The next thing she knew Williams was in, grinning, face blackened by oil and smoke, urging Bernard on as the villager tipped fuel into the filler cap behind his head. He raised a hand to Eve, waited for the tap on his shoulder to tell him refuelling was complete, and floored the accelerator.

Eve looked across at Ettore and wondered who was the man next to him, calmly meeting her gaze. Then she had him. Robert Benoist. Looking right at her, those piercing eyes fixing her, a hint of a smile playing about his mouth. Eve had smiled back then turned her attention once more to the track, counting the seconds till Williams reappeared. He did. With Caracciola on his tail this time. She hated it.

Lap 75.

Eve watched as Rudi came rumbling into his designated pit slot and his white overalled mechanics leapt out at him. Rudi was out of the car and pointing furiously. New tyres. He needed new tyres. The strain of those corners had torn through the tread, leaving tendrils of rubber hanging down. The mechanics set about the wheel change while Rudi himself poured fuel into the thirsty monster. He looked up in despair as Williams rocketed by, willing the petrol into the tank, sloshing it carelessly over the bodywork and ground. Finally it was done and Rudi climbed back in and, grim faced, rejoined the battle. Eve looked at her watch. Over four minutes. Too slow, she knew. Far too slow.

Lap 100.
Close to four hours after the start the chequered flag came down on Williams. He had averaged 49.83 mph, round the 1.97 mile course, and had the fastest lap – 2 mins 15 seconds, at 52.69 mph. He came home 1 minute 17.8 seconds ahead of Bouriano's 35C. An exhausted Rudi came home third, his arms numb from the exertion of handling the Mercedes.

As Williams pulled in after his lap of honour, the crowd surged forward. Antony Noghes struggled through with the cup and managed to thrust it into Williams' hands, while flashes detonated all around. Williams saw Eve and beckoned her over. He kissed her, leaving a black smudge on her nose, which he made worse by trying to wipe away.

'How does it feel?' she asked him.

The grin that threatened to bisect his face said it all. Eve produced the gift with a flourish, holding it above his hand and while Williams snapped at it like a hungry dog, mesmerised by the way the diamonds caught the light. Theatrically he snatched it away and looked at it. A beautiful Cartier. He turned it over, but the steel back was unadorned.

'Don't worry, darling,' she said. 'We'll get it engraved. First in the first.'

Then she lost him as everybody else pressed in to claim their piece of the day's hero.

Robert watched Williams and Rudi pose, the weary combatants of the race. Maurice had been talking to Ettore and scuttled back as fast as his limp would allow.

'Good gossip, brother. She is, or was, the mistress of Bill Orpen. The painter. He ... you will like this ... he is the chauffeur. The chauffeur.'

'Really?'

'Yes and apparently the money is all hers. He's a kept man.'

'Lucky chap.'

'But Ettore reckons that was one of the best drives he has seen. Says the man has star quality. He's invited him to Molsheim. Going to offer him a team drive.'

'Is he now?'

'He thinks he could go all the way. Champion.'

Robert watched as Eve appeared at Williams' side, now clutching a small dog in her arms, and posed for more photographs, then he turned and slipped away into the crowd.

Sir William Orpen had, of course, heard of Robert Benoist, all of France had, but he had never met the driver before. So he was rather taken aback when Robert came visiting him at his studio and asked to see some of his work with a view to purchasing one. However, as he was crating up to ship back to England, he would be more than pleased to offload a few canvases.

Orpen waited as Robert flicked through the stacks in the studio until he had found what he was looking for. As he suspected. 'Beautiful, isn't she?' declared Robert, redundantly.

'Hhmm.'

'How much is this one?'

'It's not for sale, alas.'

Robert lifted it out, tried to imagine what it would be like in a frame rather than on the primitive stretcher, admired the graceful curve of the reclining nude, the playful smile on the face. 'Why not?'

'I'm rather fond of it. It was my last portrait of her.'

'Two hundred and fifty thousand?'

Orpen coughed. 'Two-fifty? Done.'

Robert smiled and they shook on the deal. 'I'll have it picked up tomorrow if that is convenient with you.'

'Absolutely. Just get your man to call in advance. I'll have it properly packed. To protect her.'

Robert stepped back and admired his purchase, 'What's it called?'

Orpen, already regretting his hasty decision, murmured quietly: 'Early One Morning'.

Eight

Williams drove one more race at Montlhery after Monaco – a spirited second place in an all-Bugatti field, with fellow Englishman Lord Howe winning – before the journey to Molsheim. He and Eve decided to drive in their new Peugeot, heading north west from Paris, stopping at Rheims, Verdun, site of the most famous battle of the Great War, at least in France, Metz and arriving in Molsheim, to the west of Strasbourg, early on the fourth day.

Eve couldn't help but notice how relaxed and happy Williams was, as if a great weight had been lifted from him. Having proved he could actually race and win, some inner calm had finally taken over. Although she now knew him well enough to suspect that, like a slow drip, the need for excitement would build up again gradually. For the moment he had nothing to prove. He was up there with the élite.

They were astonished to find Molsheim was less a works than a grand estate. Even the factory seemed like an extension of the house, spotlessly clean, with a relaxed, friendly workforce

72

building cars – including a mock-up of the fabulous and gargantuan Royale, rumoured to be one of the most expensive vehicles ever produced – boats and the prototype railcars that Bugatti had designed using petrol engines and pneumatic tyres. Eve and Williams put up at the small hotel that had been built for customers who wished to stay over, and were then invited to join in the shoot.

'What's in season?' asked Williams.

'Pigeons,' said Ettore.

In the large pasture behind the factory twenty or so people had gathered to take turns at what the Americans called skeet shooting. Bugatti had installed a system that could hurl ten clays up at a time if required, to try to duplicate the mass explosion of birds from the undergrowth. Of course, when all ten were used it made sorting out who had hit what rather difficult.

Ettore pointed out some of the other guests. 'Bradley. English motoring journalist. Philippe de Rothschild. Banker, of course. Fine driver, too. Next to him, my son Jean. I'll show you some of his designs later. Very good. Robert Benoist I believe you know. No? I'll introduce you. Next to him, his brother Maurice.'

Bugatti was interrupted by a mass discharge of guns as the discs came arcing through the air, all but one exploding into tiny shards.

'Holtschaub. Customer. Dumas from the Ministry of Transport – here about the railcars, naturally – Meo Constantini, my race manager—' A second detonation of shotguns, more innocent clays pulverised in mid air. 'Would you like a try?'

Williams nodded and was found a place and a gun. He discovered the whole process oddly satisfying. No living creature suffered, there was an element of skill – although the line of flight was more predictable in the clay than with avian flesh and blood targets – and he found he was really rather good. Except when

73

Eve decided to tickle him or surreptitiously slid her hand across the front of his trousers.

Robert broke his gun and watched. Maurice sneered, 'I told you she was a slut.'

Robert smiled. 'Jealous?'

'Only all of me, brother.'

Lunch was called and they strolled back to the house. Ettore fell in beside Williams and Eve. 'How is my Bugatti?'

'I think one of the ends has run.'

'How do you know?'

'I can hear it.'

Ettore raised an eyebrow, surprised. It wasn't the quietest engine in the world when it was blown by a supercharger, and he thought nobody else could pick up every metallic nuance like its designer. 'We'll have to strip it down.' He looked at Eve. 'Expensive.'

'I had assumed as much,' she said with an affected weariness. 'Dogs are so much cheaper.'

'Well, there might be another solution,' Bugatti replied enigmatically and veered off to talk to Jean before either of them could ask exactly what that solution might be.

Lunch was held in the grand salon of the house, a feast of Alsace delicacies, with a foie gras pot-au-feu, spaetzlc, baeckeoffe, kugelhopf and a vast assortment of sausages. The language in the room switched rapidly between German, French and English, with Ettore occasionally using his native Italian to emphasise a point. Robert and Maurice sat opposite Williams and Eve, with Bugatti at the head of the table.

Ettore did the introductions at their section, and Robert looked at Eve and said, 'Ah. Bill Orpen's muse.'

'Ex-muse,' Williams said quickly.

'I have a fine example of your musing.'

Eve stopped short of sipping her pinot noir, puzzled. 'You do, Mr Benoist?'

'Robert, please. Yes. "Early One Morning".'

Eve felt Williams shift uncomfortably, trying to figure out where this was going. 'Really? Bill said he'd never sell it.'

'I made him an excellent offer.'

'I'll match it,' said Williams.

'With what?' retorted Maurice. Eve glared at him and he went back to his plate of snails.

Robert waved a fork airily, as if distracted. 'No, it really isn't for sale now. I do admire it so.'

Aware that some kind of tension was building Ettore interrupted. 'Williams' car needs a re-build. I was thinking of giving him a team drive. What do you think, Robert?'

'You have a place?'

'Yes. You know we do.'

Robert took a mouthful of Gewürztraminer before saying, 'I thought I might have that.'

A silence fell. Constantino began to say something and then fell silent when Robert flicked a fierce glance his way.

Ettore said quietly, with a hint of flint in his voice, 'I need you in the Paris showroom.'

'I can do both,' insisted Robert. 'We can do demonstrations before races.'

'That wasn't the agreement,' said his employer, trying hard to keep the irritation from his voice. 'Now I have two would-be drivers, one place.'

'I have an idea,' said Maurice brightly. 'How about a challenge? Twenty laps of Montlhery—'

'That's unfair,' objected Eve. 'You have raced there dozens of times, Mr Benoist. Will just once.'

Williams touched her arm. 'That's all right, Eve. A duel? Why not?' Williams watched Robert's grin broaden. Time to find out if it was true the man never backed down from a challenge. 'But let's throw in the painting. Just for the sport.'

Williams could see Robert's brain working furiously. To refuse the wager would seem churlish, cowardly even, a vote of no-confidence in his own skills. He couldn't think of a way out that would save face. Eve felt Robert's eyes bore into her as he laughed at Williams' audacity and said: ' "Early One Morning"? Why not? Just for the sport. Ettore – name the day, I'll be there.'

Bugatti hesitated, wondering if he should be part of this, then noticed Jean signalling furiously. It was a second before he understood what his eldest son was saying. Finally, he nodded his consent.

'Excellent.' Robert stood up and clicked his fingers at Maurice. 'We have to take our leave. We have a few days in the country.' He hesitated and finally shifted his gaze from Eve to Williams. 'Does anyone know where I can find a decent chauffeur?'

Nine

MONTLHERY RACETRACK, JULY 1929

The early morning sun glinted off the brace of Bugattis sitting out on the concrete, the last tendrils of a damp mist curling around the eight-spoked aluminium wheels. Both were painted in the Bugatti factory blue, each had been beautifully prepared, overseen by Jean, who had watched every last rivet being ground down, strengthened the drive train when he thought it too delicate (a source of friction with his father, who always thought his designs perfect) and tuned the vast sixteen-cylinder engines to perfect pitch.

Next to the machines, on an easel, a protective cloth thrown over it, was the prize, the one Williams wanted above all. He would always find a way of getting a drive, whether he got the Bugatti seat or not. He wanted that painting back where it belonged. With Eve.

He sat in the pits, alone, slowly emptying his mind, reminding himself of his golden rules. You can only be sure of winning if you start a race absolutely calm, your hands not sweaty. The juice in the bloodstream can come later, but there, on the start line, up to the first bend, too much means a stalled car, a bad line, an over-ambitious out-braking into the curve.

No Robert, as yet.

Williams emptied his pockets into the small wooden container he always used. Already superstition and ritual were entering his racing life. Cigarettes. Lighter. Wallet. Change. All into the box. Next, the dressing routine. Shoes off. Overalls on. Soft kid racing boots, laced. Gloves, tucked into belt. Tweed cap. Goggles. Ready. Where was Robert?

The faint buzz entered his consciousness at that point, and he knew exactly where his opponent was.

The noise grew louder, angrier, and all heads turned upwards, eyes shaded against the sun. The bright red biplane appeared over the far side of the banking, the rotary engine screaming as the plane dipped, coming in on a collision course for the two Bugattis, sending mechanics and spectators scattering. At the last second it rose up, fixed wheels almost touching the metal of the cars and sideswiping the painting, the engine straining to claw into the air once more, the propeller wash peeling back the cover off 'Early One Morning', sending it tumbling down the track. Williams could see Robert at the controls, the trademark grin across his face.

The biplane gained height, circled, did a single, lazy roll and then came in to land on the far straight, taxiing off on to the central grassed reservation. Robert leapt out and bowed to the smattering of relieved applause.

He strode over towards Williams, stripping off the heavy leather gloves, jacket and helmet as he went, to reveal his racing suit underneath. He collected his white canvas helmet and goggles from Maurice and slipped them on. 'Ready?'

Williams nodded and they went to their respective cars.

'I hope you drive better than you fly.'

Robert laughed, knowing that was nigh on impossible. 'We'll see. One last look?'

Williams stopped before the naked form of Eve in the painting and then glanced over at the real thing, who blew him a kiss. Robert signalled for the portrait to be removed and stepped into his car. With one leg in he froze, extracted himself, walked back and held out his hand. Williams took it. 'I forgot. Goodbye, Williams.'

With no further explanation Robert got behind the wheel, the mechanic cranked the engine and sixteen cylinders fired in an exuberant explosion of power. Williams followed suit, heart racing with anticipation as the engine responded to the tiniest throttle pressure, watching Ettore and Jean tussle over who would drop the starting flag. Le Patron won, of course, and took his position on the low starter's podium.

Stay calm, thought Williams. Get the heart rate down. Don't worry. He may be more experienced, but he is older, slower, less hungry. Bugatti held the flag aloft and hesitated. The engines started to protest as the rev counters crept round to the red line, the intricate mechanical innards chattering away, blurring the instrument panel. The flag twitched. Williams reached up and swivelled his tweed cap backwards, pulling the goggles in place with a fraction of a second to spare. The flag cracked down and the world around Williams became a rocketing blur.

Two cars and two drivers each perfectly matched. Glued together the Bugattis powered round the track, a mechanical *pas de deux*, sweeping along the straight and up the banking, as if choreographed, occasionally one inching ahead, but never for very long, as if afraid of hogging the limelight, the thirty-two cylinders all firing on cue.

Even Eve, who thought this whole thing a theatrical sham, had to admit it was exhilarating and beautiful.

As she watched another neck-and-neck lap she became aware of someone at her side. Maurice. He offered her a Celtique cigarette and, after a slight hesitation, she took one. 'Peace offering?'

'Are we at war?' he asked.

'I had the impression you didn't like us.'

'No, no, no. Far from it. My brother is a great admirer.'

'And you?'

Maurice shrugged. 'Haven't you heard? I like what my brother likes.'

Williams in the lead now, edging ahead, and a slight frown flicked across Maurice's face.

'Why do you say something like that?'

'Oh, it's always been the same. I am the elder, but Robert . . . in the war I was stuck in the mud at Verdun,' he slapped his gammy leg, 'while Robert was the fighter ace. After the war when we took up racing . . . well, the leg again. I am one of those miserable creatures Josephine Baker despises so much.' He said it with a smile in his eyes.

Eve shook her head. The silly Baker woman had told a journalist how war deformities made her feel nauseous, a statement she quickly withdrew after the scandalous outrage that followed. Still, being the scantily clad toast of Paris she was quickly forgiven. Except by those she defamed. 'You shouldn't believe anything Americans say.'

Maurice glanced back at the track and stretched his collar. He was fashionably dressed in a wool suit, with waistcoat, shirt and tie and the brown suede shoes that the Americans had made acceptable, but it was not the best ensemble to be wearing in bright sunshine. Eve was glad she had chosen a simple cotton dress and brimmed cloche hat.

'You know,' Maurice said in a low voice, 'no matter who wins out there, I can think of two losers.'

'Who?'

'Us.'

He stood up to cheer as Robert came home to take the flag and Eve felt her heart sink.

Williams took it well. He pulled over and climbed out to the thin applause and shook hands with Robert. Jean wanted to press him on how the car had behaved, but he strolled over to see Eve, with the young Bugatti in tow, hectoring him with technical questions.

Maurice popped the champagne and handed Robert a glass. 'Still got the old magic, I see.'

'Only just.'

'What do you mean?'

Robert stripped off his helmet and took a sip of the drink. 'How many Grand Prixes have we raced?'

'Forty . . . fifty?'

'Seventy-two. And Williams?'

Maurice shrugged.

'One. One proper race and a handful of secondary events. Yet I beat him by this much.' He held his arms out to show a metre, slopping his drink. 'Next time this much.' He narrowed the gap to half that distance. 'Then.' He handed his glass to Maurice and clapped his hands with percussive force, causing Maurice to jump. 'I don't like it.'

Robert retrieved and gulped back the remaining champagne before walking over to Eve and Williams, who were talking to Jean near the Orpen painting, its protective wrapper back in place. Jean said: 'Congratulations, Robert. Williams here was just saying he could feel a vibration at around five thousand revolutions. Front left wheel. Did you feel anything?'

Robert shook his head and a concerned Jean pulled Williams

off to examine the two cars. As he stepped away Williams hesitated and asked Robert: 'What was the goodbye for? At the start?'

'Don't you know that? All factory Bugatti drivers always say goodbye to each other before a race . . . it's good luck.'

Williams went off with Jean.

'Sounds more like pessimism, Mr Benoist,' suggested Eve.

There was a sudden squeal of rubber on concrete and a cloud of acrid smoke as Jean took out Williams' car for a few laps.

'It's like "break a leg" in the theatre. We don't mean it. Anyway, your husband is a fine driver. I suspect he doesn't need luck.'

'That might be true. But he isn't my husband.'

'Really?' he said with feigned surprise. 'I would do something about that. Or he should.'

Williams returned, wiping his face with a cloth. He held out a hand belatedly to Robert, who took it. 'I was just saying, you're not bad for a chauff . . .' He stopped himself. Time to drop that. 'Actually, not bad for anyone.'

'Bugatti says he'll build another Thirty-five C. So there's two places. One each if we want it.'

Robert threw back his head and laughed. 'Wonderful. I bet the old rogue had two places all along. I was also just saying, Williams, you should marry this woman quick, before someone else does. And I have the perfect wedding present.'

He walked over to 'Early One Morning' and yanked off the covering, leaving Eve's flesh tones glowing in the sunlight. Robert looked at the representation, the subject and finally at Williams before saying quietly, 'She's all yours.'

Ten

FRANCE, SEPTEMBER 1929

It nagged at Williams every time he saw the painting. 'Early One Morning' hung at the head of the stairs in the Normandy watermill, and, like any everyday fixture, he quickly became habituated to it. Every so often, however, maybe once a day, he saw it afresh, and felt that grip round his heart when he realised that the beauty lying naked on the rumpled sheets was his. All his.

It was at that point he wondered why the man had done it.

They were at Bricktop's in Montmartre when he finally got around to asking him. He and Robert had spent the weekend at Molsheim testing new cars, all business-like and professional, so it hadn't been the place. On the Monday Williams stopped over in Paris en route to Eve, and after a dinner at Paquin's and drinks at Le Grand Duc they had crossed over to the hole in the wall where Bricktop, the red-haired hostess, had kissed Robert on both cheeks and ushered them to a corner table, jammed between the bandstand and a coterie of Americans.

They ordered brandy and Robert frowned at the clarinettist on the stage, playing a breathtakingly fast 'Cake-Walking Babies

From Home'. Robert wrinkled his nose. He wasn't sure about Bechet, especially the small, straight saxophone he sometimes played; he found it coarse and wailing.

When Bechet finished there was a commotion at the next table. One of the men had his wallet out and was trying to tip the player twenty dollars. His wife was trying to stop him. As usual, Bricktop refereed, gliding over and giving Bechet five, but then confiscating the wallet of the patron. 'Don't worry, Scott, I'll keep the tab running.'

The wife smiled gratefully, and the Scott character slumped down in front of his whiskey. 'Sing for us then.'

'Later, lover, later,' and she waddled off, pushing her ample frame among the tightly packed customers, schmoozing and kissing and shaking hands as she went.

Williams' head had a faint buzz to it now, and he knew he was relaxed enough to broach the subject that had been worrying him. The band, minus Bechet, had begun playing a blues.

'Robert, there is something I've been meaning to ask you.'

'Why I am such a good driver?'

'Not quite. Well, that as well.'

Robert stretched his arms expansively. 'How long have you got? I could talk about myself all night.'

'Why did you give the painting back?'

Robert narrowed his eyes and Williams felt himself sweat a little. A glare from Robert was one glare too many. 'Wedding present. Which reminds me. When are you getting married?'

'Soon. Very soon. So is that all it was?'

'Rubbish.' The voice boomed over the patrons from the bar. 'Keep the rhythm, man. You're all over the place.'

Williams looked round. It was Bechet, at the small bar at the rear of the room, verbally abusing his own band. They carried on, ignoring him.

'Horace, that is some terrible bass playing.'

Horace let the big instrument fall to the stage with a reverberating crash that shimmered around the room. From his inside pocket he produced a revolver and waved it towards his employer. 'Sidney, you dumb fucker. Just shut up. Go home.'

There were squeals as people realised exactly what he was wielding in such a cavalier fashion, and heads hit tables and arms folded over them as if they could protect them from bullets. One or two patrons slithered off their seats to sit it out on the floor.

The first shot caused a puff of masonry to bloom from the stage. It was then Williams realised that Bechet had a gun of his own. Robert reached over and gripped his arm. 'Don't move.'

'I wasn't planning to.'

The exchange lasted five seconds, a fusillade of rapid fire, booming around the confined space, rolling clouds of cordite mixing with the cigarette smoke. It ended when Bricktop took the gun from Bechet's hand and slapped him about the head with it, careful to avoid his mouth. Last thing she needed was a star with a ruined embouchure.

'Sidney, go home. Go on. Out. Horace, gimme that thing. Here. Now.'

Sheepishly the big man handed over his Gat, Sidney was packed off, it was confirmed that, miraculously, nobody had been hit and Bricktop decided it was time to sing 'Miss Otis Regrets'.

Robert let out a breath. 'They are such terrible shots. Best place to be is where they are aiming. Aaah,' he said as Bricktop launched into a smoky-voiced Cole Porter medley, 'this is more like it.'

They ordered a second round of drinks. 'So it was a wedding present?' persisted Williams. 'Nothing more to it than that?'

'I said. Yes. Why are you so interested all of sudden?'

'I'd never have given it away.'

'No, I can see that.'

'Then why did you?'

Robert gripped Williams' hand and pulled him closer. 'Two things, my friend. One, you won that race and if you ever tell anyone I said that I'll rip your tongue out.'

'I didn't. You won it.'

'It wasn't fair. Eve was right. I have raced Montlhery dozens of times. If you knew that course, knew the line, like I do . . . you'd have won.'

'And the second?'

Robert smiled, a big, warm, regretful grin. 'I realised to have that painting, to have that woman on the wall and not have the real thing to touch and feel and love . . . I realised, Will . . . that way, madness lies.'

They married the following year. Deliberately low-key, because there were those in the village who had never realised they weren't already married. Just a discreet service, a few of Eve's family and a celebratory lunch.

It turned into something of a wake. Eve had just finished organising the food when the letter arrived, informing her that Orpen had died. She cried for much of the morning, and Williams offered to cancel the day, but she decided the last thing Orpen would want was people to stop drinking and enjoying themselves on his behalf. So the wedding lunch was served in the courtyard at a long table, and the racing drivers and the dog breeders seemed to get on remarkably well once they passed the couple-of-glasses-of-wine-each mark, and it was only after the heat was starting to fade that Eve realised that she had lost her husband.

She excused herself and wandered down to the river, following the sound of heated voices until she was sure it was Williams and his cantankerous friend. She found a vantage point and, feeling just a little guilty, settled down to watch and listen for a few minutes.

'You are a very stubborn man,' said an exasperated Robert. 'I think you just lack the fire in the belly.' He pointed at his own stomach and was infuriated when Williams laughed and turned away.

Robert grabbed his arm, softening his tone. 'Don't do that. I didn't mean to insult you. Not on your wedding day.'

Williams shrugged. 'None was taken.'

'I didn't mean you are a coward. I know you are not.'

'Robert, I don't expect you to understand.' He put his hand on the other man's shoulder, a gesture Eve found oddly intimate. 'You have a wife, a mistress—'

'Two, if you don't mind.'

'A doting brother. Ettore thinks of you as his eldest son. You have the showroom, your customers . . . but it's not my life. Mine is different. I am what I am.'

'And what is that?'

'Oh God, you sound like Eve now.'

She coughed to reveal her presence and they both looked round. Williams came over, kissed her on the cheek and said, 'You try and explain to him. I need another drink.'

She walked over to Robert, his hands firmly in his pockets, jaw jutting out. 'Your husband . . .' He turned to look at her. 'Your husband makes me mad. Mad.'

'Why?'

'He wants Wimille to drive in his place at Monza. But Wimille has a benefactor, he will buy a car. We don't have to give him one.'

She had heard of Jean-Pierre Wimille, a young, phlegmatic driver who Williams reckoned had astonishing natural flair. 'Why does he want him to have the place?'

Robert blew out his cheeks. 'He says the Fifty-four we want to sell Wimille is not good enough. Will also says . . .' This was clearly the part that made Robert mad. 'That Jean-Pierre is a better driver than him.'

Eve sat down on the river bank, almost out of shock. Admitting that there might be a better racer, to these men, was tantamount to owning up to poor sexual performance. 'Is he?'

Robert knelt down next to her, his knee touching her shoulder, possibly accidentally. 'Wimille is . . . Wimille is a great driver. Or at least will be. One day. Will . . .' Robert tore a reed from the river bank and began to shred it while he marshalled his thoughts. He flung strands ineffectually towards the swans gliding regally by, who returned a stare worthy of Benoist himself.

'It is as if God gives some people this gift, to be able to control machines. Will has the best ability to read a car I know. To pinpoint what is wrong, how to fix the roadholding, the corner-ing. Wonderful. But God, being God, decides that there must be a system of checks and balances. To offset such a marvellous gift. In Will's case . . . he's lazy.'

Eve watched the sun filter through the leaves and play on the water's surface and considered this. It didn't add up. 'You think Will is lazy?'

'Not lazy as you mean it. I've seen the kennels he has built. Seen him strip down engines and gearboxes. Not physically, but here.' He tapped his temple. 'You see, he wins a race, it is enough for him. He has proved something for a while. The best of them – Nuvolari, Chiron back there, Rudi . . . maybe even I in my prime, we have to go out and do it the next day and the next and the next. Will, he comes home to his new wife and plays with his dogs.'

'You make that sound like a crime. I would say that makes him a better human being.' And, she wanted to add, a better husband, but thought Robert might take that personally.

'You are right. Except at Bugatti, we don't want human beings. Too troublesome.' He laughed. 'Will thinks too much.'

'What is Jean-Pierre's flaw?'

'Wimille? He wants two things: glory and money. Wants them so, so bad. Then again, that probably isn't a flaw in this game.'

Robert stood up and tossed the last of the reed into the water, watching it spiral away in the eddies.

'And yours, Robert? How has God cursed you?'

Robert rested a hand briefly, lightly, on her head and laughed. 'Me? I fall in love too easily.'

Eleven

LAKE SENLITZ, AUSTRIA, OCTOBER 2001

The old lady sits in a canvas chair in the marquee they have hastily re-erected next to the recovered Humber. On the wooden pallet in front of her sits the trunk, scuffed and swollen and damaged. By narrowing her eyes she can see it as it was – swish and elegant, in that hotel room near Berlin, the day she packed it.

Hovering around her and the Vuitton are Warner, his technician, a bored Austrian policeman and Deakin. Rose can sense a sort of irritable excitement in Warner. He wants to see inside the trunk as much as anyone, but dislikes the way this woman has taken control in such a matriarchal manner.

'OK, Deakin. Let's take a look.'

Deakin unclips the trunk and, with great difficulty, levers the two halves apart. As the front cracks open, a thin stream of slimy water snakes across the floor on to the pallet. The technician hovers, forceps in hand. Deakin waves him back.

She can smell the long, slow decay within. As with herself, the years have taken a toll. How much of a toll though? Deakin

90

works his fingers into the opening and pulls the two sides apart so it gapes like a razor clam.

Deakin thinks at first there is nothing but mush inside, but as he pulls the rotted fabric aside he realises it is only the top layer on each side that has emulsified, the clothes closest to the perished seal. Deakin peels off the remains of a man's suit, opening the jacket to read the label. James Pyle. It means nothing to him. He hands it to the technician who carefully places it on a trestle table.

Underneath, still shimmering after all these years, is a beaded dress, the once luminous material flat and dissolved in places, but still clearly something special.

'Odd choice for our Mr Williams. Did they have, what are they called, cross-dressers back then?' he asks her.

'It's a Molyneux,' she says tartly, as the technician lays it next to the suit and takes a photograph, the flash making her blink. 'Very expensive. Or was.'

The items start to come out thick and fast. A pair of silver-backed hairbrushes, hair oil, Lobb shoes, a Hermès belt, some women's underwear, a faded photograph album and a heavy object wrapped in greased paper. Gingerly Deakin unwraps it. A gun. A Colt .45 automatic pistol, still glistening with its sheen of protective oil. All are laid out and photographed before being labelled and bagged by the technician.

Finally one other object, right in the far corner, a piece of metal, a cylinder, maybe forty centimetres high. Deakin levers it out from its nesting place, where a film of rust has cemented it to the lining. There is no top, and poking out are the slimy remnants of bundles of money, French and English. A lot of money. Enough to want to kill someone for, he thinks. At least, back when it was worth something.

'Let me see that.'

Deakin hands over the container and Warner comes across to take a look. 'Please be careful,' he pleads.

'Of course.' She looks up at him. 'But it is mine.'

'What do you mean?' snaps Warner.

'Well, I put it in the case.'

Warner opens his mouth to speak but thinks better of it. He knows his chances of getting a straight answer from a spook – even an old spook – are pretty slim.

As she carefully wipes away at the slime with a tissue, the small group huddled around her see there is a thin, fragile paper label wrapped around the outside of the canister. A skull and cross-bones slowly emerges. And just to hammer home the point, the legend 'Danger de Mort'.

'Is it safe?' asks Deakin.

'Oh yes. Emptied a long, long time ago. May I have a cloth?'

The technician obliges and carefully she scrubs away the final blobs of mud, revealing the stencilled details of the contents, the name of the producer and place of manufacture. She feels gratified at her little piece of theatre when she hears the collective intake of breath. They all know what it means. Still shocking after all these years. Good.

Rose hands the canister to a technician who holds it as if it is a bomb. Which it is. 'Can you clean that up and preserve it for me? So the label remains legible? There are some chaps I want to show it to.'

'Of course.' The man gets to work with chemical sprays and preservatives.

'Bloody hell—' starts Warner, but Rose raises a hand to silence him.

'Help me up will you, Deakin?' she asks. 'I need to take another look at the car.'

Deakin assists her out of the chair and they shuffle, slowly, out of the marquee and into the darkening afternoon light of Senlitz. Clouds are gathering over the mountains, and they seem to have taken on the black, threatening hue of the water.

Rose lets Deakin guide her round the ruined vehicle, and she squints in the windows, shaking her head. Finally, at the rear of the car, she asks him to open the boot once more and peers inside, holding her breath against the acrid smell of rapid, oxygen-driven decomposition.

She points a bony finger at a leather loop on the rear bulkhead.

'Pull that down for me will you, Deakin?'

He reaches in and tugs. The handle snaps and comes away in his hand. Rose raises an eyebrow, a silent instruction to continue. He traces the edge of the thick cardboard partition until he finds some leverage and tugs.

Deakin can't help it, he screams, or at least something halfway between a scream and a gasp emerges.

The body, trapped in the compartment for all these years, away from aquatic scavengers, has remained remarkably intact, so he can still see that it is, or was, a woman. The skin has mummified, stretched and wrinkled over the underlying bone, and there is still a mess of dirty blond hair attached to the skull. Slowly it topples over and hits the floor of the boot with a thump, sending up a sickly shower of ancient flesh particles.

'Fuck,' says Deakin quietly.

Rose, playing nervously with the elaborate watch on her wrist, nods and says, almost to herself, 'You know, I always wondered what became of her.'

Twelve

FRANCE, FEBRUARY 1937

Eve is dreaming, remembering in lurid details how they had made her husband so unhappy, so very unhappy. After all he had done for them. In reality they had been at Maxim's when it happened, but in the dream they are in a cellar, a cellar lit only by red lights that give everyone a devilish glow. Maurice is telling a convoluted joke about Satan and sex, when Robert enters, his eyes dark coals.

He orders a couple of Pernods and gives one to Williams, almost forcing him to gulp at it.

'Will. I have spoken to Ettore. He says yes. Le Mans. We can have two Tanks.'

Williams beams and Eve feels for him. The Tanks, the Type 57, are big beautiful alloy-clad racers, like something from the movie Things To Come *or* Metropolis, *which Williams has spent hours making super-reliable for an assault on the 24-hour race.*

It is at this point Robert's voice becomes oddly metallic, inhuman, as if a speaking weight machine were saying the lines.

'Ettore appreciates what you have done, Will. Without your breaking the endurance record at Montlhery, he wouldn't consider this . . .'

Williams seems to shrink, his voice growing smaller. 'But?'

'But France needs a victory. Badly. If you were to win, it would be an English victory . . .'

'In a Bugatti? Surely it's the car, not the driver. At least, that's what Ettore's always said to me.'

Robert takes a deep breath. 'He wants me to drive with Wimille.'

Williams nods, knowing that by championing Wimille he has been the instrument of his own downfall. 'And the second Tank?'

'Veyron and Labric.' Two more Frenchmen.

Williams blinks hard, downs the Pernod and leaves, squeezing Robert on the shoulder as he goes. Robert looks across at Eve and shrugs, unhappiness written across his entire face.

'How could you do this to your friend?' Eve screams at him and runs out after her husband, but the wet glistening streets are empty, just a few wraith-like wisps of smoke left hanging in the air.

Eve felt something move lightly through her hair, tickling her scalp and sat up, fearing a mouse. She squealed when the creature ran down the side of her face. Williams stepped back. 'Sorry. I frightened you. You were asleep.'

Eve looked around, momentarily disoriented. She was at the kitchen table, and had been lying with her head in her arms. The dogs lay in the dark corner, panting, having given up on supper.

'God. I was dreaming . . .'

'What about?'

'About how you should have raced at Le Mans.'

He shrugged. He was past caring now. The team had won, a French victory when the Germans were taking everything else in sight. Eve shook her head to try to clear the image of that cellar. 'What time is it?'

'Ten.'

She stretched, trying to shake off the heavy weariness of sleep.

'I thought you weren't back till tomorrow.'

'We have a customer in England. Interested in an Atlantic. I'm taking one over.' The Atlantic was Jean's astonishing sleek coupé, very low, very fast with a strange fin riveted down the back, giving it the air of some super hero's pursuit vehicle than a road-going motor. 'Coffee?'

She nodded. 'Are you going?'

'We also have an invitation to run a couple of Jean's 4.7s at Beddington.'

'Where's that?'

'Hampshire. Invitation only. They have asked Rudi and Mercedes. Stuck and Auto Union. There's appearance money. One hundred and fifty pounds a driver. Plus two hundred for the winner. Ettore says he will cover the rest of the costs.'

The last sentence faded and she smiled as she wondered if this was Bugatti's little consolation prize for depriving her husband of Le Mans glory.

'What's funny?'

'Nothing. Do you want to go?'

'To race against Rudi again? Maybe Nuvolari? Yes. Would you come?'

Eve could see the fire burning in his eyes once more, the need for the chance to feel adrenaline pump through his veins. The moronic English quarantine laws would mean she couldn't take even one of her dogs. But she could see this meant a lot to him. She nodded and he kissed her forehead.

'Beddington it is, then.'

Thirteen

BEDDINGTON, ENGLAND, 1937

The September sun bounced off the fields of wheat stubble and haystacks, bathing the English countryside in a comforting, golden glow. Eve shifted in her seat as Maurice contemplated his cards and let her eyes wander down the vista the way the designer intended, taking in the lake and its faux-Roman temple and the water gardens beyond, ending at the dark copse before the farmlands began.

Behind her was Beddington House, a grand eighteenth-century Palladian villa, trying hard to keep its dignity with a fan of rude racing cars parked on its lawns – the usual Alfas, ERAS, Rileys, Delahayes, MGs, Talbots, Maseratis and, right next to where she sat at the folding table with Maurice, a brace of gleaming new Bugattis.

To one side of the house a group of drivers and mechanics, including Robert and Williams, were playing football on a makeshift pitch. The pair of them were running that bit harder to keep up with the younger men, and she hoped they remembered they had a gruelling set of pre-race trials the following day before

97

the race proper in the afternoon.

The innocuous new asphalt road to her right snaked around the house and, out of sight, connected to the racetrack the Duke had carved out of the glorious landscape at the rear of his house, across the gardens, through the forest, round the deer park, into the field he had rented from a neighbouring farmer and back again. For three miles, 125 yards, it twisted and rolled around a slumbering English countryside unaware of the kind of mechanical mayhem about to be inflicted on it.

The course bristled with hastily constructed stands, a press box, a commentary platform, feeding into a speaker system the engineers were struggling to perfect, hence the occasional howl of feedback or a hideously distorted voice drifting over the mansards of Beddington House. Now and then they heard a bark of German. The radio station Deutschlander was due to send back bulletins of the race to the home country.

Tomorrow the crowds would start to arrive, perhaps up to thirty thousand, drawn by the carrot of seeing the new Mercedes and Auto Union Silver Arrows, scourge of the continental raceways, at work on a field of English and French rivals. They would pay their 4 shillings (children 2/6, parking 2.0s). The *Light Car*, the *Sporting Life*, *Motor Sport* and the *Autocar* correspondents – including the famous 'Grand Vitesse' – were already here, sitting in deckchairs with owners and competitors, sipping Pimms served by the white-gloved staff and waiting for the bulk of the Germans to arrive.

There were whispers, of course, that the Germans weren't coming. There were rumbles about an annexation of Austria, Sudetenland and Leipzig and ever since Hitler marched into the Rhineland unopposed, the mood in Britain had been jittery. The possibility of war was even mentioned at the wonderful RAC club on Pall Mall, where they had had dinner before travelling to Beddington.

Eve heard a strange giggle and looked up to see two young, freckle-faced mechanics sneaking away from the rear of Williams' Bugatti. She stood up and moved around to see what they had done. An L plate had been taped to the elegant rear of the car. She plucked it off, bringing a flake of blue paint with it and cursed. Some distance away the two young Englishmen guffawed at their prank.

She tore the sign into a dozen pieces and threw it on to the Duke's already ruined lawn.

'I hate this country,' she said to Maurice, 'if they're not snobs they're imbeciles.'

'Or both,' he said as he grabbed a passing Pimms and sipped. 'At last. A drink that doesn't taste as if it came straight from a tradesman's bladder.'

Encouraged, she took one from the tray just as the sound of a high-powered sports car bounced through the trees lining the driveway and off the Portland stone of the house. 'Ah. Here comes Rudi and the stiff arm brigade,' said Maurice.

The little Mercedes roadster swept on to the gravel path then bumped its way over the grass to stop near them. At the wheel, as Maurice had correctly identified, Rudi. Beside him was a uniformed officer of some description.

Rudi beamed when he saw them and climbed out. He was wearing a canvas jacket over white overalls, as if he expected to leap straight into a car and start competing. 'Eve. How nice to see you. Maurice.' He pointed at the rather stiff, correct figure hovering behind. 'May I introduce Assistant Sportskorpsführer Keppler.'

Keppler gave the soft, half-hearted version of the Heil Hitler salute, bending his elbow and nodding his head.

Maurice sniffed. 'What's an Assistant Sportskorpsführer?'

Keppler stepped forward and smiled. He was not a handsome man, his face slightly puffy and the eyes too small, but there was a liveliness about it that was somehow engaging. 'I am the person who makes sure you all lose.'

Eve laughed and Keppler beamed and went off to look at the rival cars, walking around the Bugattis with his hands clasped behind his back.

'Where's Baby?' asked Eve. Rudi's wife Alice, whom everyone called by her nickname, was famed as the best timekeeper in Europe, a devil on the twin chronometers. He rarely travelled without her.

'Switzerland.' He lowered his voice. 'House hunting.'

Eve raised an eyebrow.

'Just in case.'

'How is racing for Adolf?'

He unzipped his jacket and showed her the swastika on his breast pocket as if it were some kind of festering wound. 'They've made me a Sturmführer now.' He pulled a face but wiped the expression when he realised Keppler was coming back.

'Do these have the new rear axles?' Keppler asked authoritatively.

Eve and Maurice looked at each and shrugged. 'You need to speak to a driver or mechanic,' said Maurice. 'We're just along for the ride.'

All looked over when they heard the hiss of air brakes and a huge silver truck edged its way in through the stone gates, its sides centimetres from the twin pillars and metalwork. 'Ah,' said Keppler. 'The first of the trucks,' and strode over to direct the great lorry.

Eve looked quizzically at Rudi. 'How does he know about Jean's new axles?'

'There's a spy at Molsheim,' replied Rudi flatly.

'What? Are you serious?'

'There's a spy at every race works across Europe. And some in America.' He smiled at Maurice. 'In answer to your question, that's what an Assistant Sportskorpsführer does.'

Keppler stood proudly on the lawn, hands on hips, and waved the truck to his side. The cab doors opened and out jumped a stream of tall, handsome lads, all in steel grey overalls, who began to prepare the reception area.

'The pits are round there,' said Eve to Rudi, pointing along the slip road.

'I know. But Mercedes always has a second pits, away from prying eyes.'

Eve could see the football game was forgotten, and Robert, Williams and the others were drifting over to witness the spectacle. As the transporter ropes were untied, cords pulled and from the top of the truck a massive banner unfurled, proudly displaying the German eagle.

'My God,' said Williams when he reached Eve's side. 'What is this?'

Rudi turned and offered his hand and Williams pumped it. 'This,' said Rudi slowly, 'is the future of motor sport.'

Robert snorted. 'Well they can count me out.'

Rudi laughed. 'They intend to,' he said.

The Mercedes mechanics had produced a floor area made of strips of articulated aluminium and unrolled it. Tubular steel barriers were erected. Two ramps emerged from the rear of the trucks and down them came a covered shape, the green tarpaulin masking the outlines of some sleek, silver machine. The car was wheeled on to the metal flooring and the cover whisked back.

The W126 Mercedes seemed to suck up the rays of the English sun and fling them back defiantly. It was all riveted alloy,

101

fluted air intakes, wire wheels, a race car stripped to bare
aerodynamic essentials, a perfect synergy of form and function.
And the function was to win. The swastika on the tail told whom
that victory would serve.

As the German mechanics began fuelling, using pumps and
pressure hoses, Williams sniffed. There was a strange, sweet
aroma, not the usual benzol smell, drifting over. 'Christ, Rudi,
what does she run on?'

'State secret.'

'Probably Hitler's piss,' suggested Maurice.

'Sshh,' said Rudi nervously.

'Why are they fuelling her? You're not taking her out?'

'The Auto Unions are three hours behind. They got held up at
Dover. There was no crude oil for their trucks.' That meant
Rudi's great rival Bernd Rosemeyer would be late arriving, too.
'It'll be dark when they get here. So I can get a couple of trial laps
in.'

Rudi walked over, inspected the car and climbed in. Before he
put his helmet on he fiddled with something at each side of his
head. Rudi then signalled one of the mechanics who sprinted
forward with a small trolley and plugged a metal cylinder into the
side of the Mercedes. Robert and Williams glanced at each other
knowingly. No hand cranking. Electric start.

The first roar of the exhaust seemed to shake the very earth.
Now Williams knew what Rudi had been doing prior to putting
his helmet on. Ear plugs. The exhaust note was a deep, low
thrum, a thudding, chest-wobbling boom that powered up to an
agonising scream as Rudi pressed the throttle and the superchargers pushed air through the carburettors.

The strange odour of the secret fuel drifted across the grounds
of the house, and Rudi slowly took the car down the slip road
towards the track, blipping the throttle. Like the children of

Hamelin they all followed, mesmerised, half running, but too late, he was a disappearing speck by the time they reached the circuit proper. They could hear him, though, the angry note of the engine softening and rising again with each gear change, Rudi working hard through the box. He had what the Germans called *Fingerspitzgefuhl* – instinctive feel – and it sounded as if the car was responding to his thoughts.

In an astonishingly short time he reappeared, drifting the back end and correcting out of the hairpin, before aligning himself for the long run up the straight. Williams checked his watch. 'Two minutes fifteen,' he said, calculating that meant a lap time of over 80 mph – incredible on such a winding course.

'I had two eleven,' said Robert.

'Christ.' Williams ran a hand through his hair. 'What time is the next boat back?'

Fourteen

PARIS, AUGUST 1939

For Eve's birthday they went to La Pagode, the Japanese cinema and tea house on rue Babylone, and watched *Angels with Dirty Faces*, which made Eve sob, although Robert thought the noble ending a cop out. Afterwards the Gaumont-Pathé newsreel came on of goose-stepping German soldiers and Robert said loudly: 'Look at them. The pricks.'

A patron behind him hissed at him to be quiet and that he only wished France's army looked like that. 'Shut up,' snarled Robert, 'or I'll knock you down and piss in your ear.'

Afterwards they went for drinks at Drouand's near l'Opera, although Maurice, disliking the smug crowd the fashionable restaurant attracted, was keen to head off to the Sphinx. However, Robert protested that it was Eve's birthday and a brothel was perhaps the most appropriate of venues. Eve wasn't sure whether she was disappointed or not, as she had seen the magazine advertisements for the Egyptian splendours of the place and was curious.

Once settled, wine and brandies before them, they sat in

silence for a while, lost in their own thoughts. Eve scanned the room, looking for famous faces. Charles Lindbergh was there, with his wife Anne, no doubt back from another tour of Germany and telling anyone who'd listen about its wonderful Air Force.

'What if it is war?' asked Maurice finally, swirling the wine in his glass. 'You think the Maginot line will hold?'

Robert shook his head. Robert was sick of talk of defences, politics, was disgusted by the funeral of Rosemeyer, killed trying to break the Autobahn speed record for the Führer, which was choreographed as if he had been a war hero. He indicated Lindbergh. 'That man got one thing right. You saw what happened in Spain. They'll fly right over it.'

'What will you do?' asked Eve. 'If we fight?'

'Me?' asked Robert, as if the idea had never occurred to him. 'Grab some Chablis, head down to Menton and wait until it blows over.' He lit a cigarette and gave a thin smile. 'Or see if my old squadron will have me back. What about you, Will?'

'England. Enlist.' Firm and unwavering. 'The French don't have a war leader.'

'And England does?' sneered Maurice.

'The British are absolutely awful at having a good time.' He could see Eve nodding enthusiastically. 'Give them hard times, misery, give them war . . . they'll rise to the occasion. You want to fight a war? Over there is where you have to be.'

Despite the implied slur on his country, Robert nodded approvingly. He was beginning to feel a line had to be drawn, even though he was sure that Williams' mother country was behaving as perfidiously as always, manoeuvring to save its own neck while using France, Belgium and the others as a shield. 'Eve?'

Williams, mistaking the direction of the question, said forcefully, 'She'll come with me.'

105

He didn't catch the small, quick, rebellious wink she flashed at Robert.

Jean-Pierre Wimille spent 3 September 1939 getting slowly, inexorably drunk. It was the day he should have raced the Tank at La Baule. He had, however, declined to test the car and let Jean Bugatti do it. Late at night, on roads he thought empty, Jean had swerved to avoid a cyclist and was killed. Wimille's stubborn indolence had cost the brilliant young man his life. And, he knew, Ettore's. The old man would never recover from the blow.

Eve spent it at the desk in the bedroom, composing a long letter to the shocked and fragile Bugattis, trying to piece together some consoling thoughts, but mostly failing.

Robert was with his mistress in Nantes, a woman who adored having a sporting hero as a lover, but who at the same time demanded material proof of his devotion. He had travelled to deliver a gold cigarette lighter.

Williams worked at Avenue Montaigne, covering for Robert's absence, and although buying was the last thing on people's minds, cars were coming in and out of stock, some being shipped out of the country, others being mothballed until the political temperature fell once more.

Maurice nursed a hangover. The previous night he had spent carousing with friends around rue Blondel near Les Halles marketplace, a model of French inefficiency and bureaucracy, where goods imported from the regions were sold, and then often transported back to the very same district at hugely inflated prices. At night, filled with the calvados-breathing workers in blue salopettes manhandling vast mounds of fruit and vegetables, the Baltard ironwork of the great sheds glowing from the flames of burning crates, the streets around the metal parasols were filled with the kind of sexually licentious establishments that the bourgeois liked to dip a well-scrubbed toe in after the opera or theatre. During the course of a lesbian tableaux in a grubby bar, Maurice had made some excellent contacts in the market trade.

That day, hangover notwithstanding, over cervelat sausages at Balzar, Maurice negotiated to buy a small candle-making business. He also met with some of his friends who ran a small butcher's. Light and food, he believed, might be two important commodities soon. In the evening he began negotiations with a coat manufacturer and a coal merchant. Warmth, that would be much sought after, too.

Elsewhere, other, more important, people put the wheels of purgatory into slow, grinding, bone-breaking motion. Britain, and then France, declared reluctant war on the country already pounding Poland into submission.

Across in England, over a drink at Jules Bar in Jermyn Street, a friend of Rose Miller's mother asked if she would like to pursue some interesting work for her country.

Fifteen

FRANCE, SEPTEMBER 1939–JUNE 1940

Like waiting for test results you know will reveal a terminal
disease, the confession of an unfaithful partner, the death of a
loved relative, the announcement of war at least came with the
blessing of certainty after four years of stomach-churning vertigo
as France stared over the abyss and somehow did not fall. Now it
had, headlong, and they were all waiting for the impact.

Williams came back from the Bugatti HQ in Paris on the fifth
of September; he and Eve clung to each other for the longest
time, snuggling and pressing as if trying to fuse into a single
organism, as scared as either could ever remember.

That night he cooked a huge slab of lamb, which they
devoured hungrily with a bottle of red Loire wine, each speaking
in mundanities until they went outside to the dying day and, as
twilight faded and the first stars appeared, spoke softly in the
darkness, sitting under the big tree at the edge of the garden.

'You meant what you said that time. About returning to
England?'

Williams lit them a cigarette each. 'I have no alternative.'

A snort. 'How is Paris?'

'The theatres have closed. Cafés are busy trying to put up black-out curtains. The Louvre is being emptied. Everything shipped into storage. They've killed all the poisonous reptiles in the zoo. Nervous.'

'I can't go with you.'

'Communists are being hounded. As allies of Hitler.'

'Did you hear what I said?'

'There will be rationing I expect. To conserve stocks.'

'I can't go to England with you, Will.'

'Sirens go off so often everybody ignores them. One day they'll be for real and the entire population will be out on the streets.'

'Stay here.'

Williams turned and faced her, waiting for his eyes to adjust fully to the darkness so he could see her face clearly. There was moisture glistening in one eye. Maybe he was only worth a half-cry. She blinked and now both sparkled wetly. 'I can't. I'll be arrested. Interned.'

'You are assuming we are going to lose. Maurice says—'

'Maurice?'

'Maurice says with the British we can hold them.'

'Come with me.'

'I can't. My parents. My dogs.'

'We'll take your parents.'

'Father is too ill to uproot.'

'You don't want to go, do you?'

She hesitated, wondering whether to fudge the truth. In the end she blurted out: 'To England? No. You'll go off and fight and I'll be left alone again, just like when you were racing.'

'You'll be free.'

'Better a prisoner in France than free in England.'

'That's insane.'

Eve touched his shoulder. 'Is it? I have friends I can turn to here. Family. Over there? We could hide in France. It's a big country.'

Williams stood up. 'I thought about that. Every option. The thing is, we'd have to live with ourselves afterwards.'

'I'd manage.'

Williams flung his cigarette butt off into the darkness, watched it flare briefly as it bounced along the gravel in the courtyard. He thought about sitting and waiting, perhaps hiding for weeks, months, years while other men fought the war, the just war. It reminded him of those long hours in the pits at Le Mans while others drove the Tanks out on the circuit, itching to be behind the wheel himself. 'I don't think I could.' He pulled Eve to her feet, lifted the hair away from her face and kissed her, feeling the salt of her tears run into his mouth as he did so.

'You're really going?' Robert asked. 'Definitely?'

They were in the comfortingly ornate Ritz bar, where the very prospect of war, invasion or bombing seemed absolutely absurd. In fact, in this part of Paris it was being treated as, at worst, an inconvenience – as they passed the fashion shops around Place Vendôme they had laughed at the mannequins sporting gas masks, chicly tied with coloured bows rather than ugly coiffure-threatening straps.

Williams nodded.

'And Eve still isn't?'

Hammering started from the corner and they both looked around, irritated at the intrusion. 'Black-out curtains,' explained the barman. So it was even creeping into these hallowed halls after all.

'I think,' continued Williams, 'I have exhausted everything short of kidnapping.'

Robert raised an eyebrow. 'Well . . .'

'No. Thanks all the same. What about you?'

'Huh. The Air Ministry . . . you wouldn't believe men can be so foolish, Will.' Robert took a drink of his whisky, pausing to gather his thoughts. 'You know, I was always so jealous of you.'

'Me? Jealous of me?'

'That you had Eve. That you had such skill. That you did it on your own. A chauffeur. That you didn't need it the way I did. You had a real life . . . you always reminded me that there was another way. I could never quite reach it.'

Embarrassed, Williams snorted derisively. 'Listen, perhaps some of that is true. How do you think I felt? You were the great Robert Benoist. Just to be on the same team . . . don't get me started. Grown men shouldn't cry at the Ritz.'

He laughed. 'Well, the great Robert Benoist wants to say this. He will miss you.' He kissed Williams noisily on both cheeks. 'Now fuck off.'

Williams and Eve didn't say much at the station. Every argument had been rehearsed, every weakness probed, every possibility exhausted, but two intractable people found no compromise. She had bought him, and carefully packed, a new Louis Vuitton trunk, as if to say 'no hard feelings'. If only that were true.

The whistle blew, there were frantic goodbyes along the platform as the passengers squeezed on to the crowded train. He kissed her, a quick, glancing one this time, as if anything longer would be unbearable.

'I have to go.'

'I know.' But the voice said she didn't. They were jostled by fellow travellers, eager to be away, as if Hitler was already knocking at the door. Another whistle. Williams stepped down from the train.

111

'I won't go.'

She felt her heart lift, lost in that one moment, knowing she had him back. Then her mind quickly spooled ahead, to a pacing, angry Williams, his opportunity lost, the slow corrosion of waiting and inactivity eating into him. She spoke words that were heavy and slow to come. 'I think you must. It's too late to stop now.'

He nodded, knowing that she had seen through the gesture for what it was. The train shunted forward a few centimetres and hissed impatiently. 'I'll miss you,' he said. It didn't seem enough, somehow.

'You better had.'

Williams stepped on to the train, reached out and brushed a blonde strand from her face. The locomotive jerked once more and his hand was snatched away. She began to walk slowly alongside, trying to hold back the tears that were stinging the corners of her eyes, as he leant forward to touch her cheek once more.

'Look after Robert. He's down at the Air Ministry every day demanding a new commission. At his age.'

She stopped, smiled and raised a hand as the train took her man away, heading west with gathering speed, its carriage windows framing a flashing cavalcade of relief, anguish, despair and hope. As the guard's van creaked by her, she said quietly to herself: 'And who's going to look after me?'

As she quickly turned and strode back towards the platform entrance the familiar intense stare came back at her and she froze. Robert.

'I thought you might need some company,' he shouted over the bobbing heads.

Eve managed a grateful grin she tried to invest with at least a simulacrum of happiness. As she walked up his arm came out and she slid hers through his and wondered what was going to happen now.

JUNE, 1940

Robert came back to the workshops and showroom on Avenue Montaigne to change. It was deserted as he expected. The mechanics had been taken by the *mobilisation generale*, the secretaries to the exodus, and the customers to other countries. In his office he stripped off his Air Force uniform in disgust and threw it into the waste. He had spent days badgering officers to be allowed to fly sorties, to support the troops, but confusion overwhelmed everything. Planes that could be harassing German troops and convoys stood on the Tarmac, idle.

Finally, as the Germans came closer, Robert had asked permission to take the planes back to a safe field to continue the fight. Permission refused. He attempted to take one anyway and was threatened at gunpoint. That was when he realised it was futile. France wasn't going to fight after all, not as a cohesive force.

Changed into civilian clothes, he locked up the premises and began to walk north towards the Champs Elysées but hesitated. He couldn't stand to see the great street humbled by the ugly steel barriers strung across it to prevent German gliders landing.

Robert turned and headed south down the Avenue Montaigne, past two gendarmes, rifles slung over their backs, looking nervous and jittery, scanning him for signs of subversion, as if he might have a hammer and sickle tattooed about his person.

The pavements were gritty beneath his feet, the last of the sand that had been dumped outside each apartment, waiting for the concierges to carry it to the roof as protection against bomb blasts. Only someone who didn't live in Paris could have come up with that plan, he thought. The concierges refused to a woman and a man to undertake such a menial task. The sand was left to be dispersed by the few children left in the city and pissed in by the packs of abandoned cats that now roamed the streets.

Posters everywhere proclaimed the city's fate; those torn down in disgust stirred lazily in the breeze.

Notice

To Residents of Paris

Paris having been declared an OPEN CITY, the military Governor urges the population to abstain from all hostile acts and counts on it to maintain the composure and dignity required by these circumstances.

The Governor General of Paris

Dentz.

How, wondered Robert, can you maintain dignity and composure when your trousers are round your ankles and your arse is stuck in the air, just waiting for the German army to shaft you? He cut through to the Avenue George V and, round the corner from the Crazy Horse, found a café open. The walnut-faced proprietress glared at him when he asked for a cognac with his coffee and pointed at the sign. No alcohol, Tuesday, Thursday and Saturday.

'Aren't you Robert Benoist?' she asked.

He nodded. It was amazing people still remembered him, two years after his last, twilight victory at Le Mans.

'Why aren't you off in England with your rich Jewish friends?'

He paid for the drink without it touching his lips and crossed the river. As he traversed the Alma bridge he could see clumps of black smoke hugging the river and taste the vile chemicals in the air. The sun suddenly became as hazy as the Paris streetlamps in their blackout veils, its light and warmth turned down several

notches. It was true, then. Someone had torched the oil tanks at
St Cloud.

A lone plane flew overhead and the few people on the bridge
ducked under the parapet but Robert could see it was just a 108.
A spotter plane.

It banked over the Île de la Cité and headed north. Robert
guessed it was flying up the rue Sebastopol against the stream of
the second river Paris had suddenly acquired, the one of people,
flowing like thick molasses, coming in at the North and East
gates, moving down Sebastopol and St Michel, exiting the city at
Orleans and Italie. Cars, motorbikes, carts, bicycles, horses, all
crawling at the same achingly slow speed, driven on by fear and
desperation.

As he reached the Left Bank of the river, there were perhaps a
dozen others in view, a few strolling, like him, most grim faced,
hurrying about their business. A city of five million had suddenly
become a semi-ghost town, with perhaps 750,000 people left:
those too old, young or, like him, stubborn to move. His wife and
children were safe out in one of the Rothschild houses – those
rich Jews the café owner talked about had made sure friends were
well provided for. Maurice was still here, busier than ever, Eve
had decamped to Normandy and her dogs and he still saw
Wimille now and then, grumbling about how the war had struck
just as he was finding the best form of his life. Which was, he had
to admit, tragically true.

Some of the gutters were inky black from the millions of
singed fragments of the government papers burned by the minis-
tries on the nearby Quai d'Orsay. Now a light soot began to fall,
speckling the pavement and Robert could feel the lining of his
lungs burning as noxious chemicals attacked the tissues. The fuel
depots were blazing, bleeding their filth into the city's sky.

He looked around, wondering if the Metro was working then,

115

like an apparition came that rarest of mythical beasts, a cab. He ordered the phlegmatic driver to take him to the Dome, where the sight of Peggy Guggenheim sipping champagne convinced him he could get his cognac. The heavy black-out drapes were pulled back, but the terrace was emptying as the air became more sulphurous. Robert went inside, sat down, gave his order and listened to the radio, where the constant repetitions of the glutinous song 'J'attendrai' were interrupted by gloomy pronouncements on travel restrictions and exhortations to stay put.

Maurice, looking flushed and happy, sat down in front of him. With his pastel-coloured jacket and boater he looked like a boulevardier, in strangely gay dress for a city descending into twilight. 'Brother. I thought I'd find you eventually.'

There was a dark spot on Maurice's sleeve, Robert rubbed his fingers on it and sniffed. Gasoline. 'What have you been doing, Maurice?'

His brother looked around and from his pocket produced a handkerchief, which he slowly unwrapped. Robert caught a glimpse of brilliant colours dancing before the treasure was quickly returned to safety. 'For ten litres of petrol. The things I was offered.' He smirked. 'Including a real marquise.' A decree published in *Le Matin* had forbidden the removal from French soil of gold, platinum, silver and finished jewellery. Those heading for Portugal, Spain and Switzerland were happy to divest themselves of valuables if it meant fuel or food.

Seeing Robert's look of disapproval he changed tack. 'Who betrayed us, Robert?'

'We betrayed ourselves.'

The 108 came back, low, the engine noise thrumming percussively down the boulevard. 'Where are the English fighters?' asked Maurice.

'In England,' said Robert. 'Along with the British troops.'

'And precious few French ones.' Maurice had been assured that the British troops were given loading preference at Dunkirk, an action which simply confirmed his view that their so-called ally cared little for anything but the fate of Albion. The English will fight to the last Frenchman, was the widely held view with which he concurred. 'I suppose Williams won't be coming back now.'

Robert shook his head. 'No, even Will isn't that big a fool.'

He thought of Eve, alone, out in Normandy and tried to stop his mind wandering any further.

Sixteen

SCOTLAND, OCTOBER 1940

'Where do you think you are going with that, m'lad?'

The sergeant major loomed over Williams, almost blotting out the entrance to the Bridge End Hotel. He was tired now, and didn't need any more army games. It had taken two and a half days of riding overcrowded, delayed and misrouted trains to get up here to Kinross, and his temper was fraying dangerously.

He had been in the army for eight months, and he had hoped that Scotland would be a change for the better after the grinding, depressing uncertainty of London. They had acted as if he were an octogenarian when he had volunteered his services. After weekly, daily, then hourly appearances at the Strand recruiting office, they had found him a position in the RASC, running errands, ferrying officers, not what he had in mind at all. He was driving, at least. It kept his mind off Eve, kept away those cramping pains in his stomach, the feeling of nausea, the hideous realisation of what he had done now France had fallen.

He welcomed the transfer to the clean air and promised good, simple food of rural Scotland, and tried not to dwell on the fact it was taking him further than ever away from his wife.

'With what, Sergeant Major?'

'That.'

Williams didn't have to look. He had already received ribbing and reprimands about the fact he preferred his Vuitton trunk to the standard kit bag. If he'd been shipping overseas, then maybe he'd have acquiesced, but shuttling around the British Isles, the trunk-on-wheels served just as well. He didn't see what the fuss was about.

'It's my case.'

'Is it? And what do you think this is?' He nodded at the large, grey stone building behind him. 'The Ritz?'

It isn't the Ritz, he wanted to say, I know the Ritz. This is just some large dull provincial hotel taken over by 4th Liaison RASC and where he would be billeted in the basement while the general he was to ferry around would no doubt be swanning around in the Chairman's suite. He knew he was already two sentences beyond where Robert would have hit the uppity bastard. His snapping point was always a little further on, but it was coming up fast. He was tired. He wanted a drink. Not this idiot.

Both opened their mouths to speak at once and nothing came out but a honking sound. They both turned to stare at the source of the horn, a sleek Humber staff car that drew up a few yards away. Out stepped a brunette, in a uniform Williams didn't recognise right off, with an RAF flying jacket over the top. She walked slowly round the car, looked over at the pair of them, waiting for the salute they gave and she returned.

'Trouble, Sergeant Major?'

'This man has non-regulation kit, ma'am.'

He felt the eyes rake him. 'The sergeant major's right, you know. I don't think it's going to be a Louis Vuitton kind of war.'

119

'What sort of war did you have in mind, ma'am?'

'Corporal Williams?'

The question threw him and he could see the sergeant major frowning. How did she know who he was? Mind you, the phrase, 'can't miss him, only man fool enough to wheel around a LV trunk' might explain it. 'Yes, ma'am.'

'That's what I'd like to talk to you about.'

'Mind if I get rid of this first, ma'am?'

She inclined her head at the bolshie sergeant major who sighed and stepped aside. 'There's a pub down by the river. Four hundred yards. Shall we say half an hour?'

The warm beer tasted suspiciously thin, but Williams drank a whole pint of it before she arrived at his table in the small garden out the back with the fast-flowing river gurgling by at the end of the slope. The northern sun soon heated him up in his thick, coarse woollen uniform, and he was relaxing, almost forgetting the summons, when she slipped into the seat unheralded, gin and tonic in hand.

'Don't get up, Williams,' she said quickly. 'We won't be disturbed. I've requisitioned the garden for the war effort.'

'I didn't catch your name, ma'am.'

'No you didn't, did you?' She smiled and it transformed her face into something altogether more soft and friendly. Then it went, flicked off. What was she? Twenty-five? Six? Yet there was a hardness about her, possibly just a defensive carapace, although all of them were in the process of developing that. Her accent was top drawer, arrogant, yes, snobbish, certainly, used to being obeyed and served, but there was something else, too. The Sergeant Major, he knew, had felt it as well. An extra dose of self confidence, the assurance that comes with knowing you have absolute power on your side. 'Captain Rose Miller.'

Which outfit? He wanted to ask, but something told him he shouldn't.

Eventually she said, 'I'm with the Inter-services Research Bureau. Tell me, have you been out of France long?'

'Nine . . . no, close to eleven months.'

'Miss it?'

He nodded, thinking of the difference between London and Paris. 'Not too bad. Only every day.'

'I have had a word with your General. He was rather looking forward to having a race driver as his chauffeur.'

'Was? Or is?'

'I suggested to him you were rather overqualified.'

Williams didn't like this. Didn't like people who suddenly seemed to know an awful lot about him. Like the chap in Ireland all those years ago, he'd had the same air of authority. He began to feel uneasy, and as if reading his mind she said, 'Why didn't you contact your old friends in SIS when you got to London?'

'I don't have any old friends in SIS.'

'You helped them in Dublin.'

He laughed at this. 'Is that what they told you? They tried to get me to play piggy-in-the-middle. I didn't fancy my chances.' Then he realised she must have had access to some file about the whole affair. 'Is that who you are with? SIS?'

She shook her head but didn't answer directly. 'I am afraid we are rather making this up as we go along. We need some people who know France, who speak French like natives. We are not sure what for yet. Maybe translation, perhaps writing propaganda leaflets.' A long pause while Rose drank. 'What do you think?'

She pulled a rather crumpled envelope from her pocket and smoothed it out. 'Initially, returning to London for an informal chat. At the Victoria Hotel. Whitehall. Do you know it?'

Williams shook his head and tried to keep the exasperation

121

from his voice. 'I've just come from London.'

She smiled again, but this time he was disappointed to see her face didn't transform, but remained cold and impossible to read. 'As I said, we are flying by the seat of our pants. If it is any consolation, the chat is in two weeks' time, so no rush.'

'You came all this way for me?'

She waved a hand airily to dismiss such a notion. 'Good God, no. Several likely chaps up here.'

'Still, an awful lot of effort to pick up a few leaflet writers.'

'Hm.' He tried to interpret the expression. Nothing. 'There's something else might tempt you. If all went well, you'd be commissioned. Second Lieutenant initially. And you know what that means.'

He certainly did. No more sergeant majors querying his choice of luggage for one thing.

'What do you say?'

Williams took a big slug of beer and picked up the envelope. He rather liked the idea of any outfit that could sequester a pub at a moment's notice. The fact they knew that he'd been a driver for hire in Dublin suggested something other than leaflets was on the agenda. He slurped the last of his beer and licked the foam from his lips. 'Yes,' he said softly, 'why not?'

Part Two

From: SOE LONDON
To: Captain Rose Miller
Interim report. Stations STS 51/STS 23b/STS 51a

William Charles Frederick GROVER-WILLIAMS
General List Officer 231189
Born 16 Jan 03
Racing driver with Bugatti

Joined RASC Feb 40 as driver No T/174143. While at 4th
Liaison HQ RASC, Kinross (Bridge End Hotel) was selected
for employment in commissioned rank with SOE (Second
Lieutenant). Known as Vladimir Gatacre while training.

Initial training reports comment on his hard work and
anxiety to do well, describe him as an efficient soldier who
likes discipline, was fond of planning things and seeing that
the plan was carried out meticulously. His training as a WT

operator has been handicapped by his dislike of Morse and lack of confidence in learning it.

Further training has emphasised his loathing of signals but noted his extreme keenness on demolitions, which he considers his pet subject. He is described as a 'very good all round man' the 'star turn of this party'. Keen, shrewd and popular; strong sense of humour in adversity. A real good fellow who might overdo it if allowed to. A resourceful individual who would probably work best on his own.

Now Acting Lieutenant
Currently at STS 61c: Beddington House Finishing School

Seventeen

BEDDINGTON, AUGUST 1941

The late dusk was falling over the familiar scenery. Williams took two paces on to the asphalt of the old track and heard that terrible nerve-pinching screech of the superchargers, one which now reminded him, horribly, possibly unfairly, of the sirens attached to the Stuka dive-bombers to generate terror in the victims below. Was the Mercedes team trying to execute an early version of that terror? No, it was just a function of the blowers, surely.

The track was cracked and patchy now, part of it torn up as the farmer's field was reclaimed for cereals, the grandstands stripped down to mere wooden skeletons, the Castrol and Esso signs faded and flapping, but he could still smell the sweet, cloying aroma, like burnt sugar, of the German fuel.

All changed now. The Duke moved to London to do his bit, having lost his domestic staff anyway – a million servants suddenly unyoked and put into uniform had meant running a stately home wasn't quite the pleasure it had been – and the precious furniture and portraits had been put into storage while government oiks did whatever government oiks do. There were so many large country piles available it was no wonder that Special Operations Executive, the very name of which was meant to be top secret, was referred to by some of the instructors as Stately 'Omes of England.

Behind him in this particularly echoey shell of an 'ome, Williams could hear the gramophone music. The FANYs, the girls who were essential to the functioning of the STSs, the Special Training Schools, had reappeared in long evening gowns after a day of cleaning, cooking and driving and an ad hoc party had developed, with tangos and foxtrots.

He wasn't in the mood. And there was always the nagging thought that perhaps this was just another test, a check for sociability. Every detail was considered vital to success, and the sad fact was if you couldn't pass muster on any aspect, one morning you simply weren't at breakfast. Williams' group had already lost one chap who hit the whisky a bit too hard in Arisaig, another two who had failed the interview with the psychologists and yet another who declared that loud bangs made him jump when they were planting the new plastic explosives. The rumour was they went to a cooling-off house somewhere deep in the Highlands where they stayed until their secrets no longer mattered. Now he was left with a perfume salesman, a travel courier, a debutante, a nurse, a banker from Coutt's and a tailor.

Weeks of training had grown into months, with delays as various experts were found to fill in the gaps in their instruction – one so-called explosives expert had managed to blow his hand off, leaving a large vacancy in the ranks – as parachute courses were hastily arranged at Ringway, new safe houses brought on line.

All the time Williams was expecting a hand on his shoulder, a quiet word from Sykes or Fairburn or one of the other instructors as they finally figured out what was buried deep, deep in his psyche. Yes, he liked the action. Demolition was even fun.

Whereas the others in the group seemed driven by a desire to single-handedly liberate France and harass Germans, Williams had just one real aim, an ambition burning so bright everything else was a mere silhouette in comparison. To see Eve again.

Just to be able to do that he had lost three quarters of a stone, could strip and reassemble everything from a Sten to a Schmeisser in total darkness, knew from two old Shanghai policemen the fastest way to kill an opponent, how to derail an express train and survive in hostile country, foraging off the land for weeks on end and the simplest way to blow up a bridge. He only hoped Eve could somehow sense he was moving heaven and quite a lot of earth to get back to her.

Then he heard the soft sound, just hovering across the breeze. A sob. He walked out into the darkness and, over to his left, saw her sitting in front of a once well-pruned bush, now growing wild for want of a gardener.

Virginia Thorpe looked up and quickly dried her eyes. A waft of her Chanel perfume drifted across to him. It was not his favourite scent.

'Hello? Another one who thinks it's a vulgar charade in there? Or are you frightened you won't be able to control yourself with such gorgeous creatures?' Virginia Thorpe – or at least that was the name she used – was the deb of the party. She was beautiful in a languorous, sinuous way, but also, he was sure, a fearful snob. Being high and mighty enough to look down on the exceptionally well bred FANYs was certainly quite an achievement.

'Are you all right?'

'I just needed some air and . . . well, it gets to you sometimes, doesn't it? I saw you standing there and didn't want to disturb you. You seemed so lost in your own thoughts. So I just crept by.'

'I didn't even hear you. Nice quiet approach,' he said approvingly. 'Didn't hear so much as a twig snap.'

'Perfected when you have two older brothers. Spying on them got me where I am today.'

'Where are you today?'

She stood up. 'Cigarette?'

'Thanks.' He took a Craven A from her and lit them both.

Williams hesitated for a moment before confessing, 'I raced here once.'

'Raced what?' asked Virginia.

'A Bugatti.' Careful, man, he told himself, no good trying to impress this one. 'A car' would have done, but something made him rise to her bait.

'Really?' Just a hint of being impressed. 'Did you win?'

'No. The Germans did.'

She laughed, a deep throaty sound. 'Not very encouraging.'

'Why are you doing this, Virginia? I'm sure the FANY would have you like a shot. There's no need to risk your neck with all this derring-do.'

'Derring-do? That's a quaint expression for it. You boys all think you are Richard Hannay or Sandy Arbuthnot don't you? Isn't that the appeal?'

In the gloom she could almost pass for Eve, albeit an Eve of ten years ago. More refined and polished, with a confidence his wife didn't acquire until relatively late, and the thought made him ache for the real thing even more. But finally he said; 'I'm an Eric Ambler man myself.' The music stopped and there was a burst of applause. 'We'd best go back. Be marked down for not playing the game.'

'I don't think this is a team players' game, Gatacre. Do you?'

For once he gave an honest answer. 'Right now, I'm not sure what kind of game it is.'

They came for him at three that morning. Two big chaps he

hadn't seen before and never wished to again. It began with a shock of iced water in the face and an involuntary inhalation, which made his sinuses feel as if they were on fire. While he was still choking the blows began, one to the head and an expert one to his testicles which seemed to open up a tap, so that his strength drained from every limb. Rubber legged and confused he was dragged out and down the corridor, a third man appearing to poke him in the kidneys with a stick as they went.

Dragged downstairs he found himself in a room he never knew existed, some kind of wine cellar perhaps, the walls thick and damp, oozing a 'don't bother screaming, nobody can hear you' solidity, where he was tied roughly into a chair by the green-uniformed thugs.

Name.

Use your code name. The one on your papers. Charles Lelong.

What do you do?

Electrical engineer.

Why aren't you in Germany working for the Reich?

I repair factories after bom— after terrorism raids.

Twenty minutes of mouths shouting so close to him he could feel the warm spittle spraying him and he was back to his bed. Someone had thoughtfully changed the damp sheets and pillow-case. He smiled and snuggled down. Bet the Geheimstaatpolizei didn't do that. All in all, didn't go too badly, he felt.

Thirty minutes later they were back, rougher. No water in the face this time, just a yank on his hair and he was on the floor. Back to the same room. This time he could see blood on the floor. Was it real blood? It had the sickly claret-coloured sheen of actual arterial contents. More questions, but of a less general nature. Who are your friends in Paris? Who is Robert Benoist? Jean-Pierre Wimille? Where is your wife? And guns, pistols pressed against the side of his head, held under his nose, the

131

terrifying twin SS lightning bolts and the SD patches inches from his eyes.

By the third time, his head was completely clogged. He wanted to sleep, to feel those sheets again, to just tell them everything and get it over with, but his tongue wouldn't let him. To his horror he realised they had almost won. Even though he simply gave his false identity over and over again, he had let a small chink in, had toyed with the possibility of compromise, failure, treachery. That was how it worked. Needle away until almost involuntarily the survival centres of the brain do what they have to do. He tried to shut down his higher levels, to think about something else to mask the shouting. So loud, so piercing.

Then he had it. He focused on engine noises, the distinctive signature of all the cars he had known. He let them sing in his head, the deep throb of the Alfa, the scream of the early Mercedes, the strange ripping sound of the Bugatti, on and on they went, a cavalcade of the most cacophonous vehicles ever built, filling the room and his skull to the exclusion of all else.

Eventually, somewhere near dawn, they threw him back into bed and left him, shaking and sweating, wondering how much worse the genuine article could be. And how much weaker he would be when the time came.

Williams managed two hours of fitful, anxious sleep before the soft voice of his room-mate in his ear told him it was time for breakfast. Blearily, feeling faintly ashamed of his performance, even though his weaknesses and betrayals were all in his head, he lined up for eggs with the others. The queue was chatting and joking as usual, occasionally looking to him for a comment, but he felt dizzy and disoriented. Then he saw Virginia looking alabaster pale, her eyes shrunken, a dark crescent newly arrived under each one. They caught each other's stare and both knew. She winked first, the conspiratorial contact of fellow sufferers.

★ ★ ★

Five days and two more nocturnal interrogations later, his temples throbbing from a mild hangover, he watched Virginia doggedly swim length after length of the Beddington pool, a mock Greco-Roman temple, complete with columns, busts, and mildly erotic mosaics.

He went down on his haunches as she came in for the turn. 'Where did you learn to swim like that?'

She smoothly executed the change of direction and said over her shoulder. 'At home. In a pool much like this one, actually.'

On her return she said: 'Come in.'

'I can't swim.'

She laughed as her arms knifed into the water. They knew from parachute training that lakes make good navigational aids in a drop zone. So good, in fact, that the over-enthusiastic pilot might send you straight down into one. He had managed to avoid the inflatable dinghy training drop.

'I'll teach you.'

'Vladimir Gatacre?' the voice boomed off the tiles and he found himself springing up to almost attention. One of the gnarled instructors, this one a whippet-thin man in his fifties, strode over. 'Get your kit off, Sir. Time to earn your water wings.'

He looked down at Virginia. 'Sorry, looks like I'm already spoken for.'

After a month at Beddington there was little that could surprise Williams or his colleagues. One afternoon, following a particularly good lunch of what turned out to be wood pigeon, he was invited to the Carrington suite in the west wing. When he arrived he hesitated outside. The Sergeant reading the *Express* newspaper opposite with its usual grim headlines ('Miners' strike in Kent.

Leningrad under siege.') looked up.

'It's OK, sir. No boxing gloves this time.'

The last time he had burst into a room during an exercise a large red glove had landed on his temple, warning him always to check who is lurking behind a door. Williams, despite the Sergeant's assurances (the new motto 'Trust nobody', echoed in his brain during most waking hours), knocked.

'Come in,' said a muffled female voice.

On the other side of the door the heavy curtains were drawn, plunging the room into a curious half-light. Before him was a large desk, illuminated by an overhead light, and upon that desk was a large cloth which, judging by its contours, concealed an array of items underneath.

The woman who had spoken to him was sitting in a corner, visible mainly from the glowing tip of her cigarette. Without taking it out of her mouth she muttered, 'Remove the cloth. You have ten seconds. Put it back. Tell me what the items were and tell me how they connect to each other.'

Williams stepped forward and, feeling like a cheap vaudeville magician, got ready to reveal what was underneath the cover. He pulled it away and his eyes scanned the motley assortment, mouthing them to himself, trying to put together a little mnemonic as he had been taught, or failing that burning the image of the tray and its contents into his visual cortex.

'Ten,' said the voice, and now he realised he knew the woman. 'Tell me.'

He replaced the cloth. 'A piece of glass. Venetian. Murano? A rose. A tartan biscuit tin with what looked like red paint on it. A stuffed animal. A vole? A tape measure. Postcard of Windsor Castle. A piece of writing paper with all the words scrawled out. A couple of model village houses. A snowstorm paperweight of . . . was it the Acropolis?'

The woman stood and stepped forward so that she was at the edge of the pool of light. Rose Miller, in uniform, with flying jacket. 'Not bad. And the connection?'

His mind desperately shuffled the pack, first checking the initial of each to see if there was a word there, thinking what he would really like to do is have the Brains Trust standing next to him. A stuffed animal? Why? Then it came to him.

'It isn't a vole. It's a shrew. They are all references to Shakespeare. Merchant of Venice, War of the Roses, Macbeth, Taming of the Shrew, Measure for Measure, Merry Wives of Windsor, Love's Labours Lost, Hamlet . . . the snow thing? The Tempest?'

'Timon of Athens. But very good.'

Williams sighed with relief, suddenly wary. The constant testing and examination was draining. But perhaps that was the idea. 'So what's the point?'

'Do you know your Kipling?'

'No, I'm more of—'

'An Eric Ambler man,' she finished. Williams felt a jolt. He'd said that to Virginia out in the open air. Suddenly other little insights the instructors had had came back to him. Microphones. They are listening. All the time.

'It's a test. An observational and intuition test. We call it . . . Kim's Game. After Kipling.' She turned on the ceiling light, but it still left the room a gloomy yellow, as if smog had somehow crept in. 'Come on. I want to show you something.'

Williams watched the two Bugattis pull away from the line, marvelling at the acceleration, irritated at the puff of smoke coming from the rear wheels of the one on the left. Not enough power to the floor, too much wasted in wheel spin. Brakes too early, allowing the other to nose ahead, makes it up with fluid acceleration through the banking, and a clean exit, into top gear and along the straight. He awarded himself eight out of ten.

'How fast are you going?'

The abrasive sound of Rose's voice shocked him out of his reverie. Kim's Game was the first time he had seen her since that day in Kinross when she had commandeered the pub. Then there had been a come-hither edge to her, a spider-like seduction as she drew the potential recruit into her shadowy and beguiling world. Now that he and the others had discovered that spying, or at least the preparation for it, was, like much else in wartime, ninety-eight per cent mundanity, two per cent excitement, she was much more brisk and business-like. In front of them, projected on a small screen, was the footage shot by Maurice of the duel at Montlhery all those years ago. Now he could see all his mistakes in blurry, shaky black and white, realised how he was lucky even to come close to Robert.

'How fast?' Irritation in the voice.

'Oh. Sorry. About one-fifty along the straight.'

'Miles per hour?'

'Yes.'

'Looks bloody dangerous.'

Williams laughed. 'It's a damn sight safer than your parachute course.'

The camera jerkily swung around off the track and on to the spectators, making Williams feel slightly nauseous. His heart juddered when the image steadied and sharpened on to Eve, clutching a terrier to her breast, looking as if she was going to squeeze the life out of the poor dog in her anxiety.

'She looks worried.'

'She always did,' said Williams, thinking of how she grew to hate him risking his life. And now he was risking it to get back to her.

Rose twigged. 'Ah. That's Eve is it? She's very beautiful.'

'Yes.'

'Tell me. Why didn't she come with you? Married to a British subject, she would have had no problems.'

On screen the flag came down on Robert as Williams tried a last minute piece of slipstreaming. 'It's a long story.'

'Lights.'

Williams was suddenly blinking in the glare of bare bulbs. 'Where did you get the footage?'

'From the Prescott Hill Climb Bugatti Club. Drink?'

Williams nodded and they walked through rooms stripped bare of ancestral portraits and antique furniture to a well-appointed bar, where David, the white-coated barman, dispensed spirits, beer having disappeared a week before.

Unusually, it was deserted, the other recruits attending a lecture updating them on French politics in the thirties. Williams having been over there for all of that decade was excused in favour of the impromptu film show.

They ordered double scotches and sat down at a small table out of David's earshot, a consideration which, he was both pleased and alarmed to discover, was becoming second nature.

'I've read your interim report. Hopeless at Morse. Suspicious of all communications. Slow at lock picking. Swims like a house-brick. Runs into rooms without checking behind doors.'

'So I've failed.'

'Cheers.' She took a sip. 'On the other hand, likes blowing things up, works well alone, drives like a demon. I quote: "a tough, resourceful individual". Three nights of mock interrogations and you bore up well. You'll do, Williams. So far, at least. You have your passing-out test yet.'

Williams knew he would be required to get inside some high security installation or police station or steal a military car or a weapon, some little assignment that would show he could pull off a stunt in a country on a war footing. 'Why the movie?' he asked. 'I was there, remember?'

'So was Robert Benoist.'

'Robert?'

'You are a lucky man, Williams. You have friends in that country. Friends I think might help you. And a wife. The others will never know who to trust, will get desperately lonely . . . might make mistakes.'

She was going too fast for him. 'You want me to recruit my friends?'

'Robert Benoist. I read his press cuttings. I would imagine here is another tough, resourceful individual.'

Williams laughed. 'I can't argue with that. But he is his own man.'

'Meaning?'

'I don't know if he'd like being under anyone else's control. Especially mine. Number two driver suddenly number one? Never a happy situation in a team.'

Rose took out a Woodbine, Craven A having suddenly been supplanted in the tuck shop by those and Players. She offered him one and smiled. 'So you think he's a waste of time?'

'No, not necessarily. He's a brave man—'

Rose snorted and quoted in her very cultured voice: 'The man who can most truly be accounted brave, is he who knows best the meaning of what is sweet in life, and what is terrible, and then goes out determined to meet what is to come. Pericles. History of the Peloponnese War.'

'I'm an Eric Ambler man myself.'

She smirked. 'You get my drift. I have the feeling Robert knows the sweet things in life. Would he help? Would he put that in jeopardy?'

A few other recruits drifted in, but kept their distance. He could see Virginia talking animatedly to one of the instructors, a craggy Irishman clearly busy falling in love. She laughed, a little too loudly. 'Why Robert? I don't understand.'

'There will be missions where we need the talents of men like you and Robert.'

'Racing drivers?'

'At a hundred and fifty miles an hour, a tyre bursts, a deer runs out, you hit oil . . . how can you survive, when everything happens so quickly?'

Williams paused, wondering what she was getting at. 'It is only happening quickly to an outsider, an observer. The trick is to slow the world down, so that when things happen at one-fifty, one-sixty, they seem to be occurring at normal speed to you.'

'Precisely,' Rose said, 'that's why I want you and Robert. Men who think fast is slow.'

That's an answer? he thought, but didn't voice.

'There is one other thing.'

'What's that?'

'You drivers know what it is like to undertake a pursuit, and undertake it again and again, when you know the odds of you surviving shorten each time.'

'That was never my favourite part.'

'But it's true.'

'You never go out intending to be killed. Well, I never did.'

'Good.'

There was a silence while she considered whether to go on. 'It's started over there. God only knows it took them long enough.'

'What has started?'

'Resistance. Fourteen, fifteen months since they invaded. Since then, nothing. Then four weeks ago a German was shot at the Barbes-Rochechouart Metro. A week later someone tried to kill Pierre Laval of the Vichy government at Versailles. Another week, a German soldier shot at Gare de l'Est. Twenty killings in all, and growing. They are ready to fight now, especially the communists. We can hardly keep up with the new names being bandied about – Liberation-Nord, OCM, Front National, FTPF – they're the communists – and Armée Secrete . . .'

The list droned on and she saw his brow furrowing. It was as bad as pre-war politics. Actually, it was probably the same as pre-war politics – dozens of factions each with its own agenda. 'You'll be getting a lecture on them all, don't worry. Whoever we decide to back, they will need guns. They will need instruction. They will need examples. They might even need the odd racing driver.' She winked at him, an unnerving experience. 'So, Robert. Where is he now?'

Williams thought and replied: 'Probably brushing up his Pericles by enjoying the sweet things in life.'

Robert Benoist had grown used to the sight of Germans swarming across his city like a plague of green insects, but the shock of so many in a confined space, almost outnumbering civilians, took him aback. He looked at Eve on his arm and pulled her tight to his side. Over his shoulder he turned to the gaunt, worried-looking Dr Ziegler and whispered, 'Stay close. We won't stay long.'

Maurice's apartment was fit to burst. As Robert threaded his way through the crowd towards the drinks table he picked up snatches of conversation that went over the usual topics. The price of lightbulbs – if you can find one – the black market, how to get an *Ausweiss* – a travel permit – the new rations, the best collaborationist leaflets to make fuel briquettes out of, the coming winter. The latter exercised most people. The one of forty–forty-one had been bad, and now temperatures were dropping again. The autumn sound of Paris was no longer the rustle of leaves in the

Luxembourg garden – now given over to vegetables – but that of newspaper shoved into overcoats as insulation.

He heard his brother's distinctive low level whisper, urging a guest to come and see him if he needed . . . but at that point the words became inaudible.

'Maurice.'

'Robert. Eve.' His eyes raked her up and down with practised assessment. 'You look lovely. No trouble getting here?' Maurice had pulled some strings to arrange Eve's journey to Paris, and he beamed when she shook her head. 'Ah. Dr Ziegler. So glad you could make it. Drinks?' Maurice swept glasses of champagne from a passing tray. 'Robert. A word. Mother isn't very well again. We should have her looked after.'

'Anything I can do?' offered Dr Ziegler.

Maurice smiled: 'No, no. As you know, she's a stubborn woman.'

Maurice steered Robert to a corner and hissed: 'Are you out of your fucking mind bringing him here?'

'He's our doctor.'

'He's our very Jewish doctor.'

'Yes. And he doesn't have a telephone.'

'What?'

'They've cut off his telephone. I want you to get it back on.'

'Me?'

'Yes, you. Come on, Maurice. In return for a girl. Or a dirty show. A painting. I don't know how you do it, but you must help him. How can he work?'

'I think that's the general idea.'

Recently the first *rafle*, round-up, of Jews had occurred, with more promised. Jewish property and enterprises could now be confiscated. 'Just do it, Maurice.'

Robert glanced back over the heads of the partygoers and saw a tall, blond man had moved in on Eve. 'Who's that talking to Eve?'

'Ah,' said Maurice, relieved to be off the subject of Ziegler's telephone. 'Neumann. Joachim Neumann. Assistant to Keppler. You remember Keppler? The Sportskorpsführer? Out in the open now. SD. Neumann's not as bad as he looks. Quite a civilised chap, really.'

'We all are, Maurice.' It was Keppler, a man made doughy by many months of high living. 'Robert Benoist. How nice to see you again. The last time was in England.'

'And the last time you'll see it,' said Robert. Maurice blanched.

'Oh, I don't know. Mind you, I spend the day compiling lists of Wehrmacht men who will not use the official whores. I think we may have to postpone invading England altogether because our army have sore pricks.' Maurice joined in the laughter. 'We have decided to send anyone who catches VD to a Punishment Battalion. That should make them more careful where they dip their wieners, eh?'

Keppler followed Robert's gaze over to Eve, who was looking at her feet as Neumann spoke in her ear. 'Joachim. The ladies love him. I think it is the uniform.' Keppler patted his large belly. 'Somehow seems to fit him better than me.' He saw the look on Robert's face and said quietly, 'Don't cause any trouble, Robert. Striking a member of the SS is a capital offence. Tell me, whatever happened to that English driver, Williams? Where is he now?'

'Keeping better company than me I hope. Excuse me.' And he went to rescue Eve from Neumann, SS or no.

Eighteen

Williams had last visited Quaglino's in 1938. Then it had seemed slightly stuffy and formal after La Coupole and Fouquet's. Now, with evening dress for men the exception rather than the rule and civilians and servicemen in equal numbers, it exuded a slightly desperate jollity.

Williams, Virginia and Rose had taken a cab from the small flat near Baker Street where the women were staying – Williams was in a dingy hotel around the corner from them – and arrived to a backdrop of low rumbles and flashes as the East End of London flared fitfully under another raid. 'Don't worry,' said Rose. 'I hear if there is an alert they let you bed down in the basement.'

Virginia curled her lip. 'I'll take my chances in the street, thank you, ma'am.'

'No "ma'am" tonight. Rose.'

They checked their coats – Rose revealing a svelte black-beaded dress and Virginia a silk brocade gown with a ruched bodice – and were shown to a table. Williams, who had opted for uniform (the safest dress for a male these days), pondered the reason for the evening. They were obviously on the home straight now. Williams had passed his test of obtaining a classified document by blatant bribery of a government official – it turned out to be a vital map of the Tunbridge Wells sewer system – and had been in a holding house near Guildford for more weeks than he cared to remember, occasionally brushing up on fieldcraft and weapons, but otherwise cooling his heels and fighting boredom instead of Germans. Virginia was billeted elsewhere, but on a similar regime. At least while in the city he got to use the London Transport rifle range, which was conveniently buried under Baker Street tube station, and was able to take his frustration out on paper targets.

As they sat down Rose said, 'What a treat.'

'Is this our last supper, as it were?' asked Virginia.

'Not exactly. It's a bit of a tradition that, as your Conducting Officer, I take out my charges for an informal chat. Just to see if you have any worries. Count yourself lucky. Normally it's a ghastly bistro on the Edgware Road.'

'How do you stand it?' asked Williams.

'Well, the owner sometimes gets a chicken from his brother in the country.'

There was a pop of champagne corks and they looked over at a cheering group of young men and women. Another engagement announced, with the wedding day delayed, possibly indefinitely. 'That's not what I mean. How do you stand sending people off knowing they won't come back.'

Rose snapped a breadstick irritably. 'Might. Not won't. A certain ratio may not . . . but look at our pilots. Do they think about casualty rates every time they go up?'

'If they want to stay alive.'

'Hmm.'

Virginia interrupted by asking: 'So how is it we have been promoted to Quaglino's?'

Williams shuffled, embarrassed. It was his shout, as they say. He had access to a Bugatti entertaining account for clients held at Coutt's which had never been closed. It had sat there untouched for more than two years. Seemed a shame. But for some reason he didn't want Virginia to know that. He was relieved when Rose just glanced up from the menu and said; 'Oh, I fiddled some expenses for Vladimir here. Said he needed another bribe to corrupt yet more local policemen.'

Williams ordered a bottle of astonishingly overpriced Margaux, Orpen's favourite, and they plundered the menu. There was smoked salmon, chicken, mushroom pâté, various rabbit dishes. A cornucopia compared to what regular folk were getting, he knew. No whale meat at Quaglino's. Although if the Atlantic blockade got much worse, it might come to that, even here. Resentment against 'posh' restaurants was building, and he had heard talk of a five-shilling ceiling per person on meals. He scanned the prices as they ran through their orders with the waiter and realised they would burst well through that tonight.

The band started. Al Bowly with the Ray Noble Orchestra and 'The Very Thought of You'. A few couples from the engagement table got up to dance.

'I have something for you both.' Rose fished into her clutch bag and produced two tissue-wrapped items and deposited one in front of each of them.

'Do we open it now?' asked Virginia, already unwrapping the delicate layers. 'Oh,' she said, with an expression a few notches short of enthusiasm. 'How lovely.'

It was a gold powder compact, in a deliberately anodyne style that could have come from anywhere in western Europe. From his wrapping Williams produced equally plain but elegant gold cufflinks which he weighed in his hands. Their heftiness suggested quality.

'Thank you,' he said, and began turning one link over, trying to slip a fingernail into the hidden seam or concealed catch or whatever the boffins had dreamt up.

'What are you doing?' asked Rose.

'Looking for the gadget,' he said. 'I assumed these contain a map, a compass or our L Pill.' The latter was the cyanide suicide tablet each agent would carry, just in case.

'Sometimes,' smiled Rose, 'a pair of cufflinks is just a pair of cufflinks and a powder compact is just a powder compact. Another fledgling tradition. But one with a purpose. No distinguishing hallmarks, of course, but solid gold. You can pawn them if need be.'

The food arrived and it was clear that some kind of rationing was being applied in the kitchen after all. The portions were tiny. 'Best fill up on bread,' warned Rose.

They ate in silence for a while, enjoying flavours and textures far more delicate than they had become used to. Rose had just finished her chicken with the *Maître d'* approached and whispered in her ear.

'Excuse me,' she said, standing. 'A call.'

Virginia waited until she was out of earshot before taking a slug of wine and asking, 'What do you make of her?'

It was a very leading question. Did she mean personally or professionally. 'I wouldn't want to be in her shoes,' he finally offered, noncommittally.

No. Rather clumpy I thought.' She took another gulp. 'I think we'll need a second bottle. Anyway, I think she's a phony.'

'A what?'

'A fake. Something not quite U about her. The shoes, maybe.' He realised she was well on the way to getting drunk.

Rose strode over, her face dark, and for a second Williams thought she had heard them. He half considered checking the flower for hidden microphones. 'Look, I'm sorry, you two, but something's come up. Quite serious. I have to go back to Baker Street. You'll be all right, won't you?'

They both nodded and wished her good luck and Virginia suddenly burst out laughing. 'God, I feel like you used to when teacher left the classroom. Don't you?'

Williams couldn't help but grin. It was true, Rose Miller had the ability to be an oppressive presence when she wanted, quite the school ma'am, no matter how she wanted to be addressed. 'You still want that other bottle?'

'Oh, absolutely.'

They had taken the last Margaux, so Williams settled for a rather inferior St Emilion.

'How've you been these past few weeks?' he asked her.

'Bored. Bored, bored, bored. Bored. That about sums it up,' she said with feeling. 'You?'

'Much the same.'

'I know I shouldn't ask you this, but when do you go?'

He shrugged. She was right. She shouldn't ask.

'But it'll be soon, won't it? I think it'll be soon. This dinner. The cufflinks. The ghastly compact. Look, I know this is terribly forward of me.' More wine. 'But dear ol' Rosie had absolutely forbidden me to look up any of my old chums in town. Says I have to get used to isolation. But it's been so wretched in that bloody house. I wondered if . . .'

Williams wasn't entirely sure if he was meant to jump in here, and if so, with what exactly. But he felt the hairs on his neck prickling.

Virginia smacked the table in mock anger. 'Oh, do I have to spell it out?'

'I think we should go.'

Her face brightened. 'Now?'

'Separately.'

'Oh, for God's sake, man. We could dance. At least that.'

So he took her round the floor in a desultory foxtrot, trying hard to hold her chest away from his for fear that something might leach through to him, corroding his resolve like spiritual acid.

'Do you know anyone over there? I do. My old teacher lives in Lyons. I hope I get sent there.'

He grunted.

'Look, Vladimir. That can't be your real name, can it? You don't look like a Russian.' She said this in a low stage voice. 'Tell me the real one. At least that. Mine's really Veronica Taylor-Stapylton. I thought having the same initials would help.'

'Jenkins. Ron.'

She pinched his arm and he winced. 'No, it's not. I know it – I heard one of the instructors use it at the beginning by mistake. It's something Williams, isn't it?'

'Good Lord, no,' he said with conviction, the penny finally dropping. 'It's Seymour Kuntz,' he smirked, stealing an old punchline from a Maurice joke. Her brow furrowed as she tried to read his face.

Williams applauded as the music finished and briskly walked back to the table and asked for the bill, scribbling in the Coutt's cheque book. 'There's still half a bottle of wine,' said Virginia.

'Finish it,' he said, putting down a pound note. 'Here's the cab fare back. The *Maître d'* will look after you. Sorry.'

She jutted out her lower lip, threw the bill across the table and watched him leave in pouting silence.

He half stumbled into the fresh air, realising that he, too, was unused to such a quantity of red wine with hardly any food. Rose was across the street, leaning on her staff car, driver behind the wheel, smoking a cigarette. The air was tinged with the acrid fumes of burning buildings far away down the river, the sky smeared with red as if sunset had been called back for an encore, disrupting the otherwise velvet-black of the darkened city. He walked across to her.

'I was going to give you five minutes more.'

'And if I'd fallen for her cut-glass charms and tottered out arm in arm with her?'

'You'd be on a train to the Highlands where you'd be eating haggis and tossing the caber for the next year. Lift?'

'Another charade?'

'No. Show's over for tonight. This is off duty. What do you want to do?'

'It's your town more than mine.'

She opened the door to the Humber. 'Hop in.'

The place was half the size of a tennis court but Williams could have sworn five hundred people were crammed into the space. It was a basement somewhere not far from Leicester Square, with no external sign he could discern, and a retired pugilist with an interesting nose on the door, although he didn't seem too keen on turning anyone away.

The band, nearly all octogenarians, apart from a negro sax player, were playing fast jazz, and the crowd – everything from spivs to serving officers and all points in between, danced as best they could in the constricted space.

After ten minutes of feet and elbow they gave up and Rose shouted in his ear. 'There is a quieter bar up top.'

He followed her up a back staircase to a small, rather smelly room done out in purple velvet. The only other customer was a snoozing sailor. Rose fetched a couple of scotches from the

149

barmaid and tucked them into a corner booth and, to his surprise, whipped a curtain across. 'In case clients want a bit of privacy.' Now Williams realised the girls who looked like tarts working the dancefloor were probably just that. 'But it doesn't usually get busy till later.'

Williams looked down at the seats, but they seemed clean enough.

'No, not here, you fool. They just soften them up in the booths. Promise them the world. Deliver the rather tarnished goods next door.'

'How do you know about this place?'

'John Gilbert?'

'The lock-picking instructor?' Gilbert ran the Beddington breaking and entry course.

'The problem with the racket is that almost everyone comes from a very nice background.' She made the word harsh and truncated. 'And this isn't a nice war. Johnny is a former safe-cracker and burglar. He brought me here to meet some of his friends. When you go over your identity and ration card will look just like the real thing. One of Johnny's friends. You will have a great deal of money at your disposal, thanks to Ronnie Cann. Took him a while to switch from fivers to francs, but I think you'll agree he does a nice job. Johnny's got us a first-rate pickpocket, too. He'll be starting as an instructor. As soon as we can get him out of Dartmoor Prison.'

Williams started to laugh. 'So, you employ everyone from debs to dips?'

'Rogues to racing drivers.'

Williams swallowed some scotch and loosened his jacket. The body heat from below seemed to be bleeding through the floorboards. 'So. Is this really pleasure?'

She shrugged. 'I'm having a good time.'

'That's a nice frock, by the way.'

'Frock?' She flicked some of the beads. 'Frock? It's a Molyneux, I'll have you know. And bloody expensive.'

Williams wondered if she was drunk, or if this was an act like Virginia's. 'So no business?'

She gave a lopsided smile. 'Perhaps a teensy bit.'

'Go on.'

'Two things. What do you make of Virginia?'

'As a seductress? Or a spy?'

Rose laughed. 'I'll settle for special agent.'

'A disaster.'

'Why?'

'Too good looking. Every man in every room she enters will look at her. Germans will offer to carry her bags . . . and if the bags are full of radio . . .'

'I take your point.'

'And she's got English written through her like a stick of rock. Oh, she can speak the part, but there is something very brittle about her, something the French haven't got. Furthermore, I have absolutely no idea why she would want to do something like this when there must be a thousand other ways to help the war effort . . .' There was a silence. 'You did ask.'

'I know. Thank you.' She didn't want to tell Williams it was too late. Her own doubts, especially over why such a young beautiful girl would put herself in such danger, had been overruled. Virginia had the green light.

'What was the second thing?'

'Less tricky. Could you kill someone? In cold blood?'

The switch in tone took him aback. 'Less tricky? What's that supposed to mean?'

'Just answer me. Cold blood. No warning. No reason. We say – he has to die. You do it.'

'I don't know.'

'Your Irish friends did it.'

'I had no part of that.'

'Oh, don't be so naïve. You think you can pick and choose which parts of a struggle like that apply to you? Just because you drove on a few raids where nobody got killed, you don't think you have any responsibility for anything else that went on?'

Williams nodded. 'No, I realised that. Which is why I got out. I grew up. Fast.'

He told her what she already knew, about the envelope Slade handed a young man called Grover that was the death warrant for one of his friends. How he was sure there was more to it than the smooth-talking SIS man had suggested and had burned the package without opening it, infuriating both O'Malley and Slade when they discovered what had happened. It was the only way out – his handing over the package would have been in itself a compromised act, an act of betrayal. It was then he realised he was just a boy messing about in things that had taken three hundred years to fester and finesse. All he had wanted was an escape from the suffocating normality of his family. Afterwards, he grabbed the chance to sink into Orpen's equally claustrophobic world for a few months.

'So then I had two lots of people hating me. The Irish and the British. My family were still in France and I went back, the prodigal son with his tail between his legs, and my father knew a man who knew a man who knew Orpen . . .'

'William Grover became just Williams. And now Grover-Williams. You're not very original with names, are you?'

'Maybe not. But you can see I'm none too keen on assassination.'

'This will be different.'

'Will it,' he said flatly.

'Anyway, that's for the future. I'm sending you in, three weeks time. Full briefing starts tomorrow. I want you over there and ready.'

'Ready for what?'

'As I told you. Whatever we want.'

Williams looked at his watch and Rose grabbed his wrist with a surprisingly firm grip. She angled it so the meagre lights flickered across the diamonds.

'And you can't take that. Too damn conspicuous.'

He slipped off the Cartier and handed it over. Rose examined the back and raised an eyebrow.

'We always meant to get it engraved . . . you know how it is. I'll be back for that,' he added firmly.

Rose slipped it into her clutch bag. 'Good. Then you'll know where to find it, won't you?'

Robert sat on the edge of the terrace at the Auffargis house, pulling petals from a withered rose head, letting them drop on to the gravel, brooding over yet another row with his estranged wife. When all this was over, he would contemplate the dreaded divorce. The arguments and recriminations that would cause didn't bear thinking about. He envied Williams his simple monogamous outlook, even if it was probably being sorely tested by separation.

It was a cold, sharp day lit by a low, jaundiced sun, but he was enjoying even that feeble warmth on his face. He had spent the day polishing and checking the last Bugatti Atlantic now sitting in the garage-cum-barn out back. It should have been turned in, but the papers Maurice had secured allowed him to keep it on the pretext he would be touring the country impounding all of Ettore's cars still in France. He despised Maurice's cosying up to the Germans, but he had to admit, when it came to playing both ends against the middle, Maurice was a master.

He had thrown the rubberised cloth over the Bugatti when the

Economic Police Patrol, with a small unit of German troops, had arrived only minutes later. The Sergeant in charge had looked in the barn and moved on. It wasn't cars they were looking for, but evidence of food hoarding, provisions to steal.

The small figure who appeared at the end of the drive snapped him out of his thoughts. She hesitated at the gates, the bicycle still between her legs, as if unsure of the address. He raised what he hoped was a reassuring hand and she pedalled in, swerving to avoid the pot holes now forming in the untended road surface. No gardeners or handymen or chauffeurs left now. He'd have to get off his arse and do it himself if he wanted a decent approach to the house.

She must have been around seventeen dressed in a rather threadbare overcoat that might have been fashionable five years ago. Her red hair was tied back with a bright purple scarf, and she wore a look of determination on her flushed face as she pulled to a halt, dismounted, and carefully laid the bike against one of the terrace pillars, careful to avoid crushing the wisteria. He could tell she had come from Paris, and city folk only ventured into the countryside for one thing these days.

'You're too late,' he said.

'I'm sorry?'

'You're too late. The Germans were here an hour ago. Took away a sack of potatoes and two chickens. Cleaned me out. I have nothing to give. You could try the farm down that way.' A pretty girl had some chance of getting something from old Pierre Marchant, one of the farmers who revelled in the shift in the balance of power that meant urban dwellers went cap in hand to their rural cousins, rather than vice versa.

'I haven't come for food.'

Robert stood up, a little suspicious. Surely she wasn't... 'Coffee?'

'No thanks. I have to give you this. You are Robert Benoist?'

He nodded and she held out a thin envelope. He ripped it open. It was one of the single sheet letters introduced shortly after the occupation with options to cross out: Dear . . ., Hope you are well/better/coming here – and so on. He read it three times before the message finally clicked and he felt a grin spread over his face.

'Are you sure about the coffee?'

'I have to get back.'

He walked out on to the driveway with her as she collected her bike. 'Thank you. You're very brave.'

She flushed a little and smiled shyly. 'Oh, the Germans never stop us.' She indicated the note. 'Not for that kind of thing, anyway. Doesn't occur to them that women could be up to no good.'

Robert felt a sudden chill, an intense feeling of concern for her, this vulnerable child swimming into unknown depths. 'I'm sorry, I didn't ask your name.'

'Beatrice.'

'Well, Beatrice, long may they continue to believe that. Be careful.'

'*Vive la France.*'

Now Robert felt awkward replying after the innocent intensity she invested in the tired old phrase. 'Yes, *Vive la France.*'

Without a backward glance she was gone, pedalling furiously into the darkening afternoon. He looked at the note again. He'd have to tell Eve. In person.

Robert was aware of the envious and suspicious glances as he drove west, through Dreux and towards Alençon. The roads were mostly empty, with just a few horse-drawn carts, a smattering of cars newly converted to run on compressed coal gas, with a

155

dangerous brazier created in the boot, and, in the larger towns, the velo-taxis, an upmarket version of the rickshaw. But a man driving a car? And a beautiful streamlined car at that? Nazi bigwig, that was the assumption most people made. Or a black marketeer.

He gunned the car, letting the fearsome noise wrap around him. Above sixty kilometres an hour the lack of soundproofing made conversation difficult in the Atlantic, but, with no passenger, he didn't care. The engine made its own delicious conversation and he let it talk at length on the spookily empty roads.

He was near Alençon when he came across the convoy, a long snake of half-tracks, Mercedes trucks, Kubelwagens and staff cars, plodding along at around forty or forty-five kilometres an hour. The troops in the rear vehicle all turned to look at him, their eyes dark under their coal scuttle helmets. At one time they would have worn field caps, but now that the British were making sporadic strafing sorties across the Channel, they had armoured up.

One of them waved and gave a thumbs-up in admiration of the Bugatti, but the majority of the boys – most were less than half his age – remained stony faced. He wondered where they had been. Russia maybe, where already six inches of snow covered the countryside, slowing down an advance that had once taken Rzhev, Belgograd, Stalino and Taganrog – less than three hundred miles from the Volga – in forty-eight hours? No, Robert thought, according to reports from both the conventional and the newly emerged underground press those units were still pushing for Moscow, hoping to take the city before everything froze solid. Perhaps the look on the prematurely lined faces was the thought that they could be the next to be shipped east.

After five minutes of unrelenting staring from the back of the Mercedes, Robert, cursing the fact that every Bugatti was right-hand drive, decided to risk overtaking. He dropped a gear, pulled out, relieved to find the way ahead clear, and floored the accelerator.

The drab military colours of the vehicles flashed by, and now he just had glimpses of open jaws and scowling faces. He felt himself smile, counting off the metres till he was clear of these gormless barbarians. He was half a dozen trucks away from freedom when the lead staff car swerved out, blocking his side of the road. He automatically glanced at the speedometer even as he stamped on the pedal. He was travelling at over a hundred and the Atlantic's brakes weren't its best feature. A tall, spindly hawthorn hedge made it impossible to swerve round this sudden obstruction so he pumped the brakes, once, twice, then full down, feeling the wheels lock, correcting the skittish rear end, bracing himself as the military car came closer and closer, feeling the Bugatti decelerating with agonising slowness, until with a smok-ing screech and a stench of rubber it stopped centimetres away from the occupants of the staff car, rocking on its suspension. Robert realised he was holding his breath and let out a long thin stream of air.

The tall, elegant Lieutenant who stepped out of the rear seat of the staff car offered a thin smile as he walked over to the driver's window. Robert rolled it down. 'A Bugatti,' the German said admiringly.

'Well read.'

'An Atlantic, I believe.'

Robert allowed himself to be a tiny bit impressed. 'Indeed.'

'Lovely.'

'Aren't they?'

'Why do you have it?'

Robert handed over the *Ausweiss* that Maurice had provided and then the identity card. 'Ah. You work for the company. I see.'

Still holding the papers the Lieutenant walked around the machine admiring its low-slung lines. When he returned he bent down. 'My Colonel would love to see this.'

Robert started his cover story, that he had just picked it up and was taking it to the large warehouse in Dieppe where many of the best cars had been spirited away. 'I'm afraid it has been requisitioned by—'

The Lieutenant cut him off with a snarl and threw the papers back at him. 'Fall in, in front of that half-track. Now.'

The German walked over and spoke quickly to the half-track crew. Robert watched as the forward machine gun was manned and swung in his direction. The convoy restarted with a grinding of gears and the low grunt of engines and Robert slotted in between the half-track and a Kubelwagen.

The lumbering column of vehicles swung south, away from where he wanted to go, had to go, heading for Le Mans. Robert could feel the Atlantic juddering unhappily in second and third, gears it simply wasn't used to hanging around in.

It was ten kilometres before he hit on the solution, another five of tricky driving with one hand before he had managed to sabotage his own car and a further seven before he began flashing his lights and honking his horn. Eventually the vehicle ahead slowed and after they had all rolled to a halt, the Lieutenant strode back into view, clearly irritated.

'What is it?'

'How much further?'

'Another eighty kilometres.'

Robert tapped his fuel gauge. 'I'm all but empty. I was meant to fill up at Alençon.'

The Lieutenant put his head in suspiciously. He turned the engine on. The needle juddered but didn't rise. Which was hardly surprising because Robert had disconnected it.

'Very well. You,' the Lieutenant pointed to the truck. 'Put some fuel in this car.'

The Lieutenant went back to his vehicle as the soldiers fetched jerry cans and started to slosh it into the Bugatti's cavernous tank. Robert waited until the machine gunner slid down for a moment before he rammed the car into reverse and let in the clutch. There was a scream as both soldiers' legs were crushed against the solid girder-like bumper of the half-track. He spun the wheel, thankful for the tight turning circle Jean had given the Atlantic and accelerated out, deliberately spinning the wheels, leaving a shower of dust. The Lieutenant, leaning against his car, smoking, gasped as the low coupé rocketed by him, holding in his stomach, feeling the metal wings pluck at his trousers.

The first bullet came after Robert within five seconds, but it took time to manoeuvre the bigger half-tracks into a clear line of sight. The convoy was already receding when he saw the muzzle flashes in his mirror, but at that moment he glimpsed the farm track running off to his left and he slid the car into it, hoping the suspension could cope with barreling over ruts at a hundred and thirty kilometres an hour. The track led him to a small lane, the lane to a road heading north, and as darkness fell he switched on the blue-painted black-out headlights and hoped nobody else took a fancy to his car that night.

Arthur Lock checked his watch by the feeble light of the moon and lit the third bonfire in the triangle. He wondered if the plane was coming. This was the third time of asking. On one occasion weather had stopped the drop, on another the plane had simply not appeared. This was the last chance, he felt, tonight or it was time to think again.

He hurried over to the edge of the field to join two of the half-dozen Frenchmen scattered on the edge of this dark wood and stood with them stamping his feet. He gratefully accepted an offer of brandy, rough though it was, and shuddered with pleasure as it scorched its way down into his stomach.

What a game to play. Dropping agents into the dead of night, hoping they don't break their necks or drown or fall straight into a German patrol. Then expecting them to disappear into the populace and somehow, against all the odds, make a difference. He wouldn't blame them if they weren't coming, not one bit.

Even as he began to have his doubts, he heard the low throb of the Halifax engines and could sense, rather than see, the great four-engined plane banking to circle back round over the DZ. That was unusual. A pilot who cared enough to give the jumpers a decent chance of landing on target. Most of them seemed happy enough to turf their charges out and head home.

He waited impatiently as it made the turn, levelled, and started the dropping run. He could imagine the first agent sitting on the edge of the hatch, remembering all that training. Push forward and straighten, arms by side, clean through the hole or your face bangs on the opposite side of the hatch. Wait for the static line to pull. Hope the jump master had remembered to hook it up. Feel the painful jerk as silk grabbed the air. Check canopy. Check lines. Twist slowly. Head for the fires.

The plane flew overhead, the noise faded and he started to scan the sky. 'There,' said one of his companions, and he could hear wind through silk as the first of the delicate mushrooms turned towards them and came rushing down at the earth. The other two blossoms were over to the south, one of them perhaps a mile away. Lock dispatched his colleagues to intercept, checked the pistol in his belt for easy access, just in case, and strode out to where the first drop had crumpled into the earth.

As he approached the jumper got up rather stiffly and began

160

hauling in the chute. Tentatively he said: 'There are two tragedies in life.'

The figure jumped then spun round and Lock had two shocks. One, it was a woman, and two there was a large streak of blood down her face.

'God, you gave me a fright,' Virginia Thorpe gasped. She looked him up and down, noting his very un-French ginger hair and freckles.

'There are two tragedies in life,' he repeated.

'One is not to get your heart's desire.'

'The other is to get it,' Lock completed and held out his hand. He used his code name as instructed. 'Captain Eric Colson. Welcome to France. You all right?'

She touched her face. 'Yes. Damn thing.'

Lock reached over and gently felt her pretty, delicate nose. 'Not broken I don't think. It'll just feel like it for a while. Come on, shouldn't hang around out here.'

The fires were doused, the chute rolled and stored for later retrieval, along with the baggy overalls which she stepped out of, revealing the drab skirt and jacket she had on underneath. There were three canvas bags plus a handbag. Lock took the former, one on each shoulder, carrying the third, and ushered her away from the field down a narrow footpath.

'What about the others?'

'Don't worry, they'll be taken by a different route. Can't put all your agents in one basket, eh? Did you have a radio?'

'No. Martin—' she carefully used the code name – 'he's the pianist.'

With his free hand Lock felt the bags slung over his shoulders. No weapons. Just documents. And money. She was one of those who'd come in with payroll and bribes. Good.

It was two kilometres to the draughty old barn, full of old straw

161

and duck droppings. The ducks themselves were huddled in a metal shed to the left, keeping themselves warm. Lock flicked on a torch and indicated a corner, where there were two uninviting blankets.

'Someone will be along eventually. We have to wait here. Sit down.'

Virginia looked at the blankets closely, decided they were old but clean enough and wrapped one round her. Lock slumped down a few feet away. 'Cigarette?'

'Should we?'

'Don't worry. You think the Germans patrol every lane in France? You forget how big a country it is.'

She took one and gratefully accepted the light and felt better as soon as the smoke hit her lungs. For the past twenty-four hours she had gone over and over her reasons for doing this. Nothing made sense. It had seemed like an adventure to begin with; now she was here the butterflies and sickness in her stomach were telling her that much more was at stake.

'Marilyn, isn't it?'

'Code name. Yes.'

'What do your papers say?'

'Yolande Laurent.'

'Occupation?'

'Dress designer with Piguet.'

The name meant nothing to Lock, but he knew a story that was checkable when he heard it. 'And will they vouch for you?'

'Oh yes.' She had worked there for a year before the war, helping reinvent the house's trademark gowns, so she knew the drill. A Yolande Laurent certainly had worked there, but had moved to New York to marry one of the clients who came in to buy a dress for his wife and left with more than he bargained for.

She suddenly felt cold and flat as the cigarette finished and she pulled the rough, animal-scented blanket round her. 'How long have you been over?'

He hesitated. She should know better than to ask questions like that. 'A while.' In fact, Lock had been in France since before the invasion and stayed on after the Germans overran the country.

'How is it?'

'Grim for most people. Getting grimmer. You do what you have to do to survive . . .'

As if on cue three figures appeared at the entrance of the barn, silhouetted by the moonlight. Lock stood up and Virginia did likewise. Lock flicked the narrow beam of his torch over the men so Virginia could see the Germans' uniforms. The light glinted off the threatening barrels of the MP 38 submachine guns levelled at her. Lock heard her juddering intake of breath, imagined the cold, dead feeling gripping her insides and shrugged apologetically.

'. . . even if it means the odd sacrifice now and then.'

Eve opened a bottle of Bourgueil, recorked it, put it and two tumblers into a wicker basket, along with a piece of cheese and what was left of the bread she had made earlier in the day, threw a cloth over the contents and headed out into the courtyard of the water mill.

The four German soldiers billeted with her snapped to attention as they always did, although this time she could feel the eyes following her. The over-correct formality was slowly melting away eventually, she was sure, to be replaced by the standard issue arrogance of conquering soldiers. One of them muttered something and another laughed. Eve ignored them. It was only for a week longer and they were being pulled out to God knows where.

She cut left, down through a tangle of brambles, scratching her bare legs as she went, and picked up the river path. The ground was hard – there had been a frost the night before, and the fallen leaves were still brittle and crunchy underfoot.

Eve climbed over the low fence that marked the boundary of her property and carried on along the bank, paralleling the wide, sluggish river, now a deep, earthy brown from all the rain. The path dipped and became muddy, so she picked her way carefully until it started to climb again to firmer ground. She could smell the cigarette smoke now, and knew he'd be there.

Robert was sitting on a fallen log at the base of a soaring oak tree, just finishing the last of his cigarette. He smiled and rose slowly, stiffly to his feet, kissing her on both cheeks. He'd spent the night parked in a field, tight against the hedgerow, before daring to continue on to see her.

'Eve.' He tried hard to keep the emotion from his voice, but he was pleased to see her. She sat down next to him and he indicated his cigarette butt. 'I'd offer you one, but I think it's mainly old nettle leaves. With maybe a cabbage in there. Maurice has promised me two hundred real cigarettes by next week.'

Eve poured some wine for each of them. 'How is Maurice?'

Robert laughed. 'I tell you, thriving. He's having a good war. I found my forte before all this happened . . . he's found it now. Mr Big BOF.' Eve looked puzzled; the acronym for black marketeers clearly hadn't spread outside Paris yet. '*Beurre, Oeufs, Fromage*. Although with Maurice it's more practical things—'

'And how are you?'

'All the better for being here.' She smiled at the compliment and Robert felt the familiar wariness from her. She never quite believed his intentions were honourable. Or maybe that was just paranoia on his part. He sipped the wine. It was lightly chilled, just right and he nodded appreciatively. 'I had a visit the other day from a young lady named Beatrice.'

'Do I want to hear this?'

'Oh yes, nothing like that. She brought a message. Don't know who from, I don't think I was supposed to ask.'

'What was it?'

He slugged back the wine and held out the tumbler for a refill. 'Well, there was some good news and some bad news. Which do you want first?'

Slowly she said, 'The good.'

'OK. Will's coming back.'

She almost dropped her drink as the realisation that he wasn't joking broke over her and she found herself gasping for breath, as if all her airways had suddenly constricted. 'Will . . . when?' Then she remembered the second part of the news. 'And the bad?'

Robert's mouth turned up at the corners. 'Will's coming back.'

She leapt forward with such a force Robert barely had time to brace himself as she slammed into him, arms round his neck, her squeal of delight echoing through the naked branches of the trees, dancing all the way back to the house.

When it opened in 1932 The Sphinx was the most glamorous brothel in the world. Famed for its gilded Egyptian motifs, the giant slit-eyed cats framing the doorway, and the opulence of the main salon, it advertised widely across Europe. It was the pinnacle of a *poule*'s career to get one of the slots on the drawing-room's sofas, and such was its fame that many believed the popular rumour that when Hitler visited Paris after its fall he wanted to see the Arc de Triomphe, the Eiffel Tower, Sacré Coeur and The Sphinx.

Whether Hitler admired the exterior or not, now the salon and bar were the haunt of his German officers, not all of whom came to sample the goods, a social club where rivalries and ambitions were, more or less, put aside. On this chill October night a huge, profligate fire was roaring in the fireplace, which formed the mouth of the enormous eponymous Sphinx itself, helping to keep a rosy glow on the near-naked girls who prowled the room.

At one of the tables on the left-hand side – which denoted that they were not to be bothered by the women unless summoned across the invisible barrier – sat a group of German intelligence officers. Three branches were represented, the Abwehr, the Gestapo and the SD, all nominally separate organisations yet all overlapping in their sphere of interests, especially when it came to tracking down the British spies who had suddenly started to appear, like an eruption of acne across the face of the country. Strictly speaking the SD should concentrate on French organis-ations, the Abwehr on British infiltrators and the Gestapo on subversives and Jews but they were discovering that enemies could not be so neatly compartmentalised. And, contrary to what Berlin thought, they did speak to each other, even if it was over bottles of Taittinger.

Keppler and Neumann of the Sicherheitsdienst faced Kommis-sars Stuppel and Kock of the Geheimestaatpolizei and Staffenburg and Pitsch of the Abwehr, the military intelligence currently, in residence at the Hotel Lutetia.

They were passing round the house pillow books, loosely bound collections of erotic postcards, which were intended to help clients get in the mood. Keppler rotated his to try to find a reference point for what was going on. He was fairly sure that they could only put you into the mood for a visit to the circus or some other contortionist's venue.

'So is it true, Keppler?' asked the portly Staffenburg, puffing on a cigar.

'Is what true?' Ah, he had it now. Very athletic.

'That you have a tame Englishman.'

Keppler looked up at Staffenburg and smiled. The Abwehr

man had a reputation as something of a buffoon, a mere hedonist who got where he was because he was married to a distant relative of Admiral Canaris. Maybe so, but Keppler knew that underneath that lipid-rich exterior, there was a shrewd, and eminently selfish, mind. Like Goering, whom he resembled, Der Dicke Staffenburg had to be watched lest you allowed the clown-like behaviour to lull you into a false sense of security.

'Where did you hear that?' asked Keppler warily.

'My man Bleicher. A little pillow talk.' Staffenburg winked lasciviously.

'I should steal him from you. Neumann here has finally found a nut he couldn't crack.'

The table laughed and Neumann said: 'I haven't finished squeezing yet.' He knew it was misplaced confidence. The woman Eve had proved totally immune to his blandishments.

'So do you?' asked Staffenburg.

Before Keppler could answer, a negro waiter – tolerated by the Germans in such exotic environments – approached and bent to whisper in his ear. Keppler instinctively leant away in case any of the man's spittle should touch him. Keppler nodded and announced, 'Excuse me, gentlemen, but I have business upstairs.'

Staffenburg tipped all but the last few dregs of champagne into his glass. 'Don't worry, Keppler, I'm sure we'll still be on this bottle by the time you have finished.' They all guffawed, but Staffenburg picked up the exchange of knowing looks between Keppler and Neumann and came to the conclusion that no woman was involved in this transaction. He was wrong.

Virginia Thorpe paced the room, her head throbbing with confusion. After being handed over to the Germans she had been driven for what must have been three hours in the back of a truck, sandwiched between two big men who smelt of stale sweat and

167

rancid meat. They had not talked to her, although one of them had put a strip of plaster across her nose with remarkable gentleness. She had been kept for most of the day in a windowless room in a house on the outskirts of Paris, some kind of temporary prison. Again, no mistreatment, even some quite decent food.

Then a new set of men, two dour Frenchmen and a plainclothes German overseer, had delivered her into an alley and marched her roughly up to this ridiculous bedroom, all red velvet and purple wallpaper, with terrible reproduction furniture – if she didn't know better she would think this was some kind of bordello – and taken away her jacket and all her possessions.

Her main task now was to keep a pressure cap on the panic welling up inside her, to try to remember what the instructors said. There will be interrogation, *Anschauzen*, the yelling, bullying shouting inches from the face, mind games, intimidation, perhaps even torture. This was what went through your mind in the small, dark hours at Beddington. How will I do when it's the real thing? When there isn't a small part of your brain telling you these guys are just play-acting at being Nazis? Will she crumple and fold or keep her dignity and her secrets? Although what secrets she had, she wasn't quite sure. She must resist, she knew that. And she must try to escape. Shakily she got to her feet. Better to keep busy than start brooding on the Gestapo's methodology.

Virginia checked the wardrobe. Empty but for a feather boa and some kind of black corset. And a whip. She flung back the shutters, but the window was barred, heavy substantial rods of iron set close together.

She heard footsteps and low voices in the hall and sat down quickly on the edge of the bed, trying to compose herself. Don't look scared, they'd said. Any weakness—

'Ah. Miss Laurent. If that is your name. Welcome.' She looked up and the fleshy face beamed at her. 'I am Sturmbannführer Keppler of the Sicherheitsdienst. This –' he indicated the tall handsome man next to him, 'is my colleague Obersturmführer Neumann.'

Neumann glared at her, and she was shocked to see such hatred coming from such beautiful blue eyes.

'I apologise for the unusual surroundings,' continued Keppler, 'but you have arrived outside office hours.'

'My name is Yolande—'

'Stop it,' barked Neumann in heavily accented English, making her start. 'Do not insult our intelligence. Your name is nothing of the sort.' He pulled up a chair and sat astride it. 'You have a training name, a code name and a cover name. And a real name.' He waited for this to sink in. She was beginning to shake slightly. Above them a bed began to move rhythmically, unmistakably, as the business of the house went on as usual. 'You think you are the first spy to come here?'

There was moaning now, a woman. She tried to figure out if it was French or English moaning before she realised she was being ridiculous. Or perhaps it was the best thing to do, to keep concentrating on the absurdities.

Neumann sensed her drifting and shouted: 'Spy! What a disgusting occupation for a woman. Beneath the lowest, disease-infected whores in this place. Spies. You know what we do to spies? Do you? What fun we can have?'

Her throat was dry but she managed to say: 'My name is Yolande Laurent, I work at—'

The blow took her by surprise, spinning her half off the bed and bringing tears to her eyes. She pushed herself back up, sniffed and said, 'My name is—'

The second blow threw her to the floor and she stayed there, waiting for the stinging and throbbing to subside, coughing as she tried to catch her breath.

'Neumann,' said Keppler calmly. 'That's enough. Get out.'

'I—'

'Out. Go and enjoy yourself somewhere else.'

Then she knew what this was. Even as she rubbed at the burning patch on the side of her face, she heard the voices of the instructors at Beddington break through the shock and the terror. Expect the brutal young interrogator and the kindly older one. Except kindly wasn't a word she would apply to those piggy eyes in a jowly face. But that was the routine they were running through, for sure. Her spirits lifted a notch. Knowledge was control.

'I know what you are thinking. That old bad-man, good-man routine.' Keppler smiled weakly at her, and she felt the little knot of courage dissipate. 'Sorry. We are both bad men as far as you are concerned. Neumann, you know, was the son of a concierge in Hamburg. All those comings and goings. Grew up spying on people. And with a dislike of the rich, privileged Jews who looked down on his mother. Just think how he felt when he was given the chance to be paid for getting his own back on such people. Me? Born in Austria but joined the German police force, even though they ridiculed my accent. I was a detective in Karlsruhe before I joined the party in 1935. So, I suppose my methods are more traditional than Neumann's. But the fact is, we both want our questions answered . . .' He helped her from the floor on to the bed, and she composed herself.

'My name is . . .'

'Please,' he barked at her, raising his hand, causing her to flinch. He dropped it to his side. 'Please. If you can't say anything else, don't say anything at all.'

Keppler began to pace and allowed a warm glow of satisfaction to fill his belly. This was something he enjoyed, showing his colleagues that, although he knew their more extreme methods had their place, his ten years as a cop had taught him there were less invasive ways. The salted food/no water trick, for instance. It took a little longer than the current favourite of dunking spies in scalding and freezing baths and holding them under till they nearly drowned, but it had an elegance such crude brutality lacked. A man dying of thirst can be most eloquent when a glass of water is just out of his reach.

'The Hotel Victoria in Northumberland Avenue.'

She looked up at him.

'Interviewed there by a Major. Didn't give his name. Am I right? That was your recruitment into SOE. From there, a month or so of observation, to check you were the "right sort", fitness training at Arisaig Commando School. Then on to Guildford for tradecraft or Ringway for parachute training or vice versa. Finished at . . . Beaulieu? No, Beddington probably. Kept in holding house at Farnham. Orchard Court near Baker Street just before dispatch. Do they still have Parks the butler there? So English. Even the spies have butlers. Let's see, who would have been dispatching officer? Vera Atkins perhaps? Bodington? Miller? No matter, always the same drill – check you are French down to your fingertips.'

He reached out and snatched her hand before she had a chance to hold back and admired her nails. 'Very nice. So. You see, as my friend suggested, there is little we don't know.'

'My name is Yolande—' she began weakly.

'Your name is not important. Look, how do you think we know all these details? We have Arthur Lock, an Englishman, a hero to half the misguided Resistance, a loyal worker to us. We have at least three other SOE agents helping us. Five radio operators transmitting back under our guidance. The only reason we don't

171

arrest every damn one of you is that you would send in another lot. This way, we get to keep you under observation until we are good and ready to haul you in. It's a game, Miss whoever you are. And we are winning. Your choice is to talk to me, or spend some time with Neumann.'

The woman upstairs was panting now, loud exhalations building to a theatrical climax.

'And if I tell you to go to hell?' she said with a bravery she tried to summon up from her twitching insides.

'Ha.' Keppler threw the brown envelope on the bed next to her. He waited until her eyes flicked down to the small package. 'From your jacket lining. What I believe you call your L pill. Cyanide, isn't it? Fast and painless. At least – that's what they tell you. I wonder how they know. Who has come back to say – "actually, old chap, hardly hurt at all". But if you want to find out, be my guest. I won't try to stop you. Another drop of agents is due next full moon. I can wait for them.'

As the panting became faster she reached out for the envelope, her hand hovering over it. The L pill. All of them had listened solemnly while they were told when and where and how to use it. Better to die silent, like a good Englishwoman.

She flipped open the envelope and took the pill in her fingertips, wondering if the poison was already seeping through into her bloodstream. She looked straight at Keppler, trying to calm the howling within, so she at least looked defiant, opened her mouth as wide as she would at the dentist and tossed the cyanide to the back of her throat. He didn't so much as blink.

Her dry throat tried to swallow, get the pill down, to let it take her before she changed her mind. But her body had already decided for her. Virginia's oesophagus had crushed itself flat, refusing to accept the deadly parcel. As she gulped and gulped, pushing the tiny tablet to the back of her throat, the retching reflex kicked in and she began to choke and cough.

Her eyes felt as if they were bursting out of her head and a metal band closed on her temples. She leaned over the bed and watched the half-dissolved pill slide off her tongue and onto the carpet.

God, had she taken enough into her bloodstream? Or was she going to live after all, because suddenly, irrationally, looking at the small, effervescing white disc, she wanted to live more than ever and hated herself for it.

Keppler picked up the harmless, saliva-covered piece of chalk, smiled, and popped it into his own mouth. 'Well done. A good try. But you don't want to die, do you? It would be such a waste of a young life.'

She began to cry just as the woman overhead orgasmed with a ridiculous flamboyance, the hideous loveless sound filling Virginia's brain to the exclusion of all else.

Nineteen

PARIS, MARCH–APRIL 1942

Robert exited the Metro at Raspaill, having stayed on past Montparnasse when he saw the amount of gendarme activity on the platform. A couple of greasy-haired *zazous*, the long-haired, jazz-loving youths, were being roughed up and, as a spin-off, papers demanded from random passers-by. Not that he had anything to worry about, strictly speaking, but like most people he had no desire deliberately to expose himself to the whim of the police, especially when their gander was up after the insolence of the *zazous*.

He emerged out on to the street, his breath coming in clouds as he walked across the frost-crisped grass of the Montparnasse cemetery. Spring was a long time coming. Many months had passed since the message from Beatrice, so long he was beginning to think it was a hoax, until this cryptic message arrived to send him back to Montparnasse for the first time in over a year.

His route took him through the cemetery, past the fluttering notices pinned to the trees warning about cooking cats – the cemeteries had become a favourite hunting ground for the contents of feline stews – and past benches with their 'Forbidden to Jews' plaques and into Avenue du Maine, slowly making his way north to rue de Vaugirard.

A few foolish feeble buds were showing on the plane trees, but for the most part it could still be deepest January. It was as if Paris was hibernating. The dark mornings, thanks to the switch to Berlin time, the power cuts, the blackout, it felt like living in a city of perpetual twilight, its spark permanently dimmed. Not even the news of the Americans entering the conflict had brightened the coldest months or brought a glimmer of cheer to Christmas.

Now he was at the small series of dead-end alleys, the *impasses*, that ran off rue de Vaugirard, and he could feel eyes staring at him from the long, grey queues that had formed outside the butchers' shops as he glanced down each cul-de-sac, looking for his rendezvous. The lines didn't move, except perhaps to contract and expand slightly, like a human concertina, as gossip and rumour and innuendo flowed back and forth.

The Café Cuisse was a long, dingy corridor of a place down the last *impasse*, its presence signalled by a shabby sign of a happy butcher. Robert waited outside the entrance for a second, peering into the gloom, then entered. The smell hit him immediately, the metallic, coppery tang of blood. A few of the regular clients were at the bar, manfully sipping what passed for coffee and washing it down with rough brandy. All wore large leather aprons, stained with red blots of accumulated equine blood, and wicked-looking knives hanging from the belts that were slung under their ample guts.

One of them eyed Robert cautiously and, apparently satisfied, went back to his drink. It was a good place for a meet. Given the choice of hanging round the Coupole or Select or taking your chances with surly cleaver-carrying horse butchers who were the main clients of the local cafés, most Germans and their stooges would opt for the former.

The proprietor gave Robert a coffee without his asking and indicated towards the rear, where, past the chipped and scuffed furniture, a lone figure sat reading a newspaper, the pages held out, obscuring his face.

The first Williams knew of Robert's presence in the café was when the little yellow flame sprouted at the bottom of his *Figaro*, quickly spreading like a brown stain up the spine, and he had to leap to his feet and stamp out the conflagration.

Robert watched the performance with a bemused grin, leaving Williams almost too exasperated even to offer a greeting to his old friend. He held out his arms and Robert fell into them and Williams thumped his back until he felt his ribs would crack under the onslaught. He pushed Will away, and put his hands on his shoulders, marvelling at the physical change, the muscular, honed figure before him.

'What?' asked Robert. 'You expected me to say all that "Giraffe Has A Long Neck" shit?' He pulled out a chair and sat.

Williams hesitated and joined in the laughter, which drew a few sidelong glances from the counter. Such expressions were rare these days, as if joy were a culpable offence.

'Good to see you, Will. How long have you been back?'

Williams sat down, gave his coffee a stir, even though there was no sugar to be had for it, and hesitated before telling the truth: 'Four months.'

'Four . . . you've been here four months? And you didn't contact Eve?' Robert felt a bolt of anger as Williams shook his head. 'What the hell have you been doing?'

Williams leant forward and lowered his voice while increasing its intensity. 'I am a pestilence, Robert. A plague. A vile disease. I can wipe out whole families, whole villages, just by my presence.

Just talking to you puts you at risk.'

'But—'

Williams raised a hand to silence him. 'I had to get it right, Robert. I had to know which days you could order alcohol, that pastries are only available Mondays, Tuesdays and Wednesdays, get used to the ration books, know that only Germans can drive on Sunday. You've no longer noticed all the changes, you've come in so gradually. But it's a minefield for a new arrival. Ordering a *café au lait* can be fatal.' Robert nodded. He knew there was no milk around that month. A stranger might not. And such a blunder might draw the attention of a V-Mann of the collaborationist rue Laurent Gestapo, or the real thing.

'So, where've you been?'

'The Citroën factory. Remember Bernard the mechanic? Foreman. Got me on the assembly line for six weeks. Thanks to him all the bearings on the tank turrets go out with caccolube grease on them . . .'

'Caccolube?'

'It contains carborundum powder. The turrets work well for a few weeks, maybe months, well enough that nobody suspects sabotage, then one day . . .'

Robert slapped the table with joy at the thought of a Panzer tank seizing up in the heat of battle, jammed solid as a Russian tank battalion appeared over the ridge of the Steppes.

'Same with the wheels, with ball bearings . . .'

They both chuckled. 'What now?'

'Now I need help. Now I need a truck. *Ausweiss*. Petrol.'

'Petrol, leave that to Maurice . . .'

'Maurice?'

'Maurice. And *Ausweissen*. He has his methods.' A thought suddenly came to Robert. 'Do you have a radio?'

Williams shook his head. 'No, nor a big flag with "Secret Agent – Come and Get Me" on it.'

Robert furrowed his brow, and Williams thought that the older he got the more hawk-like he became. 'Meaning?'

'Meaning the best way to get caught is to start broadcasting your position to the world.' Williams smiled ruefully. 'Besides, my Morse is diabolical. We'll use cut-outs.' The system of couriers with limited knowledge of all parties was by no means water-tight, but it was far less damaging if a messenger was caught – he or she could only take so many down with him. 'You have a cigarette?'

'Don't you?' Robert asked disappointed. 'You didn't bring any across?'

'Yes. But too good to smoke in public. If you catch my drift.'

Robert offered him one of the *tabac national* cigarettes, appreciating that smoking real tobacco might also attract the curious. They lit up.

'I'm using letter drops and couriers to communicate with England. That way if the link is blown, we should be buffeted. So, what chance of a lorry of some description?'

'I can get you a truck. But I'll have to drive it.'

'Why?'

'Because the better driver should take the wheel.'

Williams laughed softly. 'I thought we'd settled that.'

'We did. I won.'

'Thirteen years ago, old man. Anyway, you told me I was the victor.'

'I was being kind. And less of the old man – you aren't a boy any longer. We toss for it, then. Agreed?' Williams nodded. He was surprised by the excitement in Robert's voice. He'd been expecting an uphill struggle to get him involved. 'What are we doing?' Robert asked eagerly.

'It's dangerous.'

'Good.'

'What about Wimille?'

'You got any money?'

'Around two million Francs.'

'Then he'll play. You know Jean-Pierre. He's a cash-on-delivery boy. One more thing.'

'What?'

'I told Eve I had a meeting. I suspected the message was from you. She's in the rue Weber apartment.'

Williams felt his head swirl at the thought. For four months he had kept the whole idea of seeing Eve sealed in a corner of his brain, like a trunk in the attic, full of anticipated pleasures, but not to be opened. Not yet. Now it burst the stays, spilling its contents into his cerebrum and a mixture of love and terror almost overwhelmed him. Even before he realised it he was starting to rise from the seat, drawn to her, to the thought of her. Robert, ever practical, pushed him back down.

'Are your papers in order?'

Williams nodded. Robert removed his arm.

'Then go to her. She's still the most beautiful woman in Paris.'

Now he hesitated, fearing the magnitude of the task, the rediscovery of each other, that was before him.

'Before I take your place,' his friend added.

Williams stood, squeezed Robert on the shoulder and said, 'I'll be in touch about the . . . things we need.'

'Sure. But get this one right first, eh? She's missed you.'

'Me too,' Williams replied flatly.

Robert laughed and punched him on the arm. 'I would practise saying that a few times on the way over. Now go.'

After Williams had left Robert smoked another bitter cigarette, trying to work out what he had in mind. Dangerous. Not like

racing cars then? How many people had been claimed by that
during his time at Delage and Bugatti? Soon, the Germans would
have been in France for two years. In that time they had gone
from tourists and 'very correct' to an occupying army whose real
role had become very apparent – to strip France of men and
goods and redirect them to the Reich. He stubbed out the
cigarette. The thought had been circling in his head throughout
the harsh winter – it was time to do something about it.

Hans Keppler strode across to the window of his office on
Avenue Foch and looked down on the broad double-
carriageway thoroughfare. The chestnut and plane trees finally
looked as if they were going to make an effort to pretend it was
spring after all. The roads were quiet, just the odd charcoal-
burning car chugging asthmatically by or a smoother Citroën
Light 15 arriving or departing the courtyards at numbers 72, 82
and 84 that the SD had requisitioned. He was at 82 in the best
office in the entire complex, he felt. Dominated by a huge
chandelier, with an Aubusson carpet and ormalu desk, it was
elegant and civilised, even if the business he carried out wasn't
always.

He heard Arthur Lock cough and was reminded of just how
base some of the activities were.

'Anything?' he asked.

'Personal shit,' said Lock, and sneered, 'I love you so much,
darling. Kiss little Jimmy for me. Most of their women are
probably kissing big Jimmy next door.'

Keppler drummed his fingers on the window sill. 'Show her.'

'Laurent?'

'Yes. Show her how much we know. Tell me how she reacts.
You know what I need from her.'

'Pleasure.'

The enthusiasm with which Lock ensnared his fellow country-men left even Keppler with a sense of disquiet. He had no illusions about how Lock would act if ever it became expedient to switch sides. The man had deserted even before France fell, taking with him the mess funds. He had popped up as Major Lock of MI9 helping downed airmen in late 1940, while also helping himself to escape line funds. When discovered he had contacted the SD at Lille and betrayed everyone, including his young bride and her family. Having paused only to pawn their jewels, he was taken to Keppler to see if he could be of any use.

'After you've finished with Yolande Laurent get down to the Champs Elysées cafés. I have reports of English being spoken. Pump the waiters for all you can. Take some marks with you.'

Lock nodded and made his way to the door.

'Oh, and Lock.'

'Yes, Sturmbannführer?'

'And make sure you account for every last one of those marks. In writing.'

'Of course, Sturmbannführer,' Lock said innocently.

The Germans had made Virginia relatively comfortable on the fifth floor. Her cell was small, but they had managed to squeeze in a bed and a desk and chair, a selection of books in French and some basic toiletries. She was allowed to use a sitting room during the day, and had even been offered dinners out, which she had, of course, refused.

Since the night when she had tried to swallow what she had thought was an L pill, they had treated her with surprising civility. She knew this wasn't always the case. She glimpsed other prisoners who bore marks of beatings, heard both men and women sobbing in the night, lay awake listening to the distant shouts and screams of interrogation, of the slamming of doors and the angry bark of guards. Not for her, though. Not yet.

In a strange way she wished it would hurry up and happen. Waiting made it worse. The day would come when she was tested and she needed to know how she would react, whether the training in any way helped her to face up to what was in store. The longer they delayed, the more some part of her began to hope that it would never happen, that it would all turn out OK in the end, as if this were an Angela Brazil novel. That stupidly optimistic part of her brain was, she knew, slowly corroding her resolve, weakening her.

Lock knocked on the door but entered without waiting for a reply. Instinctively she shuffled back on the bed, away from this reptilian creature. He smiled and sat, placing a pile of documents on her desk and then ignoring them.

'How are you, Yolande?'

'Please, get to the point.'

'You're his now, you know. Keppler's.'

'What on earth do you mean?'

'Once he knew you couldn't go through with killing yourself.'

'It was chalk.'

'That wasn't the point, was it? We now all know your desire to live is stronger than your sense of duty.'

She glared at him but he just smiled back in his oily way. Lock was a creature she just couldn't place, as if he was some strange new species brought back by an expedition and was yet to be classified. He looked English, he sounded English but some basic part of him was missing. The humanity, she decided. 'That is rather rich, coming from you, Lock.'

'Me? I've never made any bones about who I look out for. Your lot come over here with all this noble cause claptrap and the moment they tickle your toes, you roll over.'

'Nonsense.'

Lock tapped the stack of documents. 'Do you know what these are?'

'Your memoirs?'

'Not quite.'

He handed a sheet across and she cast an eye over it. It was a letter, a personal letter, from a husband to a wife or sweetheart. 'Very touching.'

'It will be flown out on tonight's Lysander. All of this will be. It just so happens that, in return for safe passage, the flight controller lets Keppler read the mail.'

He let this sink in.

'All the mail. All the requests for arms, radio operators, maps, advice . . . all of it. Everything passes through the SD before it reaches London.'

Virginia shook her head in disbelief. The rules they had been taught at Beddington and Beaulieu with such certainty no longer seemed to apply. Was such a sordid arrangement worth it? Compromising security in order to get agents in and out without harm, agents who may be put at risk by the very action that secures their safe passage? Her head started to spin.

'So you have to realise, being the stubborn one won't do you any favours. Not when everybody else is busy cutting a deal with old Hans. He never asks anything unreasonable, you know.'

'What does he want?'

'First of all, a list of who you trained with.'

She laughed. 'Well, that won't do him any good. We all used false names. I have no idea who these people were.'

Lock took the time to roll himself a cigarette and look up at her occasionally. 'You know that's not true.'

'Do I?'

'You were trained with the same people for what? Six months? Eight? People aren't watertight. They leak. Little snippets at a time, perhaps, but it all comes out eventually. Now, I know you don't know where they are now, don't know where or why they were sent across. That's his job. Keppler's. All we need is the list and . . .'

'And what?'

Lock scooped up his documents, retrieved the letter from her and opened the door.

'And you get to keep those lovely nails for a while longer.'

The door closed and Virginia swung her feet on the bed, staring at the ceiling, trying not to think about the clumsy threat. A terrible feeling of hopelessness descended on her, a cloud of despair that everything, all the training, the sleepless nights, the fear she battled every single waking moment, everything had been a complete waste of time. Outfoxed and outflanked, sold up the river by men like Lock and the Lysander organiser. Hopeless. She closed her eyes and felt a hot tear roll out on to her cheek. Hopeless.

Williams pulled Eve closer to him, squeezing the breath from her lungs, as if he was trying to envelop her.

'Careful,' she gasped. 'I'm thinner than when you left.'

The air was thick and swirling, as if the apartment were about to erupt into an electrical storm. Questions and suspicions and apologies and recriminations and love and lust jostled with each other for pole position, the detritus of a long separation. Williams was aware of emotions locked behind enormous gates on both sides, frightened that to open them even a crack would sweep them away under a torrent.

Then, finally, they spoke in unison.

'I'm sorry.' A moment's pause and then the first carefree laugh.

'You first,' said Eve.

'I should have stayed.'

'I should have gone with you.'

'Does that make us even?' he asked.

'I think it does.'

There was a war going on outside he reminded himself. He was in an enemy-occupied city. The Gestapo or the SD might be searching for him even now. They were certainly arresting other agents, tightening their grip on the city. Yet he couldn't make any of it register, take hold. All that mattered was the room and the woman in front of him.

He pulled her down on to the bed, and she unbuttoned his shirt and began to sniff at his chest. 'What's all this?'

'What?'

'This.' She prodded his pectorals and felt her finger bounce back.

It was a moment before he realised she was referring to a physique changed and hardened by assault courses and push-ups and old colonial hands who liked nothing more than giving their men a 5 a.m. run. 'That? I think it's called muscle.'

She sniffed at his chest again and prodded, marvelling at the elastic skin, springy again after losing the adipose layer that had slowly accumulated underneath in their years together. 'I think I like it.'

'Why do you keep doing that?'

'What?'

'Sniffing me.'

Eve pulled herself up level with his eyes and he smiled into her face, thinner, it was true, but then so was what Robert said. As far he was concerned – maybe both were concerned – she was still the most beautiful woman in Paris.

'I want to know where you've been.'

He laughed and pulled her head to his neck and said very softly: 'Don't worry about where I've been. Worry about what we are going to do.'

Eve sat up, shook her head and shuffled back to work on his belt buckle. 'I know exactly what I'm going to do, Mister Williams.'

It took Maurice six weeks to find a decent truck with adequate documentation and a supply of petrol. He seemed pleased to see Williams, keen enough to help, but there was always a bill, always expenses. To Maurice, Resistance was a business like any other.

Meanwhile supplies came in. Sten guns, two Thomsons, pistols, some plastic explosive and timers. More money, always welcome. The team grew, much against Williams' better judgement, but picking up parachute drops needed organisation. A few of Robert's old farmworkers, Jean-Pierre Wimille, Thérèse Lethias, an old friend of the Benoist family, all helped with the clandestine activity.

Most of the materiel was hidden around Auffargis, some, including nearly all of the cash, at the Lethias' villa on the outskirts of Pontoise. Until it was needed. Thérèse started calling herself Banque du Liberation. And still the coded messages came from London: you need a radio operator. And still Williams replied: no. Then one day, when winter had finally given up the ghost, the plucky Beatrice came cycling down the drive with a single word as her message. Caravan. Williams heart gave an enormous judder, a surge of excitement cut with thin veins of fear. It was time to get off their arses and do something.

'Is there a reply?' asked Beatrice, anxious to be gone. She smiled as Robert walked from the house and raised a hand.

'No,' said Williams, but as soon as she remounted her bicycle he suddenly changed his mind. 'Actually, yes. Gelignite.'

'Gelignite?'

'Gelignite and *plastique*. And more pencils.'

She couldn't keep the curiosity off her face this time. Was he

186

going to write the Germans to death?

Williams smiled. 'They'll know what it means.'

Keppler growled as Maurice won another hand of *casino*. He, Neumann, Lock – now wearing a SD uniform – and Maurice had been sitting around for an hour now, with a slow steady flow of money towards Maurice. The Sphinx was only half full this evening. Many officers and their units had been withdrawn from Paris and were heading east for the big summer offensive. Their replacements were not always the kind of gentlemen The Sphinx preferred. On stage two naked redheads performed a rather desultory version of the sand dance, accompanied by an elderly clarinet and piano duo. Keppler wondered if perhaps he should find a new venue. It wasn't as if he ever used any of the girls.

Maurice suddenly launched into one of his endless stream of jokes and Lock leant forward, his French still being a little shaky. 'So it's this guy's fiftieth birthday and he's feeling pretty good, certain he doesn't look his age. He goes to his wine merchant and says, I'll have a bottle of the twenty-seven Margaux. In fact, it's my birthday. If you can guess how old I am, I'll pay you double. Forty-five, says the merchant. Ha, no, I'm fifty, the man says. He goes to the butcher's and asks for a nice steak to go with the wine. He does the same thing to the butcher. If you can guess how old I am, I'll give you this fine claret and you can eat the steak. Forty-five, says the butcher. Ha, no, I'm fifty. And off he goes. On the Metro on the way home he says to the little old lady next to him: It's my birthday. If you can guess how old I am you can have this wonderful claret and this excellent steak. The old woman furrows her brow, unbuttons his trousers and has a good rummage around. She takes her hand out and says: You're fifty. Good Lord, says the man, how did you do that? Easy, says the woman, I was standing behind you in the butcher's.'

187

Neumann banged the table and Lock smiled weakly, possibly because he hadn't quite caught the ending when Maurice's words tumbled together into a single stream. Keppler nodded and lit a cigarette.

'By the way, Maurice, did you have any luck with that little task we talked about?'

Maurice passed the cards to Neumann to deal. Neumann raised an eyebrow in question, but Keppler waved it away.

'Not exactly, Sturmbannführer.'

'Not exactly,' he said coldly, letting his displeasure show in his voice, enjoying watching the ferrety Maurice shrink back into his scarab-shaped chair. 'Not exactly. Well, I haven't exactly got any more *Ausweissen* for you to run your little racketeering organisation.'

'Sturmbannführer,' he protested, 'I have nothing to do with the black market.'

'Your very blood runs black, Maurice. And if I choose to shut you down . . . you know the penalty for trafficking. Shall we say my office? Next Wednesday? Ten o'clock. I have the census lists, perhaps that will help.'

'Of course, Sturmbannführer,' said Maurice, as brightly as he could muster. But, from that moment on, he lost all his winnings, and more.

Twenty

JUNE 1942

Feldwebel Technician Otto Bruninghaus moved the dials in front of him, straining his ears to make out the ethereal voices that crackled and spat and drifted in and out of aural focus, as if he was eavesdropping on the spirit world. Finally he got a clear signal and flicked on the loudspeaker so the half dozen men in the room – four guards taking a break and two other technicians – could hear.

'I have a contact. Big contact. Ten thousand feet. Closing.'

And another voice. 'Something on your tail. One-ten. Break right. Break right.'

Bruninghaus said loudly, mimicking perfectly the rising panic in the voice: 'Something on your tail. A one-ten.'

Radio silence. He could picture the strange black combat, the shapes of planes barely glimpsed in the starless sky, the navigators hunched over primitive radar sets, the Me-110s swooping to protect the Dorniers and Heinkels, playing tag with the Bristols and Boulton Pauls lunging blindly into the night, the sudden glare of tracer fire and the sickening judder as cannon shells tore

189

through metal and fabric and maybe flesh.

Bruninghaus's job was simple. To confuse the British night fighters, to disorientate them even more, so they would no longer trust their eyes, their ears or their screens. He was sitting in what he thought of as a giant, angular albino insect, a metal capsule attached to a trailer, its legs formed by the struts that splayed from each corner to give stability, its head by the giant radio mast that was raised into the air, enabling signals to pass unimpeded from the bottom of the chalk quarry where it sat.

Everything was white – the scarred walls and soil of the pit, the structure itself, the tents where they slept, their overalls, a world devoid of colour, at least on the outside. Every two or three days they packed up the rig and moved to another of the big pockmarks in the earth that dotted this part of France, to the far north west of Paris, just outside the Forbidden Zone, the huge swathe of northern France out of bounds to all but essential workers. Every few days the spotter planes would come over, searching for them, to be chased away by the protecting Messerschmitts.

'Have contact.' The radio buzzed again. 'Dorniers I'd say. I'll go under. Have a go.' There was the sound of gunfire, crackling, unreal.

'Damn. I'll turn again. Watch out for one-tens.'

This was probably a Boulton Paul, a single-engined fighter with a rather ungainly gun turret placed behind the pilot whose hapless occupant managed to miss the Dorniers. Bruninghaus flicked the transmit switch.

'Am getting low on fuel here. Returning to base. Over.'

'Who's that? Say again?'

His audience began to titter and Bruninghaus turned to face them and said in a sing-song voice, 'Time for tea. Tea time. Everything stops for tea.'

The others began to guffaw.

Then, more urgently, he said: 'Dornier 17s. Dozens of them. Dive, dive.'

The radio waves became full of confused jabbering, and after a few more baffling interventions Bruninghaus stood up and stretched and gloated, 'That should make sure our boys get an easier ride through to London. I need a piss.'

He went outside into the night and unzipped his overalls to relieve himself against one of the trailer tyres, careful not to splash the electrical wires snaking across the earth to the clanking generator. In fact, the machine seemed excessively noisy tonight, its low hum joined by a tappety burbling. Then he realised that the sound was coming from behind him. He turned, felt his jaw drop at what he could just make out in the gloom, and ran for the doorway to warn his companions.

Williams eased the truck into low gear and winced as he passed the guardhouse. Two amorphous shapes could be seen in the light of the few stars that were out, the apparently black splashes on the dirty white track their lifeblood draining away. All those days and nights of practising eye gouging and throat slitting and neck snapping, and there it was before him, the first evidence of cold-blooded murder, performed by Wimille's little coterie of mercenaries.

This was it, this was real, he thought and reminded himself that the explosives packed behind him, surrounded by enough black-market petrol to keep Paris running for a month, that was real too, as were the pot holes and ridges in the crude road he drove towards the quarry.

He looked in the wing mirror as he turned on to the hairpins of the cliffside road that would take him to the bottom of the giant gash in the earth. He could just make out the low shape of the Atlantic in the glass. He was glad it was there. Eve had thought them mad. She'd suggested the Renault van or the Citroën as the follow car, but both he and Robert felt speed would be their best ally. 'You'll be spotted in the Atlantic,' said Eve, adding with impassioned crudity, 'it's like driving round with your dick hanging out.'

'Spotting us is one thing,' Robert had said.

'Catching us is another,' finished Williams.

He guided the truck round the first of the hairpins, peering through the slot cut into a piece of steel welded across the windshield, hoping that the load in the back was secure and stable. He glanced at the primitive system of levers they'd welded on to the dashboard, praying they would work as well as they had in the dry runs.

This was no dry run. Sweat was beginning to stream down his face as he took the second bend, trying to use the throttle as little as possible, hoping not to lose the element of surprise. He'd been given this target before leaving England, assured that he would only be needed if the RAF failed to find and destroy the mobile masts. They clearly had.

Next bend, and suddenly the wheels were slipping on the edge of the road, sending flurries of grit and chalk into the air. He corrected, pulled the lorry back on to the centre, settling into the ruts made by hundreds of other trucks over the years. Better to endure the bouncing than risk plunging over the edge and detonating the load without achieving anything. Final turn, then a long ramp down to where he could just make out the spectral shape of the camouflaged transmission unit.

This was the part he had been dreading. The wait.

Williams lined the truck up at the top of the ramp and wiped his damp hands on his shirt. He pulled the six make-shift levers on the dash, watching the wires pull taut, praying that behind him half a dozen pencil timers had just broken. The problem was, all that had been sent were four-minute timers. Four minutes was three minutes too long as far as he was concerned.

He sat there, waiting for the seconds to crawl by, waiting for the searchlights to suddenly blind him, the bullets to start hitting the cab, the grenades to ignite the load behind him. Then he began to breathe long and slow. This was like a race. Life or death. Similar odds. You did that for ten years. You can manage this.

One minute.

Was he crazy? Should he have just come back and stayed with Eve, and sod those mad bastards in London who think that pinpricks like this one could affect the course of the war? A symbol, they always argued. No matter what you do it will be a symbol, a rallying call. Which presumably it would be even if he died. But he wasn't going to die. He was going to slow time down. He closed his eyes, felt the tachycardia kick in as, against the constant urging of adrenaline, his heart rate fell.

Two minutes.

With measured calm and steady hands, Williams moved the throttle brace into position, the steel rod that would fix the accelerator in the fully depressed position, and slid the retaining bolt through the steering wheel, which would keep the truck on a direct course for the wireless station ahead.

Three minutes.

There was someone outside who had spotted him. A technician. Sprinting to raise the alarm. Chequered flag time. He pressed the throttle to the floor, felt the ancient engine twist and jerk in its mounting as if trying to break free, engaged the throttle brace and let in the clutch, and in one smooth, flowing movement was out the door and heading for a hard landing.

Fifty seconds left.

The air exploded from his body as he hit the ground with a puff of choking chalk dust.

193

Forty-one, forty, thirty-nine . . .

Then he was on his feet and running, counting down, sprinting up the slope towards the Atlantic, willing his legs to pump faster.

Twenty, nineteen . . .

He waited for the explosion to lick its warm breath over him. Keep running.

Ten, nine, eight . . .

He was level with the car when he heard the crumple of metal as the truck punched into the German unit, its engine screaming in its red-lined death throes, the building itself half torn from its housings with a teeth-clenching shriek, bracing wires pinging free from the ground and spinning through the air with a lethal whistle.

Three, two, one . . .

Williams ducked.

Nothing.

He stared in panic at Robert who mouthed, 'Get in.'

Williams looked again at the twisted pile of truck and radio station. He could see a figure crawling from the wreckage. Something in his hand. Gun.

Williams opened the Atlantic door and reached into the back for the Thomson. 'Will. Get in. It's a dud. The pencils mustn't have snapped.'

'There's still the gelly . . . and the petrol.'

'Get in, you idiot.'

Another figure, and Williams felt the crackle of air as a bullet flew past him. He pulled back the bolt on the Thomson. He knew you couldn't ignite petrol with a bullet. Not an ordinary bullet. But you might with tracers, and the thirty-round magazine had seven of those in there, big .45 slugs that burned bright and hot.

He set the gun to auto fire. A pain seared through his ear, and

194

his shoulder. Then he heard, way off to his left, a gunshot and saw a muzzle flash from the corner of his eye. Sniper. Wimille or one of his lads. Good people. Value for money.

Williams squeezed the trigger and felt the submachine gun judder up to the left and noticed the two fiery angels flying towards the truck.

More cover fire from the clifftop, pinning down the Germans. But still he could hear the air snapping near him.

Second burst, three tracers out into the truck. Still nothing.

Now Robert was firing, holding the Sten all wrong, hand on the magazine, sure way to jam it, but the damn thing didn't have the guts to jam on an angry Robert and the nine-millimetre slugs zinged into the wreckage ahead of them.

All or nothing. Williams squeezed the trigger to empty the magazine and at seven hundred rounds per minute the bullets were gone in an instant. Not a dicky bird. He turned to get the hell out of there.

The explosion of fuel knocked him back against the Atlantic as a fireball rolled and boiled around the truck, greedily engulfing the damaged radio station as well. Whether the timing pencils clicked in or the gelignite went – the plastic was pretty inert – a second, deeper, more energetic detonation spun pieces of metal and debris high into the air. Finally, reluctantly, with a high-pitched tearing sound, the radio mast started to lean, shift and turn as it fell on to the pyre, generating a dense cloud of metallic fireflies which spiralled up into the dark night.

Williams was already in the Atlantic, its wheels smoking as Robert yanked it round and sped up the track, sliding the back dangerously on each bend, while Williams smiled at a third explosion, consuming what was left of the complex.

They made the main road and headed into the forests, retracing their route through the backroads and unused pathways that

Robert had picked out to circumvent any patrols and road blocks. The trees blurred by at terrifying speed, Robert risking a flash of dim lights only when absolutely necessary. Williams let out a long breath of stale air, slumped down in the seat and closed his eyes, confident that his friend wouldn't wrap them round a trunk.

'Arm,' said Robert.

Williams looked down at his torn shirt and winced as his fingers found the wound underneath, a one-inch gouge through the muscle.

'All right,' he said with more hope than conviction. The trough of raw meat was beginning to sting.

Robert glanced across. 'Yeah, you'll heal.' He pointed to the cracks and starring at the corner of the windshield where two bullets had passed through and said with mock anger, 'Do you know how much a new one of these fucking things costs?'

Hans Keppler, a handkerchief over his face to try to filter out the worst of the smell of burnt rubber and human flesh, surveyed the tangled ruin of what had once been a fine piece of German technical engineering but was now a smouldering piece of scrap metal with the chassis of a truck embedded in it. Medics were extracting what charred remains they could from the mess, and laying them out on stretchers. Only one completely intact body had been located, and that was blackened beyond recognition. The day was already warm, thought Keppler, by the next day this charnel house would stink worse than ever.

Keppler looked at Neumann. 'Organised. Daring. Anything?'

'We have one sentry who saw a car. Low, fast. Two men, he thinks. But he died before he could say much more. Lost too much blood.'

'What's the nearest village?' asked Keppler.

'Place called Boissy. We've already shot four of them.'

196

Keppler raised an eyebrow. Hitler had ordered reprisals for acts of terrorism in the previous September, but this seemed a little too hasty.

'Two Jews and two Communists,' said Neumann by way of explanation. People who deserved to die whether Boissy was implicated or not. 'Just to help the recollection process of the rest.'

'I want the village fined a million francs. No more retaliatory measures for the moment.' Keppler used the approved term *Vergeltungssanktionen*, retaliation rather than reprisal. General Karl Heinrich von Stulnagel, the Militarbefehlshaber of France, had forbidden the word reprisals and even hostages from being used to describe the response to terrorism. 'If we find the expiators—' – *Suhnepersonen*, another new term – 'used the village and villagers in any way, then I suggest we transport all the males for labour work in Germany. Better than wasting bullets.'

And a safer, more elegant solution, thought Keppler. Sabotage on the scale of this attack was rare. But when it did happen, all concerned knew that the Germans would take revenge on the population. Keppler wondered if that was part of the aim of the perpetrators – to radicalise the population by having the Occupiers seen as brutal thugs. If so, it was a callous, but effective policy on behalf of the Resistance. Which is why Keppler preferred what General Keital called *Nacht und Nebel* – the disappearance of the Reich's enemies into the Night and Fog, leaving their loved ones in ignorance of their whereabouts or state of health, and as an important bonus, snuffing out the opportunity to create martyrs for their futile cause.

'Do you think the Laurent woman might have any knowledge of this?'

Keppler shook his head, disappointed. 'No.'

'You indulge her. Sir.'

'She'll break. I know the type. You don't have to touch them. Her mind does it all for you.' Keppler also quite enjoyed the rumour over at the Hotel Lutetia where the Abwehr were convinced he had acquired himself a British spy as a willing mistress.

Keppler took the handkerchief away from his mouth and walked briskly towards his white-spattered Opel staff car. He turned to Neumann. 'Everything ready for *La Grand Rafle*?'

'Yes. I have ordered a hundred extra coffins. Two hundred pairs of handcuffs. Black-out curtains for the buses which will take those not to be transported to execution and two thousand litres of fuel for burning the corpses of the dead.'

'Burning where?' asked Keppler, out of curiosity.

'Père-Lachaise. Most adults for resettlement will go to Drancy, families and children to the Velo.'

Drancy was an unfinished housing estate near Le Bourget which had been operating as a holding camp for Jews since May 1941; the Velo was the cycle track, the Velodrome d'Hiver. All would eventually be put on transports to the east, where God alone knew what awaited them. Although, in this case, Keppler could second guess the deity.

They climbed inside the car and Keppler ordered his driver to proceed. The *rafle*, Keppler had decided, was folly. The Jews were not going anywhere. They had no radios, no bicycles, longer curfew hours and, since May, all over the age of six were required to wear the yellow star. Keppler would forget the Jews for now, and work on cases such as this act of destruction. He took one last glance back at the carnage and said to Neumann: 'I don't want you wasting days on this Big Round-up. Just do it quickly. And remember – use gendarmes where you can, that way it will be seen as a French operation. And we can get on with catching these terrorists.'

Twenty-one

AUGUST 1942

In the darkness Williams pulled Eve closer to him and she stirred. More than a month since the attack at the chalk pit. No new instructions, not so much as a 'well done' from London. Probably punishment for not having a radio. Now it was back to waiting. Waiting for a young girl to turn into the drive, or a half-track full of soldiers or a black Citroën full of Sonderkommando. It was getting to Eve more than him, he knew.

Robert was travelling to Paris more and more to see his mother, who had a suspected liver ailment and was in and out of hospital. At least it kept him occupied. Wimille had gone back to living it up as best he could in Paris, swearing he would be ready whenever he was called upon. In a strange way, he said, he had enjoyed it. Nothing strange about it, thought Williams. They just all needed whatever stupid drug risking their lives generated. Some more than others, that was all.

'Will.'

Eve had opened one eye.

'Hmm.'

'I want to go to Normandy for a while.'

'Why?'

'To see the dogs.'

'They'll be all right.' A neighbour was feeding and exercising the terriers.

'They'll forget who I am.'

'They're dogs,' he said. 'They love whoever feeds them.' She poked him hard and he sighed. 'If you wish. You'll need travel documents.'

'Maurice said he can fix me up.'

'When did you see Maurice?'

'In town. A week ago.'

Williams sat up. 'You've been plotting this for a week?'

'Plotting? Don't be ridiculous. I've been thinking about it. I could go and see my parents, make sure the dogs are fine. I'll be away a week or two at most.'

'I don't want to be without you.'

'Come with me.'

He looked into her eyes to see if she was serious, but the smirk told him she was just echoing another situation where he had been the one doing the leaving. And for a lot longer than two weeks. She knew that him travelling around was an unnecessary risk. Women still attracted less attention than men young enough to be working in the Reich's munitions factories. 'How is Maurice?'

'Fine. Funny thing, he offered me a refrigerator.'

'Why?'

'He said he had come into a couple.'

'What did you say?'

'I said we'd think about it.'

'Say no.'

'Why?'

Williams slid out of bed. Dawn was breaking, streaking the sky

200

a deep orange. At one time the return of the sun meant the end of nightmares, the solar angel driving away the demons. Not any longer. The horrors seemed to go on, day or night now. Not so much here, in the country, but Paris was like a wounded animal turning on itself, devouring its own rancid flesh in a desperate bid to survive. 'Because you don't know where it's come from.'

'You don't mind taking his *Ausweissen*.'

'That's different. That's for a good cause.'

He turned to face her, and even in the gloom she could tell by the set of his jaw he was deadly serious. She decided that one victory, his acquiescence over her travelling, was enough for one morning. 'Okay, Will. No refrigerator.'

In the soft early dawn light he saw the figure at the gate and reached down for the Colt pistol beside the bed. He looked back. Gone. Then he saw her again, pushing her bicycle down the drive. Beatrice. Or one of her friends. A year ago the Germans would let a pretty young girl come and go with near impunity. It never occurred to them that young French women would be part of a clandestine organisation. Now, since they had uncovered dozens of underground printing presses and Resistance cells, they had realised the glue holding them together – the runners, messengers, lookouts, distributors – were, as often as not, the same smiling girls they whistled at in the street.

Williams pulled on some clothes, shoved the gun in his waistband and went down to greet the courier. No, he couldn't go on risking their young lives. Maybe London was right. Time to get a pianist in.

Maurice looked down the list on the desk in front of him and ticked two names, Pierre Tavel and Jean Leffe. He glanced up at Keppler who was staring out at the splendid chestnuts in the central ribbon of the boulevard and the grand *poules*, the high-class prostitutes who had always lived on Foch, sunning themselves on the grass.

'Tavel, I am pretty sure,' said Maurice softly. 'Leffe's real name is Szlifkes. Polish Jew.'

Keppler nodded. This was tedious work, but each department had been given a quota of Jews to identify. RSHA, the mother organisation of the SD and Gestapo in Berlin, estimated 800,000 Jews in France, perhaps a quarter or a fifth of that in Paris. The numbers didn't add up. The *rafles* had failed to find anything like that amount. Rather than accept that they might have inflated the figures, Eichmann had told the Gestapo and SD to flush out those hiding under aliases or being harboured by sympathetic French families.

Keppler walked over and examined the list. He flicked the pages. There were eight ticks in all. 'Not many, Maurice.'

This was the third time Maurice had visited the office, the third occasion he had had to shut his mind to the consequences of his actions, identifying people he knew were naturalised Jews, who would fail the Nazi criteria on parentage, and be resettled along with the thousands of others. Still, if he didn't do it . . .

'Well, I've already given you most of the ones I know. Surely there can't be many left in the city?'

'Berlin thinks there must be. They think they are out there somewhere, waiting to cause trouble.'

'What do you think, Sturmbannführer?'

Keppler laughed and fished himself a cigar from a beautiful red mahogany and brass humidor, recently arrived on his desk from an apartment over in the 7th that had been vacated the day before the round-up. A tip off, he suspected. Either a sentimental gendarme or one who charged exorbitantly to supply news of impending actions.

He swivelled the container to Maurice, who selected a fat

Jamaican. 'I don't think about things like this. Orders come from RSHA, I obey them, then get on with my real job. Which, I should remind you, is the pursuit of enemies of the state. At least, those more dangerous than Jewish doctors and bankers.'

Maurice nodded. He knew Keppler was a reasonable man.

'So, what is it to be this time, Maurice? Eight names . . . a couple of *Ausweissen* for you to continue your scurrilous smuggling activities or another visit to the warehouse?'

The great storage sheds near Gare de Lyon were stuffed full of the possessions of Jews who were caught in the big trawl-in on 16 and 17 of July. Sure, Maurice felt sorry for them, but there was everything from tables to refrigerators going begging. Shame to let it rot. But in the end he said: 'The *Ausweissen* would be most useful. My mother is not well and—'

'Stop. Spare me the weasly excuses.' Keppler signed the paperwork and handed it over to Maurice. 'Let's see if your memory improves next time you have to visit poor ailing Mama.'

Maurice grabbed the permissions to travel, which he would split with Robert, and hurried out, closing his ears to some of the more extreme sounds echoing down the corridors and out into the fresh air, ignoring the protests of his bad leg.

The meeting was on the banks of the Canal St Martin, up near La Villette. As with the horse butchers in Montmartre, the cafés hereabouts were the haunts of the slaughtermen and the herders, and probably as safe as anywhere in Paris, but Williams knew that the army of collaborationist eavesdroppers had grown as rations had shrunk. People had to eat, feed what was left of their families. So meetings were best arranged in the open air, away from the cafés where random raids were becoming more and more common.

Williams had to be careful in Paris for other reasons, too. As a healthy man in his late thirties he was eligible for working in the Reich. His papers proclaimed him as an electrical engineer, a reserved occupation, especially when so many factories were being hit by allied bombing or, more rarely, sabotage. Even so, one false move during a routine check and such niceties could be forgotten and he could be heading east. He slowed as he came past the gushing lock gates and into the wide Basin La Villette. An elderly couple sat on the benches on the Quai de la Seine, throwing a few precious crumbs to the pigeons.

A little cluster of teenage girls, their wooden clogs clacking ferociously to the rhythm of their gossip, hurried by. The same noise could be heard all over Paris – the Wehrmacht had taken the nation's entire leather supply, and decent shoes now only appeared for special occasions. At the far end of the Quai a lone woman studied a magazine – sunglasses, hair tied back, wearing a jacket and skirt made from thick felt-like material that were fashionable, despite their unsuitability for the summer weather.

Twenty metres away he slowed, unable to believe what he was seeing, then remembered himself. Don't act surprised. Do not draw attention to yourself. He strode up and uttered his part of the pre-arranged greeting.

'Mam'selle. I believe you have a bicycle for sale.'

Rose Miller looked up over her glasses. 'Yes. Would you like a ride?'

'I'd prefer to know how much first.'

'Sit down and we can discuss a price.'

Williams quickly took his place beside her and whispered, 'What on earth are you doing here?'

'We had some accidents at Ringway. Terribly short of people this month.'

'But you . . . if you are caught . . .'

She pointed to her brooch, a green emerald set in an arrangement of gold leaves and he understood that, somehow, it was lethal. Her L pill. 'Listen, Bodington has been over twice.'

'Bodington?'

'Nick Bodington. Buckmaster's deputy. Knows Paris from before the war. If *he* can chance it, so can I.'

Williams was unconvinced. It seemed like unnecessary bravado. Rose put a hand on his knee, briefly, as if to reassure him.

'Besides, I needed to see what it is like. Changed, hasn't it?' She waved a hand to indicate the whole of Paris. 'Even since you came over. How can I do my job unless I really know what conditions are like? You can't beat first-hand experience.'

'All right, all right. You are here now. Listen, I've changed my mind. I need a radio operator.'

Rose nodded. 'You'll have to wait. As I said, we are desperately short. The courier system is still working, obviously.'

'For the moment,' said Williams. 'I think it's time to change.'

'Have you contact with any other groups. Prosper?'

He shook his head. He had heard of one group who met in cafés in central Paris who occasionally lapsed into English. Maurice told him they were being watched, hoping to snare others. If that was Prosper, Williams wanted no part of it. 'So why are you here?'

'I need a recce done. Something funny is going on. On the railways. Some trains heading east are stopping at a factory at St Just. You know it?'

'No.'

'It's a chemical works. I need to know what's going on.'

'Is that it?' he asked, disappointed. 'You came all this way to tell me that?'

Rose snapped. 'Yes that's it. Except I want you to film it.'

'Film? With what?'

'I have the equipment. I will show you. And afterwards Robert – he's to come back with me.'

He felt a sudden panic at losing his friend. 'What? Why?'

'Training. See if we can make him a better radio man than you.' She arched an eyebrow. 'Not that it will be very difficult.'

Some way down the towpath a pair of German officers appeared, the familiar muddy green identifying them as Wehrmacht.

'Are you in order?' asked Williams, using the now automatic shorthand.

Rose nodded.

'What's your name?'

'Claudette Duclos.'

They stood to walk casually away from the Germans, who seemed simply out for a stroll. But you could never tell. 'What's your cover?'

'Typically French,' Rose smiled, and stood on tip-toe to kiss his cheek. 'You're a married man, and I'm your mistress.'

Rose Miller spread the small rigid attaché case stamped SNCF out on the table and went through the mechanism once more. Outside a ferocious summer storm raged; raindrops like lead pellets rattled the windows, and low thunder sporadically underpinned it.

Rose, Robert and Williams had before them a selection of weapons, including a new Colt .45 auto that Williams had bagged as his, and three Sten guns plus Bakelite limpet mines, pencil sticks, plastic explosive. Behind them Chiquita, Robert's Portuguese maid who had finally come back to work for him after reaching Lyons and getting stranded there during the exodus, was preparing a chicken stew with a stringy bird she had managed to barter from a nearby farm. She didn't bat an eyelid at the hardware being tossed about.

Rose pointed at the concealed camera. 'Focus, about fifteen feet. It's a fixed lens, wide angle. All you do is set the aperture according to the amount of light. Trigger here. Point the case at what you want to film. Load and unload in this bag here.' She held up the black velvet sack.

'How noisy?' asked Robert.

Rose shrugged. 'The case has been blimped. Soundproofed,' she added when she saw the quizzical look on their faces. 'I also have a new poem code. We are changing all of them. I know you don't like it, Williams, but when you get an operator, I want you to use this. Not very cheery, but they are far less likely to know it than the Yeats you chose.'

The poems were the grids upon which the messages could be coded and decoded. The Germans knew this, and were aware that some poems were more popular than others. So the more obscure the better – one chap in SOE codes was even writing his own, although he was having trouble keeping up with demand, his muse not always working to the exact period of full moons. She cleared her throat and began to recite. 'Sweet sister death has gone debauched today—'

The kitchen door flew open and crashed back on its hinges, making Chiquita jump. Williams pushed back his chair and levelled the Colt at the doorway. Eve, wet and bedraggled, stood there, eyes blazing, surveying the scene before her. Chiquita rushed over and eased her out of her coat. Williams looked at his watch. He should have met her at the station. He began to apologise but was cut off by the torrent of words spat at him.

'You know what I heard in Normandy? Oh, the dogs are fine by the way, Will, thanks for asking. Last week the Germans raided the Leroux house. The son had a radio on the table. So

207

they shot him. Shot the mother. Carted the daughters off to Christ knows where. You sit here with this pile of shit in plain view and you don't post a look-out . . .'

Rose said. 'I'm Claudette—'

But Eve hadn't finished. She strode over to Rose. 'I can guess who you are. These two idiots spent ten years trying to get themselves killed on the racetrack. Then you come along with your half-baked secret war. And they say, oh, how wonderful. An even more dangerous game to play. You, of course, think they are doing this for England and France.' Eve picked up the Colt and flung it at the window. They ducked as it crashed through the glass and into the shrubbery.

Williams glared at her then turned back to Rose. 'Finish giving me the new code.'

'Now?'

'Now.'

Rose cleared her throat. 'Sweet sister death has gone debauched today and stalks on this high ground with strumpet confidence—'

'Strumpet?' asked Robert distractedly as he watched Eve pirouette towards the doorway, her arms outstretched in some wild theatrical gesture. He wondered if she had been drinking. Perhaps that Normandy cider.

'Strumpet,' confirmed Rose.

'As in tart,' offered Eve.

Rose ignored her. 'With strumpet confidence, makes no coy veiling of her appetite but leers from you to me with all her parts discovered.'

They jumped again as the door slammed once more. Robert touched Williams' arm. 'Better go after her, Will.'

Williams, embarrassed by the wilful display, said, 'Let her stew.'

Rose got to her feet. 'She'll catch her death. I'll go.'

She opened the door and blanched at the driving rain hitting her face. The wind wrapped something round her foot. A blouse. Rose followed the trail of discarded clothing, carefully picking up shoes, skirt and underwear as she went, squinting into the blackness until a flash of lightning illuminated in stark blue-grey, the chilled flesh of Eve, standing naked looking up to the heavens, a smile on her face, imagining it was ten, twelve years ago and all she had to do in life was disrobe now and then for a nice old man to paint her.

Eve was aware of someone to her side and looked around, surprised to see Rose. She looked the woman carefully up and down in grudging admiration, and said quietly, 'He's mine. I don't care who you are. Touch him and I'll rip your guts out.'

Before Rose could give any sort of reassuring reply Eve snatched the bundle of clothing from her hands and marched inside, leaving her standing, wondering what she had just witnessed, as rivulets of water streamed down her face and into her open mouth.

Twenty-two

LAKE SENLITZ, OCTOBER 2001

Deakin could tell the old woman was tired now. She sat slumped in the canvas chair while yet another body shrouded in black rubber was taken away. She had promised the police a full and frank statement, and they were happy with that. Nobody wanted to detain a fragile old woman about crimes that may or may not have been committed fifty-odd years previously.

The technician handed her a tightly wrapped box containing the rusty canister. 'There is a plastic film over the label, which should protect it from further degradation, but I've taken photographs as well, just in case.'

'Good man. Thank you.'

She glanced up at Deakin and caught the look on his face. 'You have a question?'

'We all have a million questions. Such as what are you going to do with that?' He pointed at the box containing the cylinder.

'Oh, finish off a few things. Loose ends, you know. Been nagging at me all these years.'

'About Williams?'

'And the others.'

'How did he end up in the lake?'

'All in good time, Deakin, all in good time.'

The first heavy drops of rain splattered around them and Deakin looked up at the black sky. 'We should be going.'

Rose stood. 'I have one last thing to do. Put that in the car will you?'

Deakin took the package and placed it in the boot of the hire car while, heart in mouth, he watched Rose struggle down to the shoreline, stepping gingerly over the rough stones, any one of them capable of breaking her thin, brittle ankles. Deakin said his goodbyes to Warner, promising him a full report back in London, and waited for her to make the journey back, relieved when she reached solid ground. Exhausted by the effort, she gratefully took his arm. Deakin looked down and saw the Cartier watch was missing from her wrist.

Twenty-three

AUGUST–SEPTEMBER 1942

Williams crept up the stairs and into the spare bedroom, tiptoed up behind Eve as she darned a stocking and put his hands over her eyes. It was two days since her little exhibition. Robert had billeted Rose with Madame Lethias and gone off to visit his mother. Williams and Eve were alone, something everyone seemed to think was a good idea.

'You don't know what it's like, do you?'

She grabbed his wrists and pulled the fingers from her face and turned, the mad anger no longer in her eyes. 'To have your stomach knotted all the time? To feel the fear eating into you, lining your face, destroying your heart? I used to feel it just once or twice a month when you were racing, I could manage that. But now, every time someone appears at the door, every time you go out . . .'

'It's important, Eve.'

'How many of you do you think there are over here? A hundred? A thousand?'

Williams shrugged. He didn't know. Whenever he sat in a café he wondered if the surly, unshaven guy at the bar, the woman near the doors checking herself in the mirror every five seconds, the travelling salesman, which one of them might have passed through Arisaig and Beddington and been seen off by Vera Atkins or Rose Miller.

'And you think you can make a difference. We need an army – a real army, not a secret army – to drive the bastards out.'

'Every little helps.'

Eve stood up. 'How will it help if you get yourself killed? Help the allies? No. Help me? No.' She hugged him as hard as she could. 'Tell that woman to go away. Tell her you'll sit out the war till the second front starts. Let's go to Normandy.'

'I can't do that.'

'Which part?'

'Any of it. Look.' He turned her face up, brushed stray hairs out of her eyes. 'Robert feels the same. OK, she is sending us off to do something that looks stupid, but what do we know? Do we see the big picture? No.'

'Does that woman?' Eve spat the words out.

'That woman? Is that what your little show was about?' he asked. 'Was it about Rose?'

Eve looked down at her darning again. 'Of course not.'

'Not even a little bit?'

She looked up and held her thumb and forefinger a couple of centimetres apart. 'Maybe this much.'

Williams put a hand under her chin. 'Why? What are you thinking? That we are, were . . .'

'Don't say it. Don't. It's not that. It doesn't have to be sex, you know.' She paused to examine why her insides were still slowly, corrosively boiling. 'I suppose I am jealous because she gave you this part of your life and I have no say in any of it. I can feel you excluding me, even when she isn't here. You and Robert. It's

213

worse than when you were racing. Seeing the three of you, cooking something up like witches, forgetting all about me . . . it was too much.'

'I don't mean it to feel like that. I value what you do, what you think. You know that.'

'Then do me a favour.'

'What?'

'Stop using that stupid car.'

Williams laughed out loud. 'Stupid?'

'It's stupid to be seen in. Anywhere. Anytime.'

'That car could save our lives.'

'Or it could get you killed. I know Robert is reckless, but he really doesn't need a partner in idiocy.'

Williams ran through the task they had been given by Rose, and, it was true, speed was not going to be essential. Robert's argument would be this: driving fast cars is what we do, have always done. But Eve's was the wiser counsel. 'We'll give it a try. This time.'

Eve kissed him, hugged his chest again and said quietly, 'Thank you. And I'm sorry about the other night.'

Williams led her by the hand into their room across the landing and lowered her on to the bed. 'I'm sorry too.'

She looked up at him and smiled. 'Show me . . .'

The Alphachem offices at St Just were located upwind of the actual chemical plant, so that the exposure of the clerks and managers to the vile odours and eye-stinging emissions were minimised. The building wasn't anything grand, just a concrete box, really, but within Raymond Berri had insisted on an office every bit as well appointed as if he had been on the Champs Elysées. Heavy red curtains, leather sofas, a big desk, a wonderful padded swivel chair. The picture of him painted by Orpen had pride of place on one wall. Thinner in those days and grander. For the last five years he'd been climbing back up through Alphachem. Now he could climb no more. From the window he could see the single track rail spur that came from the mainline east of Paris and where, once a week or more, a train of boxcars would shunt down to pick up a consignment of delousing powder.

At least, that was what the inventory said. For weeks, no, months, now Berri had been having doubts, ever since he had taken a closer look at the trains and heard the heart-stopping noises from within. Sobbing. Babies crying. Low moans. The hacking of sick people. Human misery in small parcels of sound.

Whatever it was he wanted no part of it and had said so to the man sitting opposite him, Georges Legine, the owner of the company and therefore his boss.

Georges took a cigar, clipped it and lit it. 'Raymond. The things is, if we don't do it, someone else will. And someone else will make millions of francs a month. And we'll have lost that for what? Some vague liberal unease on your part.' He waved the cigar dismissively and exhaled. 'It's madness.'

'It's collaboration.'

'Oh, Raymond. You make it sound like a dirty word. Didn't Petain himself use the term? Everyone collaborates. It's just a matter of degree. Should you boycott the baker who serves Germans? Or the butcher? You'd starve if you started applying such criteria. I consider what we are doing as the necessary business to stay alive. There is only one customer now, Raymond – Germany. We supply or die.'

'There are Jews on those trains.'

'So? What concern is it of ours?'

Raymond cleared his throat. 'I am Jewish. At least, one of my grandparents was. In some people's eyes that is enough to get me a corner of a cattle truck.'

'Is that why you went to the Resistance?'

It hit Raymond like a slap and he squirmed in the chair, causing the leather to squeak. It was true. One of the foremen from before the war had been a vocal communist. Raymond was sure he would be part of this Franc-Tireurs et Partisans outfit. He'd tracked him down in Senlis and, although admitting nothing, the foreman promised he'd speak to 'some people'. Raymond regained his composure. 'Nonsense.'

'You know there is a rumour that Rene Peugeot sabotaged his own works. I wouldn't want anything like that to happen here, Raymond.'

The door opened and the swarthy officer called Meyer, who co-ordinated the Alphachem shipments with the Drancy trains, entered without knocking, two German soldiers flanking him. Berri heard the high whistle of the approaching train. He suddenly realised what was happening.

'I don't suppose I'll need to pack?' he said quietly.

Meyer shook his head.

Berri grabbed a fistful of cigars from the box and stuffed them in his inside pocket. Georges Legine shrugged, an it's-your-own-fault gesture of reasonableness and Berri walked out with his escort to find his place in the scruffy, rattling cattle trucks now slowly snaking past the window into the works' sidings.

Williams and Robert stepped out of the small car, aware of the stares of workers and German guards. The train had just pulled in and now sat four hundred metres down the track, huffing and hissing impatiently, dwarfed by the knotted steel pipework of the chemical complex and its cavernous storage warehouses. The pair were absolutely calm. Their documents said they were railways safety inspectors for the SNCF. And the documents were entirely genuine, thanks to Ettore Bugatti, who used his contacts in the industry to secure the real thing, official stamps and all.

Robert carried the blimped case, held as casually as he could, finger on the trigger which would start the film rolling. He had to use it sparingly, as there was only around five minutes of actual film time on it. He asked directions to the office from one of the workers and they entered a rather stark reception room, with a desk and two threadbare chairs. The receptionist, a small, balloon-faced woman in her fifties, was eyeing them suspiciously. Williams flashed his ID. 'SNCF Inspectorate. Can we see Monsieur Berri please?'

'Monsieur Berri is no longer with us,' said the receptionist.

'Really?' said Robert, puzzled. They had been given the name only last week, and Williams was convinced it was Orpen's old friend, a man he was sure they could trust. 'So who is in charge?'

'That would be our chairman, Monsieur Georges Legine. I shall tell him you're here. Do you have an appointment?'

'This is a snap inspection,' said Williams with as much SNCF-style pomposity as he could muster. 'Having an appointment would rather defeat the object. We'll be outside.'

They left the building and walked across to the track, slowly following it down towards the train, a ragbag of scabrous mismatched trucks. They could see a clump of German guards, including a couple on the roof of the train, all brandishing submachine guns. Williams concentrated on getting his stride as easy and unworried as possible. Robert bent down to brush his shoe and came up with a small square of paper he had palmed. After a few more metres he unwrapped it, studied the contents and passed it across to Williams.

The writing was tiny, spidery and very, very young.

I was picked up in the street in Toulouse on 12 July by the police. Held in a gymnasium there and transported to a big place called Drancy. It is near Paris. Am now on a train travelling east. Whoever gets this, please tell my parents I am alive. They will reward you. They are at 7 rue Pergola in Toulouse. There is no phone. Please write to them. Tell them I love them. And I love my sisters. God bless, Armand Simone.

Williams swallowed hard. The message was so measured, so calm. A young boy snatched before he could tell his parents, thrown into a rancid, overcrowded gymnasium with dozens, perhaps hundreds of other equally confused and scared men, women and children, then shipped north to Drancy. He knew, everyone knew, that conditions there were squalid beyond belief, that after a few days in the vast, filth-ridden dormitories, of scrabbling for inedible food, trying to use the primitive, diseased sanitation, suicide became a viable option, the best way out.

But he'd thought only Parisians ended up there. Now Jews from the ZNO – the Vichy non-occupied zone – were being brought up as well. Williams could see a sprinkling of other scraps of paper beside the track, the senders clearly hoping that friendly factory workers would find them and pass them on, a desperate dead-letter drop. Even that action spoke of terrible despair. Williams made to pick one and Robert stopped him, aware that the guard on the roof was peering down at them.

'Maybe later. There is nothing we can do. Not now.' Williams hesitated and Robert grabbed his friend by the upper arm and squeezed as hard as he could, pulling him upright. 'You want to join them in there? Don't be stupid, Will. Pull yourself together.' He said slowly: 'We're SNCF inspectors, Will. Remember. We don't care. We don't care. We mustn't care. Not now.'

Williams checked his heartbeat. It was wild and erratic, and he slowed it, taking in big gulps of air, letting the calm of the race circuit shroud him. After a minute or so he finally nodded, fully back into character and raised a placatory hand to the German guard, who waved back.

They moved close to the last two cars, new additions which had been shunted up from a siding. Beyond a ragged line of soldiers at the rear of the train they could see white-overalled men heaving a cargo into the gaping sides of these boxcars. At first the workers looked to be hideously deformed, but Williams said: 'Gasmasks.'

Robert nodded. Gasmasks. He pressed the trigger on the case handle and heard the faintest whirring as the reel started to spool.

'Hey, you two. What the hell are you doing here?' The German officer burst out of the ranks and strode towards them. 'Who are you?'

'SNCF,' said Robert coolly.

Meyer snatched the ID and flicked his eyes from photo to face rapidly. 'You have no authority over the trains of the Reich.'

'They are not trains of the Reich. They are SNCF trains while they are on French soil.'

'And we have authority when hazardous materials are transported.' Williams indicated the gasmasked men.

Meyer dismissed the idea with a wave and handed the IDs back. 'Not hazardous. The masks are just a precaution. Delousing powder.'

'Gentlemen, gentlemen.' The soothing voice of Georges Legine came from behind them. 'Excuse me. Herr Meyer, is there a problem?'

'Yes. This train has to be on its way in,' he checked his watch, 'twenty minutes. Exactly'

'It will be. Allow me to talk to these gentlemen.' Meyer turned

219

on his heel and went off to shout at the workers to get a move on. 'Ah, the Germans. Such slaves to the timetable. Now, what can I do for you?'

'We wish to check that the safety regulations as regards the transportation of toxic material are being adhered to.'

'Of course. Come.'

He led them through the line of soldiers, who grudgingly parted. Robert was now next to the men and the cylinders they were loading and pressed the trigger once more, rotating the case to catch the label, with its prominent skull and crossbones, on film. He hoped.

'As you can see,' said Legine, 'proper padding between layers and netting to hold them in place. This stuff isn't that lethal in fresh air. Only in confined spaces. So once the clothes are treated, and the lice dead, they are laid outside and the toxin evaporates.'

They walked on to the second truck and ahead the battered old cattle cars stretched, the stench of human waste and sweat and fear oozing from them. A barrier of four soldiers standing abreast prevented them going any further along the low platform, but the expression on their faces told Williams they could smell it too. Robert nudged Williams ever so gently. He was staring at one of the Germans, his eyes boring into the man, as if he was personally responsible. Williams broke off contact.

Beyond this barrier of soldiers, four gendarmes walked the train, occasionally stopping to shout or bang their sticks on the side of the trucks. A voice occasionally reached them, a plea, asking, Robert could just make out, for water. More thumping on the sides, fresh threats from the gendarmes.

Now Williams could hear terrible coughing from within the nearest boxcar, a thin feeble sound, the sound of small lungs infected with something slowly filling them up with mucus. The youngster began to cry, a little girl, and he could hear soothing

220

words from an adult. Still no response from anyone else, not Legine, not the guards. A gendarme was up to the chained doorway now, and he rapped on the side. 'Quiet in there. Be quiet.'

The hacking became muffled as if a hand was over a mouth. The gendarme moved on. Robert thought of the gun in his inside pocket, constructing a dangerous fantasy of him and the policeman and a dark alley.

Legine, alarmed by the pair's excessive interest in the trucks, steered them away. 'Just these two trucks are our responsibility, gentlemen. Not the rest of it. Now let me assure you about safety. We've been making this stuff for five years. Never had an accident yet.'

The wailing started slowly, this time from a truck some distance away from them.

'This stuff being?' asked Williams.

Now the wail was echoing along the platform, climbing the register.

'Zyklon B, they call it. Prussic acid. A delousing agent. Heading for the Russian front, I believe. I'll show you the dockets.' Legine was agitated, anxious to move away from the chilling sound. 'They're in my office.'

'Shut that damned woman up.' It was Meyer, irritated at the commotion.

Legine started to fuss, ushering them away from the train, but the screech of metal rollers as a cattle truck gate slid back made Williams stop and spin round. The cries of relief from those within as fresh air flowed into the truck were drowned by the cries of the hysterical woman, but again, the workers refused to look up and carried on loading.

Within the mass of vertical bodies, where faces crushed against faces, limbs entangled with each other, chests were pressed tight, and everyone breathed only the exhalations of their neighbour, there was a ripple as the woman forced her way to the front, her baby clasped in her arms. The gendarmes screeched at her to shut up, but she carried on wailing.

Her companions slowly prised the dead child from her arms, pinning her limbs as she thrashed about in the madness of grief, and passed it down to a gendarme, who, with surprising gentleness carried it across the platform and laid the body down in the shadow of the factory wall covering the tiny body with a paper sack.

The screams lessened then, spiralling down into sobs. The gate clanged home, the bolts were secured, but the image of those haunted faces framed in the doorway wouldn't leave Williams. It was burned on his cortex in stark black and white, a composition of faces, hollow-eyed men and women who have already passed beyond this life and are waiting for death to save them.

Twenty-four

MAY–JULY 1943

The eight months were purgatory for Williams. Robert went back with Rose to England, picked up by a Hudson near Le Mans. Sporadic drops of weapons and supplies came in and had to be intercepted and dispersed around the estate with the help of Eve, Maurice and Jean-Pierre Wimille. However, stashing supplies for some vague far-off event was hugely frustrating – and judging by the débâcle of Dieppe, the second front was a very long way off indeed.

It was getting more dangerous to move around. The occupiers had introduced a scheme, the Service du Travail Obligatoire, the STO, forced labour for nearly all able-bodied men. Now Paris was a city of women, old people and young children, the middle band of males gone, as if wiped out by an age-sensitive plague.

With agonising slowness, that savage snapshot, the faces at the door of the cattle truck, slowly faded, to the point where Williams could close his eyes at night and not have it leap out at him, not cause the anger to rise again. He just hoped that one day, when he needed it, it would be there again to remind him.

Robert returned in March, leaner and fitter, with the new, lighter B2 radio, a decent enough grasp of Morse and a welcome innovation – codes on silk sheets and one-time pads. The poem codes were quietly being retired for something more professional and harder to break.

Maurice, Eve and Williams celebrated Robert's return with a meal at the restaurant in Dreux that Maurice supplied with decent wines. The owner, a man of surly demeanour, explained that, by sheer luck, he had a decent cassoulet they could share with real, not sawdust sausages. And to follow, a *tarte tatin*.

Maurice, of course, knew what was in the cellar and ordered Brouilly and Pouilly Fumé, in a voice that caused the owner to shush him. Exactly what was and wasn't in stock was a closely guarded secret, to be manipulated according to the cut of the customer's jib.

There were a few other clients, all of them smart businessmen, who, thought Williams, looked as if they wouldn't know a ration book if he slapped them round the face with one. He had misgivings about even being there, but the others had overruled him.

'How is it over there?' asked Eve.

'Well, the food is worse than ever. And there's hardly any of it,' smirked Robert. 'I saw Philippe Rothschild.'

'Ah,' said Williams. 'How is he?'

'Well. He's working with a similar outfit to us. Urged me to join them. Gaullists.'

Williams knew this was the SOE branch under the control of the Free French, the one that was supposed to have the pick of French nationals. Robert would be quite a prize. 'What did you say?'

'I said I didn't care for de Gaulle. Just because he was right about tanks, and actually did some fighting against the Germans, doesn't automatically make him the best man to lead France.'

'What did Philippe say?'

'He understood. He told me to be careful. Of SOE. We aren't always told the full story.'

Williams laughed. 'It's a secret service. That's what they do. Keep secrets.'

Eve asked: 'How is the city?'

'London . . . well, London's taken a pounding. Makes me glad that it didn't happen to Paris.' He looked at Williams. 'Don't believe all that pulling-together propaganda shit. People are dying. There are deserters robbing banks. Food shortages like France . . .' He tailed off while wine was poured then continued. 'But there is a feeling since Africa that the tide has turned.'

'Doesn't feel like it here,' said Maurice.

'I don't know,' said Williams. 'You look for the signs you'll see them. Maybe you should lift your head from the black-market trough now and then.'

Maurice furrowed his brow. 'Listen, without me—'

'Without you what?' Williams snapped, pushing his plate away. 'We might not get to eat this shit? All it does is give me gut ache anyway . . .'

'It's not gut ache, it's your prissy guilty conscience—'

'Stop it,' said Robert firmly. 'Just stop it. What's got into you two? Don't fall apart now.'

There was a silence while wine was twirled in glasses.

'What's next?' asked Williams. 'For us? More waiting?'

'Mostly. Two things. There is a line of pylons that feed power to dozens of factories, from Michelin to Aluminium Nord. We are to blow those at some point.'

Williams broke into the baguette, wondering about its strange flaky consistency. You just didn't know what you were eating these days. 'And?'

'Georges Legine has to die.'

Eve asked: 'Why? They'll only replace him.'

'Then we do the next one.'

'And the next?'

'If we have to. As an example to others. And, being a French-man, it's unlikely there'll be reprisals.'

Williams said: 'Why don't they bomb the St Just plant if they want to do some real damage?'

'I suggested that,' said Robert and affected an English accent. ' "Not a top priority, old boy", apparently.'

No, trainloads of Jews heading east, just a fact of war. And, thought Williams, it ties up all those guards, all that rolling stock. Jews heading east meant no fresh units heading west, he supposed. 'Do they know where the trains go?'

Robert shook his head. 'Like here. There are rumours.'

The cassoulet arrived and they ate for a while in silence. It was good. Better than any of them had tasted for a long time. Even Williams, despite his earlier protest, tucked in, earning himself a smirk from Maurice which he ignored.

'Did they have any suggestions as to how to get to him?' he asked.

'Oh yes,' said Robert quietly. 'He's been assigned a Milice escort.' The Milice were the volunteer militia formed in what was once the unoccupied zone, a ragbag assortment of thugs, bigots and criminals. 'There is only one time in the week when he dumps them.' Robert went back to slurping his food.

'And?' asked Williams.

'And I think we'd better toss for this one.'

Georges Legine peered into the darkness and damned the black-out lights of his car, sending their feeble slits of blue-ish light into the gloom and fading away to nothing. As he dropped down to second gear he spotted his first one in the trees, just a glimpse. Big, maybe too big. The last one had been unshaven and stank of cheap perfume and he'd felt like he was fucking a docker. Not the idea at all. Something more delicate. But it looked like a bad night tonight. Perhaps there had been another raid by some high-minded Germans or the gendarmes were out to extort some more protection from the girls' purses.

It wasn't fair. He had one simple pleasure in life, a quick taste of anonymous transvestite sex and that was it. Back to the wife, children, work, the unholy trinity of his life. He was just contemplating giving it up as a bad job, when he saw her.

Tall again, but not too heavy, a muscular body sheathed in a yellow dress, his favourite colour. A shock of curly hair, and from what he could see, nice legs. Not as petite as he was hoping for, but this was no night to be fussy. He gave two flashes of the lights, the agreed invitation and she raised her arm in agreement. He pulled over.

Georges stepped out and looked around. Nothing, possibly the shape of another car in the gloom, but it didn't look like cop or Gestapo. He squished across the wet grasses to the bushes and his quarry. Skittishly she stepped back into the shadows of the tree.

'How much, Madame?' he asked.

'Two thousand,' said the low voice, trying hard to climb to a higher register, but failing.

Extortionate, but it was a seller's market tonight. 'Show me your arse,' Georges said matter-of-factly.

She turned around, stuck her rear out and slowly wiggled the dress up and over her hips, to reveal the lace-covered buttocks underneath.

'Lovely. It's a deal. Come here.'

Georges took off his overcoat, stepped to the shrubbery he knew so well and selected a small, well-trammelled clearing. He laid the coat on the ground and beckoned her over. She hesitated and he wondered if this was his/her first time.

It was sheer stroke of luck that Georges stumbled on a root just as the knife flashed out, grazing his adam's apple rather than opening up a second mouth. Mary, Mother of God. A robbery. Georges tried to shout but only a dry, strangled yelp emerged and she was back on him.

'Help.'

Georges lashed out wildly with a strength born of desperation, catching the creature a good solid blow in the face. Ha. Another. He swept a short, heavy branch from the ground and began to swish it back and forth. Williams waited until it was at the far arc of travel, confidently stepped in and drove the blade up under the ribs and twisted. He felt the warm blood trickle over his hands. Already the light was fading in the man's eyes and Williams made sure he got the dedication in before the curtain fell once and for all. 'This is from Raymond Berri.'

The Atlantic started up and purred down the road and Williams sprinted to the kerbside as best he could, the blood spatters on his dress glistening black in the moonlight. Wimille and friends had done a good job of driving off all the competition, leaving him the only show in town for Legine, but he knew the creatures would be back soon. He fell into the car beside Robert, panting, and they drove off. Robert glanced in the rearview mirror. He could see a couple of dark figures on the road. The curious, alerted by Legine's cries, coming out once it was safe.

Out of the park and heading south, back towards Auffargis, Robert taking the car on to the warren of backroads he knew so well. Williams tore off the wig and rubbed his chin where Legine had managed to hit him. He was rusty. He would have done better than that at Arisaig. But then that was all make-believe, with rubber knives. How did he feel now he had done it for real,

knifed a human being in cold blood? Rose Miller had asked him if
he could. Now he knew. He tried to examine his thoughts.
Nothing. Except for the burning anger a scribbled, despairing
note could still ignite in his guts. It had to be done. It was done.

'Next time,' Williams said wearily, 'you get the frock.'

'But, darling, it was your arse he liked.'

Williams punched Robert so hard his upper arm went numb,
but that only made him laugh even harder.

Twenty-five

FRANCE, JULY 1943

'Life must go on,' said Maurice as they were waved through a roadblock after he had produced his travel pass. They were in a Hotchkiss tourer, another of Maurice's recent acquisitions, with the hood down, as they headed north to the picnic site at the Forest of St Germain.

Williams and Maurice were in the front, Eve and Robert in the rear. Williams had suffered a restless night, because inside he wasn't as at ease about the death of Legine as he had thought he should be. He was sure it would pass. That morning Robert showed him a badly printed copy of *Combat*, the underground paper. In it were strange pictures of the camps that the paper suggested were the final destinations for the trains, camps that made the hellhole of Drancy look like the Elysian Fields, so it claimed. It could be propaganda of course. The thought of those trains told him otherwise. Exactly why they took so much delousing powder along, though, was a mystery to him. Probably to stop typhus outbreaks.

'Did you hear about the guy on honeymoon in Mexico?' began

Maurice. 'Well, the local police chief, he warns him, he says, Señor, Speedy Gonzales, the fastest dick alive, is in town. It is essential that you sleep the night with your hand firmly planted upon the pussy of your beautiful bride. So the guy does exactly this. But in the middle of the night he needs to scratch his nose. When he puts his hand back a voice says: "Please-a Señor, to take-a your hand-a off-a my arse." '

Robert and Williams laughed despite themselves – Maurice's jokes may not have been top notch, but his delivery was. Then Eve said quietly: 'I don't get it. Why didn't he scratch his nose with the other hand?' At which point they all guffawed.

Williams pointed when he saw the line of pylons marching aggressively across the countryside. 'Those?'

Robert nodded. 'That line. But we have a problem.'

'What?'

'Tell him, Maurice.'

Maurice became serious for a second. 'Berlin has ordered fifty hostages for each act of sabotage. Ten to be executed. Forty to be transported to Germany. Which, I have heard suggested, is much the same thing. Only slower.'

Williams nodded.

Robert leaned forward. 'Which means we are looking at a large number of avoidable casualties.' He put his hand on Williams' shoulder. London had urged him to destroy the line as soon as possible, but that seemed ridiculous to him. The Germans were becoming very adept at carrying out running repairs. Bombed factories were up and functioning again within days, sabotage often corrected within hours. Surely if it was all co-ordinated properly, if the Resistance attacks were timed across the country to coincide with the second front, that would make any blow twice as effective. 'Oh, don't worry, Will, you'll get your big bang OK. But not until the Allies have landed. You'll just have to wait.'

'Wait, wait, wait. That's all we fucking do. Wait.'

'Yes and you could be in Paris getting your toes tickled by the SD. Plenty of people will be. I met Madeleine the other day, SOE's radio operator. Beautiful, too beautiful for this job, and not overburdened with brains.'

'What were you doing? Swapping Morse tips?'

'I was trying to tell her not to write the messages down every time. And to keep moving. They'll DF her before long if she carries on with her routine.'

'I told you,' said Williams. DF was the aggressive direction finding the Germans were indulging in, along with tricks of sequentially cutting the power supply to streets and even houses in an area where a pianist was operating, knowing that when the radio went off air, they had pinpointed the agent. At least Robert had bought one of the newer sets, which could be operated from batteries. 'Every time you use that radio, you make sure you go as far away from the house as possible.'

'Don't worry we've got a proper operator coming. Name of Chandler. I'll put him in Pontoise with Thérèse Lethias. Is that far enough away for you?'

Williams grunted. The real answer was no, but he couldn't see any alternative.

Maurice took a small track into the forest that had closed around them, bumping the Hotchkiss down a rutted sand road, churning up a plume of dust. The trees parted almost theatrically to reveal a wonderful, almost perfectly circular lake, with a dilapidated wooden jetty running from the shore and a tethered swimming platform bobbing in the centre.

Eve squealed in delight and Maurice crowed: 'Welcome to Chez Maurice, a spot known only to the fortunate few. This is an official no-war zone, mention of the Germans is forbidden, as is brooding too much.' He turned to look at Williams. 'This means you.'

Williams managed a smile. They had decided the previous night that the Atlantic had to go. Eve had won. It was to be put out of action for the duration of the war, safe from plundering Germans. 'I hope you don't mind,' continued Maurice, 'but I borrowed your portable gramophone.'

There was five minutes of furious activity. Eve unloaded the player and cranked it up to give them a soundtrack of Jean Sablon. Maurice spread out the blankets while Robert and Williams unpacked, with increasing disbelief, ham, chicken, a pie, tripe sausage and four bottles of wine.

Eve, revelling in the feeling of hot sun on her pale skin, took off her blouse. Then her skirt. And her slip. The water was calling her. The first the others knew was when they heard the splash of a body knifing into the lake and the heartfelt gasp as she surfaced, shaking the water from her hair.

'Maurice,' she shouted, 'you could have heated the damn thing!'

He shrugged. 'Too early in the season.'

Williams stood and undid his trousers, stepped out of them and unbuttoned his shirt. Robert looked on, puzzled, wondering what he was going to do. He answered by waiting until Eve had struck out for the platform then sprinting along the jetty, picking up a couple of splinters as he went, performing a rather heavy, inelegant dive into the water and striking out crudely but strongly.

Eve heard the splashing behind her, and redoubled her effort. She felt vulnerable in open water with what had to be Robert closing on her fast. She started to scream a little, like a pursued maiden, and in her haste her strokes became ragged. She was aware of the splashing directly behind her, could feel the hand scything through the little waves the breeze was creating, the hand almost touching her feet. Then he was alongside. She

233

turned to say something and swallowed a great gulp of water, spitting and coughing and hacking and managing to splutter in surprise: 'Will . . .'

He trod water while she recovered her composure and they did the last fifteen metres in parallel, Williams hauling himself on to the platform and holding out a hand for her. He jerked her out of the water and they stood there, dripping and drying in the sunlight.

'I thought you couldn't swim.'

'I have to have some mystery in my life.'

'Not from me.'

He kissed her. 'Especially from you. Don't want you to take me for granted.'

The crooning of Sablon came across the water intermittently as the breeze blew, like a radio going in and out of tune. She could see Robert opening the wine and helping himself to a large glass.

'I feel sorry for Robert,' Eve said.

'Why?'

'He should have a woman.'

'He has a wife, a mistress in Nantes and the odd "friend" he can call upon.'

'Wife in name only. The woman in Nantes is a bitch. Robert told me he thinks she has a German lover, which is why he no longer travels there. And "friends"? Pah. No, he needs someone to love him properly.'

'Are you offering to fill the post?'

Eve slid an arm through his, leant on his shoulder and said teasingly: 'Would you mind?'

'Maybe after I'm gone.' He pulled her face round. 'Or have you comforted him already? While I was in England.'

She slapped his face lightly.

'And what about that Rose Miller woman with the big eyes and big chest?' Williams knew better than to protest that her chest wasn't all that big. That was a pit with sharpened stakes in the bottom, just waiting for him to stumble. 'There must have been many lonely nights in London.'

'There were,' he said, and kissed her again. 'And they stayed that way.'

She pouted to let him know she was prepared to accept this for the moment. 'She likes you. I can tell.'

'Everybody likes me.'

'Yes, everybody finds someone to like because there are so many of you. Irish gangster, faithful chauffeur – oops, chauffeur – top racing driver, dog breeder, secret agent . . .' She traced a line on his chest and Williams shuddered. He held her close, feeling her nipples pressing into his flesh and, as blood flowed into his groin, wondering how much they could see from the shoreline. 'I still don't really know your secret, Mr Williams.'

There was no build up. No faint whisper growing louder. The roar of powerful engines suddenly engulfed them, assaulting their ears with a thudding ferociousness. The Mosquito came over at tree-top level, the propeller blades almost crowning whole swathes of the forest, and burst over the lake. They could see the pilot, briefly, but he was looking straight ahead, all his energy and concentration focused on keeping the machine low and level.

Then it was gone, leaving only a ringing in their ears and their hearts pounding. 'That's it!' exclaimed Williams. 'What if we get the RAF to do a dummy raid on the pylons while we blow them. That way the Germans blame the airforce, not the locals. And no reprisals. What do you think?'

Remembering Maurice's restrictions on topics of conversation she turned and pushed him as hard as she could. Williams stood for a second balanced on the edge, windmilling his arms theatrically before allowing himself to topple.

'You broke rule number one,' she shouted as he crashed into the lake. 'No war talk.' Even so, she couldn't help considering it. No reprisals, she thought. As if anybody could guarantee such a thing these days.

In the sun-dappled courtyard of the Avenue Foch SD headquarters, Hans Keppler leant against his powder-blue Opel and lit a small cheroot. He had started smoking them to try to cut down on cigarettes. And he was perhaps drinking too much. A bottle of excellent wine seemed to be permanently open in his office. The belt of his uniform was beginning to slide under his burgeoning gut, as if he was an old man.

On the far side of the yard, Neumann paced up and down in front of the six men they had plucked from the streets of Villers, near where Legine had been assassinated. Six months ago they would not have bothered, but now there was an epidemic of clandestine killings – even the Milice were being targeted.

The firing squad marched out and assembled in front of the prisoners, some of whom only then began to appreciate just why the wall behind them was so badly pock-marked and stained. They weren't the first prisoners to be lined up here. They certainly wouldn't be the last.

'I have given you every opportunity to help,' announced Neumann in the pompous voice that made Keppler's teeth grate. 'One of you must know something. Gossip. Hearsay. Anything.'

The six, their jaws slack, their eyes full of pain from beatings, merely shuffled. 'Fine. Sergeant.'

The soldiers shouldered their weapons. Virginia looked at the floor. 'Take aim.'

'Nobody?' asked Neumann.

'Fire.'

Even though he had seen this pantomime dozens of times, Keppler still flinched at the sharp metallic click as firing pins fell on empty chambers. As expected, the men were quaking. One of them had lost control of his bladder. Ashamed, he stepped forward.

'I . . . I would like to talk with you.'

Neumann frowned. 'You left it a little late.'

The squad chambered the rounds into their Mausers and prepared to fire for real.

The short Frenchman shuffled forward, the ankle chains preventing him from making much headway. 'First save these men. Let them go back to their families.'

Keppler was suddenly interested. Neumann was not a man to let people go back to their families if he could help it. He saw that as defeat, evidence of weakness, rather than good public relations. Entrance to Foch should be a one-way ticket as far as he was concerned. 'Bring him here, Joachim,' he shouted.

Two of the firing squad frogmarched the man over to the Opel, his chained feet dragging on the brick flooring. Most of his top teeth were missing and livid bruises criss-crossed his cheeks, as if he had been whipped. One eye twitched uncontrollably. And he smelt of fear, sweat, blood and piss. Keppler stepped back from him in case some of the odour clung to his uniform.

'What do you have?' asked Keppler. He could see Neumann pacing, irritated that he had been usurped.

'A car. A very low car. Knee-high to a grasshopper, they said. Two men in it.'

'Did you see it?'

'No. A friend.'

'Which friend?' Keppler asked casually.

The eye starting twitching faster. 'I mean a man I met in a café. Didn't know his name.'

237

Keppler didn't have time to waste extracting the name of his gossipy chum from him, and admired the man for trying to protect him, so he simply asked: 'Anything else?'

'No.'

Keppler sighed. 'Back in line then.'

'Except he said, it was very strange. It had a fin down the back.'

'A fin?'

'Yes, like a fish. Big metal fin.'

'Back in line.'

He was dragged away and Keppler felt the old excitement rise in him, the kind of thrill he rarely felt these days, the frisson of the chase and the kill that had made him want to be a policeman. The solution to this matter was nearly all there in his head now, he knew it. He just had to order his thoughts. Plus he had a hunch, a strong instinct about where he could find the missing elements.

As he turned to hurry inside he hesitated and shouted across to his junior. 'Neumann, you can stop. Send them for labour duty—'

The flat slap of the rifle shots rang out around the courtyard, making Keppler start, and the six jerked grotesquely, before slumping into a heap, some of them still twitching. Neumann pulled out his Walther pistol to administer the *coupe de grâce* and shouted: 'Sorry, Sturmbannführer. What were you saying?'

Keppler flung open the door to Virginia's cell with a force that made her jump. Behind him stood Obst, his stenographer, a plump bespectacled man who looked as if he should be in a tax office in some provincial town.

'I didn't mean to startle you, but time is short.'

Virginia looked up at him and tried to compose herself. So this was it. She felt the blood drain from her face. 'Time for what?'

Keppler clicked his fingers and Obst handed over a light blue

238

document, with black carbons attached. 'Do you know what this is?'

She shook her head.

'It is a *Nacht und Nebel* order. Filled out in your name. What it means is very, very simple. You go to Germany. You don't come back. We don't care what happens to you in the meantime. Here.' He held out the pages. 'How is your German?'

'Poor.'

She took the document and scanned it, from her cover name, Yolande Laurent, printed at the top down to the flamboyant signature of the Sturmbannführer.

'As you see, ready to implement.' The voice was harder than she had ever heard, making sure she knew the time for bluffing was over.

Virginia pointed to her spare dress and the toiletries. 'Can I take some things?'

'You can tear it up.'

Virginia waited, knowing that Keppler was about to offer her something, some way out.

'I have been looking at dates. There is someone I am after, someone I am fairly sure went through with your batch of agents. Had to have. It fits in with the time we started to see . . . to see a pattern emerge.'

'What pattern?'

He ignored her. 'I need that list. Just the men. Now.'

'I can't do that.'

Keppler sat down next to her on the bed. 'Listen, what you do will make no difference to my actions. I know exactly how to proceed. However, I just want some confirmation of a suspicion I have.'

'I can't give you a list.'

Keppler snatched the *Nacht und Nebel* order from her and

239

handed it to Obst. 'I have seen where you will end up, you know. Or at least, something very similar. The Kommandant was most proud of his work. I made my excuses and left. On the way home I had to stop my car to be sick. What happens here is as nothing. Nothing.'

Keppler watched a spark of fear flash in her eyes. It was there for a second, but he knew he had her, knew her imagination was doing his job for him. Slow it down, soften it. Play the trump card. 'Look, Virginia . . .'

Her head snapped up. Her Beddington name. How could he know that?

'Virginia Thorpe. We showed your picture to one of your fellow agents. He identified you not as Yolande Laurent, but Virginia Thorpe.'

'Then why not ask him for the list?' she said.

Keppler had anticipated the question. He flicked the *N&N* form. 'He is rather difficult to get hold of at short notice.' In fact he was extremely difficult to get hold of because the man from Coutt's was dead, falling from the roof of number 84 while trying to escape. All I need to know is this – was there a man who raced cars? A racing driver? A man couldn't keep that quiet for ever. Nothing else, that's all I need. No name, nothing. Just confirmation.' He let his voice harden slightly. 'In ten seconds Obst here will implement the order.'

Five of them ticked away.

'All you have to do is nod if I am right.'

Three more went by.

'A racing driver.'

The inclination of the head was sharp and fast, as if that somehow made it better.

'And he was called Williams, wasn't he? Not there and then, but that was his real name. Wasn't it?'

240

Another brief nod and even as he watched her blanch with self-loathing, inwardly Keppler gave a whoop of joy and let the warm glow of victory wash over him. The knee-high to a grasshopper car was a Bugatti Atlantic and the two men had to be Benoist and Williams. Now all he had to do was find out where they were hiding themselves and that car. And that was the easy part.

The day after the picnic Williams slapped thick grease over the bodywork of the Atlantic, thick gloops of it running off down on to the gravel driveway and lying there like so many beached jellyfish. Robert was inside, covering the seats with oiled tarpaulin.

Eve emerged from the house swinging the keys to the Renault van. 'I'll see you later,' she said, and they both raised a hand as she drove off.

'I'll miss her,' said Williams.

'Me, too,' said Robert. 'But she'll end up getting us both killed.'

Williams finished the protective coating and peered in at Robert. 'One last blast?'

'We shouldn't. But . . . you want to do the honours?'

Robert started the engine and moved across to the passenger side. Williams jumped in beside him, the tarpaulin crackling beneath him. For the last time for a long time he let the rear wheels spin on the gravel, splattering the entrance like buckshot, let in the clutch and took the car out on to the road, watching the speedometer swing up until they were going at more than a hundred and twenty kilometres. The countryside flashed by in a blur. Williams judged the turn perfectly, letting the back end drift as he took them on to the forest track, correcting the oversteer and accelerating again, until the trees became a solid wooden wall of trunks.

241

'We'll have to move as well,' shouted Robert.

'What?'

The noise was frightening, the whoosh off the vegetation mixed with the raucous scream of the engine.

'We'll have to move house. Been there too long.'

'Any idea where?'

'Uh?'

'Where?'

'Tahiti.'

'Sounds good to me.'

Realising that meaningful conversation was impossible, they both fell silent while Williams took them on a circuitous route through the forest, only stopping once to take a nasty dip in the road very slowly, rather than risk tearing off the exhaust as the suspension bottomed.

As Williams eased off the pedal on the final leg, they began to see figures in the trees, barely glimpsed flashes of sheepskin and sten guns. Mostly local farmers, the ranks had been swollen recently by the little team Robert had cautiously assembled from the waifs and strays from the forests around Auffargis. Eventually they arrived at the clearing.

Eve was stomping up and down, occasionally glancing at her watch, furious at what she saw as reckless tardiness. She stabbed a finger at her wrist in silent admonition. Around her were four of the farmers and six of their big, muscular shirehorses, harnesses attached to long ropes disappearing into a long, shallow pit which had been crudely excavated by the tractor-dozer at the edge of the clearing.

Williams guided the burbling car down the long slope, feeling the chill of the freshly uncovered earth as they reached the bottom. It was a little too like a grave for comfort, he mused, and one that could hold an awful lot of people. The top of the trench was about a metre above the precious car's roofline. He wondered how much a metre of earth weighed. Not too much he hoped.

The two drivers loped quickly back up the ramp and Eve got to work. She signalled the horses to be driven forward, and the sagging ropes tightened and hummed as the heavy tarpaulin was dragged over the car, wrapping it in a green cocoon.

'When do we move?' asked Williams.

The dozer started up, a raucous rasping sound, and it chugged forward, pushing the mound of excavated earth back into the hole, the soil forming the rough shape of the car, like an unfinished clay model.

Williams looked across the hole at Eve on the far side who shrugged in sympathy. Williams passed the key on its silver chain to Robert who looked at it thoughtfully and kissed it before tossing it over to Eve. She caught it and carefully looped it round her neck.

Robert looked at Williams. 'My mother has been moved to hospital in Paris. I must see her. But I'll take us to our new home after that.' He put an arm around Williams and steered him away from the burial. 'Tomorrow. We move tomorrow.'

243

Twenty-six

JULY–AUGUST 1943

Eve slumped down next to Maurice on the terrace of the café near Etoile, breathless and sweaty, and ordered a coffee. When it arrived he offered her a flask. 'Armagnac. Complements the taste of acorns perfectly.' She helped herself to a generous dose.

The day was cooling now. As if to mock the deteriorating fabric of daily life in the city, the summer of 1943 was turning out to be glorious. She shouldn't complain – the airless heat was preferable to the icy winter it had suffered. At least living was cheaper than in the cold months.

A charcoal-powered car chugged by, belching its filthy fumes, a billboard strapped to the top advertising that evening's perform-ance by Maurice Chevalier at Odeon.

'Is it true?' she asked.

'Is what true?' He looked at her admiringly. She looked good in the simple summer dress with the high neckline, a new silver chain round her neck disappearing into her hidden cleavage. Maurice had always been indifferent to Eve's charms, or at least more immune than his brother. He liked his women to be beautiful – Eve certainly fulfilled that criterion, even twelve years after he first met her – but she remained something of an innocent. Not stupid, not naïve, but she exuded a more wholesome view of humanity than Maurice could possibly countenance. He liked his women somewhat more earthy, soiled, compromised. Like himself.

'Sicily,' she said quietly.

Maurice shrugged. Rumours were rife that resistance to the landings in Sicily had collapsed, that Mussolini was finished. Even the word armistice was being bandied about. 'Ask them.' Maurice pointed to a group of two couples at a far table, laughing a little too loudly.

'Who are they?'

'I don't know,' said Maurice. 'But if I were the Gestapo I'd have them in the cells of rue des Saussaies in a flash. Every day they meet here. Sometimes one brings a case which the other leaves with. Stupid.'

Maurice lit a cigarette and offered Eve one. She refused. They were normally so adulterated – the smugglers like to boast 'as long as there is grass in Belgium, the French shall have tobacco' – that she had decided to give up.

'I asked you to meet me because perhaps you could convince my pig-headed brother it is time to give up his . . . pursuits. And your husband.'

'Why?'

'It is getting far, far too dangerous. Those people at Foch have stopped beating about the bush. The honeymoon is very, very over. Yet those two race around in that car as if they can whistle their way past the graveyard.'

'Not any longer.'

Maurice raised an eyebrow. 'Really? They got rid of the Atlantic?'

'They're in mourning for it.' She took a hit of the coffee and shuddered. She'd been over-generous with the Armagnac, and it wasn't the subtlest example of the liquor. She waited for the searing trail down her gullet to subside before she asked: 'Why the sudden concern, Maurice?'

'I saw a DF map in Keppler's office.' He caught the look of distaste that was clearly more than the effect of the brandy. She found it hard to accept that dealing with the enemy wasn't the same as supporting them. To him it was all a matter of checks and balances, and as long as the correct column came out in profit, then compromises were tolerable. 'I saw the areas they are concentrating on, where they have transmissions they cannot pinpoint exactly, but know someone is operating. A lot in Paris. One in Pontoise. Isn't that where Robert put the Englishman? And a few on the edge of the Rambouillet forest.'

Eve nodded. Robert always left the house to transmit, always drove into the forest, but clearly had a few favourite spots. Repetition, the radio man's worst enemy.

'Eve, you would be shocked if you knew how much they know.' He looked up as a car pulled into the kerbside. A powder-blue Opel. He felt a bolt of white hot pain shoot down his bad leg. He quickly whispered: 'Go inside. Now.'

Without asking for an explanation, Eve turned her face away from the car, stood, grabbed her bag and headed inside.

The window rolled down and there was Keppler, smiling. 'Maurice. We have a date.'

'We do?'

'Who was that with you?'

'My wife. She's just gone to . . .'

'Your wife? I didn't know you were married.' Neither did Maurice till that answer popped out of his mouth. 'I am afraid I only have one ticket.'

'For what?'

'Your namesake. Chevalier. Come along.'

Maurice stood and limped slowly over to the car, his leg more painful than ever. The door opened and he slid in beside Keppler. Framing the SD man on the far side was Neumann, expressionless. In the front, next to the driver, Arthur Lock, busy rolling a cigarette, turned and gave him a smile that made him wince. Arthur Lock was not the kind of man who you wanted smiling at you. At Keppler's signal the driver pulled away.

'We don't have a date, do we?'

'Only with destiny, Maurice,' Keppler replied sardonically with a little high laugh. 'And how is Mrs Williams?'

Maurice's mind raced. He sped it forward to the worst possible scenario. Why didn't they pull in Eve if they were after the Chestnut circuit? Because picking up Eve might forewarn Robert and Williams. This way, all Maurice had done was accept an invitation from his old chum Keppler. Nothing suspicious about that. Maurice felt his forehead prickle hot and cold, as if he was about to vomit.

'So where are we going?' asked Maurice. Because he knew if it had been straight to Foch or Saussaies, there would have been none of these niceties.

'To see how your poor old mother is.'

Sitting in the small café opposite the St Stephanie Clinic in the Republique district, to the south of the city, where his mother was being treated, Robert sipped at his third bitter coffee of the morning, trying to lift his energy levels. Despite a large quantity of red wine he'd been unable to sleep, his mind spinning about what he suspected. And about the dangerous game Maurice had embarked on. Three years previously the Germans had arrived behaving with an almost serene *noblesse oblige*. Now that the *noblesse* looked distinctly shaky, the rules had changed. He just hoped that Maurice had noticed.

Robert tried to stop the gnawing in his stomach, as if the acid was corroding the fleshy walls. Like everybody else, he didn't eat anything like as well as he had pre-war – although he did well in comparison to most – but it wasn't hunger causing his dyspepsia. It had been writhing away ever since he got back with his orders. Blow this, damage that. Meet the radio operator Madeleine – a woman so beautiful as to draw the attention of the dumbest of Germans. And once they got over that face, they were bound to wonder about that big case she was lugging around. Link up with this group there, bury more arms here. Something was very wrong. He just didn't know what it was.

Down the street the last of the housewives departed with a precious slice of bloody flesh. One of Paris's many overworked horses had collapsed between the shafts, and while the owner had gone off to seek help, a swarm of two-legged vultures had descended, brandishing their sharpest knives and largest enamel bowls. Great steaks of the stringy flesh were quickly sliced off, leaving the carcass glistening sickeningly. As the women scurried away, so a cloud of crazed flies descended. When the owner returned he would find his horse reduced to an undulating mass of black, interspersed with islands of darkening crimson.

The girl made him start. It was Beatrice, no longer the child who had once cycled up his path, but a young woman, albeit one with a lined, hollow face and eyes that darted jerkily from side to side. This time she was keeping an eye on her bicycle, her most precious possession. He hoped that the damage caused by fear and subterfuge and privation to this young lady was reversible and that once this was over she could go back to being frivolous and carefree. Somehow, though, he doubted it.

'I have a message from Jester.'

Robert nodded. Jester was in charge of the dead letter drops, and someone Robert trusted. Mainly because he had never met him, didn't know where he lived and had never met anyone who did. That was his kind of agent.

'Maurice is ill.'

Robert tried to keep his face impassive. The phrase meant Maurice was taken. It was known that a few brave Frenchwomen who worked in Foch and Laurent and Lutetia, the other Gestapo strongholds, kept their eyes and ears open and reported to Resistance contacts. But Maurice was a familiar figure around Foch at least; something must have changed to make them assume he was there under duress.

'Is it serious?'

'It could be terminal. You should go now.'

With that she mounted her bike and pedalled off, not looking back. One day, when all this was over, he must find that Beatrice and do something for her. Maurice taken. Go now. He scanned the street for suspect cars, men with hats pulled low, as the V-men did whenever they thought they needed to look inconspicuous. Nothing. Robert looked at the hospital opposite. Still nothing untoward.

He decided to take a chance, grabbed the precious chocolates he had found at a stupendous price – his mother had an astonishingly sweet tooth, and had suffered these last few years – and hurried across the road, bounding up the steps to the entrance.

Madame Benoist was on the third floor, but rather than encase himself in the claustrophobic lift he took the stairs, two at a time, occasionally glancing behind him. It may be early, but the hospital had been up for hours, and he could smell fresh carbolic almost masking the fading aromas of an untempting breakfast.

Robert stopped at the entrance of the room. A group of nurses were round his mother's bed, fluttering and twittering like sparrows. 'What's going on?' he boomed inadvertently.

'Ssshhh,' said the Sister. The group parted and when he saw her face he gasped. A livid bruise ran left to right, the ancient skin glowing hideously purple. One eye was closed, red and swollen, the lid marbled with veins.

'Robert,' she said thinly.

He walked over and held her and he was aware of the sister shooing the junior nurses away. Robert could feel the bones through his mother's nightdress and the wild beat of her heart. He fought hard to stop crying, to keep his voice steady as he held her at arm's lengths and forced himself to examine the poor, defiled face. 'Who did this?' he demanded.

'It was the Germans,' said the sister.

Robert spun round. 'And you let them do it?'

'It isn't a matter of letting them or otherwise, Monsieur Benoist,' she replied with surprising passion. 'Not with the SS. Your mother was very brave.'

He turned back to the bed. 'But why?'

'They had Maurice with them. Don't blame him. You'd have done the same.'

'Done what? Done what, Mother?'

'Please, he had no choice but to tell them.'

Robert felt the colour drain from his face and he laid her back on to the pillow as gently as he could, his arms shaking with the tension of not lashing out at something to vent the anger he felt building. He turned to the sister. 'I need a telephone. *Now.*'

Twenty-seven

Williams woke with a slightly thick head. Rather than transport the by-now meagrely stocked wine cellar of Auffargis they had decided to try to drink it. He, Eve, Robert and Jean-Pierre Wimille had got through far too many bottles. Wimille had finally volunteered to join Chestnut full time. Like many other Frenchmen, he was now beginning to think sabotage and subversion wasn't all pissing in the wind. With the Allies ready to take on the Italian mainland, perhaps they really could make a difference.

Eve had told them about Maurice's chummy exchange with Keppler, which she had heard from within the café. 'If you dance with the devil, sooner or later he gets to call the tune,' Williams had slurred enigmatically at this point.

Still, they were moving now. New house, fresh start, time to regroup. Wimille was sleeping it off across the hall. He was to help them move essential belongings to the new house Robert had chosen near Houdan, but he and Robert had carried on drinking after Eve and Williams had excused themselves to go and make lazy, drunken love and fallen asleep entwined. He untangled her arms from him, slipped out of bed and poured himself a large tumbler of water.

'Good morning, Mister Super-lover,' she said.

He glanced over to see if she was being sarcastic.

'I'm serious. You should drink two bottles of wine more often.'

He threw the dregs of water at her and she squealed and dived under the covers. He pulled on trousers and a shirt. 'I'll get the coffee.'

He went downstairs, shaking his head, checking the physical damage of their late night, holding out his splayed fingers at arm's length, examining them for tremors. Not too bad. The house smelled, though, of stale cigarette smoke and vinegary wine. Chiquita, the maid, was already up trying to clean up the mess.

'Morning,' he said.

She nodded back with a smile.

'Robert up?'

'Monsieur Benoist has gone to Paris. See his mother at the clinic. Left very early.'

Williams walked over to the window and looked out across the lawn to the stand of trees that formed the edge of the forest. He thought about the men out there somewhere, scattered across the thousands of hectares, waking stiffly after another night in the open, quietly seething about what had become of them, vaga-bonds in their own country.

The phone rang and Chiquita went to get it. He looked back at the woods one more time, and was halfway through turning to take the call when his brain finally put together what the early morning sun had caught at the very edge of the tree line, his cerebrum magnifying it until he could see the air-cooling holes around the barrel.

Chiquita had picked up the phone. 'Hello?'

'Get down!' Williams yelled as he dropped to the floor, but it

252

was too late. The heavy machine-gun slugs ripped into Chiquita's body and flung her back against the wall, sending big spurts of her blood across the rough white surface. The window imploded, showering him with glass and he shuffled to press his back against the heavy outside wall, feeling it shake and shudder as round after round blasted it, splintering the terrace, and he imagined the dancing rose petals torn from the trellis, floating on clouds of brick- and sawdust.

Even above the sustained racket of bullets he heard something upstairs. Wimille. He hoped he had the sense to get out the back. There were bicycles, a motor bike, places to hide. He also hoped he took Eve.

The upstairs window blew out as the gunners started to rake the rest of the building, and through the open doorway he saw Eve rolling down the stairs, falling into a heap at the bottom as the banisters and rails flowered into raw shards.

'Eve. Eve.'

She began to move, slowly at first, then quickly on all fours, ignoring the glass and debris that sliced through the flesh of her hands and knees, heading for him.

'Stay back. Stay down.'

More bullets hammered into the wall and through the window, zinging as they went, smaller calibre now, rifles and Schmeisser fire. Eve reached him and crawled up his body until she was level with his face. 'Always say goodbye. Isn't that what Robert used to say?'

The gunfire stopped, leaving their ears buzzing angrily after the onslaught they had suffered. Some crockery items fell lazily to the floor, smashing into pieces. Williams brushed the hair away from Eve's face. 'No more goodbyes.'

Then he heard the rumble of the half-track coming up the drive.

★ ★ ★

Keppler's blue Opel led the way. He was in the back seat with Maurice, who stared at the floor, ashamed even to set eyes on the house. In the front was Neumann, whose idea the fusillade had been. He was convinced that if this Chestnut circuit did have all the arms that Maurice had suggested, there was a good chance they might use them. Best soften them up first. Behind the Opel was a half-track with a contingent of troops to mop up the pieces.

They slewed to a halt outside the house and the soldiers were out and inside within a few well-drilled seconds. Good men. SS men. Not like some of the scum arriving these days, thought Keppler. Romanians, Croatians, Hungarians, all pouring in to defend the Atlantic wall from whatever it was the Allies were up to this summer. Something, that was for sure.

Keppler stepped out of the car and glanced down at Maurice. He wasn't moving. Neumann was already out, picking his way around the destroyed Renault van, collapsed on its frame after the machine guns had reduced the body to a metal mesh, across the ruined terrace and into the house.

Soldiers were breaking those big flower urns that hadn't been shattered by the gunfire, and every so often guns, explosives and timing sticks would fall out. A concrete trough yielded an intact parachute container, full of Stens and ammunition.

Keppler walked around the side to the barn-cum-garage which he had ordered not be targeted and threw open the doors. Empty. No Bugatti. He stifled the disappointment. This wasn't about such booty, this was about breaking a spy circuit, he reminded himself. He slammed the doors shut. Owning an Atlantic, one of just three ever made, that would be a bonus, though.

Williams and Eve were dragged out on to the terrace, where they were thrown down on the torn boards, the soldiers aiming machine pistols at their heads. Both glared at Keppler with hate, until Williams spotted Maurice in the car and his jaw began to work, clenching and unclenching, his teeth grinding noisily.

Williams wasn't scared now. This was like just before a race. He had to stay calm, detached. Every time he let that clutch in, he was embarking on a journey that could end in pain or injury or death. Now he was doing it again. And he had training to fall back on. But Eve. Please, God. Not Eve. If they laid a finger on Eve he'd make sure Maurice died, one way or another.

'Just these two and one dead girl, sir,' said the sergeant. So Wimille had made it.

As the man talked he heard a clink. The Bugatti key and chain had slipped from Eve's neck and fallen down through the cracks in the terrace. She'd undone it. She winked at him and he thought his heart was going to explode.

'No Robert Benoist or Jean-Pierre Wimille?' asked Keppler.

A smiling Neumann emerged with a gramophone and a stack of records. 'A miracle. Not one broken.' He proceeded to load it into the boot of the Opel. 'So the brother has flown the coop?' Neumann asked Keppler.

Keppler strode up and stared down at the pair, and signalled them to be dragged to their feet. 'No,' he said as ominously as he could to Williams' face. 'Not exactly.'

Robert listened to it all. Chiquita had picked up the telephone, he had heard her greeting and then that sound. At first he had thought it was interference on the line, a common enough occurrence these days, but then it resolved itself into the sound of a room, a house suffering a holocaust of gunfire. And some masochistic part of his brain, some evil primitive part, made him hold the phone to his ear for what seemed like hours, flinching as he heard the detonations and destructions and imagined what those bullets were doing to the flesh of his friends. To Eve.

With exaggerated care he put the phone back on its cradle and slumped in the chair at the nurses' station, putting his head in his hands. For a moment he began to cry, then caught himself.

'Are you all right?' asked the sister. 'Can I get you anything?'

Robert sat up, blinked, and took a deep breath. From his jacket he took a Browning pistol and checked the action, much to the young nurse's horror. 'Yes. Please. A glass of water.'

Robert gulped it back, dragged a forearm across his mouth and stood, his emotions in check again, all but for that bright, white spot of anger burning near his heart. Keep in there, he reminded himself, feed off it. The brighter it glowed, the easier this would be. 'Tell my mother I'll be back.'

He retraced his steps down to the entrance and stepped outside, hesitating for a second at the top of the steps. The first cosh hit him a glancing blow on the shoulder and he spun around, reaching for the Browning. The second caught him on the bridge of the nose, blinding out daylight with its wash of pain, and a third and fourth sent him crumpling down the stone steps into oblivion.

Twenty-eight

The police Citroën van came screeching from where it had skulked round the corner and the two gendarmes rushed down the steps after Robert and pulled the dazed man to his feet. Blood streaked his face from his contact with the rough stone, and, thanks to the lead-filled coshes, bruises more florid than his mother's were already blossoming across his face.

A brusque search revealed Robert's gun, which the gendarme called Didier slotted into his belt. He opened the rear doors of the van and with the help of Farnoux, his partner, they flung Robert in the back of the paddy wagon, stepped after him and banged the sides to tell the driver to go. Siren blaring it headed north, from Republique, heading through the heart of Montmartre, skirting the Les Halles markets, on its way to the Arc de Triomphe, and, ultimately, the deceptive grandeur of Avenue Foch.

Robert pulled himself up slowly, scrabbling for some kind of hold as the van swung this way and that. There were no benches or seats of any sort for prisoners, just some worn leather straps hanging from the roof and metal rings for attaching handcuffs. Painfully he slid himself up the bulkhead and managed to hold on.

The two policemen dangled at the far ends, like experts, swaying with the rhythm of the Citroën. Farnoux pulled a small folding metal seat down from the wall and perched on it. Didier looked the wild-eyed, blood-stained prisoner up and down. 'That's just for starters, Monsieur Big Shot,' he said, and grinned.

Robert examined Didier's bulging gut, and the Browning stuffed against it, and wondered how much the man weighed. More than he should as a police officer in these austere times, that was for sure. Himself and Didier probably made one-eighty, maybe even two hundred kilos. Robert waited until the van slowed, probably working its way around a velo or a horse-drawn cart or a knot of pedestrians – with only light traffic, people wandered into the road with impunity these days.

Robert already knew the man in the cab's clumsy driving style. He would jerk away from a near standstill and accelerate furiously until the poor engine ran out of steam, then brake with an equally heavy foot as soon as he saw some obstacle. He waited, letting his weight pull on the strap, trying to look suitably beaten and cowed. They mustn't notice. They mustn't realise. Until the moment came.

It came with an unexpected judder and screech of tyres, even though he had tried to anticipate the lumpen responses of the driver, and he hit the bulkhead with a painful thud. Using the momentum, Robert bounced back as the van picked up speed again and pumped all his energy into the two or three strides he would have before they finally cottoned on to the fact that, in the heady flush of a successful apprehension, they had forgotten to handcuff him.

He saw the shock in the faces as he came down the length of the van at them, the desperate scrabble for the gun holsters, Farnoux trying to rise from the seat and then Robert hit Didier like a sack of bricks, throwing all his mass straight into the gendarme's chest, their combined weight punching open the unsecured lock on the rear doors and sending them as one diving out on to the road.

Robert was on top when they hit the ground with a bone-jarring crunch and he felt the air explode out of Didier, ribs straining and snapping as his full weight drove the man into the road surface. Already he could hear shouting and banging as Farnoux screamed at the driver to stop. As he pulled himself up Robert jerked the Browning pistol free from the belt and levelled it at Didier.

Didier, sweating with the knifing pain in his sides and breathing hard and shallow, looked up in terror and began to push with his boot heels, crawling on his back to get away from the figure standing over him with the pistol, the man who looked as if he might just be crazy enough to kill a cop. The gun was rock steady, tracing his movements as he cockroached backwards.

'Please,' Didier gasped. 'I am only doing my job.'

Robert's eyes glanced down at a uniform defiled and degraded by what the *flics* had done for their masters over the last few years. He thought of those pathetic, heartbreaking little notes from the train, the swaggering cops banging on cattle trucks telling the starving, thirsty inhabitants to keep quiet.

'And I'm only doing mine,' said Robert softly before he shot him twice in the heart.

The first police bullet smacked past him and down the boulevard. Robert began to look around. Pedestrians, mostly old women, were frozen in position, wide mouthed with a mixture of horror and excitement, unsure of how to react.

The Musée Grevin, with its waxwork tableaux, was opposite. No escape that way. Another bullet. A shrill whistle summoning help, blast after blast. Robert raised the Browning and shot at the van where Farnoux and the driver were crouched, both blowing for assistance at the top of their lungs. A crowd was gathering. A charcoal-powered car had stopped, the driver unsure what to do about a gunfight in the Boulevard Montmartre. Sirens. Lots of them. Robert ran, south, through the art nouveaux-covered Galeries, elbowing aside the first shoppers scurrying out to snap up the day's meagre produce.

The noise and shouts behind him told him the police were giving chase. His heart thumping, he swerved left and right until he emerged from the arcade into a long, narrow street running east towards Boulevard Bonne Nouvelle, Williams' old stomping ground.

He began to run straight ahead, down the road, picking up his feet to make sure he didn't trip on the uneven paved surface. Another shot. Robert risked a glance behind and saw maybe six or seven uniforms powering after him. A round burned through the outer part of his leg and he felt himself stumbling headlong as the muscle jerked in pain. He hit the road, rolled, and came up with the Browning outstretched. Think. How many rounds? It's a High Power. German model. Nine millimetre parabellum round. He'd reloaded the bloody gun time and time again but his brain was mush. Seven . . . no, thirteen. Thirteen rounds. He'd already used three, or four. He had enough left to take a few with him.

On they came, eight of them, slowed now, getting ready to close in for the kill, like a pack that knows it has its prey cornered, relishing this moment. He had slain one of their number. They weren't going to take him alive. They weren't going to let him go slowly. No quick bullet for him.

Robert pumped two rounds at them and the cops stopped, hesitating. No hits. They were crouching, difficult targets at this range. He stood, ignoring the flash of agony in his leg. Look at that later. If there was a later. He fired another shot. One of the police groaned and clutched his shoulder.

The other seven started to yell and came at him, firing as they went, caution gone, bullets splaying round him. Robert dived to the wall as if it could wrap and protect him.

A vase came first. It shattered in front of the lead policeman and he blithely carried on, unaware of its significance.

The gramophone hit the cop full on with a deadly inert impact, sending the man to the floor as if poleaxed, a huge flap of red scalp dangling free. Robert looked up. A table was arcing through the air. Books. Another vase. All rained down like some strange biblical plague of household objects. Robert smiled to himself. Resistance.

A full chamberpot smashed into the cops, who began to huddle together like a Roman tortoise formation, but without the shields to protect their backs. A guitar. More vases. A sewing machine, breaking bones as it slammed into a shoulder. The air grew thick with domestic detritus, some of which must have been of great sentimental value. A small cupboard. Bottles of cleaning fluid exploded around them with muffled explosions. Some kind of caustic soda detonated in their midst and there were screams. Robert fired again, joining in the ritual assault on the men with something more lethal than bleach. One of the cops hit the floor, rolled and was still. A washstand hit him and the body arched, but no more. Dead. A radio, a precious radio, eviscerated itself on the cobbles.

From the apartments above more and more rained down and Robert backed off, heading for the streets where he knew he could find safety. There was an enormous groaning sound and a balcony gave way, an upright piano heaved over the edge tearing the metalwork and huge lumps of concrete free, disintegrating with spectacular echoing dissonance.

The police began to retreat, walking at first, then running, back to get their colleagues and return in greater numbers,

261

leaving three sprawled in the road, slowly disappearing under random cairns created from the bric-a-brac of other people's lives. The shutters and windows began to slam shut, the stories of innocence already being concocted, the occupants only now beginning to wonder just what they had done. Robert raised his arms, tears in his eyes, proud of his countrymen for the first time since he knew not when and shouted: '*Vive la France!*'

Keppler took his charges to the police station at Rambouillet and Williams was transferred to a windowless van, chained to a ring in the side, two German soldiers guarding him. Keppler had said he would talk to him when they got Robert. 'When?' Williams had laughed. 'If.'

Keppler smiled back. 'When,' he repeated. Eve was loaded separately. The Women's Section was in a different building.

After a slow, jolting drive through the southern suburbs of Paris the van drew to a halt. He knew where he was. Fresnes Prison, the great hulking fortress on the outskirts of the city, was taking on the same symbolic mantle as the Bastille. This was a place where awful injustices happened, where all flesh was corruptible, malleable, where you lived and died by the whims of jailers more evil than any of their charges.

Williams was unlocked from the ring, handcuffed, and led into the outside world. The large cobbled courtyard was surrounded by towering walls with tiny slit windows. In the little amount of bright summer sunshine that managed to penetrate this well, the walls' rancid, diseased surfaces looked vile enough, thought Williams. God only knew what this place was like at the dead of night when most inmates arrived. In the corner were two bodies, crumpled and ignored, both bearing the marks and strangely angled limbs of savage beatings.

Williams was pushed firmly through the huge, over-sized

metal doors, clearly designed to make the prisoners feel insignificant, as if giants really walked this earth. He was marched into a cold, echoing hallway, where his details were entered into the prison log while a selection of French and Germans eyed him up, as if vying for the chance to lay into him. Williams stayed calm, answered the questions curtly but correctly, giving his name as Charles Lelong. He was then taken by a German NCO and two French warders downstairs, along a grim, sweaty passageway, and into an internal courtyard, this one lined and criss-crossed with galleries and gangways, resounding to the crunch of hobnailed boots, shouted orders and the odd thunk of wood and rubber on flesh.

Williams' cell was on the lower level, which meant it had no window. The darkness was probably a blessing. The NCO delivered a heavy punch to Williams' face and he stumbled inside, crashing into the opposite wall.

The door slammed on him, the NCO looked through the peephole and marched off. Williams checked his face, but the blow had merely cut his lip. He sucked back the blood and, still handcuffed, groped his way around his new home, locating a WC, a tap and an iron bed with a straw mattress. He sat gingerly on the latter, and, despite the near certainty that there were lice just waiting for him, he sank back and closed his eyes, trying to still his racing mind so he could get some sleep. Astonishingly, he dozed.

He was woken by the sound of a trolley rattling across the steel latticework of the galleries. An elderly German was escorting two orderlies who were dishing out soup and coffee, although, as Williams discovered, it was difficult to be sure which was which. More visits gave him a grimy blanket and some newspaper, which was torn into small squares in case there was any doubt about its intended use. Finally, his

263

handcuffs were removed and he massaged some life into his numb wrists.

Nothing too drastic yet, he thought. But he knew what might be awaiting him. Suspension from hooks in the ceiling with his arms behind his back, constant beatings, the famous and dreaded *baignoire*, where victims were repeatedly held under water until they lost consciousness, a torture that could be repeated for hours. A torture that was rumoured to be something of a spectator sport at rue de Saussaies – the German female clerks were often invited to watch.

The afternoon passed slowly, the anticipation of Gestapo and SD delights eating at him, so Williams tried to get his mind off torture and began to play mental games, trying to recall every winner of every grand prix since 1925, something to stop him thinking about Eve, to leave no room, no part of his brain that dared dwell on what he had got her into.

At around four there was a commotion. Voices shouting in French. Then English. 'Is there an Englishman here?'

'Yes,' yelled another voice.

'Quiet.' Guards were trying to silence everyone, but the voices radiated off the hard metal surfaces so much it was hard to pinpoint who was speaking unless you were right next to the cell, and the conversations bloomed and died within seconds, everyone knowing they had two or three short sentences to make their point. Williams walked to the bars to listen, but not participate.

'Who are you?'

'Conrad. Vincent Conrad.' Code name, thought Williams.

'Chalambaud. You in the Racket?'

Williams knew what this meant, and so did Conrad. Wisely, he chose not to reply. Then the first voice said; 'Don't let the bastards break you, Vincent. The Allies have taken Sicily. It's started.'

264

So Sicily really had fallen? Christ, from there Italy. So not Calais or Normandy. Jesus. The news both exhilarated and depressed him. Fighting their way up Italy, through Hitler's heavily defended back door, meant they could forget the second front for at least a year.

An orderly appeared at the door, glaring. 'Was that you?' Williams shrugged, not wanting to give them an inch. 'If it was, just shut up. Last time we celebrated some Allied victory Fritz shot five of us. Just shut up.'

The noise gradually subsided, to be replaced by the odd muffled scream from somewhere down a subterranean passage. Then singing, in both French and English. Except the lyrics to the songs were coded stories of missions, betrayal, escape, recapture. There were a lot of agents in the prison, thought Williams, a hell of a lot.

As he sat down on the bed again Williams thought about his wife. Damn. Eve, alone in a cell like this, waiting for . . . he squeezed his eyes shut. Go away, he told the images. Go away. He lay down and began to chew the inside of his cheek till it bled.

Across at the Women's Section, Eve had been put in a higher, lighter cell with a scrawny, pinched woman who, the trustee delighted in telling her, was a prostitute, who looked at her with scant regard, and made it clear that over half the cell and all its contents were her property. Eve sat down quietly on her tiny cot and hoped Williams was OK. She couldn't help feeling that men risked being treated much worse in this hateful place. Although she had already seen women being dragged off by their hair and kicked and beaten as they were pushed along the gangways, so perhaps this was leaping to a false conclusion. For the first time in a long time, Eve began to feel scared for herself rather than Will or Robert.

'Resistance?' asked the prostitute.

Eve shrugged, aware that the woman could easily be an informer. 'A mistake. It'll be cleared up.'

The woman grunted. 'What's your name?'

'Eve.'

'Renée. You won't be here long.'

'Why not?'

'Resistance are usually taken to Saussaies or Foch. Sometimes they come back, sometimes they don't.'

'Why are you here?'

'Resistance.' Eve's expression must have shown her disbelief. 'Why do you look like that? You think only the bourgeoisie are allowed in?'

'No, I . . .'

'I heard what the trustee said. Whore. He's right. And I have a disease. And now so do twenty, thirty, forty German soldiers. And they'll be sent out of France to die on the eastern front. Tell me, Eve, how many Germans did you get rid of?'

Eve burst out laughing and when she realised she wasn't being mocked, Renée joined in. 'I'll make sure you get the Croix de Guerre.'

'Just get me some of that penicillin, dear.'

Eve stood up and crossed over to the other woman's bed. Renée hesitated and moved up. 'Listen, I am new to all this, Renée. Forgive me, I have a feeling you . . .' Eve stopped, struggling to find the expression.

'Know the system? Like the back of my hand.'

'My husband is also in here somewhere. I'm going to get him out.'

Renée rubbed finger and thumb together in the age-old symbol for money, but before she could elaborate, a key turned in the lock, the door swung out and in stepped Neumann, his gleaming, immaculate uniform and boots a stark contrast to the cancerous surroundings. Renée couldn't help an intake of breath.

'Eve.' He glanced around at the cell, which was clean and neat by Fresnes standards. He placed a block of grey, gritty soap on her bed, along with a toothbrush, a hairbrush and a tube of toothpaste. 'I brought you some things.' He looked at Renée and his lip curled with distaste. 'I will arrange for you to get your own cell.'

'I'm happy here.'

'I'm not happy you are here. I can get you out, you know. Very simple.' Neumann raised a querying eyebrow.

'And my husband?'

Neumann stood staring for a second, his face impassive, those blue eyes flashing, turned and left, slamming the cell door, bringing a fine shower of dust from the lintel.

Renée made the money gesture again, then pointed at her crotch. 'I was forgetting. There are two ways out.'

Twenty-nine

The shredded remnants of the *Nacht und Nebel* order were still on the desk in Virginia's cell. She had spent much of the last twenty-four hours in a coma-like state lying on the bed, refusing all food and offers of companionship. Now she wished she had an L pill; she would take it like a shot. She felt she had been bamboozled into a betrayal. But what had she done? What had she really done? Confirmed simply that Gatacre was Williams. Yet she had only discovered it by chance, she could have pretended the information had never come her way, but something, something weak inside had made her head nod of its own accord.

She looked over when a knock came at the door and stared back at the wall when Lock entered.

'Go away.'

'Keppler wants you.'

'Tell him to go to hell.'

She was aware of him moving closer. 'Look, little lady, you might as well face up to it. You're in as deep as me now. Thing is, Neumann has got your pal Williams. You know what that means, don't you? All you have to do is tell him he's wasting his time playing the silent hero. The game is well and truly up.

Save him a lot of pain. You owe him that.'

She snapped round and glared at him. Maybe he was right. Maybe she did owe him that. Virginia sat up, feeling her head swim as she did so and swallowing hard.

'You all right?'

'I need some water. Perhaps something to eat.' If you were going to be a traitor, she reasoned, you might as well do it on a full stomach.

It was nightfall by the time Robert reached Auffargis. He had come a very circuitous route over the back fields, looking for signs of sentries, an ambush, but there was none. He had managed to escape from the cops by taking to the rooftops, and eventually descending into an apartment block when the wound in his leg became too painful for the scrabbles and leaps. The concierge had surprised him on the second floor, pinning him to the wall, an ornate poker in hand.

'I am not a housebreaker.'

The elderly man had peered into his face and whispered, 'No. But I believe you are Robert Benoist.'

Robert swallowed hard and said: 'Yes, I am.'

The concierge had let him go. 'Then it would be an honour if you would join me for a drink in my room.'

After being forced to drink too much brandy and reminisce about his racing days while the man cleaned and dressed the wound in his leg – which was effectively a very deep rip through muscle – the concierge had loaned him his bike and sent him on his way. He had cycled slowly and stiffly out to his old house.

Robert had a torch but did not use it. There was a moon – more poor souls would be coming in from SOE, he thought – and he knew the paths well enough. He approached through the woods and sat on the flattened grass and broken ferns where the machine gunners had lain half a day before him. He imagined the fire raking the house, the van shuddering as bullets wrecked it, the terrace collapsing, the plants torn asunder. Were they alive? He'd called in to see Bugatti's old secretary, Madame Teyssédre, a brave woman who he knew had links to the Resistance, just as she suspected his, although they never discussed them for security reasons. Find out for me if they are alive. She said she'd try. Then she whispered, 'Have you heard about Sicily?'

As he lay there watching his poor shattered house, waiting for signs of a trap, he thought about Sicily. A sudden influx of agents in Paris and northern France with orders to begin sabotage. Massive drops of weapons. Radio sets. Explosives. That would convince the SD and the Abwehr that something big was afoot. Messages would dribble back to the Wehrmacht and the RSHA where a picture would emerge of the Allies planning to attack northern France. While all the time they were sneaking up the back alley.

So London lost a few spies in the deception, a few tonnes of materiel, a dozen radio sets. Which the Germans turn. Or think they . . . his mind spun. Who knew the truth? Not him, not any of them.

After waiting thirty minutes Robert crept across the lawn, gun in hand, down to the last two bullets in the magazine. But nothing stirred except for an owl way back in the forest. He felt sick as he got closer to the house and saw the damage the heavy calibre guns had done, atomising huge sections of the wall, smashing every last piece of glass in a window frame. He sat down on the terrace and, beneath the broken boards, he saw something gleam. Reaching down between the splintered wood he managed to pull up the silver chain with the Atlantic key on it. Eve must have deliberately dropped it down there. He kissed it and placed it over his own neck.

Inside the wrecked kitchen he cleared the debris from a section of the floor and levered up one of the flagstones. Beneath was the B2 transmitter. He lugged it outside, strung the aerial over the wooden trellis half hanging from the wall and set up to transmit. This wasn't his sked, but he inserted the emergency crystal. Someone would be listening. And the Germans. Out there in the night a DF van would prick up its metal ears and slowly turn its attention to him. Let them try. He used the one-time pad to create the short, sharp communication.

He transmitted, received a recognition, did his security check and sent the message in full. Don't trust this radio any longer. Chestnut blown. Last secure transmission. A reply. He quickly put it into clear. We'll send a plane. He roughed out a final goodbye: Thanks. Perhaps later. Have housekeeping to do. Out.

Afterwards he took the B2 back inside, returned it to the hiding place. In the sink he burned the silk code sheet and the one-time pads while he smoked a welcome cigarette. Finally he put the crystals, two regular and one emergency, in their black velvet bag and, using the butt of the gun, smashed them to useless bits and hurled them through the open window. Ready. As he had said, time to clean house.

Some figures are so strange as to be unnoticeable, invisible. It was Madame Teyssédre's idea and Robert embraced the surreal-ness of it. So, late in the afternoon, a man in a stove-pipe hat and black frock coat cycled rather stiffly along Boulevard Capucines, looking neither right nor left, not bothering to take in the wonderful confection of Opera, the young men being dragged from the Metro by Gestapo, the Light 15s prowling past him, the rickshaws and charcoal cars that crossed every intersection ahead of him. Paris was imploding now, the hated regime had become more violent, wild, thrashing out to try to suppress the groundswell building and building; but instead of suppressing it was compressing the people like a spring. Sooner or later they would bounce back.

The chimney sweep turned right by the Opera Comique, ignoring the Germans mingling on the pavement sipping pre-show drinks, past the row of horsedrawn taxis, and the little cluster of emaciated, desperate prostitutes hoping to catch an officer's eye.

Robert reached the apartment block, dismounted and locked the bike up with a chain. He rang the bell for the concierge. Nothing. He waited ten minutes until a young mother came out to give her baby some air before curfew and he slipped in as the door almost slammed shut. He climbed one flight of stairs, slowly, because of the still aching wound, found himself a deep, dark doorway and settled down for however long it took.

It wasn't a lengthy wait. He heard the door close softly and the lock being turned and the distinctive foot-dragging gait of his brother. He smiled bitterly to himself. Now they both had matching limps. Maurice descended the stairs, his stiff leg thudding down first each time. As he passed him on the landing Robert gave a low whistle and he saw his brother start and turn. Robert stepped into the light, the meagre bulb throwing the stove hat into a gross, elongated shadow.

'Williams?'

The sound of a guilty conscience. A man with something terrible on his mind. Robert stepped forward and raised the Browning. 'You know it isn't Williams. You know it can't be Will, don't you?'

272

'Rob—'

'Hush.' Robert came close, put a hand behind Maurice's head and forced the gun into his mouth.

'I coubbnnmmm,' Maurice tried to say.

'Hush now, brother. You broke my heart. Broke my heart. Just two bullets left. I hope the first one kills you, I really do. It'll be better than you have given Will. And Eve.' He pressed the gun down, forcing Maurice to his knees.

'Theyadmmuuvvver.'

'Hush. Doesn't matter now. Whatever.'

The gun began to shake. Slowly at first, then quite violently until it was banging against Maurice's teeth and Robert fought to pull the trigger against the sound of his mother's pleading. 'You'd have done the same,' her weak voice said. Would he? *Would he?*

Robert wrenched the barrel from Maurice's mouth, brutally cutting his top lip with the fore-sight, swung the gun back and slashed it across Maurice's temple, sending his brother sprawling to the floor with a groan. He lay there, panting, not daring to move, knowing the moment of blind hatred had passed for ever, unless he said or did anything to provoke Robert. He'd won. He'd survived. Do nothing.

Disgusted as much with himself as his brother, Robert repocketed the gun, went down the stairs and stepped out into the glare of headlights from SD cars. He thought about running back inside when he heard a Schmeisser being cocked somewhere behind him in the hallway. No doubt the soldier would love him to try something.

'Robert.' It was Keppler, taking in the strange disguise. 'A new career. Very good. Well, you'll be pleased to know the chimneys at Foch haven't been done for some time.'

Williams had lost sense of whether the water pouring down on him from the overhead spigot was boiling hot or freezing cold. His raw, pummiced skin reacted in the same way – screeching out in agony. In the interrogation cell of Fresnes the music played softly in the corner, one of his Jean Sablon records, while Neumann paced up and down in front of him, occasionally regulating the water that cascaded on to his head, running into his nose and mouth. Williams felt as if the constant streams had runnelled his face, etching deep furrows into it.

He couldn't actually see Neumann because, after binding him into the heavy wooden chair, they had slipped blackened motorcycle goggles on to his head. And then the water started. Cold, hot, freezing, scalding. In a strange way, Williams could relax now. After all the gut-wrenching anticipation of torture, after thinking perhaps they weren't such bad guys after all, and it wouldn't happen, here was the proof that they deserved whatever they got.

His whole upper body was screaming out and he was compartmentalising the pain, trying to make it distant, happening to someone else, cursing God, simultaneously denying Him and praying to Him that this wasn't happening to Eve.

Suddenly the water was turned off and the sickly crooning became much louder. Williams breathed a soft sigh of relief, but now the skin began to prickle and itch, something he could do little about with his hands firmly tied. Which was just as well, because within seconds he wanted to rip into his scalp and tear it off.

'Better, eh?' Neumann said. 'Now. You know what we need. Your contacts. The radios. Are you still using a poem code? If so what is it? If not, where are your one-time pads? Who is Jester? Where is Madeleine?'

The smell that drifted across to him seemed so out of place

here, so alien, he had a moment placing it. Then he had it. Perfume. Chanel. Number Five. From Coco who, of course, lived at the Ritz with her German lover. How appropriate. 'Williams,' said Virginia. 'Remember me?'

'I always hated that smell.'

'Chanel?'

'Treachery.'

Neumann laughed and Williams felt hands grab his arm and his fingers being splayed out on the arm of the chair. Virginia felt sick to her stomach. She had to convince him this was all for nothing, pointless. Lock was right, they were being played for fools.

'Williams, they are going to smash your right hand. Tell them,' Virginia pleaded. 'You know they know everything. Please.'

Williams was aware of cold metal on the back of his hand. A hammer face.

'Let me out,' Virginia said. 'Let me out, I want no part of this.'

Williams felt the hammer lift anyway. 'You are already part of it,' said Neumann.

He braced himself, wondering what would be left after it pulverised bone, snapped tendons and crushed muscles. Would he be able to drive again?

The door opened and Williams heard a heated, whispered conversation. A decision was made. He slowly let the tension drain from his body. He was being untied and unmanacled. He was dragged up and pulled out into the corridor. Neumann whispered: 'You're a lucky man, Williams. Keppler wants to see you. And he doesn't like damaged goods.' Foch, he thought. They're going to Foch.

Robert sat on the chaise longue in Keppler's office, his bad leg stretched out. It had been re-bandaged by the warders of the tiny cell on the fifth floor where he had spent the previous night. Nobody had really tried to pressure him to talk so far. He had a visit from an Englishman called Gilbert, who had done his best to convince him that co-operation was the only way. Then a more insidious conversation with some slippery sack of shit called Lock. That hadn't lasted too long.

But he had seen other men who bore the signs of heavy beatings, and he'd heard the guards in action, shouting and slapping and whipping. Clearly, the message was there are two routes we can go here. Your choice.

At a small fold-out desk next to Keppler's ormolu sat Obst, a stenographer. Two armed soldiers were on either side of the door, just in case Robert felt like walking over and strangling Keppler there and then. It was a tempting idea. He watched as the Sturmbannführer decanted a bottle of red wine, poured a glass and nodded appreciatively. 'Château Corton André. Superb.'

Robert asked, 'What year?'

'Thirty-seven.'

'Too young. You mustn't be impatient. Or do you think you're running out of time?'

Keppler smiled. 'Sicily?' He shook his head. 'It's a long way up Italy, let me tell you. A long way.' He sipped again. 'Six years. I think it's time enough.'

The door opened and in came Williams, still damp from his soaking, skin blotchy from scalding, the goggles firmly in place. Neumann pushed him into one of the gilded Louis XV chairs and snapped handcuffs in place. Virginia went and sat quietly near Obst.

Robert looked at Neumann and hissed: 'What's wrong? Run out of little old ladies to beat up, arsehole?'

'Perhaps. But their sons will do just as well.' He took a step

276

towards Robert who swung his leg off the settee and half rose to meet him. The guards stirred, wondering how to react to the looming confrontation.

'Neumann. Enough. Go and send Lock in.' There was a beat before he added, 'And make sure Mrs Williams is comfortable.'

The junior officer hesitated and looked at Williams, hoping for a reaction to the news that his precious wife was in the building. He left disappointed.

Keppler took out his Luger pistol and laid it on the desk in front of him. 'When Virginia was turned over to me, I told her more about SOE than she knew. I could do the same for you. Prosper, Autogyro, Donkeyman and now Chestnut . . . all gone. We nearly caught Bodington last month. That would have been a prize. Your head of clandestine flights gives us these—' from his desk he produced a pile of mimeographed letters and communications. 'Everything going out on the Lysanders, copied to us. Very polite, eh? We know who is doing what where. Except you two decided that the normal methods of communications were unsafe. You were right. So you kept us in the dark. Very, very rude. Time to make amends.'

The door opened and Lock slipped in and stood next to one of the guards. Robert looked across at him with his hawk-like stare until the Englishman's eyes went down.

'What's going on here, Keppler?' Robert asked, 'Why don't you just pull out our toenails and have done with it?'

Keppler shuddered. 'My God, the very thought of it. That doesn't happen here. Not in this room.' He smiled. 'Not on this carpet. We can take you to eighty-six or seventy-two if we need to do that. But I prefer not to use such methods.'

'So what am I doing here?' asked Williams.

'Well, every now and then Neumann has to be allowed to

prove he can do better than me. I'm just an old copper to him, outdated, outmoded. He has science on his side, I have reason. Every time he proves me right.'

'How gratifying,' croaked Williams.

'Yes, I think so,' said Keppler as he sipped the wine again. 'You see, there isn't much I need from you. Arms dumps? Got them. Contacts? Got those, too. Wimille? Well, he'll have gone to ground. All that is left is just a few details, really. Not worth the effort of beating you all up.'

Robert got up, walked over to Williams and took the goggles off. Nobody tried to stop him. Williams blinked in the sudden light and his eyes began to water. Robert touched the burns on his head and smiled at his old friend. 'These need dressing.'

'They will be,' said Keppler.

'Now.'

'You are in no position to make demands.'

'And you think you are? They'll go septic. They need something on them.'

Keppler hesitated and clicked his fingers at Virginia. She went outside, fetched a first aid kit. On her return she began dabbing iodine on the wounds. Williams, wincing, avoided her gaze.

'So,' continued Keppler, 'there are three things I need.'

'Just three?' asked Robert.

'Yes.'

'And in return?'

'You go east as POWs. Not *N&N*.'

'*N&N?*'

'*Nacht und Nebel*. Night and Fog. *Veruckt unerwunscht*. Return not required.'

'*Nacht und Nebel*. Nice,' mused Robert. 'So why should we trust you, you cunt?'

Lock couldn't help a smile at the sheer audacity. Even Keppler was too taken aback to react angrily. 'Ask Arthur over there. Ask Virginia. Starr. Gilbert. Suthill. A dozen others. Look, Neumann is our resident thug. I make deals. And I keep them.'

'It's not good enough.'

Keppler banged the table in mock disgust. 'Benoist, you really are the absolute limit. Can I remind you, you are my prisoner, I have the power of life and death, yet you sit there as if it is the other way round.'

'I think it is.'

'Please, explain for us.'

Williams cleared his throat and answered for Robert. 'The Allies are in Sicily. Next Italy.' He looked at Robert, 'And if I got it right, the Germans seem to have been hammered at somewhere called Kursk. So now we know that one day, one day soon, you and your chums here will be called to reckon for us. How you treated us. Now, I can guess what will happen to Lock. But you . . .'

Keppler shrugged. 'So, my life in your hands? An interesting thought. Let's pretend you are right. How do we proceed?'

'Tell me the three things you want,' said Robert, 'and I'll tell you what I will trade for them.'

Keppler stood up and paced in front of his desk, a small smile on his face, fascinated and amused by the calmness of the man. 'I want your radio. Its code. And . . .' He looked a little embarrassed. 'The Bugatti Atlantic.'

Robert nodded. 'Seems reasonable.'

'Robert—' Williams croaked, suddenly disliking where this was going.

'No, Will. Let's see how it goes. Roll the dice, Keppler.'

The German nodded. 'The radio? I assume you have a radio?'

'Yes, I have one. And for that I want Eve Williams released.'

Keppler clapped his hands in delight. 'Very good . . . although

279

why are you bargaining for another man's wife?'

'*In loco maritus*,' said Williams.

'How modern.' Keppler took the yellow release form and signed it, handed it to Virginia and said, 'Do it.'

'But—'

'Just do it.'

Five minutes passed while Keppler paced and hummed tunelessly to himself. Eventually he went over to the window and looked down. He beckoned Robert to his side. Below he saw Eve and Virginia reach the high metal gates at the front. Eve, looking tired and bedraggled but as beautiful as ever, hesitated as she stepped through the small door cut into the larger one and scanned the building. Robert wasn't sure she caught the two-fingered kiss he made as Virginia bundled her out into the street. He imagined he could hear her running on the other side, sprinting for the small apartment round the corner, and sanctuary.

'You know that was easy for me. I hate women being involved in this,' said Keppler: 'So?'

'Don't do it, Robert,' said Williams.

'She can be picked up again very quickly,' snarled Keppler.

'A deal is a deal. And she's out, Will. That's all that matters,' said Robert heavily. 'Here we go. Go back to the house in the forest. Kitchen. Fourth flagstone from the door. You'll find a B2 transmitter.'

'And the frequency?'

Robert glanced at Williams and said: 'Over to you, Will.'

Williams tried to stay calm. There was a message here. Robert knew perfectly well what the frequencies were. He could tell Keppler. Unless he wanted to make him complicit in this dreadful compromise. Or was trying to tell him that it really didn't matter. Williams caught the softest, fastest of winks and, taking it as reassurance, said quickly: 'Four point five to nine megacycles. Three crystals. Two normal, one emergency.'

Keppler smiled and went back to his wine. 'Now let's try . . . for the coded poem. You are still using the poems?'

Both nodded at once, a tad too enthusiastically, but Keppler failed to notice.

'You want the code? You'll leave my family alone, once, and for all time,' said Robert.

'Maurice included?'

'Fuck Maurice. I should have shot him.'

'Did you know your brother helped us compile lists, lists of naturalised Jews in Paris? I gave him a travel pass for every ten names.'

Robert felt his spirits sink. They moved around on the backs of denounced and deported Jews. He felt sick to his stomach. He repeated softly: 'I said, fuck Maurice.'

'OK. You have my word. The family, left in peace.'

'No matter what?' insisted Williams.

'No matter what.'

Obst, the stenographer, asked: 'Which of you is the poet?'

Williams began the defunct code: 'Sweet sister death . . . has gone debauched today, and stalks on this high ground . . .'

'Repeat the last five words please,' requested Obst.

To Williams' surprise, Virginia picked up: 'Stalks on this high ground . . . with strumpet confidence . . .'

Obst stumbled at the sudden change. 'Strumpet?'

'Yes, strumpet. With strumpet confidence makes no coy veiling of her appetite . . . but leers from you to me . . . with all her parts discovered.'

Obst asked: 'Who wrote this?'

Virginia answered: 'David Jones. He saw you lot in action last time.'

'I prefer Irving Berlin,' said Keppler offhandedly.

'He's Jewish,' said Williams bitterly.

'I won't tell if you don't.' Keppler drained the last of his wine and said triumphantly, 'This seems to be going rather well. So finally, we come to the Bugatti Atlantic. What do you want for that?'

Robert pursed his lips and clicked his fingers, as if seeking the right conditions that would satisfy him before he said slowly, in his most cultured voice: 'How about you suck our cocks?'

Thirty

PARIS, LATE MARCH 1944

Eve let the feeble spring sun warm her back, stroking deliciously through the thin linen jacket she wore over a faded cotton dress, as she leafed through the postcards and books on the banks of the Seine, moving from stall to stall, marvelling at the pictures and prints of a city that seemed to exist in a half-remembered time, as if it really was sepia and brown tinged, the way her memory tended to play it back these days.

Eight months since the arrests. Eight months of arguing, cajoling and – above all – bribing. So many thousand francs to make sure they had decent cells, another ten for better rations, twenty for a message, a scrap of paper with almost illegible scrawl, written in the depths of winter with numb fingers, but still strong, the big X, the kiss, still defiant. Five thousand to take them new clothes. Twenty-five for a passage into that hideous inner courtyard and glimpse at a cell window, so high and so far it could be anyone, but she knew it was Will.

And she got a message from Robert. It told her he had spent the last two weeks inscribing something on his wall. Something he still believed, something for her to cling on to. Never give up. Never confess. Never surrender. That he would look after Will for her, no matter what. It had made her weep for her friend.

Now, the ultimate bribe.

Paris felt like a powder keg or a steam cooker with no safety valve, heading for an explosion. More desperate deportations of Jews and undesirables, more workers for the Reich, more reprisals not only in the capital but at Lille and Tulle. There was a strong anticipation of ultimate liberation now. That included kicking over traces, losing any little conveniences. Like SOE spies. And of feathering nests. Hence the greed of guards and gaolers in Fresnes, there to be exploited.

So she had to make sure Will and Robert were on the right train, not labelled *N&N* but POW. So she had a deal, of sorts.

She felt a tap on her shoulder and turned round to see Neumann beaming at her, in sober civilian clothes for once. She managed to smile back with what she hoped was enthusiasm. He kissed her cheek and she tilted her head as if she welcomed it.

'They went out last night. To Germany. Both to Stalags for officers.'

Inside she felt like crying, the thought of Will and Robert moving even further from her, but she managed to say, 'Thank you, Joachim.'

'All this could have been done long ago if you had just come to me earlier.'

'I know. I was . . . stubborn. Silly.'

He held his arm out and she slipped hers through his. They began to walk north, crossing the river at the Pont Royal and wandering through the Tuileries, its once immaculate beds now churned up for precious vegetable production. Nobody seemed to notice the pair of them, nobody stopped and pointed, or hissed, 'Whore, slut, traitor', as she half expected. Just two lovers of indeterminate nationality out for a walk.

'You know, I don't always approve of Hans Keppler's methods,' said Neumann. 'But he has taught me two things. The power of negotiation, especially if you are doing so from a position of strength.' He bent down to kiss her again, this time on the lips. 'And patience. And I have to say, Eve, you were well worth the wait.'

Across the Rivoli, heading for Place du Vendôme to his apartment on rue de la Paix.

'Can I ask you about something? If you promise not to question me on it?'

'Questioning is my job, Eve.'

'You're out of uniform. And all this isn't really part of the job. Not strictly speaking.'

'True.' He considered for a moment. They were on the Vendome now, the shops that had been swarming with German officers and their mistresses two years before looking a little shabbier, more desperate now. The age of frivolity was over. Buying couture dresses and hastily pawned Jewish jewellery was no longer the priority it had been. Still, as ever, a line of Hotchkisses, Rolls-Royces and Delages attended upon the Ritz, where a form of good life continued apace, day and night. 'OK, no questions.'

She began to relay the rumour she had received from a sceptical Madame Teyssédre. 'An acquaintance told me an astonishing story. They heard that a group of French Canadian agents were met at Gare d'Austerlitz by someone who they were assured was a friend. The friend betrayed them to your people.'

'Go on.'

'The agents got word out of Fresnes—'

'How?'

'Uh-uh. You know Fresnes leaks like a sieve now. Anyway, no

questions. You promised.' She pinched him hard on the arm.

'Very well,' Neumann laughed.

'The message said their betrayer was a man called Williams.'

'Really?'

'Was it?'

'Was it what?'

'Was it Will?'

'What do you think?'

'I think you had someone impersonate him. It wouldn't be the first time, would it? You set up the meeting on a turned radio and sent a stand-in.'

He shrugged noncommittally. 'Such as?'

'You are about the right height and build. A little younger. Wrong colour hair. But with a hat . . .'

'Here we are.' Neumann stopped and opened the solid, ornate door of a grand apartment block. 'No questions and no answers either I am afraid. But I will tell you this.' She felt his hand low on her back, sliding on to her backside as he propelled her in. 'I have no objection to being in your husband's shoes right now.'

Eve had to gasp when she saw the scale of the apartment itself. An enormous living room, full of good-quality furniture, all in heavy reds and golds, with two bedrooms and a bathroom leading from it. 'My God.'

'Yes, excellent isn't it. I've only had it a month. The contessa had to, um, leave at rather short notice. There's a good view of the Opera from that window there. Drink?'

'Gin?'

'Uh, no. Scotch?'

'Perfect.'

'Coming up. Make yourself at home.'

Eve slipped off her jacket, draped it over a sofa and began to walk around admiring the furnishings.

'Music?' asked Neumann rhetorically. 'Strauss. "One Thousand and One Nights". You like Strauss?' She nodded. 'Good. I can see we are going to get on brilliantly.'

'Joachim. Do you mind if I take a bath first?'

The thought of Eve in a tub made him flush and he said, 'If you leave the door open for me.'

'Of course.' He watched appreciatively as she went in to the big marble space, bent over the bath and began running the water. 'My God, it's so hot,' she shouted over the gushings. 'I haven't seen such hot water since . . . since before you people came.'

'Well, you should have spent more time with us people.' He clinked ice in the glasses but hesitated while she unbuttoned her dress and let it drop, revealing underwear that had seen too many washes. He would do something about that. The drawers of the apartment were stuffed full of enough lace and silk to cause a riot along Avenue Montaigne.

'Can I have it in here?' she asked, snapping him out of a daydream of Eve in the finest of lace camisole tops.

He picked up the glasses and hurried across to her, not wanting to miss the final moment of the striptease. Her smile faded as he stepped across the threshold, and he thought perhaps she was frightened or modest but then he felt the metal snout of the Welrod against his temple and heard the hiss of the bullet as it brushed through the silencer baffles on its way to his brain.

The bullet exploded out of his temple, punching slivers of bone and eye socket out, leaving the eye itself dangling crazily in its ruined housing. The whisky hit the floor in a fury of glass and ice and Neumann buckled at the knees.

Rose Miller waited for him to fall, wishing the Welrod came with a second shot, reaching for another round when Neumann slumped into Eve, his head lolling to one side, slowly sliding down her, leaving a trail of bloody gristle down her front, until he lay curled at her feet, the last of life leaving him in two quick, powerful spasms.

Eve opened her mouth to scream but managed to suppress the urge and muttered a heartfelt: 'Jesus.'

Rose rolled the body to one side, turned the bath faucet off, pulled two towels off the neat stack on the shelf, laid them across the smashed tumblers and said: 'Mind the glass.'

'Oh yes,' said Eve slightly hysterically, 'wouldn't want to get blood on the towels.'

Rose looked at the gore congealing on Eve's body. 'We'd best get you cleaned up. There's a shower in the master bedroom.'

Sensing the numbness enveloping Eve, Rose took her by the hand, led her away from the gruesome body, through to the big glass cubicle in the bedroom, pulled off the remains of her underwear and pushed her under the wonderfully hot stream coming from the enormous shower head. She soaped the blood and bone and brain specks from Eve's neck and shoulders.

'What animals,' said Eve flatly.

Rose stripped off and climbed in. 'Us or them?'

'Both. God.'

'Well, the alternative was a piece of German sausage up your fanny.'

Eve looked shocked. 'I'm not saying . . . I just . . .'

Rose raised a hand. 'Neumann was becoming a threat. He'd begun to use his brain as well as his brawn.'

'At least he got Will and Robert out as POWs.'

Rose just nodded, as if she believed this were true. Keppler at least had some intention of keeping his invidious deals. With Neumann, she wasn't so sure. For the next few minutes there was only the hissing of water and the squelch of soap.

'Listen, Eve,' said Rose eventually. 'I know you wondered.

288

About Williams. And me. In London. Nothing happened.'

'Something happened to him there. He wasn't quite the same person.'

'Something has happened to all of us. You weren't the same. France wasn't the same. He loves you. Did then, does now.'

'Then I owe him an apology.'

To her own surprise Rose took Eve's face in her hands and kissed her on the lips, feeling for all the world at that moment like a protective mother to the older woman. 'The wardrobes out there are full of Fortuny, Balenciaga, Molyneux, Lelong, Paquin. Help yourself. When you see Williams, you can apologise in style.'

Eve turned off the water, stepped out and quickly wrapped a towel around herself, flustered and embarrassed. 'What now?'

'You go to Normandy. Stay out of Paris. I go back.'

'And then?'

'Then we wait. Wait for the Allies and Russians to meet up in Berlin.'

Eve nodded. 'And pray he lives that long.'

Rose accepted a towel from Eve and touched her face lightly. 'Let's pray they both do.'

Thirty-one

MARCH–APRIL 1945

The wind sliced through the coarse, blue-striped uniform and straight into Williams' bones. Not that there was much flesh to act as a barrier, that had progressively fallen away over the last ten months since his arrival at this place. Sachsenhausen–Oranienburg. May its name be spat upon for years to come, he thought.

Unusually, six of them from the officers' detention block had been assigned to repair a broken water pipe, and they hacked their way into the frozen earth still not touched by the spring thaw. At least he hoped it was a repair detail. Williams had seen many, many men digging their own final resting places over the last few weeks. But none this close to the elaborate main entrance. He stopped for a second and looked up at the guard and his three Lagerschutz – trusties – in charge of this bedraggled Kommando. One swing with the spade and he could take the German's head off. Robert would.

He thought about Robert a lot. He'd last seen him at Gare de l'Est, chained with other officers, being herded into a train, dozens of them into small carriages built for eight or ten. He himself had boarded a different train, for a different destination. Even the opportunity to die together had been denied them.

After Robert's arrogant rebuttal of Keppler, the Sturmbannführer had washed his hands of them. There were beatings, solitary confinement, the usual casual brutality, withdrawal of rations and finally a ten-day transportation to Germany, during which any remaining valuables they had managed to cling on to were looted. They had been packed into a tiny hut on arrival before sorting into various groups, being shaved, showered and given the hideous uniforms and the chafing clogs. There had been nineteen of them in his shipment to Sachsenhausen. There were four left now. Some executed, some lost through illness, a few victims of the internecine fighting between rival groups of inmates, mostly over the dwindling food supply. But he'd survived.

He still had that picture in his head, the one of the faces at the cattle-truck doorway at St Just. And now he knew why it had seared its way into his visual cortex. To keep him alive. Those people, they had already crossed over. They had been through Drancy and the Velo and other tortures and they had accepted that they were simply on a long, slow road to death. And whenever he remembered those stares, the vacant, let's-get-it-over-with gazes, they jerked him back every time he felt like curling up and dying. Not yet. Not yet, damn you. Those people, he owed them a lot, they'd given him a touchstone for life. Had Robert got it, too?

One of the trustees motioned to continue digging. Had he been a Jew or a Russian such a pause would have caused Williams to have been shot there and then. But the group kept in the big concrete block that housed him were different.

291

Commandos, spies, politicals, some with *N&N* on them, true, others, like Williams, just with a letter displaying their nationality.

He went back to scraping at the earth, trying to minimise the jarring effect of permafrost on his shoulders and elbows. He had noticed three loose teeth that morning. His body had held up well, but unless it got better food soon it would start to digest itself, he knew, to the point of no return. Again, he'd seen that. Men locked in cages in the courtyard, weakening every day as the *Apells*, the roll calls, came and went, allowed to rot in full view as some kind of warning. As if anyone needed reminding just what a tenuous hold they all had on life.

Sachsenhausen was not one camp, but forty-four separate units, including satellites at the Heinkel factory and the grenade manufacturers a few kilometres down the road. Stories reached them from the latter of prisoners purposefully detonating explosives and taking guards with them. Now only trustees were allowed to do the final assembly.

A late flurry of snow began, bleakly beautiful swirls, dancing through the Breughelian landscape, mocking the grey-fleshed inmates with their dazzling purity. Williams' teeth started to chatter, loosening them further, no doubt. He could taste blood, too, where his gums had started to bleed. And still, he had to count himself lucky. All around him were the field of low, wooden huts, the various sections of the camps for Jews, and Russians and Gypsies and anyone else the Reich despised.

The Russians had always been killed on a savage scale, casually, brutally. Some went to the block known as Station Z, ostensibly for medical examination, actually for a bullet in the head, others were herded into the underground chamber on the corner opposite his cell window, where they were gassed. The smell of burning bodies was so all-pervading that few of them noticed the once-nauseating stench any longer.

Since the beginning of February, when a high-ranking Gestapo man called Müller had visited Commandant Kaindl, the killings had increased to a frenzy. A mobile gibbet had been constructed, which Jewish trustees had to wheel from end to end of the camp, hanging four inmates at a time and then moving on to their next appointment, like some grotesque telegram service. The guards had invented the 'hat' game, snatching prisoners' hats and throwing them over the do-not-cross line in front of the wire fences. Not going to get the hat, you were shot for disobeying orders. Stepping over the line to get it, you were shot for attempting to escape.

They were trying to empty the camp, to kill them all. He knew that now. There was another volley of shots from somewhere over in the Russian section. Firing squad. One every twenty, thirty minutes throughout the day. There were thirty or forty thousand prisoners, Williams had estimated. They were killing two or three hundred a day, perhaps more. The sheer scale of the undertaking was demoralising the guards, who seemed to be making hardly a dent in the morning and evening roll-calls, despite their best, murderous efforts.

Planes flew high over head, their frozen exhaust plumes vivid in the ice-blue sky. USAF planes probably, and perhaps up among them the new Nazi secret weapons the guards sometimes boasted about. They knew they were planes of some sort, fast and lethal, but could offer no more details. But, V-weapons or not, still the Flying Fortresses and the Superfortresses and the Lancasters came on, day after day, sometimes bombing the Sachsenhausen satellite factories, more often than not trying to find a target left untouched in Berlin.

The gates opened and a dilapidated truck limped in, its

canvas sides ripped and torn, one wheel on the rear double axle flat, floundering on its rim. Williams realised it had been strafed, casually sideswiped by a Mustang or a Typhoon or one of the other tank busters skimming the countryside like marauding bandits seeking prey. The tailgate came down and half a dozen bodies were thrown on to the hard ground with sickening casualness. The survivors stepped slowly down, hurried by impatient German guards, as if there was something worth rushing to, anything to achieve in Sachsenhausen other than your early death.

The men looked about as fit as he did, scrawny and bony, in the emaciated condition of most camp inmates that stripped away individuality, made it hard to recognise one human being from another. It was more like a medical syndrome than the mere result of starvation, all united in the same stance, the stoop, the slack jaw, all with the dull stares of men who had seen more horror than they could ever communicate. More than they would ever want to.

Then a pair of eyes that didn't look glazed or drugged. A pair that flashed and pierced and told you to go and fuck yourself. The frame was shrunken, how could it not be, but Robert was as straight backed and defiant as ever.

Williams dropped the pick and stood, stepping out of the shallow trench, aware of the guns swivelling to point at him, knowing he was taking a hell of a risk.

'Robert,' his voice felt weak, underpowered, smaller than he remembered. Years of whispering had left his vocal chords stiff and useless. He cleared his throat. A gun barrel was in his stomach.

'Robert.' The yell finally carried, flapping slowly across the yard, hitting Robert as he was about to pick up one of his dead companions to take to the crematorium. Benoist let go of the arm which flopped back to earth, straightened and stepped forward. A grin split his face when he recognised the voice, if not, yet, its owner. He took two fingers and raised them to his lips in a kiss and blew it across just as the rifle butt hit the side of his head and he spun down on to the bodies.

At the same time Williams was struck in his shrunken stomach, the blow punching straight through to his spine, causing him to fall to his knees in coughing agony. He heard a bolt pulled back on a machine pistol.

'Stop.' A voice rang out as a man stepped down from the cab of the truck and straightened the jacket of his SS Untersturmführer uniform. The guards froze, not used to being halted in the middle of their work. The newcomer looked at Robert, snapped his fingers and told him, in French, to get up. He waved the guard away. Then he strode across towards Williams, who was slowly unfolding himself from the bent double position. He looked up and the man said in English: 'Get up, Williams. I need you alive.'

Lock. Arthur Lock.

Except now, they discovered, he was Heinrich Locke, the new identity a reward for loyal service to Keppler at Avenue Foch. Along with Virginia and a few other traitors, Lock had managed to avoid the transports and had skipped Paris just before Liberation, to carry on the good work in Germany. Which meant camps, and more camps.

Sitting on the other side of Williams' bars – one wall of the cell was a grid of metal-framed squares which opened on to the concrete gallery – keeping an eye on Robert, whom he had put next door, Lock shamelessly explained that he had wanted to change sides before the Allies reached Paris, but knew that too many people in the city had a grudge against him.

He had put them on SS rations and offered them decent cigarettes which they consumed hungrily and guiltily, especially when fellow prisoners demanded they pass them along. They took three or four big drags and did so. There were other Allied officers in the block – RAF, SAS, SBS, SIS, Commandos, Parachute Regiment, all those whom the Germans thought deserved harsher treatment than a POW camp. But out of all of them, what did Lock want with Robert and Williams? On the third day he began to tell them, after a fashion.

'The Russians are coming. You know that. You can hear their guns at night. A week. Maybe two. Before the month is out, certainly. This uniform will be a death sentence when they get here.'

'You'll be here?' asked Williams.

'I hope not. I hope not. We'll talk again.'

'Lock?' asked Williams as he turned to go.

'What?'

'Keppler?'

'Oh, he's around. In charge of "liquidating" several camps. Keep out of his way. He's not the nice man you once knew.'

Williams heard Robert's snort of laughter.

Through whispered conversations and Morse tapped on the pipes or bars, Williams pieced together where Robert had been. Buchenwald, mostly, a grisly camp whose main aim was to provide labour for a munitions factory and to get rid of Russian prisoners. As in Station Z at Sachsenhausen there was a *Genickshuss*, a measuring device for checking height, which concealed a small calibre pistol in the wall, with which the prisoner was shot in the back of the head. The small, soft bullet never exited, so blood was minimal, and German patriotic songs drowned out the shots. But, as at Sachsenhausen, this was deemed too slow and hanging, shooting and gassing were stepped up.

A week previously he and thirty-six other Allied officers had been selected for slow hanging with piano wire. Several managed to swop identities with men who had died of TB or typhus in the infirmary. Robert hadn't. But Lock got him on a convoy transferring prisoners between camps. As far as he knew, the others had gone to their terrible deaths, strangulation that lasted ten or more minutes.

'Then we got shot up on the way here. Ironic, eh? Survive a year or more of German prisons. Get blown to bits by your own side. But one thing worried me. When I was checked in here, my name was logged in pencil.'

Williams laughed. 'Mine too. We all are. It means we can be rubbed out at a moment's notice. God, my stomach aches.'

'Too much food. Eat it slowly.'

Williams lay down on his bunk and said softly, 'What's Lock up to?'

He could almost feel Robert's shrug in the darkness. 'We'll find out soon enough.' There was a pause. They could hear the usual sporadic coughings and sobbing, the intimidating sound of hobnail boots, distant gunshots, the crump of bombs falling on some hapless target. 'Will.'

'Quiet!' A guard.

'It's good to be with you again.'

Williams smiled to himself. 'Yes. Yes it is.'

There were no more work details. For the next four days the pair were allowed exercise, food as good as the guards, even coffee, although it was all but undrinkable. They saw Lock looking at them every now and then, smiling as if at some kind of private joke.

That evening he came to them, had them released and

marched down to the interrogation cells, where he dismissed the guards and gave them both another cigarette. American cigarettes.

'God,' said Williams as the real tobacco made his senses explode. 'Where did you get these?'

Lock shrugged and said cautiously, 'We have some contact with the Americans. Go-betweens. Just putting out feelers.' He lit his own cigarette. 'It has some side benefits for the runners if they make it back. They get to sell us these. At prices that'd make you weep.'

'What could the Americans want from you?'

'Oh, they have a list. People they want to put on trial, people they want to find and keep from the Russians, people who can help them identify the good and bad Nazis.'

'And that would be you?'

'It would. I have been in what they call deep cover since 1940. An audacious agent of the crown. Burrowed deep into Gestapo HQ. Saved countless lives.'

'This is a joke, right?' asked Robert.

Lock shook his head. 'No,' he said with practised sincerity. 'I can prove it if some idiot doesn't lynch me first.'

'You were a double agent?' asked Williams, almost believing him.

'Of course. What kind of monster did you take me for? Who do you think told Keppler that deals were the best way of interrogation? Not torture.'

There was a snort of disbelief and derision from Robert. 'I wish you'd told Neumann,' said Williams rubbing his still scarred scalp.

'So. Gentlemen. I need character witnesses. People who saw me at Foch. Who will say nice things about me. Fellow secret agents.'

Williams put his bony elbows on the table. 'Why should we?'

'Because I can get you out of here. Over the next twenty-four hours thirty thousand prisoners will be marched north to the sea. Those that make it will be loaded on to ships. The ships will then be scuttled. Himmler's orders. You do not want to be on that trip, believe me. The remainder of you have been marked for special treatment. That's . . . well, you know what that is. I can keep you off that list as well.' He leaned over and said pointedly to Robert, 'Can't I?'

Robert nodded and said: 'Go on.'

'We take a half-track. There is one in the storage sheds. The morons they use for guards can't get it going. You two, I would think, easy. We head west to the Americans. You confirm my story, I join OSS, you go home. How does it sound?'

Williams closed his eyes and imagined Eve, at the kitchen table, looking up at the ghost in rags, unshaven, bleeding gums, protruding ribs, shot libido, wondering why this old, old man was bothering her. He opened his eyes. 'How does it sound? Sounds good to me.' But Robert just ground out his cigarette and sniffed.

Sleep was never very deep, but the roaring from the courtyard woke them, and the deep crimson shapes dancing across their cell walls took them to the window. A huge bonfire of documents was piled in the centre of the yard where the hated roll-calls usually took place, and they were being consumed by a gasoline-fed conflagration, the most damning of documents turning to ashes and floating up into the night sky. Williams watched the small figures moving around, throwing more and more files and directories on to the bonfire in an increasing frenzy.

Down in the yard itself Keppler stood back away from the heat, keeping to the shadows, selecting which documents were to be incinerated and which packed into the special steel containers he had been issued with.

Lock looked perplexed. 'Why keep any documents at all?'

Keppler shook his head. 'I don't know. Orders. Perhaps they want to learn from their mistakes for the next time.'

Lock laughed. 'You think you'll get a second chance at this?'

Keppler looked affronted. 'Who knows? We should be ready for the eventuality. Now, I want the huts emptied before dawn and the march to begin. You will then execute the remaining terrorists. Do you have a list?'

Keppler took the clipboard from Lock and ran his eyes down it, recognising several names, those who passed through his hands in Paris, and some later in Berlin. The squeamishness had long gone from him. He now knew what had happened to most of the men and women he had promised good treatment at Foch. Lethal injections. Shot in the head. Slow hanging with piano wire. Once it had happened to a few, who would believe him that it was beyond his control? 'I thought Williams was here? And Benoist, you told me?'

Lock cursed his big mouth. 'They are.'

'Add them, add them. I want them all dead. I'll be back to check after I have liquidated Eberslitz.' Another camp, just to the east, almost within sight of the Russians. 'Then we can plan our escape and our story. Agreed?'

'Agreed,' said Lock, as if he would be waiting for Keppler who, he was certain, had no intention of going to another camp and certainly no intention of returning. He knew he wouldn't in Keppler's place.

Williams and Robert were locked in their cells all the next day as they watched the camp emptied of most of its population. Not from the big cell block, but from the huts, Jew and non-Jew herded into raggedy lines and propelled forward through that hateful gate with its clocktower and its vile slogans exhorting work and cleanliness. Those who could not walk were shot on the spot.

All day long, the men and women in striped uniforms were lined and moved forward, too weak to resist, and driven forward by randomly wielded clubs, pushed to their death along the road. Even the hospital and guinea-pig blocks were emptied, their inmates contriving to make even the usual skeletal souls look positively healthy. It was amazing that such creatures could move at all.

As each column marched off they could hear an accompanying tattoo of pistol and machine-gun shots as every few yards another man or woman was murdered. And so, as dusk approached, the last stragglers left and the doors finally closed on the camp, now strangely silent for a moment, with no more wheezing and pacing and coughing and the million other little sounds of misery that filled every moment. Thirty thousand out on the road, a shuffling column of death. Perhaps three or four thousand left in the camp, mostly those too weak even to leave their filthy bunks. Some had been shot where they lay, and with the *Totenrager*, the corpse shifters, gone, they stayed there.

Now the dogs began to bark with a worrying urgency, picking up their handlers' mood. Williams heard the running crunch of boots and the opening of cells, the swish of clubs and the confused screams of men being dragged away. He ran to the doorway and shouted, 'Robert. What is it?'

'Don't worry, we aren't on the list.'

Gunshots, loud in the confined space. A ripple of machine guns. Someone had tried to jump a guard. More barking, getting closer on this landing. Williams backed away from the entrance, waiting for them to pass, like the Angel of Death, hoping he had a symbolic cross of blood on his cell. Next door now. No. Not next door.

'Robert.' He flung himself against the bars. He could hear the dog, snarling. 'Lock, Lock. Where are you, damn you? Lock.'

He glimpsed Robert being bundled out, his face set in determination. They caught each other's eye and Robert shouted his watchwords: 'Never give up. Never confess. Never surrender.' The club hit him between the shoulders and he slumped forward and was gone, whisked away.

Six SS guards appeared outside Williams' cell, two rifles poked through the grill. The door slammed back and the alsatian was in, teeth bared, rearing up on its leash, willing its handler to let it loose. Clubs were raised and he ducked and instinctively raised his arms to protect himself when the sergeant shouted an order he didn't catch. As rapidly as they had entered they withdrew, locking the door and moving on.

'Wait. Wait. You've made a mistake. Both of us. Two of us.' He fell to his knees. 'We're together. We stay together.'

The noises switched to outside his window. The big sodium lights came on and bleached the courtyard in their dazzling glare as the men were herded into a rough formation. Williams pulled himself to the bars and shouted Robert's name again. His friend looked up, shading his eyes against the dazzle and raised a hand.

'Goodbye,' said Williams softly.

The group were turned by the guards and marched across to the bunker in the corner, where the studded steel gates with the big rubber seals had been drawn back to welcome them into the dark tunnel.

Schutzhaftlagerführer Ressen stepped into his white overalls with the elasticated arms and legs and slipped the gasmask over his head, checking the fit carefully. He wriggled his hands into the big red rubberised gloves, put on the heavy boots, scooped up the canister and stepped out into the eerie silence of the courtyard. The only sound was the muffled yells of the men in the bunker, now closed tightly shut, and some lunatic yelling from the cell block. Damn fool. Should count his lucky stars he wasn't in there with the rest of them.

This was to be Ressen's last task. Do this job and catch that truck heading for Berlin, ostensibly for the final defence of the capital and the Führer. Ressen would make sure he was over that tailgate well before they reached the city limits. He might not be the sharpest dagger in the SS, but he knew when it was time to cut and run.

He climbed the six rungs of the steel ladder that took him on to the roof of the bunker and walked across to the nearest square wooden chimney. The voices were louder now, the sounds carrying up the ventilation shaft. They sounded calm, resigned, but he couldn't be sure. Ressen didn't speak English.

He reached the first chimney and levered off the big square cap. From inside he pulled up the long pole connected to the wire basket and set it down next to him. He took the steel canister and unscrewed the lid, holding it at arm's length. The moment the pellets hit air they began to smoke as the sublimation process began – straight from solid to gas.

He shook out half the pellets into the basket, then lowered it down into the darkness below, closing his ears to the sudden panic that ignited below, the yells and the shouts and curses and then the screams. They wouldn't last long. Ressen quickly replaced the cap and strode across to the second shaft, where he repeated the process. After the canister was emptied and the lid replaced he took it and flung it across the rear of the bunker to the pile of identical containers that had grown larger and larger over the last few years, a mass of yellow labels, some peeling and faded, others still bright yellow, but the type on most quickly fading, so that it was almost impossible to read all but the most recent, like the one he had just used: Danger de Mort. Alphachem-IG Farben, St Just, France.

Thirty-two

APRIL 1945

As much as anything was registering on nerves anaesthetised by sorrow, Williams was aware of Lock standing at the metal trellis work that formed the front of the cell. He didn't look up. Robert had been through so much, fought in the skies above France, raced at a time when the attrition rate was horrendous, resisted to the best of his ability. To die like that . . .

He mustn't dwell on it, on the airless chamber, its walls and floors stained with excrement and blood, marks that could never be rubbed clean. The smell of sweat and fear, the stoicism mingling with the panic. Those last few minutes when the air shaft opened and in came the pellets and the poison fumes ripped into the throat of the first man.

'Williams,' Lock said, and waited for a reply. 'Williams.'

It came through the cloud of grief like a dim, distant voice at the end of a tunnel. His own voice sounded metallic, inhuman. 'Fuck off.'

Not to see him again. Not to feel the power of that stare, not to hear him tell some fool he would knock him down and piss in his ear, not to watch him take a car into a bend at a speed that was far too fast and bring it round like a lamb. Not to share a glass of wine and a joke. It was corrosive, the very idea of a permanent separation, and it was burning through his insides.

'I couldn't save him, Williams.'

Neither could I, he wanted to shout. Neither could I. Why not? Why couldn't I save Robert? He kept asking himself.

'I said fuck off.'

'Keppler—'

That made his head snap up. 'Keppler?'

Lock was glad to have his attention and he spoke quickly before that bitter, tear-stained face went down again, back into catatonia. 'Keppler was here, yes. Not now. I think he's gone to the Americans.'

'Why would he do that?'

'Americans or Russians? Which would you choose? The Russkies are due within forty-eight hours. We have to go.'

'Fuck off.'

'No, wait. Look, he made me put you both back on the list. Both. I couldn't take the pair of you off. Too suspicious. I told the sergeant you were needed for further questioning. Williams, the guards are going. There are three thousand people busy dying in the huts out there. Don't make it three thousand and one.'

'If it's three thousand and two I'll be happy,' and he looked up at Lock from under heavy lids.

'I say the word and someone will come and shoot you where you sit.'

'No they wouldn't. Not for you. You'd have to do it yourself.' Again those brimming eyes, brimming with hate and tears. 'Could you do that?'

'It won't come to that, man. Look, we go west. You say nice things about me. You can get Keppler. We both win.' He tried to keep the desperation out of his voice. They'd abandoned him now. After all those years of service, he was just another Englishman they couldn't be bothered to waste a bullet on. 'What do you say?'

Slowly and stiffly Williams got to his feet, the inertia of many hours having almost fused his joints, and brushed himself down. 'I'll say nice things about you, Lock.'

'I have your word?'

Williams said evenly, the madness gone from his voice now: 'You have my word.'

Lock banged the bars in delight. 'Wonderful. I'll get the key.'

The vast barns at the edge of the camp held an astonishing assortment of booty. Williams estimated they were over a kilometre long, piled high with furniture, purloined art, clothes, jewellery, carpets, great mounds stacked indiscriminately, waiting for the day when they could be sorted. Which would never happen now.

He and Lock walked the length of the treasure trove, and Williams stopped to select a herringbone coat from a pile and slipped it on. Warmth. Real warmth. For the first time in a long time. He grabbed a scarf and wrapped that round his neck, relishing the feel of rough wool against his skin.

Lock had civilian gear over his arm, a smart tweed suit, plaid shirt and knitted tie and trenchcoat. But for the moment he kept on his uniform, his passport through the wreck of Germany until they reached the Allies. His manner was cheery, upbeat, as if he wanted to keep Williams on song too, keep him focused, make him realise that it was all about concentrating on getting out of this hell hole.

The half-track was at the very end of the warehouse, a scabby, neglected-looking thing, with empty gun mounts like missing teeth sprouting across the strange framework erected over the rear of it. Williams indicated Lock should get in and he lifted the bonnet. 'You tried it?'

'Yeah,' said Lock. 'Turns over. Won't fire.'

Williams quickly went through everything just in case, sucking fuel up the line, cleaning the carb, the points and checking the distributor. When he gave a thumbs-up, the motor lazily did a couple of revolutions, stuttered and then burst into noisy, clacking life. Timing was shot, one cylinder was misfiring, and blue oil was pumping out of somewhere, but it'd do.

'Excellent. I knew you were the man for the job.'

Williams slammed the bonnet down and moved to the door. 'Move over,' said Williams. 'I always drive.'

It gave Williams great pleasure to steer the half-track straight through the wooden gates of the entrance and feel them tear from their mountings and twist and buckle under the weight of the troop transport. It was the closest he had come to a happy feeling since he first walked through the same joyless portal. Apart from the moment he saw Robert.

He spun the lumpen beast through ninety degrees and headed west, trying to comprehend that this was the outside world. Except it looked like a continuation of the camp, desolate and foreboding, as hellish without as within. The road was lined with those executed on the death march, bodies carelessly tossed on the verge. A couple of miles down the road carrion-pecked bodies swung from the lampposts, illegible signs hung round their neck. Williams looked at Lock.

'It's what the SS do to deserters, mate,' he explained. There was other traffic on the road – carts, horses, the odd civilian car – but nobody paid any attention to them, except to move out of the way, unsure who was inside. Each was in their own cocoon, on a mission, trying to save their neck. They had no desire to find themselves dangling from a lamppost.

Occasionally they heard shots, or the whumpf of an artillery shell landing, sending up a thin plume of black smoke. At one village Williams stopped the half-track and ran into a still-smoking house, emerging with a white sheet which he tied to one of the heavy duty aerials that sprouted from the cab. And on they went, thankful that the all-terrain machine could take to the fields when the road was blocked by refugees or burnt-out military hardware.

The landscape grew increasingly blasted and bombed, trees carelessly strewn across meadows and roads and houses, more bodies, some of them half chewed by scavenging dogs and rats. In the corners and shadows of the building shapes scurried. Children, he thought.

'What will you do now?' asked Lock as they hit an empty stretch of road at last. 'Williams? What will you do now?' He carried on regardless of the silence. 'You know I always wanted to be a writer. Funny, eh? Me? Hoxton lad writing books. Murder mysteries, I fancied. Your Agatha Christies. Shit, couldn't do that now. A body in the library? Big deal. We got three thousand behind the wire over there.' And he laughed until Williams silenced him with a hard glance. 'At least we know whodunnit, eh? No mystery there.'

On a long, steep hill Williams ground a gear, felt it jam and punched it irritably. The knob and the top of the shaft sheared off and he cursed as the remaining spike slashed open his palm. He looked at the stream of crimson blood, checked the wound wasn't too deep, wrapped his scarf around the stem and carried on.

'You all right, mate?'

Williams nodded.

The Mustang came out of nowhere, right down the road, head on, its belly bulge almost skimming the tree tops, the Pratt and

Whitney engine screaming. The half-track rocked in the prop wash and Lock ducked as the machine thundered overhead.

'Jesus. I thought we were dead.'

'He'll be back.'

They trundled on, weaving across the stumps of villages, and clusters of red-eyed inhabitants. There were the occasional Volk-sturm units, the home guard, but nothing threatening, mostly boys rattling around in men's helmets, clutching ancient Mausers. A cluster of Hitler Youth eyed them suspiciously, but did nothing. Lock made the bent-arm Heil Hitler, and several returned it, some with wild-eyed enthusiasm. Williams was glad to see the back of them. Their luck was holding out.

The Mustang returned, running at right angles this time, low and sleek and beautiful, its silvery skin aglitter as the low winter sun caught the thousands of rivet heads stitching it together. Williams shoved his hand out of the window and raised it in salute. The pilot stared impassively for the fraction of a second he was level with them, then gained height, banked and headed off.

Williams rewrapped the scarf around the jagged gear lever and pushed forward as fast as the terrain would allow, wincing as the potholes and shell craters threw them about, the vibrations passing straight from seat to spine, thanks to the scant muscle cushioning still clinging to his frame.

With the road clear of civilians and troops, Lock began to strip off his uniform, transforming himself from SS to escaped British agent. Williams wondered if he thought anyone would fall for such an idiotic cover story. Well, maybe. No crazier than the idea that racing drivers would become SOE agents.

The first indication that there were no American lines as such, just a fluid, mobile bridgehead, came with the still-smoking ruin of a carbonised Eager Beaver, the US workhorse truck, which was twisted and shattered at the roadside. Maybe a mine, thought

Williams, and instinctively slowed. The Yanks must be near, though. As if in answer two rounds zinged against the bodywork.

'Put both hands out in surrender,' said Williams, looking down at Lock, who had slid off the seat.

'And get my head shot off?'

More rounds, and a heavier thunk, maybe a BAR. Williams could see a muzzle flash from a stand of trees in the centre of a field off to their right. Just lazy potshots perhaps. A splattering of detonations hammered against the body work and he felt the door buckle inwards. Light machine gun, a Johnson or the like. Maybe they were serious. 'Sooner or later they're going to find a bazooka or something.'

Lock reluctantly pulled down the flimsy side pane and stuck the top of his body out, yelling, 'Don't shoot, don't shoot! English. English prisoners.' A bullet smacked into the corner of the windshield and he slithered back in but Williams pushed him back out. He yelled more desperately this time, and the firing stopped.

They rounded the bend and Williams could see two Shermans parked nose to nose across the road, a ragged pile of sandbags stacked up their sides. The sun flashed back from the lenses of binoculars being trained on them. One of the Sherman turrets slowly cranked and elevated its gun, drawing a bead on the half-track. Williams stopped, exhausted, letting the engine idle, feeling it pop and splutter roughly under his feet.

'That's it,' said Lock exultantly. 'You did it. You did it. We did it. Just remember the deal. You say nice things, we're both in clover.'

Williams turned off the ignition and the half-track engine ran on for a second before juddering to a grateful halt.

'What? What are you doing, man? Look. Four hundred yards. Home. Free. Drive on.'

Williams took a breath and willed strength into the poor abused strings of muscle he had left as he yanked the protective scarf away from the gear lever. In a movement as fast as a snake strike he reached up and grabbed the back of Lock's head, taking a handful of hair and forcing his face downwards in one smooth, fast arc. Lock screamed as he saw the bloody spike rearing up at him, but it was too late, there was a horrible squelching sound as it pierced his eye and the momentum took it on deep into his skull. He began to thrash, but that only mixed things up more, and the razor-edged shard sliced its way through nerves and capillaries and brain matter until the thrashing became a mad twitching and then he was still, a last groan as the air leaked from his lungs marking the passing of Arthur Vincent Lock.

'Don't worry,' said Williams quietly, patting the head, 'I'll say nice things about you.'

Williams opened the driver's door and slid out on to the road, his legs wobbling as they hit the ground. He steadied, pulled the coat around him and began to walk, raising his arms as he did so. He could see a flurry of activity ahead, observers, stepping from behind the tanks, a few with carbines levelled, and among them a woman.

His legs went and he hit the asphalt, the roughened surface gashing the skin from his chin. Strange. After all this time. That he should fall now, he thought. Up. Get up. He pulled himself to his feet, swaying, stepping backwards when he wanted to go forward. Almost two years since his capture. Now free. All those things he had done. And seen. Robert. He fell again, on to his hands and knees, almost not noticing the searing pain in his cut hand.

Robert. Couldn't save him. Could save himself, but not his friend.

On his feet again, but the world was spinning, the sky and

312

ground switching places with dizzying rapidity. His vision was imploding, as if someone were closing the world's aperture down, shrinking it to a tunnel of light, and the only thing coming up the tunnel was a woman's voice. Funny, he thought, as the ground rushed up once more, it sounded just like Rose Miller.

Thirty-three

APRIL-MAY 1945

The wind snapped at the thin canvas that formed one side of the bathroom wall, making it sing a mournful, icy song. The first signs of spring had retreated, winter was having a last rally before handing over the reins. Williams turned on the spigot and let more hot water run over his body as he sat in the tub, inspecting the damage of two years' incarceration. He was a horrible yellowy, parchment colour, with a mottling of bruises covering him. His ribs looked like a xylophone, and his knees and elbows seemed swollen to twice their normal size, but he was eight or ten meals down the road to recovery and already he could feel tissues rebuilding. Lucky. Lucky man.

In the other room he could hear Rose Miller sorting out his belongings. The woman was amazing. She'd cleared the way for his release from the Americans within hours, convinced them that Lock was a legitimate SOE target, managed to produce his Vuitton case, which he suspected she had been travelling with as her own anyway, and taken him through to a hotel around twenty kilometres west of Berlin. The city itself was still in its death

314

throes, the Russians crawling all over the eastern districts like insects, the sounds of their artillery clearly audible. Two or three days and it would all be over. Or at least, the fighting would. There was lots of unfinished business.

'Do you mind if I put some things of mine in your trunk?' shouted Rose from the next room.

'No,' he replied, puzzled. 'What kind of things?'

'I have an Alphachem Zyklon can. Gold dust.'

'What will happen to Alphachem?'

'We'll see. The Degesch directors are to be put on trial. War crimes.'

'Degesch?'

'The people who discovered what you could do with the Zyklon B. To people, I mean.' That snapshot started to form in his brain again, the cattle truck and the faces at the St Just sidings, but it failed to hold, as if the fixing solution were defective. He knew why. He didn't need those people any longer to remind him where the French poison gas ended up. He had Robert.

'But Alphachem will plead ignorance,' Rose continued, mimicking their whinings. 'How were we to know what it was being used for?'

'If you'd seen the trains, you'd know.'

'Well, Alphachem were well aware they had something to hide – you know they buried thousand of tonnes of the cyanide pellets at St Just just as the Americans rolled up?'

'Christ. And when it leaks?'

'Ah. That's another story. For now we nail them for what happened to the canisters you saw going east on the trains.'

'You want me to testify?'

'If it comes to it. Although there is a slight problem there.'

'What?'

315

'Get out and I'll tell you.'

Williams heaved himself from the bath and wrapped a thin, threadbare towel around himself and looked at the collection of hollows that was his face in the mirror. 'Who are you going to be now, Mr Williams?' he asked of it.

Towel tied firmly in place he went through and stopped in the doorway to the austere room, with its peeling brass bed and grubby kitchen area. When he saw Rose twenty minutes earlier she had been wearing a WAAF uniform, rank of Squadron Leader, with a flying jacket over it. Now she was just wearing a flying jacket and nothing else.

'Aren't you cold?' he asked.

She laughed, embarrassed. 'Is that all you can say? Oh dear. Looks like I have lost all my charms.' She began to pull the sheets round her.

Williams felt blood move in ways and to places it hadn't for many, many months and his throat was suddenly dry. He took two steps towards the bed. 'No . . . I . . . It's . . .'

Rose held her arms out. 'Shut up and come here.'

Eve Williams paced the clearing, marvelling at how quickly nature had recolonised the ground. A small clump of local farmers waited for her decision, their horses' breath cloudy in the cool morning air. From her coat pocket she took the telegram and re-read it. Missing in Action. Regrets. She tore it up and threw it at the bushes. Williams wasn't dead. There was still something inside her breathing, waiting for him. He wasn't dead.

'Eve?'

She turned and saw the familiar figure of Wimille. 'Jean-Pierre!'

He took her by the shoulders and hugged her. She hadn't seen him since that night when he had escaped from the house, but she'd had messages. He had stayed active, building up weapon stocks for D-day. Nothing flashy, nothing too glamorous. No Gestapo chases, no torture cells, no big explosions. But the guns had been there when they were needed.

'How did you find me?'

'Madame Teyssédre.' Bugatti's old secretary had survived imprisonment and worse for her efforts. Many of her family and friends hadn't.

'How are you, Eve?'

'They say he's probably dead. Somewhere called Sachsenhausen.'

'Robert?'

'Buchenwald they think. One of . . .' She shuddered. 'One of thirty-seven.'

'Can I help?' asked Wimille.

'Can you dig?'

He laughed. 'I can dig, why?'

She pointed at the ground. 'The Atlantic is down there.'

'Where?'

'Under your feet.'

'My God. What state is it in?'

'We're about to find out.'

'Well, if it is even halfway decent, I can clean it up. I'll have it ready for when he comes back.'

'He is coming back, you know.'

Wimille kissed her lightly on the forehead. 'I know.'

Eve took a deep breath, pointed to the ground and said in a loud voice, 'OK, gentlemen. We excavate here.'

At the camp the libido went some time after the intangibles – dignity, shame, faith and hope. But disappear it did, as survival of the individual, rather than the species, took precedence. Even as he realised what was happening, part of Williams' brain questioned what Rose was doing. Was she trying to restore confidence to a starved, damaged man, or was something less altruistic at work?

But those questions got fainter and fainter, and an unfamiliar machinery kicked into action, hormones pumping, blood moving, and even the little voice telling him it was wrong, a mistake, was snuffed out for a while.

Afterwards she lay on top of him, humming a tune he didn't recognise. Rose looked at him and said, 'How do you feel?'

The voice was back, the same voice you heard after a long drunken night, admonishing you for the rubbish you talked, the idiotic things you did, making you blush with shame and remorse at the memory. Except this time there was no alcohol to blame. 'Better and worse. Guilty as hell.'

Rose kissed the end of his nose and rolled him over. Sitting astride his back she began to knead at the thin shoulders, her fingers seeking out the muscles, pushing blood into them. 'How's that?'

'Well the guilt's still there. But it feels great. Ow. Careful. Where did you learn that?'

'From my father. Or rather doing it to my father. After he came in from the fields.'

'What, beating the peasants?'

'No. *He* was a peasant. A Hungarian peasant.'

Williams half turned but she pushed him down.

'We came to England in nineteen-thirty. My father knew things were going to get bad. He wasn't prepared for the prejudice he found even in London. So he told me, the only way to deal with snobbery is to be more snobby than they are. He set up a restaurant in Knightsbridge with his brother. Made some money. I went to Roedean. Learned to speak like this . . .' She came down close to him. 'We are all fakes, Williams.'

318

Rose rolled off him and scrabbled in her bag, producing a jar of coffee beans and shaking them with glee. 'Look. How long since you had real coffee?'

'Even longer than I had a good fuck.'

'Mr Williams. Language.'

'Come on, you must have heard worse in the fields.'

She pulled on the flying jacket and went over to the kitchen area, searching for a coffee grinder. 'You tell anyone else that story and I'll throw you back to Keppler.'

The name gave him a jolt. 'Keppler? Is he still alive?'

'Look in my bag.'

He reached over and unhooked it from the bedpost and rummaged around until he found a framed photograph of a small cottage next to an Austrian lake. 'This was in Foch.'

'It was. It's his bolthole in Austria.'

'He's there now?'

She began to grind the coffee and he tried to stop watching the cute way her bottom wobbled as she did so. The windows rattled as something exploded near by and dust sprinkled from the ceiling. 'How did he get away?'

'The French had him. There was nothing on him. No torture, no executions. So he walked away, scot free.'

'That's absurd.' Keppler's little ploy of distancing himself was just that. A ploy. A way of making him seem above all that barbarity, while reaping its reward when need be. He had to pay.

'Plus, of course, the French are busy trying to forget the number of people who dealt with Foch. Put Keppler on trial, let him list all his informers and it'll be a can of worms for them.'

'Talking of worms . . . Maurice?'

'Ten years.'

'He should swing.'

'You can't hang every French collaborator. Not enough gallows. Not enough trees.'

Williams looked down at the photograph one more time. 'Why are you carrying this?'

'Rat week.'

'What?'

'Rat week. Keppler may not have done any killing himself, but he certainly sent dozens, maybe hundreds, to their death. But there is something else you need to know. I said there might be a problem with you testifying against Alphachem?'

She came over with the coffee and he sipped, blistering his lips but not caring because it was so rich and wonderful and pure. She saw the look of pleasure and said, 'American. I knew you'd like it.'

'What's the problem?'

'Keppler said you were under Gestapo direction for six months after your arrest.'

He felt his throat constrict. 'What?'

'Virginia Thorpe confirmed it. Obst, too.'

Williams was speechless.

'Deuxième Bureau have put a price on your head. You can't go back. Not yet.'

'Rose. I—'

'Don't say anything. Listen, I read the French interrogation transcripts. Rubbish. I could get more out of him in ten minutes than they did in two days. I had Gestapo officers like him crying like a baby within half an hour, begging to be hanged. But they wouldn't let me at Keppler. Denazified and sent home, quick as you like.'

'So what can I do?'

'FX has a station at Vienna—'

'FX?'

'My section.'

'I thought you were F section.'

Rose laughed. 'That was the idea.'

'What was FX?'

'Best you don't know.'

Williams spun the possibilities over in his mind. FX. Then he recalled how much she knew about Dublin. 'You were SIS? A plant in SOE by the secret service?'

Rose took a breath and let it out slowly. 'Kind of.' At a bar in Jermyn Street in 1939 a friend of her mother's had put her on the SIS payroll, while directing her towards employment with MI(R), one of SOE's prototypes, to keep a weather eye on it. When she joined SOE proper, her loyalty to SIS remained more or less intact.

'Kind of? Bloody hell. So tell me this. Robert was convinced that SOE sent in its agents willy-nilly in forty-three to bluff the SD and Abwehr into thinking some sort of build-up was taking place. A landing in Pas de Calais maybe. While really Sicily was where the blow would fall. I said SOE wouldn't do that, wouldn't sacrifice its agents. But, of course SIS might.' He thought of that slippery bastard Slade back in Ireland. 'Why should MI6 give a flying fuck about a few bumbling amateurs being snared. Is that right? Was Robert right?'

Rose drained her coffee, got up and washed the cup. She didn't turn when she said, 'Utter bilge. We never sacrificed anyone. My job was to work for SOE to the best of my abilities, except on the rare occasion when it conflicted with an SIS operation.'

'Bollocks.'

Rose spun round, tears in her eyes. 'No, not bollocks, the truth. You asked me once what it was like sending people off. People you got to know. Like. Love. It was bloody awful. Every minute of it. Ask Bodington or Buckmaster or Atkins. And I don't need you making pointless shitty accusations, thank you very much.'

If it was a performance, it was a good one, and Williams muttered an apology. It probably didn't matter now. They did what they had to to win. In the long run, he guessed the alternative was even worse than what a few hundred agents went through.

'You were saying. FX.'

She sniffed, recovered her composure and began to get dressed. 'Obst we've lost track of. Thorpe and Keppler, we know where they are. If you pick them up, I . . . can interview them. Off the meter, you understand. I can get signed depositions clearing you. And we can go dancing in Vienna to celebrate.'

'And I thought this was a one-night stand?'

'What sort of girl do you take me for, Mr Williams? You can take my Humber. I'll get the papers drawn up and weapons issued. They'll say you're on War Crimes Tribunal business. Which is pretty much the truth. Can you manage it?'

He thought for a moment. The hatred would get him through it, no matter how weakened he was. He nodded. From her pocket Rose took out the diamond-encrusted Cartier watch and held it out to him. 'Before I forget.'

And the voice in his head was loud and clear and it was his own, from many, many years ago: *If you were mine I'd never betray you.*

Williams watched the diamonds dance and sparkle and said slowly, regretfully, 'Keep it. I'm finished with it.'

Williams focused the binoculars out on the lake, bringing into sharp relief the face of the man he was after. The two others in the small boat were unknown to him. All were well wrapped against the wind rippling the lake surface, so he couldn't be absolutely sure he had never seen them before. But he really didn't care. Keppler was the one.

Awkwardly, like tired old men, they manhandled the steel cylinders that were at the bottom of the craft and heaved them overboard, a dozen in all. There were satisfied smiles all round and Keppler, dressed, rather incongruously, in an old British army greatcoat, restarted the engine and headed off back to shore.

Williams had pulled the Humber over to one side of the road which led down from the mountains to the dark, bowl-like Lake Senlitz where Keppler was depositing whatever records and goods they thought should be hidden from the Allies, yet saved for posterity. The alpine flowers were out, blooming across the upper meadows, where cows, released from winter quarters, were now roaming contentedly. Williams barely registered the stunning backdrop. He only had eyes for ugliness.

Williams ignored the desperate, muffled kicking from the boot and refocused on the party below.

The two unknown men leaped out of the boat as Keppler beached it on the small shingle shoreline that had been carved out of the low cliff that ran round this southern part of the lake. The trio shook hands, and his companions climbed into a battered Skoda and drove off, leaving Keppler to stow the gear. He only had a short walk, maybe two kilometres, to the small cottage so familiar from the photograph. It showed signs of repair – a freshly patched roof, a new coat of paint. No doubt it had been sadly neglected while the owner was off doing the Führer's work in Paris. Now he had all the time in the world to fix it up.

The kicking again and a muffled scream. Virginia. The drug had worn off. He'd have to readminister. He had picked her up near Salzburg and she had come quietly, convinced he was going to kill her. Instead, he had tied her, gagged her and injected her with the sedative Rose had provided while he went to complete the pair. She could breathe in there, he was sure. She could wait.

323

His heart racing at the thought of the confrontation, Williams pulled back the slide on the Colt pistol and laid it on the seat next to him, beside the handcuffs and a US army burp gun, the sort of machine gun that was a lethal shredding machine at close range. He hoped he didn't have to use it.

Williams selected first and set off down the hillside, carefully taking the bends at sensible speeds so no tyre squeal would alert the man busy stowing oars and ropes in the shed by the roadside.

He drove to within a hundred metres, then something made him pull over. Keppler. That stooped, arthritic creature, his skin grey, his hair thinning, that was an SD man? The man who sipped fine wines while he conjured up some new Faustian pact?

Yes it was, he reminded himself. The very same. The man still blighting his life with his lies. As he pulled away, Keppler, warned by the canny survival instincts that had kept him alive these last few months, looked up. He peered at the windscreen and again, although there was no way he could recognise Williams, he knew he had to defend himself. Calmly, Keppler pulled out a Luger pistol, levelled it and fired.

The bullet shattered the screen, and tiny slivers of glass peppered Williams' face, each one hot and stinging. He punched out the remnants of the windshield and headed straight for Keppler, foot flat down now, wheels spinning, engine protesting, right at him. A second shot. A third, and part of Williams' ear flapped open, squirting blood across the upholstery. Rose won't be pleased, said a stupid irrational voice in his head.

He hit Keppler full on, snapping a tibia with the bumper, and sending the man careering over the bonnet towards him. Williams raised his arms as the figure suddenly filled his vision, crashing into the space where the glass had once been. The car slewed to a halt.

Williams reached for the gun, but a bloody claw grabbed his

wrist. Keppler twisted in the space, bringing another arm on to his face, scratching at Williams' eyes. He felt a lid tear, and lashed out, punching, but the massive woollen coat absorbed his blows.

Now Keppler was also scrabbling for the gun. With his elbow Williams knocked the gear stick into reverse and floored the pedal as he let in the clutch. The car careered wildly backwards, bumping up the grass verge, and still the SD man clung on. Williams stamped the brake hard, but felt the wheels lock on grass made slippery by the recent thaw. The Humber slithered on, slipping and sliding, back towards the edge of the low cliff where it tipped over into the black waters with a stomach-turning free fall. Even as the icy mass closed over him, Williams could still feel the German's hands desperately trying to find his windpipe, to earn the satisfaction of choking the life from him before the lake had a chance to drown them all.

Thirty-four

Deakin has forgotten how ear-piercingly raucous Brighton's seagulls can be as they swoop down to dive bomb a ragged old man who throws bread on to the shingle for them. The sea is lively, the tide running and waves leaping up around the pillars that support the skeletal remains of the West Pier, now slowly being restored.

He is sitting in the Victorian shelter alone, watching the families enjoy what may be the last fine weekend of the year before winter closes in. He scans the promenade and finally sees the old lady appear in the distance, propelling herself along the prom towards them, threading through rollerbladers and dog walkers. She had told him on the telephone that she has finally had to accept a wheelchair.

She whirrs up to him, a smile on her face as if she is genuinely pleased to see him. She holds out a bony blue hand and as he takes it he is shocked to see the Cartier watch on her wrist. She catches the glance.

'Oh I know. I was going to do something melodramatic,

but . . . well, it's rather nice isn't it? Too nice to waste on a lake. Shall we walk? Or rather, you walk, I'll roll. We can get a cup of tea along there.' She points to the café at the end of the prom.

He stands and paces alongside her. 'Still on the payroll, Deakin?'

'Part time. Good to be back.'

'I told Sir Charles he was a damn fool letting people like yourself go.'

'I appreciate it.'

'I trained him you know. Back in the fifties.'

'Ah.' That explained his loyalty and indulgence.

'It's very kind of you to come down from London, Deakin.'

'It's not entirely a social visit, Dame Rose.'

'No?'

'Two things. The French have started digging up the Zyklon B at St Just.'

Rose chuckles. 'Good. You told them about the film?'

'I told the Alphachem CEO you still had Robert's images of St Just trains being loaded. And a genuine canister. All they had to decide was, did they want us to announce to the world what had happened? They decided full disclosure was the best policy. Caused a bit of a stir, I hear.'

'Excellent. Well done. And secondly?'

Deakin takes a deep breath, wondering whether he is going to shatter an old woman's sense of closure. A spanner into the works. 'We've checked the dental records of the bodies from the Humber. You were right about Virginia Thorpe. The man, however, didn't check out. It seems it wasn't Mr Williams after all.'

A rattly laugh. 'I know that.'

He can't keep the surprise from his voice. 'You knew?'

'Suspected shall we say. Why do you think I didn't throw the watch into the water? I had a feeling Williams didn't die in that lake. Not that easy to kill a man like Williams, Deakin. They were extraordinary men, both of them. But chalk and cheese. With Robert, what you saw was what you got. Charming, cultured, refined, a lovely man, a real gentleman. Apart from the language. Whilst Williams . . . brave, resourceful, talented, certainly. But, of course, he turned out to be anything but a gentleman. As you will see.' She peers ahead to the café. 'Good. She's there. There is someone I would like you to meet.'

Deakin is trained not to like surprises and she hasn't mentioned a third party before. 'Who?'

'My granddaughter. Evie. Lovely girl.'

Deakin looks down at her and up at the café, where a woman, perhaps in her twenties, sits cradling a coffee, smiling at her approaching grandmother. Granddaughter? Deakin has checked the files on Rose, at least those sections he was allowed to access. She never married. There were no children. Deakin lets the news sink in, trying to get the flailing loose ends to knit together. When they finally do, he asks: 'Did you ever hear from him after Berlin? Did you ever hear from Williams?'

Rose shakes her head and the cloudy eyes look wetter than usual as she says quietly: 'Not a whisper.'

Thirty-five

FRANCE, SEPTEMBER 1945

Rose Miller consulted the map on the passenger seat and took a left at the cross roads. A few signs had been tacked back up, but for the most part the Normandy countryside was still denuded of decent directions. Occasionally she could spot the jagged stump of poles where the Germans had snapped off signposts to try to baffle the advancing Allies some fourteen, fifteen months previously. She had thought the place would be back to normal by now, but no, the fields had a sad, untended look, apple trees seemed to be growing through a dense carpet of rotting fruit, and precious walnuts lay uncollected on the ground. Too much land, too few people left.

Rose ground a gear as she slowed for St Arraton, taking in the little cluster of white houses, their stonework marked by the smallpox of rifle and machine-gun fire. On the far side of the village lay a scorched Sherman tank, its tracks unravelled like giblets, a gaping wound in its side.

He's dead. We have no idea where. I'm sorry, Eve.

Would she be able to say her name without her voice breaking?

Rose Miller rounded a bend and cursed when she saw a slow-moving lorry ahead, almost filling the narrow Normandy lane. Just what she needed. She accelerated towards the tailgate and then eased off when she saw the eyes looking at her. Peering over the top of the roof, heads swaying in rhythm with the truck, were two giraffe heads, attached, she assumed, to two real live giraffes. She burst out laughing. Here she was in so-called war-ravaged Europe, and someone was moving giraffes around?

Maybe they were there to restock the zoo. She hadn't heard of anyone eating giraffes in the desperate days of Occupation, but there was much went on that the tight-lipped French would prefer not to mention. A few cafés suddenly finding themselves with *fillet de giraf* on the menu would not surprise her one bit.

The truck belched smoke and wheezed as they hit a slight incline and the driver changed down, dropping to below thirty kilometres an hour.

'Come on, Noah,' Rose found herself saying. She pressed the horn and a hand appeared from the driver's window. For a moment Rose thought she was going to get an obscene gesture and she felt her anger rise, the fury of someone used to getting her own way, but the truck slowed even more and the hand waved her on. She went down to second and floored the Jeep, brushing within inches of the truck's side and flinching as the tendrils of the uncut hazel hedgerow flicked at the other side of her vehicle. She poked a hand through the space where canvas roof met door and waved her thanks. There was an answering flash of lights.

He's dead. No, we don't know . . .

Rose looked down at her wrist and gasped at her own stupidity. The diamond-encrusted Cartier winked at her, as if party to her near-miss. It was Rose's turn to slow down. She worked the watch from her arm and pushed it under the buff folders in the Jeep's map pocket. She suddenly felt her mood lighten. That was what had been worrying her, not her over-rehearsed speech to Eve. Some part of her subconscious had been sending alarm signals, trying to warn her, telling her she had to take off the watch. Relieved, she settled back and pressed the accelerator and watched the giraffe-truck recede in the rear-view mirror. Soon be over, she thought to herself. And then they could all get on with their lives.

She pulled into the driveway of the converted watermill and waited, the Jeep's engine ticking impatiently. Eve emerged from the kitchen, a couple of those hideous little dogs yapping at her feet. Rose climbed out, adjusted her jacket carefully, and approached Eve, shocked at how she'd let herself go. Where was the radiant beauty? The Yvonne Aubicq that men had supposedly done battle over in fast cars. Ratty hair, a shapeless housecoat, a tired, washed-out face.

'Hello, Eve.'

Eve smiled weakly and nodded. 'Any news?'

'None. I've just come off the line with Vera Atkins. If anyone knows what happened to our agents, she does. The trail ends at Sachsenhausen. I'm sorry. I've brought you a few of his things.'

Rose reached into her shoulder pack and produced some letters and photographs, one of which – the standard SOE head and shoulders shot, the one that would line the stairwell of the Special Forces Club like so many frozen in eternal youthful sepia – fluttered to the ground. They both bent to pick it up, but Eve followed it all the way down, collapsing on to her knees, impervious to the sharp gravel. She looked at the photograph and began to weep, bowing as if praying and then, with a sickening thud, banging her head rhythmically on the drive, picking up small pieces of stone every time she did so, driving them deeper and deeper into her skin with each blow.

'Eve,' said Rose, touching her shoulder. 'Eve, stop it.'

She began to wail and Rose looked around, desperate for relief, some kind of saviour. In the garage she glimpsed the unmistakable curves of the bodywork of the Atlantic. 'You dug it up? My God . . .'

'Could you go now please?'

'Eve, I miss him too. And Robert—'

'Go. Please. Leave me.' She looked up, the thin streams of blood running into her eyebrows and creeping down her cheeks. 'Please.'

Rose deposited the rest of Williams' things on to the ground beside Eve and backed away, suddenly anxious to be away from this crazy woman. She climbed into the Jeep, started it, and, careful not to spray Eve with gravel, turned it in a large circle and drove out of the courtyard, making a right.

A great feeling of relief washed over her, relief and guilt. It was over. Done. What did it matter where she thought her husband died, or what he had got up to in a half-ruined hotel in Bad Bleibau? In many ways Williams did die in Sachsenhausen, and died a hero. This way the Deuxième Bureau suspicion would be quietly buried, as would the Rat Weeks, all lost in the confusion of the post-war turmoil. Forty-two thousand airmen had not returned from missions and their fates were not known. What was a handful of SOE operatives against that?

Except the thousands were faceless. She had known the handful. It made a difference.

She came to the slow-moving lorry of giraffes bumping up the road, glanced at the bearded driver, and pulled over to let him pass. Return the favour. He honked as he slid by. The feeling of nausea hit her as the belch of exhaust filled the Jeep. Rose opened the door and vomited across the asphalt, once, then again, her stomach heaving on empty.

Rose took a slug of water from the canteen, washed it around her mouth and spat. She looked down and felt at the tiny lump swelling under her waistband. She knew what she had to do. Couldn't go home as an unmarried mother. So, a nursing home in Brittany. A change of surname for the baby. Adoption to a nice English family, maybe one which lost a child in the Blitz or the youngest son to the Germans. That would be good. Maybe even replace one of those thousands of missing airmen. Then back to work. She pulled the Jeep off the verge and on to the road. Rose Miller had a feeling that Europe was about to enter a 'peace' that didn't really deserve the term and she wanted to be part of the next battle.

Eve Williams was sitting cross-legged on the gravel when the big lorry inched its way in, indicators flashing, air brakes hissing as the driver sought to edge it in without demolishing the stone pillars. Clear of the gateway he edged forward, pulling the truck tight in against one of the paddock fences, away from where she sat. With a final shush the engine stopped and the driver climbed from the cab.

She looked up at him, then at the four wonderful doe-like eyes staring down at her from their crazy-paved necks. Giraffes. She pulled some specks of gravel from her forehead, feeling silly now. 'The zoo is another fifty kilometres.'

'I know.'

He stood there, arms folded, and Eve read the tag stitched on the overall's breast pocket. Tambal. 'Well, Mr Tambal, if it's coffee you want, I can help. Anything else . . .'

She held out her hand and he strode over and pulled her to her feet. As she came up his arms went round her waist and for the first time she looked beyond the beard and the thin network of scars and the bent nose and the misshapen ear and felt as if she were going to be sick. 'Ah . . .' was all that came out.

333

He reached up and pulled the hair from her face, the way he had seventeen years before on a lonely beach in the headlights of a Rolls-Royce. 'Hello, Eve.'

'Will.' Her voice was a frightened whisper. 'Will?'

'I was.'

'No, no, you are . . .' There was pleading in her voice. 'You're alive?'

'No. Will's dead.'

She took a step back, looking at him, making sure he was solid, not some tormenting spectre. 'Why?'

'Too many things. Just too many. Time to start over.' He had done it before, he could do it again. Grover became Williams who became Grover–Williams. Now he had to die, for the terrible things he had done. Rose, Lock, and . . .

'Robert?'

The worst sin of all. He shook his head.

'Tell me.'

And he did, mostly. A friend given and then taken away, leaving him behind. After he had finished he said quietly: 'Fresh start, OK? No questions, no recriminations. That's the offer.'

'I'll think about it,' she said and grinned. When he didn't react she pinched him. 'I'm joking.'

It would be a long time before he could really laugh out loud again, he knew. It was like after the King had died when he was a boy, and his father had turned them into a house full of whisperers. Now he felt the entire world should lower its voice in respect for and remembrance of what had happened to his friend.

'The giraffes?' Eve asked.

'Long story.'

Then he saw the Atlantic. She noticed his eyes dart over there, saw the small, expectant smile on his face. Knew he was recalling the madness of driving it with Robert, risking their lives because they wanted that speed. It was a kind of insanity, he could see that now, but in a world gone completely mad, it was difficult to pick out what exactly was sane and what wasn't. He looked at Eve again, disbelieving, and echoed Rose's words: 'You dug it up?'

'Long story. But it works.' She took him by the hand and pulled him across to the garage, yanking the barn door fully open and revealing the long, low shape he never thought to see again.

Eve climbed in, turned the key, pressed the ignition and the engine ripped into life, the familiar Bugatti signature, loud and raucous, in total contrast to the elegant wrapper. 'Move over,' he said.

She looked up at him and shook her head. 'Uh-uh. Dead men don't drive.'

Williams hesitated a moment, then jumped in the passenger side. Eve let in the clutch and the car leapt forward, wheels throwing up a storm of gravel, causing the giraffes to pull back in shock as she bumped the Atlantic out of the courtyard and turned left, away from Rose and everything she stood for, flooring the accelerator, throwing him back in the seat. Williams watched hypnotised as the line of plane trees rushed towards them, blurring together as the speedometer crept round the white face of the dial, the only evidence of gaps between the fat, peeling trunks the semaphore flashing of the early morning sun.

Author's note

Early One Morning is a novel and should not be regarded as a historical document, but at the core of it are a few remarkable truths. Williams (aka William Grover aka William Charles Frederick Grover–Williams), a former chauffeur for Sir William Orpen, Robert Benoist and Jean-Pierre Wimille really did form a Resistance circuit in France in 1942–3. The idea of the fastest men in the world against the German occupiers is what sparked this work. Like so many other clandestine groups, they were betrayed to the Germans, and many people suffered and died as a result.

Robert Benoist was actually apprehended much later than Williams. His escapades herein, driving a Bugatti from under the noses of a convoy he had been forced to join and leaping from a moving police car (it was a Hotchkiss, not a van), are true. There were so many other tales of Robert's bravery and resourcefulness that, for a while, SOE were suspicious of a man who could escape from the clutches of the Germans so often, until Robert came to England for training and they saw what he was made of. As far as we know, he was hanged by piano wire at Buchenwald, alongside 36 fellow Allied officers, by the SS on 12 September 1944.

Maurice Benoist was tried by a French court for collaboration. Due to ill health, he served only five years of a ten-year sentence. Still protesting his innocence, he died in 1955.

Some suspicion of betrayal also fell on Jean-Pierre Wimille, who was acquitted and exonerated by the court. After the war, racing for Alfa Romeo, he was well on his way to being belatedly recognised as one of the greatest drivers of his era, when he was killed at the 1948 Argentinian Grand Prix in Buenos Aires.

Yvonne Williams became a well-known dog breeder and a judge at Crufts Dog Show in London. The two Scotties on the Black & White whisky bottle were reputed to be hers. She died in 1973.

Although Williams was officially notified as executed at Sachsenhausen in March 1945, in May 1947 a communication was sent from Berlin by MI5 to SOE asking for help in relocating a former Bugatti race driver, Grover–Williams, to the USA. Sometime later a man calling himself Georges Tambal, closely resembling Williams, an expert on race cars and with the same date of birth, moved into Yvonne's farmhouse. She was to claim he was her cousin. Tambal was knocked off his bicycle and killed by a carload of German tourists in 1983.

Keppler is modelled on Hans Kieffer, who was hanged by the French. His crime was signing the execution order for a group of British commandos later in the war, not running the SD in Paris. SOE admitted there was little they could have pinned on him for his activities at Avenue Foch – he really was a man who preferred a deal to torture. Of course, that certainly wasn't true of all Gestapo, SD and Abwehr officers.

Rose Miller is in no way based on the wonderful Vera Atkins of SOE, whom I had the privilege to meet shortly before her death. She told Jack Bond and I that she interviewed Kieffer after the war and managed to reduce him to tears within a short time. This did not endear him to her. Jack asked her over dinner at the

Special Forces Club how she viewed the Germans sixty years after the events. There was a long pause while she drew on a cigarette and she eventually said, very softly, with great feeling: 'As disagreeable as ever, really.' Out of Williams and Benoist, both of whom she met, we got the impression that it was Robert she admired more.

Vera would not have approved of the way I have played with dates, for instance for how long the deeply flawed poem codes were used and the timetable of SOE operations (I have them up and running a little faster than reality). She would certainly have exploded at the suggestion of an SIS plant in SOE. I can only plead, once more, that this is a fiction with a bedrock of actual events.

However, a French company (which survives today as part of a US multinational) did manufacture Zyklon B during the Second World War as well documented in France by journalist Annie Lacroix-Riz, who has suffered much vilification for this and other exposures about industry's role in the occupation.

Arthur Lock is based on Harry Cole, a British renegade, his career much as described, apart from his death.

It is likely Williams escaped from Sachsenhausen by striking a deal with an SS officer called Meyer to give a testimonial to the Allies. The famous Yeo-Thomas (The White Rabbit) used a similar method, as described in Mark Seaman's excellent book *Bravest Of the Brave* (see below).

Virginia Thorpe is a total fiction, but several SOE agents did find themselves relatively comfortable homes in Avenue Foch and appeared to have a far too cosy relationship with the SD. Henri Dericourt ('Gilbert'), who controlled Lysander flights for SOE, certainly did let the SD look at the mail. The debate over whether he was simply a traitor, a double agent or a triple agent has raged since the 1950s. There is no doubt, however, that being shown such documents seriously weakened the resolve of several agents when they were in Avenue Foch.

Around 480 SOE agents went into France by plane, parachute or boat. One hundred and thirty were captured. Twenty-six returned. This is thought to be the tip of a very large iceberg – the official numbers take no account of collateral damage to the French population caused by a circuit's collapse. There were many brave French and English men and women involved in the Chestnut circuit, including Lieutenant Roland Dowlen, an SOE radio operator who was sent to help Chestnut on 31 March 1943 and was billeted with Thérèse Lethias in Pontoise, away from the house at Auffargis, for security reasons. Nevertheless, he was captured on 31 July by DF vans, and his radio was subsequently operated by the Germans until 31 October. Dowlen was executed at Flossenburg. Other circuit members, too numerous to mention here, were also arrested and many died in concentration camps and prisons. *Early One Morning* is dedicated to all of them.

Both Benoist and Williams, whose enigma survives him, were awarded the Croix de Guerre and to this day trophies in both men's names are raced for.

Sources

My initial research into the Williams/Benoist story was with Gervaise Cowell (now deceased), the SOE advisor for the Foreign and Commonwealth Office, and Richard Day, curator of The Bugatti Trust in Gotherington, Gloucester. The results were published in *Arena* magazine as the short story *The Man With One Name*, for which I am grateful to the then editor Peter Howarth, who encouraged me to present it as fiction.

That was 1995. Two years later, after a meeting engineered by Duncan Stuart of SOE, I was fortunate enough to have use of the unstoppable energy and drive of the inimitable Jack Bond, film director and producer, who worked closely with Beatrice van Lith, Robert Benoist's granddaughter, to uncover many of the details used herein, principally Williams' survival of Sachsenhausen plus Beatrice's insights into the character of Robert. Jack also showed a remarkable facility for prising out information from both the UK and French security services, the latter regarding the Zyklon B issue (and picked up a warning that digging too hard might be detrimental to his health). Jack also unearthed, from Eve's neighbours, the tale of Tambal turning up with the giraffes.

Richard Smith, a man with a mission if ever I met one, trawled through the Public Records Office at Kew and dropped many pieces of the jigsaw puzzle into place, proving beyond any doubt that Williams was not executed at the camp. To get an admission from SOE/MI6 that the files are wrong is a remarkable feat.

Again, I have played fast and loose with all these people's exemplary work.

For those who wish to find out more about the characters and events without the gloss of fiction, I would direct you towards the bibliography which follows.

Bibliography

Orpen: Mirror to an Age by Bruce Arnold

The IRA by Tim Pat Coogan

Memories of Montparnasse by John Glassco

Americans in Paris by Brian N. Morton

The Twilight Years: Paris in the 1930s by William Wiser

Paris and Elsewhere by Richard Cobb

The Josephine Baker Story by Ean Wood

Driving Forces by Peter Stevenson (a book about the Silver Arrows).

Hitler's Grand Prix in England (Donnington 1937 and 1938) by Christopher Hilton

Ettore Bugatti by W.F. Bradley

Bugatti, The Man and The Marque by Jonathan Wood

The Bugatti Story by L'Ebe Bugatti

The Power and the Glory, History of Grand Prix Racing Vol 1 1906–1951 by William Court

The Monaco Grand Prix by Craig Brown/Len Newman

Alfa Romeo: The Legend Revived by David G. Styles

London at War by Philip Ziegler

SS Intelligence by Edmund L. Blandford

Occupation: The Ordeal of France 1940–44 by Ian Ousby

Occupied France by H.R. Kedward

The Fall of Paris June 1940 by Herbert Lottman

The Prime of Life by Simone de Beauvoir

Swastika over Paris by Jeremy Josephs

SOE by M.R.D. Foot

SOE in France by M.R.D. Foot

Inside SOE by E.H. Cookridge

Noor-un-nisa Inayat Khan by Jean Overton Fuller

Secret War by Nigel West

Between Silk and Cyanide by Leo Marks

Flames in the Field by Rita Kramer

The Secret History of SOE by William Mackenzie

An Uncertain Hour by Ted Morgan

The Death of Jean Moulin by Patrick Marnham

Bravest of the Brave by Mark Seaman

Sabotage and Subversion: Stories From The Files of SOE and OSS by Ian Dear

Undercover: The Men and Women of the SOE by Patrick Howarth

Industrialists and Bankers Under the Occupation by Annie Lacroix-Riz

Sisters in the Resistance by Margaret Collins Weitz

Paris After the Liberation by Antony Beevor and Artemis Cooper

THANKS TO: Jack Bond, Richard Smith, David Miller, Bill Massey, Martin Fletcher, Peter Howarth, Don Hawkins, Susan D'Arcy, Dylan Jones and Christine Walker. Extra thanks to Rita Kramer for inspiration and the Pericles.

GHOST HEART

Cecilia Samartin

BLACK SWAN

GHOST HEART
A BLACK SWAN BOOK : 0 552 77145 7

Originally published in Great Britain by Bantam Press,
a division of Transworld Publishers

PRINTING HISTORY
Bantam Press edition published 2004
Black Swan edition published 2005

1 3 5 7 9 10 8 6 4 2

Set in 11/12pt Melior by
Falcon Oast Graphic Art Ltd.

Black Swan Books are published by Transworld Publishers,
61–63 Uxbridge Road, London W5 5SA,
a division of The Random House Group Ltd,
in Australia by Random House Australia (Pty) Ltd,
20 Alfred Street, Milsons Point, Sydney, NSW 2061, Australia,
in New Zealand by Random House New Zealand Ltd,
18 Poland Road, Glenfield, Auckland 10, New Zealand
and in South Africa by Random House (Pty) Ltd,
Endulini, 5a Jubilee Road, Parktown 2193, South Africa.

Printed and bound in Great Britain by
Cox & Wyman Ltd, Reading, Berkshire.

Papers used by Transworld Publishers are natural, recyclable
products made from wood grown in sustainable forests. The
manufacturing processes conform to the environmental
regulations of the country of origin.

For all the cousins.

Dear Alicia,

I'm told this letter may not get to you as the communists will cut it into shreds, but when I saw the picture of us together at Varadero beach, I knew I had to write anyway. I look at it every night and remember what life was like when I was alive. I do not belong to this place, and every morning when I wake up and find myself still here I want to close my eyes and sleep for ever.

All I have now are memories. I love them and hate them for what they do to me. I love them because when I'm lost in their vision, this hollow pain in my heart goes away for a while. I hate them because they are so beautiful they fool me into believing I'm really home, and then I must leave all over again.

I wish I was with you. I wish we were packing a bag for Varadero right now, without a worry in our heads except whether or not it will rain before noon . . .

CUBA

1956–1962

1

WHAT I LOVE MOST IS THE WARMTH, HOW IT REACHES IN AND spreads out to the tips of my fingers and toes, until it feels like I'm part of the sun, like it's growing inside me. Have you ever seen the ocean turn smooth as a sheet of glass or curl up on the shore with a sigh? If you knew my country then you'd know that the sea can be many things: faithful and blue as the sky one moment, and the next a shimmering turquoise so brilliant you'd swear the sun was shining from beneath the waves.

I often stand at the water's edge, digging my toes into the moist sand, and gaze out at the ghostly grey line of the horizon that separates sea and sky. I close my eyes just a little so I can no longer be sure which is which and I'm floating in a blue-green universe. I'm a fish and then a bird. I'm a golden mermaid with long flowing hair that flies in the wind. With a flick of my tail I could return to the sea and explore the shores of other lands. But how can I leave this place that quietens my soul to a prayer?

Better to stay and lie on the blanket of fine white sand, gazing up at the royal palms for hours as we do. They sway in the ocean breeze and I could almost fall asleep, if not for the constant chatter of my cousin, Alicia. She's hardly a year older than me – in fact for thirteen days of the year we're exactly the same age – but she seems much older and wiser. Perhaps it's because she's so sure of what she likes. She has no doubt that she prefers mango ice cream to coconut and that her favourite number is nine because nine is the age she is and if nine were a person it would be a glamorous lady, a show girl with long legs and swinging hips. I, on the other hand, have a hard time choosing between mango and coconut, and if you throw in papaya I'm completely overwhelmed.

Alicia squints up at the sun with eyes that are sometimes gold, sometimes green, and tells me what she sees. 'Look how the palms move in the wind.'

'I see them,' I respond.

'They're sweeping the clouds away with their big leaves so we can look straight up to heaven and see God.'

'Can you see God?' I ask.

'If I look at it just right I can. And when I do, I ask Him for whatever I want and He'll give it to me.'

I turn away from the swaying palms to study Alicia's face. Sometimes she likes to joke around and doesn't tell me the truth until she's certain she's tricked me. But I know when she's hiding a smile because her dimples show. They're almost showing now.

'Tell the truth,' I prod.

'I am.' Then she opens her eyes as wide as she can and stares straight up at the sun, then shuts them tight until tears slip past her temples. She turns to face me, eyes sparkling and lips curled in a triumphant smile. 'I just saw Him.'

'What did you ask for?'

'I can't tell you or else He won't give it to me.'

I, too, turn my face towards the sun and try to open my eyes as wide as Alicia's, but I can't keep them open for even half a second and I certainly don't see God or even the wisp of an angel's wing. I conclude that brown eyes are not as receptive to

12

heavenly wonders as her magnificent golden eyes.

Alicia sits up suddenly and looks down at me, blocking the sun. 'What did you ask for?'

'I thought you said we couldn't tell,' I object, not wanting to admit I'd failed to see anything at all.

She settles back down onto the sand and full sun stretches over us once again. Soon we'll have to head back for our afternoon meal. These morning hours at the beach slip away so fast. I was hoping we'd get a chance to go swimming, but we aren't allowed in past our knees without a trusted adult nearby to keep watch. Ever since a little boy drowned at Varadero beach three years ago that's been the rule and there's no use trying to change it.

'I want to go swimming,' I say.

Alicia turns to survey the ocean. We see the waves lapping the white curve of the beach and know the sea is a warm bath. We'd float easily in the calm waters and maybe even learn how to swim more like the grown-ups, moving our arms like steady and reliable windmills. And maybe our grandfather, Abuelo Antonio, undoubtedly the best swimmer in all of Cuba, will come out with us and we'll take turns venturing into deeper water while riding safely on his shoulders.

'Let's go!' Alicia cries and we spring to our feet and run as fast as we can, leaving a wake of powdery white sand floating behind us.

All of the rooms in my grandparents' large house at Varadero overlooked the sea, and the dining room was no exception. Abuela kept the windows open most of the time as she believed fresh air to be the best defence against the many diseases she worried about. The lace curtains fluttered on the incoming ocean breeze as Abuelo said the blessing over our meal. It wasn't until he lifted his head and took up his fork that we were allowed to do the same.

13

I was lucky to be sitting closest to the fried bananas, my favourite, and to have Alicia right next to me as well. At home, our parents knew better and always separated us so we wouldn't talk and giggle when we should be learning proper table manners. It seemed that Mami was more concerned with what fork I used for the salad than with my school work. Most of the time, Abuelo and Abuela were amused by our antics and laughed at what our parents called 'foolishness'.

'Look at how dark you're getting,' Abuela said as she handed me a large bowl of fluffy yellow rice. 'People will think you're a mulatica and not the full-blooded Spaniard that you are.' Being a full-blooded Spaniard was also a very important thing, even more important than proper manners.

I helped myself to a generous serving of rice. 'Look at Alicia. She's almost as dark as me,' I shot back.

'Alicia's a Spaniard through and through,' Abuela said. 'With those light eyes and hair, there's no mistaking her heritage. She can get as black as a ripened date and she'll still look like a Spaniard.'

At these moments, the only thing that kept me from envying Alicia for her superior colouring was that she always came to my rescue. 'I think Nora looks beautiful, like a tropical princess,' she said.

'That's right, Abuela, I look like a tropical princess.'

Abuelo laughed. Having been born in Spain, he was more Spanish than anyone, but he didn't care as much as Abuela about where people came from or who their parents were. And even though he never bragged, everyone knew he was a real Spaniard because of his accent and eloquent speech, so different from the brusque Cuban style. 'Would the princess mind passing the platanos before she eats them all herself?' he asked with a slight bow of his head.

Later that afternoon, after we'd had our mandatory naps, Abuelo was easily persuaded to come out to the beach and continue his swimming lessons. I'd promised Papi I'd learn to be a good swimmer during this week's vacation, but I hadn't progressed nearly enough to impress him.

'Too much time playing around and not enough time practising,' Abuelo declared as he stood with us on the shore in his dark-blue swimming trunks and white guayabera shirt, perfectly pressed by Abuela that morning and every morning.

Alicia and I stood on either side of him, each clasping a big hand as we gazed out at the peaceful sea. Together, we stepped into the water and felt the waves caress our feet. We ventured in further and the silky blanket swirled up to our knees and then to our waists, but we could still easily see our toes wiggling in the sand.

We stood silent and nervous, waiting for Abuelo's instructions to begin. Perhaps he'd have us float on our backs as he usually did. Maybe we'd practise kicking our feet with our heads underwater while he taxied us around by our hands, grasping at him for dear life when he dared to let go. Or he might dive into deeper water while we clung to his neck, laughing and sputtering when he came up for air. 'Not so deep, Abuelo!' we'd cry, hoping he'd go a little deeper still.

Instead, he pointed to the platform that floated a hundred yards from the shore. 'You see that out there?'

We were quite familiar with the platform. This was the famous place to which both our fathers had had to swim as children in order to be declared real swimmers and be allowed in the ocean without adult supervision. We'd heard the story a million times, and when our parents dropped us off we'd bragged that by the time the week was over we would've conquered the platform.

On most days, older kids were on and around it, diving into the water, lifting themselves easily onto the wooden planks and jumping off again like loud, happy seals. But this afternoon the platform bobbed about without a soul upon it. In fact, except for a couple very far off holding hands, the beach was empty. Everyone seemed still to be resting after lunch.

'Well, do you see it?' Abuelo asked again, still pointing.

I felt the butterflies begin to stir. 'Yes, I see it,' we both replied. I detected a slight tremor in Alicia's voice as well.

He squeezed our hands. 'Today you're going to swim out there all by yourselves. Who wants to go first?'

Neither of us spoke. 'What? Nobody wants to go first?' Abuelo smiled down at us and then, with an exaggerated expression of concern and surprise, 'You're not afraid, are you?'

'I think I'm a little bit afraid,' I said.

Alicia thrust out her chin. 'I'm not. I'll go first.'

'That's my girl!' Abuelo dropped my hand and held Alicia's up in the air as if she'd won a prize fight. 'Now follow me and try to move your arms like this when you kick.' Abuelo circled his arms over his head and Alicia imitated him as best she could, while I stood with my arms glued to my side, aware that this lesson wasn't meant for me. Abuelo pulled his guayabera up over his head and threw it onto the sand before diving smoothly into the sea with hardly a splash. Three or four strokes of his powerful arms and in no time at all he was pulling himself up onto the platform and waving for Alicia to follow.

She began with an awkward dive, but it roused a cheer from Abuelo just the same. Her head dipped in and out of the water with jerky motions as she swam slowly but steadily towards the platform. She tried to swing her arms over her head like Abuelo had instructed, but she floundered a bit and resumed her less than graceful but reliable doggy-paddle. She'd never swum this far without stopping in her life, but she kept going well past the point where the water turned from a light green to an ominous deeper blue.

And Abuelo kept cheering her on, standing on the very edge of the platform and reaching for her even when she was too far away. Her neck craned with the strain of her effort as she neared the platform and she was barely inching forward when Abuelo reached down and pulled her up easily by both arms. She collapsed onto the platform with a thud, panting and laughing and holding her sides. Once she'd caught her breath she stood up next to Abuelo, triumphant and glistening – a real swimmer.

She called out to me. 'Come on, Nora! You can do it.'

Abuelo turned his attention to me now that Alicia had proved herself. He wanted to be doubly proud. 'Don't think about it any more. Just dive in like your cousin.'

They looked so far away on that platform of champions, but I could see their smiles bursting out at me even from there. They believed in me. They knew I could do it too.

I dived in and felt the familiar warmth that, for the first time, failed to calm my heart. My feet kicked and my cupped hands shovelled in a valiant doggy-paddle. Suddenly the water felt as thick as jelly and it filled my ears, my nostrils, my mouth, dulling my senses in an alien way. I filled my lungs with dry air in pockets and spurts between gulps of salty water as encouraging screams broke through the monotony of my laboured breathing. I looked towards my goal and caught their smiles, their arms waving wildly against the bright blue sky. Momentarily blind and deaf, I tried desperately to find a rhythm for my arms and legs that would propel me forward. I had to make it. I had to prove I could do it too.

Listening for their calls, reaching for Abuelo's big hands that should be only inches away, I looked up again. But they were still waving, no closer than before. Could it be that I was actually further away?

I pointed my toes towards the sandy bottom. If I

reached it, I might push myself up and catch my breath; but the bottom was much further down than I'd thought. I knew suddenly that I should not be trying to go forward any more, just up. Up to the sun that was a splash of watery light, up towards the birds watching me as they flew in gentle circles above my thrashing attempts to stay afloat – for even a bird would know that whatever I was doing, it wasn't swimming.

Somehow I managed to force my nose and mouth above water one last time, but then the sea covered my head and there was no sound, no sky, no wind, just the rush inside my head as I sank deeper in the quiet blue. It was cool and dark, only bubbles, clear white bubbles, spinning me around.

I awoke on the sand with the afternoon sun full upon me. I felt my chest rise and fall in shallow spasms, but when I tried to breathe deep I coughed up enough sea water to fill a good-sized pitcher. Abuelo's face was very close and I detected the sweet fragrance of cigar on his breath. Alicia was crouched next to him, but he held her away from me with a protective arm. Their mouths moved, but there was only silence. Finally the faint hum of their familiar voices grew into clear and understandable words.

'Nora, can you hear me?' Abuelo was asking, although his voice was firm, as though directing rather than asking me. 'Oh yes, you can hear me. She's OK now,' he said to Alicia, then chuckled nervously, as he did when caught by Abuela in a white lie of some sort.

He allowed Alicia to peer in closer, with instructions that she should give me room to breathe. I wanted to turn and smile and say I was fine, like I did when I fell off my skates, but I could hardly move.

'You almost drowned, Nora,' Alicia said in wonderment.

Abuelo came in close again and they both dripped on me, forcing me to blink. 'Now, now, Alicia, that isn't true,' he said. 'I was watching her every minute. There's no way she could've drowned.'

'But her hand went up like this, Abuelo,' Alicia said, thrusting her hand up in the air like a claw grasping at nothing. 'And she had that horrible look on her face.'

'You were always safe, Norita. I would never let anything happen to you.'

I tried to nod and felt my head shift in the sand, but this small movement caused their faces to start spinning and I had to close my eyes to settle my stomach, which felt as if it was still sinking to the bottom of the sea.

In a few minutes, I felt much better and was able to sit up and look around. The world was still the same as I'd left it, except that Abuelo and Alicia were watching me as if I'd just hatched out of an egg or grown horns on my head.

Abuelo directed Alicia to bring me an ice-cold coke from the house, and when she returned I drank it down. Soon I was able to stand, and we sauntered back towards the house hand in hand, just as we'd arrived. Abuelo reminded us that Abuela had promised to welcome us back from our swim with a piece of her delicious rum cake.

'By the way, there's no reason to tell your grand-mother what happened here today,' he said. 'She'll only get very upset and worry for no reason.'

We needed no convincing of the need for secrecy. We could well predict our grandmother's reaction and were quite familiar with her particular brand of worry. It was the kind that made the world stop until it was finished. And it usually involved complicated promises to various saints to cut off all her fingernails and eyelashes, or never wear lipstick again. Perhaps this time our eyelashes would be cut, and we couldn't risk the possibility of never wearing lipstick. We'd already chosen our colours for when we were old enough. At the very least, we'd never be allowed to go swimming with Abuelo again, of that much we were sure.

2

THE FRANTIC CLICK-CLICKING OF MAMI'S HIGH HEELS ECHOED down the tiled hall towards my bedroom. We were back in Havana, and it was well past the time when I should've been having breakfast. She burst through the door to find me lying on top of the bed, my school books tossed next to me in disarray.

'Beba spread your toast with marmalade the way you like, and it's just sitting there dying of laughter.'

I lay very still in my grey jumper and starched white shirt. Beba had arranged my hair in a tight ponytail with an enormous red bow at the crown of my head. She'd be upset if I messed it up.

'For goodness' sake, Nora, get up, you're going to wrinkle your uniform.'

'I don't feel well,' I said, raising my head slightly.

'What's wrong with you?'

'I think it's my stomach. It's been hurting since yesterday.'

Mami's face puckered slightly as she studied me in the doorway, but I couldn't see any sign of motherly concern. She stepped in and swiped my forehead with her hand, barely touching me. 'You're fine. There's nothing wrong with you.' She gathered my books together and placed them on my stomach. 'Your sister's waiting for you.' I had no choice but to force myself out of bed and join Marta by the door to wait for the driver.

It's not that I hated school. I just knew it would be more interesting to stay at home and help Beba cut up vegetables and fold laundry, while she told amazing stories of the black people who lived in the country and of African spirits with exotic names like Ochun and Yemaya. They had ritual ceremonies in humble huts in the jungle or around a fire where people danced in frenzied circles for hours at a time. Beba told me about them when Mami was out shopping or visiting friends, because we both knew she wouldn't approve. Later she'd make a big flan and save a bit to make me a little one, because she knew I liked to eat it while the cream was still warm and wobbly.

Mami leaned over the railing on the balcony over-looking the wide avenue below and the Caribbean in the distance. 'The driver's here,' she called. This was Beba's cue to leave whatever she was doing in the kitchen and walk us out to the elevator, down seven floors and then out to the car that came for us every morning at eight a.m.

I looked forward to spending even little bits of time like this with Beba. As tall as Papi, with broad shoulders and an amazing deep golden voice, she was the most fascinating person I knew. She always wore white: white dress, white shoes, white stockings, even a white handkerchief.

She used to dress like all the other maids, with regular clothes, an apron, and a starched little hat perched on her enormous head, but one day she asked Mami if she could come to work all dressed in white because of her religion. Mami said she could as long as she didn't bring any of that Santeria business into the house. 'We're all Catholics here. Just remember that,' Mami said sternly.

I was mad at Mami for talking so mean to Beba,

because, after Alicia, I considered Beba to be my closest friend. She was probably Mami's best friend too, because I often caught her whispering to Beba in the kitchen and telling her secrets. I even overheard her complaining about Papi and the way he controlled her spending. Beba just nodded and clicked her tongue in all the right places, like she did when I complained about Marta. Then somehow we'd end up laughing and crying as we helped her to cut the onions and all the upset would be gone.

I felt safest when I held Beba's hand, and I tried to hold it as often as I could. In the evenings it smelled of onions and garlic and green peppers and olive oil, and in the mornings of lavender soap and fresh bread and butter. I was fascinated, too, with the luminous beauty of her dark skin. There weren't any freckles or veins like I had, just a perfect smooth darkness like strong coffee with a little bit of milk.

I nuzzled against her skin, and breathed in deep. This made Beba laugh out loud. 'Why do you do that, Norita?'

'Because your skin is beautiful. I want to go to the beach every day so that I can have skin like you.'

'I think you're beautiful too,' my sister chimed in. 'I want to have hair like you and part it in the middle with clips on each side.'

Where Marta had got this hairstyle from nobody knew, but it always launched Beba into a fit of laughter that made both of us squirm with delight and forget our competition for her love and attention. When Beba was happy, all was right with the world. Even the weather was more agreeable. And when she was sad, although she seldom was, we were afraid that the sun might fall out of the sky.

'Thank the good Lord he made you how he did,' she often said. 'You girls just thank the good Lord.'

It was a mystery to me how the nuns at El Angel de la Guardia School walked about without making a sound. One might steal up behind you and you wouldn't know until it was too late. Not that we had much to hide; there was little trouble to get into except when one of the older girls was occasionally caught wearing lipstick. The sisters would march her straight to the bathroom to wash her face, and it always seemed that she was redder than her lipstick for an entire week. That was the extent of our sinfulness.

Nevertheless, we filed into the chapel for prayers every morning at ten o'clock sharp to confess our sins and pray for forgiveness. Most of the other girls disliked chapel time and I pretended to dislike it too, though actually it was my favourite part of the day. I loved the way sweet incense drifted about in hazy clouds, rising along multicoloured beams of sunlight that filtered through stained-glass windows high above. Hundreds of small white candles wavered at the bare feet of saints, their wax dripping like liquid lace as they carried their smoky messages to heaven. All the sisters, even the quick ones with eagle eyes, hung their heads low as they whispered their prayers with steady precision, lips hardly moving in strings of half-formed words.

I was particularly fascinated by the Stations of the Cross carved in white stone that hung over the closet confessionals. I gazed at the depiction of Jesus hanging with his arms outstretched as he looked up to heaven, asking God to forgive all sinners. I thought of Abuela and her promises. Would it be wrong to ask Jesus to help me learn how to swim? Perhaps if I made a promise to him right now, He'd fix it so I could go to the beach every day and practise. I could promise to cut off my hair like a boy's and give my new skates to Marta. I could promise never again to ask Beba questions about the African saints; but surely this was asking too much? The thought of never talking to Beba again about what I knew she loved most brought tears to my eyes, and it was as I wiped them away that I caught Sister Margarita watching me from the other side of the chapel. I dropped my head. Interrupting prayer for anything at all was forbidden.

Sister Margarita was one of the most important and feared nuns at the school and she rarely had time to talk to any student individually, addressing us in large formal assemblies instead. But as we were filing out of the chapel, she touched me on the shoulder and ushered me into a small vestibule away from the others.

In the semi darkness her round, wrinkly face looked down on me. It was as sacred and fragile-looking as the old Bible they kept behind glass in the library. A shaft of light that came in through the half-open door illuminated fine dark hair sprouting over her lips, lips that were smiling when she should have been preparing to reprimand me for my misbehaviour. I braced myself.

'Why were you crying during prayers, Nora?' I was surprised that she knew my name.

I could recite the Lord's Prayer, the Hail Mary and the Act of Contrition, and list the Ten Commandments and the Stations of the Cross without blinking an eye. If she'd asked me to tell her about any of those things, I could have answered confidently. But how could I tell her I was sad about not talking to our maid about Santeria?

I said the only thing that came to mind, the only thing that might save me and my family from the ultimate disgrace of expulsion, which I knew would surely follow. 'I was sad because of what happened to Jesus. It must've hurt really bad when they put those nails in his hands.' My face burned and I thought I might start to cry again.

Sister Margarita smiled a knowing smile, as if that was exactly what she had expected me to say. She bent her head closer to mine so that her dark robes brushed my cheek. 'You know,' she whispered and I smelled the aniseed on her breath, 'we're called in many ways. I sense that a religious life may be in your future. Have you ever thought about that?'

'A religious life?'

She nodded gravely. 'Yes, Nora. Have you ever thought about being a nun?'

My heart beat so fiercely that I thought I might be having a heart attack. Was there a chance that Sister Margarita would sequester me to some secret chamber where I'd be forced to sign my life away on a ready-made contract from heaven? And how did a girl become a nun? I hadn't really thought about it, even though I'd been surrounded by nuns all my life. Surely this was the way it happened. Right here, right now.

'Did you hear what I said?'

'Yes, Sister Margarita.'

'I was about your age when I received the calling, and it scared me a little too.'

'Yes, Sister Margarita.'

'I think I'll talk to your parents about it.' She placed the large hands that she kept tucked under her robes on my shoulders. 'I am right about you, aren't I?'

I braced my knees to stay standing beneath the weight of her hands and took a deep breath. 'Yes, Sister Margarita.'

I lay on my bed, staring up at the ceiling. My parents were devout Catholics. We went to Mass every Sunday, even when it was raining as hard as a hurricane and the windows were rattling in their panes. My mother always looked like the Virgin Mary herself, in a black lace veil that draped over her shoulders as she lit many candles with a long taper. I knew her prayers were for me and Marta and all the people she loved, and she would let me light one, maybe two candles, of my own. We followed all the Catholic rules, like not eating meat on Fridays and making the sign of the cross whenever we passed a church. And Papi and Mami always agreed with the nuns. When they said I should take piano lessons, they agreed. When they said I needed a tutor for maths, they agreed.

A holy life – what did it mean? I wouldn't be able to go to the beach ever again or learn how to roller skate fast downhill without falling. I'd never wear lipstick and high-heeled shoes with smooth stockings. Instead I'd walk along darkened corridors, with hands hidden and head lowered, praying constantly as I practised how to walk without making any noise. And I'd take baths in the dark just in case I saw my body by accident, because everybody knew that nuns weren't allowed to see anybody naked, not even themselves.

There was a soft knock on the door. I knew it was Beba, wondering why I hadn't yet asked her to prepare my afternoon snack.

'What's wrong with you? Aren't you hungry today?'

'No, I don't feel too good.'

'I heard,' Beba said, opening the door wide and narrowing her eyes to a comical glare. 'Your mother said you were faking something this morning to get out of going to school.'

I turned away. It was easy for Beba to make me smile. All she had to do was stare for a while with mock seriousness. It worked every time, but any temptation to smile vanished when I remembered my dilemma.

'OK. Let's see if you got a fever.' She placed her large hand on my forehead and I closed my eyes, comforted by her touch. Everything seemed better when Beba was around. She didn't take anything too seriously, and her solution to most problems involved a good dose of laughter accompanied by something sweet and delicious to eat. The only things Beba took seriously were her religion and politics. When she talked about Batista, her eyes rolled in their sockets so hard I was afraid they'd get lost in the back of her brain somewhere. She hated him with a vengeance and didn't mind who she told. Luckily for her and for us, there weren't any Batista fans in our household.

She removed her hand from my forehead and placed it on her ample hip. 'Well, you don't got a fever. I'll make you some tea anyway. Maybe then you'll eat a little something.'

Beba left and I clutched my pillow. When I became a nun, Beba wouldn't be there to make me tea or take my temperature. Nuns had to do all that for themselves.

Papi arrived home from work at the usual hour, just past seven. He would sit in his chair with the evening paper until Mami called us all for dinner. I knew that sometimes Papi wasn't as agreeable as Mami, and there was a slight chance that if Sister Margarita talked to him alone, he might not agree that I should become a nun. But Papi and Mami rarely went anywhere without each other, and it was a sure thing he'd agree with whatever Mami thought, because he loved her so much. He couldn't stand to see her upset, even for one second. He told her she was beautiful all the time and ran down to buy sugar-cane juice or fresh guayaba whenever we heard the little bells and calls from the street vendors. She'd just flutter her eyelashes at him and he'd jump off his chair and rush to the elevator before the vendors had made their way down the street.

He even told her she was beautiful on the day she tried on the polka-dot two-piece bathing suit. She stretched those two pieces of fabric so hard I was afraid they'd snap like rubber bands. When she was finally into it, her cheeks pink from exertion, Marta giggled and I stared at her in horror and pleaded with her not to show Papi.

'Why shouldn't I let your father see me? I had two children with him.'

'Because you don't look like those ladies on TV, Mami. Maybe he won't love you any more.'

Mami ignored my warning as she evaluated her plump pale body in the full-length mirror. She looked like bread dough that had risen too far out of the pan. I grabbed her hand and pulled her away from the mirror towards the bed, where she'd discarded her dress. There was no doubt in my mind that her best physical attribute was her lovely face, with large dark eyes and long lashes that curled just right at the corners like delicate fans.

'Put your dress back on, Mami. You look really pretty in it.'

She snatched her hand away from me. 'Don't be silly.' Then she marched straight out to the living room, where Papi sat reading his paper, Marta and I following her wiggling bottom.

'Well,' Mami said in a seductive voice as she struck a bathing-beauty pose. 'What do you think?'

Papi's eyes opened wide and he let the newspaper drop to the floor in a heap. 'You're an angel, Regina! A beautiful angel.'

'Not exactly the young girl you married. I'm afraid these two babies changed my figure a little bit.'

'You're more beautiful now than ever, my love.'

Marta and I stared at each other in utter disbelief. This was yet another confirmation of Mami's amazing powers. All she had to do was look at me with those piercing eyes to know what I was thinking, especially if I was thinking something bad. And all she had to do was wink at Papi and smile a little to make him think whatever she wanted him to think. The only people who had more powers than Mami were the nuns; and this was the problem.

I hovered about the other side of Papi's newspaper, waiting to be noticed. He lowered the paper and motioned for me to come closer so he could plant a firm kiss on my forehead. 'How's my girl?'

'Fine, Papi.'

'Will your mother be home soon?'

29

'Yes, she's visiting Tía Maria, but she'll be home soon.'

He returned to his paper and I leaned against the back of his chair and studied the dark gloss of his hair, the matching polish of his shoes. The gold watch Mami had given him for Christmas last year peeked out from beneath his white-cuffed shirt.

I walked around to face him. 'Papi?'

He grunted without looking away from his paper.

'Do you think that priests and nuns are always right?'

'I'm not sure what you mean, Nora. Right about what?'

'You know, like about what to do in life?'

He lowered his paper again, intrigued. 'That's an interesting question. Now that you mention it, I think that's exactly what they're there for – to help us live better lives. The answer is yes, they do know about what we should do in life. Absolutely.'

I dodged Sister Margarita for the rest of the week, but everywhere I turned it seemed her brown steady eyes were hunting me down and trying to capture me in another moment of mysterious understanding. In the chapel, my head hung lower than anybody else's and my lips moved rapidly in constant prayer. Glowing streams of rainbow-coloured light might have swept me off the bench, but I wouldn't have so much as blinked. The Stations of the Cross could have come to life, dancing and singing all around me, and I wouldn't have missed a bead on the rosary.

I began to feel some relief by the end of the week. I'd walked past Sister Margarita in single file twice without her noticing me. Being the head nun, she had many more important matters to attend to than my conversion to a holy life. I was convinced that the whole matter had been forgotten, and by Friday my appetite returned.

'It certainly looks like you're feeling better,' Beba said as she served me an extra piece of guayaba paste and cream cheese. How could I not? I had my life back. Alicia and I could dream once again about being night-club performers with feathers in our hair and long-tail capes. Anything was possible.

3

AFTER CHURCH ON SUNDAY, WE ALWAYS WENT TO MY Great-Aunt Tía Maria's house for lunch. I always looked forward to this, but never more than on this Sunday, when I was still rejoicing in the glory of my escape from nunhood. All the family would be there, cousins, aunts and uncles, gathered for the weekly feast of arroz con pollo and brazo gitano made by Tía Maria. More than anything, I was looking forward to seeing Alicia and telling her about my near miss with a fate worse than death.

As the adults sat outside on the porch playing dominoes, talking over each other, laughing, and occasionally raising their voices about the 'plundering Batista supporters' and the need for 'democratic elections', we'd sneak off and wander about the big house, hiding in wardrobes filled with old clothes and pretending we were eluding an evil man who was trying to kidnap us. Marta would follow us around, with no idea that we'd cast her in the role of the baddy. When she finally figured it out she'd start bawling at the top of her lungs and several adults would come to her rescue, with Mami leading the pack. If Juan, our oldest cousin, was around, we'd allow him to lead us in a rousing yet confusing game of baseball that he was happy to play with his girl cousins because he always won.

Alicia and I were hiding from Marta under the porch when we overheard Mami. 'José, do you remember Sister Margarita?'

'I believe I do,' my father replied. 'She's the sister with the moustache.'

'Seriously now, she called me yesterday and said she wanted to talk to us about Nora.'

'Is there a problem?'

I clamped my hand tight over Alicia's mouth. 'Did you hear that?' I asked her.

She nodded her head and I removed my hand. 'Are you getting in trouble?' she whispered.

'Worse than that. They want to make me a nun!'

The horror registered on her face. 'Why?'

'I don't know. But Sister Margarita thinks I should be a nun and she's going to tell Mami and Papi.'

'How do you become a nun?'

'They send you to a special nun school where they cut off all your hair and fingernails and eyelashes. All you do is pray and light candles and dust the statues of the saints.'

We crept out to the far end of Tía Maria's backyard and crouched behind her biggest rose bush to think about what we were going to do. This was a real problem that required a real solution, and the adult nature of our discussion quickened my pulse. We almost sounded like our parents on the porch when they talked about the government problems in tones that alternated from exuberant to resigned.

'There's only one thing to do,' Alicia said as she tossed a stone from one hand to the other. 'You have to run away. And it has to be today . . . before you go home.'

Alicia and I had fantasized about running away for years. We'd join the circus and learn how to balance on the high wire and ride elephants as though they were ordinary horses. We'd walk along the railroad

33

tracks and live off figs and bananas, our favourite food. We'd build a raft and go anywhere in the world we wanted, starting with New York, where we'd heard everything was bigger and brighter and better.

'Don't worry,' Alicia said, sensing my fear. 'I'll go with you.'

'You will?'

'Of course I will. You need company.'

Marta eventually found us crouching behind the rose bush. She sensed there was something different about our play and began to whine and beg to be let in on our secret, even after we'd banished her and threatened to feed her to the sharks next time we went walking on the malecón. She crept up one last time with an offering in hand: cookies hastily wrapped in a paper napkin. Suddenly, and quite unexpectedly, I felt sorry for her and noticed that her large brown eyes were swimming in tears.

'Our parents will be worried when they can't find us,' I appealed to Alicia. 'After a week, Marta can tell them why we left.'

'Can Marta keep a secret for a week?' Alicia asked, with hands on hips and doubt lurking in her golden eyes.

Marta jumped with every word. 'I can, I can keep a secret for a week! For a whole week!'

We made space for her behind the rose bush and settled ourselves down in the stillness of the late afternoon as we whispered our plans into her ear. She didn't understand at first and giggled as we tried to whisper more loudly. Finally, after three more attempts, there was no doubt she understood, because she started bawling again. 'I don't want you to go away, Nora. I want you to stay with me and Mami and Papi for ever.' She threw her arms around me in a desperate display of affection.

I peeked around the rose bush, expecting to see Mami's high heels marching towards us, but all was clear. Alicia rolled her eyes. 'I knew we shouldn't have told her anything.'

I patted Marta's back. 'Marta, listen. You know all those times we fight because you want to play with my stuff? Now you can play with anything you want and you'll have Beba all to yourself too.'

This seemed to calm her a little. 'I still don't want you to go,' she said more quietly.

'We have to,' Alicia replied for me. 'It's Nora's life if we don't. You don't want her to become a nun, do you?'

Marta shook her head and clasped my hand possessively. Normally I would've wriggled away, but it was very comforting to feel her warm hand neatly tucked into my own.

The three of us walked back towards the house ready to begin the first phase of our plan and Marta pulled on my arm to indicate that she needed to whisper something meant for me alone.

Again, indulging her far beyond what I was accustomed to, I bent down and offered my ear.

She cupped her hands. 'How long is a week?'

We found an empty burlap sack in the pantry normally used for raw sugar and packed the provisions for our escape. The happy sounds of conversation and laughter drifted in from the porch, along with the toasty sweet fragrance of cigars and strong Cuban coffee. Whatever hesitation I felt about our plan had quickly escalated into a quivering sensation in the pit of my stomach. I stood paralysed in the middle of the kitchen that still smelled of Tía Maria's arroz con pollo, with Marta clutching at my hand and taking full advantage of my unusual kindness towards her.

Alicia hummed to herself as she tossed cheese, bread and bananas into the open sack. 'This should do it,' she said brightly, wiping her hands on her skirt. 'We can't make it too heavy or we won't get far.'

I helped her move the sack from the chair onto the floor. 'Do you really think we should go? I mean, you're not the one they're trying to make into a nun.'

Alicia grabbed my shoulder and shook me a little. 'I won't let you go alone.' Her cheeks were flushed and her mouth twitched as she tried to suppress a smile, for she knew it would not be seemly at such a serious moment. Then she turned to Marta, who was watching us with a glum expression, almost on the verge of tears again. 'Now, Marta, when they start looking for us you have to tell them we're playing a hiding game. This will keep them from really looking for a while. You have to be strong, OK?'

Marta nodded and tightened her grip on my hand.

I squeezed my legs together for fear of peeing right there on the floor, wrenched my hand free from Marta and ran to the nearest bathroom. Perhaps if I took long enough, Mami would come looking for us before we had a chance to run away. But as I listened through the open window, I realized they weren't going anywhere soon. They were in the midst of one of those conversations that had grown more animated as the cigars were lit and little cups of cognac passed around. I hoped Papi and Alicia's father, my Uncle Carlos, wouldn't start arguing again. Last time they did, Papi fumed all the way home. He kept talking about 'revolutions' and 'free elections' and 'that bastard Batista' as Mami shushed him to be quiet. I asked him what a revolution was, but he refused to explain and only became more irritated that I'd been listening as Mami shot him a knowing glance.

'This isn't anything you girls need to worry about,' Mami had said in her overly soothing way that really meant I'd stumbled onto something only meant for grown-ups. 'All you need to worry about is doing your school work and being well behaved.'

That was simple enough, and sitting there with my cotton underwear around my ankles I felt anything but curious. Tomorrow morning, as my fifth-grade class was filing into the chapel, there'd be a space between Maria Luisa and Carmen where I should be. Sister Roberta would wonder if I was sick and she'd probably say a special prayer for me to Our Lady of Fatima. And instead of doing my maths problems after lunch, I'd be sitting barefoot on the side of a dusty road eating a banana or a few figs. Then I'd have to look for a place to sleep where the mosquitoes wouldn't get me, or the hairy spiders of the jungle.

Alicia and Marta were waiting for me at the back door. Alicia had slung the food sack over her back and waved several pesos at me as though she were a Spanish señorita flirting with her fan.

'Where did you get all that money?'

'I went through the handbags on the bed,' she said, fanning herself with the cash and batting her eyelashes prettily. Marta giggled at Alicia's antics and tried to jump and reach for the money, but Alicia raised it over her head, out of Marta's reach. 'Hey, don't touch. We need this money to survive.

My palms began to sweat and my mouth went dry. 'Put it back. You're going to get in so much trouble if you don't.'

'We're leaving. We can't get in trouble any more.' Alicia's golden eyes were filled with resolve and she stuffed the cash into her pocket.

I looked over at Marta, hoping for the first time in my life that she'd tattle on what I was about to do, but she no longer looked so sad. Alicia's thievery had titillated her senses and moved her to new thresholds of excitement. She even opened the back door for us, honoured to be participating in our escape in some way.

Outside the evening breeze was heavy with moisture and the mysterious buzzing sounds of the night: crickets and thick-winged beetles that could smack you on the face if you didn't watch out.

Alicia was impatient. 'Come on. Pretty soon they'll say it's time to go home because tomorrow's a school day.' She stepped out into the night. The porch light reflected softly off the undulating waves of her hair; a few wisps escaped her ribbon and unfurled in the breeze. 'Come on,' she whispered loudly, not turning around but tiptoeing down the back steps like a burglar, the sack of food bouncing on her back.

I followed her across Tía Maria's yard, an anxious spirit being led to the edge of the world by a girl with messy golden hair and bobby socks. We padded our way across the grass, beneath the darkening sky sparkling with stars and veiled by the delicate pink remnants of a dying sun.

We plunged forward into the restless night and reached the fence that separated Tía's yard from the rest of the world. We'd never been allowed to go any further than this, yet Alicia had already lifted one leg boldly over the fence with barely a thought. I stood back and allowed the force of my fears to untangle the words and feelings stuck in my throat. If I didn't say anything now, I never would.

I touched Alicia's arm as she reached for the sack of food. 'I think we should go back.' My voice was quiet, yet clarified with a knowing that I did not completely understand myself.

Alicia turned to face me, and in the thin starlight I saw fear crouching in her eyes. She looked away again, but didn't move any further over the fence.

We stood at the edge of the world, our bag of provisions between us, Alicia's leg still propped on the fence, as we contemplated the rest of our lives. Then I heard Mami calling for me from the porch. She was in a good mood and the sound of her voice warmed my insides with nostalgia, as if I had already been away from home for years and was reliving a precious memory of my previous life, the only thing I had left of it. It took all my energy to keep from running back as fast as I could.

'Don't be so scared,' Alicia said.

'I'm not . . . I just . . .'

Mami's good mood was quickly eroding. 'Marta, where's your sister?' This was followed by Marta's anxious and squeaky reply, which I couldn't quite make out, but it was unconvincing even from such a distance.

Alicia took hold of the sack of food and swung her leg off the fence. 'Maybe if we wait until next week we could take more stuff with us.'

Papi's voice boomed over the night sounds. 'Nora, you get over here this instant!'

We bolted back across the yard and up the steps of the back porch in five seconds flat, almost losing our shoes in the process. We opened the back door cautiously and peeked in to find the kitchen empty, but the growing agitation of the adults was clearly audible in the front room. Alicia silently motioned for me to go in and face the adults alone while she took care of returning the food and money. There was no time to argue.

My lies had known little success in the past and my heart throbbed as I entered the living room. Marta was huddled in the corner of the couch with a cushion over her face, sobbing uncontrollably. My uncles and aunts were circled around her and Mami was kneeling on the floor, her face twisted in an anxious knot.

I took a deep breath and attempted to look innocent. 'I'm here, Mami.'

She turned towards me with dark, devouring eyes. 'For God's sake, where have you been?'

Marta threw the cushion aside at the sound of my voice and sprang off the couch, flinging her arms around me for the second time in one day, with a confusion of sobs and words no one could understand.

'What have you done to your sister?'

I threw my arms around Marta and buried my nose in her hair, which smelled of lilacs and cigar smoke. Alicia's parents, Uncle Carlos and Tía Nina, stood together in the doorway.

'If you know what's good for you, you'll answer me this instant, young lady.'

'We weren't doing anything. We were just ... playing.'

'What were you playing to upset your sister so much?'

I stared back at my mother's face and felt guilt gurgling up from the soles of my feet. I had just opened my mouth to tell all about our plans to escape when Alicia skipped into the room, laughing and calling out, 'I won! I won, Nora! Now it's Marta's turn to hide.'

Alicia's parents stepped forward. 'Were you playing hide-and-seek, honey?'

'Yes. It was really fun and I won.'

'You see, Regina? It was just a game, you can relax,' Uncle Carlos said, placing a soothing hand on Mami's shoulder.

Mami considered his appeal briefly, but then turned on me with fresh doubts. 'If it was just a simple game of hide-and-seek, then why was your sister so frightened?

'Because,' Alicia piped up, 'we told her that if she couldn't find us it meant we had turned into ghosts and that we'd come back and haunt her for the rest of her life. I think that scared her too much.'

'I should say so,' Mami said, scooping Marta up in her arms and flashing me one of those looks that meant I'd go straight to my room when we got home. But at least I was going home. I'd hug my pillow all night long and Beba's laugh would wake me in the morning like it always did.

We drove home in silence and Marta fell asleep with her head on my lap. I let my own head fall back on the seat while I stared out at the darkness through the windshield. The lights bordering the malecón whizzed past like angry comets rising up from the sea as the motor's drone lulled me into a semi sleep. I heard the rush of the waves, and distant voices calling me from the deep.

My parents spoke in hushed tones to one another. 'Carlos doesn't know what he's talking about,' my father said. 'People wouldn't support a revolution right now. The economy is too strong, too many people are making money like they never have before.'

'People like us are making money . . . but Carlos wasn't talking about people like us.'

'I'm not saying it's all perfect.'

'Then what are you saying, José?'

'It's not enough – a few rebels in the hills making trouble. I want Batista out as much as anybody, but it won't happen like that. I just hope that crazy brother of mine doesn't do anything foolish.'

'I hope not,' Mami says.

A few more minutes of silence captured in the drone of the motor. Papi spoke again. 'I think Nora spends too much time with Alicia.'

'Oh, I don't know. Alicia's a good girl. She's very clever and pretty.'

'Too clever and too pretty, I'd say. I don't like the way Carlos and Nina are bringing her up, spoiling her the way they do. She's too free spirited for her own good and I don't want her to influence Nora. Maybe that's what this meeting at the school is all about.'

'Sister Margarita assured me Nora wasn't in trouble.'

It was my father's turn to say, 'I hope not.'

Free spirited – what wonderful words. I closed my eyes and the lights of the malecón glowed through my eyelids, pink and purple and green, and I thought of long sunny days at the beach with nothing to do but swim, roll in the sand and drink ice-cold cokes. And there was the corner ice-cream stand, El Tropicream, crowded with laughing children who had ice cream painted all round their happy mouths like clowns at the circus.

I was there, too, hanging in a birdcage from the highest palm, somewhere between heaven and earth, wearing a black dress all the way down to my ankles and praying that a swift wind would come and knock me back down to the sand where I belonged.

We passed under the gentle gaze of the Virgin. Her statue, holding rosary beads that lit up at night, was perched on top of the main gate of El Angel de la Guardia School and welcomed all who entered. In years of passing under her, this was the first time I had prayed for her intercession. 'Please, dear Virgin, let Sister Margarita be sick today. It doesn't have to be a serious illness, just something small that can only be treated in New York or Chicago or some place really far away.'

Marta kissed Mami and Papi goodbye, then ran off towards her classroom, the red ribbon in her hair streaming behind her like a kite tail. 'Remember to walk,' a normally silent sister said when Marta whizzed past her; she slowed down to a brisk walk until she was outside, then raced to her classroom faster than before.

The three of us were escorted past the formal salons where the piano recitals and graduation luncheons were held, down a dark wood-panelled corridor. At the very end was Sister Margarita's office, the only office in the school with double doors. I imagined it to be full of wondrous and exotic things. Instead I was surprised to find a simple yet spacious room, filled with hundreds of leather-bound books on shelves reaching from floor to ceiling. The only magnificent thing was the enormous arched window, behind a large desk strewn with stacks of papers and the occasional sweet wrapper.

Through the bevelled glass students could be seen

filing to class, and for once I longed to be with them instead of sitting there on a straight wooden chair where my feet didn't quite touch the floor.

Mami and Papi watched me curiously, while talking about our new neighbours who had moved in three floors down. They'd asked me several times what the meeting was about, but I didn't have the nerve to tell them. I wanted to stall my fate as long as possible. I'd lost the battle of the piano lessons and the maths tutor but I wasn't about to lose this one, and I needed more time to figure out my strategy.

Sister Margarita entered the office through a small door between the bookshelves, and floated silently across the floor. She sat at her desk and folded her hands in a smooth and commanding gesture of sacred authority. With sunlight streaming in through the window behind her, she looked like an archangel guarding the entrance to heaven.

'Has Nora told you why I asked you to come in today?' she asked.

'No, she hasn't,' my mother replied.

Sister Margarita turned to me. 'Would you like to tell them now, child?'

My throat was tight and dry. I gripped the seat of my chair. I couldn't speak. I could only shake my head and swing my legs back and forth.

'Would you like me to tell them?' Sister Margarita smiled down on me and I was momentarily awestruck. A smile from Sister Margarita was a gift bestowed on precious few, and for a split second I thought I should just go ahead and become a nun so as not to disappoint her. I nodded that she could speak for me and felt an intense heat rising up from the furnace in my stomach.

She looked at my parents, glowing with pride. 'It seems that little Nora has been called.'

'Called?' Papi asked with a half smile.

Mami leaned forward in her chair and touched my

knee lightly to stop me from swinging my legs. 'We don't understand, Sister.'

'I've been watching Nora for many months now and I believe she's been called to follow Christ in a holy life.' Sister Margarita's words rang clearly like a bell striking the hour, and her eyes lifted towards the ceiling as if she were in ecstasy.

I dared not follow her gaze lest I see the face of God Himself confirming my appointment. I felt dizzy. I gripped the chair tighter and looked straight ahead, past Sister Margarita's smiling face and out of the window, towards the girls laughing in the sun. A bright beam of light hit my eyes directly, but I couldn't even blink as tears began to well in them.

All three were watching me now. My parents appeared startled, as if they'd never seen me before. Sister Margarita looked as if she expected me to sprout wings and a halo.

Papi broke the silence. 'Is this true, Nora? Do you want to be a nun?'

I blinked once and looked at him, then over at Sister Margarita, whose smile had only intensified in sweetness. How could I disappoint her? She seemed so sure I wanted to be like her and not a chorus girl with bright pink feathers sticking out of my head, or a wife and mother who dressed her babies in soft embroidered clothes.

Mami's neatly painted brows lifted in a curious arch and she placed her hand on Papi's arm when he was about to speak again.

My bottom lip began to quiver. I tried to make it stop, but the more I tried the worse it became. No longer able to tolerate their probing gaze, I dropped my head. I saw Mami's high-heeled shoes press down on the floor as she moved to stand, but I jumped down from my chair and ran across the room before she could reach me. Flinging open the office door, I raced down the corridor and burst out of the main doors, nearly knocking over Sister Roberta in the process.

'Nora, what's the matter?' I heard her call after me as I jumped down the steps two at a time, not stopping until I reached the lawn below. I stood with my back to the school, panting and staring at the sliver of ocean that glinted through the pastel collage of buildings before me. I could keep running past the gates and under the Virgin and never again return. I could find my way to Alicia's school and convince her to leave with me now. The train tracks didn't seem so bad, after all. A few nights in the jungle wouldn't kill me.

I heard spongy footsteps on the grass behind me. With his long legs, Papi could walk almost as fast as I could run. He turned me around by my shoulders and crouched down so we were at eye level. 'No one's going to force you to do something you're not happy with.'

I looked into Papi's dark eyes and breathed in the reassuring smell of his aftershave.

'Do you really want to be a nun like Sister Margarita?' he asked, with a slight shake to my shoulders.

My answer came out with such force that I almost knocked him over onto the grass. 'No, Papi. I don't want to be a nun ever! I think Sister Margarita wants to steal me away to a secret nun school.'

'Don't be silly. Even if you wanted to be a nun, you couldn't really begin to study seriously until you were much older.'

By now Mami had begun her tiptoeing journey across the lawn, taking care not to spike her heels in. Sister Margarita stood in the doorway of the main entrance, but she didn't come down the steps to join us and although she was too far away for me to read her expression, I knew she was no longer smiling.

Mami looked down on us, squinting in the morning sun and searching for her sunglasses in her bag. 'Nora, running away like that was extremely rude. I want you

45

to go and apologize to Sister Margarita immediately.'

A huge weight began to lift off my shoulders as we made our way back across the lawn.

'She doesn't want to be a nun, Regina,' my father said.

'Of course she doesn't,' Mami snapped. 'Who ever heard of a nine-year-old nun?'

4

TÍA PANCHITA WAS MY GREAT-AUNT ON MY FATHER'S SIDE. She had a great head of silvery hair she pulled into a tight bun at the nape of her neck, and she wore thick cat's-eye glasses that made her eyes so huge it was possible to count the flecks of green in the brown, like leaves floating on a murky river. She lived alone in a sprawling house on a sugar-cane plantation in the heart of the island near a little town called Guines. I always knew we were getting close when the car started rattling over roads that were either unpaved or rarely repaired. As Marta and I sang and laughed our voices bumped along, making us sound like tipsy opera singers, while Papi cursed and predicted the need for new shock absorbers when we got back to Havana. Trees stretched their limbs overhead, occasionally dipping to brush the car roof in greeting.

Tía Panchita had never had children and her husband died many years before I was born. She explained to us, while pointing to his elegant portrait over the piano, that he'd been a very important man because he'd used the most modern technology and was known to have the best-quality sugar cane for miles around.

It was strange that an important man like him should die from a mosquito bite. It became infected and they ended up having to cut off his leg, but they weren't able to save him even then. Tía told us this story many times, and whenever I looked at the picture of him sitting with his legs crossed, a Panama hat resting casually on his knee, I was tempted to ask her which one they cut off. Of course I never had the nerve, but one day Marta did it for me. And Tía didn't, as I expected, collapse in a pool of tears. She simply blinked her enormous eyes once and said, 'You know, I truly can't remember.'

In Guines, everybody knew everybody. And nothing was liked better than lounging on the wide porches for most of the warm days, waving to friends and conversing with whoever decided to stop by for a cup of Cuban coffee or a cold glass of guarapo. The only problem with this was that Tía always insisted we look as though we were going out for a party, even if we were just relaxing and going nowhere at all. This way, she said, she could impress whatever visitors she had with her beautiful sobrinitas.

Although we'd been visiting Tía Panchita ever since we could remember, it was only when I was eleven and Marta nine that we were allowed to spend the night there by ourselves. By then our parents thought our manners were good enough to render us pleasant company for an old and elegant person like Tía Panchita. It also helped that Tía was always asking, 'When are the girls going to visit me?' When she said 'girls' she meant Alicia too – sometimes she forgot that the three of us weren't sisters, which delighted us all the more.

Tía usually gave Marta and me the room right next to hers. It had two very high double beds, surrounded by a cloud of mosquito netting that she pulled aside during the day with a satin sash. The sheets were white linen that she'd embroidered herself during endless hours of drinking coffee and rocking back and forth on the porch.

All the rooms were interconnected, just like a train,

and every room had a door that led to the porch, and the fields and forest beyond. To get to the kitchen from our bedroom we had to walk through Tía Panchita's room, then through the empty bedroom, then the dining room and the big living room, and finally we'd get there. The only way to do it any faster was to run along the porch until you found the door you needed. Marta and I had fun opening and closing doors and Tía Panchita didn't seem to mind as long as she knew where we were. She told us that the old house had been in the family for generations, ever since the war with Spain in the mid 1800s, and that we could explore and do as we liked as long as we didn't mind running into the occasional ghost.

'What if we do?' we'd ask her, horrified.

'Just offer him a good cup of coffee. That usually takes the fight out of ghosts and people alike.'

But most of the time we preferred to be with Tía Panchita, sitting on the porch and watching the people who came by to visit her. Visitors who came on horseback especially fascinated us. They'd swing off their horses and tie them to the porch railings, then sip coffee with Tía and make conversation for hours. Marta and I took turns inching up to the horses and daring each other to touch their velvet muzzles, which were so unpredictable with their constant chewing and sudden snorts. We'd jump back, giggling nervously, before we inched forward again, only to be startled into another round of giggles. Alicia had the nerve to approach the horses with a steady calm and stroke their noses lovingly, while whispering sweet talk that made them still.

'This one doesn't act like a city girl,' the visitors commented approvingly.

Like everybody else, Tía Panchita had a black maid, but sometimes it was hard to tell who was the maid and who was the patrona. Lola, a slight woman of about Tía's age with wiry salt-and-pepper hair, came every morning before anyone was up and started the coffee. Sometimes she made bread and sometimes she brought it already made from the bakery. Either way it smelled delicious.

Marta and I loved to sit in the kitchen with Lola and watch her make butter. First she skimmed the cream off the top of the milk and then she'd add salt and stir it for hours. Lola wasn't a talker like Beba. Mostly she liked to listen, which was great for Marta, who'd chatter her ear off about silly things. But Lola always appeared to be interested, nodding her head and widening her eyes when Marta asked her, 'And then guess what happened?' I'd have lost interest long ago and figured Lola would have too, but she must have really been listening because most of the time she guessed right.

Often Tía would burst into the kitchen and snatch the spoon from Lola. 'Lola, I've told you before there's no need to make butter from scratch. I can buy it already made and you're too old to be working so hard.'

Lola would shake her salt-and-pepper head and chuckle, complaining that store-bought butter wasn't the same. I agreed.

Both women would sit out on the porch together for hours, each in her own wicker rocker, talking and laughing and greeting visitors like a pair of old hens. They'd take turns preparing refreshments, and if they were too tired they'd enlist our help, issuing directions through the open kitchen window. We'd emerge from the house feeling quite accomplished, as we balanced trays of coffee cups, spoons, sugar, cookies and guayaba paste.

When night fell and most of the visiting was over, Tía Panchita and Lola always ended the day in the same way. Tía went inside and took the wooden cigar box from the shelf in the dining room, then placed it on the little table between their rocking chairs. She insisted that Lola select first. They'd roll the cigars between their fingers and tap them next to their ears. Then they'd light each other's cigar and puff and rock for at least another hour, until the stars made their appearance in the blue-black sky above.

On one of our visits, just as the cigar ritual was about to begin, Alicia's parents dropped her off to spend the rest of the week with us. Tía was delighted, and together she and Lola moved the rollaway bed into the large bedroom that Marta and I shared. With Alicia's bed right next to mine, the mosquito netting could easily cover us both.

When it was time for bed and Lola had gone, Tía tucked us in. But before she arranged the mosquito netting and inspected it for holes, she locked the doors leading outside. It took quite some time, because every room had an identical door that required bolting with a heavy wooden plank. Echoes sounded throughout the house each time she dropped a plank into place. She secured the windows in similar fashion, except for those that were locked with a metal latch which was easy to close. Once she was finished, she checked every door and window again to make sure she hadn't forgotten one. The entire process took almost half an hour.

'It looks like you're getting ready for a hurricane,' I said.

Tía sat down on my bed and looked at the three of us with her magnified eyes. 'It's worse than that. Listen.'

At first I heard nothing but the chirping of crickets that always comes up as the sun goes down. Then I heard it – a quiet, rhythmic thunder that seemed to emanate from the ground all around us, everywhere and nowhere at once. My heart beat a little faster to the quickening sounds of what I knew to be the African drums, as they grew louder and faster.

Alicia jumped from her bed onto mine and scrambled underneath my covers. 'Tell us about the drums, Tía,' she begged, even though we had all heard talk of these before. We knew the stories of people falling to the ground overcome by evil spirits and writhing like snakes. Those were the lucky ones. The less fortunate were turned into goats or even into rocks and trees. The most frightening stories were of the bloody sacrifices. They'd kill chickens and pigs and . . . and white children, who'd misbehaved so badly that their parents didn't want them any more.

Marta threw her covers off and ran over to sit on Tía Panchita's frail lap. She clung to her like a baby, and I rolled my eyes, although a chill had crept up the back of my neck as well.

Tía stroked Marta's hair. 'Don't be afraid, little one. I was teasing you. Those are just the drums of the Santeros. They're playing loudly tonight. It's the music of Africa from long ago and the black people believe it has special powers.'

'What kind of powers?' Alicia asked.

Tía thought carefully. 'They're powers I don't completely understand. But if you're afraid when you hear the drums you must say the Our Father and Hail Mary and pray for Papa Dios to keep you safe. You have to say it over and over again until you fall asleep. Come now, get into bed and we'll say it together.'

Marta scrambled back into her own bed and we pulled our linen sheets up under our chins and put our hands together. We prayed softly over the beat of the drums, which sounded deep and full, as one would expect the heart of the jungle to sound in far-off Africa. We tried to ignore the intoxicating rhythm that forced us to pray to its exotic cadence.

'Our Father,' (boom) 'Who art in Heaven,' (boom) 'Hallowed be Thy name' (boom boom) . . . Our prayers had never sounded so beautiful before. I wanted to say them again and sing in a loud voice. For the first time,

I wanted to dance to the Hail Mary and sing my Amens in keeping with the joyful and mystic glory of the drums. All at once, I was rushing barefoot through the green canopy of the countryside, hungry for the wild spirit to take me and teach me the ways of the underworld. The place Beba had told me about had to be beautiful, and sleep must come easily in a place where dreams followed the rhythms of the night.

'Good night, my dear sobrinitas,' I heard Tía Panchita say as she closed the mosquito netting and turned out the light.

Ever since I was a little girl, I had wondered what it would be like to become a woman. I'd imagined the transformation would happen gradually, in the same way that a rosebud opens its petals one by one until the fullness of its splendour is revealed. And when I asked Mami and Beba if this was so, they confirmed that it was, then quickly changed the subject. But that's not how it happened for Alicia. Alicia became a woman all at once, before my eyes, and after that day she was never quite the same.

It was the next morning, and we were sitting on Tía Panchita's sun-flooded porch, chatting in the warmth and watching the wasps hover about the empty guarapo glasses that were still on the steps. Tía and Lola were rocking in their chairs, drinking coffee and commenting on the unusual heat of the day.

'We won't get many visitors today,' said Tía, squinting out at the road through foggy glasses.

'Anyone who has any sense will stay indoors,' Lola agreed.

It was then that we saw the outline of a young man on horseback take shape beyond the heat of the dusty road. He looked like a wavering ghost, floating in a brown haze. At first we couldn't be sure he was riding towards us, but with a flick of his wrist he deftly manoeuvred his auburn horse onto the narrow path that led up to the house. As ignorant as we were about horses and as far away as we were from this particular specimen, we could tell that it was not like the other horses we'd seen. It was young and full of fire, the kind of horse only an expert should ride.

'Tony! Hola, Tony!' Lola stood up from her rocker and waved both hands at him.

'It's nice he's come. It's been a while,' Tía Panchita said, gathering the empty glasses together and tidying up a little for this new visitor – new to us, at least.

The young man rode his horse up to the railings and in one smooth motion swung his leg over and dropped to the ground. The auburn horse raised his great head in protestation at being tied up and not allowed to munch on the grass beneath his hooves. Even I could see that this was a horse that needed to move and run, not watch people nibble on cookies. I was fascinated by the clean perfection of his muzzle and spirited precision of his every move, so fascinated that at first I didn't notice the amazing young man who'd been riding him.

But when I did, I no longer paid any attention to the horse. Tony was beyond beautiful. His mulatto skin was the colour of burnished gold; I imagined that if I touched the tip of my tongue to his cheek it would taste of honey. His light eyes were the colour of the shallow sea close to shore, where the water turns blue to turquoise to blue again, and they held a dreamy sort of gaze, as though he were contemplating pleasant thoughts.

He bounded up the steps of the porch two at a time, clearly comfortable with his body and unaware that his every move possessed a grace and strength beyond that of ordinary people, and kissed Lola and Tía Panchita warmly on the cheek. I don't remember what he said, only that his voice was deep – but not deep like Papi's, for there was a sweetness suggesting that boyhood hadn't completely left him. Yet the width of his shoulders and the hint of the well-muscled body underneath his clothes left no doubt that he was not like our same-age boy cousins whom we could still push around with encouraging success.

He hadn't noticed us staring at him and I preferred to watch from a safe distance, fearful that the strange sensations coursing through my body should become noticeable. An unusual warmth had collected in the very deepest part of my belly and floated down to create a tingling between my legs I'd never felt before. It was like the heat of being discovered in a fib, but strangely pleasant and reminiscent of the intoxicating rhythm of the drums.

Alicia straightened her skirt, smoothed her hair back with one hand and walked straight up to the grown-ups without a word to Marta and me. Tony was sitting with his back to us when Alicia introduced herself and we could see her above the broad curve of his shoulder.

Her face glowed and her lips were shining and red, as if she'd just eaten fresh strawberries and hadn't bothered to wipe her mouth. Several strands of hair had escaped her ponytail and framed her face like corkscrewed ribbons of gold. Her golden-green eyes were swimming with allure and confidence as she rested one hand on her hip and played with a strand of hair that had fallen over her shoulder with the other. Never before had I noticed the swelling beneath her blouse or the way her hips flared when she put more weight on one leg like she was doing. Alicia had walked to the other side of the porch and become a woman.

'Come over and meet Lola's nephew,' Tía Panchita called over to Marta and me.

We dragged ourselves over to the other side of the porch, but there was no similar transformation in store for me. I felt fantastically awkward when Tony stood and offered me his hand in greeting. It was firm and slightly callused, and his touch and gaze together rendered me speechless. Marta giggled and asked questions about his horse, while I attempted to strike the same sort of womanly pose as Alicia had, but my socks had fallen down to my ankles and my blouse, which Tía had reminded me to tuck into my skirt, billowed about, effectively hiding any semblance of a waist. And when Tony smiled at me and winked one of those incredible eyes in my direction, I felt my knees turn to jelly and my tongue to stone.

'Tony, why were the drums so loud last night?' Panchita asked.

Tony's eyes twinkled with amusement. 'Were you scared, Doña Panchita?'

'I certainly was. I thought Satan himself was dancing on my bed. I could hardly sleep!'

At this both Lola and Tony laughed, and I noticed that Tony's teeth were perfectly straight and white. Mami always said that black people had the best-quality teeth of any race. She also said that mulatto people are sometimes the most beautiful because they have the best features from both the black and white.

'Don't be scared. Satan was far away last night. They were preparing for the initiation ceremony tonight.' Tony was still laughing as he said this, and even though he was talking with Tía, he was turned towards Alicia.

'Oh dear Lord, that means there will be more drums tonight! I need some more coffee, good and strong this time.' Tía left to prepare the coffee and Alicia swiftly sat in her rocking chair.

She crossed her legs and fingered the hem of her skirt. 'Will you be there tonight?'

Tony's smile was soft, and his voice softer still. 'I'll be there.'

'And what will you do?'

'I'll dance with friends . . . have a good time.'

'I bet you're a good dancer.'

Tony's smile lit up once again and for a moment he seemed to lose his composure as his gaze quickly swept across Alicia from head to toe, lingering on her bare knees which now pointed straight at him, ever so slightly parted so that only the finest writing paper could have passed between them, but parted nonetheless. It happened so fast that in a blink I would've missed it. But I didn't miss it, nor the slight trembling of Alicia's hand when she swept an errant strand of hair behind her ear.

I felt suddenly guilty, and was turning to join Marta who was slowly inching her way towards Tony's horse when Tía Panchita returned, balancing a tray loaded with cookies and three cups of coffee. Tony stood up and helped her with the tray, but then expressed his apologies, saying he had business to take care of in town. I was glad to hear it.

With hasty goodbyes to all and a lingering smile for Alicia, he sprang back on his horse and headed down the path. He was almost at the road when Alicia snatched a handful of cookies and hastily wrapped them in a napkin. She jumped down the steps and ran after him, and even though his horse shied a little, she didn't hesitate as she reached up to offer him the cookies. When he took them from her she didn't release them right away and their hands touched. I saw this, too, even though I was pretending to be distracted by the horse dropping that Marta was pointing out to me and listening to her chatter about the hay sticking out of it.

I was glad to see the shiny bronze rear of the horse, its tail swishing like a broom as they headed out. And I was relieved when the strange sensations I'd felt since Tony's arrival began to fade and I was myself again. Alicia, however, seemed possessed, and alternated between melancholy and jubilation for the rest of the day. She ignored Marta and me, preferring to sit with Tía Panchita and Lola on the porch all afternoon, asking them endless questions about Tony. How old was he, where had he learned to ride so well, what kind of business did he have in the city, what word would best describe the colour of his eyes. She must've spent an entire hour pondering this one, finally concluding that they were the colour of the sky at twilight, just before the stars appeared.

Marta and I attempted to entice her with a walk through the sugar-cane fields or a game of dominoes, but she turned us down, gazing out towards the road Tony had taken into town.

Eventually, when Alicia was convinced that she'd learned everything she could from Lola and Tía Panchita, she stood up from her chair, sighed loudly and wandered back into the house, smiling to herself and humming along to music only she could hear.

'I believe your niece is in love,' Lola said as she helped herself to the last of the cookies on the tray.

Tía Panchita nodded and chewed her own cookie pensively. 'No doubt about it.'

That night we said our prayers over the drums once more. They were louder this time and faster too. It was easy to imagine the dancers swirling around a huge bonfire, their giant shadows playing against the trees, the beads around their necks swinging and catching the light like miniature planets on a frenetic orbit. I imagined their heads wrapped in hand-kerchiefs, some all in white like Beba, dipping and swaying to the hypnotic rhythm. Even from such a distance, it was impossible to keep from moving my toes under the sheet to the delicious beat that pounded out its cry like a wounded heart, begging to be loved, trading life for the promise of seduction. Any price could be paid for a moment of bliss. That's what Beba said, and even though I had little idea what she was talking about, I liked the sound of it better than anything else.

As soon as Tía turned out the lights, Marta's breathing grew heavy and regular. But I sensed that Alicia was still awake, waiting in the dark and holding her breath. I'd been angry with her ever since Tony left and had refused to answer her when, posing in front of the mirror, she'd asked me which way I preferred her hair: up in a ponytail or loose around her shoulders. I looked over at her bed, but she was lying well below the only stream of moonlight that came through the window slats, and I couldn't see her.

I closed my eyes. The sound of the drums slipped into my dreams and the anger began to melt away with the promise of a new day. Surely tomorrow things would be as they always were. After breakfast, we'd sit on the porch and invent a new game to play. Marta would follow us into the sugar-cane fields and Tía would warn us not to get dirty just in case visitors came by. A smile had already curled the corners of my lips when I heard Alicia speak to me. At first I thought I might be dreaming, because her voice was so soft. But I heard it again, a desperate whisper, 'Nora, I'm going there.'

I opened my eyes to see her sitting up in bed, her face glowing in the thin ray of moonlight, her eyes huge with excitement. She was wearing the white dress she normally wore to Mass on Sundays.

'Why are you dressed like that?'

'I'm going to the drums. I'm going to see Tony.'

I couldn't believe it. Going to the drums? Going to see Tony? The huge doors of Tía's house were locked and bolted, every one of them. And the drums . . . the drums were not for us.

I was about to protest when she leaned over and placed her hand over my mouth and I tasted the bitterness of Tía Panchita's expensive perfume on her fingers. 'Be quiet and don't bother trying to talk me out of it. I have to see Tony. I know you don't understand.'

She was right. I couldn't begin to understand what

would possess her to go out into the night and risk her life to see this man, any man. She was still a child. Yet at that moment, sitting in the moonlight with her hair loose around her shoulders, she looked remarkably like a full-grown woman. It wasn't her face or the emerging maturity of her body, but the expression in her eyes: determined, self-assured and glowing with a light from within.

She removed her hand from my mouth. 'You're going now? In the middle of the night?' I whispered.

'I know Tony will be there. You can come with me if you want.'

I shook my head, horrified at the prospect of venturing out into the night. This was beyond the realm of forbidden, far worse than our old plan to run away. It was lethal to the soul. 'I . . . I can't go.'

Alicia moved aside the covers, smoothing out her skirt, and I noticed she was already wearing shoes, but no bobby socks, her bare ankles reflecting the moonlight. Silently, she approached the door leading outside to the porch and the field beyond. Placing her hands on the heavy wooden plank, she paused briefly, then lifted the plank deftly and leaned it against the wall without the slightest sound. Marta did not stir, despite the creaking of the floorboards and the groaning of the door which Alicia slowly, almost imperceptibly, opened.

The sound of the drums flooded our bedroom. Alicia stood breathless for an instant, before stepping over the threshold and slipping out into the night.

Although it was warm and humid, I trembled beneath the covers for what seemed like hours. I stayed in bed, straining my eyes against the dark and praying as intently as any nun could have prayed, abandoning the verses I'd memorized over the years and speaking to God in my own words in a desperate plea for help. But mostly I just listened to the sounds drifting in through the night. Were those footsteps outside? Had Alicia come to her senses and returned, or were her captors searching out fresh victims?

I shut my eyes again. 'Make this nightmare go away, Papa Dios,' I prayed fervently. 'Please make it go away and let the sun come up over the ridge of the green mountains so we can have our café con leche like we always do and play dominoes on the porch.'

But the drums grew louder, to what I had no doubt was the rhythm of death. They'd captured Alicia and were preparing her for sacrifice. Tony was smiling and his ghostly green eyes gleaming at the sight of his perfect prey. How could I just lie there and allow this terrible thing to happen? I had to rescue Alicia. She would do as much for me, I knew she would.

I pushed back the covers and emerged from the mosquito netting, my knees quivering as I searched for my slippers under the bed. With excruciating caution, I walked to the door and stuck my nose out. The air was cool and forbidding now that the wind had changed, and the sounds of the drums vibrated through the air, the trees, the ground and every blade of grass.

Out on the porch, I surveyed the shadows of the night. All was dark and misty green. Stars blanketed the tropical sky. I looked back into the room to make sure Marta hadn't stirred, and proceeded to step slowly off the porch. I made it to the second step, knowing there were three more to go. And then what? The vast field lay ahead of me, then the grove of trees that were shadowed even in the daylight. Beyond these was San Nicolas, an all-black village where Lola lived, and Tony, no doubt. Alicia would have taken the dirt path through the woods, and if I wanted to find her I had to allow myself to be swallowed by the void of blackness before me.

Then I saw movement. Black upon black, moving and shifting. Was Alicia returning? My heart leapt with the possibility and I almost called out. But what if it wasn't Alicia? What if it was one of the evil spirits of the night that Beba had told me about? Cutting onions and green peppers in the bright sunny kitchen, I was never afraid; but here in the clutches of the night, while everyone slept, an evil spirit could easily devour me.

After several minutes of heart-stopping paralysis, I saw the movement in the blackness get closer, bobbing up and down in a familiar way that I would've found comforting if I wasn't frozen with fear. It was Alicia, walking absent-mindedly, as if kicking shells on the beach. Her loose hair floated on the night air, catching the light of the stars. She didn't see me, and I would have yelled at her to hurry if I hadn't been frightened of waking Marta and Tía Panchita.

When Alicia finally did look up, she froze and gasped faintly. Then she realized it was me and quickened her step. I looked behind her to see if anyone or anything was following her, but she was quite alone.

'What took you so long?' My fear had turned to anger.

She half smiled when she spoke. 'I was with Tony. He kissed me.'

Her lips were swollen, as if she'd eaten something she was allergic to.

'On the lips?' I asked, incredulous. Only grown-ups kissed on the lips.

Alicia nodded and rubbed her eyes. She walked past me and opened the door casually, as if she'd just returned from a long and relaxing day at the beach. She kicked off her shoes and pulled her dress up over her head, letting it drop to the floor in a heap. Then she fell into bed and was instantly asleep.

Taking care to re-bolt the door without making any noise, I hung Alicia's dress back in the wardrobe and tiptoed about the room, arranging everything just as it had been when Tía turned out the lights a lifetime ago.

She'd never know anything had happened. Alicia was back and everything would be all right.

When I awoke, I could tell by the way the sun shone full and bright on the wooden floor that it was almost halfway up the sky. Marta and Alicia's beds were empty and I could hear the sounds of plates and spoons clinking over breakfast in the kitchen.

I kicked the mosquito netting open and ran out to the kitchen, to find Tía and Lola fussing over the coffee and the bread and butter as usual. Marta had her elbows on the table and was munching happily on a steaming slice of bread dripping with butter.

'Where's Alicia?' I asked, noticing that a place hadn't been set for her.

Tía didn't look at me, and Lola silently pulled out my chair and started to butter a piece of bread for me.

'Your Uncle Carlos came for her early this morning,' Tía finally said.

I was shocked. 'But she was supposed to stay for two more days. Why did she have to go so soon?' The possible answers to this question caused the hair on my neck to bristle, and I hastily stuffed my mouth with bread and butter.

Tía Panchita stirred her coffee vigorously, then shovelled in three teaspoons of sugar, although I knew she only liked one. The clinking spoon silent, she studied me through her thick glasses, her huge eyes unblinking and calm. I knew there was no need to repeat my question, and I squirmed under her hot gaze.

She took a sip of coffee, then placed her cup down on the saucer with a clang. 'It was time for Alicia to go home.'

5

WEEKS WENT BY WITHOUT WORD FROM ALICIA. EVERY TIME I asked Mami if I could call or go for a visit, she turned away and mumbled something about her being sick, or them being out of town. But nobody went out of town during the school year. When I reminded her of this, she looked at me like Tía Panchita had done the morning Alicia had left, as if she could determine my innocence or guilt by the way I held up to her stare. I passed these tests, but it was difficult, and I dared not attempt it often. So I silently worried and wondered about Alicia and when I'd see her again.

I felt more hopeful about seeing her when Christmas Eve arrived. On this day the entire family always got together for a pig roast at Tía Maria's house in Havana. We roasted it in a big pit in the ground filled with hot coals and rocks. It was a full day of cooking that started first thing in the morning. The men stood in a circle around the pig out back, smoking cigars, laughing and talking about things not meant for women's ears. I wasn't a woman yet, but when I walked up to see how the pig looked, all splayed out like a thick rug, and to inhale the enticing aroma of pork fat sizzling on hot coals, they poked each other with their elbows and coughed. This served as some kind of code, prompting them to make polite comments about how tall I was getting and that Papi would have trouble on his hands when I was older because I was so pretty that all the boys would come calling. I didn't listen much to them; I just inhaled deeply and asked if I could poke the pig with a stick like I'd seen them doing.

The household help was given the day off on Christmas Eve, so the women were all inside, cooking the rice and black beans and yucca with mojo sauce. They laughed and gossiped about whoever wasn't there at that moment, complaining and bragging about their men, while wiping their foreheads with the backs of their hands and their hands on their aprons, which covered fashionable dresses made by their personal seamstresses for the occasion. They didn't stop their conversation if one of the men wandered inside to get a cold beer or taste the black beans. In fact they raised their voices a bit, grinning boldly if he attempted a sheepish defence.

'I'm outnumbered,' he'd declare before beating a hasty retreat. 'And besides, we're working very hard out there.'

One of my favourite places to pass the time while the feast was being prepared was outside, with Alicia's father, my Uncle Carlos. He liked to sit on the porch with his small guitar, strumming away while the family sang along to old Cuban songs. He had a beautiful voice, and expressive eyes that shifted from sad to happy depending on the song he was singing. I often asked him why he wasn't a star on TV, because he was a better singer and more handsome than any- one I'd seen. This always earned me one of Uncle Carlos's brilliant smiles and the opportunity to make a special request. And then he would sing 'Piel Canela' only to me, which made me feel that perhaps I was pretty after all.

I knew I wouldn't have Alicia all to myself. There would be too many other cousins vying for attention, creating new alliances that would be broken in a matter of hours or minutes, and doing everything they could to maintain or improve their position in the pecking order. I knew, too, that Alicia was the most popular girl in the clan. The little girls wanted to be just like her and most of the boys had a crush on her and sought her approval; even Juan, who was the oldest.

Normally I wasn't bothered by any of this, but ever since Tony's arrival at Tía Panchita's, things had changed for Alicia in ways I couldn't understand. I was desperate to talk to her without interruptions from the other cousins. If we had a few moments alone, I knew she'd confide in me like she always did – and I'd never felt so ready to listen.

As we waited on Tía Maria's porch for the rest of the family to arrive, I kept a special watch for Alicia's white Chevy. Juan, who was unofficially in charge, had decided we should explore Tía Maria's backyard shed, which was reputed to be haunted by the ghost of Tía's great-aunt Carlotta. The door, normally locked, had been left open after some extra chairs had been retrieved to accommodate the growing number of guests. Excitement was in the air as we formulated our plans. We had the whole day ahead of us and much of the night. The younger children squealed with delight and waited for instructions, each wanting to be the first to follow their older cousins into the chamber of horrors.

Alicia and her parents finally showed up well past noon. The pork was already half cooked and I'd managed to postpone our visit to the shed until Alicia arrived, knowing it wouldn't be as much fun without her. Juan and I both smiled at the sight of their car, but when Alicia stepped out she looked as though she'd faded into an old black and white photograph, where the people just stare into the camera like they're already dead.

She wore a brown dress almost down to her ankles and her hair was drawn back in a stiff-looking braid.

Alicia hated brown. She liked pink and light blue and yellow. Perhaps Mami was right and Alicia had been sick. In fact, she looked as though she was still a little bit sick. We waved excitedly to her and she barely lifted her hand in return.

When she approached the gathering on the porch, everyone crowded around her. I wasn't the only one who'd longed for her, and for a few minutes her old smile returned and her eyes shone brilliantly, sometimes golden, sometimes green. She was just as beautiful as ever.

I noticed her figure was more like a grown-up woman's than before, with breasts that stretched the stiff fabric of her dress. And her fingers were long and graceful as she patted the heads of our younger cousins and accepted chicken croquettes from my mother, who planted a firm kiss on her pale cheek.

'We missed you,' I heard my mother whisper.

Alicia and I found a moment to speak alone after our exploration of the shed, which proved much less exciting than expected. Even Juan had become bored and was stealing puffs from his father's cigar when he wasn't looking.

We sat on the steps of the porch. The heat of the day was cooled by an ocean breeze that swept up the avenue and swirled about the big house, seeking out the delicious aroma of the pork that was almost ready. Alicia tapped her black shoes against the step and looked out towards the street with an absent expression on her face.

I always knew how to start a conversation with Alicia. It was just like breathing. But this time my mind was blank and my mouth dry as I stole uneasy glances at her.

'Alicia . . .'

She turned to me. Her eyes were unfocused and she seemed to be distracted by the thick buckle of her shoe, which she began to adjust with great concentration.

'What happened at Tía Panchita's? Why did you leave so soon?'

Alicia shook her head. Her eyes watered suddenly and I noticed a shiny film that reflected the light like a magnifying glass. 'I'm not supposed to talk about it,' she whispered.

'Why not?'

'I made a promise.'

'To who?'

Alicia's face flushed and her eyes bore through me with conviction. 'To God. They made me promise to God.' She turned away and began to pull at the buckles of her shoes with both hands this time.

'Have you seen Tony?' I asked.

Alicia jumped at the sound of his name, then became very still. If I hadn't been studying her so intently, I would've missed the almost imperceptible shake of her head.

'I have,' I said. 'I saw him at Tía Panchita's just last week.'

Her voice wasn't even a whisper. It was a fleeting thought, lifted by the lingering ocean breeze that surrounded us. 'How is he?'

'I don't know. He didn't stop. I saw him ride by on his horse and he waved.'

Alicia nodded slightly without looking at me. And no matter how much I pried, she refused to say anything more about where she'd been or what had happened to her. She avoided me for the rest of the night and stayed close to her parents. How could she change so completely in so little time, I wondered. My best friend was gone, or hiding somewhere underneath a brown dress and sombre grey face.

I saw Alicia again two Sundays later at Tía Maria's house. She wore a long navy-blue dress this time with the same black shoes, and her hair pulled away from her face and twisted so that not a curl could be seen. She looked less serious, however, and when she saw me she smiled with that familiar cleverness that always meant she had something fun planned and wanted me to join in. At the first possible moment, she whisked me away to our rose bush.

Reaching down into her sock, she produced a small white envelope. She was solemn as she held it out to me like a communion wafer. 'If anyone sees what's inside this envelope . . . I'll be sent away for ever. You have to promise complete secrecy.'

'What is it?'

'Do you swear not to tell anyone?'

'Yes, I promise.'

Alicia took hold of my hand and put the envelope in it. 'This is for Tony,' she said. 'You have to give it to him next time you see him; next time you go to Tía Panchita's house.'

'Why don't you give it to him yourself?'

'Because I'll never be able to go there again. That's part of the agreement.'

'What agreement?'

'I told you, I made a promise to God.' Alicia's brows knitted together with such force that they produced a deep wrinkle in her forehead. I'd never seen a girl with lines like that on her face.

I folded the envelope twice and stuffed it in the pocket of my blouse, pressing it down hard on my chest so that it would show as little as possible. 'Isn't giving this envelope to Tony against the promise you made God, too?'

Alicia wrung her hands and glanced nervously over the rose bush towards the house. 'Yes,' she whispered, 'it is.'

'Then tell me what happened.'

She attempted to sit Indian style, but the narrowness of her long skirt prevented her and she had to sit like a lady with her legs to the side. She folded her hands, looking more like a nun than ever. 'Lola was there that night; the night I left to see Tony. She saw me, but I didn't see her.'

'Lola . . . saw you with Tony?'

Alicia nodded. 'The next day, very early, she called Tía Panchita and told her everything. It was probably still night because Tía called my parents and they came right away to take me home, before anyone was awake. They had me checked by the doctor, this old man with bad breath and a red spotted nose. He made me lie on a table and open my legs wide so he could look inside me. After that, they sent me away to stay with a priest and some nuns. We prayed all the time and ate beans and rice with a little meat. We went to church twice a day and they made me talk to the priest over and over again about what had happened with Tony, but they didn't believe me when I told them he didn't do what everyone thought he did. He only kissed me on the mouth and told me that he loved me. He didn't violate me like they said.'

'Violate you?'

'You know, like when a man and wife make a baby. When they have sex.'

I was stunned. How could Alicia be denying anything about sex when I still wasn't exactly sure how the act was performed? Seeing my hesitation, Alicia sighed. 'When they're alone in bed at night, and married – because they're supposed to be married – the man puts his pito inside the woman's hole down there. There's a hole down there where the blood comes out.'

I knew about the blood from Mami. She'd blushed when I'd presented her with my blood-spotted underwear one morning, convinced I was dying. But I was not yet twelve and there hadn't been any blood since that day, even though I'd checked my underwear rigorously since she told me about it. I was glad it hadn't come again, even though Mami told me it would and that it meant that I was officially a young lady.

'Did you get the period blood yet?' I asked, interrupting Alicia.

'Yes. How about you?'

I nodded, ashamed, but not sure why.

'They made me promise before God that I'd never talk to Tony again or be with any man, especially a black man.' Alicia looked up, her eyes clouded with shame. 'I can't really explain what I feel. It's a strange pain in my heart whenever I think of him or say his name. It makes me feel like I'm the luckiest person on earth just to have known him, and other times I feel like I want to die. I've prayed so hard for this feeling to go away so I can feel how I did before I knew him, but I can't stop thinking about him. That's why you have to give him the letter. Will you give it to him, Nora?'

'If they catch you again, then what?'

'I don't care.' Alicia drew several quick circles in the dirt near her feet and smoothed her skirt, leaving a light trail of dirt with her fingers. 'If you don't give it to him, I'll have to run away and give it to him myself.'

'No . . . I'll do it,' I said quickly, helping Alicia to stand in her narrow skirt.

As we walked back to the house, I asked, 'Do you always have to wear those clothes?'

'I have to wear them for a year to make sure that God forgives me for my sins. I made a promise.'

I shook my head in disbelief at the number of promises flitting about like fireflies that glowed in the night and, like Alicia's vows, vanished in the light of day.

It was several weeks before I managed to fulfil my promise to Alicia. I sat on Tía Panchita's porch like an anxious sentry, waiting for Tony with the envelope, already crumpled and sweaty from continuous handling. This day alone, I'd moved it from my drawer to my pocket, from my pocket to my bag and then back to my pocket again. I couldn't wait to get rid of it, and although I'd seen him ride by on his horse twice during our stay, Tía Panchita or Lola were always on the porch and would've seen me pass him the note. It was during his third pass that I had my chance. Both had gone inside to fix the afternoon meal and I ran down the porch steps and along the path to the main road, pulling the letter from my shirt as I did so and waving it like a white flag.

Tony looked suspicious as he saw me running towards him. For a moment I thought he was going to urge his horse into a gallop, but he waited, looking down at my letter as if it were a gun instead of a simple white envelope.

'This is for you from Alicia,' I said, panting and nervous.

Tony made no move to take it from me. A fine vein running down the smooth brown skin of his neck throbbed steadily and his hands fumbled with the reins that rested on his thighs. He was without a doubt the most amazing boy I'd ever seen, and at that moment I could easily imagine Alicia risking all to be with him again.

Finally, he reached down and took the letter up to his lips and inhaled deeply. Then it slipped out of his fingers and fluttered down to the ground, settling on the dirt near his horse's hooves. 'Tell your cousin not to write me any more letters, unless she'd like to see me hanged from the nearest tree,' he said with sad resignation. He prodded his horse with his heels and started to ride off. 'Anyway, I can't read,' he added, turning back one last time.

I returned the dusty envelope to Alicia behind the rose bush at Tía Maria's the following Sunday. She implored me to recount every detail of my encounter, the exact words Tony spoke, the expression on his face, the clothes he wore, and then I had to repeat it all over again, at least three or four times.

'Do you really think they'd hang him?' I asked.

The deep line in her forehead returned as she gazed at the rejected envelope. 'Do you really think he can't read?'

6

I HEARD THE DRUMS IN MY SLEEP AGAIN. THE DREAD I'D FELT at Tía Panchita's house settled on my heart with a heavy and startling thud. I was still waiting for Alicia to return from her encounter in the forest with Tony. Time froze, and I began to shiver as I struggled to breathe in the thin air around me. I'd lose her for ever and have to explain through lying, rattling teeth what had happened. Worse than that, I'd have to live with the knowledge that I could've saved her.

But there was something different this time. The sound of the drums was deeper and the enticing rhythm that made my toes twitch, even when I was afraid, was replaced by a haphazard pounding that woke me with a start.

I was not at Tía Panchita's, but in my own room seven storeys up in Havana. The drums were never heard in the city, only in the deep forests at the edge of small towns where the sugar cane grew thick in backyards and plantations alike. And the sound that made the windows tremble in their panes wasn't like any drums I'd ever heard. Instead, a low blasting sound spread out across the silence of the city. I bristled with fear, and dared not get out of bed and peek out of the window into the night.

The switch in the hall clicked on and my room

glowed with the faint light fanning under my door. Mami's slippers padded down the hall. She opened the door to Marta's room first and then closed it promptly. Marta could sleep through anything. We always joked that a hurricane could blow her windows open and swoop her out into the storm, and she'd still sleep through it all and wonder what had happened the next morning when she found herself lying amongst the trees in the street.

My door opened slowly. 'Nora, are you awake?'

'What's that sound, Mami?'

'It's OK. It's far away.'

'But what is it?'

Mami entered and sat on my bed. In the half-light, the delicate crease between her eyebrows, which appeared when she contemplated such simple worries as who to invite to her next dinner party, or whether or not Marta and I should wear the same colour dress for Easter, had grown into a cavern. She spoke with careful and measured words. 'Somewhere in the city, angry people are setting off bombs.'

'Why?'

'They want a different government.'

I sat up in bed, feeling safer now that she was in the room with me. 'Does it have to do with what Papi said yesterday about the people who were killed?'

'It might.' The crease shifted and smoothed out slightly. 'They were also against the government. You see, there are many who want Batista out. They want free elections.'

I'd heard about this from fragments of conversation I'd gathered over the years as adults argued on the porch, debated over coffee at the dining-room table, or when Mami and Papi were talking in the car. Everyone we knew was opposed to Batista and wanted a new and better government. There'd been talk about revolution and free elections for as long as I could remember, but nothing had ever really happened.

Now it seemed things were happening all at once, frightening things.

'Do you and Papi want Batista out too?'

'Not like this. Free elections like they have in the United States, that's what we want. Now go to sleep.'

I could tell by the way she bit the inside of her cheek that she didn't want to talk about it any more. 'You have school tomorrow. You're safe here and you'll be safe there too.'

She kissed my forehead and closed the door behind her. I heard another distant boom, but it was no longer the sounds outside that kept me awake. It was the image of my mother's face, shifting and vague, a smile flickering on her lips as she tried to comfort me. She was pretending to be strong instead of just being strong, and this made me worry in a new way.

I closed my eyes and wondered if Alicia could hear the explosions from her house. Was she trembling in bed like me? No; she was probably hanging from her window, almost falling out onto the street below, straining to see what was going on. If Alicia was here she'd turn it into an adventure. We'd become under-world spies, eager to save our country from Batista, beautiful heroines who'd snap our fingers and command the revolutionaries with our cunning and beauty. And after a night of death-defying adventure, all would be still and calm in the morning. There would be café con leche waiting for us on the kitchen table, and fresh bread and butter, and Beba would smile her expansive smile with teeth as white as sugar cubes, and tell us it was going to be another beautiful day.

Marta and I arrived home from school to find Alicia and Tía Nina sitting on our living-room couch. Never before had they visited on a weekday afternoon. Stranger still, Papi was home, although it was hours before he was due back from the office. And instead of

76

her school uniform, Alicia was wearing a pair of white pedal-pushers with her loafers and a yellow sweater, clearly weekend wear. Tía Nina looked ill. Her hair was in disarray, falling out of a hastily made bun. Her red-rimmed eyes darted about the room, focusing on nothing in particular as she toyed with an unlit cigarette. She fumbled with a lighter, then tossed it and the cigarette on the table and began to sob, her head in her hands.

Papi sat next to her on the couch, still and pensive. Mami hurried in from the kitchen when she heard Tía Nina's sobs. A cup of hot tea rattled in her hands and she winced when it spilled a little over the sides and burned her fingers.

'This will help you to calm down,' she said, placing the cup in front of Tía Nina. Then she gave us her sit-down-and-don't-say-a-word look, so we dropped our books and sat right there on the floor. Marta and I became very obedient when we were scared.

Alicia's eyes were puffy from crying too, but she kept her hands neatly folded in her lap and smiled weakly when she saw us. She wanted to speak, but Marta and I both knew that we had to be quiet and still and simply listen, lest we be banished to our rooms. I was aware of Beba, who kept poking her head through the kitchen door while she prepared dinner, trying to hear what was going on. Her eyes were flashing with anger and she frequently shook her head in disgust and loudly grumbled her disapproval of the whole situation.

Tía Nina took a tremulous sip of tea. The cup and saucer rattled all the way up to her lips and back to the table. Then she retold the story she'd been telling all day, as though she herself could hardly believe it. 'The sun wasn't up when they came looking for him. I'm telling you, he barely had time to throw on his clothes.' Aunt Nina glanced at Marta and me, pausing as she noticed us for the first time. Then she tore her eyes away and continued. 'The police came fifteen, maybe twenty minutes after that.'

'What exactly did they say?' Papi asked, his face cold, his eyes dark with a fear I'd never seen before. Papi was never afraid; he was angry sometimes, and impatient, but never afraid.

'They suspect he was involved in the bombing last night. But he was with me all night. He never left home. They wanted to know where he was now, and I told them I didn't know . . . And I don't know, that's the truth.'

Papi raked trembling hands through his hair. 'The less you know the better, Nina.'

'My God, will they kill him if they find him?' Tía Nina slumped back on the couch, almost landing on Papi in the process. He jumped and glared at Mami as if he expected her to do something.

Beba poked her head out of the kitchen door. 'They're common criminals and they should be shot,' she shouted, before disappearing once again. I could hear her grumbling in the kitchen as she threw pots and pans around.

Mami kneeled next to Tía Nina and gently stroked her hair back into place. 'Everything will be all right, Nina. We're all praying. Everything will be OK.'

Alicia took hold of her mother's hand. 'Papi knows how to take care of himself. Don't cry any more.'

'She's right, Nina. Carlos knows how to take care of himself, he always has,' Papi said with a certainty that was reassuring. But I could see by the way his gaze turned inward and his jaw tightened that he was thinking about things he couldn't discuss here, things that would make Nina worry more.

We stayed in my bedroom for the rest of the day. It was a brilliant afternoon and the sky was as blue as ever; from the balcony we could see the ocean twinkling playfully, as it always had. But an unusual stillness had settled on the street below, as if all was not as it seemed. The constant drone of cars on the wide avenue had dwindled to an occasional whirl. Last night's bombing had kept many people home and the merriment that was peculiar to Havana streets was absent. It was so quiet that we could hear the birds on the roofs and the occasional tinkle of someone selling tamales or sugar-cane juice down below. But even their cries were different. It was as if they weren't interested in making any sales, but in getting home to their families in case they were caught on the streets during the explosions.

'If Batista catches my father, he'll kill him,' Alicia said matter-of-factly as she sat on my bed, her bare feet dangling. I detected cracking patches of pink polish on her toenails. When did she start painting her toenails? It wasn't even close to a year since she'd made all those promises to God.

Marta gasped in horror as Alicia went on. 'They'll kill him, just like they killed those other men. That's why he has to hide. Then when Batista's gone, he can come out again.'

'Some people say he'll never leave,' I said.

'Then I'll go and find Papi in the mountains and live with him.'

It was upsetting to think of Tío Carlos in such a predicament. I imagined him strumming his guitar and singing Cuban folk songs to his companions, telling them jokes; and as he did so, everyone would laugh, slap him on the back and tuck cigars in his shirt pocket because he was so clever and fun to be around. It was hard to imagine him doing anything so serious that he would need to hide from the police. Even when he was serious, which wasn't very often, his eyes smiled. He'd escape their capture, I was sure of it. He could slip through anything with his slick sense of humour that could charm a man out of his own shirt, not to mention a box of cigars. And Alicia knew this better than I did, which is why she wasn't afraid.

But Tía Nina was not so confident. As the days went by without word, her desperation intensified. She lost so much weight that her nice dresses hung on her shoulders as though they were still on the hanger. She talked constantly in a shaky voice and smoked so much that the tips of her fingers started to turn a dark yellow. We'd sit at the table to eat the wonderful food Beba made – chicken and plantains, yucca with mojo, the best flan in all of Havana – and Tía Nina wouldn't eat a thing. Beba shook her head when Tía Nina passed on the meat and potato stew, her favourite, muttering that she couldn't eat.

Eventually it was decided that Tía Nina should go somewhere far from Havana so that her nerves could heal, and Alicia would stay with us so she could continue to go to school. We hadn't spent this much time together since we'd stayed at Tía Panchita's house. Now we'd gaze at ourselves in the mirror while listening to Elvis Presley records and pretend we were on our way to grand parties to meet the most wonderful boys, who immediately fell in love with us because of our amazing beauty and dancing skills. Marta, who was still happy just to be included, often played the role of the matronly chaperone who'd accompany us on our dates and scold us when we allowed the young men to hold our hands or peck us on the cheek. Alicia and I took turns playing the young men's role, and I suspected that no matter how I played my part, she always cast me as Tony. It was always Tony who asked her to dance, Tony who fought off the rivals when it was time to go home. Once, when I pretended to have been thoroughly beaten by another boy and was lying flat on my back begging for mercy, Alicia corrected me. 'Tony would never give up like that,' she said. The game went on for hours and evolved into the most fascinating variations, the magic following us to the dinner table, out with Mami to run errands, even to school. I completed my lessons happily, knowing that in the afternoon I'd be rewarded with the delight of Alicia's company.

Three months passed and still Uncle Carlos did not return. We heard occasional explosions in the middle of the night and during the day as well, but by now we'd become accustomed to the booming that had frightened me so much the first time I'd heard it. It didn't get in the way of our usual routine of school, homework, dinner and girl talk. Quite the contrary: it made us feel we were invincible. When we encountered the rubble produced by an explosion the previous night, we were intrigued rather than frightened, as if we were passing the ruins of some ancient city, not the pharmacy we'd walked by for so many years. But Mami tensed up and began to walk very fast, so we could barely keep up with her, and behind her sunglasses her eyes were moist with tears. I knew she didn't want Alicia to see her crying for fear that it would make her worry about Tío Carlos, so I didn't ask her what was wrong.

Alicia still talked to her mother on the phone every day. One afternoon, almost four months after she'd moved in, she hung up looking rather sombre. 'Mami's coming back next week and I'll be going home,' she said, jumping up on the bed and sitting cross-legged. The phone call had interrupted a fascinating lesson: Alicia and I were telling Marta about the facts of life. This had started when Marta bragged that she was already beginning to develop and was a little girl no longer; she unbuttoned her blouse and showed us the tiny buds on her chest to prove it. But when Alicia opened her own blouse in response, Marta and I were awestruck.

Her breasts were contained within a seriously functional bra, much like Mami's complicated undergarments which I'd seen drip-drying in the bathroom.

They seemed a grown woman's breasts, not like my own that swelled pleasantly enough and knew their place, sensible little mounds easily tamed in the world of one size fits all. As Alicia unclasped her bra, we were dumbstruck, frightened even, by the size of her nipples, large pink saucers with raisin peaks. I could easily imagine a whole brood of children suckling happily, growing fat and strong and healthy.

Marta closed her shirt demurely. 'Wow,' she said, clearly impressed. 'Does it hurt when they get that big?'

Alicia fastened her bra and winked at me. 'It doesn't hurt at all, does it, Nora?'

'Let's see yours,' Marta demanded. 'We showed you ours. Now you have to show us yours.'

My face turned red and my hands flew up to my chest defensively. I would've been happy to display them if not for the amazing show that had preceded me. I was suddenly a little girl again, pretending to know how to read the newspaper.

'We won't laugh,' Alicia said kindly.

'I know . . .'

'I've already seen your tetas before, anyway,' Marta said, waving her hand in the air. 'Who cares?'

'They don't have to be big to look good,' Alicia said. 'Juan told me that some men like it better when they're not too big.'

Cousin Juan? Why was Alicia talking with Juan about such a thing? And who cared what men liked or didn't like? Whenever I caught a man looking at me, I cringed with embarrassment. And if he dared say something like, 'So young and fresh, just like a rose,' or 'Your smile is more brilliant than the sun,' I wanted to yell at him to leave me alone.

Mami said men always did things like that and worse, and I should simply keep my eyes averted and ignore them. Of course, if Alicia should be walking next to me, the looks and comments were always directed at her. One time, I even caught her smiling back at a particularly handsome young man who had complimented her hourglass figure. I could see she wanted to say something as well, and probably would have done if Mami and I hadn't been there. Perhaps Tía Nina had never taught Alicia how to be a lady. But when I told Alicia that she shouldn't look at men who said things to her, she shoved my shoulder playfully and laughed, 'Oh Nora, maybe you should've become a nun, after all!'

Uncle Carlos reappeared a few weeks later, thin and easily startled, but in a very good mood nonetheless. Batista had left Cuba for good, driven out by a handsome man with a bushy black beard.

After that, Fidel Castro and the Revolution were the only things anybody talked about. Of course, we'd all heard of him before. He'd been fighting in the mountains with a few rebel supporters for years, but nobody had paid too much attention. Now, whenever we turned on the TV, Fidel was there. If we changed the channel, Fidel was there. If we turned on the radio, Fidel was still there, preaching about a new Cuba that would grow stronger and richer and take its rightful place in the Americas.

It all sounded very good, and for the most part the adults in my family liked what they heard. And Papi was so happy to have Tío Carlos back that I think it helped them finally agree on something. They stood around the TV during Fidel's speeches like soldiers standing to attention. Papi was particularly pleased about his promise to reinstate the process for free and democratic elections. Uncle Carlos was simply overjoyed that Batista was out and that he'd had something to do with it, although he was very mysterious about just how much.

'Nothing could be worse than that bastard,' he said over and over again; his eyes were smiling and his shirt pocket was never without a cigar.

All the while, Beba stood in the doorway of the kitchen, surveying the scene with arms folded, shaking her white turbanned head in disapproval. 'I've got a bad feeling about that man.'

'About Castro? Why?' I asked.

She narrowed her eyes at me suspiciously, like she did when she thought I'd sneaked a spoonful of freshly made flan she was saving for dessert. 'Someone who can stand in one place and make speeches for that long – there's got to be something wrong with him.'

All I knew was that the bombing had stopped, and the only things to worry about were completing homework, weekend plans, and whether or not Mami and Papi would allow me to shave my legs like the other girls.

'You're too young to shave your legs,' Mami said.

'My legs are as hairy as Papi's, and all the other girls at school shave.'

'OK, but only up to your knees, do you understand me? Only girls on the street shave their legs above their knees.'

Here was yet another rule I couldn't understand. But I welcomed it, along with Mami's usual attention to my grooming and appearance. It seemed that things were finally getting back to normal.

7

ALICIA AND I WERE TO ATTEND OUR FIRST FORMAL DANCE AT the Varadero Beach Club. Abuela selected our dresses and brought them home one afternoon as we sat with Abuelo, drinking cokes frothing over with sweetened condensed milk. Marta scowled at the sight of the boxes; there'd be no dress for her, as she was still too young to attend a dance.

'Don't be sad. We'll have fun together, Martica,' my grandfather said, poking her in the arm. 'While they're at that silly dance I'll take you out for a night swim. Have you ever swum in the ocean at night?'

Marta shook her head, intrigued but still pouting.

'It's magical. The moon lights the water with a silvery glow and the—'

'You're not going on any night swim with that child, Antonio,' Abuela interrupted as she fumbled with boxes and shopping bags. 'It's far too dangerous.'

'I guess we'll have to settle for a walk and an ice cream, then.'

Marta gazed longingly at the boxes and flying tissue paper. Abuela produced a blue-green dress, the colour of the ocean at twilight, and held it up against Alicia, who batted her eyelashes playfully. Instantly, her eyes assumed the same misty colour and her hair shone like the sun in golden waves across her shoulders. We stared at her silently, not gasping only because we were accustomed to her beauty, which grew more alluring with each passing day. I had no doubt she'd be the most beautiful girl at the dance. She was always the most beautiful girl wherever she went.

'I knew that colour would be perfect for her,' Abuela said, well pleased with her selection. 'Now, let's see about Nora.' She opened the second box, which contained a delicate cream dress with an embroidered light-blue sash. Next to Alicia's brilliant dress it looked horribly plain and childlike, more of a confirmation dress than a grown-up dress for a dance. I felt like crying at the sight of it, but I didn't want to hurt Abuela's feelings. I could see that she loved this dress as well.

I could already picture us walking into the dance. We'd make our entry into the hall chaperoned by Abuela, and Alicia would be mobbed by every boy in the room. They'd step on my white patent-leather shoes in a desperate attempt to get a place on her dance card, while Abuela pushed me forward, trying to entice the boys like a street vendor selling over-ripe mangoes.

'This light colour will look beautiful on you,' Abuela said, but there were no gazes for me as there had been for Alicia, no flash of time standing still for my beauty. Abuelo was already setting up the dominoes to play with Marta, and Alicia was busy examining the length of her dress, which hit right above her well-shaped calf.

'Try it on,' Abuela said. 'I wasn't as sure of your measurements as I was of Alicia's. There's still time to make adjustments if we need to.'

'I'm sure it'll fit just fine.' I dropped the dress back onto the tissue paper, eager to get it out of my sight. I needed to be out in the sun and the wind, away from this shameful stage where I always came second. I didn't understand why all of a sudden these things mattered to me, but for the first time I wanted to be beautiful and draw the admiring gaze of the boys and feel the powerful rush of my own femininity. I wanted to cross my legs and catch the world with the tilt of my ankle, as I'd seen Alicia do while we waited for the bus downtown. I wanted to pretend not to notice how every man I passed held his breath in the hope of possessing me.

I mumbled a hasty excuse and left Abuela standing with my cream dress in her arms. My feet dug deep as I marched across the beach towards the ocean. I kicked off my sandals and stepped into the warm water, wiggling my toes in the soft sand. I longed for a long cleansing swim, but that would involve going back to the house for my bathing suit and I didn't want to face anyone at the moment. The only thing more shameful than being second best was letting them see how much it bothered me.

Alicia's toes appeared next to mine, pink toes wiggling next to my brown ones.

'Why are you so mad, Nora?'

I continued to stare at my toes, now covered with ten little mounds of fine white sand.

'It's because you don't like your dress, isn't it?'

Again, I remained silent.

'You can have my dress if you want. If you like it better, that is.'

I stepped back and sat by the water's edge. 'No. Your dress is beautiful on you. I just get tired of it sometimes . . . being the plain one.'

Alicia sat next to me. 'You're not plain, Nora. You're beautiful. You just don't know it yet.'

I felt irritated by her lack of understanding. 'But everyone always tells you how lovely you are, with your green eyes and all. The only thing I'm told is to stay out of the sun so I don't look like a guajira.'

Alicia laughed. 'Don't pay attention to Abuela. She doesn't know everything. Besides, some dresses look better when you wear them than they do on the hanger. I think yours is one of those.'

'Maybe it is,' I respond, feeling sleepy all of a sudden.

There's a spicy fragrance floating on the breeze today. Does it come from the vendors selling their garlic tamales or is the sea in a mischievous mood? My head falls back and the ends of my hair brush the sand. I let the full force of the sun hit me, unconcerned that my tan should deepen before the dance so that I look like a shadow lurking about in a white dress. When I glance at Alicia, her face is also turned to the sun, like a sunflower smiling into her mother's face.

I don't need to go to the dance. I'm not a dance type of girl. I don't need to whirl about and be noticed and crooned over. I just need this moment on the sand. To know that the ocean will always be blue or green or somewhere in between, and that I can turn my face to the sky and find a moment's peace.

Alicia was right. My dress did look better on than it did on the hanger. And Abuela was right too. The delicate cream colour contrasted nicely with my dark hair and complexion.

Before we left for the dance, Abuelo stood before us and smiled proudly. 'Two beautiful princesses,' he said. 'One as lovely and bright as the Cuban days, the other as mysterious and alluring as the nights.' Then he turned to Abuela. 'And let's not forget the queen of them all, who graces us with her beauty, be it day or night, rain or shine.'

Abuela laughed happily and patted his cheek. She wore a navy-blue polka-dot dress, and her generous mane of grey wavy hair was moulded artfully to her head. She smelled of soap and lavender, and her black box-bag hung neatly over her arm.

'How about me, Abuelo? You forgot me,' Marta said, running in from the porch.

'You aren't merely a princess,' Abuelo said, putting

his arm around her chubby shoulder, 'you're an angel from heaven and your beauty is beyond description.'

Marta smiled in spite of her bad mood.

We walked to the dance along the sidewalk that followed the water's edge. The sun had almost set and hung low, wavering in the misty warmth of the tropics. The sea was a smooth silver tray that received its nightly offering of heavenly gold with unusual grace.

Tiny lights started to blink and glimmer in mesmerizing patterns along the distant shore. They reminded me of the glamorous parties my parents used to attend, with Mami in her swirling skirts and Papi in white linen, crisp and cool. They'd kiss us good night in a haze of perfume and tinkling bracelets and slip out into the night, giggling like children. They were going out into those beautiful lights, and even though it looked like a fantastic carnival, children weren't allowed to go there. But on this night we were entering the world of those magical lights that glimmered on the shoreline.

I was surprised so many boys had asked me to dance. I accepted, a little awkwardly, and allowed them to lead me to the dance floor with sweaty palms that trembled ever so slightly when we touched. Cologne and perfume had been applied with such vigour that I felt I might be overcome in a forest of exotic flowers which writhed erotically at times, hesitantly at others, to the mambo beat of the orchestra swaying on stage. And the chaperones, mothers and grandmothers, chatted along the perimeter of the room, pointing to their daughters and granddaughters as they held their handbags on their laps.

I hardly had a chance to talk to Alicia, who was continually surrounded by a throng of young men, who looked a bit older than the boys who asked me to dance. Alicia wasn't awkward at all on the dance floor. She smiled and moved with the grace of a woman born to royalty, at ease with being the constant centre of attention. She was the star of the ball, and she left a wake of turned heads behind her each time she walked out onto the dance floor, her companion beaming as if he'd just been crowned king of the world. Other girls shot envious glances and quickly turned to see if she'd caught the attention of their partners, which of course she had. One of my dance partners, a tall pimply boy with sweaty hands, asked me if Alicia was my cousin, and his eyes turned glassy as though he was talking about Marilyn Monroe.

On the walk home, Alicia giggled about the boys who'd professed their love for her, how they'd gone on and on about the beauty of her hair and her skin and her eyes. I was able to share a couple of stories of my own, but nothing like Alicia's volumes. At one point, a boy had even tried to kiss her cheek when she offered him her hand.

Abuela listened with a serious expression and slowed her footsteps considerably. Then she stopped in her tracks and turned to face Alicia, even though she was speaking to us both. 'You're very beautiful, and boys and men are naturally drawn to beauty, but you mustn't be fooled by their flowery compliments.'

'They're just trying to be nice,' Alicia said, still smiling.

'Nice!' Abuela barked as she pushed her glasses up her nose with a quick thrust of her finger. 'A man would be nice to a mule if he was desperate enough. Never, never allow a man who is not your father or grandfather to touch you or kiss you in any way. There are places men can go if that's what they need.'

I knew Abuela was referring to the brothels in the Barrio de Crespo, where the prostitutes were said to saunter around the streets wearing next to nothing, smoking long cigarettes. It was well known that this was where young men went to learn about the arts of love and physical pleasure. And it was also understood that young girls didn't require a similar education. They would learn from their husbands on their wedding nights. Chaperones were there to make sure that the education didn't begin before the wedding.

We were almost home when I asked the question that upset my grandmother the most. 'Abuela, who are those ladies, the prostitutes? Where do they come from?'

Abuela stopped dead in her tracks and stared at me with incredulous eyes. 'How can you talk about such things? That is nothing that a young girl like you needs to worry about. You shouldn't talk about such things, do you understand me?' The colour in her cheeks was clearly visible in the pale moonlight. 'Those women have sold their souls to the devil. They're worse than dogs. That's all you need to know.' She was walking ahead of us now, as if she'd suddenly become concerned to be out in the night with such ignorant young ladies.

I dared not ask her about the men's souls, but I could well imagine her answer. The men checked their souls in at the door along with their hats, and claimed them unharmed at the end of the evening. Once a woman lost her soul, it could never be regained.

Alicia opened the window in the bedroom we shared, after Abuela had closed it for the night. We listened to the waves rolling up on the beach as we laughed and whispered about the boys we'd met and which ones we liked most.

'Do you think our fathers went to the prostitutes before they got married?' Alicia asked.

To think of my wonderfully correct Papi, with his perfectly pressed trousers, his hair never out of place and his undying love for Mami, with one of those soulless women Abuela had talked about was inconceivable. 'Of course not. Are you crazy?'

'Well, I think they did. And some men still go, even after they're married.'

Alicia wanted to talk, I could tell. She wanted me to ask her how she knew this, so she could tell me fantastic stories about illicit sex and women of the night, which would go on for hours. I was too tired to listen this time.

I heard the creaking of bedsprings as Alicia sat up to look over at me, although I'd already turned away from her and was pretending to be asleep. 'Did you know that a lot of married men have mistresses? Sometimes they have whole families their wives don't know about.'

I sighed. 'Go to sleep, Alicia.'

Alicia lay down and was silent, but she wasn't sleeping. She was thinking and dreaming, her eyes intent upon the sky as she looked for shooting stars. Even after a night out dancing with countless young men, each more handsome than the next, I knew it was Tony she thought about, and what she might do if given a chance to lose her soul.

8

THE EXPLOSIONS STARTED AGAIN. AND THIS TIME THERE WERE gunshots. Sometimes it sounded as if the shooting was right outside our window, not far away in some other part of the city. More than once the shots came in the middle of the day, and we dropped to the floor below the windows like soldiers in a war movie, trembling and waiting for the silence to return. One afternoon, Beba and I dropped to the floor in our kitchen. On the way down, Beba knocked over the tomatoes and onions she was preparing, and we lay in them for several minutes. When it was over, we carefully collected every piece of onion and tomato that had fallen and washed it off. With the shortages getting worse every day, we couldn't afford to throw anything out.

We crowded around the television set at all hours of the day and night, trying to learn some new bit of information that might offer hope or alleviate our growing despair. The prevailing mood was cold and suspicious, as if we were at a funeral for somebody who'd been murdered and whose killer was still on the loose, maybe among us, maybe next door or down the street. It could be anyone in this shifting and un-predictable climate, but one thing was certain: Castro was no longer the redeemer; the man who could save

Cuba and put her on a level playing field with the United States; the man who would clean up the corruption of Batista and his super-rich cronies, and paint the country new with a sparkling coat of democratic ideals. Suspicion and fear abounded that Castro's promises were false and that his sudden sweep to power was being supported by the least democratic people of all.

We knew that the explosions we heard were caused by those against the Castro regime, and the discord between Papi and Tío Carlos began anew. Tío Carlos believed Castro's militant position was necessary during these uncertain times, and that it would change once stability had been established. He believed there was still hope for a democratic solution. But Papi had lost all hope. He sat in his chair in his immaculate suit and polished shoes, listening to the demolition on the streets and watching Castro gesticulating on the screen. His eyelids were heavy from lack of sleep. 'It's only a matter of time,' he said to Mami, who had nothing to say herself, but who shared his vacant expression.

In spite of the sounds of war, and the intolerable tension that ensued as the adults discussed politics and the inevitable choices some were bound to confront, we tried to live our lives as before. And on most days I managed to forget there was any trouble at all.

Alicia and I returned to the beach as often as we could. We talked about what would happen if we had to leave Cuba; but in our usual way, that left room open for the possibility of adventure. We lay on the white sand as we had done as children, gazing up at the palms swaying in the wind. We swam to and from the platform like a couple of dolphins, and laughed as we shook the wet hair out of our eyes, always composing ourselves when good-looking young men came into view. As usual, most of the looks and comments were for Alicia, whose voluptuous figure was a beacon for any male nearby. I had to settle for the occasional leftover remark or compliment when they noticed the dark girl alongside the beauty.

'I don't ever want to leave Cuba,' Alicia said as we lay drying in the sun.

'I don't either.'

'There could be no better place than this in the whole world. I could never be happy anywhere else.'

If I hadn't been on the verge of falling asleep, I would've told her that 'anywhere else' was an impossible thing to consider. We were Cuban and this was our country. Things would get better, because they always did. If you couldn't count on the ground beneath your feet, then what did you have? But why say all this when the wind caressed our bodies with such perfect warmth? Why interrupt the chorus of the sea that said it all much better than I? We were home, and this was where we'd always be.

Papi arrived home early from the office and didn't sit in his usual chair. Instead, he went straight to the bedroom without a word to anyone, not even a kiss hello for Mami, who'd been anxiously waiting for him since early that afternoon. Mami followed him, and Marta and I went straight to Beba, as we always did when we wanted to get the straight story of what was going on. Political issues weren't discussed at school, in fact they were avoided, and Mami and Papi still protected us from the truth whenever they could. But Beba had special X-ray vision that could see beyond the complicated surface of things and understand the simple truth, without fancy explanations or excuses. She'd say, 'Your mama doesn't want you to shave above the knees because no man should be looking any further than that. And if he doesn't like what he sees, he isn't likely to touch.' Or, 'Your figure will fill out when it decides to. Besides, some men like their women skinny. No use worrying about the good Lord's plan. It's always best.'

We went into the kitchen and found her chopping onions with such force that it looked as if she might cut right through the chopping board. Her eyes were dampened by the onions, which were fresh and strong, and soon my eyes began to water as well.

'What's happening, Beba? What's wrong with Papi and Mami?' Marta asked.

Beba dried her eyes with the back of her hand, then wiped her hands on her apron. She leaned on the counter, like she did when her knee was hurting her from standing too long, so I pulled a chair over for her and she sat down with an audible and weary sigh. 'The world we know is changing. Some people think it should change. Some people think it should stay the same.' She shook her head slightly, and I saw that the tears in her eyes were not because of the onions.

'What do you mean?'

'While you were at school today, that man gave another one of his speeches that lasted more than six hours. Holy Lord, how that man can go on for so long without losing his voice I don't know.' Beba had refused to say Castro's name for weeks now, believing that simply uttering it would give him more power. 'He said what I knew all along: that he was a communist and that Cuba would be the most powerful socialist state in the western world.'

Marta and I were silent. Although we weren't exactly sure what communism was, we knew from conversations we'd overheard that this was the worst of all the possible outcomes debated during the past months.

Mami and Papi finally emerged from their bedroom. Mami's face was tear-stained and red. Papi sat at his place at the head of the table, after placing a weary kiss on each of our foreheads. In the kitchen, Mami whispered that we should refrain from asking any questions. 'Your father is very upset and I don't want him to get more upset.'

'Mami, is it true? Is Cuba communist?' Marta asked.

Mami turned on her suddenly as if she might slap her across the face, although I'd never seen her slap anybody ever in my life. But she just pushed the hair out of her face and turned to help Beba set the table for dinner. She gave two plates to Marta and two to me. 'Castro may be communist, but Cuba is not communist,' she said with a conviction that was chilling. 'Cuba will never be communist.'

'May God hear you, Doña Regina. May your words go straight to heaven,' Beba said from the other side of the kitchen, and we all prayed the same.

Sunday dinner at Tía Maria's had become a sombre occasion, but one that became more meaningful as we held on to what we knew of the world that was crumbling around us. There was no laughter on the porch, with clouds of cigar smoke generated by a circle of happy, back-slapping men in guayabera shirts, and no domino sets being arranged after dinner with good-natured banter about who was the best player and who was the cleverest cheater. Although there was much less meat to go around, the chicken and rice were as delicious as always, and Tía Maria received her compliments with a sad bow of her silvery head and no promises of the feast she planned to prepare next week. And we cousins didn't separate ourselves from the adults as we had used to do to make our own fun. Instead, we hovered nearby to learn from our parents, aunts and uncles, to try to understand the state of affairs and what would happen next. Juan seemed better informed than any of us, even Alicia.

'The government's taking over everything,' he said authoritatively. 'They've taken over the sugar mills already. The banks are next.'

I wondered how it was possible for a government to

do such a thing. Did they simply stroll into all those hundreds of sugar mills, kick out the workers and assume the controls? Would they open all the giant bank vaults, where I imagined a little man lived with rolled-up sleeves counting money, and shove him off his chair so someone else in green army fatigues could start counting where he'd left off? It seemed impossible and not at all real. And how about Papi? He was an important person at the National Bank. Surely they wouldn't kick him out? The bank couldn't run without him, of that I was sure. And he'd never wear one of those green uniforms. He'd die first.

'I think we're going to be leaving,' Juan said as he took a big spoonful of flan.

'Leaving where?' I asked.

'To the United States, of course. New York or Miami. You'll all be going too, sooner or later, I bet you.'

We all looked at each other, shocked, some more horrified than others. But Alicia was calm and smiled serenely. 'I won't ever go. If they try to make me go, I'll run into the hills and hide like my father did.'

'You're crazy,' Juan said as he scraped up the last of the sweet caramel sauce with his spoon.

I thought a lot about what Juan had said about going to the United States, and I listened carefully to everything Mami and Papi discussed, but I was relieved to hear no word of leaving Cuba. In fact, they seemed more hopeful that things would change. Everyone seemed to agree that the United States would never tolerate communism so close to their democratic shores, now that it had been so clearly spelled out by Castro himself. They'd consider it a disease that could infect their capitalistic ideals. Everyone knew that Russia and the US were the worst of enemies, and rumours had already been confirmed that Castro was collaborating with the Russians on his new socialist state. There were too many reasons to believe that

Castro's days were numbered and that we'd soon be back the way we were; too many days and nights spent glued to the television set as if our lives depended on its eerie glow. For the first time in my life, I'd grown pale and yellow from lack of sun. At least Abuela would be happy with my lighter complexion.

Mami cried every day. At first she didn't want us to see her and she'd withdraw to her room, returning to the business of her day with swollen eyes and a tremulous smile. But as the days went on she lost all concern for appearing weak, openly sobbing whenever and wherever the feeling took over: on the couch while watching the news; in the kitchen, while helping Beba put together a meal with scant provisions; or out on the balcony, as she watched the sun disappear into the wide stretch of ocean before her. She avoided shopping as much as she could, and if she did venture out she'd return worse than she left, the sour mood of her experience causing her face to wrinkle with disgust and her unpainted lips to pucker as if she'd been forced to suck on a bitter lemon all day.

One afternoon she came back with a small bag of rotting potatoes and dropped them on the dining-room table with a thud. 'I stood in line three hours for these,' she said, then locked herself in her room for another long cry.

Eventually, she refused to do anything but stay at home and talk to Beba. It seemed that Beba was the only one who could calm her down, with her straight no-nonsense talk about government and society and the way things should be. All of this would go down very well with a cup of strong cinnamon tea. Mami sat at the kitchen table, bobbing her head as Beba talked to the rhythm of her knife coming down on the chopping board. Sometimes Mami laughed through her misery when Beba said things like, 'That man should be taken to the deepest part of the shark-infested ocean and sunk with a weight around his neck. Then we'll pass out his bones, picked clean, and use them to play the drums during the big party we're going to have because Cuba is free.'

But there was one day when even Beba wasn't able to calm her down. We were driving to one of the few restaurants still serving dinner, for many had closed due to the shortages. The string of lights that always blinked merrily along the malecón were blowing out one by one, leaving a silent grey sweep of oceanfront. Where once could be heard music and singing, there was now an empty and silent stage, strewn with the debris of happier times.

Papi said we had to use as much cash as we could, because it would soon be worthless. He spent it on anything he could find: two full boxes of corn oil, which we could use for trading on the black market, along with ten expensive pairs of women's shoes in all different sizes, which he bought from an old toothless man in an alley in the oldest part of Havana. He also paid Beba twice her usual salary, which she accepted sadly while clucking her tongue and shaking her head. 'I'd trade all the money in the world for that man to leave. Lord knows it's true.'

We drove the usual route down Carlos Tercero that passed by our home parish. We knew it well, the little fountain where we'd thrown our pennies, the corner where the man usually sold the ice-cold mangoes we enjoyed after Mass on Sundays.

'You're going to stain your Sunday dresses with mango juice,' Mami would say.

'We'll be careful, Mami. We're not little girls any more, you know.'

As we drove past the church, Mami was raising her right hand to make the sign of the cross as she always did, when she choked on an agonizing scream. Papi slammed on the brakes with such force that Marta and I were thrown against the back of the front seats. I looked to see if we'd run someone over or if we'd hit a dog. They sometimes ran loose through this part of the city.

'No! Dear God!' Mami wailed, her hands flying to her face.

At first I didn't understand what I saw. The black people in the church courtyard looked so happy, dancing and laughing as though they were having a big party, the kind we often saw in the country when the drums pounded their infectious rhythms and smiles flashed like beautiful crescent moons. Perhaps they were happy because Castro was gone and Cuba was free again. My heart leapt at the possibility.

I hung out of the window to get a better look. Young men swung on the carved wooden doors, wearing the rich-coloured robes of the priests and pulling them off each other, tossing them up into the air in a frenzy. One man with bare feet pretended to be a matador, waving the drape used on the altar during communion at his companion, who sported two crucifixes on his head like horns. Several women had wrapped their bodies in embroidered capes and were gyrating their hips to the sound of the congas being played from the sacristy. The pounding spilled out onto the street, echoing with mystical and evil enchantment.

My own heart beat with rage at the sight. This was our family church, the place where my parents were married, where Marta and I were baptized. This was the place where I'd learned about God and His benevolent and unchanging ways. I expected a lightning bolt to rip open the sky and incinerate these blatant sinners for their blasphemy. But the sun shone and the breeze was as warm and sweet as always.

Marta's face was streaming with tears. 'Where are the priests, Papi?'

'They left,' he answered, shaken but composed. 'Some of them went back to Spain. I don't know where the others went, but they're not here any more.'

101

'Why can't there be any religion? It doesn't hurt anybody,' Marta asked.

'A communist state is an atheist state,' Mami whispered with venom in her voice. 'The only thing that can be worshipped in this country now is that man.'

9

SCHOOL HAD BECOME OUR SANCTUARY, THE ONLY PLACE where we could pretend things hadn't changed. Whenever we passed underneath the sacred Virgin clutching her rosary, I knew I could look forward to a few hours of peace and sanity. We went to the chapel at the same time every day and ate lunch at the same time. The sisters expected behaviour and academic performance to be absolutely perfect, as if the world weren't falling apart outside the school's wrought-iron gates. We all pretended together, and when the large paned glass rattled with the explosion from somewhere deep in Havana while Sister Roberta read Shakespeare to the class, she didn't flinch. She just kept reading in her sweet even voice, and we all listened probably harder than we ever had before.

The prayers in the chapel were heavy and long, and for the first time it seemed that everybody was praying for something that truly mattered. I prayed that life would return to the way it had been before, that I would be able to graduate from El Angel de la Guardia, that Alicia and I would go to the university together and go shopping by ourselves for the first time at El Encanto. I prayed that my mother would stop crying every day, that Papi would come home and read the paper in his chair like he had

103

always done, and not just sit there silently as if he was waiting for his own death. I prayed that we would be able to buy food at the market, fresh beautiful food, enough to feed an army of friends and family, so that Papi would never have to go to the black market and trade secretly for food and risk being arrested. Most of all, I prayed that my home would always be right here, and that I could be close to all the people I loved.

Within the solid walls of El Angel de la Guardia, it seemed right that God should answer our prayers and that our previous way of life should continue as it always had. It was only when Papi came to pick us up at the end of the day and we passed under the gates of the Virgin back out into the world that I'd begin to feel the cold dread creep into my body again. Outside the gates, there were no longer any rules we were familiar with. We had to be watchful constantly and scramble from school to home in case the unforeseeable should happen while we were out.

I was beginning to feel the reassuring calm of the school day come upon me when Papi stopped just outside the gate, underneath the blessed Virgin. He cocked his head to one side and his eyes filled with an unspeakable torment.

'What's wrong, Papi?' I asked.

His face had turned from a light tan kissed by the sun to a chalky white, and his jaw was clenched tight, but he said nothing. I looked out towards the simple two-storey structure that was our school, the broad green lawn split in two by the path leading up to the double doors of the main hall. At this hour the doors should have been open, and girls of all ages wearing the same beige and brown uniforms should have been buzzing about the lawn and steps, waiting for classes to begin. But the doors were closed and not a soul could be seen anywhere.

'Are we early?'

Then I turned again to see that Papi wasn't looking

towards the school, but upwards. I followed his gaze. The Virgin with her rosary was gone. We saw her later at the side of the entrance road, broken into pieces, her severed hand still clutching her rosary. In its place, piercing the tropical blue sky, was a strange angular metal crescent with a hammer in the centre of it, looking heavy and ominous.

Papi reversed the car with a screech of the tyres and headed back for home. El Angel de la Guardia was gone, along with every other Catholic school in Cuba. There would be no more sanctuaries.

Every day we listened to Beba's powerful golden voice defame the man who'd become synonymous with the devil. 'He's a lying pig who deserves to be shot in the head. He says he wants to take care of the black folks. Do you see any black man standing next to him up there? I sure don't, and my eyesight's pretty good. He says we were enslaved before and now we're free. Shit, if this is freedom then give me slavery any day of the week. I can't even buy a piece of bread for my breakfast with all this freedom I got.'

Papi was no longer able to work after he'd applied for our visas. But he said he was glad, and that he no longer worked in a bank but a circus run by clowns controlled by the communist party. And we were glad he was out of the bank too, because several employees had been imprisoned for counter-revolutionary activities. Papi described how one of the clerks had entered the bank one morning with a Castrista soldier at his side. He made his way slowly through the offices, pointing his finger at those he suspected of being actively against the revolution. Every one was led away for questioning and several had yet to return home. The jails were full of political prisoners and everyone was suspect.

With our visa application in process, we'd literally

thrown off our red revolutionary bandanas and become 'gusanos', worms betraying their homeland and the revolution of their people for their own personal gain. Gusanos were publicly derided and it was not unusual, if you were lucky enough to find a few precious gallons of gasoline for your car, to discover you could not drive it because your tyres had been slashed or your windshield smashed. In this beautiful land where the sun shone every day and the breezes called you to walk along the shore at any time of day or night, we were forced to stay inside our apartment and avoid taking any unnecessary risks.

'If we're worms,' Mami said with her fists clenched and her eyes watering with fury, 'then the idiots who support this godforsaken revolution are cockroaches, and may they rot in hell!'

Juan and his family were the first to receive their visas. They had plans to move to Miami, and were already taking English classes to be as prepared as they could to succeed. But it was harder for the older people to consider leaving. We visited Tía Panchita at her house and tried to persuade her to apply as well. A few months earlier, the government had given her plantation to Lola's brother Pedro, saying that he worked the land so it should belong to him. Mami and Papi begged Tía to apply for her visa. Marta and I sobbed as we imagined her there by herself, but Tía wasn't moved by our arguments or our river of tears.

'I won't leave my home,' she said resolutely. 'I won't spend my last days in some foreign place where they don't speak my language, shut away in a one-room apartment where I can't look out on my fields. I'd rather go hungry at home.'

Then she poured herself another cup of weak coffee and stared out at the dusty road, rocking on the porch and blinking behind her thick cat's-eye glasses.

Lola reached across from her rocking chair and

patted her hand kindly. 'Maybe you should think about it, dear. Don't you want to be with your family?'

'I have thought about it. I'm staying here with you.'

One afternoon, Tony came by while I sat on the porch with Tía Panchita and Lola. He'd grown to well over six feet and was more handsome than ever. All that had occurred between him and Alicia seemed to have been long forgotten by the adults; but Alicia had never been allowed to return to Tía Panchita's, in case memories should become inflamed. And I knew that Alicia still compared other men she saw to Tony and invariably concluded that he was the most beautiful man of all. I could hardly disagree. When he bounded up the porch steps two at a time with that sparkling smile, my breath still caught in my throat and my heart pounded a little more vigorously, as it had on the first day I saw him.

Under his arm he carried a thick book, and his wide eyes danced with light and amusement. 'I'm learning how to read,' he exclaimed proudly, holding out his book for our inspection.

Tía put down her needlework and repositioned her glasses to get a better look at the kind of book communists would use to teach reading. Her face betrayed nothing, for she already knew, as we all did, that Tony fully supported the revolution. 'You're a smart fellow. You'll learn fast,' she said severely, and promptly returned to her needlework.

'You'll only learn what they want you to learn, boy,' Lola said to her nephew.

'I want to learn how to read. This is my chance to do something better than just work the sugar cane.'

'Sugar cane?' Lola laughed a dry throaty laugh, which ended up with her coughing more than laughing. 'You don't have to worry. Pretty soon there won't be any sugar cane left to work.'

'That's the problem with you old people,' Tony said,

inflating his muscular chest. 'You've already decided the revolution is a failure. Maybe for those who never wanted anything to change it is, but for me it's a chance to better my life.'

Lola got up slowly from her chair to go inside. 'I'm just a stupid old woman. What do I know?'

Tony turned to me with eyes pleading for sympathy. 'What do you think, Nora?'

I struggled to find the words to respond. I couldn't imagine a life without books and my heart went out to him. 'I'm glad you're learning how to read, Tony. That's a good thing, if you're happy with it.'

Tony cocked his head to one side and smiled sadly. He had been hoping for more support than this and his eyes searched my face, causing me to blush and squirm. Then he jerked his head away, as though ashamed of my lack of courage, and stepped slowly off the porch, each step representing yet more miles between his world and ours.

Lola came back out to see him leave, on foot this time, as his fine horse had been commandeered by the government almost immediately. None of us waved to him or called out, wishing him a good day. Never had there been such silence on the porch.

Mami developed a bad case of nerves. She jumped if there was a knock at the door, convinced that soldiers stood behind it ready to search our apartment and take us all to prison because of our black-market dealings and desire to leave the country. We heard that our neighbour downstairs had been recruited to spy on the other tenants for just that purpose, so Mami persuaded Papi to pour the entire remaining box of cooking oil down the toilet. It was also rumoured that executions were being aired on television, but Beba was directed to scurry us away to our rooms when television programmes became questionable. She placed one strong hand on each of our shoulders and escorted us there while we complained. Then she'd rush back to the living room so she could watch it herself.

On one occasion, when passing from my bedroom to the kitchen in search of Beba, I saw that the rumours were true. Papi and Uncle Carlos didn't notice me standing behind them. In the grey light of the television I saw it all: the men, already skeletal and half dead, lined up against the wall, wearing stained and torn prison uniforms. They were blindfolded, with their hands tied behind their backs, even though they obviously lacked the strength to take even one step towards freedom. Gun shots sounded like a huge firecracker echoing on and on, and the men collapsed to their knees before spilling onto the ground like half-empty sacks of potatoes. The revolutionary music played, the flag was flown, and Papi's face was ashen when he turned around and saw me standing there.

'Why did they shoot those men, Papi?'

He took a moment to answer. 'Because they're suspected of being anti-revolutionaries. They're martyrs and they have their place in heaven.' Papi sat down in his chair, his eyes red and pained. He put his face in his hands. 'Go to your room now, Nora.'

I spent many long afternoons lying on my bed waiting – waiting for the visas to arrive, waiting for someone (especially Alicia) to come and visit, waiting for the silence and the dread to be interrupted by anything. One day I spent an hour watching a spider in the corner of my room spin its web. Where once I would've felt the immediate need to scream and have Beba squash it with her bare hands as she often would, I now felt peaceful watching it spin to and fro, up and down, swinging on its invisible tether. The revolution didn't bother the little spider. It continued spinning and crawling around as it always had. Watching it, I could make myself believe that things weren't really so bad. Even if the explosions continued to sound throughout the day and night, maybe it would all soon be over. Even if the Bay of Pigs invasion had failed and everyone had given up hope that the Americans would save us from communism, I still prayed that they'd try again. I prayed that the next bullet I heard would shoot straight through that man's head, blowing off his green army hat so that it landed in the mud and was trampled by every man, woman and child in Cuba. Spin, little spider, spin your web of dreams and hope.

Months passed and we heard nothing of the visas. Food was getting scarcer and lines formed all over the city for milk and bread and even toilet paper. Mami forced herself to stand in them with the hated ration book in her handbag, and Beba still came over every day, even though we were only able to pay her in pesos, which were worthless even when there was something to buy. She was willing to come for food and company and for something to do. We were grateful for her presence.

Beba had just arranged the silverware on the table when there was an unexpected knock at the door. Mami nearly dropped the plates she was holding, and when she set them down on the table she faltered on her feet as though she was drunk. Beba answered the door and we all stiffened at the sight of a severe-looking woman carrying a clipboard.

'Are you the domestic?' the woman asked.

Beba wiped her big hands on her white apron and eyed her suspiciously. 'I am. I've been working for the Garcia family for almost twenty years.'

The woman was unimpressed. 'I'm here to offer you reading lessons.'

'Reading lessons?'

'Yes. Don't you want to learn how to read, so you can improve your station in life?'

Beba placed her hands on her wide hips and glared

at the woman without shame. 'What makes you think I can't read?'

The woman appeared shaken, but quickly regained her composure. 'Well . . . can you?'

'No, but that's none of your business,' Beba replied in a voice loud enough to echo through the entire building.

The woman's face dropped, but once again she resumed with resolve. 'The party is offering this opportunity—'

'I don't care what you or the party is offering me. I do what I please and I don't want to learn how to read. And when I decide I do, I'll find my own teacher and I'll read the books I want to read.' Beba slammed the door in her face and sauntered past all of us, chuckling to herself and humming a tune. I imagined that she'd be able to render Castro helpless given an hour alone with him, and I would have let out a cheer if not for Mami's slumped body on the couch.

'What have you done?' she whispered. 'What have you done?'

'Don't worry, Doña Regina,' Beba said, setting the plates Mami had abandoned at the table. 'They won't do anything to me. They don't do anything to the coloured people.'

It was late Sunday morning when Papi managed to find a leg of pork on the black market. It was a bit scrawny and said to come from a pig that was too old to eat, but it was meat and we'd had precious little of that lately. He wrapped it carefully in many layers of newspaper and placed it in the bottom of a shopping bag, preparing it for its journey to Tía Maria's house, where most of the family was assembled. Even though everyone did it, buying on the black market was considered an anti-revolutionary crime and Papi could've been arrested. But the gnawing in our stomachs made us courageous and I felt like an

111

underworld spy as we drove the five minutes or so to Tía's house.

The pork leg was cooked indoors and all the windows were closed, lest the wonderful aroma escape and proclaim our find. No neighbour could be trusted. You could never be sure about who had aspirations to join the party, and fear and the greed for power motivated many to point their finger at friends they'd known all their lives. And it wasn't just neighbours. Children denounced parents and parents children. Everyone had a heartbreaking story to tell about a child who'd turned his own parent in for a crime against the state, often something considered less horrendous than Papi's delectable purchase on the black market.

The aroma of pork skin sizzling with lemon and garlic almost brought tears to our eyes, and fear of being caught didn't dampen our delight. On the contrary, this was our secret way of snubbing the party and all its informants. With each delicious bite of pork we were declaring our hatred for Castro and the communist party, a private gastronomic counter-revolution!

Alicia and I sat together on the porch, savouring our few pieces. (One leg of pork didn't go very far.) All of our conversations of late had been clouded by our inevitable separation. Alicia's parents wouldn't be applying for visas, because Tío Carlos was convinced that the present circumstances were only temporary and Castro would soon be ousted. Many agreed with him, but Papi considered Tío Carlos to be as stubborn as he'd always been, and too proud to admit that the man he'd once supported into office had ruined our lives.

'Maybe the visas will never come,' Alicia said, as she mopped up every last bit of pork juice with a stale crust of bread. 'And even if they do, you don't have to go, Nora. You're already fifteen. You can say you want to stay here and live with me and my parents.' She offered this possibility even though we both knew it was inconceivable that I should do anything but go with my family. I nodded glumly and watched the fire-flies dance and flicker.

We remained out on the porch after we'd finished our meal, wondering if this might be the last time we would be together at Tía Maria's house. Lately I'd been wondering if everything I did was my last time: my last time walking around the corner with Marta to buy a loaf of bread or an ice cream; my last time waking up to the sound of Beba singing in the kitchen, banging plates and dishes around as she did when she wanted us to wake up; my last time standing outside on the balcony, waiting for the sun to go down so I could see the city glow pastel pink in the twilight.

But how could I measure a week without Sunday at Tía Maria's house? It was as central to our existence as the rising and setting of the sun. No matter what happened during the week, there was always dinner at Tía Maria's house on Sunday. Our difficulties would be sorted out, the harsher edges of life softened by the laughter and music on the porch and the promise of a delicious brazo gitano to come after dinner.

And how could I live without Alicia nearby? She was my mirror, my inverse self. She had secrets of mine in her heart that I could never share with any-body else. And living in any place other than Cuba was tantamount to saying I was going to go and live on the moon. How could people survive in a place where it was cold; where tropical breezes didn't warm your soul on a daily basis? How could people live in a place that was so enormous? Cuba was small and cosy. Like my bedroom, I knew where everything was. The United States, spanning three thousand miles across an entire continent, would be like sleeping in an auditorium, my tiny bed minuscule and insignificant in the corner. This I could not imagine. Even less could I imagine speaking English, even though I'd studied it in school. It seemed right that this strange and complicated language with its thick 'th' sound and irreverent vowels should come from an icy place where everybody was shivering and hurrying to get somewhere.

We spoke very little about our impending separation, almost not at all, as if fearing that talking about it would somehow make it happen. Perhaps Beba was right. Better to talk about the strong Americans and their hatred of communism, and about a thousand planes buzzing over our heads like a swarm of angry bees aiming their stingers at the capped and bearded head of that man. Better not to talk about anything at all.

10

BEBA WAS KNEELING ON THE FLOOR AT MAMI'S FEET AS THEY both wept with the same agony Tía Nina had unleashed a few years earlier. Marta and I were speechless and numb at the sight of Mami and Beba in such a state. We couldn't comprehend the reality that, with our visas granted, we'd be leaving our home very soon.

Papi stood apart from us, hands stuffed in the pockets of his linen trousers as his black shoes tapped out an erratic rhythm on the tiled floor. He was somewhere else, way ahead of us and unable to offer any consolation to the wailing women before him.

He walked to the centre of the room and spoke only to Mami. 'Beba isn't the only one who won't be leaving, Regina.' The wailing stopped and silence spread over us like death.

Mami straightened up and wiped her eyes with the back of her wrist. 'José, what are you saying?'

For a moment Papi couldn't speak.

'For God's sake, tell me!'

'Regina, calm down. There's a solution for this, I'm—'

'What is it?' she screamed and sprang from the couch to lunge at Papi.

Gently, he placed his hands on her shoulders and

115

eased her back down on the couch. 'My visa will be granted shortly, I'm sure.'

'Your visa wasn't with ours?'

'No, but it'll come.'

Mami stood up again, clear minded and chipper. 'Then we'll wait until it comes and we'll all go together. That's what we'll do,' she said in her most reasonable voice. Her solution sounded logical enough; and perhaps while we waited for Papi's visa Beba's would come too, and if we waited longer still, the government would change again and we wouldn't have to go at all.

We patted Beba on the back and told her, with trembling voices, that it was going to be all right. But she stayed on the floor, quietly weeping, her face covered by her hands. Beba never gave her grief up easily and she wasn't prone to hysterics. My dread returned at once.

Papi took slow steps to the window and gazed out at the glittering Caribbean in the distance. He kept his hands in his pockets, but I saw them ball up into fists and the linen expand as he did so. He walked back, and his words were strong and clear. 'You have to leave with the girls as soon as possible. If you lose these visas, you'll lose your chance for ever.'

'But it could be years, José. We might be separated for years.'

Papi was silent. A fine mist of perspiration glistened on his forehead. 'It won't be years. Don't you see?' He turned to Marta and me, attempting a smile that looked more like a half-hearted grimace. 'This is their ploy to make us stay. They think you won't go without me. But it won't work. You three will be on that plane if it kills me. And if my visa doesn't come, I'll swim to Miami if I have to. I promise.'

Mami collapsed on the couch once again. 'You can keep your promises. This is too much for me to bear.'

Beba collected herself and retreated to the kitchen without another word.

We were scheduled to leave in a week, which was the same as saying tomorrow, in an hour, this very second you'll walk out the door and leave the life you've known for ever. There were no elaborate preparations for our departure, no packing to be done because we were only allowed to take one change of clothes, no pictures or books or jewellery or anything that might remind us of the home we were leaving behind. We simply floated about the rooms of our apartment like ghosts wandering through a museum of belongings that were no longer ours. Our heartache settled like fine dust on every stick of furniture, on the corners of every tile. It blew like a silent storm out of the windows and blended with the moisture of the sea. We took pictures with our hearts and minds, and the little time we had expanded into an eternity of tomorrows we would never have. I found myself gazing at the Caribbean for hours at a time, trying to make up for a lifetime of lost memories.

Mami and Papi were even more inseparable than usual, and Mami cried constantly while Papi held her. When her head was on his shoulder so she couldn't see his face, he looked as though his big heart was rotting and shrivelling into a small dry raisin. I tried to interpret the despair I saw in his eyes, for I knew better than to ask directly. Did it mean we'd never see him again? That he couldn't bear being apart from us? Was he keeping a secret too dangerous or painful to share?

Marta and I stood around the apartment, too weak from the shock of what was happening to do anything else. We hovered about Beba, who'd regained her composure, but her strength was no longer warm and familiar; it was cold and resigned. She had stopped singing and telling stories. Her pure white clothes appeared crumpled and occasionally stained. We sat together in the kitchen with no food to prepare and waited for the days to pass and the world to end.

Alicia and I were together at Varadero beach two days before we left. Even here, where the breeze had always floated through our childhood dreams and scattered our fears into the brilliant sky, the air felt heavy and difficult to breathe. I could feel the sun pulsating angrily as it looked down upon its favourite island falling into ruin.

Alicia's parents had still refused to apply for visas, certain that the political climate would change. Although I didn't dare say anything, I believed secretly that they were right. Why should we leave our home because of the capriciousness of one man? It seemed like an incredible overreaction to leave our lives, our families, everything that made us who we were, when so many other proud Cubans were willing to wait and pray for change. Wasn't that the most reasonable thing to do? Hadn't Papi and Mami and the sisters at El Angel de la Guardia always told us to be patient? Didn't the Bible say that patience was a virtue? Why were we willing to abandon our home when there was still hope?

All these questions I longed to ask, but dared not when I saw the anguish in Mami and Papi's eyes. I didn't want Mami to go weak and crazy like Tía Nina had when Uncle Carlos went away. I knew that it was better to remain silent and hold my breath and pray that things wouldn't get any worse.

Alicia and I sat on the soft white sand, resting our eyes on the turquoise blueness spread out before us, allowing the tepid water to moisten and tickle our toes.

'We learned to swim together here,' Alicia said, still staring out at the sea. 'Remember the day Abuelo made us swim to the platform?'

The platform was still out there, bobbing peacefully,

unaware of the grand role it had played in training generations of swimmers in our family and other families as well, no doubt.

'As I remember, you were the one who learned how to swim. I learned how to sink to the bottom like a big rock.' I laughed at the memory, but I wanted to cry.

'You were brave, Nora. You tried even though you were afraid.'

'I was definitely afraid.'

'How about now? Are you afraid?'

I buried my toes and studied the thick drips of sand and water that spilled over my feet like hot fudge. 'Yes, but I don't feel like I did when I was little. I just feel this frozen kind of sadness that doesn't let me cry.'

Alicia nodded in a way that showed me she knew exactly what I meant. 'It doesn't seem real. We've grown up together our whole lives. How can we just keep growing up apart?'

'Maybe we won't. Everybody says this can't last much longer. I think we'll only be gone a short while.'

We lie back and gaze up at the palms sweeping the sky as they have since we were little girls, and forever before that . . .

'Can you see God today?' I ask. Alicia takes hold of my hand, and the warmth of her love and sadness fills me like the sun overhead.

'Oh yes,' she whispers. 'He's looking right down on us at this very moment.'

'And what did you ask Him?'

'Well, you know I can't tell you that, Nora,' she says, and we both smile through our tears.

José Marti Airport was a confusing throng of young soldiers with enormous guns slung about their bodies, who surveyed anxious and miserable people of all ages running around with their one half-empty suitcase, bawling like babies as they hugged family members they might not see for years, if ever again.

119

Children looked up at the adults with wide eyes, curious about this sudden reversal of roles.

'Don't cry,' we heard an irritated soldier instruct a woman old enough to be his grandmother. 'If you cry like that it means you're against the revolution, and that's a crime, or haven't you heard?'

The old woman wiped her eyes under her spectacles with her handkerchief and turned away from the soldier, her bottom lip trembling. 'Cabron,' she muttered as she walked past us.

The four of us waited against the wall as Abuelo went to check on the status of our flight. Mami was a zombie, which was quite a change from her usual hysteria, but I preferred hysteria to this death mask. Papi whispered into her ear and she nodded as she listened, blinking slowly like a child learning the rules for hide-and-seek. I imagine he told her what he'd been telling her all week: that everything was going to be fine, that we'd be together soon, and that nothing could keep our family apart.

Arrangements had already been made for our arrival in Miami, where we were to stay with friends until we were reunited with Papi. The longest he'd wait for his visa was one year, and if it didn't come he'd start looking for other ways to get out. There were many reports of people stowing away on boats and planes. And the US was accepting anyone from Cuba, with or without a legal visa. It seemed a reasonable plan; a year wasn't so long. But Papi might as well have been talking to the wall that Mami leaned on.

She mumbled what she'd been saying for two weeks. 'I can't believe this is happening to us.'

As I looked at Papi, tall and strong, his eyes bright with emotion, I had no doubt our separation would be a brief one. But what would we do until then? At fifteen, I was already taller than Mami, and when I took her hand she let her head drop on my shoulder. 'You have to help me, Nora,' she said in a voice weakened by pain. 'I need your help to get through this.'

'I'll help you, Mami, don't worry,' I said, trying to sound strong, although I too wanted to break down and weep like everyone else. I wanted Papi and Mami to take me in their arms like they had done when I was a little girl, and tell me it was all a bad dream and that things would be fine in the morning. I'd wake and see the light streaming through my window. I'd smell the coffee brewing and I'd hear Beba singing merrily from the kitchen in her beautiful golden voice.

'We're planning a trip to the beach,' my mother calls brightly. 'Get up before we lose half the day.'

'I'll get up right now,' I want to call back, but I can't because I'm leaning against a grey wall with Mami's head on my shoulder, holding an empty suitcase and wearing three pairs of underwear.

'I'll help you too, Mami,' Marta says as she takes the suitcase from me.

'You see, Regina? You have two wonderful daughters to help you be strong. And I'll be there soon.'

'I don't think we should go,' Mami says. But the strength has gone out of this argument and it is now only a hollow whisper.

Abuelo was weaving his way swiftly through the crowd. His face twitched when he neared and his desperation swept over us like a furious wave. We were no longer sad and contemplative, but energized with the need to get on with it, this business of saying goodbye: to our home, to Papi, to everything we were.

Abuelo was so nervous he could hardly speak. Sweet calm Abuelo was never nervous, and the pit of my stomach fell to my feet. Everything was falling down around me, but I still wanted to stay with all my heart.

He pressed Papi's shoulder. 'The plane is boarding.'

Papi looked at his watch. 'They shouldn't be boarding for another hour, Papa.'

'Look at this place. Does it look like anyone knows what they're doing? This is a madhouse and I'm telling you that your plane is boarding now!' Abuelo never yelled, but he did so now and his face assumed a tightness that pulled the corners of his mouth down taut.

Mami straightened to attention and her eyes cleared. She shook herself. 'We can't miss the plane, you heard what he said,' she snapped, looking straight ahead. We almost ran behind her and Abuelo to keep up.

We arrived at the gate out of breath, our hearts in our mouths as we joined the end of the line snaking through the door out to the plane, which reflected the tropical sun like Beba's sparkling pots and pans. A middle-aged lady in front of us wept as a female official inspected her suitcase. The official took great pleasure in ripping the photographs she found one by one and tossing them onto the floor. She had a full mouth and wide-set almond eyes. She would've been considered very pretty if not for the sneer that cut across her face.

'Get in line right there,' Abuelo commanded, unmoved by the scene before us. 'Give me your visas.' Papi handed him the three visas and stood with Abuelo outside the rope.

We looked at the flight number on the board. This was not our flight, but we got in line anyway when we saw the look on Abuelo's face. He wasn't confused at all. He knew exactly what he was doing.

When it was our turn to give the clerk our tickets, Abuelo stood close to him and passed him the visas so that his body blocked what he was doing. But I saw him slip several foreign bills into the front flap of one of our passports, and remembered that Abuelo had money invested in an American bank account.

The clerk examined the passports and visas, then glared at Papi. 'Sir,' he said, 'didn't you read the sign?

Passengers boarding the plane must stand inside the rope.'

Papi looked confused, but when he saw Abuelo nod and lift the rope so he could pass beneath, he scrambled under without a word.

We knew we had to look natural and normal in every way. We couldn't risk calling any attention to ourselves, when we wanted more than anything to leap out of our skins with joy. The uniformed boys with machine guns strapped to their fronts and backs were everywhere. Anything could lead to an arrest. And this was much more serious than buying meat on the black market.

Together the four of us walked out of the door in single file with our heads down, lest anyone read the apprehension in our eyes as something more than the sadness of leaving our homeland. We almost ran across the tarmac to the plane and climbed up the steps, and I realized that in our haste we'd forgotten to give Abuelo a hug and a kiss goodbye.

I turned around to see if I could catch a glimpse of him at the window and he was there, standing as straight as a royal palm, his hands stuffed in his pockets and his guayabera crisp and white in the sun.

We had all been dreading this moment, but now we couldn't wait for the plane to lift off the ground so there could be no doubt that we'd made it. The plane was full of screaming children and sobbing women and nervous bug-eyed young people paralysed with shock, but we couldn't relate to their misery or their fears. We had our Papi back. Does anyone have some champagne? How about a cigar?

There were more passengers than seats, and several people had to sit on the floor during the short flight to freedom. Mami and Papi sat near the back, huddled together with their hands intertwined. Mami wept and laughed and then wept some more, while Papi held her close to him. Marta and I held each other too, as we heard the faint and mumbled prayers of the other passengers hum all around us.

'Please, Heavenly Father, let us return soon . . . Blessed Mother, have mercy on us and keep us safe . . . Dear Jesus, don't forget our brothers and sisters who stay behind. Let us be together again soon.'

The roar of the engine silenced the prayers and the sobs and the complaints of the children who weren't really sure what was happening to them. In the next few minutes, over two hundred hearts would be ripped from their homeland. Who might survive the trauma, nobody knew. And who might be lucky enough to return and feel the warmth of the Cuban sun course through their veins once again, no one could say.

The plane charged down the runway, rattling and skipping as it went, then lifted its beleaguered cargo up into the Cuban sky. Our swollen eyes peered out of the small windows and watched the green of our island home diminish to a jewel embedded in a glistening sea. It grew smaller and smaller until it was barely a twinkling mist, a memory lost to the harshness of the glaring sun.

And then it was gone.

THE UNITED STATES

STATES

1962–1981

11

November 1962

Dear Alicia,

We haven't landed yet, but already I know . . . I will never be American.

Everyone around me on the plane is happy and talking about how they can't wait for their first American meal with plenty of American meat, and how they're going to drink American beer until it comes out of their ears, when the only thing I can think about is my last conversation with Beba.

She slipped into my room while we were waiting for Abuelo to take us to the airport. As long as I live, I will never forget what she told me. 'When my people came to this country from Africa, many lost their souls, but some survived, Norita. They never forgot who they were and where they came from. They were the strongest ones, and I know you'll be strong like them.'

I told her I felt as weak as a baby, and I was crying like one, too, so she took a white handkerchief from her apron pocket and wiped my eyes. 'You aren't weak, Norita,' she said. 'You're strong and you have a beautiful heart. But people in America will try to steal it from you, and you must resist or you'll lose yourself.'

I asked her how I could keep them from stealing my heart and she said, 'Just as my ancestors did. Give them your ghost heart, for they'll insist you give them something, but keep your real heart for yourself . . . always.'

When the world was as it should be, I would've asked her a million questions about what a ghost heart was and where it came from and how to tell it from my real heart. And she would've explained it to me in her way, which helps me understand just about anything. But just then Papi burst through the door and announced that it was time for us to go. We barely had a chance to say goodbye to Beba, but as I'm writing this letter I see her face in the clouds, and I'll be thinking about her and you when I catch my first glimpse of the land that might steal my heart if I'm not careful. It won't be long now.

I never thought I'd do this, but I made a promise to God like Abuela likes to do. I promised that every day I wake up in this place, the first thing I'm going to do is get on my knees and ask God to end the revolution so we can go home. I won't cut off my eyelashes the way Abuela does, but I'll cut my nails very short and keep them that way until we're back. If you make a promise too, then maybe soon we'll be listening to our Elvis albums in my room, and walking on the beach early before the wind picks up. We'll go shopping at El Encanto to buy new dresses, because there should be many more dances and celebrations when the revolution is over.

Once we find a place to live, I'll write to you again on proper paper (these immigration forms were all they had). And I will keep my heart safe, just like Beba said.

Nora

When we stepped off the plane onto American soil, I hoped the ground would quiver and bolt me off like an angry horse. But I wasn't so lucky. We were immediately directed to form a line against the wall in a large building away from the main airport. For a moment I felt like one of the poor souls lined up against the wall at El Morro, waiting to be executed.

I whispered this to Marta, but Papi overheard and shook my shoulder roughly. 'You listen to me,' he said. 'This is your country now. It's gratitude I want to hear from you and nothing else.'

Poor Papi. There was such fear in his eyes. And it didn't go away, even when we found ourselves in Little Havana, in the heart of Miami, the next day. We were surrounded by Cuban refugees, eating Cuban sandwiches, drinking Cuban coffee and listening to Cuban music blaring from speakers onto the street.

Mami and Marta and I would have been happy to stay in this place, as close to Cuba as possible, but Papi's fear grew worse. He told Mami about his friend at the National Bank, who had found a good job in California. His friend said that in California it wasn't like Miami, where compassion for refugees was wearing thin and opportunities were getting harder to find. And in California there weren't any Cuban ghettos.

A few days later we boarded another plane for California, and the only thing that kept us from complaining was the look in Papi's eyes. They sparkled as I hadn't seen them do since before the revolution. It was a comfort to see, even though I knew that in this new place there'd be no mini Cuba to welcome us when we arrived.

Our new home in California was an apartment, even smaller than Tía Maria's shed out back. Marta and I slept in the living room on a couch that folded out into a lumpy bed, and Mami and Papi slept in the only bedroom. Every day for a week after we arrived, a lady from the church with amazing blond hair, which looked like a stack of hay piled high on her head, brought us a meal. In broken Spanish she explained that the ladies at the church were taking turns making us special dinners so we wouldn't feel homesick.

The first time she made this announcement, we excitedly uncovered the casserole dish and peeked underneath the foil to discover cheese bubbling over brown beans and meat. We'd never seen food like this before, but somehow it was supposed to ward off homesickness.

'Enchiladas,' the blond lady said. 'Mexican food to help you feel at home.'

Nobody had the heart to tell her that we'd never had this strange food in our lives, and that Mexican food was very different from Cuban food. But the enchiladas were pretty good and we ate them around the small kitchen table barely big enough for two people. Our knees bumped into each other, but we tried to make light of it and focus on how lucky we were to have enough food to fill our stomachs. I tried to feel grateful, but everything seemed odd and disjointed: the food, the weather, even the way the leaves fell from the trees one at a time, as though to remind me that I was dying a little every day.

Sometimes after dinner Papi and Marta and I went for walks while Mami did the dishes. She told us she didn't need our help cleaning up, but I knew she didn't want us to see her crying. All of a sudden, she'd become private with her tears.

During one of our walks, I detected a burning smell in the air, similar to the burning of coals before a pig roast. I knew it was impossible, but the mere thought of it warmed my heart with thoughts of home.

'What's that smell, Papi?' I asked.

Marta and Papi sniffed the air, puzzled too.

'Maybe they're burning trash,' Marta suggested.

We walked a bit further and Papi pointed towards

the window of a big two-storey house standing in the middle of a green yard with a white fence all around. There we saw the source of the smell: a fire burning inside the house, right in the middle of the living room. I'd read about this in books, but to see it in real life was strange. How could a country this big and modern still use wood fires to keep houses warm? It seemed illogical to me, when everybody knew that the United States was the richest and most powerful country in the world.

Not that the heater in our own little apartment made me feel any better. For a whole week Mami refused to let Papi light it, because she thought it would blow up in the middle of the night. But we didn't have enough blankets to ward off the cold, so she finally allowed him to turn it on. She then sat vigil next to it all night, watching the blue flame flicker behind the grate.

I could tell Papi liked the house with the fire inside, because every time we walked by he slowed down a little and gazed at it. 'How would you girls like a big house like that some day?' he asked us. I wanted to remind him that we already had an apartment in Cuba overlooking the sea that was just as big, and that Tía Maria's house was twice the size, but I stayed silent.

'I don't want a big house,' Marta said on the verge of tears. 'I just want to go home.'

Papi gave me a knowing look. Now it was just he and I left to be strong. I swallowed my own tears as best I could. 'That big house would be nice, Papi. I'm sure Mami would like it too.'

January 1963

Dear Alicia,
   I dreamed of you for the first time since we left. You were walking along the rim of the island, dragging your feet on the sand and wondering why I hadn't come home yet. You didn't realize I was

sitting at the top of the tallest palm tree watching you. I tried to yell down to you, but my throat was stuck and I couldn't make a sound. My only chance was to throw myself down. I was getting ready to jump, but I wasn't afraid. Even in my dream I could feel the warmth that rescued me from the nightmare of this cold country.

When I woke up and realized where I was, I shut my eyes, hoping that if I didn't move a muscle and went back to sleep, I'd be able to talk to you before the dream ended. But I couldn't do it.

I hadn't cried since the day I left home. I've been trying to be strong for Papi and Mami and Marta, but on that morning, before anyone was awake, I buried my head in the pillow and sobbed so hard it was difficult to breathe and my lungs strained with the hurt I'd kept inside since we arrived. Beba would be disappointed to know that in so little time I've allowed my heart to become as brittle as the crunching leaves beneath my feet.

Marta and I started school last week. Here, boys and girls go to school together. The girls streak their eyes in thick black liner and paint bright frost on their lips, making them look like voodoo dolls, and the boys wear their hair long, almost to their shoulders. Even the teacher's assistant, Jeremy McLaughlin, wears his hair long. All the girls think he's handsome. I suppose he is, if you don't mind that he's probably never once put a comb through his hair because it's so curly. But I shouldn't criticize him. He's been very nice and takes extra time to explain things to me without making a big fuss and drawing attention to the fact that my English is not so good. Everyone here is American and we are the only Cubans in the entire school.

I try to say as little as possible while in class. But one day my teacher decided to begin the day's lesson with a discussion on current events. She showed the class the front page of the newspaper and the headline that read, 'TRADE EMBARGO: THE US RESPONDS TO CASTRO'. Then she asked me to tell the class what I thought about it.

I couldn't think of what to say right away. For me this is more than a current event, it's my home, my heart and my life. Finally, I stood up to speak, even though my teacher said it wasn't necessary. To practise, I will write what I said in English.

'The Trade Embargo with Cuba . . . it is not enough to make change. Castro does not have hunger even though the people have hunger and much fear. They go to jail if they are against the communism. I miss my country and I pray every day I can go back home. There are some things worse than hunger.' Nobody said a word and when I looked over at Jeremy, his eyes were red.

It's so strange to hear myself say to strangers what I can't say at home. I miss being home, and I miss you.

Nora

I wasn't ready to admit, even to Alicia, that I looked forward to school for one reason and one reason only. Jeremy would be there, sprawled behind his desk wearing his blue jeans with a shirt and tie, diligently grading papers and answering questions asked by the mostly female students who found any excuse to be near him. I could hardly blame them. His quiet gaze and unpretentious good looks were irresistible, and I too found my eyes wandering towards him from my front-row desk several times an hour. More than once I caught him watching me, but he didn't look away, embarrassed to be caught, as I did. He smiled sadly, probably pitying me in my starched clothes and knee-high socks, studying me as though I were an odd creature from another world. It was painful to see my awkwardness reflected in his eyes.

133

I was leaving campus that first week when I heard him call my name the way he did, forcing himself to use proper Spanish pronunciation. As I watched him approach, my stomach tensed and I'm sure he noticed the redness gathering about the borders of my face and spreading like a storm of infatuation all over me. He was used to it, of course, used to being adored by every girl who saw him. And so he had many opportunities to practise pretending not to notice. He was doing a very good job of pretending with me.

Slightly out of breath, he said my name again. 'Nora, I hope you don't mind if I ask you something.'

'I don't think so,' I replied, rather stunned to be talking to him at all. I couldn't help but notice Cindy, the pretty blond girl in my homeroom class, staring at us from her locker.

'What's worse than hunger?' he asked, and then expelled a sigh he seemed to have been saving for a week.

Nothing came to mind right away and I became distracted by the intense expression in his eyes, as though he was trying to read my thoughts as they formed.

'I'm sorry to catch you off guard like this. It's just . . . I've been thinking about what you said and I was just wondering . . .' His words trailed off.

'It is easy to find food,' I said cautiously. 'Maybe you don't like it, but you eat it and the hunger goes. When you lose hope . . .' I looked into the soft palette of his hazel eyes once again. 'You wait and hope finds you, but sometimes it doesn't find you.'

Jeremy thought about my answer and slowly nodded his understanding. 'You know something?' he said. 'I'd like to improve my Spanish a bit. If I tutor you in English, will you tutor me in Spanish?'

'You want to learn Spanish?' I asked, smiling now.

'Oh yes,' he said seriously. 'I'm planning to join the Peace Corps and live in South America some day.'

* * *

It was impossible to get to my classes without passing Cindy's locker. I wondered if she'd requested a centrally located one so it was necessary for every member of the student body to notice her at least once during the day. And she took full advantage of her exposure too. She kept herself surrounded by friends who laughed incessantly as they looked out of the corners of their lavishly painted eyes to see if they were creating enough of a spectacle, sharing conversation and gossip without concern for who should hear them. I never paid attention myself; it would've been difficult to capture their words and phrases and put them together in a way that made any sense. The only reason I took half an interest was because more than once I'd seen Cindy strolling with Jeremy as he headed for the teacher's lunchroom. She chattered away and walked kind of sideways so she bumped into his shoulder as though by accident, but I could see by the sparkle in her eye it was not.

'Greasers!' I heard her scream from her locker to the semicircle of friends gathered round. 'He likes greasers!' and she convulsed with a series of high-pitched giggles that infected the rest of the group.

I had almost slipped by, invisible and silent as always, when she addressed me for the first time. 'Hey, your name's Nora, isn't it?'

'My name is Nora Garcia.'

More giggles from the rest of the group.

'Now, why do you suppose a fox like Jeremy likes greasers?' She cocked her head to one side and studied me from head to toe as I tried my best to understand the unusual context in which she used the familiar words 'fox' and 'grease'.

I shook my head, confused and red-faced.

'I thought you'd know, since you're a greaser.' She smiled prettily, while her eyes glared.

This sparked another burst of hysterical giggles and incoherent commentary from the others. I remembered

Beba and her cold stare that could silence the worst of storms. I felt it surging up from the centre of me and filling my eyes, hot and clear. It captured Cindy's watery grey eyes and she blinked curiously once and then twice, flustered to see I hadn't blinked at all.

'What are you staring at?' she mumbled.

I waited a few moments longer before I released her, then walked away without saying a word.

After a brief silence, I heard one of her friends call after me. 'The greaser doesn't understand. Hey, you're in the US of A now, so learn English, why don't you?'

I kept walking until I reached my homeroom class. Jeremy was sitting at his desk and smiled up from his work when he saw me enter. I set my books down in front of him and wasted no time. 'Am I a greaser?' I asked.

He seemed confused and a bit annoyed. 'I hate that word.'

'Some people just called me a greaser.'

Jeremy's concern became tinged with shame. 'It's an insulting term fools use to describe people with a Spanish heritage.'

'Then I am a greaser,' I said, delighted and smiling with the warm knowledge that Cindy said Jeremy liked greasers. I was almost positive that's what she'd said.

'I don't like hearing you say that, Nora.'

'I am a greaser,' I replied, quite satisfied. 'I am Spanish, like you say. And Spanish people are greasers, so I am a greaser.'

Jeremy shook his head, half smiling at me, and swallowed his amusement. 'OK, if you say so, but you don't have to keep saying it over and over, do you? How about referring to yourself as Latina or Hispanic or just . . . Cuban?'

12

May 1963

Dear Alicia,

Papi finally found a job at a bank in downtown Los Angeles. He has to get up at four-thirty in the morning to catch the bus and make it to work on time. It's not a prestigious job like he had in Cuba. He's a low-level accountant and I heard him tell Mami that he reports to a man with a fraction of his education and experience, but they say that's no reason not to be grateful. When he came home with the news, Mami was outside hanging laundry, and she got down on her knees to thank God as the wet sheets flapped in her face. Later she told me that if Papi hadn't found this job he would've had to take another job in construction, laying tiles with someone he'd met on the bus who offered to teach him how. I wanted to ask Mami if she considered chopping sugar cane in the fields to be more dishonourable work than laying tiles, but it took me several days to get up the courage. When I finally did, she answered without getting upset or breaking down as I feared she would. She said, 'Neither type of work is dishonourable, but if your father's going to break his back for a living, it should be to feed

137

his family and not for that man.'

I must begin my homework before it gets too late, as I have an early morning English lesson with Jeremy.

Every day I check the mail, hoping there will be a letter from you, and every day I'm disappointed. Please write soon.

Nora

'What are you doing?' Mami asked me early one Sunday morning. I was settled on the kitchen table, the only writing surface in our tiny apartment.

'I'm writing to Alicia.'

Mami raised her eyebrows in surprise. 'You can write if you want, but she probably won't get it. They're intercepting the mail, cutting it up and censoring it so that sometimes there isn't anything left.' She yawned and shuffled across the kitchen – two shuffles would get her to the coffeepot. I shuddered to think she was starting to get used to the watery American coffee that she claimed helped her digestion.

She beckoned that I follow her back into the bedroom where Papi was snoring peacefully, and pulled out a large cardboard gift box from under the bed. Inside was a disorderly array of photographs and envelopes. I took one, held it to my nose, and the homesickness I'd been feeling since we left rolled over me like an enormous wave. I could smell garlic and onions and sweet tobacco and lilac perfume and the sea itself. I felt I might stumble, so I sat on the bed with the letter still held up to my face. How could our home be over there and we be over here? How did this absurd thing happen?

'I thought we weren't allowed to bring photographs with us?'

Mami sat down next to me and lowered her voice. 'Your father got so mad at me when he saw them. I smuggled them out inside the lining of the suitcase.' She shook her head. 'I know it was a risk, but I couldn't leave without taking some memories with me.' She reached for a photograph and showed me. It was their wedding photograph, which had always lived in an elaborate silver frame on the shelf by the window. The line where the sun had faded the picture was clearly visible. Their smiles, once innocent and beautiful, now inspired sadness.

Then I found the picture I'd been looking for. I could kiss Mami's feet for including it. It was of Alicia and me, hand in hand, the ocean swirling about our ankles on the day we celebrated Alicia's tenth birthday. The whole family had gone to Varadero beach for the day and we'd just completed our swimming lesson with Abuelo. We looked exhausted but elated as we smiled into the camera. I looked closer: our skinny limbs were still shiny from the sea, my hair was plastered against my cheek in an unflattering mess, but Alicia looked beautiful as always, chin up and golden hair lifted by the wind. I wished I could dive into the picture and never come back.

'You can keep it if you like,' Mami said softly.

'Thank you.'

'Actually, this is what I wanted to show you,' she said, holding an envelope out for me to examine. I could see by the signature that it was a letter from Tía Maria, but it was peppered with square cut-outs throughout, so if you held it up it looked like the snowflake decorations I'd seen hanging in the American classrooms. I tried to read it, but it was difficult to understand and I kept falling into those little holes. The only message that came through loud and clear was that Tía's arthritis was getting worse.

'The communists are censoring everything,' she said with palpable disgust. 'Even letters from little old ladies who complain about aches and pains and not having enough coffee for their breakfast.'

I placed the photo in the drawer of my nightstand, and looked at it every night, wondering if Alicia had received even one of my letters. I planned to show this photograph to Jeremy. We'd been meeting regularly for our tutoring sessions and I knew he'd be fascinated to see Alicia, who I'd told him about, and to see us at the beach that I tried to describe with my limited English. 'It is so beautiful and warm and my words are not enough. I can only say it is the place where my heart belongs.'

September 1963

Dear Alicia,

Of all the letters I've written so far, I hope this one reaches you more than any of the others. Perhaps that isn't quite true, but I'm so upset right now that it feels true and the only thing I can think of is to write to you, and pretend that you're here, or better yet, that I'm there.

There's serious trouble with Marta. It started when I noticed her leaving for school a good fifteen minutes earlier than necessary, saying that she wanted to get to school early so she could get a 'jump start' on her studies, whatever that means. She likes using American phrases like 'get off my back' and 'don't have a cow', and she tries to act as if she was born here, which I believe only makes her look foolish.

I always walk the same route to school, but one morning they were digging up the road so I had to take another. That's when I spotted Marta sitting on somebody's porch, and she wasn't alone. She was with a boy. I've seen him at my school, so I know he's a couple of years older than Marta.

They didn't see me, even though I was stomping my feet so hard that I could feel my soles tingling. I can't begin to imagine what Marta was doing. She knows she shouldn't ever be alone with a boy. But I could see by the familiarity in their eyes that this was not their first meeting.

I called out her name just as he was bending down to kiss her, and she jumped, obviously horror-stricken to see that I'd caught her in the act. But when she stepped off the porch and walked towards me, she looked just like the little girl I'd known in Cuba. I wanted to whisk her away back home and hide her under the bed and slap her cheeks until she came back to her senses.

She told me his name is Eddie and that he's her boyfriend. Can you believe that? And then she told me that things are different here and that people don't follow strict rules like they do in Cuba.

And I said, yelling right in the middle of the street, 'I don't care what people do here. You can't change the fact that you're Cuban, even if you change your hair and clothes, kiss every boy you see and eat hamburgers for breakfast, lunch and dinner. You can't change it.'

Marta stared at me for a few seconds and I thought she might cry, but I know she was only worried that I'd tell Mami and Papi about what I'd seen. I thought long and hard about what I should do. And I finally decided not to tell them, because I don't want them to send her away like your parents did to you. But I might change my mind.

We walked the rest of the way to school wordlessly. And when we parted at the corner, I didn't answer her when she said goodbye. And I refused to speak to her later that day after school as well.

Perhaps you will read this and think I was too harsh with Marta. But the way I see it, she's betraying who she is, and for what? An American boy whose life revolves around football. I bet he doesn't even know where Cuba is on the map. If you were here and living in this place, I know you'd understand. I miss you now more than ever.

Nora

I posted the letter to Alicia the next morning and arrived at class one or two minutes late, to find Jeremy not waiting for me as usual, but talking with Cindy. She glanced at me, then at the clock on the wall, annoyed that I'd interrupted them. But she was the one interrupting us. Jeremy and I met daily for our Spanish/English lessons and he was learning quite rapidly. He always told me what a good teacher I was and that I should consider taking it up as a profession. When he said this, his hazel eyes softened with appreciation and his hand seemed to move just a little closer to mine. Our hands had been accidentally touching quite a bit lately, as had our knees when we fumbled to get comfortable around the little table we shared during our lesson.

But Cindy was leaning on our little table and sticking her backside out while she continued chattering and laughing away, oblivious to me and my heated glances. I sat at my desk and pretended to be absorbed in my books and papers, turning the pages of my notebook this way and that. How long was I expected to wait? Jeremy hadn't even said hello to me yet.

I glanced at him once again and my heart broke, just like that. The softness I had seen in his eyes when he had looked at me had intensified into a smouldering heat and he was slightly flushed. She probably didn't notice, because she hadn't memorized the creamy tones of his face as I had. She didn't know that when he didn't shave in the mornings there was a delicate bridge of hair that appeared just above his jaw line, which rippled like the sea when he chewed gum. And he loved to chew gum in between classes, the only time it was allowed. Spearmint was his favourite. He'd probably treated me to three or four packs during our lessons.

Still, I couldn't deny that Cindy was beautiful in the way American girls were considered beautiful. She always wore her hair loose around her shoulders, like a golden shawl. It glistened spectacularly in the sun as well as under the glare of fluorescent lights, and she swung it around as often as she could and on the most unnatural of pretexts. When searching for a book under her desk she'd have to swing her golden mane. When raising her hand in class or entering a room and deciding where to sit, swoosh would go her hair and the effect was like a red cape on a mad bull ... all the boys were transfixed, just as Jeremy appeared to be at that moment.

Yet if you examined her closely, you'd see that her nose was slightly raised so you could see into her nostrils, and although her smile was cute and her laugh infectious, her lips were thin and her teeth tinged yellow-grey from the cigarettes she liked to smoke when she walked home from school. Had Jeremy noticed this?

He must have whispered that he had to help this Spanish girl with her English, and I noticed him glance at her rear end, tightly packaged like a pair of oranges, when she left. That was another thing: American boys preferred skinny women, while in Cuba Cindy's figure would've been rejected as unwomanly and unattractive. They even had butt pads for people like her. I heard Beba telling Mami one day when they were chatting in the kitchen.

I focused on the English lesson that followed more intensely than ever. I made absolutely certain that our hands and knees never touched accidentally. I had planned to show Jeremy the photograph of Alicia and me at Varadero beach. I'd told him about it the day before and how dangerous it had been for my mother to smuggle it out of the country the way she had done. He was very keen to see it, as I knew he would be.

'So where's that photograph you were going to show me?' he asked once we'd settled in for our lesson at the little table.

I avoided his gaze and pretended to look for a

143

particular page in my book. 'The photograph . . . I forgot to bring it.'

He cocked his head to one side. 'How could you forget, Nora?'

I felt a surge of indignation. The photograph was tucked into my Spanish–English dictionary. I could've opened up the page and shown him the splendour of my previous life, just as I longed to open my heart, but I quickly dropped the dictionary into my bag instead.

'I think I may have lost it, because it isn't where I left it.'

'So you didn't forget it?'

For the first time since I'd met Jeremy, I wanted to run away with my books and never return. These Americans can't get a subtle hint to back off. They hunt you down with their questions and wide-eyed curiosity as if they have a right to know everything.

'I just didn't bring it,' I muttered. 'That's all.'

The next day I was relieved to find Jeremy alone, but I felt my mouth and eyes tighten as I avoided his gaze. He was watching me with concern. Even out of the corner of my eye, I detected a smile playing about his lips and this unnerved me even more. He hadn't even opened his book, although we'd decided to begin with his Spanish lesson for a change, as I'd concluded I was moving along with my English more quickly than he was with his Spanish.

'Something is wrong?' I asked as he sat twirling his pencil in his fingers.

'I was going to ask you the same thing.'

I felt my ears go hot and a flush spread towards my cheeks. Once again, I had to fight the sudden urge to run out of the room.

He placed the pencil on the desk and leaned forward so he was near me, so near I could count the fine gold stubble on his upper lip. 'Nora, I may be only a few years older than you, but I'm still a teacher here and there are certain things a teacher shouldn't do . . .'

'I know what you do here.'

Jeremy appeared flustered too now and he pushed his long hair out of his eyes. 'The girl you saw me talking with yesterday . . .'

'Cindy.'

'Yes, Cindy.' He nodded. 'She's a student and I'm a teacher. And you're a student . . .'

'And you're a teacher,' I said, acting as if we'd just begun our lesson.

He smiled with me, but placed his hand on the dictionary I was preparing to open. 'If I wasn't a teacher . . .' His eyes searched my face as he summoned the courage to say something, but then thought better of it and sighed. 'I think we understand each other, don't we?'

I matched his smile and nodded. 'You are a very good teacher, Jeremy.'

13

December 1963

Dear Alicia,

The other night I heard Mami and Papi talking
when they thought I wasn't listening. Our apartment
is so small that the only place for privacy is in the
bathroom or outside the kitchen on the back step.
The window over the sink was open so it was easy
for me to hear them. Papi said that he'd heard your
father had disappeared, like he did before. He was
trying to keep Mami from worrying and I was worried
too for a moment, but I felt better as I kept listening.

Papi also said he was certain that what happened
with Batista before would happen with Castro now,
and there was such hope and affection in his voice.
Papi has always been very realistic about the
revolution and the chances of our going home, not at
all like the rest of us who constantly wish for the
impossible. If Papi says that things with Castro are
going to change then I believe him, and I salute your
brave Papi for helping this to happen. You must be
very proud to be his daughter.

I have a wonderful feeling that this Christmas we'll
be all together again. Don't be surprised if the next
time you hear from me I'm standing at your front

door with a car waiting at the kerb to take us to the beach. I suggest you tell Abuelo that next time we go swimming I'm going to beat him to the platform and back again.

It's late and I must get up early for my English lesson with Jeremy. I never thought I could like an American boy as much as I like him, and if I let myself, I could even fall in love. But Jeremy, like all Americans, prefers skinny girls with blond hair. I'm still skinny, but last time I checked my hair was blacker than coal. Nevertheless, I'm learning English very quickly and I'll put it to good use when I return. I'm certain the new government will need plenty of translators. Perhaps you can investigate this for me when you have time.

This is the happiest I've been for a long time.

Nora

'Eddie and I broke up,' Marta announced on our way to school a few weeks later.

I was so surprised to hear her speak his name so casually that I didn't say anything right away.

'Don't you want to know why?' She kept her eyes on the sidewalk. 'He told me I was a prude and he didn't want a prude for a girlfriend.'

I searched my memory bank for the word 'prude', but it was nowhere to be found. I hated to ask Marta what it meant; it made me feel small and unworthy to show her she was learning better English than me. Anyway, I could ask Jeremy what it meant later.

'I thought I should tell you, so you could stop worrying about me,' Marta added.

And so you don't have to worry about me telling Mami and Papi any more, I thought.

We were almost at school when I held onto her arm for a moment. 'Marta, please don't do this again. It'll be so much harder when we go back . . .'

147

'What makes you think we're going back?'

'I heard they're trying to get rid of Castro and . . .' I stopped myself. 'I just know it, I feel it inside.'

Marta shook her head and rolled her eyes. 'Don't fool yourself, Nora.'

Jeremy looked startled to hear my question and he turned the same rosy colour he had when talking to Cindy. He tapped his pencil on the desk. 'Let's see, it's kind of like . . . Well, it sort of depends how you mean . . . or . . .' Then he turned to me boldly. 'Why do you need to know this?'

'My sister broke up with a boy who said she is a prude. I don't know what it means, but she should not be with him and I have to be careful for her because I can't tell my parents because they might send her away and—'

'Wait a minute . . . What happened with your sister and this boy?' Jeremy looked serious, and although I had forgiven him for his attraction to Cindy and decided that a trusting friendship with him would be better than nothing, the way he stroked his chin and nodded his head made me reconsider how I felt about him all over again.

'I don't know what happened. She is not supposed to have a boyfriend.'

'How old is she?'

'Almost fifteen.'

'It seems to me . . . Why isn't she supposed to have a boyfriend?'

'She is too young. She has not even introduced the boy to my parents.'

Jeremy's eyebrows lifted. It seemed as if there were many things he wanted to say.

I inched closer to him and lowered my voice. 'In Cuba a man and woman are not ever alone until they get married.'

'Are you serious?'

148

'It is true. Everywhere they go before they are chaperoned to make sure.'

'To make sure of what?'

'That nothing bad happens between them.'

'Oh, man,' Jeremy said, shaking his head in amazement. 'I never knew that stuff still went on.'

'If a woman is caught alone with a man who is not her brother or father, people will think she is bad like a prostitute and then no man will marry her.'

Jeremy almost jumped in his seat at the word prostitute. 'I can see why you're so worried about Marta, then.'

I nodded, glad that he'd understood. 'So what does it mean . . . prude?'

Jeremy readjusted himself in his seat and faced me, his eyes sincere and open, but once again there was a smile lurking. 'Before I tell you, would you answer a question for me?'

I nodded, eager to get on with our lesson.

'Do your parents know about our meetings?' While he waited for my answer his eyes positively sparkled. He seemed to enjoy the dilemma he'd created for me.

I tore my eyes away from his. My hands were hot as I fumbled with my books. 'It's different for us.'

'Why? I'm not your father or your brother, am I?'

I felt as though he was playing with me, using his knowledge of my attraction for his amusement, and it maddened me. 'You are the teacher and I am the student. Your words.'

'I remember them.'

'And,' I looked him straight in the eye this time, unconcerned with whether my face was on fire or not, 'you are not how Eddie is with Marta.'

'You mean I'm not your boyfriend. How do you say boyfriend in Spanish again?'

'You know how.' I felt flustered.

'Tell me anyway. I like how you say it.'

'*Novio.*'

He said the word to himself several times, perfectly imitating my accent and not removing his eyes from my face.

'So are you going to tell me what it means, this word? Prude?'

His eyes fell away from my face and he cleared his throat while shuffling his papers. 'Well, it's . . . Let's just say it's the opposite of a prostitute.'

I heard him calling my name a few days later when I was walking home from school. He ran to catch up with me, his long legs and arms pumping like an athlete's. I rarely saw him outside the classroom – he was panting slightly and squinting in the bright sunlight. He was so different from any boy I'd known in Cuba. I'd have to find a way to describe him better in my next letter to Alicia.

'Nora,' he said, laughing a little and shaking his head so that his curls bounced and bobbed. 'I thought I'd have to call you tonight and I don't have your phone number.'

'What's wrong?'

Jeremy grabbed my arm. 'I got my assignment. I'll be going to Peru in a few weeks, but I have to leave immediately for the training.'

'I don't understand.'

'The Peace Corps. Remember I told you?' Jeremy spoke with such enthusiasm and delight that it looked as though his eyes were going to pop out of his head.

I smiled and congratulated him and said all the things I knew I had to say to make him believe I was happy. I couldn't let him see that with this news he was taking away the only thing that made getting up in the morning to go to school worthwhile. How could he know that I'd come to depend on him in the way that I'd depended on El Angel de la Guardia during the early months of the revolution? He was my sanctuary. And now, once again, there were no more sanctuaries.

'I'm going to miss working with you . . . and seeing you.' He was still smiling and looking into my eyes. My sadness intensified. I was at the airport leaving my country all over again and there was a deep pain in the pit of my stomach that left me fluttering and vulnerable and lost.

Jeremy cocked his head to one side as he did when he didn't understand my English or Spanish, depending on who was teaching who. His smile faded and he seemed to be a little lost as well. He placed an awkward hand on my shoulder and left it there, so the warmth penetrated through three layers of clothing and stamped my shoulder with his touch. 'Thank you for being such a good teacher,' he said.

I was about to thank him too, when she swept down upon us. Cindy, with her turbulence of blond hair, her yellow smile and exceptional energy. She circled Jeremy, prodding and touching him repeatedly so he had to remove his hand from my shoulder.

'Hey, that's great news! I just found out,' she said, and Jeremy smiled and turned that amazing shade of red. 'Come and tell me all about where you're going.' She pulled possessively on his arm. As always, I was invisible to her.

They were already across the street and Jeremy kept turning around and waving while Cindy jumped all over him, like the aggressive cheerleader she was.

'I'll look for you when I get back,' he called out, holding Cindy at bay, causing her to freeze for a moment.

'How long will that be?' I called back.

'Two years, give or take a few weeks.'

I smiled and waved. We'd be back in Cuba by then. I'd be walking on the beach and attending chaperoned dances by the dozen. Abuela would buy me dresses that accentuated a figure that was beginning to fill out quite nicely. Not as dramatically as Alicia's, but soft and feminine just the same.

I wrapped my coat tighter around me and wondered if the Peace Corps ever sent people to Cuba. I should've asked Jeremy when I had a chance. I should've suggested that he consider going to Cuba when he talked to me about joining months ago, but I hadn't liked talking about the possibility that he would leave, and it was too late to worry about this now.

I'd never see him again. Of this I was certain.

14

IT WAS HARD TO BELIEVE WE HAD BEEN AWAY FROM OUR country for more than two years. In some ways, the time had gone by quickly in our struggle to adjust. In others, it felt as if we'd been gone for decades, and I feared that in spite of my promise I was forgetting how to be Cuban. My English was fluent, although I still had an accent. Marta and I almost always conversed in English now, but when we argued or confided our most secret feelings, we switched back to Spanish.

We'd saved enough money to move out of our one-bedroom apartment and into a two-bedroom house, complete with a little yard at the front and back that Mami wanted to convert into a beautiful garden, even though she'd never touched earth in all her life. But she was true to her word and the garden of our little house flourished. Almost every afternoon when I came home from school I'd find her digging the flower beds, pulling out weeds, pouring in plant food or selecting roses for the table. She was happiest when gardening, but it was disturbing for me to see her hunched over in the dirt with a handkerchief tied around her head and her face smudged. She'd long foregone the habit of dressing well even if she was staying at home, and had adopted her own version of American casual: a stretched polyester tracksuit one of the church ladies had given her when we first arrived, and tattered house slippers. This was something a respectable Cuban woman would never have done, but Mami happily waved her gardening tools at passers-by without the slightest concern for her appearance. And if it was the little old lady, Mrs Miller, who lived next door and who Mami said reminded her of Abuela, she'd find a perfect rose to give her as well.

I liked Mrs Miller too. She always told me I was an elegant young lady and too smart for the crazy boys of today. Perhaps she'd seen Marta walking home with different boys who'd disappear the minute they turned the corner, whereas I was always alone. Or maybe she just said those nice things because I put her newspaper on her porch when it landed out on the grass, as I knew she had arthritis in her knees and going down the front steps was difficult for her. Whatever the reason, I felt good in her company and found the smell of soap and baby powder that lingered about her comforting, and the slow deliberate way she planned all of her movements, like opening her purse for a cough drop.

The cold winds warmed steadily through spring, and by summer, if it were not for the dryness in the air, I could almost imagine I was in the tropics again. Mami was especially proud of the way her roses were coming along. But one afternoon when I arrived home from school, she wasn't in the yard, although her gardening tools were scattered on the ground and a bag of topsoil had fallen over, making a tremendous mess on the steps. The front door was open, and when I entered I heard Mami's low mournful wails, and Mrs Miller's frail voice trying to console her. I threw my books down and ran into the kitchen to find Mami with her head on the table and Mrs Miller stroking her back with a trembling hand.

'Your daughter's here, Regina,' Mrs Miller said,

obviously relieved to be sharing this burden. But Mami didn't look up. She simply stopped sobbing and became very still.

My heart froze with fear. 'What happened?'

Mrs Miller reached for a yellow paper from the table to give me, but Mami snatched it back. 'I don't want you to see this. Your Tío Carlos is gone. That's all you need to know.'

'Gone?'

'Dead. He's dead.' Mami's eyes challenged me to keep my distance. She was lying, I knew she was. How could Tío Carlos be dead? He was younger than Papi. Handsome and smart and strong. He'd never been sick a day in his life. Why would Mami make up such a thing?

I took a step closer. 'Let me see the letter.'

She clutched the envelope tightly in her hand and shook her head.

'Mami, you can't protect us from everything. We're not little girls any more. Please.'

She dropped her head and began to sob silently once again. Without looking at me, her hand released the yellow paper on the table. It was a telegram and the Spanish words read, 'CARLOS ALEJANDRO GARCIA DIED ON 2 JUNE 1965 — STOP. EXECUTED BY FIRING SQUAD — STOP. A TRAITOR TO THE REVOLUTION — STOP.'

A trembling, aching feeling overtook me. I sat next to Mami and felt Mrs Miller's hand on my back this time. I read the telegram over and over. *Executed by firing squad.* I saw his sweet smile, and the way he played his guitar, taking requests while relaxing on Tía Maria's porch. *Executed by firing squad.* He was never angry, and even when he and Papi argued about politics, he maintained a hint of a smile and he'd end the exchange with a friendly slap on Papi's back. *Executed by firing squad.* Alicia was his princess. His eyes lit up whenever she came in the room and he used to tell her to stop growing so fast, that he wasn't ready for a big girl yet. *Executed by firing squad*. Alicia, oh my God, Alicia. I still hadn't heard from her, and by now I feared that I never would. How could she find the strength to live? Tía Nina could never survive it.

Mrs Miller sat down at the table beside us. 'What's wrong, dear?' Poor Mrs Miller. The telegram was in Spanish and Mami and I had been talking in Spanish too. She had no idea what was going on.

Saying the words out loud made it real in a way that burned through my soul, a branding of hatred and pain that I knew would never go away.

'They killed my Uncle Carlos. They murdered him, because he stood up for what he believed in, because he had the courage to speak against injustice, because he loved his country, our country. They stood him up against a wall and shot him like a dog because they knew that as long as he lived, their lies would be discovered. They murdered him because he was too strong for them.'

Mrs Miller gasped. She may have expected a death in the family, but nothing like this. The fine trembling in her hands grew more pronounced and her touch was jittery and warm on my arm. 'Oh my. I'm sorry, I'm so sorry.'

She made us tea and we sat silently in the darkening kitchen for some time. Marta should've come home an hour ago and Papi would be home soon, and I knew this was Mami's primary concern now.

At last, we walked Mrs Miller to the door and thanked her for her help. Then we turned on one light and waited in the living room.

The phone rang. It was Marta asking if she could stay for dinner at Debbie's house. 'You need to come home,' Mami said. 'No, you need to come. Something's happened and we need you here. I can't tell you over the phone.'

We heard Papi's car in the drive and looked at each

other, knowing the worst was yet to come, wishing we could do anything to spare him this pain.

He saw us sitting in the semi darkness, waiting for him with swollen eyes. Mami stood up, the telegram in her pocket. Her lips began to tremble. 'José, something has happened.'

He dropped his briefcase to the floor and together they walked to their bedroom. The door closed and with a pillow pressed to my belly, I waited. I heard his scream in the very core of my soul, in a place where the worst of humanity can be imagined and where the idea of hell was conceived. My own sobs exploded from the back of my throat – I couldn't prevent them, and I almost stopped breathing before I realized I'd been suffocating myself in the pillow in an effort to stifle my crying.

I heard him again: 'Dear God, oh Dear Blessed Mother . . . Not Carlitos . . . please God . . . not my brother . . .'

I wanted to go in and help comfort him, but I knew Papi would allow only Mami to see him like this. For everyone else, he must always be strong and in control. I must respect this.

Then Marta came through the front door ready to offer excuses for her lateness. I told her what had happened and her face twisted in agony. She heard Papi scream from the bedroom, dropped her bag and ran to their room.

'Marta, you can't go in,' I said, running after her. I grabbed her arm, but she wrenched it free and burst through the bedroom door. Papi was lying on their bed in his suit, his knees up to his chest, sobbing as Mami stroked his hair, talking softly with a gentle strength we only saw when he was unable to be strong.

Marta threw herself on the bed and curled up next to him with her arm around his shoulder. He didn't seem to notice her at first, but then his hand came around and touched her cheek. Mami saw me standing in the doorway and motioned for me to enter as well.

'We need to pray,' she whispered, but only Mami and I were able to say the words of the Our Father without sobbing.

'Tell your father what you said to Mrs Miller today,' my mother asked. And so I tried to remember and to make it sound eloquent and real, but I stumbled a bit, so eager was I to make it somehow better.

As I talked of Tío Carlos's courage and strength, Papi gazed up at me and nodded slowly. He took my hand and pressed it to his lips. 'Thank you, Nora.'

After a few weeks, we stopped speaking of Tío Carlos's death. It was like talking about the air that we breathed, or the ground beneath our feet. It was always with us, and the sadness we felt pushed us deeper into the American way of life. Even I had to give in a little and concede that my dream of returning home was fading past the point of recognition. But sometimes, as I walked to and from school on my usual route, the realization of what was happening came upon me like the sudden rainstorms of the tropics. I used to love the rain and the way it washed the world clean. But these storms were of a different sort. They were filled with the tears I was too tired to shed myself and they fell upon soil I could no longer feel beneath my feet. But the more I sank into my cautious understanding of survival, the more Marta seemed to bloom. She flourished in this strange weather, and I watched her unfold as though she were not my sister, that little girl that had scuttled after me and Alicia in my other life. She was changing as surely as if she'd shed her old skin and slipped into the pale freckled hide of the Americanas who were her friends.

Sometimes when she talked about her friends and the boys she liked, I felt a deep sorrow in the pit of my stomach. But at least with Marta I wasn't forced to pretend, and I scowled fiercely at her.

'You're such a drip, Nora,' she'd say with her crisp American pronunciation that was a marvel to my slow tongue.

I'd answer her in Spanish. 'I'm not what you say. I keep my real heart safe. I don't give it away so easily like you do.'

'That's a really strange thing to say. Have you taken a good look at how weird you're getting? I'm embarrassed that people know you're my sister sometimes. I feel like telling everyone my sister is a nun or that she's dead.'

'Maybe that's exactly what you should tell them: that I'm dead.'

I couldn't explain in either language this peculiar pain that refused to heal. It was always there, and I had eventually grown to love it as the only reminder I had left of who I was, the only certitude that I had once belonged to my life and my world.

Marta's eyes filled with tears and she switched to Spanish. 'Nora, don't talk about being dead. It makes me sad and I hate feeling sad.'

I waited for her to wipe her eyes. The sun had started to set, and because the window of our room faced west, for just a few minutes every afternoon the walls were bathed in golden light and we became translucent.

Marta's dark eyes opened wide as she absorbed the light. 'I miss the way you used to be, Nora. You were so happy and fun and all I wanted to do was be with you. Remember?'

'I remember.'

'Why can't it be like that again?'

I couldn't think of an answer that would make any sense, so I stayed silent and we watched the golden light slip from the room and the quiet grey of twilight fill the space of our dreams.

The envelope, worn and creased at the corners from its

long journey, was propped on my pillow when I arrived home from school. I immediately recognized the writing on the outside, always graceful and neat, but slanting to the left instead of the right. My fingers trembled as I eased open the seal and Alicia's voice floated up from the pages like a beloved melody from long ago.

March 1966

Dear Nora,

I finally found the strength of heart to write back to you. I also found a way, through an old friend of Papi's, to send you this letter so that words aren't cut out here and there as the government does. And believe me, if not for that there'd be only one big picture window, a frame for your beautiful face that I miss so much.

It's been nine months since they killed Papi. We were allowed to send one telegram after his death. Those words 'traitor to the revolution' were not our words, but considering the choices we were given, 'traitor to his country and his people' and others just as bad, they seemed like the best option. The truth is that Papi would've been proud to be considered a traitor to the revolution. Soon after you left, he came to understand that Castro was never going to allow for free and democratic elections, especially after President Urrutia was removed.

Papi was gone for weeks at a time when things got bad. He wouldn't tell us what he was doing, or where he was going, but we knew it was more dangerous than before. Mami became very sick during this time. She had to go to Abuela's. We both went. Towards the end we hardly ever saw him. We'd hear how he was doing through friends who'd come to our door in the middle of the night and leave us whispered messages or scribbled ones on scraps of paper. Mami burned them in the ashtray right after she read them, crying all the while. She was unable to get out of bed after we heard Papi was captured.

Abuela tried to pull me away from the television when we saw him, but she would've had to tear out my eyes to keep me from watching. He stood together with the others and he was so thin, I almost didn't recognize him. During that last moment of his life, he turned his face to heaven and called out, 'Viva la libertad! Viva Cuba!'

I screamed it with him and for hours after they killed him. Until my voice was hoarse and I could hardly breathe, I screamed. Abuela closed all the windows for fear of the spies that are everywhere, but I didn't care then and I don't care now. Even after so many months have passed my heart is still screaming with him, Nora. They're silent screams that become great hurling sobs in the middle of the night when no one can hear. Every day I have the feeling he'll be home any minute and then I realize I'll be waiting for my father the rest of my life.

I can't explain the sadness that's lodged itself in my heart. I no longer feel the need to function as a human being, to bathe, to eat, to brush off the flies that land on my face and arms. I'm a paper doll, flat and empty, pretending to be like everybody else only because I'm tired of explaining why I'm not.

Mami stopped speaking altogether after Papi died. The doctor sent her to the Sanitarium and said that with medicines for her nerves she'll get better, but I'm not sure there's any cure for what she has or that she wants to be cured. Tía Panchita sent for me after Mami went away. She thought it would be better for me in the country away from the madness of the revolution, but there's no getting away from it. This disease has infected every person, every bird, every grain of sand. The island has detached from its usual place and drifted to some other spot on earth, where life means something different than it used to.

I have read your letters, each one a thousand times, and pretend all the while that you are here with me still. Please keep writing and don't interpret the length of time it took me to write back after Papi's death as anything other than the weakness of a frail heart.

Alicia

I refolded the letter and tucked it underneath the picture of Alicia and me in my nightstand drawer. Every night for weeks I took a moment to visit it. It was no longer necessary to read the words, for I'd memorized every one. Instead, I studied Alicia's script and felt the pain in every curve of the line, every tenuous crossing of the pen. Although thousands of miles away, we were together again and the understanding between us was stronger than ever.

I began to feel more like myself, and more alive than I had since leaving my country. And with every letter that arrived, I thanked God for granting me the peace of yet another sanctuary.

June 1966

Dear Nora,

I'm going to write to you about the day I came back to life. I pray with all my heart you understand how close to death I actually was and that my will to live goes beyond politics and fear and even the memory of my father, may he rest in peace. I don't understand all that is happening to me, but writing to you about it and imagining your quiet way of listening helps me beyond what I can express.

I hadn't been outside the house for weeks. I feared that if sunlight touched my skin I'd be turned to dust or if it hit my eyes I'd go blind. I was so weak that even thinking about whether or not I should eat made me tired, and often I'd go back to bed for the rest of the day when I'd only been up for an hour or two.

I was sitting in the shadows of the kitchen when Tony came in. He was even more beautiful than I remembered him, and I felt my heart move the instant I saw him. For the first time since Papi died, I became aware of the breath entering my lungs and the mild aching in my legs that were folded underneath me.

He sat down and told me Panchita and Lola were worried about me and that I needed to eat and get well for many reasons. His voice was like warm honey and right away I felt the rumbling of hunger in my stomach. He took a loaf of bread from the cupboard, broke off a piece and handed it to me. I ate it completely, and the next, and the one after that. Then he peeled the last banana Tía had, and I ate it straight from his hands. A delicious energy coursed through my veins and I felt how a little baby must feel when he's born fresh into the world.

He came to see me every day after that and every day I got stronger. We went for walks into the forest, he read to me from his revolutionary books and I listened to his voice and tried to ignore the words. Tony believes in the revolution with all his heart and soul. He's taken me to his village and I've seen the way the poor children live, without shoes, without food and clean water. Most of them can't read or even write their own names. Tony believes all children should be taught how to read and have the chance for a decent life.

He tells me these things while we rock on the porch or walk through the sugar-cane fields hand in hand. He also says that he's loved me since the first day he met me and that I'm the most beautiful woman he knows. He doesn't say this as I've heard other men tell me, Nora. I can just see you shaking your head. He says it with true light in his eyes, so I know he sees beauty in my heart the way I see it in his. And because of this, when we stroll beyond the grounds of Tía's house and wander behind the trees, I let him kiss me on the lips like we did so many years ago. I press my body against him so that my chest melts into his and I feel the strength of his desire for me right on my belly. The only nourishment I need is to drink from his lips and to feel his arms around me. I'm not ashamed to say that I want nothing more than to lie with him and give him all that I am. I never knew I could love a man or anyone the way I love Tony. He has become my life, Nora, and I have become his.

He wants me to go with him to work the sugar-cane fields when I'm stronger. The party is asking people to sign up in support of the revolution, even pregnant women and sick old people. I can't imagine supporting anyone or anything that killed my father, but I can't bear the thought of being away from Tony even for one day. I haven't told Tía Panchita yet, but I'm sure I will go with Tony to the sugar-cane fields or to the ends of the earth; it's all the same to me.

Do you suppose Papi would forgive me? Sometimes I imagine him up in heaven watching me and weeping for the decision I've made to love Tony. At other times I believe he's happy that I'm alive again and able to love, when I was sure my heart and soul had died. Perhaps he can see from heaven that right and wrong aren't as important as happiness and love. Or perhaps I'm simply a fool, too weak and shallow to care about anything but my own survival.

You wrote before that you didn't think me capable of betrayal. Yet isn't this the worst betrayal of all? Do not spare my feelings. I've always been able to hear the truth from you, if no one else. Please write to me again soon. I'll be waiting.

Alicia

15

MAMI TOSSED THE PAMPHLET I HAD GIVEN HER TO REVIEW back on the kitchen table. 'What's this Peace Corps business?' she asked, pronouncing 'Corps' as if it were a dead body and with as much disdain as if she could smell it rotting.

'It's a government organization that trains people, mostly young college-age people, to go to other countries and help with—'

'Oh yes, I remember hearing about this now,' she said, getting up from her chair to attend to the stew she had on the stove. 'Kennedy started all this, didn't he?' She nodded severely, like a detective who had just figured out who committed the murder.

'There's nothing wrong with it, Mami. It's a very good cause and poorer countries benefit from the help that's brought in.'

She stirred with one hand and placed the other squarely on her hip. 'When do you go to college? What happens to your scholarship?'

'I won't lose my scholarship if I wait a couple of years, and then I'll have more life experience. When you have life experience it helps you do better in college. That's what my counsellor told me.'

She started to mutter, which I knew wasn't a good sign. It meant she was trying to keep the kettle of anxiety she always had simmering in her heart from overflowing. 'Life experience, eh? Why don't you go down to skid row and take a good look at what life experience can do for you?' She waved her spoon in the general direction of where she thought skid row would be.

'That's hardly a fair comparison.'

She turned to face me, her cheeks flushed from more than the steam rising from the stove. 'Don't talk to me about what's fair, because I know better than anyone that nothing's fair in this life. Is it fair that you have an opportunity to go to one of the best colleges in this country and that you'd rather go traipsing through the jungle instead? Is it fair that you sleep in clean sheets every night with a full belly, when other young people your age can't be sure where they'll sleep or where they'll get their next meal? They make it sound real glamorous,' she said with an all-knowing roll of her eyes, something she'd recently picked up from Marta. 'Taking young people from their comfortable lives and out to the sugar-cane fields, putting guajiro hats on their heads and machetes in their hands and making them believe they're supporting some great cause for humanity.'

'I never said anything about going to Cuba, Mami.' I could hear my voice rising in spite of my effort to remain calm.

'Maybe not, but those corpse people go there too. I saw them on TV not long ago, and it made me sick to my stomach to hear the reporters talk about sugar-cane production and increased profits when everybody knows the people are hungry enough to eat their own shoes if they had any.' She pointed the spoon directly at me this time. 'If you even think about going back there to help that man, then you're no daughter of mine. Do you understand what I'm telling you?'

'I understand perfectly,' I said, almost yelling. 'But

you don't understand that I'm not going to Cuba. This has nothing to do with Cuba.'

She held the spoon steadily at me. 'Don't you forget who you're talking to, young lady. I'm your mother and you need to show some respect.'

I lowered my eyes and she lowered her spoon. After some more muttering, Mami put the lid back on the pot and forced herself to sit back down at the kitchen table to take another look at the pamphlet she'd dismissed so easily before. She turned the pages, squinting at the pictures of people raising livestock and digging ditches alongside the natives, smiling all the while as if comforted by the knowledge that they were single-handedly saving the world.

She was making an effort to be reasonable. She'd made some progress when dealing with Marta lately, but she'd never expected any trouble from me. 'Now tell me honestly, Nora,' she said, studying me with sincere curiosity. 'What do you want with all this? I could understand if you had always enjoyed camping or if you had a great love for cows and dirt, but the truth is you won't even help me plant a rose bush out in the yard when I ask you to.'

Encouraged by the disappearing crease between her brows, I made a brave attempt at explaining my humanistic sensibilities. I'd even managed to speak for three or four uninterrupted minutes when Marta came home from school, sniffing about for a preview of the evening meal. She only needed to listen for thirty seconds or so before folding her arms and making her declaration.

'Oh, I know what this is all about,' she said with a self-satisfied smirk. 'It's about that guy who used to tutor you, isn't it?'

'What are you talking about?' Mami asked, suddenly alarmed at the mention of some guy she knew nothing about.

'This has nothing to do with Jeremy,' I shot back.

'Jeremy? Who's this Jeremy?' Mami's cheeks were reddening once again.

'Oh no?' Marta replied, ignoring Mami's question. 'He's the only person you know who ever went to the Peace Corps. You wouldn't admit it, but I know you were in love with him. Not that I blame you . . .'

Mami threw the pamphlet on the table for a second time. 'Do you mean to tell me that you want to put off your college education for a boy? Is that what this is about, Nora Garcia?'

I sat red-faced and silenced by my shame. I hadn't stopped thinking about Jeremy since he left, and I couldn't deny I'd been nurturing visions of finding him in the steamy jungles of Peru ever since reading about Alicia's plans to follow Tony to the ends of the earth, if need be.

'Really, Nora, I thought you were different. If Marta came up with something like this I'd understand, but you—'

'Hey, what's that supposed to mean?' came Marta's half-hearted complaint, but she was far too satisfied to see me squirming to take it any further.

With head hanging low, Mami placed both hands palms-down on the table, as if ready to conduct a séance. Then she raised her head slowly and glared at me. 'I'm not going to tell your father about this, Nora. Because if I did, the disappointment would surely kill him. I don't have the heart to do it, and I certainly hope you don't either.' She turned to Marta, her tone somewhat fiercer. 'And that means you too, young lady.'

University life was as comforting as it was desolate. I sat in huge auditoriums with no fewer than 150 students and took feverish notes, barely raising my head to look at the professor for fear that I might miss an important point. Once again, I was invisible, like the black hole in space described in my astronomy class, absorbing and sucking in everything around it without ever revealing itself.

And yet there were some definite improvements to my life. Something about the anonymity of the place made me feel freer than I ever had done in High School. Since I was never required to speak in class, nobody heard my accent. I could be whoever I wanted to be. I took to wearing jeans and Mexican sandals every day, varying only a sweater or shirt. Even when it rained, I wore socks with my sandals and carefully avoided puddles. I let my hair fall loose around my shoulders without brushing out the waves. One day I caught sight of my reflection in a window and actually liked what I saw. I looked again. Was it really me? It was the same narrow face and serious expression, but there was another presence behind the eyes ... my timidity had been replaced by a self-satisfied independence that went very well with my appearance. I fancied myself a wild and exotic creature, from nowhere and everywhere. Mami wasn't much concerned with my change in style, and even purchased a few oversized sweaters for me. She'd seen Marta transform herself so often that my evolution was like the receding of the Ice Age in comparison.

My vague dissatisfaction with life, coupled with a lack of social distractions, gave me a distinct academic advantage and I managed to land on the Dean's List at the end of my first quarter. I even received an invitation to attend a Chancellor's reception at Royce Hall, along with other honorees. Instinctively, I hid the invitation from Mami and Papi, aware that my anonymity would be challenged at such an event. I'd have to talk about where I came from, faltering while my listeners nodded and smiled that obligatory smile of feigned understanding. They'd ask me if I was Iranian or Egyptian, because they couldn't place my accent and weren't accustomed to Latinas in their circle of academic excellence.

There was no doubt in my mind that this was an event to be avoided at all costs, and on the day of the reception I ensconced myself in the most remote corner of Powel Library to read Alicia's most recent letter. I had already planned to reward myself with it if I could get through a third of my reading for the Medieval European History class. As it turned out, I finished with enough time to read Alicia's letter and respond with one of my own as well.

December 1967

Dear Nora,

I'm starting to believe that God purposely partners good with bad so we can understand that life is never simple and is sometimes more confusing than a Chinese recipe for kimbobo.

I'm writing this letter from a small hut Tony and I share with two other couples in the heart of the jungle in Matanzas. We've been living here for about five months, ever since we were married. That's the good news: Tony and I are married, and we'll be blessed with a child in seven months. Can you believe it? I'm going to be a mother, Nora! And I pray that our baby will have Tony's pure heart and strength. He's already begun building a sturdy crib from straight pieces of wood he collects in the jungle around the village. He wants to finish it as soon as he can because (and this is the bad news) he'll be going away to Africa soon. They're putting together troops of the strongest and most intelligent men for the cause in Angola.

I love him more every day. With this life we made growing inside me, I feel I'll go crazy with love for him. Every night since I found out he was leaving I cry myself to sleep. It's almost as bad as when Papi died, that dark pain gripping the very centre of my heart and squeezing it until I can hardly breathe.

Tony tells me I have to be strong for the baby, otherwise it'll sense my sadness and be born cranky and weak instead of happy and strong. I try, Nora, believe me I try to hold back the tears, but whenever I think about being alone again, I can't help myself. The other night I was glad when a storm blew through the village, so Tony wouldn't hear me sobbing again. I don't want him to think I'm weak, but I'm afraid I am. I can no longer put on that face I used to have. Remember it? I could make anyone believe I wasn't afraid of anything and that I could calm a hurricane by shaking my finger at it. All of that stubborn strength has now left me, and I feel more lonely than I ever have before.

Lola and Tía Panchita were happy to hear about the baby, but no one else in the family is, I'm afraid. They still believe a white woman has no business with a man who isn't as white as she is. It doesn't matter if he's kind and intelligent like my Tony. I thought Abuelo and Abuela would be different, so I took him to Varadero to show him the house where we spent so much of our childhood, our beach and our palm trees. We knocked on the door, and when Abuela saw Tony standing next to me she slammed it in our faces, but not before saying that I shamed the whole family and the memory of my father by this marriage. I don't think Abuelo was home, but it's too painful to think of going back. I won't put Tony through that again. I wouldn't hurt him for a lifetime of conversations with people who've turned their backs on me.

Tony's greatest hope is that he'll be invited to join the party. Even as I write these words and feel the hot wind of the jungle surrounding me, I shudder. How can I forget that the party killed my father? I don't forget and I'll never forgive them . . . yet I see goodness here. I see people working harder than they ever have in their lives to improve a village where

171

there was never running water. I see a medical clinic being built next to a schoolhouse and if all goes as planned the children and adults in the village will be immunized against major diseases and be able to read in one year's time. It's happening all over Cuba.

Sometimes I wake up in the middle of the night and wonder what's happened to this world. It's as if God and the Devil are the same man, depending on how you look at him, and so I try not to look too hard or else I will go back to how I was, a hopeless and pitiful woman.

The sun has gone down and Tony will be home shortly. We don't have much for dinner, a little left-over beans and rice. It's amazing how a bit of food can seem like a feast when you're sharing it with the one you love. After we eat, I'll settle myself into his arms and watch the stars come out over the treetops. If my life never changes from this moment on, I'll be the happiest woman on earth. I hope and pray that some day you can say as much and more.

Some of my new friends say I shouldn't write to you any more. They say you and your family are traitors for leaving, but I defend you most of all. You had no choice but to leave and now your life has changed as much as mine.

I miss you, Nora. More than ever, I miss you now. I promise you as I promise Tony to be strong. I hope you do the same. May I hear from you soon.

Alicia

16

'HOW DO I LOOK?' MAMI ASKED, SURVEYING HERSELF IN THE full-length mirror in the bedroom. 'Your father said he wants me to wear something youthful.'

I studied her with an objective eye. Red was always a good colour on her, and although she'd put on a few pounds, the overall effect was very flattering. I told her so.

'You're not just saying that?'

'You look great. Papi will love it.'

For some time now, Papi had been able to budget for the occasional dinner out at a restaurant, and they'd been looking forward to this date all week while reminiscing about how it was in Cuba before the revolution. Their plan to try a small Italian place in town could hardly compare to the opulent nightclubs and seaside resorts they had frequented there, but they weren't complaining.

'Do you ever think of going back?' I asked Mami as she stepped into her new red shoes. She wavered a bit and reached out to the bed for support.

'Going back where?'

'Home, of course. To Cuba. I hear a lot of people are visiting now.'

She turned to me, her eyes more fiery than her crimson dress. She kicked off her shoes and padded across the thick carpet in her stockinged feet. 'Cuba isn't home any more, Nora. And those fools who go back to visit forget they were called traitors and gusanos when they left. They forget everything to set foot in their homeland again before they die. They want to look upon their green island and pretend they never left. I will never go back while that man is there. Do you understand me?'

'Alicia says it's not so bad. That there are good things happening too.'

Mami spun around. 'Alicia? What does she know?'

'She lives there. She sees it all with her own eyes.'

'I'll tell you about Alicia. She's taken up with that black boy. And if that weren't bad enough, he's a communist. He's brainwashing her to think the way he thinks and to do the things he does. Next thing you know, he'll turn her into a Santera. He probably already has.'

'How do you know about Tony?'

'Alicia's not the only one writing letters. Your Abuela wrote all about the disgrace Alicia's made of her life. She and Abuelo can't wait to leave. Just pray their visas come up soon.' Mami continued to mutter as she looked for a pair of earrings in her drawer. 'The only person who's seen that girl lately is Tía Panchita. But everyone knows she's a little crazy and doesn't understand the problem between black and white people. Black people don't believe in interracial marriage either, let me tell you.'

There was no use arguing with Mami when she got onto certain subjects, and racial relations was certainly one of them. I dared not tell her that Alicia and Tony were married and expecting a baby.

'Is Abuelo coming too?'

'They're both planning to get out of Cuba as soon as their visas are ready.'

My heart leapt at the thought of seeing Abuelo again. I pictured him with his soft smiling eyes staring out at the sea, studying the rolling surf and undercurrents to determine if it was a good day for swimming. We walk into the warm clear water side by side and swim at an easy pace to the platform. We pull ourselves up and wait until the sea has dried like flat crystals on our skin before we dive in again and head for shore. I hear him next to me, breathing steadily, his arms arcing in perfect smooth circles that slip in and out of the water without so much as a ripple. We walk back along the shore and I marvel at his youthful physique. He's almost seventy, but his back is as straight as a board and his chestnut hair, barely frosting at the temples, falls full and thick on his forehead.

'That was a good swim, Abuelo.'

He turns to me and smiles with a warmth that outshines the sun beating down upon our shoulders. 'Yes, the water was fresh and smooth today. It was a good swim.'

I follow him back to the house, where Abuela is waiting with our afternoon meal.

Just a splinter of this memory fills me with a quiet joy for what was, and a deep sadness for what will never be again.

In a crazy way, even Mami's outdated and glaring racism touches me in a tender way. I don't agree with it, but the fact that I remember her expounding those same views while standing out on our balcony in Havana with friends and family, not at all concerned that Beba was in and out freshening drinks and emptying ashtrays, makes me love it a little bit. Beba often agreed with her on the subject.

'Black folk get along better with black folk,' she'd say with a swaying nod of her turbaned head. 'Nobody can argue with that. I don't see any reason why it should be different with white folk.'

Mami applied her hairspray in quick bursts about her head. 'I always thought Alicia was a little crazy,' she said, her mouth taut, her eyes squinting against the fumes. 'She's crazier now than ever, I think.' She applied her lipstick in one tidy sweep across her lips. 'Keep your head on straight, Nora.'

September 1968

Dear Nora,

Everything you heard about childbirth is a lie. It's much worse than they say. I felt my body ripping open from the inside out and all of my parts falling out of place. After the baby was born, I asked Tony to look and see if my legs were still attached, and if my navel was where it had been before, because I was sure I looked like a rag doll pulled apart by an angry gorilla. Tony laughed so hard he cried huge tears as he held Lucinda in his arms for me to see for the first time.

Isn't Lucinda a beautiful name? I think of the soft light that reflects off the ocean when I say it. Tony says she looks like me, but there's no doubt that Lucinda is his daughter. I prayed our baby would have her father's eyes, and my prayers were answered.

Today is the kind of day I'm sure you treasure in your heart. The breeze is lifting the trees and carries a fragrant warmth you can taste, like honey and mint. The sun sparkles off every leaf and every particle of dust that floats by, and the stillness reminds us that days like this should never change. We've come to stay with Tía and Lola, and sometimes I sit on the corner of the porch where I first met Tony and pretend nothing has changed for us. But it has, Nora.

The party has assigned six families to live with Tía and Lola. They were sharing the kitchen and the bathroom when we arrived and didn't even have one of the bedrooms to themselves. They were living in the little pantry room off the kitchen, where Tía stored sacks of sugar before. There's just enough room for a cot and for an old mattress next to it. Thank God there's a window, but the screen was broken and Tía and Lola's legs and arms were covered with mosquito bites. I couldn't stop crying when I saw them.

Less than an hour after we arrived, Tony selected two of the least dilapidated slave shacks behind the fields and was out there with an axe, a hammer and a huge broom, which he used to kill the rats before he could get to any sweeping. He said there were hundreds of them as big as little dogs, not to mention scorpions and spiders of every size. Every time he talked about it, Tía and Lola gave out little screams that made him laugh like a schoolboy. I laughed too. Living in the jungle has cured me of these womanish fears.

Within a week, we moved into our new houses. Tía and Lola's house is right next to ours. They're simple, but clean and a definite improvement on where Tony and I spent our first year of marriage. The windows have little shutters we can close at night to keep out most of the pests, and when I look outside I see Lola and Tía on their new porch, rocking away in their chairs.

The family that took over the pantry was so grateful for the extra space that they gave us a mattress they weren't using. Tony placed it right under the window, so when we lay together at night we could still see the stars, like we did in the jungle. Tía found a roll of mosquito netting and we fixed up our little bed so that it's actually quite pleasant. We enjoy quite a bit of privacy because the sugar-cane stalks block the view from the main house and hardly anyone bothers to cross the field unless they need to go to the river, which isn't very often.

This is where I gave birth to my beautiful Lucinda and where we spent the first few weeks of our life together as a family. She slept between us as we watched the stars – with each one that appeared we whispered a new blessing for our daughter, and we fell asleep with such love in our hearts.

But the dream is over, Nora, at least for a while. Tony's been gone for weeks and I don't know how much longer it'll be before he returns. I could say I miss him, but that's like saying I can live on a single breath for the whole day. Tony has taken my soul with him to Angola. I spend most of my day praying for him and imagining what expression is playing on his face at that moment. Mostly, I imagine the look in his eyes when he wants to make love to me. His eyes caress me first with such longing that my heart flutters and my knees go weak. Then he smiles so slightly that I can't be sure it wasn't just a shadow brushing his cheeks. That's all he needs to do and I'm his, however and whenever he wants me.

I try to stay strong by reminding myself of the process of change and that, with a revolution that challenges the philosophy of a whole country, things always get worse before they get better. There are great agricultural works being planned. Rivers are being dammed all around the island to harness power, and soon they tell us there will be prosperity for all, not just for a few like before.

There's a place for Tony and Lucinda and me in this future. We'll be together again and live in a house right on the shores of Varadero. I dream that some day you'll come to visit us and we'll sit on the sand under the palms for hours and watch our children play.

Alicia

We rarely ate dinner as a family any more. Papi frequently arrived late from the office, sometimes I didn't get home from the university until well past seven, depending on traffic, and Marta always had something going on. I wasn't surprised, therefore, to find Mami sitting alone at the kitchen table with a plate of leftover stew from the previous night.

I took a plate from the cupboard, served myself and sat next to her. She was moving the chunks of meat around on her plate without eating.

'I talked to Marta today,' she said, not looking up. 'Or rather, she talked to me.'

I began the painstaking task of separating the raisins from the rest of the meal and waited. Mami often complained to me about Marta. She'd describe her antics in colourful detail and defame her latest boyfriend, who was always unworthy of her. Her most recent concern had been that Marta wasn't interested in continuing her education after High School at all. 'Can you imagine?' Mami had said. 'What's she going to do? Flip hamburgers for a living?'

I looked up from my plate and noticed her red-rimmed eyes. 'What is it?'

Her tears flowed. 'I don't know what your father's going to do. Marta says she's getting married to that boy – that boy with no education, and no way to support a family. She hardly knows him, for God's sake. How long have they been seeing each other? Six months?'

'I believe it's been five years, on and off.'

Mami grabbed her napkin and blew her nose loudly. 'Anyway, she's still a child. I don't care if the law says she's old enough to be married. Everyone who knows Marta knows she's still a child.'

'I thought you and Papi liked Eddie better than the others.'

'We do. It's not that he's a bad boy, but he's a boy,' Mami said, leaning towards me on her elbows.

'And didn't he get accepted at USC?'

'Yes. But does he have a job? No, he doesn't. You know what Marta says? Just listen to this.' Mami waved her napkin in the air. 'She says that she'll support Eddie while he studies and then he'll support her when he's finished. Have you ever heard of anything so preposterous?'

'That sounds kind of nice to me.'

'I can just see Marta working her fingers to the bone. Once he's got his degree hanging safely on the wall, he'll find somebody else and leave her planted.'

Mami wanted nothing less for us than the fairy tale she used to tell us of her own courtship and marriage. Tucked in for the night behind a cloud of mosquito netting, we'd beg her to tell us the story.

'Again?' she'd ask, laughing with pleasure. 'I've told you that story three times this week.'

'We want to hear it again,' we'd wail.

She's a cameo silhouetted in the moonlight as she speaks. 'I was very young when your father and I met, no more than nineteen, and I was tiny, but I had a very nice shape!' We laugh and giggle our approval as ritual demands. 'Your Abuelo made arrangements for a grand party to be held in honour of your Tía Griselda, who'd just returned from Europe. There were tables set on the sand and boleros sung by a trio and bright flowers everywhere. Of course, I was excited to see Tía Griselda and hear about her trip, but I was especially excited to meet the young man I'd heard so much about from my cousins. This young man, whose name you already know,' (more giggles) 'was the good friend of my cousin Alberto. He came from a well-established family in Havana. They had a beautiful house in Varadero, and if that wasn't enough, he was already a rising star in the National Bank. You better believe all my cousins and I were carefully selecting what to wear that day.'

'What did you wear, Mami?' we ask.

'I decided that whatever I wore, it had to be white. I wanted this young man to notice right away what a good colour it was for me.' It takes us a few years to get this joke, but we laugh along anyway.

'When I first saw your father, he was wearing a linen

suit and a Panama hat as he looked out at the ocean. He didn't have to turn around for me to know he was handsome. I could already tell by his posture and the breadth of his shoulders. But when he did turn around . . .' Marta and I sit up in our beds and poke our heads through the mosquito netting so we can clearly see Mami's eyes light up brighter than the moon floating outside the window. '. . . I almost fainted.'

'Why did you almost faint, Mami?' we ask, already having memorized the answer.

'Now, I don't just say this because he's your father, but he was the most handsome man I ever saw in my life! All my cousins fell in love with him instantly, but—'

'We know, we know! He only had eyes for you.'

'That's right. And he didn't leave my side the entire afternoon. Every weekend after that he invited me to go somewhere: the movies, or to see a beautiful show at the Copa Cabana, or to a magnificent dinner. Six months later, he asked your grandfather for my hand, and we were married at the Church of the Sacred Heart, the same church where both of you were baptized. I was the happiest woman on earth and I have been ever since.'

Mami closes the blinds so the moonlight lies in luminous bars across the floor and wall all around us. 'Now I don't want to hear any talking, just sleeping,' she says before kissing us each good night.

Now Mami twisted her napkin so that it fell to pieces on the kitchen table. 'What am I going to tell your father?'

I took hold of her hands to still them. 'Weren't you just a little over nineteen years old yourself when you got married?'

'Yes, but a girl didn't need an education like she does now. A pretty face could get you a lot in those days, but it's a different world here.'

'That's exactly right,' I told her. 'It's a different world.'

Heated arguments followed, some lasting well into the night and concluding with the slamming of doors and a few threats thrown in for good measure. 'If you think we're going to spend a fortune on your wedding when we should be paying for your college education, you're crazy,' Mami would yell.

'Then I'll elope,' Marta countered. 'And we'll move away and have many children – your grandchildren – who you'll never know.'

This was usually followed by Papi's more reasonable plea. 'Now let's not talk this craziness, both of you. Let's calm down . . .'

I was impressed with Marta's fortitude. She had to endure both Papi and Mami's onslaught for days. They made a formidable team: Mami a volcano of emotions, erupting with an irregular but agonizing rhythm; Papi, like the relentless drip of a leaking tap. I tried to intervene once or twice, but was quickly put in my place.

'Nora,' Papi said, his anger controlled. 'You may be in college and getting good marks, but you don't know everything yet.'

I was ready to turn out the light after a particularly tense day when Marta came in and sat down on my bed. She looked like a wounded puppy as she scrambled up next to me. We could've been in Cuba, watching the stars through our bedroom window, feeling the warm breeze wrap itself around us one last time before we retreated to our tented beds.

'Thanks for trying to help with Mami and Papi.'

'I'm afraid I wasn't much use.'

Marta punched the bed with both fists at once. 'They think we're supposed to do things their way until we die. It's my choice who and when I marry, not theirs.'

'Of course it is.'

'But it's so hard, because much as I want to say, "The

182

hell with you, we're not in Cuba any more," I can't. It feels like I'd be cutting out my own heart.' Marta buried her face in her hands and began to sob for the seventh or eighth time that day. She reminded me so much of Mami.

'Have you talked to Eddie?' I asked gently.

'I don't want to hurt him. He thinks Papi and Mami like him so much and everything . . .' Marta looked at me, her brown eyes swimming with tears. 'What should I do?'

Two days later, Eddie showed up at the front door wearing a suit and tie. His freckled face was flushed and his hair slicked back with the broad stroke of a very wet comb. I hardly recognized him. No one had ever seen Eddie in anything but a pair of faded jeans and a football jersey. With barely a hello to anyone, he asked to speak with Papi.

Mami glared at Marta, who was curled up on the couch leafing through one of the many bridal magazines she enjoyed flaunting. We followed Eddie into the kitchen, where Papi sat reading the evening paper.

'Excuse me, Mr Garcia . . .' Eddie shoved his hands in his pockets and then pulled them out again as if he'd touched something hot.

Papi lowered his paper. A slight redness began to glow about his ears as he surveyed the scene before him; I was afraid he might throw Eddie out of the house or explode in his face. He said nothing.

Eddie cleared his throat. His voice wavered, stringy and high. 'I owe you an apology, sir, and I hope that you'll accept it.'

'I don't understand.'

'I love your daughter, Mr Garcia . . . Marta.' He coughed. 'I asked her to marry me, because I want to spend the rest of my life with her, but I didn't ask you first. I didn't realize . . .'

I glanced at Mami, who was smiling through her tears. Papi stood up from his chair, his eyes also brimming.

'Mr Garcia ... I'm asking you for permission to marry your daughter.'

Marta slipped up next to me and squeezed my hand. 'Thank you,' she whispered.

17

Dear Nora,

So much has changed since my last letter to you.
Some of the changes I saw coming, but others fell on
me like a wall of bricks, and each brick has inflicted
its own particular pain.

Lola died last month and Tía didn't speak for days.
She just sat in her rocking chair with Lola's empty
chair next to her. For a long time she wouldn't let
anyone sit in it, except for me when I needed to feed
Lucinda. She hardly ate and never cried in front of
me, but at night I heard her. She sounded like a little
girl sobbing and suffering from a kind of pain she's
too young to understand.

The government's ploughing over all the sugar-cane
fields and planting a new kind of hay for cows. The
plan is for Cuba to become the top dairy-producing
country in the western hemisphere. What that means
is that we had to move out of our houses in the field
and now we live in a little apartment in Havana, near
the malecón. The rains have come and they haven't
stopped for days. Tony's not back yet, and the aching
in my heart has spread out through my entire body so
that I'm just one giant ugly sore of a person. Some

days, I don't think I smile even once. Tía says my sadness is affecting my little Lucinda, because she hardly smiles like other babies do. She doesn't play with the little toys we make her or the brightly coloured flowers I show her. All she likes to do is sit and stare at the sun.

But I wish you could've seen her the first day I took her to the sea. It was one of those days when the sun explodes in the sky and lights everything up to ten times its usual brilliance. The greens were greener, the blues were beyond heavenly and the sand whiter than I imagine snow to be. Tía sat on the sand as I took Lucinda down to the water. As always, she raised her head to the sun and would've been happy to do just that, but when we entered the water she splashed and bounced up and down with such happiness that I cried and cried as she laughed and laughed.

I've had this secret fear, Nora, and you're the first to know. Sometimes I wonder if there's something wrong with my little Lucinda, because she's not like other children. She's so serious all the time, like she's thinking these important thoughts instead of exploring with her little hands and feet, the way I see other babies do. But when I took her to the village doctor in Guines, he told me she was fine and very healthy and that I shouldn't worry. But I still do. When I saw her frolicking in the ocean, all my fears lifted from my heart and I felt light enough to fly to the top of the palm trees.

I received a box of letters from Tony last week. He's been writing to me regularly, but with mail backed up the way it is, they all came at once. It was like a feast for my heart. And I was most overjoyed to read that he'll be coming home soon. This strengthened me, and I found the will to visit Mami in the Sanatorium, but as before, she didn't recognize me. And when I spoke of Papi she thought I was referring to the man down the hall who she says is her husband. They tell me she is not likely to improve, and my only comfort is that she appears happier than most.

You may have heard that Abuelo and Abuela's visas finally arrived. What you don't know is that tomorrow Lucinda and I will take the train to Varadero, where Abuelo will secretly meet us at the beach where we used to go swimming. I haven't been there for years. Do you think it's changed?

I must bring this letter to a close. Tía's waiting for me. She's better now, even stronger than she was before. It's as if she swallowed up all of Lola's strength, so that now she's as strong as the two of them put together. We go out every afternoon before the markets close, to see if we can find a few bananas or maybe a bag of rice at a lower price. I've managed to get a few things free. Tía says it's because of my looks, which still aren't too bad, even though I don't have a proper dress to wear. It's almost an adventure. We take our ration books, and even if it's not our day we show up and stand at the end of whatever line we find, which sometimes wraps around the block. When we get to the front (this only works with men), I ask in my sweetest voice if there's anything left. Everyone knows that even when the shelves are empty there's always something left. So I bat my eyelashes, I toss my hair this way and that, and even smile seductively. In this way I've been able to get three cans of milk, a loaf of bread, half a bag of rice, and once, when this man told me that I looked like Botticelli's Venus, a whole chicken. Most days, though, I don't get anything at all, and I'm afraid that soon I'll have to jump on the counter and dance like a showgirl. I'm a little ashamed to admit this even to you, but hunger can lead a person to do things they would've once considered impossible.

I'm afraid that I'm not much of a revolutionary. I

think too much about myself and my needs and not enough about what's good for the country. Perhaps it would've been better had you stayed and I left. But you are still here, Nora, I can feel it in your letters. You never left.

Alicia

When Abuelo and Abuela descended the steps of the plane, I hardly recognized them. They looked as though they'd lost 100 pounds between them. Abuelo wore a faded suit somewhere between green and grey, which was obviously made for a man twice his size, and Abuela's normally plump cheeks were sunken, giving the impression that she'd lost most of her teeth. We managed not to gasp at the sight of them, but inside we were flooded with tears. For years we'd comforted ourselves with the thought that perhaps things weren't as bad in Cuba as we'd heard. After all, when people are missing their loved ones and adjusting to great social changes, they can be prone to exaggeration, and Cubans love to tell their stories with a flare for the dramatic. We only had to take one look at the hollow sadness lurking in Abuelo and Abuela's eyes to know that even our worst fears couldn't compare to the reality of their suffering.

We hugged them cautiously, as if they might disintegrate in our arms if we weren't careful, and they looked upon us as if we were strangers. Was it the shock of it all? Was it like opening your eyes and realizing that the dream and the nightmare have suddenly reversed?

When we got home, Abuelo sat on the white couch and moved his rickety hands up and over the soft cushions. He gazed about at the pictures on the walls and stared at Marta and me with the same vacant appreciation.

'We missed you, Abuelo,' we said. But this old man sitting in front of us wasn't my Abuelo who had taught me how to swim. Those weren't the tranquil eyes that surveyed the ocean, the solid arms that cut easily and steadily through the crystal-blue waters. Abuelo had sloughed off his skin like a snake and sent it on the plane without him.

Abuela picked at the cheese plate on the coffee table and chattered non-stop like an angry bird, her bony ankles crossed and her stockings rolled down below her knees because of her bad circulation. The red crease across her forehead created by her hair net turned redder as she talked about the plane trip, how it had pitched and how she'd feared Fidel himself would shoot the plane out of the sky, just because he could.

For days they wandered about our house, as though searching for something they weren't sure they wanted to find. It wasn't unusual for Abuelo to walk into a room and just stand there watching us, as if he couldn't be sure whether we were real people or ghosts playing with his imagination. They didn't like to go out much, and Abuela contented herself with making Cuban dishes she hadn't been able to cook for years, due to the lack of ingredients.

One evening, she presented us with a giant roast leg of pork on a silver platter. She placed it in the centre of the dining-room table, sat in her chair, and began to weep.

'What is it, Mama?' Papi asked.

'For years I prayed that one day I can cook a leg of pork like this for my children again. Now I'm crying with gratitude. Forgive me.'

The pork was unusually delicious that night, the way we remembered it in Cuba. Abuelo said it was so good because it was seasoned with our tears.

Summer turned into autumn, and Abuelo began raking the leaves on our front lawn in the afternoons. He marvelled, as I once had, at the falling leaves, the russet and yellow carpet crunching beneath our feet. Abuelo told me that raking the leaves and smelling the earth on his hands reminded him that he still belonged to the land, even though he was so far from his home.

'Are you sorry you left, Abuelo?'

He laughed at little at this question. He was looking much more how I remembered him, robust and confident, and he didn't slow his brisk pace with the rake. 'I'd be lying if I told you that I didn't go to sleep every night with the sounds and smells of my country pulling at me like a stubborn dream. But I'll tell you this: it's much easier to sleep with the pain of nostalgia in your heart than the pain of hunger in your belly.'

We played dominoes after dinner almost every night. I looked forward to this ritual, and imagined we were sitting on the porch at Varadero, gazing out at the Caribbean, rather than on our redwood deck overlooking the valley filled with a sea of smog. It was at these moments, when we were alone, that I dared ask him about Alicia and Lucinda.

'Oh, yes, we met at the beach,' Abuelo whispered, casting a wary eye over his shoulder in case Abuela should hear him. 'Alicia is as lovely as ever, but thin like everybody else. She's doing better than most,' he added, when he saw my concern. 'And Lucinda is a beautiful child. Her eyes are more captivating than the ocean and sky put together, but so sad. I've never seen anything quite like it. When I held her and tried to make her smile, she looked through me straight to my heart.' He shook his head sadly and turned his attention back to the dominoes.

'Do you think Alicia will ever leave Cuba?'

He clucked his tongue with certainty. 'She still believes in the revolution, that child. And Tony's a good man. He saved her after Carlitos died, but he brainwashed her in the process. She's forgotten all about her father, and her mother, who's still locked up in the hospital. She doesn't seem to see the country falling to pieces around her. I don't know if it's the revolution or the obsession she has for her husband, but there's no talking to her about emigrating. She looks at you in much the same way Lucinda does, and says she'll never leave her home.'

The north campus café was a crowded blur of commotion, but I managed to feel peaceful in the midst of such frantic activity. I always sat in the far corner and sipped my coffee until about nine o' clock, depending on the time of my first class. It was a strange place for an education major to spend time, because all my classes were at the opposite end of the campus, but that's precisely why I preferred this spot. It was a small reminder that I had choices and space and freedom.

I'd been on a couple of dates since starting at the university, but had managed to end the exchanges efficiently enough. Perhaps Sister Margarita knew what she was talking about all those years ago. It seemed that the religious life was a pleasant one, with few worries. Mami and Papi might be proud to have a daughter committed to the Church. Mami could write to all the family and brag about me, as if now her place in heaven was secured.

'Nora, is it you?'

Startled, I spilled coffee over the table, creating a hot waterfall onto my jeans in the process.

'Oh, no, I'm sorry . . . I . . .' Jeremy rushed to grab a handful of napkins from the dispenser and I stared after him, hot coffee dripping off my thighs. Time suddenly spun around and did a flip. Jeremy was no longer real to me, but a legend from some distant time and place. Now here he was, blotting the table with a wad of napkins, laughing and shaking his head just like I remembered.

I placed my hand on his shoulder. 'Jeremy . . . you're

here . . . I mean, what are you doing here?' A flutter in my throat made it difficult to swallow, let alone speak.

He laughed again and gave me a warm and friendly hug. 'Nora, my God, it's good to see you.' He held me out at arm's length. 'You look different than I remember you . . . but the eyes are yours.' He gave my shoulders a squeeze. 'May I sit with you a while?'

'Of course.'

I moved my books off the table and blushed when our knees touched by accident, just like in High School. He explained that he was considering an assistant professorship in the anthropology department. He'd been travelling for the last couple of years, mostly in South and Central America.

'I dare say my Spanish is as good as your English now,' he bragged with an impish grin.

'Show me,' I challenged in Spanish.

Jeremy's eyes sparkled, and he began to chatter about the weather and about the different countries he'd visited and his hope to return soon. I listened politely and nodded with genuine approval at his fluency and accurate accent. Some words he spoke almost like a native.

'I was looking for you,' he said, reverting back to English.

'You were?'

Jeremy finished his coffee and tossed the empty cup into a nearby bin. 'About two years ago. I saw your name on a list of students invited to a reception of some sort, but you didn't show up.' He looked past me, as if trying to remember a dream, then shook the fog out of his head and laughed. I held my breath and waited for my life to change in the instant it took for his eyes to flicker and his chest to fall. 'I remember that reception well.'

'Really? Why?'

'It was just a few days before I got married.'

Long seconds passed before I was able to congratulate him and smile, but it was a far from convincing smile and best attempted while sipping coffee and hiding behind my cup. 'Any kids?'

'No, not yet. Jane has a few health problems. She came down with malaria on our travels and it's weakened her a bit.'

I tried to express my sympathy, while concealing the fact that I was quite pleased his wife's name was Jane and not Cindy.

'Do you have a class now?' he asked.

'Yes, I'm late.'

'Come on, then,' he said, grabbing my backpack and making a show of how heavy it was. 'I'll walk you.'

We chatted about academic life and how he preferred travel and fieldwork to the office. He asked about my family and my studies. I told him I was planning to be a teacher and he was delighted to hear this. There was so much more I wanted to say, but we arrived at the lecture hall and he handed over my backpack. 'You didn't mention if you were married or anything like that.'

As he waited for me to respond, I felt the spinning truth of the moment. It could be years before I saw him again, if ever. I had to seize the moment. What would Alicia do if Tony were about to slip through her fingers? She'd throw herself at his feet and declare her undying love for him. She wouldn't care if he was married and had children, or grandchildren, even. She'd just look him straight in the eye and say what she had to say.

'I'm not married,' I answered.

'Of course, I forget how young you are. There's a seriousness about you that fools me sometimes. It always did.'

'My mother married my father when she was barely nineteen. I'm older than that.'

Jeremy nodded politely and took a step back. 'That's

right. I remember you told me before.' He raised his hand to wave goodbye.

'Maybe we could have coffee again when . . . when you're not too busy,' I blurted out.

His face lit up. 'I'd love to, Nora.'

When I got in, I found Mami and Abuela in the kitchen, hunched over their coffee in the classic gossip pose. Mami straightened up. 'Have you heard from Alicia lately?'

'Not for a while.'

Mami nodded her head in her solemn all-knowing way. Abuela folded and unfolded her napkin and added more sugar to her coffee.

'What is it?' I asked.

'We called your Tía Maria in Cuba today. She told us she'd had a visit from Tía Panchita recently. She lives with Alicia, you know, and her baby . . .'

'What's wrong with Alicia?'

'It's not Alicia exactly, it's her baby. I forget her name . . .'

'What's wrong with Lucinda?'

'They're not exactly sure, but it's fairly certain the baby is blind. They don't know why . . .'

I felt dizzy and sat down at the table. A heated anger surged within me when I thought of the way Alicia had been ostracized by the family for marrying Tony, the suffering she had endured, and now this. I pictured her wandering the dilapidated streets of Havana, carrying her blind baby on her hip, looking for a leftover crust of bread some shopkeeper might give her for a smile. I winced at my own helpless frustration. It could take weeks for her to receive my next letter.

Abuela shook her head sadly. 'I knew nothing good would come of this marriage. It wasn't meant to be, and when things aren't meant to be and you do them anyway, this is what happens.'

I swallowed my rage. I couldn't be disrespectful to Abuela, but at that moment I felt as though I was being forced to be nice to Hitler himself. My jaw clenched as tears pushed through. I could burst. I could burst from the sheer inability to move.

I hadn't noticed Abuelo walk up behind us and I didn't know how long he'd been listening, but no doubt he was already well aware of the news. Abuelo never raised his voice. His disposition was as sunny as the tropical skies he'd lived under for most of his life. But when he spoke this time, he seemed a different man. 'Don't talk nonsense, old woman,' he retorted. 'You're talking about your granddaughter and great-granddaughter. Don't forget that.'

Abuela was about to protest, but he shot her down again. 'You turned your back on your own blood, and for what? Because you don't believe white people should marry black people. When I told my family in Spain that I wanted to marry a Cuban girl, they tried to talk me out of it. They wanted me to marry a Spanish girl from my village. What if I'd listened to them?'

'It's not the same thing, Antonio. You can't compare it.' Abuela waved her hand in the air as though she was swatting a fly. 'Black people and white people shouldn't be in the same family. It's not natural, and black people feel exactly the same way too.'

Abuelo crossed his arms. 'Not natural? When I held that child in my arms, it felt like the most natural thing in the world.'

Abuela's mouth dropped open. 'You saw her? Even when you promised me you wouldn't?'

Abuelo stood tall and proud, every bit the man I remembered at Varadero and at the airport all those years ago. 'I did, and I don't mind telling you that Lucinda is the most beautiful of us all.'

18

WE'D BEEN MEETING FOR WEEKS.

Jeremy arrived at eight o'clock on Wednesday mornings without fail and insisted on buying my coffee, even though I protested. For an instant when he approached, balancing the tray with two large coffees, his briefcase slung over one arm, I could pretend he was mine. I wouldn't dare pretend when he sat so close. At those moments I had to concentrate on remaining friendly and light and avoid looking at him for too long, for fear that my eyes would turn into two adoring hearts.

Our favoirite topic of conversation was Cuba. Jeremy had always wanted to visit, but had never been able to because of the travel restrictions. I spoke freely about how going back was a forbidden topic with my family. This was the unspoken rule, because the suffering and regret such talk would bring was too much for Mami and Papi to bear. Oh, we could talk about the beauty of the beaches, the unsurpassed quality of the seafood and shopping at El Encanto. It was the sense of having lost our souls we had to keep quiet about, the pain of our transplanted roots craving their native soil. Nobody else would probably ever notice, because we Cubans were so good at adapting and accommodating, but I told Jeremy that if you looked really close, you could see it, like invisible scotch tape on a beautifully wrapped package, or the strings on Peter Pan when he's flying across the stage.

'Why can't you go back?' Jeremy asked. 'They're lifting the restrictions now. Lots of Cubans go back to visit family. Nothing happens to them.'

I pulled my backpack up to my lap and zipped it closed. It was getting late. 'My parents wouldn't hear of it. They promised they would never set foot on Cuban soil again until Castro was gone.'

Jeremy placed his hand on my arm. 'We're not talking about your parents, Nora. Did you make any promises like that?'

'I guess not.'

'Well, then.'

'It would destroy them if I went against their wishes . . . I know it's hard for you to understand.'

Jeremy removed his hand, leaving a cold spot that missed his touch. 'It just seems to me that if you want to go back and see your cousin, who's going through such a hard time right now, it shouldn't be the end of the world.'

By our third meeting, I was in love with Jeremy all over again. And every day, ten times a day, when my mind invariably wandered to him, I reminded myself that he was a married man.

I contented myself with our once-a-week coffee meetings. By Monday I would be agonizing over what to wear, how to do my hair, what book to be reading when he approached with his tray of coffee. When we went our separate ways, I replayed every second of our time together and filtered each word that came out of his mouth, every subtle expression on his face, for the possibility, however fleeting, that he might consider me as something more than a friend who reminded him of his fascination with the Latino culture.

My life revolved around Wednesday mornings from eight to nine a.m. And I was quite happy.

September 1970

Dear Nora,

Forgive me for not having written in so long. I received your last letter and it's given me unimaginable comfort during these trying times. I thank you with all my heart for offering to help, but I don't know what you or anyone could do now. After many nights of endless tears and self-torture, I've come to accept that I can only wait and see what happens with my precious Lucinda. I put her name on the waiting list at the Havana Eye Clinic. In some ways it's a miracle that one of the most renowned eye surgeons in the world is here in Havana. Did you know that people come from all over the world to receive treatment from him?

In the meantime, I try to be Lucinda's eyes. When we go to the beach, I describe the sand and the ocean and the palms that sweep the sky clean. I've learned how to keep my voice clear and bright while tears stream down my face. How to find the words to describe the beauty of our home? I struggle with this every day and feel like I'm trying to paint a masterpiece with a box of broken crayons. But Lucinda appreciates my effort; I know she does because she smiles more these days, and she tells me she loves me as she touches my face and feels for my smile. Every day she calls for her father and asks when he'll return. For now I can only hope that soon she'll feel his arms around her and hear his deep reassuring voice telling her how much he loves her. Tony knows nothing. As far as he's concerned, our daughter is a normal and healthy two-year-old who's saying the most adorable things as she runs around discovering her world.

Instead of looking forward to seeing Tony again, I worry. I can no longer imagine his joyful face at the sight of his wife and daughter, but only the horrible pain I know too well. As strong as he is, I'm afraid this will destroy him. I just hope the love we have for each other will help him through this, as it has me.

The only time I feel free from my worries is when I go to the church on the corner of our street. Perhaps you remember it? La Iglesia del Carmelo, with a little fountain in front where we used to throw coins as children and make our wishes. Abuela would scold us and say we shouldn't make wishes to a fountain when we could be praying to God. I go to this place every day. It's always empty, except for a couple of elderly ladies who sit in the shadows with their veils, lighting candles off to one side. Mass hasn't been said for years.

Hunger is growing, and many people have become like starving hawks that take any opportunity to strike for a meal. I try to watch out for the desperate ones and, most of all, avoid becoming one of them myself. Desperation steals up in the night like a disease and creeps into the heart. The most honourable of human values are crushed under the weight of it, and when it's taken complete possession of a person you smell it on them, like the putrid filth that collects in the alleys of Havana. This filth flows out onto the streets and collects in the gutters. If you're not careful you can step in it and carry it home on your shoes. I know desperation breeds most in the hearts of those who've lost all hope in the revolution and the ideals of change. Tony reminds me in his letters that we have to remain strong, and understand that for even a single person to change it takes an enormous amount of effort, so for a whole country to change its ways . . . well, you see where I'm going with this.

I'm closing my eyes now with happiness in my heart, and thoughts of you and Jeremy finding a way to make the love you have for each other grow. I'm not advocating adultery, but I believe all things happen for a reason and I hope the reason Jeremy is in your life is made known to you and him very soon. I pray for you every day.

Alicia

Marta and Eddie announced they were going to have a baby at about the same time that I began my last year in college. Jeremy was fascinated to hear how Mami was going to Marta's new house almost every day to help with the details of her home and with her preparations for motherhood. And I almost began to get used to the fact that I was in love with a married man. But he rarely spoke of his wife. The only thing I knew was that her name was Jane, they'd met in Peru, and that she suffered from bouts of malaria. I believed he was trying to spare me painful details, but he didn't understand that I'd learned to manage my secret obsession for him very nicely. Whereas before it might've been painful, now I wanted to know everything about him . . . even his choice of spouse and all that went along with it.

Even so, I managed to meet somebody else. He was a business associate whom Papi invited to Marta and Eddie's house-warming party. His name was Greg, but Papi called him Gregorio. He was nice looking, with reddish hair, and was a hard worker with a good future, which Mami and Papi liked most of all. What I liked best was that I could look him straight in the eyes without blushing, which I could never do with Jeremy.

Throughout the party, Abuela watched me talk to him. But her eyes were far away, and I knew she was thinking about how it would be if we were still in

Cuba. I don't know if it was the wine, or the bougainvillaea blooming outside the window, but it was as if we'd never left.

In an instant I'm at a garden party at the ocean's edge, not quite on the sand, but close enough to see the breeze sweeping translucent swirls out to sea. Everyone is vibrant with laughter and warmed by a good-natured sun that knows its place in the blue expanse above.

But the surf doesn't pound; it's the tempered beating of our hearts. The sea breeze doesn't blow; it's the resonating essence of a lilting flute. All our worries dissolve in rainy intermissions that evaporate up to heaven three or sometimes four times a day.

Greg pours me another glass of wine, and again I am far away. A lady does not drink too much. Mami and Abuela have always told me that a lady must be able to think on her feet and balance on slender heels, while strolling the malecón arm in arm with the man who is her destiny.

While I was daydreaming, Greg asked me out to dinner. We began to go out most weekends and sometimes during the week as well. Although I knew I shouldn't be, I was afraid to tell Jeremy about Greg. But I knew I'd soon have to find the courage.

I saw Jeremy stretched out on a warm patch of grass. But he hadn't seen me yet, and I thought about walking away before he did. I was embarrassed for him to see me not in my usual jeans and sandals, but wearing a new coordinated outfit with matching shoes and bag. I was planning to meet Greg after class for a drive along the coast and dinner at our favourite seafood restaurant. He was expecting me to be at the university entrance in five minutes.

I was stepping away when Jeremy turned and spotted me. Now I had no choice but to join him, and I felt my cheeks flush as I approached. He gave my new look a curious glance, but said nothing as he turned his face back to the sun.

I patted the grass to make sure it was dry and sat down next to him. We didn't say anything for several minutes. This was customary for us. We were like a couple that had grown comfortable with our silences over the years.

My eyes swept over him. I tried not to notice that he was still beautiful to me, and to suppress the profound sense of belonging I always felt when I was near him. I cleared my throat, breaking the warm buzz between us. 'I'm afraid I don't have much time.'

His eyes fluttered and he grunted his acknowledgement low in his throat. I knew that sound well. It usually made the lower half of my body grow warm and tingly, but I fought the sensation this time and tightened my stomach.

'I have a date,' I said, 'and I need to be at the other side of campus in five minutes.'

He sat up slowly and rubbed off the blades of grass that were stuck to his palms. He hardly looked at me. 'You should probably go, then,' he said.

I stood up and backed away as though it was some kind of trap. 'Yes, I probably should.'

He glanced up then, his eyes kind and mild as I retreated. 'Have a good time, Nora.'

June 1971

Dear Nora,

My angel is home! It's only been two weeks since Tony returned, but already our life has changed in amazing ways. He found us an apartment two blocks from the sea. In the middle of the night we hear the waves like distant sighs. And there's so much more to eat. He brought boxes of dried milk and bananas with him, which we trade for meat and toilet paper. You have no idea how long it's been since we've had toilet

202

paper. I think it's far too fine for its intended purpose, so I'm saving it to barter with later if necessary.

Lucinda loves bananas, just like we did, and she eats one every day now. The very sun shines brighter than it used to, Nora, and colour is returning to a city that was fading under its glare.

I heard him before I saw him, asking the neighbours which room was ours. I bolted out of the door, leaving Lucinda spinning on her feet and so confused about my sudden departure that she started to cry — and Lucinda hardly ever cries.

I saw the outline of his broad shoulders coming up the stairs. His eyes were searching for me, wild and hungry with the pain of too much loneliness. I ran into his arms and we clutched at each other's hair and clothes. I pressed against him so hard that I almost disappeared into him, and tears poured out of my eyes and every part of me, it seemed. If that moment had lasted any longer, I probably would've died from too much happiness. Is there such a thing?

I never saw Tony cry, not really cry, until he looked upon his daughter with the knowledge that she couldn't look back. For several days he held her as though she was an infant and not a little girl. He kept gazing into her face and passing his hands across her eyes, over and over. I know what this is. I used to do it myself, hoping she'd blink at just the right moment and give me that little bit of hope to comfort me for a couple of hours, until I'd be forced to accept her blindness all over again.

Almost every night at sunset, Tony and I go down to the beach. We lie on the sand without clothes and it's the most wonderful feeling. The breeze is cool, but the sand is still warm from the sun. We play like children, naked and free, and we make love until we're too tired to move. Back in our new apartment, we fall asleep in each other's arms like we used to. To open my eyes and see him by the open window

203

fixing our morning coffee is like waking up in heaven every day.

Just yesterday, I sneaked away to the church again. I had to go back to thank God for answering my prayers and bringing my husband back safe. I lit a small white candle at the altar like I always do, and stayed for a few minutes watching the flame. It gives me such peace to see it waver and dance in the darkness. I have only one prayer left: that Lucinda's blindness be cured. God heard me, because just as I was praying, the windows lit up and filled the church with streams of coloured light, when it had been dark for more than an hour.

Don't laugh; you know I'm always looking for miracles, and if they don't find me, I'll find them, even if they're in the headlights of a passing car.

Alicia

19

SUMMER WAS ONCE AGAIN UPON US, AND MAMI HAD BEEN bustling about the house with nervous anxiety for almost a week. Visitors were coming from Miami and it was important that everything was in perfect order. She hired a window cleaner, and carefully selected blooms from the garden to arrange throughout the house. The bathroom was equipped with new brightly coloured guest towels and bowls of pot-pourri. Mami and Abuela cooked into the night, making croquet as and stuffed potato balls, and Papi readied the pit outside to roast the pork.

Mami was at her happiest when preparing for guests. She'd thrown dinner parties as Papi advanced in his career, and she enjoyed those, but with Cuban friends and family she rolled up her sleeves and dived into the process with abandon. She played her favourite danson on the stereo and gyrated her hips to the music as she dusted. She could be persuaded to have a glass or two of wine and enjoy the sunset out on the porch, even though it was Wednesday night and there was still so much to do before the guests arrived.

'Do you remember your cousin Juan?' Mami asked me.

'Of course. I was fifteen when we left. I remember everything.'

'He's an attorney in Miami. Quite successful, I hear, and he's coming out with his mother, your Tía Carlotta, for some kind of conference.'

Mami proceeded to inform us of all the recent family gossip. I listened with half an ear, while Papi read the paper, not even bothering to appear interested. Mami spoke vehemently about Juan's foolishness in having joined a Cuban Brotherhood association aimed at hastening Castro's demise. 'I don't want him talking about that nonsense in my presence. All it does is make me upset and get my hopes up for nothing.'

Juan and Tía Carlotta showed up that Friday in a black limousine from the airport. Tía Carlotta wore the Cuban uniform of success – an elegant beige linen suit, with a designer handbag and pounds of gold jewellery dripping from her hands and neck. Her red-toned hair (I remembered her as a brunette) was stiffened with hairspray, and it almost scratched my cheek when I gave her the obligatory kiss on the cheek in greeting. Juan was twice the size I remembered him, contained within the tailored perfection of an expensive grey suit. But he had the same flush about him that I remembered when he spoke about his life and his work with the Cuban Brotherhood.

Mami put her hands over her ears, although she was still smiling. 'Please, Juany, I don't want to know.'

Tía Carlotta shot Juan a stiff look and he obliged, as the good son that he was. It was no secret that he took care of his mother (his father had died of cancer soon after exile), and that she'd been able to resume, if not surpass, the lifestyle she'd had in Cuba, because of him. Even so, she hadn't lost her authority as a mother.

We were sitting in the living room amongst the blooms from the garden, sipping wine and nibbling on Cuban delicacies, when Juan leaned over, straining his impressive girth, to speak only to me. He addressed me in Spanish, and I realized how long it had been since I'd spoken my native tongue with someone of my generation. Marta and I had been speaking English with each other more and more over the years, and now I spoke Spanish only to my parents and grandparents. Speaking Spanish with Juan made it feel as though what we had to say was more important, somehow.

'Have you heard from Alicia?' he asked.

'We keep in touch through letters.'

'Then you know she's a communist, and that she married some communist who's literally brainwashed her.'

'I know she loves Tony very much. They have a daughter, Lucinda.'

'I heard she's blind.'

'They're hoping for an appointment at an eye clinic in Havana.'

Juan popped a potato ball in his mouth and chuckled as he chewed. It seemed like he was swallowing all joy and hope along with the potato. 'They'll never get in there,' he said, and took a swig of wine to clear his throat. 'It's well known that the better clinics only serve the needs of foreign dignitaries and high-ranking party members. Ordinary citizens never get to the top of the waiting list.'

I didn't know what to say. Juan was confident about his information. He lived in Miami and, with his ear to the ground and his heart fully engaged in the struggle, was steeped in the latest news. We were removed in our Californian environment, where Latino issues focused on problems with migrant workers from Mexico and bilingual education in the inner city. I wanted to argue otherwise, but I had no ammunition and Juan had quite an arsenal available to him.

'You can help her, Nora.'

'How?'

'Convince her to apply for a visa. I'm sure I can do something this end if she does.'

'She won't leave Tony. She won't leave Cuba.'

We could've been in Tía Maria's backyard. 'Just play one game of baseball with me, Nora,' he'd say, squeezing his chubby hands together as if in fervent prayer.

'You always throw the ball too hard,' I'd respond.

'I promise I won't this time.' He tosses his glove at me and I try it on. It's about three sizes too big, but I give in because I'm the closest thing Juan has to a male companion at the moment, and because I know he won't give up until I do. We play in the yard until the shadows lengthen and engulf us, until I can no longer ignore Mami's complaints about getting dirty, or until Alicia comes and lures me into something more interesting.

'She's the only one of us left over there,' Juan added, perhaps remembering that I always gave in to his pleas.

'She is?'

'Of our group, she is. The only others who stayed were the old people.'

'Like Tía Panchita.'

Juan furrowed his fleshy brow and glanced at his mother, who'd been listening to our conversation without meaning to look as though she was. She mirrored his confused expression and turned back to Mami, who was rearranging the croquetas and potato balls on the tray.

'Tía Maria said she'd call you,' Carlotta said.

'About what?' Mami asked, dropping a potato ball on her foot.

'Panchita died two weeks ago. They say she died while smoking a cigar even though the doctor had told her she couldn't smoke cigars and that the best thing that had happened to her was the shortage of tobacco in Cuba.'

Mami's eyes watered as she leaned back, the potato ball still resting on the tip of her brown pump. 'May she rest in peace.'

'She was a good woman,' Tía Carlotta added with a solemn nod of her stiff auburn head.

'She cared about the black people like they were her own flesh and blood.'

'Sometimes to the detriment of her own people . . .'

'If she'd guided Alicia differently, she'd be free and not in the grip of this communist lie,' Juan offered.

'They say that before the revolution, the plantation would've gone much better if she hadn't given over the control of it to her black friends.'

'They say Lola's the one who got her smoking every day like she did, and that Panchita spent money she didn't have to maintain their cigar habits.'

Mami picked the potato ball off her foot with a napkin and carefully wrapped it up. 'She may not have been very smart, but Panchita was a good woman.'

'She was a good woman,' everyone chorused.

The doorbell rang and Mami opened the door to find a smiling Greg standing on the threshold. Mami proudly introduced him as my 'novio', which I still wasn't too sure I liked hearing. After a robust handshake with cousin Juan, he sat in the chair next to me. Although we'd had sex a half dozen times already, he wouldn't dare kiss me or even place a hand on me in the presence of my family. I ignored him, still upset and confused about Tía Panchita's death.

I stood up, knocking a glass of red wine off the table and onto the white carpet. Mami gasped and Greg hurriedly began to blot the stain with his napkin.

'Tía Panchita was a great woman. She was the only one who didn't turn her back on Alicia when she married Tony,' I declared to a bewildered group.

'Calm down, Nora,' Mami said.

'You're criticizing Tía Panchita because she helped black people, because she loved Lola better than most people love their own sisters and brothers . . . This is why the revolution happened in the first place.'

Mami stood up. 'You don't know what you're talking about, foolish girl.'

Tía Carlotta cleared her throat. 'Maybe we should leave, Regina. Nora's upset.'

Mami held out a firm hand in her direction. 'You're not going anywhere,' she said, taking a step towards me. 'You watch what you say, young lady. While you're in this house, you show respect.'

I marched out of the front door and heard Greg's strained explanation as I left. 'She's very stressed with her job hunt . . . She's been getting upset easily . . .' I could picture his face, red as the stain on the carpet he was blotting.

'She's spoiled,' I heard Mami reply. 'She thinks she's smarter than everybody.'

'She definitely has the Garcia smile,' Papi said, peering into the crib.

'Don't be silly, José. She can't smile yet.'

'I'm telling you, I saw her smile just a minute ago when you weren't looking.'

We'd grown accustomed to Mami and Papi's good-natured arguing since Lisa was born. It seemed their entry into grandparenthood had caused them momentarily to forget how to get along. Mami could talk of nothing else but the baby and how Marta was doing and whether or not she and Eddie were dealing well with parenthood. Anyone would think that Marta and Eddie had contracted an exotic and incurable disease that required everyone's constant vigilance. And for the first time in years, Papi was coming home early from work so he could accompany Mami on her daily visit, before Lisa was put down for the night. We'd hear him whistling a tune as he came in through the back door, with a smile from ear to ear.

But Mami's joy over Marta's domestic good fortune wasn't enough to distract her from the disappointing developments in my life.

'I don't understand why you let that nice young man go, Nora. He had a good job and very decent sensibilities. Even more than that, I'd say he was quite in love with you.'

I wondered if Mami was suffering from premature dementia when she brought the subject up again. We'd already talked about it at least twenty times. Several weeks earlier, I'd spoken to Mami and Papi separately and explained that I was no longer seeing Greg. Papi accepted the news with a blend of surprise and curiosity, and then made a simple statement that reflected his acquired American ideals more convincingly than his evolving preference for American football over baseball. 'As long as you're happy, Nora. That's what your mother and I want for you more than anything.' He thought for a moment. 'If you haven't told your mother, I suggest you do so as soon as possible. She's grown quite fond of Greg.'

Mami stared at me as if I'd told her I'd become an astronaut and was leaving for the moon the next morning. 'Was this your decision?'

'Yes. I just didn't feel comfortable with him, Mami.' I could've told her that his touch had begun to repulse me and that the last time we made love I'd found myself thinking about a back pain I'd developed and the dreadful fact that I'd plucked out my first grey hair the day before.

She smoothed out Papi's shirt on the ironing board, but the crease between her brows deepened and began to redden. 'I hope you thought carefully about this. Greg's a good man. He has a good job and a very promising career and you can't find that every day, you know.'

'I know, Mami.'

'And he understood things . . .'

'Yes, Mami.'

'About our culture and respect and . . . I'm telling you right now, I think you're making a big mistake.'

She began to iron furiously. 'Oh, I know the American way. Parents aren't supposed to interfere in their children's lives. They're just supposed to smile and nod and say, "That's fine, dear. Whatever makes you happy, dear."'

'Actually, that's exactly what Papi said.'

Mami stopped ironing and glared at me. 'Your father's a man and he doesn't understand that the older a woman gets the fewer her choices.'

'For goodness' sake, I'm barely twenty-four years old.'

She nodded and resumed her ironing as though she'd been ironing for twenty years without a break and couldn't possibly stop now. 'When I was twenty-four, I was married, I had two children, a house and a servant to help.' She looked back up at me from her task, her eyes round and accusing. 'What do you have?'

'A college education.'

'A lot of good it's done you,' she muttered. 'You don't even know a good man when you see one.'

August 1971

Dear Nora,

I knew how upset you would be by Tía Panchita's passing. I thank God Tony was here when it happened, because I know I wouldn't have survived it alone. Before she died, I took her to Guines one last time. The bus was three hours late and the road had so many potholes I thought it was going to fall apart piece by piece, but Tía didn't notice. She just looked out the window through her big glasses and sighed the whole way there. It actually seemed she was getting better with every mile.

When we finally arrived at the house, she didn't say a word. The roof over the porch had partially caved in and crushed most of the front steps. I tried to talk her out of climbing up, but she insisted, so we

212

sat on a crate as I prayed the roof wouldn't fall in completely and kill us both. We looked out upon the forest, the only thing that hasn't changed.

She'd hardly spoken all day, but at that moment she said that this was the only place where she could look out at the world and understand it. 'When I sit here in my place, I know who I am,' she said.

Later, she tried to convince me to let her spend the night right there on the porch. It took a lot of persuading, but finally she understood it was a bad idea, or maybe she was too tired to keep arguing. She fell asleep on the bus and when we got back to Havana she was gone. A few weeks later I sprinkled her ashes on her porch, because I have no doubt that's where she left her soul.

I still go to church when I can. I haven't seen the elderly ladies for months, so I sit in the corner by myself and pray until my heart runs dry. Mostly I pray that Lucinda be given her appointment at the eye clinic soon. Tony tells me it'll be any day now, because party members have priority and he's been invited to join. He believes in the revolution as much as he ever did. He reads his books and devours Castro's speeches on the radio as if they were food, which grows scarcer every day. He wants me to read to him sometimes when he's tired, but I hardly listen to the words coming out of my own mouth.

Before, Tony could say things had to get worse before they got better, and I believed. He could say capitalism is the religion of the rich and powerful, and that the pure heart of socialism will triumph in the end, and I believed. He continues to say these things, and I listen because I know he needs me to listen, but I no longer believe.

We walk along the wide boulevard of the malecón every Sunday with Lucinda between us. I look into the eyes of others doing the same, walking past buildings that were once sparkling and beautiful and are now like enormous tombs haunted by hungry rats. The sun has become a bare glaring light bulb that accentuates the ugliness of our lives. Only at night does pretending hold any comfort. I look at the lights blinking on the malecón and remember. Was it all a dream, Nora? Did we ever laugh together on the beach without a care in the world, certain our lunch would be ready, with plenty left over for the servants to take home? I could feed my family for a month with the food I left on my plate. I could live for a day on the crumbs that fell to the floor.

Forgive me for complaining, but one of the few comforts I have left is knowing that you'll read these words and understand me as no one else can. I know you're thinking that I've become one of the desperate people, but I assure you my sadness no longer consumes me like it used to. Strangely enough, it has become my strength, as it reminds me that I can no longer get lost in fanciful dreams if I hope to survive. I don't know if I'm growing up or simply getting tired. Perhaps a bit of both.

Before I close, I must let you know how proud I am of you for breaking things off with Gregorio. It took courage that your mother doesn't understand. Your heart will guide you to your destiny and you must write me soon and tell me where it leads.

Alicia

I found a job teaching first-graders in East LA who were just learning English. I loved the children and kept myself busy with work and school and spending as much time with my niece, Lisa, as I could. Time passed quickly, with barely a thought about men or dating. I forced myself to accept a couple of dinner invitations, including one from a friend of Eddie's who Marta insisted was a match made in heaven just for me, but I declined second invitations from them both.

Marta and Mami warned me that I shouldn't be so picky, but I didn't feel I was being picky at all. I was simply waiting for what felt right. Waiting for hope to find me, as I always had. Once again, my thoughts turned to Sister Margarita's invitation so long ago. Perhaps she had possessed the wisdom to look into my future and see the romantic calamities I might avoid if I only followed her holy example. Perhaps Sister Margarita had been right all along.

My academic efforts had always proven successful, and by the fall of the following year I was beginning my preparations for graduate school. It was necessary for me to return to the university on a few occasions to gather documents in order to complete my application. I was surprised by how good it felt to be back, and I was even more surprised to find myself standing outside Jeremy's office door one afternoon, holding two cups of steaming coffee. I could hear him on the phone, his calm voice trying to reassure one of his students, who was obviously unhappy with his grade. I didn't wait for him to finish his call before knocking and peeking in. He seemed surprised to see me, and stumbled a bit as he found a way to end the call. I placed the coffees on his desk, and sat down next to him. We gazed at each other, smiling, in silence for almost a minute.

'How's it been going?' he finally asked.

'Fine. And you?'

'Good, good.'

We smiled a while longer and then he shook himself and began to rearrange some papers on his desk. 'Let me guess,' he said. 'You came by to personally invite me to your wedding.'

I laughed, strangely delighted that he should say such a thing. 'What makes you think that?'

'I got the distinct impression you were involved with somebody and on your way to blissful matrimony last time I saw you. How long has it been?'

'Almost two years . . . I think.'

'A lot can happen in two years,' he said, still fussing with his papers and hardly looking at me.

'Yes, well . . . I'm definitely not getting married. I may never get married.'

Jeremy folded his arms and nodded slowly, but his dimples flickered as though he was trying not to laugh. He sat back in his chair, still studying me.

'What's so funny?'

He shook his head. 'You sound so American when you say that.'

'Is that bad?'

'No, it's not bad,' he said, still smiling.

The glow had begun in my middle again and I was feeling a bit delirious. 'What's been happening in your life?'

Jeremy uncrossed his arms and leaned back in his chair. 'Nothing much.' Then his fingers floated up to his face and he began to stroke his chin, as he used to do in High School when he was working out his translation. His eyes wandered about the ceiling and then landed resolutely back on my face. 'That's not really true . . . Jane and I got separated a while back. The divorce should be final any day. I thought of calling to let you know, but it just didn't seem . . .' He stopped himself short and leaned forward to place his hand over mine, which were folded on my lap. This time it was no accident. His voice was gentle and clear as he spoke to me. 'There's no reason I shouldn't tell you now – I may not get another chance.' He squeezed my hands as though to gather courage before going on. 'Ever since the first day I saw you all those years ago, with your ponytail and knee-high socks, I . . . I loved you, Nora. I looked for you when I got back from Peru, but you'd moved and I figured you'd gone back to Cuba like you said you would. Then I met Jane and I thought it best to get on with my life. But

216

when I ran into you again, I knew I'd made a mistake.'

Tears floated in my eyes, so that his image became blurred and dream-like.

'I didn't mean to upset you . . .'

My heart pounded harder than it ever had in my life and I felt I might faint if I didn't concentrate on inhaling and exhaling one breath after the other. 'Years ago, I told you that when you lose hope it's worse than hunger, because you have to wait for hope to find you, remember?'

'I remember.'

'I was wrong, Jeremy. I was so wrong. I wasn't supposed to wait for hope to find me, I was supposed to go out and find it for myself. And Sister Margarita was wrong, too.'

'Who's Sister Margarita?'

'Didn't I tell you about her?'

'No, but I'm listening.'

I began to tell him about Sister Margarita, but my words were a jumble, and every time I looked at him smiling so tenderly, it became impossible to make any sense at all. Still trembling, I reached for the coffee, hoping that it might calm me, but Jeremy took the cup from my hand and placed it back on the desk. He scooted his chair forward so that our knees were touching, and leaned towards me, his eyes awash with peaceful longing.

'I've always wanted to ask you something,' he said.

'Of course.'

He inched closer still. 'How do you say, "May I kiss you?" in Spanish?'

'You know how,' I responded, blushing like a high-school girl.

'But I like how you say it. Won't you say it for me?'

He was so close, I could feel the warmth of his breath on my lips. '*Te puedo besar?*' I said.

He touched my cheek and repeated in perfect Spanish, '*Nora, te puedo besar?*'

217

'Yes, Jeremy,' I said. 'For you the answer will always be yes.'

I wrote to Alicia immediately to give her the good news about Jeremy and me, but months passed without another word from her. I was frantic that something might have happened to her and Lucinda and Tony. As Juan had pointed out, Alicia was the last one of the family left in Cuba, so there was no one to call or write to to find out. The only way to calm my fears was to tell myself that if she were in serious trouble, I'd know it. We'd always been able to guess what each other was thinking, and somehow I was sure I'd feel the truth in the same way that I'd known in my heart of hearts she'd survived her father's death years ago.

I convinced myself she was well, and pictured her digesting my letters like little snacks that kept her going in the midst of her difficulties. But the letters were more for me than for her. They reminded me of who I was. They were my psychological trip home and I felt incomplete without them. And so I wrote again and again, even though she didn't write back.

November 1974

Dear Alicia,

Jeremy and I bought a little house in Santa Monica Beach. It's not on the ocean, like Abuelo and Abuela's house in Varadero, but if I stand on tiptoe on the toilet in the bathroom, I can just catch a glimpse of it over the rooftops. We take frequent walks, regardless of the season, as Jeremy believes the ocean is beautiful in any kind of weather. He's convinced me to take a few months off while I get my teaching credential, so we've had more time to spend together.

Mami's teaching me how to cook too. Most mornings, after Jeremy leaves for the university, I

218

drive to her house for a lesson. So far I've learned
how to make arroz con pollo, picadillo, kimbobo,
platanos fritos, leg of pork with mojo sauce, and flan.
I remember spending hours in the kitchen helping
Beba cut onions and tomatoes and garlic until we
reeked of the stuff, but we never talked about cooking.
Beba liked to talk about the spirits that lived out in the
forests and evil that befell foolish people who didn't
respect them as they should. Mami's pretty much the
same, so I have to pay careful attention to what she
does, while she gossips about Eddie's sister, who's on
her second marriage.

I know now how you felt years ago when you wrote
that if your life didn't change from that moment on,
you'd die happy. Every day is a perfect flower that
begins with Jeremy in my arms and ends the same
way.

I don't know if you felt this way as well, but I'm a
little scared to feel this happy. I'm afraid that one day
I'll wake up and find that I've lost Jeremy and our
little house and our afternoon walks and everything. I
tried to explain this to Jeremy, but he doesn't
understand. He just says, 'I'm not going anywhere.
You're stuck with me.'

I lie awake at night long after Jeremy's fallen asleep
and worry anyway. I realize how silly I'm being.
Jeremy hasn't given me any reason to doubt him. He's
as kind and thoughtful a husband as he was a friend,
even more so. But my worrying has nothing to do
with Jeremy; it's a part of who I am, and it doesn't
fade away like my accent did.

One day, Mami asked me about my tense
expression and I told her about my crazy fears and
how childish I was being. She told me what I guess I
knew all along. 'That's not childishness,' she said, as
certain as if I was mistaking a mango for a banana.
'When your father got his first job over here, I was
sure he'd lose it in a week. And when we bought the

house, I constantly scanned the street, expecting to see some American man in a dark suit walking up the drive to tell us there'd been some mistake and we'd have to give it back. When you lose everything once in your life, the chances are it will never happen again, but it's impossible to forget and it's natural to worry.'

So now that I have permission to worry, let me tell you again how worried I am about not receiving a letter from you in so long. I'm certain you must have my new address by now. Perhaps you moved again and forgot to forward your mail? Please know that no matter how much time goes by, I always keep you and Lucinda and Tony in my prayers.

Nora

June 1976

Dear Nora,

Forgive me for taking so long to write you back. I've read every one of your letters over and over. I wept with joy when I read about your marriage to Jeremy and I'm so happy to know of your wonderful life together. It is as I always knew it would be.

I don't know where to begin or where I left off in my last letter. My life is like a complicated recipe, where you can't remember if you already added the sugar or the salt – oh, just go ahead, it doesn't matter, it's ruined anyway.

You see, Tony is once again gone from my side. It's not his love for the revolution, but his growing hate for it that is the culprit this time. He didn't change one day to the next. His enchantment began to erode as his anger grew steadily over time, like the relentless beat of a drum that grew louder and louder until he was screaming with the agony of it. That hopeful light that always danced in my man's eyes was replaced with a black rage, seething and unpredictable.

Tony had been going to the eye clinic every week to inquire about the waiting list. He was always told the same thing: that Lucinda's appointment would be scheduled as soon as possible and that a notice would be sent to our home. One day, he was told that Lucinda's name was no longer on the list. He had to be dragged away from the clinic by two police officers. He would've been arrested if one of the officers hadn't been an old friend of his from Angola.

Tony was a different man after that. He sat for hours at a time, staring out of the window at nothing. He reminded me of myself after Papi was killed, except I couldn't reach him the way he reached me. Only Lucinda was able to bring a faint smile to his lips, and then only sometimes.

Then his policeman friend returned and told Tony that a neighbour had seen me going to church with Lucinda, and that this was why her name had been removed from the list. You may ask how ten or fifteen minutes a day spent in an empty church can ruin your life, but in the communist party religious inclinations of any kind are considered a weakness that violates the integrity of communism and threatens the revolution. We tried to go on with our lives as usual, but our desperation grew. Lucinda sensed it too, and she cried for little things.

One night, Tony slipped into bed and whispered in my ear. He was out of breath and his voice trembled as he spoke. He said he couldn't wait around and watch the world fall apart as the life drained out of Lucinda and me. We made love with such passion that night, as if it was the first time – as if it would be the last.

Tony was arrested a few weeks later along with other demonstrators and journalists at the Plaza José Marti. It's been over six months now and nobody can tell me if he's dead or alive, or if I'll ever see him again. I go to church in the day now and I don't care who's watching. Lucinda comes with me; she sits very still in the light of the windows and prays with me. She prays out loud for her father and for her country, in a voice as sweet as an angel's.

This may sound strange to you, but even with all that's happened, I'm hopeful again. Although Tony and I are physically apart, our hearts and minds are more united now than they were when we were within arm's reach of each other.

I was allowed to take Lucinda out of school, because she is still too young to go to the government school for the blind. I'm teaching her myself with the help of a new friend, Berta. She works in a hotel and is very funny. It is more important now than ever to laugh when we can.

I promise to write more often, for both our sakes.

Alicia

Christmas was approaching, and we scrambled, as we did every year, to find a place that would sell us a whole pig for roasting. Jeremy was fascinated with this holiday tradition, and it could've been our most joyous Christmas in a long time if Abuelo hadn't started to experience heart trouble again, requiring his second hospitalization in a year.

I visited him daily; we spent time watching his favourite Spanish soaps, and he laughed and complained about the outlandish behaviour of the actors as if they were his neighbours and friends. But as soon as the programmes were over, his sombre mood returned. He told me that this time he wouldn't be leaving the hospital. I reminded him that he had said the same thing during his previous stay a year ago, but he shook his head and sank deeper into his pillow. His strong frame was slowly collapsing, like the beams of a sturdy pier giving way to the constant barrage of the ocean. As I looked at him, I remembered Abuelo's strength in the water, the best swimmer in the world. He had laughed in the face of the most serious arguments and his presence had added reverence to everything we did, even if it was just drinking a coke together.

I was getting ready to head for home and start dinner when he asked, 'Have you heard from Alicia?'

We hadn't spoken about Alicia for some time, but he asked me to update him, and made it clear he wanted me to spare him no details. When I had finished relating the contents of her latest letter, he nodded slowly. 'What are you going to do?'

'I'm going to send her more money.'

He nodded again. 'What else?'

'I don't know what else I can do, Abuelo.'

'You can go to her, can't you? She needs your help.' His words stung me and I squirmed under the heat of his glare.

Abuelo had heard the arguments and Mami's outbursts at home. He didn't like conflict, and it wasn't like him to make a suggestion that could create more of it.

'But Mami and Papi, you know how they feel about it . . .'

'You and Alicia are as close as sisters. She's alone again and I worry about this new friend that works in the hotel.' He sighed and reached for my hand. His felt as fragile as paper. 'You haven't changed, Norita. You think too much when you would do better to just dive in and do what you know you must.'

I smiled and held his hand in both of my own. 'Last time I followed that advice, I almost found myself on a permanent vacation at the bottom of the sea.'

'I was right there, Norita. I never would've let you drown, and you know it.'

'I never doubted you, not for a second, Abuelo. I knew I was safe.'

He closed his eyes. 'And I'll be there with you next time. Just dive in. You're a wonderful swimmer.'

On his tenth day in hospital, soon after he'd finished watching his favourite soap, Abuelo took his usual nap and never woke up.

I like to think that he was dreaming of the warm blue seas of home, and relishing the way he slipped into the water and propelled himself through it, so smooth and perfect – the best swimmer in all of Cuba.

20

SUNDAYS BEGAN TO REMIND ME OF SUNDAYS IN CUBA SO many years ago.

Marta and I were both married and settled into our lives with our American husbands. Mami and Papi were able to count their brood on more than one hand and set the table using almost all their good china. The meal began at around noon. Marta was pregnant again, and liked to sit outside on the deck under the tree that had always been Abuelo's favourite spot, while Eddie kept an eye on Lisa, who was quite fond of picking the fresh buds off flowers and handing them to Papi, who was not quite so delighted. We nibbled on Cuban delicacies intermixed with American cuisine, of which we'd become increasingly fond. Jeremy had taken to cooking a bit himself at the weekends, and thoroughly enjoyed surprising my family with some new dish out of an obscure ethnic cookbook he'd found during his travels.

We drank wine and beer into the afternoon. We listened to Benny More and Celia Cruz, alternating with New Age elevator music – the opiate of the yuppie generation, Jeremy liked to say, although he owned and listened to quite a bit of it himself.

Mami and Papi marvelled at their grandchild and how fair she was. 'Who'd think she had any Cuban blood in her at all?' Mami said, smiling, obviously quite pleased by the fact.

'You know who she looks like, don't you?' Marta said, gazing lovingly at her daughter, who was scrunching her nose at the olive she'd tasted.

'She looks like Alicia,' Mami said nonchalantly. She hadn't mentioned Alicia since her outburst, too long ago to think about any more. 'Alicia was a beautiful girl. I'd say she was even blonder than Lisa.' The unspoken question hung in the air like a black rain cloud, but nobody dared say anything lest it burst and soak us all. I knew they were wondering if I'd heard from her and how she was doing. And what of her blind, racially mixed daughter, whom Abuelo had believed to be one of the most amazingly beautiful children he'd ever laid eyes on?

Jeremy brought in a tray of Greek houmous with neatly sliced wedges of pitta bread on the side. He winked at me when he set the tray down, then made himself comfortable at my feet, his head on my knee. 'Nora received a letter from Alicia just a few months ago. It was a long one, wasn't it, honey?'

I felt my back bristle and was immediately annoyed with Jeremy for bringing it up, even though I knew he wasn't being thoughtless, but quite deliberate. I coughed and reached for the pitta, flicking Jeremy's head as I did so. 'It was a very long letter.'

Mami reached for some pitta and houmous as well. 'This looks interesting, Jeremy.' She popped it in her mouth and nodded approvingly. Papi opened another bottle of wine and poured himself a glass, swishing it around and holding it up to the light.

'How is she doing?' Mami asked, as she fished around for another pitta wedge.

'Who?'

She looked up from the tray, her face flushed and anxious. 'Alicia, of course.'

'Not so well. There are problems.'

Mami sat back in her chair with a huff. 'That doesn't surprise me at all. They're finding rafts full of people every day trying to escape. They say the prisons are full of those who try to leave illegally. The very same people who supported the revolution are now being thrown in jail for trying to get out.'

Jeremy squeezed my ankle. He wanted me to speak, but I stayed silent. He sat up and away from me. 'Alicia and Tony have renounced the party. Tony's in jail for taking part in a demonstration against the government. Nobody knows when and if he'll get out.'

Mami gasped and dropped her pitta and houmous on the floor. 'Oh, dear God.' Now she was full of questions, and as I answered them she began to cry. Papi tried to calm her down, but she continued to grow more agitated, and trembled as she spoke. 'We must send her money, José,' she kept saying over and over again.

August 1977

Dear Nora,

I light a candle at the church for Abuelo every day, may he rest in peace. And as I watch the flame flicker in the darkness I thank God he died in freedom, near you and the family. I pray that the years he lived in abundance and joy erased the years of hunger and fear he knew here.

I must extend my gratitude to you and your family. You don't know what a difference your generosity has made to us. Tony is still in jail, and I use most of the American dollars you send to bribe the guards into allowing me to bring him food. There is one guard with kind eyes who tells me he delivers my packages to him personally, and I have no choice but to believe him.

It was necessary for us to move out of the apartment Tony found and into a smaller one on the first

227

floor. At least we're still close to the malecón and Berta has moved in. She was with a horrible man who beat her black and blue almost daily. When he came around looking for her, I told him she'd moved to Russia with a soldier. I even supplied the name of one of Tony's old friends, who I knew had recently gone, in case he bothered to check. Berta was very grateful; she's turned out to be a marvellous friend, and very resourceful as well. We've been able to eat regular meals and find meat at least once a week since we met her. She works in tourism at the hotels and promised to find a job for me soon. I wish now that I'd taken my English classes more seriously, but Berta assures me I don't need to know English and that working in tourism is the surest way to leave Cuba. I won't go without Tony, but I need to have a plan ready so we can leave as soon as he's out. Ricardo, the guard who gives things to Tony, tells me he's been hearing rumours about Tony's release, and I want to believe him, because when I do I feel I have two hearts pumping bravely inside my chest instead of one squeezing out its weak existence.

Time is running out for many reasons. Lucinda's been out of school for so long, I'm afraid soon they'll come looking for her and force her to attend the educational camps, as they do all the other children. She'd be away from me for weeks at a time and they'd programme her mind and her soul to give up our hope of freedom and build tolerance for this unrelenting frustration we live with.

I wonder sometimes if I shouldn't leave with Lucinda as soon as I can. When I think of how I'd suffer if my daughter were taken from me, ninety miles on a raft doesn't seem like such a risk. I hear that if you leave at the right time when the currents are flowing south and the wind is behind you, you can make it in two days. Two days to freedom, Nora, what a beautiful thought.

I must bring this letter to a close, as I've run out of paper. One last thing: you wrote that Abuelo's last words to you before he died were of me, but you didn't tell me what they were. I would like to know when you get a chance to write back. I'll write again soon. I feel so much better when I do.

Alicia

I awoke with the image clear in my mind. Two white and wavering faces, ghostlike and tranquil, emerging from the sea. They walk hand in hand across the ocean bottom to reach the shores of freedom. They pass through the horror of a thousand deaths to reach me, and I'm waiting on the shore when the tops of their heads emerge from the water like two rising moons. Their bodies glisten with the ocean, but there's a brittleness about their souls, a dried-up misery that calls to me more poignantly than any cry or complaint. Their bare feet sink into the sand as they stand on the water's edge.

Lucinda walks towards me, takes my hand and calls me Tía Nora. She tells me I look beautiful, just as she knew I would, and she blinks every time I pass my hand over her eyes. I turn to see if Alicia is amazed by her daughter's miraculous recovery, but she is well accustomed to miracles and I decide to leave this one to its own enchantment.

I take them home to my house, which is right on the beach, so close that the waves wash over the threshold of my front door. We eat ripe sweet apples and oranges, which grow on trees that lean into my windows with such familiarity that I need not even get up from my chair to pick them. We chew more than we talk. And when we do talk it is only to say that the weather is good and that the fruit is sweet and that the water in these parts is far too murky for swimming.

21

May 1978

Dear Nora,

Ricardo tells me Tony will not be released as soon as he thought. I didn't want to believe him when he first told me. I preferred to think he'd confused him with somebody else or that he'd been drinking, but then he gave me the note from Tony himself. It was very brief, but I wept with joy at the sight of his lovely writing, which still looks like that of a little boy. He wrote that although prison life is harsh there are a few guards who make his imprisonment tolerable, and Ricardo is one of them.

I realized I had to do something to thank Ricardo for his kindness and to ensure he continued taking care of my love. I began bringing him food I buy with the dollars you send. One afternoon I brought him a fresh mango. It was so ripe and sweet I could smell its perfume in the bag. There was one for him and one for Tony. He took the bag from me and stared at me as he never had before. To be honest, Nora, it's been such a long time since anyone's looked at me that way that at first I wondered if I might have something stuck in my teeth.

I'm not such a fool as I used to be. I didn't for one

minute believe Ricardo had fallen in love with me, but I understood that how I responded to his declarations had everything to do with whether or not Tony ever tasted the mango that hung between us.

Did I mention that Ricardo's face is rough and scarred, and that with his hairy fingers his hands look like two giant spiders? The kindness in his eyes grew into a glare and I soothed him with a slight stroke on his spidery hands. That was enough for the moment, but the next week I allowed him to touch my hair and whisper silly things in my ear while he peeked down my blouse. On that day I brought Tony a loaf of fresh bread Berta had taken from the hotel.

Ricardo informed me Tony was being moved to another section of the prison and it would be difficult for him to keep taking him food, but that if I allowed him to slip his hands under my blouse, he'd arrange for a transfer.

I've been paying the ultimate price for my peace of mind for months now. Once a week at eleven, after Ricardo's shift, we meet at the north end of the malecón. He tells me not to be late, because his wife is very ugly and very jealous, and if he's late she'll wonder where he is and probably eat his rice and beans, because she's fat, too. He tells me that having me is worth going hungry for one night, but if he can have me and a plate of food, why not?

I wrote before that desperation changes people. Hunger, like alcohol, has a way of lowering inhibitions so that what was once impossible suddenly becomes not only possible, but likely. I know now that I'm capable of doing anything to protect Lucinda and Tony. The problem is that there are fewer and fewer desperate acts to choose from and we're left with nothing but the most common degradations.

I consider the offer you made me so long ago, to apply for visas, and that Juan would help in whatever

231

way he could. Then I believed I'd die if I left Cuba, but today I'd leave on a floating tree trunk if I knew Tony would be safe. I'm a prisoner with him, and the only peace I get these days is from knowing that Lucinda is with me and not in the educational camps. I received word just last week that she's excused for now, but I don't know how long this reprieve will last.

I will leave this place. I promise you with all the love and strength I have in my heart that even if my daughter never knows what it is to look upon the royal palms or the beauty of her own face, she will know freedom.

Alicia

Jeremy held me as I cried.

'You must go to her,' he said with a firm grip on my shoulders. 'Maybe you can convince her to stop what she's doing to herself.'

'All she cares about is keeping Tony safe. It doesn't matter if I'm there.'

Jeremy and I never quarrelled. If I had a tendency to raise my voice to the Cuban pitch I was accustomed to in my home, his steady rational responses always smoothed my ruffled feathers.

But this time, he was the one heating up. 'Other Cubans go visit their relatives, why can't you? Just tell your parents you're a grown woman and you've made up your mind.'

I turned away from him and felt numbness creep over me, as it always did when I thought about going. I saw my mother's face twisted in agony when Castro declared Cuba a socialist state. I saw my father curled up like a baby on the bed, sobbing when he learned of Tío Carlos's death. 'It's not that easy,' I said.

'It is, but you make it difficult.'

I turned to face him. 'You don't understand, because

you never stepped out of your life as though you were stepping out of a pair of comfortable shoes, only to find yourself banging around in heavy boots that don't fit and never will.'

Jeremy cocked his head to one side. 'You're right, I don't understand, Nora. I don't think I ever will.'

We first heard news of the balseros on TV. Desperate Cuban men, women and children flinging themselves into the sea, hoping that the tyres and scraps of wood they'd tied together with rope would transport them to freedom. We talked about it during Sunday dinner and, as usual, Mami was leading the conversation.

'Nobody here cares about what happens to those wretched souls,' she insisted. 'The Americans have forgotten about Cuba. What is it, after all? Just a little island in the middle of the ocean that makes no difference to anyone. It matters to us, but nobody else.'

Papi, Marta and I had learned over the years to keep our mouths shut whenever Mami went on in this way. There was no convincing her of anything that was even slightly hopeful when it came to Cuba and Cubans. She was hopelessly pessimistic and became offended if one attempted to offer a slightly sunnier view. Eddie caught on years ago, but Jeremy either didn't know or didn't care.

'I think there are some Americans who care. I do,' he said, dismembering the roast chicken before him.

'Of course you do, you married a Cuban woman,' Mami said as she waved a fork in his direction. But he wasn't finished.

'I cared before I married Nora.' Jeremy placed his fork down and cleaned his hands on his napkin, considering his words carefully. 'I wish Cubans could experience the freedom of democracy, Regina. I'm just not sure that the way to bring it about is to keep distancing ourselves from Castro.'

If I'd been close enough to pinch Jeremy's knee, I

would have. As it was, I wanted to dive under the table for cover.

Mami's rage was red and profuse; it travelled up from her belly, making itself seen as flames peeking up over her blouse, engulfing her neck, her ears, until finally her whole face was ablaze. 'Distancing ourselves? Did you say distancing? They've been inviting that murderous criminal to European summits and South American meetings all over the place. Meetings attended by American politicians, including our President. Meetings in which that man is officially acknowledged as the President of Cuba. Have you ever heard of anything so stupid in all your life?' She spat the words out like venom. 'President! As if he were elected, as if they had more than one name on the ballot during the circus they called an election. Did you know that people who didn't go out and vote were denied their ration books for God knows how long? Did you know that?'

Mami pushed herself away from the table. She was still steaming. 'This government has taken a hard stand against communism everywhere in the world, but right next door it does nothing. Cubans have died alongside Americans in Vietnam because of this country's hatred of communism. But can they go next door and get rid of that raving lunatic who uses Cuba as his personal playground?'

Her eyes were bulging at Jeremy, who sat silent and unflinching. Only I could see the shadow of disappointment on his face. And I alone knew that his disappointment was directed at himself and his own insensitivity.

I cleared my throat. 'Don't get so upset, Mami. There are lots of ways to look at it . . .'

Jeremy interrupted me. 'That's OK. You don't need to defend me. Your mother's right.'

'Of course I'm right,' she huffed, not easily swayed into a truce.

'Please forgive my rudeness.' Jeremy directed his apology to both Mami and Papi. Papi nodded, although he hadn't said a word.

Mami looked around at all the faces at the table, obviously relieved that the explosion had passed without any fatalities. She turned sombre eyes back towards Jeremy. 'Of course, you're allowed to have your own opinion, Jerry. I'm just telling you what I think. It's not like we're in Cuba, you know. You can think what you want.'

Jeremy nodded and Mami smiled as she went into the kitchen. She returned in less than a minute, carrying a beautiful golden flan dripping with caramel sauce. She placed it in front of Jeremy, knowing that flan was his favourite, and cut him a huge piece. Then she kissed him on the top of his head and left to start on the dishes without cutting pieces for anybody else.

Jeremy held me close and whispered in my ear, and nuzzled the base of my neck until I was giggling like a child. We made love by the moonlight that glowed through the open window. Sometimes the ocean breeze found our little house through the maze of neighbourhoods and houses in between. We breathed in the cool freshness and allowed it to dry the perspiration on our skin.

Jeremy fell asleep with his arms wrapped around me, and suddenly we're floating out in the middle of the sea in a small sturdy raft. The ocean is rolling pleasantly while the mist sprays over the sides, caressing us. I see the stars blinking overhead. This is the most beautiful night of my life. My fortune is determined by the strength of my faith and my dreams. It's the wind in my sails, the circular force of the currents, the beating of my heart. What an amazing feeling to risk all that I am and all I believe in for this sense of hope. The growing pitch of the sea doesn't bother me. It will calm soon and the sun will rise out of the sea as it always has. We're on our way to a better life.

Jeremy and I see the rising sun together. It starts as a tremulous light that spreads in soft ribbons against the dark of the passing night. The ocean glows deep and warm as it smiles up at the sky. Another day has begun.

'We're part of this now, Jeremy,' I say, and his face is golden with the sun. He holds my hand with loving delicacy, as if it were a flower. A sliver of land floats on the mist beyond. It would be difficult to see if not for the hint of brown contour, immovable against the flow of the sea. We're headed right for it and as we get closer the mist burns away to reveal the solid hills, the swaying palms, the broad calm harbour that destined the land for greatness in the New World. Once again I gaze upon the beauty of my beloved Cuba.

22

Dear Nora,

I'm proud to say that I now have a job at the Hotel
Nacional. They've renovated it beautifully, and as I
walk on the marbled floor and smell the rich food
coming from the restaurant, I can pretend everything
is as it used to be. But I can't pretend for long,
because the hotel is full of tourists from many
countries, like Canada and Germany. Nobody speaks
Spanish, but thankfully my job doesn't require that I
say much. I just smile politely and show them the
way to the lobby, and sometimes take them to their
rooms. I wear a lovely uniform. It's blue with gold
trim on the sleeves and the bottom of the skirt, and I
have matching shoes as well.

Lucinda stays home by herself when I work. I don't
know what else to do. She is not quite eleven, but
she's very mature for her age and knows where
everything is. During blackouts, which come very
often these days, I rely on her to find things in the
dark. I don't want to waste the few candles we have,
so we sit for hours in the dark and I tell her about
you and your life. She knows all about Jeremy and
she wants to learn how to speak English to impress

237

you. I've begun to teach her the few words I know, like 'Hello, my name is Lucinda,' and 'Can you tell me the time?' She's very good at remembering these phrases, but I'm afraid her accent is terrible, even worse than mine.

She tells me stories, too. Last week she heard that one of our neighbours left the country in a small boat. He applied for a visa years ago, but he got tired of waiting. It's amazing the things people say to my Lucinda, as if they believe her blindness will keep their secrets safe. Normally, plans to escape aren't shared openly, because anyone caught trying to leave can go to prison for many years. But more and more are taking the chance. Life for them here is more frightening than the possibility of jail, drowning or even getting eaten by sharks.

People here have become desperate for things like soap and toothpaste and aspirin. A stash of soap under the bed is the best cure for insomnia. Last year I was able to get hold of a box. It was rose scented and each piece was wrapped in very thin almost transparent paper; so delicate. I used to count them every night, and feel the heaviness in my hand as if they were gold bars. I was forced to exchange the last few bars for medicine when Lucinda was ill recently, and then I knew how a millionaire must feel after he loses everything. It is a feeling perhaps worse than hunger; an emptiness that sours the heart.

There are some who find this situation thrilling. The woman across the street leaves her house every morning with a straw bag hanging from her arm. You can see the excitement and spring in her step, like a hunter heading out for the kill. Her husband is not quite so animated. He hasn't left the house for months and slumps around the front steps waiting for his wife to return. When she does, he sniffs out her bag as if he were an old hound dog looking for a bone. I'm not lying to you when I tell you that a few times I've actually seen her smack him on the nose when he gets too close to her bag, and he paws her all the way back into the house. It's very sad to see.

I sit in the dark after Lucinda has fallen asleep and think of how easy it would be, Nora. How easy to float to freedom . . . to paradise. I remember the splendour of my life before the changes. I had a new dress almost every week and the maid would brush my hair in the morning until it shone. The bread was always fresh and warm and the butter dripped off it onto our plates, and there was meat every day and fish until it was coming out of our ears. There was a new bar of soap by every sink and bathtub. There was lilac water to splash on our hair after a long warm bath. There was music on every street corner and the musicians were plump and merry and laughed along with their melodies. The children were as crisp as paper dolls new out of the box. I remember how good it felt right after a bath when I was going out to dinner with my parents. My skin was just a little tight from the soap and my scalp felt cool in the breeze.

If all of this was possible then, then isn't it just as possible now to find my way into a raft or a banana boat and float to freedom? Just last week I learned of a freighter that was willing to take those who had the cash to Jamaica. If it were not for Tony, I would've left with Lucinda and never looked back.

Enough. Tomorrow is a working day. May God bless you and Jeremy in many ways. Remember I love you.

Alicia

We were late for Sunday dinner because Jeremy had many papers to grade.

Expecting to see everyone sitting around the table, we were surprised to find Mami still in the kitchen, wearing her apron and sniffling into a tissue as she worked. She lit up when we walked in and almost dropped the salad in her excitement. She grasped my shoulders. 'You'll never guess who called!'

I looked at Jeremy, who shrugged, just as bewildered as I was, eyes still red from hours of reading term papers.

'Aren't you going to guess?' she asked, giving me a little shake as well.

'I have no idea.'

'Alicia! It was our little Alicia!' Mami dropped her hands, raised them, dropped them again, and then wrung them nervously. 'And you could hear her clear as a bell, the connection was so good.'

'Alicia . . . you actually spoke with her on the phone?' I felt Jeremy's hand on my back.

Mami nodded and swallowed hard. 'We talked for several minutes about so many things. She asked for you. I gave her your number and she said she'd try to call you at home.'

'Does she have a phone?'

'Apparently there's one at the hotel where she's working, but it sounded like she couldn't talk for very long.' Mami didn't seem to know whether she should continue with the salad or stir the beef stew. 'She sounds just the same, Nora, just the same. She has the same little voice and . . .' Mami leaned on the counter and began to sob. I ran over to her, my own eyes watering, and held her as she spoke. 'I could see her so clearly. That last time we said goodbye to them at Varadero, remember? She was a beautiful girl and so sweet and smart.' She turned to Jeremy and sniffed loudly. 'She had golden hair, beautiful and curly. Nobody would think she was Cuban. And her eyes were green.'

'Her eyes are probably still green, Mami. You're talking about her as if she's dead.'

Mami returned to her cooking. 'People I know who've gone back to visit describe it like a cemetery full of walking corpses, a living death.' She sniffed loudly.

We spoke of little else during dinner. Mami recounted her five-minute conversation with Alicia at least twenty times. Each recounting seemed to uncover one more detail or nuance of how her life was, and what she would do next. Of course, I already knew all these things, but I didn't share what additional information I had. What Alicia had written in her letters was sacred and meant just for me.

'She's working in a fancy hotel,' Mami said. 'Tony won't get out of prison for a couple of years, but she's hopeful it could be sooner. It seems she has a friend who watches out for him. She's saving the money we send and that tourists give her. She says that with this money she'll be able to leave once Tony gets out.'

'So they're definitely planning to leave?' Marta asked as she attempted to feed her baby son Michael, who was spitting out his black beans, behaving as American as he looked.

'It certainly sounds that way.'

'Are they planning to get visas?' Papi asked.

'She says they're going to try, but if they can't they'll get out however they can.'

The table was quiet at these words. More reports of drowned rafters were being confirmed every day.

'Did she say she'd call me?' I asked for the tenth time at least.

'She took your number down and repeated it twice. She said she'd call you as soon as she could.'

Papi was quiet during dinner. He couldn't hear about Alicia without thinking of his brother. He ate very little and left the table early, saying he needed to finish some reading before Monday. Mami apologized to Eddie and Jeremy. 'You see, he had a terrible loss. Actually, we all did . . .'

'They know, Mami,' Marta said. And Mami was

silenced, relieved to be spared the recounting of Uncle Carlos's death. We all were.

I waited for days and then weeks. Every time the phone rang I snatched the receiver, hoping to hear the thin crackle of static and Alicia's distant voice balancing precariously on the wire. Would I recognize it after so many years? I heard a child's voice when I read her letters, a lovely flowery voice full of clear light and possibilities. The kind of voice that could only belong to a beautiful girl. But she was now a grown woman, and she'd suffered so many things. It would be different; it had to be.

Jeremy teased that my desperation to hear from Alicia was starting to make him feel like a jilted lover. And my desperation fuelled the dreams that came almost every night. I'd wake up clutching Jeremy, his T-shirt moist with my tears. I was looking for Alicia with Tony at my side. We were walking along the beach and he was telling me how much he loved his wife, and his green eyes were glowing as he stared out at the sea wondering where she might be. We were both saddened by her absence, and I placed my hand on his shoulder to express my compassion. Suddenly, we were both naked and twisting into each other like snakes embracing in the sand.

Jeremy always wanted to hear about my dreams, but I didn't share this one. He'd never been a jealous man and he'd probably give me a curious smile if I told him. In the darkness his eyes would penetrate me and he'd smile and hold me with a chuckle because I looked so damn guilty.

'I love you so much,' I said as I laid my dampened cheek on his chest and felt the comforting rise and fall of his breathing.

'Don't worry. She'll call,' he whispered, half asleep.

23

November 1980

Dear Nora,

Your last letter was tucked unopened in my purse
for many weeks before I had the heart to read it.
Please forgive me, but my life has taken another
drastic turn. If I'd written to you earlier you would've
wondered who that strange person was signing my
name. Perhaps you'll still wonder, but I have no
choice but to be honest with you. I know now more
than ever why Tía Panchita needed to sit on her
porch before she died. It is the same for me when I
write to you.

I go to church and I talk to God amidst the silence
of the statues covered with dust and cobwebs.
Lucinda and I pray together and I suppose our
prayers make it to heaven, but it's been a long time
since I heard God's voice. I used to hear Him all the
time, loud and clear in the wind and in the roar of
the sea. Now all I hear is noise, noise that keeps me
from my sleep.

Berta has been teaching me about her work. She
comes home with beautiful things almost every day.
Last week she had a bottle of lemon-scented
shampoo. The week before that a big square box of

243

tissue paper for blowing your nose. The week before that two pairs of brand-new stockings as sheer as glass. We laughed as we threw them up in the air and watched them float down to the ground like feathers. You put just one toe into them and you feel like Cinderella, and that beautiful feeling travels all the way up your body.

For some time now I've known that Berta is one of those ladies Abuela wouldn't let us talk about. She wears her best clothes and sits in the lobby of the hotel or in the bar, smoking cigarettes and crossing and uncrossing her legs until a man buys her a drink or asks her for the time, even though she doesn't wear a watch. Often I see her working from my place at the door. She throws her head back and laughs the way I remember I used to do when in the company of admiring young men. She tugs on her tight skirt so the men can't help but stare at her legs, which are bare all the way up her thigh. Before long she leaves on the arm of one of them. Sometimes they go to a restaurant and a show, but the younger ones take her straight to their rooms.

Berta says this is the only way to make real money. Did I tell you she has a degree in engineering? She studied in Russia for a while and can order a drink in three languages, not including Spanish.

About three months ago, I went to work as usual and the manager called me to his office. I'd never been to his office before. It still smelled of fresh paint and the window looked out on the ocean and framed it so beautifully. He asked me to sit down and offered me a coke. Do you know how long it's been since I had a coke? My hand trembled as I took the glass and brought it to my lips and I couldn't hold back the tears that ran down my face.

Then he whispered in my ear. A week before I would've stormed out and left him with his words hanging in his mouth, but on this day they sank into my soul. I've become the worst thing a woman can become. And I do it as easily as I swam to the platform so many years ago. I just close my eyes and dive in. I don't feel the men touching me, I don't hear the ridiculous things they say. I'm doing my job, taking advantage of an opportunity that allows me to go home to my Lucinda at the end of the day or night with a bag full of milk and toothpaste and soap and meat and cans of vegetables and fresh fruit.

I still love only Tony and nothing changes that. Others may possess my body for a short while, but it's only with Tony that my spirit has danced. I continue to send him packages every week with Ricardo, but I'm thankful he no longer requires additional payment as I believe he's taken up with someone else.

I'm now able to save money to escape, and when we leave I'll erase everything from my mind and heart. This is the one thought that keeps me alive.

I will wait for your letter as I wait for news from Tony every day, with one hand on my heart and the other raised to heaven.

Alicia

Mami collapsed on the couch sobbing, and Papi stood glum and stoical beside her. It was exactly as I had expected, but still my palms were sweaty and I felt a new fear gurgling in the pit of my stomach. Jeremy stood next to me, a few steps back. Even after more than seven years of marriage, he wasn't used to these emotional outbursts, and he'd learned the hard way that it was useless to respond like an objective anthropologist studying a strange tribe somewhere in the jungle. Whether he liked it or not, he was one of us now, a bit more cerebral and contemplative than the rest, but one of us nonetheless.

'Do you know how I feel?' Mami asked, lifting her

tear-stained face from the cushion. 'I feel like my country was taken away from me and now my honour has been as well, because my own flesh and blood is going back to pump American dollars into that criminal system. Every penny you spend will end up in the pocket of that man.'

'Regina, please calm down,' Papi said, placing his hand on her arm; she flinched it away, but shifted her gaze downwards like a scolded child.

Papi cleared his throat. His eyes were unwavering, but as sad as they'd been during the worst moments of his life. 'You know how we feel about this, Nora, but you're a grown woman now and we can't tell you what to do. Maybe one day you'll have children and you'll . . .' Papi stuffed his hands in his pockets and shook his head as tears swam in his eyes. 'One day you'll understand.'

We left Mami and Papi without our usual Sunday meal warm and heavy in our bellies. Instead, we had sushi at a little place near the oceanfront, and took a walk on the pier afterwards. Few words passed between us. Jeremy held my hand snugly in his coat pocket, for the wind was blowing cold.

'So are you still going?' he asked when we'd almost reached the end of the pier.

'I'm still going.'

We stopped for a moment and leaned against the railing as we gazed at the sea beneath us. The wind was full of mist and filled our noses and eyes, washing us clean and blowing us dry at the same time.

'Good,' he said, wrapping his arm around my shoulder and pulling me towards him so that I was standing on only one foot. 'You're sure you'll be all right alone? I can try to get away, but it's just hard in the middle of the quarter.'

'I'm sure I'll be fine.'

We stood watching the waves rolling forward in rounded symmetry, continuous bands of unimaginable strength pounding at the foundations of the pier. The water was a deep and ominous green, opaque and glossy like very thick glass, its edges sharp and pointed, lifting huge crags up towards the sky and swallowing them again in violent spurts. How different from the ocean I'd soon be seeing in my homeland. I tried to explain this to Jeremy as we stood in the mist, and as I spoke, it was as if the sea's jealous roars were trying to drown me out.

'It's quiet, for one thing,' I said. 'The waves don't pound, they glide over you like a soft breeze. And you can see all the way down to your toes, even if you're standing in water up to your shoulders. Sometimes when you're suspended in perfect warmth, a rain cloud will float by out of nowhere and it'll start raining thick warm drops of water right on your head. Alicia and I liked to pretend we were washing our hair in the middle of the ocean like mermaids. Or we'd dive under the surface, thinking ourselves so clever to escape the rain for the few seconds we could hold our breath. Just as suddenly as it started, the rain would stop and the sun would shine even more brilliantly than before. In this way we experienced several mornings and nights in a single day.'

He was watching me, smiling that curious smile that makes my heart melt every time. 'Really? So then you only need to go for one week instead of two. After all, if you have several mornings and nights in one day . . .'

I threw my arms around his neck and whispered in his ear, which was chilled from the wind. 'I'm going to miss you too, Jeremy. I'm going to miss you so much.'

Jeremy passed the phone to me, half asleep, and when I heard her voice on the line I bolted straight up in bed.

'Listen to you answering the phone like una Americana,' she said.

'Alicia, is it really you?'

She laughed. 'Of course it's me, silly.'

'I don't believe I'm actually talking to you! I don't believe it's you!'

'I can see you haven't forgotten your Spanish. I was afraid I'd have to talk to you with the little English I know, and that would make for a very boring conversation.'

'You sound just the same, Alicia. Your voice, it's . . . it's the same.'

She sighed. 'If only everything was the same. You know me, I have a tendency to wish for the impossible. But then some of my wishes do come true. Are you really coming home?'

'I'll be there in a few days, just like I said in my letter.'

'It's too wonderful to imagine.'

I heard noise in the background, and then a pause. When she spoke again, Alicia's voice was muffled. 'I hear someone coming and I shouldn't be using the phone.'

'Is there something wrong?' I asked, sensing the fear in her voice.

'Not a thing. All that matters is that you're coming home. I'll be waiting for you at the airport. I love you, Nora.'

'I love you too, Alicia.'

HAVANA

1981

24

TWO HOURS INTO THE FLIGHT FROM LOS ANGELES TO MIAMI, I forced myself to drink a glass of red wine in an effort to calm my nerves. Liquid tranquillity and finally sleep overcame my anxiety, and I found myself standing with several others in a circle of light.

The fire is brilliant, licking our toes and caressing our bodies as we move into it and away from it like the shifting of the tides. Our hips jerk to the rhythm of the drums. It's Beba who plays them and she smiles with big beautiful teeth, even whiter than her snowy turban. She beats the drums so hard I'm concerned she'll grow tired, but she's glowing like an angel.

'I've been waiting for you, little girl,' she says, without skipping a beat. 'Where have you hidden yourself all these years?'

'I was far away, but now I've come home.' I move nearer to her. I want to see the polished smoothness of her skin up close. I want to smell the onions and the peppers on her hands and hear the deep and golden timbre of her voice, which is more reassuring to me than my own mother's voice.

I look into her eyes and she stops playing. They are as I remember them, alive with the knowledge of a secret joke, poised on the verge of tears and laughter. She can make all the hurts and fears of childhood disappear with a single embrace, a wave of her hand, the wink of an eye.

'Everything's going to be OK, little girl. Don't be afraid.'

'Do you promise?'

'Has Beba ever lied to you?'

'No, Beba. You never lied to me or anyone. That I know as surely as I know my own name.'

Satisfied with my response, she begins to play again, moving her enormous head that sways and dips to the rhythms floating round us and through us. She's no longer paying attention to me. She knows I'm here. She knows I'm safe.

Lucinda takes my hand and brings me back to the fire. She leads me closer and closer to it. 'It's OK, Tía Nora. It won't hurt.' And she steps into it herself to show me.

Flames shoot through her body and she lights up, the fire curling up in her eyes and her mouth like an oven of hot embers burning and smouldering. Her hair is golden light floating on the heat. She smiles a brilliant burning smile and holds her small hand out to me, which glows gently from the inside out so the veins are clearly visible. I reach out to take it, and the darkness sweeps me away, silencing the wind and the whisperings of my mind.

I trembled when the plane touched down in Havana, and when I stepped onto Cuban soil the prayers I remembered saying as a child formed on my lips. I was not alone. Many other passengers wept for joy, and thanked God and all the saints for allowing them to return to their homeland before they died. One older woman collapsed on her knees, her face pressed to the ground. Her young companion, who looked like her granddaughter, was embarrassed by this display of emotion and attempted to raise her by one arm, but her grandmother refused to move.

I walked past them, preparing to tell the girl she should be patient with her poor grandmother, when the tropical fragrance in the air forced me to stop dead in my tracks as well. After so many years of empty remembering, my heart leapt. Like words to a song I'd long forgotten, it was suddenly upon me; every chord, every phrase, every turn of the melody was singing to my spirit, 'You're home, you're finally home where you belong.' I felt the petals of my heart shift and loosen; another breath and they'd be completely open. A few more seconds of warmth from the sun that hits this land from its unique angle and distance in the sky, and I would be as I was meant to be.

My feet shuffled forward and I heard the sounds of Cuban Spanish spoken all around me, the dropped s's and slurred consonants making every word sound like the erratic beating of a drum. Rhythmic and alive, broken with laughter and wild gesticulations, it said more to me than a thousand words.

My head spun with the whirl of commotion. Entire families were at the airport to welcome their Americanized relatives. In their haste to get to them, they stumbled over each other, heavily laden bags of soap and toilet paper tumbling to the dirty floor and quickly recovered by eager relatives, whose emotion was momentarily suspended by the sight of such rare luxuries.

I scanned the crowd, sniffing and waving my hand-kerchief in the air for Alicia to find me. Several people bumped into me as I made my way through the throng, searching my eyes as I searched their faces. Although I didn't know them, their expression of longing and hope was one I was all too familiar with.

I spotted them leaning against the very wall where I'd waited to leave my country so many years ago. Alicia's face had hardly changed. Her fine and perfect features, her almond-shaped eyes dancing with intelligent light, full of inspiration and wonder. She was still a child. Her golden hair was back in a ponytail, wisps of curls framing her face like the most delicate lace. But she was thinner than I remembered and her shoulders slumped beneath the crisp shirt she wore. Her skirt would've fallen to her feet if not for the belt cinched tight around her tiny waist.

My gaze shifted down and I beheld one of the most beautiful children I'd ever seen. She was quite literally a golden child, and appeared much younger than her twelve years. Her hair fell in ringlets of dark gold, and her skin, although lighter in tone than her father's, still retained the burnished warmth that filters through the trees at sunset. Her turquoise eyes gazed straight ahead, but they were not vacant. They were mysteriously calm, as though she were in constant prayer and meditation. She smiled brilliantly in response to something her mother said to her. Mesmerized by Lucinda, I hadn't noticed that Alicia had spotted me in the crowd and they were walking towards me.

We stood for a moment, and I was in Tía Maria's garden once again. I was looking to Alicia for guidance or at least a funny joke that could transport us into the trance of endless giggles that irritated everybody but ourselves. But this close up I could see that she had changed. The once fine texture of her skin had been degraded by time, and although still beautiful, it was far from the porcelain perfection I remembered. Her hair, which could once capture every beam of sunlight, was dull and dry, and as she pulled me into an embrace I realized that it was none too clean either.

We held each other for a very long time, and in her arms my shock melted into tears which streamed down my face, dampening Alicia's hair. She was crying too, and her skinny shoulders trembled against mine.

'You're here,' she kept whispering. 'You're really here.'

We stood at arm's length, holding hands. Memories

had been much kinder than this moment, for as I looked upon this fatigued woman approaching middle age, I was suddenly faced with a stranger. This wasn't Alicia, unless I looked at nothing but the golden light of her eyes, which wavered with the shifting grace of the ocean.

'You've grown into such a beautiful woman,' she said. 'Such a beautiful and elegant woman.'

Lucinda stepped forward and took my hand. She stepped closer still, so that her head was next to my heart, and hugged me tight. I let go of Alicia's hands, wrapped both my arms around Lucinda and kissed the top of her head. I loved her instantly.

'Tía Nora, you smell so good,' Lucinda said, and I held her even more tightly.

Berta was waiting outside for us in a borrowed car. She was a large, attractive woman with thick black hair and full lips painted hastily in fuschia. She wore a tube top that barely covered her ample bust, and a smooth roll of honey-coloured flesh escaped over her skin-tight shorts.

She drove a 1955 powder-blue Chevrolet with a visor, just like Papi used to have, and handled the oversized steering wheel like a pro, yelling profanities out of her window at offending drivers with the same dexterity.

Between shouts and crazy manoeuvres, she managed to snatch glimpses of me and my clothes and shoes. Her questions were pointed and not in the least bit apologetic. 'I bet you paid more than twenty dollars for those shoes, didn't you?'

'I think so.'

'So, what do you do to make money?'

'I'm a teacher. I work with young children who are still learning English.'

She flung her head out of the window for the tenth time and her raven hair streamed out like a flag, nearly blinding her in the process, not that this prompted her to slow down at all. 'Get out of the road, you worthless piece of shit!' she shouted to another driver.

'So, you have to go to school for a long time to do that or what?'

'A little bit. It's not that bad.'

'How much you get paid?'

Alicia leaned forward from the back seat and placed a cautious hand on my shoulder. 'I may have forgotten to tell you how forward Berta can be.'

Berta cackled behind the steering wheel and I couldn't be sure if she hadn't just spat out of the window as well. 'That's right,' she said, grinning from ear to ear and showing a remarkable set of large and perfect teeth. 'But you can tell me to shut up and I won't be mad at you, not even for a minute.'

'We wouldn't make it without Berta,' Alicia said, leaning back again, obviously exhausted. I noticed perspiration lining her mouth.

Berta yelled through the window again, this time at a group of young men standing idly in the street and blocking the flow of traffic. 'If you don't move your butts, I'm going to serve them up for dinner and your balls for dessert!' This brought a series of even more colourful comebacks from the young men and a sparkling eruption of giggles from Lucinda in the back seat, who, until then, had been silent.

I heard Alicia exhale from behind me. 'I told you things had changed, Nora.' I knew what she meant. Never would vulgarity of this sort have been tolerated openly on the streets, but it now fell from the windows of once elegant buildings like confetti. It was obviously the order of the day, for women as well as men. Perhaps it was necessary for survival, for Berta used it as one would wield a huge rifle, and her efforts cleared her path as well as if she'd strapped one to the hood of her car.

We drove through the potholed streets of Havana,

dodging young and old alike. Many rode on rickety bikes, sometimes two or even three at a time, their limbs splayed out in an effort to balance like a circus act on a high wire. The majority of the buildings we passed had fallen to ruin, like enormous wedding cakes decomposing in the sun, their former glory strewn about the sidewalks like so many crumbs. Coloured glass that had once graced the most elegant of windows must have fallen upon those below like heavy tears.

I had walked this street as a child many times. The driver had often dropped us off at the far corner near the pharmacy, and I had held on tight to Mami's hand as we crossed the busy road. Could this be the same place? Yes, it was. And around the corner was the Woolworth drugstore, where Alicia and I loved to sit at the counter and order our favourite avocado and shrimp salad. When Mami wandered off to look at this or that, we'd spin on the seats so that sometimes we were too dizzy to eat. Or we'd watch elegant ladies strolling past in their high-heeled shoes, with matching bags swinging from their crooked arms. We dreamed of how we would dress and walk when we were old enough to shave our legs and wear stockings. We listened to the street vendors, who called out their wares with a dignity that blended nicely with the musicians serenading us.

But now the skin was being stripped off my beautiful memories. People didn't stroll any more; they shuffled in ill-fitting shoes held onto their feet by a fraying strap. Many children were barefoot. They were at the age when feet grew quickly, and I imagine they were lucky if the one pair of shoes they received a year lasted more than a few months.

I studied the faces of my countrymen as they ambled about the decomposing city, their eyes turned inward as if they were lost in a dream from which they did not want to wake. They stepped over the garbage and debris without noticing. Perhaps they were, as I was, trying very hard to remember the way their city used to be, so they didn't have to see it now falling down around them.

I turned back to look at Alicia, who was smiling a small sad smile. 'Things have changed,' she said again with a slight nod of her head. 'Don't cry, Nora.'

Was I crying? Were the tears on my cheeks my body's reaction to the thick tropical weather so unlike the dry Californian climate? I rubbed my arms with both hands at once. I could feel the damp softness already, the sensuous experience of mild humidity that made my skin feel as soft and smooth as the finest silk. I could feel the creases around my eyes and the corners of my mouth, even my scalp, begin to loosen and smooth out like glass. The air was heavier, but fragrant and soft.

Lucinda was leaning forward in her seat towards me and a smile had drifted across her face, like the sun peeking out from behind a cloud. 'Mami and I have been dreaming of this day for so long. We talked about it since I was a little girl.' She reached out her small hand and began to stroke my hair. 'Tía Nora?'

I took her hand and kissed it. 'Yes, my love?'

'Don't ever leave us.'

At this Alicia straightened up and placed a gentle hand on Lucinda's shoulder. 'We talked about this. Nora has a husband and a job in the United States. She's only coming for a visit.'

'He can live here too. Jeremy even speaks Spanish, doesn't he, Tía Nora?'

I smiled at the way Lucinda pronounced Jeremy's name, with the J sounding like an H. I rather liked the sound of it. I took hold of her hand once again. 'If there was any way we could live here with you both, I would stay. But I'm afraid your Mami's right. I'll have to go back soon.'

Lucinda settled back in her seat with a solemn nod.

At this moment the ocean appeared ahead of us between two buildings, like a jewel sandwiched between two dry and moulding pieces of bread. It sparkled and winked its turquoise perfection at me, and the waves rolled in graceful and gentle bands onto the beach beyond the malecón. I gazed at the sky and ocean as they floated together where heaven meets the earth. This point on the horizon, where my Cuban soul lives, this place had not changed at all. It was exactly the same, and all the depressing ugliness I'd just seen faded away.

'Stop the car, Berta,' I said and she nearly careened into the sidewalk of the malecón. I got out of the car and walked to the wall that held back the sea. The wind blew back my hair and the ocean spoke to me as it rolled forward. The warmth of the sun reached in and touched my heart and soul so that they glowed. 'Welcome back to the only place your heart can ever truly call home. Go ahead, breathe in. With every breath it becomes more and more difficult to deny that you're a daughter of the island. The passion in your heart belongs here.'

My knees were weak when I walked back to the car, as though I'd been administered a strong drug.

'We'll have time to spend at the beach,' Alicia said soberly. 'Now you're tired and we should go home to rest for a while. Berta and I made you some good Cuban food. You must be hungry.'

I realized suddenly that I was. 'I don't think I've ever been hungrier in all my life,' I told them as Berta burst away from the kerb and back into the traffic.

25

THEIR HOME WAS ONLY A FEW BLOCKS FROM THE SEA. IT WAS actually a two-room apartment within what had once been a lovely townhouse, with rose-coloured walls, terraces spilling over with geraniums and lacy banisters of intricate wrought iron. With time and neglect, the plaster had peeled off in large curling strips, exposing the powdery flesh beneath; but the iron, like the teeth of a corpse consumed by fire, was true to its past.

What Alicia referred to as the kitchen was in reality a small broom closet. It contained a double-burner hot plate and a small refrigerator barely big enough for a couple of cartons of milk. Several boxes stacked against the wall served as shelves, in which were kept two bags of rice and a large bag of black beans, a few onions and a box of powdered milk. The only window – in the upper corner – had no screen, and could only be opened during cooking, otherwise the kitchen would be overcome by the prodigious flying insects of the tropics. The effect was a room so stiflingly hot that it was a wonder the rice and beans didn't cook all by themselves in their bags.

When Alicia and Berta disappeared into the kitchen to finish my homecoming meal, I sat with Lucinda and listened to her sweet singsong voice. She sat on the couch, which also served as a bed, and looked at me with such tenderness that I felt she could not only see my skin, but see all the way through to my soul as well.

'I always took care of Mami when she worked,' she said simply. 'Now that she doesn't work, I still take care of her.'

'Your Mami isn't working any more?' My delight at hearing this made me sound almost shrill.

'Mami's been too tired to work lately, but I make sure nothing disturbs her at night when she sleeps, because rest is what makes her feel better. When she's had a good night's rest, we go to the beach and that's my favourite place in the world.'

I nodded my agreement. 'This country has the most beautiful beaches in the world. Back in California the beaches are beautiful too, but very different.'

'Aren't all beaches the same?'

'My goodness, no. Over there the water is cool, even cold. And the ocean is dark green and so deep that the sun can't light it up and warm it like it does here. If you could give the sea emotions, the sea over there is a sombre and serious sea, but here it's playful and rather vain. It's in love with its own beauty, which it sees reflected in the sky. But who can fault the ocean, when there is none who can even come close to her?'

Lucinda nodded eagerly, and I thought sadly of how she'd never be able to look upon the blessing of beauty that was her own face. She showed me the books she kept underneath the couch. They were obviously her pride and joy, and she ran her fingers over the pages tenderly, reading to me her favourite passages from *Jane Eyre* and *Oliver Twist*. She read very well, with feeling and maturity, but I soon realized she had most of these passages confined to memory, because her fingers no longer touched the pages as she spoke but hovered at least two inches above.

At a word from her mother, Lucinda put the books away and set the small table in the centre of the room, with no difficulty whatsoever. She knew exactly where the dishes were kept, and every spoon and fork. It was quite amazing, and for an instant I doubted she was blind at all. Perhaps, I thought, she could see just a little out of the corner of her eyes. But when I studied her movements closely, I noticed that her hands hesitated briefly to be sure they'd touched what she intended before she took firm hold of the object. In these dreary little rooms, Lucinda wasn't blind at all but completely in control, and it was a joy to watch her.

She whispered to me as we waited for the meal to be served, 'Mami's happy because she found three fresh tomatoes yesterday.'

'That's wonderful. I love tomatoes.'

'I'm lucky that I love bananas best, 'cause they're easier to find than tomatoes. Is it hard to find tomatoes in California?'

I took her hand. 'Not as hard as it is here.'

Alicia and Berta emerged from the tiny kitchen, beaming and dripping with perspiration. Between them, they brought a meal that was simple but delicious. A whole chicken had been slowly stewed in its own juices with onions and garlic. The black beans were the best I'd tasted since leaving Cuba, and the rice was fluffy and perfect, with tomatoes sliced on the side in thick rounds and lightly salted.

Berta turned on the radio and we listened to the crackling sounds of mambo music as we ate. The breeze from the ocean circled the apartment and settled upon us like an old friend. I closed my eyes. We could've been at Abuelo and Abuela's house at Varadero, eating arroz con pollo after a long swim. After the meal we'd take a leisurely stroll and reward ourselves with coconut ice cream or a freshly cut mango.

I opened my eyes to find Alicia studying me. She appeared more tired than worried, and although dark circles were evident beneath her eyes, she was still beautiful. The weight she'd lost only accentuated the chiselled perfection of her cheekbones, the perfect line of her nose and the delicate sweep of her jaw, which flexed as she chewed. Seeing daughter and mother side by side was quite astounding. Lucinda resembled her father, there was no doubt about that, but her aquiline features were almost the exact replica of her mother's.

'You've come so far and this is all we have to offer you,' Alicia said, setting down her fork as her eyes filled with tears. 'I'm ashamed to tell you how long it took us to find this chicken . . .' She shrugged off her sadness and winked in Berta's direction.

'Well, I sure don't mind telling you,' Berta countered with a flick of her head that swung a shock of black hair across Lucinda's startled face. 'What we should've done with this chicken was dress it up in new clothes and take it dancing for the evening. It's almost a shame to eat it.'

We all laughed, and I realized that Berta helped Alicia with much more than her talent for finding chickens and toilet paper. In some ways, she reminded me of Beba. Her no-nonsense humour seemed to beckon hope and forward thinking as resolutely as a good strong heat could boil water. There was no time to worry when you knew that day would follow night and that you had to continue breathing and living and laughing and crying today, just like any other day.

After dinner, Alicia collapsed on the couch while Lucinda did the dishes in the bathroom sink. I offered to help, but she refused with a casual wave of her hand, as though she were a middle-aged lady quite territorial about her work in the kitchen. Berta retired to her room, complaining that she would need to get up early the next morning. The radio was hers and she took it with her.

Alicia insisted we go for a walk while Lucinda

finished the dishes, and in less than a minute we were walking arm in arm towards the malecón. We were silent as we walked, listening to the sounds of the city: children being called in from the streets for the night, pots and pans clanging as they were washed after dinner, the scuffling of brooms sweeping the grime of the day out into the streets. Few cars could be heard or seen. Alicia explained that it was next to impossible to find headlights for them, so they couldn't be driven at night. If you saw a car at night, it was almost always a taxi or a Russian-built government car.

We reached the malecón in a few minutes, arriving at almost the same spot where I'd stood earlier that day. But the difference was dramatic. A blinking necklace of lights spread out before us, tracing the line of the shore. The curve and sweep of the lights conformed exactly to the memory I cherished. The music of the sea, the mist against my cheeks, Alicia's voice speaking to me, telling me whatever came into her head, as she was prone to do. I held onto the concrete wall for support. My eyes were aching from the effort of trying not to cry, as tears sprang to my eyes for the third time that day.

I heard Alicia's voice carry on the breeze behind me. 'This is what I wanted you to see.'

'We shouldn't have come when you're so tired. We could've come tomorrow.'

'I wanted to see it tonight.'

I turned to Alicia, who was gazing and smiling at me. 'You can see this every night, silly.'

'No. I wanted to see the expression on your face when you saw it.' She shoved my shoulder playfully. 'Silly.'

We walked on a few blocks further and crossed the street arm in arm. Hardly speaking, she guided me past the corner where the pharmacy had been and on towards the street that I knew we must visit. My senses became enlivened, and I felt like an old horse heading back to her stable. We stopped suddenly, my eyes lifting seven storeys to our apartment, and the years swept away as if we had just been sent on an errand. I expected to see Beba's white turban out on the balcony at any moment and Mami watching and waving like she did when we went to the corner for an ice cream. 'Bring back some coconut for after dinner,' she'd call. 'And be careful crossing the street.' My eyes strained against the shadows, hoping to catch a glimpse of a ghost or anything that could make it all come back again. Perhaps if I looked at it hard enough and long enough.

'Who lives there now?' I asked, trying to keep my voice steady.

'Nobody. The building's been condemned for years.'

I looked more closely and saw the windows boarded up and other balconies stripped of their railings. I felt a sudden urge to run up the seven flights of stairs and see it all again: my room, the kitchen and the chair where Papi used to read his paper. I might even find my Elvis albums where I'd left them by the window. I began to walk forward to do just that, but Alicia held on to my arm. 'It's not a good idea to go in, Nora,' she said softly.

'Why not?'

'It's very dangerous,' she said, leading me away. 'More than you know.'

We walked back home slowly, Alicia leaning more heavily on my arm. 'Have you seen a doctor yet?' I asked.

'A doctor? For what?'

'You're obviously not feeling well and you've lost a lot of weight . . .'

'I suppose you're going to tell me next that a woman should be round and plump with a big butt if she wants to look good.'

I laughed, remembering the traditional Cuban

abhorrence of skinny women. 'I'd never say such a thing, I just think you should see a doctor. Maybe he can give you an antibiotic or some kind of medicine . . .'

'Doctors here don't have much medicine to give, Nora. Besides, all I need is rest. Now that you're here, that's medicine enough for me.'

I called Jeremy from a pay phone down the street the next morning. Alicia said it served most of the neighbourhood and that I should get up early if I didn't want to wait in line for too long. Lucinda asked meekly if she could accompany me, and this surprised and pleased Alicia.

She held my hand tightly and matched her steps precisely to my own, and she never stopped chattering away about her books and how she wanted to teach blind children one day. She stopped in the middle of the sidewalk next to the phone before I'd spotted it and stood close to me, under the shadow of the phone booth, as I dialled and spoke to the international operator. She smiled when she heard my English, and I believe she was proud.

It was still very early in the morning, but Jeremy answered the phone before it had a chance to complete the first ring. He sounded delighted to hear my voice, and said many times that he missed me, and asked even more times how I was and how I'd found everything.

'Have you talked to my parents?' I asked.

'They called last night, wanting to know if you'd made it OK, but I told them I hadn't heard from you.'

'How are they doing?'

'They seemed a little worried about you, but they'll be fine. The important thing is that you take care of yourself and come back soon. I miss you, you know,' he said for the tenth time, but I didn't get tired of hearing it.

I felt Lucinda tugging at my sleeve. 'Can I say hello to Heremi?' she asked with a shy smile. I passed the phone to Lucinda. 'Hello. How are you?' she asked in her best, most carefully pronounced English. Then her eyes flew open and she giggled as she answered Jeremy's questions in Spanish and gave him a blow-by-blow account of all we'd done since I arrived.

'. . . And we're taking her to our special beach today or tomorrow. It all depends on how Mami feels.' Lucinda nodded. 'No, she's been sick for a long time and she needs to rest all the time, but I take very good care of her. She tells me no one can take as good care of her as me.' She nodded again. 'Yes, I'll take good care of Tía Nora, too. I'll make sure she's always with me, except when she takes a bath or goes to the bath-room. Even then, I won't be very far away at all.' After several goodbyes, she handed the phone back to me, quite satisfied with herself.

'Looks like you have an able little bodyguard there,' he said, still chuckling.

'She's precious, Jeremy. I feel as though she's been with me all my life. I really don't know how I'll manage to leave her.'

'Are you trying to scare me? You said you'd be back in two weeks, and I don't believe I'll be able to stand it for a minute more than that.'

I held Lucinda close to me as I answered him. 'I miss you too, and I'll be home very soon. I promise.'

As it turned out, Alicia did feel better and we managed to get to the beach several times that first week. Alicia and Lucinda called it their secret beach and it took some doing to get there. It was at least three miles further than our childhood beach, and we needed to arrive between nine and ten in the morning and enter through an opening in the barbed-wire fence that ran for at least three or four miles further down the road. We took a picnic of bread, cheese and ham, all items I could purchase at the tourist market without difficulty. I was also able to find a beach umbrella, ridiculously priced, but worth the expense, because the secret beach provided no shade whatsoever.

Alicia eased back on her elbows with an audible sigh. The shadows under her eyes had grown more pronounced and I wondered if she'd become even more tired since my arrival.

'Why don't we just go to the usual beach? It's so far to come all the way over here.'

Alicia shook her head and sputtered a dry laugh. Her eyes were on Lucinda, who waded in the warm water without a worry in the world. Whenever she stepped on something interesting, she reached down to pick it up and hold it to her cheek.

'That beach is closed to us,' Alicia said matter-of-factly. 'You can go if you want.'

'What do you mean?'

Alicia allowed fistfuls of sand to slip through her fingers before answering. 'Ever since they started building the hotels, they closed the best beaches to the people – the Cuban people, that is.'

'That doesn't make any sense.'

Alicia kept pouring her piles of sand. 'This beach is technically closed as well. That's why they have the fence up. They'll start building the hotel in a few months and then we'll have to find somewhere else. Right now they don't really enforce it, but they will.'

I was silent while I thought about this. 'It's hard to believe that when we left here they called us gusanos and traitors to the revolution. Now they let us have the best.'

'Ah, well . . . You may have been worms when you left, but now you're butterflies, and better than that, your wings are made of American dollars. That's all the Castristas care about.'

Alicia spoke with little emotion. She'd obviously accepted this reality long ago. But I was angry and had a good mind to march straight to the nearest hotel and complain. I told Alicia this and her eyes flew open in alarm.

'That's the worse thing you could do,' she said. 'I don't care about all that. All I care about is Lucinda and Tony and leaving here when we're able.' She turned to me, her eyes alive with fear. 'Promise me you won't make any trouble at the hotels.'

I nodded and she relaxed.

Lucinda called out from the water's edge that she was collecting perfect shells to give us each. Alicia smiled and lay down in the sand. She wore an old smock shirt and a pair of baggy shorts. She looked like a pubescent girl, with barely the suggestion of breasts. Her once-shapely legs were knob-kneed and thinner than Lucinda's, and her skin was so fragile and pale that I could see the delicate tract of veins pulsating in her throat.

Alicia's eyelids fluttered. 'I wish we could look up at the palms like we used to. Remember?'

'I remember,' I answered, still startled by her appearance.

She opened one eye. 'Lie down next to me, Nora.'

I lay down and closed my eyes, feeling a chill despite the warmth of the sun and the sand beneath our bodies. It came from somewhere deep inside me, but I dared not examine it any further. Better to listen to the sigh of the ocean and Lucinda's giggles floating above it.

26

THE HOT WIND CAME IN THROUGH THE OPEN WINDOW AND moaned. I had difficulty breathing as I waited for morning. Alicia was sleeping on the couch and Lucinda slept peacefully next to her on a roll of blankets.

It had been three days since I'd spoken to Jeremy. Had he forgotten me? What silly thoughts popped into my head on sleepless nights. He couldn't possibly forget me in a week. He loved me and had pledged to be with me always, and I was painfully aware of a desire to be with him in our little house. I looked out of the window at the stars, the same stars I'd gazed at as a child from this particular angle in the sky. I'd be home in less than a week. I'd be lying with my sweet Jeremy in our king-size bed, his arms wrapped around me as he liked to do before he fell asleep. If it was Saturday, we'd go for our morning walk and return to our house for the breakfast of eggs and bacon we allowed ourselves only on weekends. Weekdays were dedicated to healthier breakfasts of low-fat cereal and fruit, with maybe a sprinkle of sugar.

The little hand on my forehead startled me. Lucinda was crouching next to me. The moonlight illuminated her angelic features and reflected off her small teeth. She appeared to be looking into my eyes. At first I thought she was smiling and playing a trick on me, but then I realized it was agony I saw on her face, a mature pain not appropriate for one so young.

She inched closer to me and whispered in my ear. 'Tía Nora, are you awake?'

'Yes, my love. I'm awake.'

'I must tell you something, Tía Nora.'

'What is it, sweetheart?'

'Mami is very sick.'

The elbow on which I supported myself threatened to give way. Perhaps I was still sleeping. I blinked, but Lucinda remained as she was, with her little hand on my shoulder, her corkscrew curls catching the moonlight through the window, her wondering gaze quite at home in the dark.

'Lucinda, you must be having a bad dream.'

'No, I'm not. They don't think I know.'

'Know what, exactly?'

'Mami has the disease.' Her face contorted in pain. 'I heard Berta and Mami talking when they thought I was asleep.'

Her hands reached for my face as she tried to read my expression, her fingertips gently exploring my eyes for tears. Relieved to find them dry, she continued. 'They take people who have it far away because they don't know how to cure it. They're keeping it a secret so Mami doesn't have to go away from me.'

I sat straight up and held Lucinda close to me. 'Don't worry. I'll help your Mami, Lucinda.'

Her arms reached around and I felt her tremble with sobs, but she quickly recovered and smothered the sounds of her pain for fear that she'd wake her mother. As I held her, I was hardly able to breathe, as if I'd been kicked in the stomach.

'Can I sleep with you, Tía?'

I threw the sheet back and made room in the narrow bed for her, and she nestled into me like a warm kitten, whimpered and fell asleep in less than a minute.

* * *

Alicia explained she'd been making this short trip out of town on a weekly basis for almost five years, and that for the last year or so Ricardo hadn't required any special favours. She'd told me about it in her letters, but I sensed she had a need to tell me again. We walked slowly through the narrow streets, trying to stay on the shaded side as the heat was suffocating. The drying laundry swinging in the hot wind above our heads was the only movement, and our pace was slow.

Alicia spoke while looking down at her feet. She allowed me to carry the bag of provisions, which contained items that were difficult to find such as aspirin, a box of saltine crackers and the inevitable tube of toothpaste, which had nothing but the world 'Dental' written on it.

'It gives me so much peace to do this,' she said. 'To know that these items can keep Tony more comfortable and safe. Maybe he'll have a letter for me.' She brightened up at the prospect.

'Does he write to you every week?'

'No. I wish he did, but it's not easy to get paper and I suppose that sometimes he's just too tired. They take prisoners out to work in the fields, you know, especially the strong, capable ones. One day I sat out in the sun for almost half a day watching a line of men working in the field. I picked one man out of the group and pretended he was Tony. His shoulders were broad and he swung his arms the way I imagined Tony would, and he held his head up high as I hope Tony still does. Then he spat down at his feet and I knew it wasn't Tony. He'd never do that.'

We walked for another half-hour in silence, our feet pounding the broken sidewalk like hot pancakes on a griddle. My throat was dry and I suggested we stop at the next market for something to drink. We sipped lime sodas under the shade of a tattered awning, while sitting on the kerb. The road was bright with heat and I wondered if even the ocean was boiling.

'How long have you had it, Alicia, the disease?'

She stared straight ahead at the empty road as if in a trance. Her soda was getting warm, and the condensation of the glass moistened her fingers. 'Is it so obvious?'

'It's obvious you're not well.'

She nodded, still not looking at me. 'I've known for a few months now.'

'And you haven't seen a doctor?'

'A doctor can't do anything for me now. Nothing that will do me any good.'

Alicia finished her soda with long slow swallows, the muscles in her thin neck rolling with every gulp.

'Are you just going to wait around to die? You have to do something. We have to find a way to get you out of here now. Tonight!' My empty glass slipped out of my hands and rolled into the gutter. 'Damn it, Alicia. You should've left on the freighter with Lucinda when you had a chance.'

'I couldn't leave Tony.'

Alicia stood up and I followed her. She was walking down the street, calm and slow, with me weeping like a baby next to her. It had cooled off a bit now and some people were venturing out of their crumbling houses. By now I was hysterical as I begged Alicia to do as I said. People threw me incurious glances. They'd seen despair grow into hysteria as often as they'd seen the dawn grow into the glaring scorch of midday. There was nothing unusual in my emotional display, and it did little to move Alicia. She nodded and patted my shoulder as we walked, much as she would a child crying over an ice cream.

I stopped and sat down on the kerb with my head in my arms. I stared at the dust covering my feet, my tears streaking water trails down to my ankles.

Alicia sat next to me with a sigh. I was tempted to

tell her that Lucinda knew everything. That in trying to protect her precious child she was actually torturing her.

She whispered in my ear, as she had when we were children and she'd wanted me to follow her in some childish antic. 'I'm not afraid to die, you know.' I turned to see her peeking at me through my arms. 'I knew the risk I was taking, but I was so crazy to make money I didn't care. I always considered myself to be lucky, but I guess this time my luck ran out.'

'Are you sure you have it? It could be something else . . .'

Alicia shook her head resolutely. 'Berta and I have seen it too many times. Many people we know and many more we don't have been sent away. There's a hospital where they go, but it's really a camp that holds them so they can't infect anybody else.' Alicia stretched her thin legs out in front of her so they were poking out into the narrow street. I remembered how her legs had looked at fifteen, shapely and strong, the legs of an excellent swimmer. 'You may not believe this, but I knew a man who tried to get it on purpose so he could be assured three meals a day and a clean bed at night. I'd never do something like that, but I know how he feels.'

'There may be medicines that can help, Alicia.'

'Not here, not for me. The only thing that matters now is that my Tony and Lucinda are safe. The rest will take care of itself, as it always does.' She placed her hand on my knee. 'Let's go, or Ricardo will be gone and I'll have to come back tomorrow.'

He was waiting at the end of the path leading to the side entrance of the prison, his greasy face contorted as he tried to make out who I was in the glare of the sun. He cocked his head to one side and rested his right hand on his pistol. In his left hand he held a white envelope which flashed like a mirror. As we got closer I could see his heavily pock-marked face, and his eyebrows joined in the middle of his forehead to form a perfect V. His smile revealed yellow teeth and thick swollen gums speckled with tobacco.

Alicia greeted him like a sister, with a warm hug and a kiss on the cheek. She was genuinely happy to see him, and presented me as the cousin from the United States she'd been telling him about. We shook hands, and I handed the bag of provisions to Alicia, who promptly turned it over to Ricardo.

'I brought him an extra roll of toilet paper this time,' she said, happily eyeing the letter that was still in Ricardo's hand, but he was busy inspecting the bag. His eyes widened when he saw the soap I'd put in: Irish Spring.

'Oh, I almost forgot. Here you are,' he said, handing her the letter. 'He finished it this morning.'

Alicia took the letter and tucked it inside her blouse. 'How is he this week? Have you heard any news?'

'I hear rumours all the time, but who knows? They might let him out tomorrow, or maybe next year.' He turned back to the bag.

'There's a letter for Tony at the bottom,' Alicia said.

Ricardo peered at us both. Sweat was creeping into his eyes, causing him to blink nervously. With the bag slung over one arm, he took several steps back towards the shade of the guardhouse. He pointed to me with his thick hairy finger. 'How long you staying?'

Alicia answered before I had a chance to. 'She'll be leaving next week, so I might send Berta with next week's package.'

He nodded his approval upon hearing this, and waved us off.

Alicia walked back home with renewed vigour. She was delighted to have a letter from Tony over her heart, pounding new life into her, but the meeting with Ricardo was holding me back from my usual pace.

'Do you think Tony gets the things you send him?' I asked.

Alicia smiled. 'You must think I'm pretty stupid, don't you?'

'I would never think that.'

She laughed and patted the letter over her heart. 'I know Tony gets some of the things, because he's written me so, though I'm sure Ricardo keeps the best for himself. But even if he kept it all I wouldn't care, because I know that, if nothing else, he keeps an eye on Tony for me.'

'Has it ever occurred to you that Ricardo might never want Tony to leave, so he can keep getting his packages?'

Alicia stopped in her tracks. 'I never thought of that.' Then a smile shot across her face. 'What if I offer him a reward when Tony is released?'

'I didn't mean you should do that . . .'

'Of course. It's a splendid idea. If what you say is true, then my Tony will be out very soon. And I have the money, Nora. I'll give Ricardo his reward. I've given him everything else.'

When we arrived home, Alicia closed the curtain of the only window, went directly to the couch and pulled it back. In the wall behind the couch was a small hole stuffed with wadded napkins and tissues, discoloured yellow from the constant moisture in the air. She quickly picked out the paper and shoved her hand inside. After very little probing she retrieved a small metal box. Beckoning to me to come closer, she opened it. It was filled with banknotes, mostly American, but some Canadian and German as well. She insisted I count them, and I estimated there to be close to five thousand dollars.

'I told you I can afford it,' she said proudly. 'Aside from Lucinda, you're the only person who knows about this money.'

'How about Berta?'

Alicia shook her head, looking a little ashamed. 'It's not that I distrust her, but I've seen desperation do things to people. I can't take any chances with this money.'

Carefully, she put the box back in its place and re-stuffed the hole. I helped her push the couch back against the wall and she promptly collapsed onto it.

By the time I'd finished helping Lucinda prepare a supper of cheese and crackers, Alicia had fallen asleep. We ate quickly, and I covered her with a light blanket before tiptoeing out into the balmy evening.

The music from the hotels reached us soon enough as we walked arm in arm along the malecón. Lucinda skipped next to me when she wasn't shuffling her feet to the rhythms. The mist of the ocean reached over the wall and enveloped us. My feet began to follow Lucinda's, and soon we were dancing together by the dim light of street lamps, which illuminated the mist like tiny crystals suspended in air. From a distance could be seen the arched windows of the Intercontinental Hotel, with guests dancing on the polished dance floor to the same music.

I pictured Alicia arriving at work in a place like this, turning the eye of every man in the room as always, tolerating their disgusting caresses for the hope of escape.

'What's wrong, Tía Nora?' Lucinda was tugging on my arm. Without realizing it, I'd stopped dancing.

'I'm sorry, honey. I guess I'm a little tired too.'

We strolled back slowly, with our backs to the lights along the malecón. Soon we heard only the crashing of the waves and the occasional cry of a seagull.

'Tía Nora?'

'Yes, my love?'

'Is Mami going to die?' She asked the question so lightly that it almost floated off on the breeze coming in from the sea.

I struggled to find an answer that would be honest, but not cruel. 'We all have to die sometime.'

'I know. That's what Mami told me when Tía Panchita died, but Tía Panchita was old and Mami isn't old yet, and she wants to go to the United States even more than I do.'

My throat tightened with sadness as I tried to find my voice. 'Why do you want to go there?' I asked.

'Because Mami says hope died in Cuba a long time ago. She always says it's possible to live without soap and toothpaste, but you can't live without hope.'

27

I SLIPPED OUT IN THE EARLY MORNING TO CALL JEREMY. HE'D
be in a dead sleep, but I couldn't take the chance he
wouldn't be home. During our last phone call he'd
said he missed me so much he was almost driven to
writing poetry, and that I should spare the world this
tragedy and get home soon. I pictured him in our bed,
sleeping with one arm under his head and the other
clutching the pillow where I should be. He wouldn't
like my phone call; in fact, he'd hate it.

'You're staying how long?'

'I'm not really sure. All I know is I can't leave
Lucinda like this to take care of Alicia by herself. And
I'm afraid they're going to take her away and lock her
up somewhere. If they find out Alicia's infected, God
knows what they'll do to her. It's crazy, Jeremy. It's
crazy what they do. And—'

'OK. Calm down, sweetheart. Let's just think about
this for a minute.'

My heart was racing as I waited for a solution to
spring from the silence on the other end of the line.
The sun had risen from the sea and a brilliant ray of
intense heat was burning the top of my ankles, and it
wasn't even seven yet. The phone was sweaty in my
hand. 'Are you there?'

'Yes, I'm just thinking . . . What if you come home as

you planned, and then go back when it seems that Alicia is . . . When it seems that she needs your help more than she does now?'

A sob exploded from the back of my throat. 'I want to be with you more than anything, but I can't leave them. Please understand. I'm all they have. I can't let them take Alicia. I can't let them take Lucinda.'

As I spoke, a line was forming behind me and I was reminded that this was the only working phone for several blocks.

'Please, Nora, call me tomorrow or as soon as you can. We have to talk about this.'

'I will. I promise.'

'I love you.'

'I love you too.'

I hung up and turned around to find a group of tattered Cubans watching me through the fog of a poor night's sleep in stifling heat. They studied my new sandals and clean clothes. My slim watch flashed in the sun, and I could sense them wondering what this foreigner with plenty of money for a hotel room with its own phone was doing using the public one. Why wasn't I frolicking on the best beaches with my over-sized beach towel and a chilled fruit salad waiting for my breakfast? Why wasn't I smiling like all the other tourists they saw stumbling about the streets after a night out, throwing change at the street musicians as though they were skinny little birds? Instead, I stood before them whimpering like a child.

An older black woman approached me. She'd been waiting in line with the others and I could see that she was going to scold me for taking so much time. I began to search my bag for something I might give her. I'd used all the money I'd brought with me on the phone call, but even a pack of tissues or a stick of gum would be better than nothing. I produced a pen and a roll of mints and held them out for her, but she made no move for them. She was gazing at my face and looking me up and down and shaking her head in disbelief. I waited for her reprimand and hung my head to see her bare feet and bony ankles, swollen and flea-bitten.

'If I weren't looking at you with my own eyes, I wouldn't believe it!' The golden voice flowed like honey into my ears; warm sweet honey that makes everything taste better and makes all the cares of the world float away on a soft current.

I looked up and stared into the crinkled black face and black shiny eyes that were already alive with tears. I clasped the large rough hands held out to me and buried my head into her shoulder as her arms came around me and patted my back reassuringly as they had so many years ago.

'Oh Beba,' I cried. 'Where have you been?'

'Right here, child. I've been right here all the time.'

Beba lived only a few short blocks from Alicia's house, in a small one-room apartment that overlooked a narrow alley. She was on the third floor and as we climbed up past the second floor the heat became suffocating. Because of the continuous heat and humidity, mould had stained the inner corridors an earthy blend of green, brown and rust, like the moss that grows in the deepest regions of the jungle; it was the colour common to most old buildings that hadn't been painted since the revolution. Finding Beba was a miracle I hadn't dared hope for since we'd left, although I still thought of her when I felt most alone and afraid. How many times I'd imagined myself with her at the sink, slicing onions and humming one of her exotic African tunes, I did not know. By the time we reached the third floor, I felt a calmness I hadn't felt since I was a child.

She told me to have a seat on one of two metal folding chairs, and busied herself at the single burner by the window. Her hands trembled as she measured out the coffee and sugar for our café con leche. As she worked, she told me that for the past ten years she'd been living in this apartment and observing, through her one window to the alley, the neighbours that came and went like noisy spirits. She'd had a good job rolling cigars in a factory just outside Havana until three years ago, when the factory closed down. But she added that her arthritis would've forced her to quit anyway, and now she got by on a measly pension and her monthly rations, which amounted to barely ten dollars a month.

'I thought of the Garcia family often,' she said in a shaky voice that I didn't want to hear.

'We thought of you all the time, Beba. I know Mami tried to find you during the first few years after we left, but nobody knew where you were.'

'People get lost here very easy,' she said with a sober shake of her head.

She walked slowly across the small room with a cup in each hand, careful to give me the one that wasn't chipped. I accepted it gratefully, knowing that the coffee, sugar and milk were difficult to come by and carefully rationed. She didn't skimp at all on the ingredients, however. The café con leche was thick and rich and perfectly balanced, as I always remembered it to be when she made it. Tears welled in my eyes. This was the home I remembered: sitting with Beba and waiting for her to tell me what was on her mind, as I'd always done. Her way was as direct and delicious as the hot cup of milk and coffee that I held in my hands. It cleared the head and the heart more efficiently than the strongest caffeine.

'You're a woman, Norita,' she said, gazing at me with misty eyes. 'A beautiful woman, like I knew you would be. How's Martica?'

'She's married now and has two children. She gave us a hard time during her teenage years.'

Beba laughed and slapped her knee. 'And how about you? Did you give anyone a hard time?'

'Oh no. I was a very good girl all the time. You wouldn't have recognized me.'

Beba was thoughtful. 'I imagined it the other way. Maybe something in that new country made you trade places. Maybe it confused you in your head a bit, like it does when you hit strange weather. When it's too hot, like today, I can't think. I can't think at all.' Beba sipped at her café con leche, peering at me over the rim of her cup all the while.

I told her about life in the United States, and about growing up there and Jeremy. I told her how Papi and Mami didn't want me to come, but that all the years I'd been away I'd thought of little else. The morning passed like a tropical storm as I told her all these things, and she listened with a wise nod of her head and a flickering smile that was more sad than happy. Then she told me of her life, as she stared out of the window at the moulding wall. She spoke mostly of her difficulties finding food, and of her shrewd friends in the black market.

'I get along all right these days, but I have to be careful,' she said. 'Two years ago I almost got arrested. Too many people still getting stirred up by that man, let me tell you.' Beba waved a crooked finger in my direction and I couldn't help but smile. It amused me that she, like Mami, still referred to Castro as 'that man'.

'I should call him that dog,' Beba said when I mentioned this to her. 'Even that's too good for him. He's shit on this country worse than any back-street dog would do.'

I told Beba about Alicia and Lucinda and she nodded gravely, not in the least bit surprised. 'She's right not to see the doctor. They'll just send her away and God only knows what'll happen to her child. I've seen it many times.'

'Their only chance is for Tony to get out of prison soon.'

Beba pushed her chair back against the wall and

leaned back, crossing her arms and locking her gaze onto me as she would when she'd caught me in a lie. 'What makes her think he's getting out?'

'Alicia gets letters from him all the time and he seems to think he has a chance. It's the only hope that keeps her alive, Beba.' Just saying her name made me feel like I was ten years old again.

'Could be,' Beba said, pushing out her bottom jaw. 'Maybe he'll be one of the lucky ones. I hope so, for her sake.'

I didn't want to leave, but it was almost noon and I knew Alicia and Lucinda would be wondering where I'd been all morning. I promised Beba I'd return soon and bring her many things.

'Don't bring me nothing. If there's one thing I've learned all these years, it's that I don't need much. Just bring yourself, Norita. And the rest of your family, if you like. I'll be here.'

28

ALICIA WAS UNABLE TO GET OUT OF BED FOR THE NEXT FEW days. A mild storm swept in as Lucinda and I tended to her. Berta blew in and out with the gales, wearing her stretchy clothes, her hair a mass of black frizz and curls impossible to tame in the humid weather. She barely glanced at us, muttering a hasty greeting before going straight to her room.

'She gets like this when there's a lot of work,' Alicia said one afternoon when she appeared to be feeling stronger. 'Bad weather means more work because the ... clients have less to do ... more time on their hands.' She shrugged and sipped the cup of tea she'd been nursing for the past hour.

With the covers pulled away from her, I had to make an effort not to stare at her emaciated form. If she'd been skinny before, she was now a wisp of smoke, curling and fading as I looked on. We heard Lucinda in the kitchen, cleaning the dishes and bustling about. I knew better than to try and help her. Only one person could work comfortably in the kitchen at a time, and Lucinda was able to manage much better than I.

'It's been so much better since you've been here,' Alicia said when she had finished her tea. 'Lucinda's happier than I've seen her in a long time. She smiles more and she sleeps as a child should sleep, all through the night and not waking up every half-hour to make sure I'm OK.'

'She's an amazing child.'

Alicia nodded and looked at me, her golden-green eyes huge in her pale face. 'I know you're leaving soon, but you won't tell me because you know I'll be sad. You have to go home to your husband and your beautiful life. I'm happy to know your life is good, Nora. It's almost like it's my own life. Does that make any sense?'

I smiled. 'When we were growing up, I felt like the wonderful things happening to you were happening to me. Like when we walked down the street and every man alive couldn't take his eyes off you. I might as well have been your shadow trailing behind, but I was happy too, as I had a taste of what it was like to feel beautiful.'

'It's hard to believe that was ever me.' Alicia pulled the sweater she wore over her shoulders around her more tightly, even though it was well past eighty degrees. 'I think I feel well enough to go and see Beba. Lucinda would like to meet her and I'm sure you want to say goodbye before you go.'

'I'd love to go see Beba, but not to say goodbye. I've decided to stay a bit longer.'

Alicia brightened noticeably. 'Are you serious?'

I glanced at my watch. 'My plane left an hour ago and I'm definitely not on it.'

Alicia threw her head back and laughed out loud, as I hadn't heard her do since my arrival. 'What's there to eat? I feel suddenly hungry.'

As we made our way to Beba's house, I held Alicia by one arm and Lucinda by my other free hand. It was only three blocks away, but it took us almost half an hour to walk one of them. Alicia concentrated on every step she took and was clearly exhausted by the time we got to the corner. It would have been so easy if she had a wheelchair, but of course that would require, at the very least, a doctor's referral, and after confirming it with Beba, I was convinced that this was an option to be avoided at all costs.

Alicia's breath was deep and laboured and she suddenly chuckled. 'I feel like I'm learning to walk all over again.'

'Maybe this isn't such a good idea. I can ask Beba to come over to our house instead.' I shivered in the heat at the term 'our house'. Had this become my home? Wasn't my home in Santa Monica with Jeremy? That sweet yellow house with white shutters that captured the afternoon breeze. What did a cool breeze feel like? I felt suddenly nostalgic for my uncomplicated life in California.

I felt Alicia's grip tighten on my arm. 'It's good for me to get out of the house,' she said. 'Maybe we can just rest for a while.'

We stopped in the shade of an abandoned building that appeared to have once been a bookstore. Inside I could see shelves draped with cobwebs, holding nothing but empty rum bottles. Most likely men sneaked in to drink and gamble after curfew. Some of the bottles looked new and shiny next to the soot of two decades. The back door was open a sliver, but wide enough so an overgrown patch of yard was visible. Through an entanglement of weeds I noticed a small wheel.

'Lucinda, wait here with your mother. I'll be right back.'

It was some time before I could uncover the mysterious item hiding in the weeds. It was rusty and needed a bit of adjusting, but it was exactly what I hoped it would be.

I made my way back to the front of the building, rolling my prize before me triumphantly.

Alicia cocked her head to one side, amused. Lucinda did the same. 'What's that funny squeaking sound?' she asked.

'What in the world are you doing with that old wheelbarrow, Nora? You don't think I'm getting into it, do you? I'd rather walk to Tres Pinos and back on my knees than be seen in that.'

Lucinda jumped up and down excitedly. 'I'll get in! I'll get in!' she cried, nearly bursting with excitement.

'Maybe later, sweetheart. Right now your Mami needs to be reasonable and let us push her in this. Isn't that right, Mami?'

Alicia crossed her arms and pouted. 'It's dirty.'

'That's true, but we can clean it up later. And look how well it works.' I rolled it back and forth. 'We can go lots of places with this.'

'People will laugh at me.'

'Nonsense. Nobody laughs at five people hanging onto a bicycle for dear life, so why would they laugh at this? Besides, I wouldn't mind seeing a few smiles from time to time.'

Alicia hobbled over to the wheelbarrow, touched the rim, then felt down to the base where she would sit. 'Filthy, just filthy,' she muttered as she turned around and carefully lowered herself to a sitting position. Lucinda stroked the wheelbarrow – the sides, the handles, the wheel, and finally her mother's form tucked inside like a baby chick.

She giggled with delight. 'Can I help push, Tía Nora?'

'Of course. We can push together.'

'Take it easy, you two. We don't need to go very fast. It's not like we have a train to catch.'

The wheels caught and wobbled as we made our way down the sidewalk. The wheelbarrow had a tendency to veer towards the right and the broken wood of the handles splintered the flesh on my palms, but it was much easier for all of us to travel this way. We passed the malecón, and the breeze rising off the ocean was surprisingly cool. Alicia dropped her head back slightly and let the wind brush through her hair. Her eyes were closed and a serene smile was on her lips. The tight grip she'd had on the sides of the barrow loosened and her hands slipped down to her sides.

'It's a nice day, isn't it, Tía Nora?'

'It's a beautiful day.'

Lucinda had stopped trying to help push after a few minutes. She slipped her little hand around my elbow and kept in step perfectly, while her face was straight ahead like a soldier.

When we arrived at Beba's apartment building my hands were sore, but our spirits were shining. We parked the wheelbarrow safely in the dark narrow passage that led to her door, so no one could see it from the street.

Beba was startled to see Alicia in her current state, but she recovered quickly and almost carried her to the couch near the window. She rattled about her sparse cupboard for some crackers and a little coffee to offer us, despite our protests. Of course she wouldn't hear of not offering her guests a little something, and she was able to come up with a plate of stale crackers spread with a thin layer of strawberry jam, and coffee with a little sugar, but no milk. Lucinda enjoyed them immensely and it was clear that Beba was taken with her. As Lucinda hugged her and touched her wrinkled face, Beba scooped her up and insisted she sit next to her. We talked and laughed for hours.

'Oh yes, I remember hearing about that boy,' Beba said with a sly smile. 'I never met him myself, but Doña Regina told me about him when it all happened. They say he was one of the most handsome men around, black or white.' She chuckled and shook her head so that her once-full cheeks wiggled a bit. 'You,' she said, pointing her finger at Alicia, 'were something else. When I heard about what happened, I thought to myself, now that girl is either a fool for love or just a plain fool. I don't know which is worse.'

'Why were people mad at Mami and Papi?' Lucinda demanded.

'Now you have to understand, little one,' Beba said, lightly stroking Lucinda's hair, 'The world was different then. Today coloured people and white people get together and get married or don't get married, and nobody says much if they even notice, but in those days people had a lot to say.'

Beba delighted us all, especially Lucinda, as she rocked back and forth on her little stool and laughed with her mouth so wide we could see all the spaces where her gleaming white teeth used to be. Her smile was as radiant as ever and her piercing gaze just as persuasive. 'It was a good life, wasn't it?' she asked, gazing out of the window and smiling past the cracked and peeling plaster. We answered her with a silent but collective sigh.

'Why don't you come with us?' Lucinda asked, jumping up to the centre of the room.

'Where are you going, child?' Beba was still looking out of the window.

'We're going to Los Estados Unidos. Just as soon as Papi gets out. We have the money all saved, don't we, Mami?'

Beba tore her gaze away from the window, focusing on Alicia with questioning eyes. Alicia smiled sadly at Beba and shook her head just a little. She hadn't yet explained to Lucinda how her illness changed all the plans they'd been making.

'Mami?' Lucinda took several steps towards Alicia. 'Mami, why don't you answer me? Are you there?' As she moved forward, she stumbled on the leg of a chair and fell to the ground. Alicia attempted to go to her, but Beba was still spry for her age. As she picked Lucinda up and wiped the dust off her knees with her arthritic hands, she muttered that she should be careful because she was too old and tired to keep picking children off the floor. How many times she'd done the same for me as a child I couldn't say.

'I wish I had straight teeth like you, so I don't have to wear braces, Beba,' I'd tell her as she brushed my hair out in the morning and made the simple ponytail I preferred to Marta's fancy braid.

'Now, don't you start complaining so early in the morning.' She'd stop brushing and stare at me hard in the mirror. 'You know what they say about complaining, don't you?'

'What, Beba?'

'Complaining gives you a hard heart and soft bones. Just the opposite of how they should be.' She continued brushing my hair so hard that my head pulled back every time she took a stroke, but it felt so good, as if she was brushing all the bad thoughts out of my head. 'Try gratitude instead. It'll make you strong,' (stroke) 'wise beyond your years,' (stroke) 'a lover of life,' (stroke).

Lucinda nestled herself next to Beba again. 'I want you to come with us,' she said, hugging both her legs.

'Beba's too old to go anywhere.'

'Don't you want to see what it's like? Markets full of any kind of food you want, hot water and soap every day of the week, and some people have more than three pairs of shoes.'

'I'd sure like to see that again,' Beba said with a solemn nod of her head and a wistful grin that eased across her face. 'Believe it or not, I used to have six pairs of shoes, every one of them bright white. Most of them were gifts from Doña Regina. She was a good and generous woman, God bless her.'

'Six pairs of shoes?'

'That's right.'

'Why would anybody need that many shoes?'

Beba shook her head, lost for an answer. 'Maybe twenty or so years ago I could've told you, but the truth is I forgot.'

* * *

The next morning, Lucinda and I scrubbed the wheel-barrow on the inside and out until not a fleck of rust or dirt could be seen. We lined it with a blanket and two pillows and thought hard about how we might create some shade. I attempted to attach an umbrella to the barrow, but I couldn't figure out a way to have it remain open without restricting the view of the driver. We finally concluded that whenever possible we'd walk in the shade.

The problem with the wheel proved to be the trickiest part. We borrowed tools from the neighbour, Pepe, and I busied myself trying to straighten it as Lucinda stood by. Pepe peered out of the window at us as I banged at the wheel with a wrench, but my efforts resulted in very little progress.

Before I knew it, Pepe was standing over me. He was a small thin man with skin the colour of ripe olives. The nostrils of his aquiline nose flared wildly when he inhaled, giving him an intense and angry appearance. Yet his eyes glowed the colour of soft amber and always appeared to be swishing with tears. He shook his head disapprovingly. 'That's not gonna work, Cousin Nora.'

'Why not?'

'You got to take the whole thing apart and put it back together again. It's the only way.'

Pepe was an expert on the subject of wheels, because he'd worked at a bicycle factory for many years. Now he worked one or two days a week if he was lucky, and he spent the rest of his time sitting on the stoop of his front door, watching the comings and goings of the neighbourhood as he smoked his rationed cigarettes as far down as he could. The fingers of his right hand were permanently stained with nicotine.

'I don't know how to do that.' I rolled back from my hunched position and sat with a plop on the ground, stretching my sore legs out in front of me. I picked up the wrench again and dropped it with a start. How could it get so hot in less than a minute in the sun?

Pepe clicked his tongue and flicked his head, indicating that I should get out of his way. He picked up the wheelbarrow with one hand, scooped up his tools with the other and settled down on his stoop, which was significantly shadier than the spot I'd chosen. I took Lucinda by the hand and we hovered about as he worked.

'It's very nice of you to help us,' I said.

He grunted. Pepe was not a man of many words, although when he looked at Lucinda it was the closest I'd ever seen him come to a smile.

'Señor Pepe, Mami says you know how to fix everything. Is that true?'

He'd already removed the wheel and was re-securing it by turning the bolts with quick and dexterous hands. 'I can fix most things, I guess.'

We brought him a glass of cold water flavoured with fruit powder mix that turned the water a blood-red colour. He accepted it without a word and drank it down very fast, his nostrils flaring like fish gills gasping for air. He set the glass down and grunted his thanks. After a while he stood up and stretched his lanky frame. He rolled the wheelbarrow back and forth to test it and then passed it over to me. It rolled smoothly and perfectly.

'It's like new. Thank you so much.'

Pepe shrugged and his mouth flickered into the suggestion of a smile.

That evening, after our meal, Lucinda and I took Alicia out for a stroll in her new wheelchair. The sky was scattered with gold ribbon clouds and children were laughing and playing baseball in the middle of the street. Rarely did a car drive by to interrupt their game. We headed, as always, towards the ocean to catch sight of the darkening sea and the first twinkles of lights on

293

the malecón. The fragrance of night jasmine floated about and mingled with my memories.

No one had spoken for some time and when we stopped I looked down to see if Alicia might be asleep again. But her eyes were open wide and more alive than I'd seen them in days. Smiling, she pointed up towards the curve of the malecón. The lights had begun to pierce through the mist of the encroaching evening.

She took my hand. 'I'm so happy right now.'

'I'm glad.'

'When you left, I worried you might forget me. I could never forget you, because everywhere I turned I saw things that reminded me of you: girls with long black ponytails, Tía's porch, even the palm trees themselves. This view right here,' she said, raising an arm as delicate as a wisp of smoke, 'is the one that reminds me of our plans to become chorus girls at the Copa Cabana, remember?'

'As I recall, that was your idea.'

'Perhaps it was, but you went along with it without too much argument.'

I adjusted Alicia's pillows so she could sit up higher. 'There was no arguing with you, dear cousin. I tried a few times and I always ended up wrestling with myself while you continued with whatever little scheme you had going at that moment.'

Alicia laughed. 'I must've been impossible – a spoiled brat.'

'You were amazing. Correction, you are amazing.'

Alicia sighed and I heard the pain in her breath. 'I wish Tony was here. I believe I'm ready to tell him everything now. I feel strong enough.'

The sun had set and the lights of the malecón twinkled at full force, like a diamond necklace on the throat of the most beautiful woman in the world.

29

WE LEFT EARLY THE NEXT MORNING, BEFORE THE HEAT OF THE day had a chance to dig its nails into the concrete and broken earth. Alicia was tired as she bounced along in the wheelbarrow with the letter clasped firmly in her hand, as though it were a ticket she had to show at any moment.

She'd dictated it to me the night before, after Lucinda was asleep, in whispered words that sometimes got lost in the whirl of the fan. It was more of a declaration than a confession. Although this was the first time Tony would learn of her work at the hotel, she expressed guilt only about not staying healthy. Her one regret was that she wouldn't join him on his escape to freedom.

> . . . I respect the choices you've made now more than ever. I hope you can forgive me mine and remember me as I was when we first fell in love. That is how I always picture you, a handsome young man sitting in Tía Panchita's rocking chair and giving me such a smile that I thought my heart would stop beating. What a blessing to know that the only man who makes me feel this way is also the man I call my husband, my most precious love.
>
> Although we haven't slept in each other's arms for

years, I can't close my eyes without whispering my good night to you and remembering that nothing, not even the sinking of this beautiful island, can destroy our love for each other.

Nora is still here with us. She hasn't gone home as I wrote you she would in my last letter. Everything is better with her here. Lucinda smiles more, and sometimes behaves as a young girl should and not like a middle-aged woman with a thousand worries. What should I do, my love? How should I talk with her? Can I tell her that her Papi will be home soon to take care of her?

Ricardo eyed the wheelbarrow with a frown as he stuffed the letter Alicia held out to him in his pocket and took the plastic bag from me.

He shoved his face into it without a word and sniffed loudly, sweat dripping into his eyes. 'Something wrong with your legs?'

'I've been tired and Nora found this barrow to help me get around.'

He took a step back. 'Are you sick?'

Alicia laughed drily and attempted to swing her legs out of the wheelbarrow, but she only succeeded in propping herself up straighter on her elbows. 'Not to worry, Ricardo. Anything I have I got long after you and I decided to be . . . friends.'

Ricardo relaxed and dropped his hand from his holster. He took a more studied look inside the bag. 'Tony likes fresh fruit. I don't see any fresh fruit here.'

'It was impossible to find this week, but maybe next week.'

Ricardo grunted and began to saunter back towards his post.

'I'll pay you good money when Tony gets out,' Alicia said abruptly.

Ricardo turned slowly and squinted in the heat. 'What do you mean?'

296

'I've been saving money for when Tony gets out so we can leave this place.'

He nodded pensively, chewing the inside of his cheek. 'I'll let you know when the time gets close.'

'Don't you have a letter for me?' Alicia asked.

He didn't turn around when he answered. 'Not this week.'

'Why not? Is something wrong with Tony? Is he sick?'

Ricardo stomped his feet, creating a cloud of brown dust about him. It was obviously taxing him to get up the hill and he resented having to turn around again. 'There's nothing wrong with him that a doctor can do anything about.'

'What's that supposed to mean?'

'Look, woman, have you ever been locked up?'

'No . . .'

'Have you?' he asked, pointing a hairy finger at me. I shook my head.

'It changes a man. They can go dead inside after a while.'

'My Tony would never go dead inside. Tell him I expect a letter next week.'

Ricardo turned on his heels and kept walking as he waved us away with one hand. 'Bring some fresh fruit and maybe he'll feel like writing. Some cigarettes wouldn't hurt either.'

'My Tony doesn't smoke.'

'Your Tony's been smoking for years.'

Alicia worried about Lucinda all the way home. We had planned a surprise trip to the beach and a picnic as well, but when Lucinda heard that her Papi hadn't written, she was very disappointed. It was only at the suggestion that Beba join us that she brightened a bit.

Beba was happy to come when we appeared at her door, and Lucinda insisted on holding her hand on the short walk to the public beach. Nevertheless,

297

her head hung low and she stumbled more than once.

'I should've written a letter myself and pretended it was from her Papi,' Alicia whispered.

'She'll be fine when we get to the beach, you'll see.'

I was right. Once Lucinda was able to dig her toes into the sand and feel the coarse heat sliding between her toes and the cool dampness beneath the surface, she raised her head to the ocean and walked confidently towards the sound of the waves. Beba wasn't able to keep up with her and had to let go of her hand or risk falling face-first in the sand. Lucinda walked on, and Beba helped manoeuvre the wheelbarrow to a shady spot beneath a squat palm tree. We spread out a blanket and assisted Alicia out of the wheelbarrow and onto the sand, where she settled in comfortably.

Her eyes were on her daughter and they glittered with love and fear. 'Anyone who saw her right now would think she was a beautiful young lady spending time with her dreams, her whole life ahead of her.'

'That's exactly what she is,' Beba retorted as she plumped up the pillows behind Alicia and covered her feet, which were always cold.

'She doesn't have girlish dreams, Beba,' Alicia said with a quiver in her voice. 'She has adult worries. She worries about me and her Papi and about being taken away.'

'Nobody's going to take her away,' I reminded her.

Alicia's eyes were grateful. 'I know you'll do everything you can to see that that doesn't happen, but you've only been here a short while. Soon it'll wear on you, as it does on all of us. The power this government has to stop your throat and steal every breath you have is something you haven't experienced yet, and I'm afraid that when you do—'

'I won't let them take her away,' I repeated.

'And what about Jeremy? What about your husband who's missing you every minute you're here with us?'

'He understands.'

Alicia scowled as she did when she thought I wasn't being honest. 'If I knew my Tony was waiting for me somewhere, what I wouldn't do to go to him! A man who really loves you is a blessing you shouldn't play with. What if he gets tired of waiting?'

'If he really loves me, he won't get tired of waiting.'

Alicia rolled her eyes and coughed. 'He's angry with you now, I know he is.'

Beba was listening to us, while keeping an eye out for Lucinda, who was walking along the water's edge, carefully feeling her way with her toes. Beba placed a hand on Alicia's knee. 'Rest now, child. Nora knows her man better than you do, and you can believe what she tells you about Lucinda. Beba's going to see to it that nobody ever takes Lucinda anywhere she doesn't want to go.'

This was enough assurance to calm Alicia and allow her to doze under the shade of the palm.

This was the third attempt I'd made to contact Jeremy. The voice on the answerphone I listened to was mine, but it didn't sound like me any more. The woman requesting I leave my name and number reflected a light-hearted innocence that came from having too few worries and an overabundance of solutions. The voice of the woman leaving the message was heavy and rest-less, and brimming with the kind of anxiety that weighs on your heart and mind so heavily that your feet ache to their soles.

Again there was no answer and I calculated the hours quickly. In Los Angeles it was eleven in the evening. Where was he? He wasn't one to stay out late. I contemplated calling my parents. I'd been gone for almost a month now. Surely they'd be over their anger by now and able to speak to me in a reasonable manner. I thought about this with my hand on the receiver of the public phone.

Thank God for the light of the moon, which

illuminated the streets after the lights had long gone out. It was a dangerous time to be out. Crime was increasing, especially in Havana, and theft was not as uncommon as it used to be. Tourists were told to be particularly careful, but I comforted myself with the knowledge that I didn't look like a tourist any more. I'd given away most of my clothes, just saving one good dress for my return home. I now wore stretchy shorts, a long T-shirt of Jeremy's and plastic flip-flops on my feet. This was the uniform of the Cuban woman who'd resigned herself to the fact that there was no reason to be elegant any more: she won't be invited to the parties she hears bouncing off the malecón, which glitter like a distant universe.

Everyone was sleeping comfortably when I arrived home. It was the first night we hadn't needed the fan in a week. I heard the dripping of the tap in the kitchen, and reminded myself that we were lucky to have running water in the house, that there were many who lived in apartments where the plumbing had corroded after years of disrepair, and where inhabitants relied on public water mains in the street. Did I really have a dishwasher in my kitchen, which I rarely used because there were just the two of us? Was it true that I'd been known to take two showers a day? Since I'd arrived, I'd managed to wash myself every two or three days with cold water while standing in the tub.

I pulled back the thin sheet of my bed and lay down quietly, so as not to disturb the soft cadence of sleep in the room. Tomorrow I'd get up early and heat water on the stove for a proper warm bath. Then I'd do the same for Alicia and Lucinda. We'd be fresh and ready to go wherever the day dictated.

30

IT TOOK FOR EVER FOR THE WATER TO BOIL, BUT ONLY THREE large kettles converted the tub of cold water into a pleasant frothy warmth, into which I submerged myself with incredible delight.

'Why are you doing that, Tía?' Lucinda asked, a curious expression on her golden face. Her eyes still reflected the soft swelling of a peaceful night's sleep.

'It feels good to have a hot bath. When I'm done I'll make one for you.'

She giggled and shook her tangled head of curls. 'Mami says she used to give me a bath when I was a baby, but not lately.'

'You'll love it. Is your Mami still sleeping?'

'She just woke up and I made her some breakfast. Do you want some?'

'In a little while.'

Lucinda closed the door behind her and I soaked for a while longer. The peeling paint in the bathroom curled down in long mouldy ribbons that reminded me of the moss which hung from the trees on the way to Tía Panchita's house. Perhaps that would be an interesting trip to make today. I'd ask Berta, who'd been home for the last couple of days, to give me the name of the person who'd lent her the car. We'd stop at the tourist market on the way out and I'd pack a picnic. I hoped that Alicia was feeling up to the trip. The fact that she was eating breakfast was a good sign.

Lucinda soaked in the tub even longer than I did. She held onto the sides for a long time, as she experienced for the first time in her life the soft silky feeling of the bubble bath I'd brought with me from the States. She smiled with wonder at the sensation and her turquoise eyes flashed with life. It was still hard to believe that eyes so beautiful couldn't behold the world around her.

'Tía, this water is even warmer than the ocean.'

'Isn't it wonderful?'

I gently placed my hand on the top of her head, so she knew I was near. 'Now tilt your head back a little and I'll wash your hair.'

Lucinda did as she was told and shut her eyes tight. Washing her thick curly hair was a formidable job and my knees were aching by the time I was finished rinsing. I imagined that Lucinda's neck was sore as well, but she never complained.

Alicia was feeling better and she allowed me to help her into the bath and wash her hair as well. I tried not to shudder as her golden locks slid down the drain. She had half the hair she used to have; I twisted it into a tight and fashionable knot at the back of her head so it would be less noticeable.

We were all dressed and ready to go when Berta emerged from her room, her thick black hair grizzled into a mane of unbelievable proportions. She blinked and propped her hands on her generous hips. 'What's this? Are we all ready for catechism?' She chuckled to herself as she sauntered to the bathroom.

'Berta, we want to rent a car for the day. The car you used to pick me up at the airport would do well. Could you tell me how to find it?'

Berta looked momentarily confused. She tried to remember as she examined her cuticles. 'It's this guy who lives down at the end of the street. I had to pay him . . . You know . . . not with cash.'

I blushed. 'I understand, but I imagine he'll take cash.'

'Probably. It's the house with the blue door,' Berta said as she disappeared inside the bathroom, where she would undoubtedly remain for most of the morning.

Lucinda and Alicia waited for me while I ventured out to search for the house with the blue door. It was easy to find, and as I knocked I realized I hadn't asked Berta for the name of the car's owner. After a few seconds the door was opened by a tired-looking woman in her mid to late thirties, missing a tooth in the very front of her smile. Eyeing me suspiciously, she shrugged her thin shoulders. 'Carlos went out last night and he hasn't been home. He's probably drunk as a skunk and sleeping it off somewhere. I don't know when he'll be back.'

'Can you help me?'

The woman waved me into the house and beckoned me to follow her through dingy rooms cluttered with broken furniture and tools, out to the small yard at the back of the house. Without looking to see if I was following her or not, she kicked open the back gate to reveal the shiny blue Chevrolet that had transported us all from the airport on my first day here. It looked freshly polished and the chrome shone in the morning light, making it look like a bright cartoon in the middle of an old black and white photo.

'This car is my husband's heaven and my hell. If you want to take it and drive it into the ocean, I couldn't care less.'

'Actually, I just wanted it for the day to take to Guines. I'll have it back before nightfall.'

'I don't care,' she said.

'I'll pay you for the use of it.'

'I said I don't care.' She walked back into the house

303

with me following close behind, and rummaged through a drawer before producing a set of keys and tossing them at me. 'Finding gas is a lot harder than finding a car, you know.'

I looked down at my plastic flip-flops, almost identical to hers, and my stretchy shorts and tank top. My hair was pulled back into a ponytail and I wasn't wearing a scrap of make-up. 'How did you know I was visiting?' I asked.

The woman smiled for the first time. She'd once been beautiful, and I imagined her, elegant with her matching shoes and bag, sauntering down the avenues as men craned their necks to catch a glimpse of her. Carlos had no doubt been one of them and had pursued her with a vengeance.

'I can always tell the Cubans that come back,' she told me. 'First of all, they always have cash to spend on things like a car or prepared food. A Cuban would offer me soap for the car or a bag of onions, or . . .' She sniffed the air with a sour expression, 'other things too. But how I can really tell is by your hands. May I?' She took my hand and held it next to hers. 'I don't think I'm much older than you, but see?' The difference was dramatic. Hers were swollen and cracked, with thick knuckles and nails that were grey and mouldy near the base. 'It's from using cold water and bleach to wash the clothes and dishes. When I run out of soap I have to use bleach or nothing at all. The only women who don't have hands like this are visitors and prostitutes.'

The woman told me her name was Lourdes, and we talked for a bit about her two children, who were away at school and came home only one weekend a month. She wanted to know about the United States, and said she had friends who had escaped on a raft several months ago. 'I don't know if they made it.'

I was ready to leave, the keys dangling from my fingers like a prize. All I had to do now was find gas.

How hard could that be? 'Will Carlos be mad if he comes home and finds the car missing?'

Lourdes threw both hands up in the air. 'His anger doesn't scare me. Besides, he didn't remember he was supposed to show up for his construction job at the hotel this morning. Why should he remember he has a car?'

Lourdes told me of some people in the neighbour-hood who might have gas for sale and suggested I find it before taking the car, as I could easily waste the quarter-tank left trying to find it. I agreed and set out on my quest. Immediately I discovered that Lourdes was not exaggerating. The first two men promptly informed me they wouldn't have gas until the middle of next week, but that if I paid them in advance they'd give me a discount. I declined their offer and continued down the list towards my next lead. It was almost noon before I resigned myself to the fact that our plans would have to wait until next week, and I considered returning to the one person who seemed the most decent and least likely to cheat me if I pre-paid. I could ask Lourdes if this was customary.

I decided to drop by the house first and inform Alicia and Lucinda of the situation, but I was surprised to find nobody home. Even Berta was nowhere to be found, although the door to her room had been left open and her radio was blaring. In the kitchen I noted the dishes had not been washed. Lucinda always washed the dishes before leaving, for fear that ants would find their way in.

I walked outside and spotted Pepe sitting on his front stoop, squinting out into the perpetual haze of endless summer while smoking a cigarette stub. He barely glanced at me as I approached, already knowing what I was going to ask.

'They went down the street that way,' he said, flick-ing his free hand in the general direction. 'Right after a man I never saw before was knocking on doors asking about a blind girl. I sent him that way.' He pointed in the opposite direction to the apartment. 'And then I told them it would be a good time to go for a walk.'

My heart constricted with fear. Had they come looking for Lucinda? Or perhaps Ricardo had informed the authorities that Alicia was ill and they'd come to take her away to the concentration camp. I was almost choking, my throat was so dry. 'Did he look official?'

At this question Pedro looked somewhat dazed. 'Official? He had good shoes and a clean shirt.'

My worst fears confirmed, I dashed down the street in the direction Pepe indicated they'd gone. I peered down narrow alleys piled high with garbage, almost tripping on my flip-flops in the process. I imagined how frightened Lucinda must feel, how desperate and confusing this must be for Alicia. Berta was probably doing her best to help, but she didn't know how to deal with people like this. She was probably making matters worse by offering sexual favours to set them free. I was nearly hysterical when I reached the malecón.

I heard Lucinda's voice first. A soft sweet melody, floating as if from the sky, and when I turned to the sound of it, I almost fell to my knees. She walked confidently, smiling to herself as she chattered, holding onto the handle as Berta wheeled Alicia in the barrow. Berta was the first to spot me and she looked grim.

When I reached them I held Lucinda tight. 'We climbed out of the window of Berta's room,' she said excitedly. 'We had to help her escape from her husband, because if he finds her, he might turn her eyes black and blue like he did the last time.'

I studied Alicia's expression. She seemed relieved and grateful for my silent understanding, but there was a resignation settling into her I'd never seen before. I turned my attention back to Lucinda. 'That was good of you to help, but I just spoke with Pepe and he told me the man is gone, so we can go home now.'

Later, when Alicia was sure Lucinda wouldn't hear her, she whispered to me and confirmed my suspicions. 'I saw him when he was down the street. I'm sure he's from the Federal Office of Education and he was coming to take her.'

'Don't worry about that now,' I said, startled by how much she'd weakened during that single morning; her eyes were shadowed and hollowed with fatigue.

Alicia awoke later that afternoon to the company of Beba, who'd stopped by to see how she was doing. Beba was concerned to hear about the day's events, but even more so to see Alicia's physical deterioration.

She spoke with gentle authority. 'If you come to my house tomorrow, I will help you with your pain.'

I could see Alicia ready to protest that she felt fine, but Beba raised her long bony finger to silence her. 'Your eyes are full of pain. Come see me tomorrow and you will feel better.'

31

LUCINDA AND I SAT IN METAL CHAIRS AGAINST THE WALL. THE thin curtains were drawn and, since sunlight had difficulty making its way down the alley into Beba's window, the room was as dark as it would've been in the middle of the night. Numerous candles provided the only light necessary. Beba wore a white turban twisted high on her head, the one she'd worn before the revolution, and around her neck hung red and yellow beads that clacked as she moved about the small room.

She'd placed a large metal tub in the very centre of the room, in which Alicia now sat. Eyes lowered, Beba passed her hands over Alicia's head and body without touching her. This went on for several minutes before she began to chant softly as she poured fragrant oil on Alicia's head.

At first, Alicia had been reluctant to participate. When she'd woken up she'd said she didn't feel well enough to do anything but lie in her bed and look out of the window. Every breath caused her to wince with pain and she looked like someone waiting, simply waiting because there was nothing else she could do. Lucinda sat next to her in the bed and tried to persuade her to eat, but Alicia refused even a little water and a few crackers. In just one night she seemed to have slipped further away from life. Her skin was yellow and tight over her beautiful cheekbones, the skin on her shoulders like gauze.

'You should go,' she said with a cough. 'You should go out and enjoy the day.' She said nothing about Lucinda joining me. It was clear she wanted to keep her daughter by her side. She closed her eyes and lay very still. Then she opened them wide and looked at me with sudden alarm. 'Why do you say that Beba is always right, Nora?'

'She's always been right. She knows things; she sees things.'

Alicia closed her eyes again. 'I'll go see her, then. I'll go and see if she can make this pain go away.' It was the first time Alicia had admitted to feeling any pain at all.

Beba scooped warm water out of the tub in a perfect pink seashell and poured it over Alicia again and again. Alicia closed her eyes, and Beba chanted a song deep in her throat which seemed to emanate from deeper still, from the pit of her belly, until the music filled the room and all the spaces within us. The words weren't Spanish but African, and the sounds were round and liquid and beautiful. We began to sway in the flickering candlelight until we were all quite relaxed. I had closed my eyes, but opened them every now and then to check on Alicia, who was crouched in the tub, shoulders stooped, looking as if she had drifted off to sleep, which she tended to do more and more. Suddenly she sat up straight, as though a current of electricity had shot through her spine, but Beba didn't change the pace or rhythm of her chanting. She didn't even seem to notice this change that to us seemed so profound.

I sensed Lucinda shiver next to me and took hold of her hand. It was warm and dry, not sweaty and clammy like my own. Beba's eyes opened a sliver and she sprinkled a variety of sweet-smelling herbs into the tub. Her chanting grew more intense and her face began to contort as though there were invisible hands pushing at the loose flesh of her cheeks and forehead. Producing a butcher's knife from the pocket of her skirt, she held it out so that the blade gleamed in the flickering candlelight. She then proceeded to slice away at Alicia's dress one piece at a time until Alicia was quite naked, with strips of wet fabric clinging to her, to the tub, and to Beba as well.

Even in the dim light it was difficult to look upon Alicia's emaciated body and I was grateful that Lucinda couldn't see her. She was a whisper of human form, a fragile collection of bones spotted with sores the colour of raspberries. In that instant, my once-beautiful cousin became aware of her nakedness, and covered herself where breasts had once graced her sensuous figure. She glanced shyly at me, and saw my eyes filled with tears.

'The pain will leave you, child,' Beba said in her singsong voice, eyes closed once again. 'Ask me what you want to know.'

I had no idea what Beba meant by this, but Alicia did. 'Will I see my Tony before I die?' she asked, her voice full of courage.

'Not as you hope to see him.'

'I hope to see him healthy and well.'

Beba began to sway and then she knelt and placed a hand on Alicia's shoulder. 'He is well. You will see him well, and you will see him free.'

'How about Lucinda? Will my Tony and Lucinda live together free in America?'

'It is not meant to be; it cannot be,' was Beba's quick reply. Too quick for the cruel blow it delivered.

'Why can't it be, Beba? I have the money. Why can't it be?'

Beba opened her eyes and stared straight through Alicia. 'Tony cannot be free with both you and Lucinda.'

Alicia began to whimper and tremble and I stood up to go to her, but Lucinda squeezed my hand and I held back.

Beba raised her gaze to the ceiling. 'Tony has been waiting for you a long time. Almost two years. He sees you now and he's waiting for you to cross over and be with him.'

'That can't be. Tony's here and . . .' Alicia let her words and thoughts float and dissolve in the warm water that surrounded her. 'Tony is already dead.'

'He's been waiting for you, my child,' Beba said.

Alicia slept soundly as Lucinda and I hovered about Beba's apartment, whispering, for the rest of the day. We were both shocked by Beba's revelation, but when I questioned her, she was vague.

'When I'm in a trance I don't plan what I'm going to say, Nora.'

'But what if Tony isn't dead?'

Beba was not in the least bit concerned about this possibility. She blew out the candles one by one and shook her head resolutely. 'What is done is done,' she said.

I turned my attention to readying Alicia for our short walk home. With blankets tucked in and pillows adjusted, the three of us headed down the hall.

'Let her sleep as long as she needs to,' Beba said, her white turban gleaming in the darkened hallway. 'She'll wake before midnight, and things will be better.'

Alicia woke up at precisely eleven forty-five p.m. Her eyes opened suddenly and they were bright, as if she hadn't been sleeping at all, but engaging in the most animated of conversations. She placed her hand on Lucinda, who was lying next to her, and Lucinda woke up as well. She'd refused to leave her mother's side since we got back and had asked constant questions about her father: if he was really dead and

311

what the whole thing with Beba meant. I hardly knew how to answer her.

'I'm thirsty,' Alicia said. 'May I have some water, please?'

Lucinda sprang up from the bed and scuttled to the kitchen.

Alicia beckoned for me to come and sit next to her. 'I feel as light as a feather. The pain that used to wrap around me tight, squeezing the life out of me, is very far away, like a little star that blinks at me but can't do me any harm.'

'I'm so glad, Alicia.'

I took hold of her hand and she squeezed it with amazing strength. 'And Tony's eyes are closer than the pain. I know he's there and I can see them. I dreamt about him just now. We were dancing on the sea together. We were floating up above the palm trees and we saw Cuba down below us flowing like a fragile leaf in the river. She was floating towards a giant waterfall and then she rushed over the top and landed at the very bottom far below.' Alicia smiled and closed her eyes. 'She was fine when she landed, just fine.'

'Rest more, Alicia. That's what you need to do right now.'

Her eyes flew open and she was a child again, bright and amazing with a mind as quick and agile as a tiny bird flittering among the flowers. 'Everything's going to be OK, Nora. Don't worry any more.'

The next morning I set out early to find Ricardo. It wasn't the usual meeting day and I had no idea whether or not he'd be at his post, but I decided that if he wasn't there I'd inquire about Tony at the prison office myself. I had nothing to lose, and nothing to hide.

When I arrived, I saw no one at the guard post, but then Ricardo emerged from behind the building zipping up his fly. I shuddered to think of how many times Alicia had seen him in a similar situation. He straightened when he saw me, sniffed loudly and flicked his hairy hand over his revolver to make sure it was still there.

'This isn't the entrance for visitors,' he informed me gruffly. 'You have to go around the other side.'

'I'm not a visitor. I'm Alicia's cousin. We met before.'

Ricardo eyed me closely under bulging sweaty brows. He rolled his tongue over something in his mouth and spat it out, leaving a wad of spit glistening on the dirt. He spread his legs, his hand firmly on his revolver. 'What do you want? This isn't the day to come.'

'I have reason to believe Tony Rodriguez is dead and has been for some time.'

Ricardo blinked the sweat out of his eyes, but said nothing.

'You can tell me the truth yourself or I can go inside and find out myself, but I don't think you want any trouble.'

Ricardo bared his big yellow teeth and his lips twitched. 'What kind of trouble can you make for me?'

I stepped forward. 'I can tell them you've been extorting a helpless widow, and forcing her to bring you food and perform sexual favours.'

Ricardo's grin widened into a dry laugh. 'How are you going to prove that, huh? Nobody gives a shit about things like that. They won't do nothing to me.'

I had no doubt he was right, and the helplessness I felt, combined with the hate I had for Ricardo, was almost too much to bear. Suddenly a thought occurred to me, prompted by my memory of Ricardo's face during our earlier visit, when Alicia mentioned that Berta might be making the next delivery.

I lifted my head high. 'I believe the prison officials will be interested to know you have the virus.'

'What are you talking about?' Ricardo's black eyes ricocheted in their sockets. 'Alicia said she got it after—'

I took another step forward and captured his darting eyes in my steely gaze. 'I'm not talking about Alicia—'

His beady eyes flew open and he stammered for the first time. 'Berta's healthy, like a young cow, and I . . . I feel fine.'

'Then how do you explain the sweat running down your face, and the yellow colour of your eyes?'

Ricardo's hands fell limply to his side as he considered the possibility of death and detainment in the sanatoriums created for young and old, criminal and saintly. We both knew that anyone suspected of being ill with the disease was forced into these modern-day leprosy colonies, where they wasted away and waited to die.

He leaned on the guardhouse, a man suddenly aware of his impending doom. 'Tony Rodriguez died about two years ago. He was caught trying to escape and they shot him.'

'Don't they send notices to the family?'

'It's easy to intercept the mail. I paid a friend to help me out.'

I clenched my fists hard upon hearing this and my nails bore deep into the palms of my hands. 'You took advantage of the love and faith of a good woman. You're worse than a rat in the sewer.'

'It was a good thing and I didn't want it to end,' Ricardo said, pumping up a bit. He licked his lips. 'She got something out of it, too.'

'You're a pig.'

'I'm a survivor,' he corrected, glaring at me from head to toe. 'Look at you, standing there with your plastic shoes pretending to be one of us. You don't know what it's like. In a few days you'll go home to your easy life, but the rest of us will still be here rotting away. We do what we have to do, just like you would.'

My eyes became blurry and hot, and my ears began to hum and pop to the erratic pace of my heart. I wanted to run and beat my hands against a wall until they were bloody, I wanted to feel the pain Alicia had been suffering. Most of all, I wanted to kill Ricardo.

I reached down for one of the many stones that lay on the rough road, but Ricardo had already turned away from me. He believed that he too was dying, that before long he'd be carted around in a wheelbarrow, if he was lucky. I threw the stone at him with all my might, but it landed several yards away, not causing enough of a stir to distract him from his torment.

This time I was successful in finding gas, and Lourdes handed me the keys after we'd shared a quick cup of very strong coffee. 'Don't drive at night if you can help it. The lights don't work,' she warned.

The blue Chevy lumbered down the broken road like an old man with a cough. The gas was cheap and the tyres worn, but it would get us where we had to go. Alicia had weakened since the previous day and it was becoming more difficult for her to find the energy to speak. Mostly she watched Lucinda, her impossibly large green eyes trying to take in as much of her as she could. Lucinda was always nearby, within touching distance of her mother. More than once I saw her smile back when Alicia smiled at her.

Alicia stayed awake once we got on the road, but she asked no questions about where we were going. The three of us sat in the front and Alicia clung to her daughter's hand.

It took almost two hours on the coast road to get there, but when we did, there was no mistaking where we were. The royal palms welcomed us like old friends, the white expanse of talcum sand fanning out towards the sea. There was a sparkling new hotel crawling with tourists in brightly coloured bathing suits, towels slung about their shoulders or wrapped around their waists like sarongs. It was obvious we were not tourists.

I parked the car a few blocks away from our final destination and settled Alicia into the wheelbarrow. Lucinda took her post next to me, one hand on the handle, her eyes straight ahead and unwavering.

They'd built an impressive fence along the perimeter of our beach with thick curving poles that looked like the inverted ribs of a whale. It would have been very difficult to climb by myself, but with Alicia and Lucinda in tow it was impossible. Our only hope was to wait discreetly near the entrance of the hotel for a moment when we might pass the main entrance unnoticed. We waited on a nearby bench for almost an hour, but the moment never presented itself. I surmised that it was probably easier to escape from the federal prison than it was to get onto our beach. I reminded myself that no matter how many new hotels there were, or regulations about Cubans not being permitted to use them, Varadero belonged to us, and it always would.

I was starting to feel that our situation was hopeless, when I noticed a group of workmen passing through the gate, loaded down with building equipment and supplies. One fellow even carried his bricks in a wheelbarrow very much like mine. The guard never asked who they were and hardly blinked as they passed. I gave Lucinda explicit instructions not to move from that spot next to her mother until I returned, then I ran back to the car. Never was I more grateful to see a pile of dirty clothes in my life. It was obvious that Lourdes' husband had finally shown up for work, and luckily for us he'd forgotten to take care of his laundry. I threw on a pair of his baggy pants covered in grease and paint, and a large T-shirt stained deep yellow under the arms. There were even two hats to choose from. I chose the one with the widest brim and grabbed as many greasy towels as I could hold.

I bundled Lucinda into the barrow next to Alicia and covered them up with the towels, arranging them this way and that until I was satisfied they could pass for a pile of lumber or bricks. It was then a matter of waiting for the right moment to step in line behind the crew of workmen. My opportunity came soon enough and I lowered my head and hunched my shoulders up to appear bigger. Momentarily distracted by a group of scantily clad female tourists, the guard waved us by with a flick of his hand.

We were on the sand almost immediately and the wheelbarrow became extremely difficult to roll, but I couldn't risk Lucinda getting out from under the towels until I was sure we wouldn't be seen. Once we were several hundred yards from the gate, I gave Lucinda the word and she scurried out from beneath the towels, surprised to feel the warm sand on her feet.

'Where are we, Tía?'

'This is home, *mi cielo*. This is where your Mami and I grew up. Where we learned how to dream and how to pray.'

Slowly, we made our way towards the water's edge, where it would be easier to roll the wagon.

'The sand is so soft here, Tía. Much softer than at the other beach we go to.'

'This is the best beach in the whole world. Even though I haven't seen all the other beaches in the world, I can tell you it's true.'

Lucinda smiled and tossed her hair to the wind. Her springy curls bounced as she kicked at the rolling waves. Her hearing was so precise that she caught the crest perfectly every time with the tip of her toe.

Alicia spoke for the first time since we'd arrived, and the clarity and strength of her voice surprised me. 'Have they cut down our trees, Nora? I'm afraid to look.'

'I see them just as they were. Don't worry.'

Lucinda stayed near the water as I carefully placed Alicia on the sand directly under our palms. Beyond Lucinda, I could see the platform to which Alicia and

317

I had swum as children bobbing peacefully, the curve of the pure white sand spreading out like two loving arms reaching towards heaven.

Satisfied that Lucinda was safe and that we wouldn't be discovered as trespassers, I lay down next to Alicia. We looked up at the impossibly blue sky as the sun bathed us and winked through the palms.

Alicia sighed, shifted in the sand and turned towards me, her green eyes reflecting the crystalline sand like jewels embedded in her skeletal face. She was lovely still and the tenderness in her expression was so fragile and intense I could hardly bear it. I knew she was watching me and loving me with her last ounce of energy.

The corners of her mouth flickered into a faint smile. 'You know, Nora, if you stare straight at the sun without blinking, you can see God.' Alicia opened her eyes wide at the sun and then shut them tight. She turned to me again, her eyes glistening.

'What did you ask Him for?' I asked.

She smiled and closed her eyes. Her breathing grew shallow and rapid and her words escaped through her tangled breath like tiny butterflies. 'When you're with me I'm not afraid.'

I held her close. 'I'm here with you, Alicia, I'm right here.'

Above us the royal palms swayed, their shadows drifting over us as quickly as the time which had passed with such ruthless indifference across our island and through our lives. We're little girls again with our hearts set on an afternoon swim, tingling with the thrill of the warm clear waters. We're learning how to skate over the rocks without falling down and scraping our knees, because scars would be unseemly on a young lady's legs. We're pressing our hands against our chests, afraid and curious about the painful little buds that grow with each passing day. We stare at the movie stars on TV and see how they kiss with their mouths barely open. Soon we discover for ourselves that sex is much more than kissing and kissing is much more than sex. We're grown women lying on the sand between heaven and earth, broken by the effort of trying to understand our incomprehensible friendship and the love that is slipping from life into forever.

I move closer to whisper in her ear. 'I'm glad we're here together, Alicia. It's just how I remember it.'

Eyelashes flutter over eyes that are fading to a quiet, sombre green, and I am not sure that she's heard me. 'Take care of my Lucinda,' she whispers back. 'Promise me . . .'

'I promise.'

Her eyes close and I feel I should be quiet now, but I want to tell her how much I love her, and about everything in my heart and all that she means to me. As I start to speak, she releases my hand and turns her face to the sun. I see her let go and lighten with the peace of the warmth all around us. Never has she looked more beautiful than she does at this moment. I realize that she's gazing into the face of God, and that this time He's taken her home.

32

ALICIA WAS BURIED IN A SMALL CEMETERY ON THE OUTSKIRTS of Havana. Aside from Beba, Lucinda and me, there were only a few neighbours gathered at her graveside. Berta complained that her work made it impossible for her to attend the simple funeral and that she didn't believe in them anyway. 'I said my goodbyes when she was alive. That should be good enough for anybody.'

The sombre mood contrasted sharply with the glorious tropical sky. When she was healthy, Alicia would've insisted that a day like this should not be wasted, and she would've organized a trip to the beach or the countryside or anywhere she could soak up the beauty around her. I only had the strength to sit on the wall of the malecón and stare out at the sea. I had never felt so lost, so incapable of understanding what I should do next. Alicia was gone, and this immutable reality crept over me like a slow freeze, so that even the warmth of the sun couldn't reach me any more.

Beba was a rock of strength and compassion. After the burial, she came to the house every day to check on Lucinda. We both feared for Lucinda's health and general well-being. She hadn't spoken a word for three days after Alicia died. She hardly ate and she slept fitfully, waking suddenly and calling for her mother.

I'd go to her and remind her gently that her Mami was gone. She'd lie back without a word, no longer requiring any comforting, at least not from me.

In the house, she began to stumble into furniture and tripped several times, once bumping her head hard enough to produce a black and blue lump on her forehead. Beba kept ice on it most of the day. She was the only person Lucinda allowed near her. When I tried to get close, she flinched and turned away from me. This is how it had been since she heard I was planning to leave Cuba without her.

I had gone to the American Embassy to inquire about the status of Lucinda's visa, hoping I'd be able to take her with me. I was confronted by a middle-aged woman with sagging cheeks and teeth stained dark yellow from too much coffee and smoking, a sure sign of someone who'd had steady employment for a while.

'When are you leaving?' the clerk asked as she shuffled through a stack of papers that looked as though they'd been weathering on her desk since before the revolution.

'In five days.'

She stopped her shuffling and stared at me in disbelief. 'Five days? You'd better pray for a miracle.'

I tried to explain I was Lucinda's closest living relative and that I wanted more than anything to adopt her, but the clerk wasn't impressed and waved me off with a well-rehearsed click of her tongue.

I phoned Jeremy for the third day in a row, hoping he'd help me find a solution to what was becoming an impossible situation, and he remained calm and logical in the face of my growing hysteria. I clung to his every word. 'Lucinda will come and live with us when her visa comes through. It's not going to happen now, the way you'd like, but it'll happen. We can even get your attorney cousin to help us.'

'It could take a year, maybe more. What about the promise I made Alicia?'

'You promised you'd look after her and you still are. You've made arrangements with Beba.'

'It's not the same.'

Jeremy's sigh was lost in the static of the connection. 'Do you think Alicia wanted us to be separated so you could look after her daughter?'

'I know she didn't want that.'

'Do you trust Beba to take good care of Lucinda?'

I laughed in spite of my turmoil. 'Beba will do a better job than I or anybody else could do.'

'There you have it, then. Beba will look after Lucinda while her visa is being processed. And you'll come home to me because . . .' He paused for a moment. '. . . Because I love you and need you with me.'

'I love you too, Jeremy.'

'Promise me you'll come home.'

'I promise.'

'Promise me you'll come home next week and that you won't let this plane leave without you.'

'I promise, my love.'

It all seemed so clear and sensible after I spoke with Jeremy. I tried to explain this to Lucinda as she sat on the couch where Alicia had spent her last days. She barely raised her head to acknowledge I was speaking to her and her hair, which she refused to let anyone comb or wash for her, hung down like overgrown ivy. She kept her hands folded tight in her lap so her nails lit up like bright little crescent moons. Tears splashed on her wrists as she nodded her understanding, but she wouldn't accept a hug.

'I've started the paperwork to send for you. You'll be with me as soon as possible,' I said.

She nodded and reached out a probing hand for Beba, who had left the room. 'Where's Beba?'

Beba appeared soon enough to comfort her.

Even though I believed what Jeremy said to be logical and sound, there were brief moments when I resented him, and I felt an uneasy distance building in my heart, the same as I'd felt towards my parents before deciding to go against their wishes. And Lucinda was beginning to hate me as well. I could feel it thick and heavy in the air whenever I came close to her. I only reminded her of the agonizing loss of both her parents. The best I could do was to keep a distance and spare us both any more pain. Never in my life had I felt so alone.

Beba spoke to me plainly on the day I announced the date of my departure. She'd finally coaxed Lucinda into the bath and had her soaking in my lemon-scented bubbles. 'You're doing what you have to do, so you don't break in two, Norita. You're only one person and you can't be both places at once.'

'I wish I could be here and go, Beba. I wish I could more than anything. Now Lucinda hates me.'

'That sweet child isn't capable of hate. She's doing what she has to do to stay whole, just like you are. It's too much grief for one person to take.'

Beba was right, as always, and I tried to remember her words when Lucinda asked me if she could go home with Beba for the night. I was so happy she'd spoken to me that I wasn't able to respond to the question or understand that it meant another rejection. She'd been staying with Beba ever since.

I preferred sleeping on the couch, which still smelled of the body lotion and perfume I'd given Alicia on the day I arrived. It seemed like a lifetime ago; several lifetimes. She appeared one night in my dreams, her hair floating on the wind like golden clouds suspended in air. She was as beautiful and vibrant as I remembered her being before I left Cuba, and she danced with Tony above the palm trees, which tickled their feet. They laughed as they looked down on me, and I was angry that they should be so carefree when I was so shackled to my problems.

* * *

323

There was a knock on the door the day before I was scheduled to leave. My large suitcase lay on the floor of the small living room so it was difficult to open the door completely, but when I finally did, I stood face to face with a small man wearing black-rimmed glasses. They seemed to do little to improve his eyesight, for he persistently peered over my shoulder to see who or what was in the room. As he did so, I took note of his clean shirt and good shoes.

'It's been reported to me that there's a child here. A . . .' he consulted his notebook more carefully, '. . . a Lucinda Rodriguez.'

I stepped forward so he couldn't see into the room. 'Is there a problem?'

The man continued to consult his notes. 'It says here the child has been recently orphaned. It's the obligation and authority of the state to evaluate the caretaking and education . . .'

I opened the door wider so I could stand outside the threshold. 'I'm Lucinda's aunt and I'm caring for her just fine.'

He glanced at the suitcase on the floor. 'But you're leaving.'

'The child will be well taken care of.'

'May I ask by whom?'

'A close family friend.'

The man jotted down something in his notebook and shook his head. 'I will report this to my superiors. However, I must inform you that it is not customary for orphaned children to reside with non-relatives. Our reports indicate that the child is blind and has had no formal education to speak of.'

'I assure you that she's been very well educated, even if she hasn't attended the state school.'

The man's grimace became a thin smile. 'We have schools for disabled children.'

'I'm sure you do.'

'Where is the child now?'

'I'm afraid she's not here at the moment.'

The man jotted some more, ripped a leaf of paper out of his notebook and gave it to me. 'Her whereabouts must be reported to this office. If I don't hear from you in a couple of days, I'll be back.'

Beba listened gravely as she measured out the sugar for our coffee. 'Did you tell them she was here?'

'Of course not.'

'Good.' She handed me my coffee and the cup rattled on the saucer. 'She can never go back there now. We have to stay indoors for a while, especially in the day.'

I showed Beba the paper the man gave me and she promptly crumpled it up into a small wad and tossed it in the bin. 'I never did learn to read.'

Next I handed Beba the box of money Alicia had been saving in the wall. When she saw how much there was, she placed a hand over her chest and collapsed on her stool. 'Good Lord, child, are you walking around the streets with this? They'll slice your throat around here for ten dollars.'

Lucinda had been asleep on the floor on a bed Beba had made for her. As she stirred I whispered, 'Alicia was saving this money for when Tony got out, so the three of them could find a way to the States together. Use it for whatever you need to take care of Lucinda, and I'll send you money every month. For you and Lucinda.'

'You don't have to pay me to take care of that child.'

'I know I don't.'

I told Beba I'd be back later in the day to say good-bye, because the next morning I was leaving very early. As I hugged Beba at the door, I saw Lucinda's small face reflected in the cracked mirror leaning against the floor next to her. Her eyes were wide open, and her face was tight with the strain of trying to muffle the sound of her own weeping.

Berta came to see me that afternoon, taking the opportunity to say her goodbyes, as she'd be gone for work before the end of the day. I'd been meaning to thank her for helping Alicia with Ricardo, but didn't quite know how to bring it up.

I offered her my shoulder to lean on as she removed her bright-pink high-heeled shoes. 'I know how you helped Alicia with Ricardo.'

'How'd you find out?'

'I figured it out by the look on Ricardo's face when Alicia mentioned you'd be making the next delivery.'

Berta cackled and collapsed on the couch. 'If it wasn't for Alicia, I'd never let a man that ugly get near me, no matter how much money he had.' She raised her painted eyebrows. 'Well, maybe . . .'

'I think you should know . . . I told him a little lie. I was so angry for what he did to Alicia that I told him . . . he was sick because you were sick too. You see, Alicia had already told him that she became ill after she and he . . . well, I had to get back at him somehow.'

Berta was still and thoughtful for a moment, and then she looked at me and said, 'Alicia always said you were smart, but that was brilliant. If I know Ricardo, he'll be crapping his pants for the next ten years.' She broke out in a fit of laughter. 'And he deserves to suffer, that bastard.'

'But it could jeopardize you . . .'

'He may be a devil, but he's no fool. He won't say anything.' Berta thought for a moment longer. 'Besides, it might be true. Alicia took a lot better care of herself than I ever did.' She shrugged off the few seconds of doubt she'd allowed herself and stood up to give me a strong hug, almost drowning me in her jungle of hair, stiff with sprays and potions that did little to calm it down.

I'd already told her three times before, but just to make sure I told her once more that no matter who came to the door, she was to tell them Lucinda had moved and that she didn't know where. Each time, Berta agreed, but I worried. In spite of her generosity, she wasn't immune to bribery, and she'd succumbed to the illness caused by desperation long ago.

I decided to take the longer walk up the malecón to Beba's house. The temperature had cooled and the ocean swelled its turquoise perfection against the cobalt sky. This was the Cuba I had dreamed about. For an instant, I envied Alicia for having lived all her life in the midst of such beauty. She was more a part of Cuba than I could ever be, and her sweet-hearted music was leaving me and slipping away as surely as the tide.

At this time tomorrow I'd be back in Los Angeles. I'd wake up and take a steamy shower as American coffee brewed in my automatic coffee-maker. I'd settle into my tidy Honda and drive down smooth streets lined by manicured lawns. I'd park in my reserved parking space and work for exactly eight and a half hours, and then drive home and order Chinese because I was too tired to cook. And Jeremy would come home to me as he always did and fall asleep in my arms.

Lucinda was sitting primly in her chair when I arrived. Beba had taken special care to comb her hair into ringlets and dress her in one of the dresses I'd brought for her. It was the yellow one with delicate embroidery on the collar, and in it she looked like one of those collectable dolls you place high on the shelf because they're too beautiful to play with.

I chatted with Beba a bit as I watched Lucinda by the window. She slowly turned to face the sound of my voice. Her eyes were soft and beamed with a lovely light. She hadn't looked this open since before Alicia's death and my throat was tight with hope and emotion. Without thinking about it, I went to her and knelt before her so we were at eye level. Immediately, her hands floated up towards my face and she smiled.

'Tía Nora,' she whispered, and I hugged her so tight that this little china doll could break, but she hugged me back every bit as tight. 'I'm sorry, Tía Nora. I'm sorry I've been so mad at you.'

'No, *mi cielo*, don't apologize for anything. Please don't . . .'

'I want to, because I truly am sorry and because Mami said I should.'

'Mami?' I looked at Beba, who shrugged, while squinting at the paper on which I'd written my home address and phone number. It was then that I spotted the metal tub in the corner of the room and became aware of the faint smell of sulphur.

'Beba gave me a bath today like she gave Mami, to take away the pain, and it worked, Tía Nora, it worked. I don't feel mad or sad any more, because I know Mami and Papi are happy together in heaven and I know you'll come back for me. You won't forget me?'

'Of course I won't forget you, my love. How could I ever forget you?'

I held her as Beba looked down upon us. For the first time, I felt unsettled by those eyes that seemed to know and see so much, but I decided not to ask her what she felt, or exactly what had happened with Lucinda. I didn't want to taint the moment with doubts for any of us.

Beba pressed her beautiful dark hands against my face and I breathed in the fragrance of coffee and lemons and salt crackers and deep abiding wisdom. Then I kissed her on both cheeks and said goodbye.

I tried to sleep, knowing I had to be up early to catch my flight, which was scheduled to leave José Marti airport at eight in the morning. I gazed out of the window at what had been Alicia's view during the many months of her illness, as she dreamt of being with Tony again and prayed for Lucinda, once she'd

328

accepted she would never recover her sight. I could see a once-elegant apartment building, and in the evening light its former glory seemed almost restored, its wrought-iron railings adorning the balconies like curling eyelashes heavy with paint and glitter.

I saw the glowing light of a cigarette floating about on one of them, and could just make out the figure of a young woman leaning back in a chair, her legs crossed as she gazed up at the night sky. Even in the dim light I could see she was lovely. Her slender limbs caught the light of the moon in narrow ribbons and her hair was awash with golden light; she began to glow as if a stage light had been placed on her and was gradually starting to intensify. I blinked hard. I was tired and needed to sleep, but I couldn't tear my eyes away from this young woman. I tried to discern what she was doing, but as the light grew brighter I realized she wasn't smoking at all. In her hand she held a candle, and she was moving it up and around, trying to get my attention. She was motioning, beckoning to me. Was there something wrong? Was she stuck up there?

I remained in my bed, watching the young woman, transfixed by the circular movement of the candle and the way her hair floated away from her face as though there was a breeze stirring about her. But the night was still. The motionless curtain against the open window confirmed this.

I concluded that she thought I was Alicia and was trying to communicate something to her. I should go out and tell her that Alicia had died. All the neighbours knew this. Why didn't she?

I got out of bed and threw on another shirt over my shorts and T-shirt. The girl was only three floors up on the other side of the street. It would be easy to shout up to her and see if she was OK. I opened the door and went out into the road. She was still there, holding her arms out towards me as though she was in trouble.

'I'm coming,' I yelled up to her and rushed to the

main door of the building. It was not only locked, but boarded up with planks that appeared to have been rotting there for years. Then I remembered that the building was condemned and hadn't been occupied for some time. The girl must have found her way inside and didn't know how to get out. I was about to call to her again; but when I looked up, she was no longer there.

I tested the main entrance and concluded that she couldn't possibly have entered or exited through there. I walked around the building several times, but all the windows and doors were hammered shut with layers of old boards, just like the front door.

Perplexed about her disappearance, I had begun to circle the apartment once more when I caught sight of something gleaming out of the corner of my eye. Perched on the gatepost was the white votive candle the girl had been waving about on the balcony, its delicate flame still flickering in the night. I walked closer to examine it and finally picked it up. How, I wondered, could she have come out without my noticing? The windows and doors were boarded up from the outside. She would've had to jump down three floors.

I took one final look down the street before heading back to my bed. It was already late, and I tried to put any thoughts about the mysterious girl out of my mind and focus on Jeremy, who'd be waiting for me in Los Angeles in less than twenty-four hours. Would it be the same for us after almost two months apart? I was giddy with anticipation, and yet my heart sank with the realization that this was my last night in Cuba — my last night at home.

33

I ARRIVED AT THE AIRPORT AT SIX IN THE MORNING, KNOWING it would be a mass of confusion. I carried one empty suitcase: I was wearing the only dress that remained of the clothes I'd brought. I had decided to leave my other suitcase outside Berta's bedroom door as a gift.

I'd been in such a rush to get to the airport that I hadn't had time to think about the events of the previous night. And there was a part of me that didn't want to think about them at all. It was time to get on with my life. I was the wife of a wonderful and loving man who was waiting for me. I should be thinking about how much I wanted to make love to him, instead of what had happened to that girl on the balcony. I'd tucked the candle safely in my bag, and now I poked my hand inside to make sure it was still there. If only I'd had time to talk to Beba. I was sure she'd have an explanation involving the 'call of one's dreams' or the 'power of the lesser-known spirits'. However far-fetched, I longed to hear something that would make sense of the lingering doubts that had preoccupied me all morning.

I was near the front of the line and was preparing to hand over my passport to be inspected for the third or fourth time since I'd arrived. I closed my eyes and forced myself to picture Jeremy waiting for me, so happy to know that soon I'd be there with him and all would be well with the world. We'd take care of Lucinda's papers, of course we would. She'd be with me in no time. Beba was more than capable of making sure she was safe. She was more ingenious and savvy about life since the revolution than I could ever be. And Lucinda didn't hate me. She knew I'd be back for her, Alicia had told her so herself.

My head and my stomach jolted, and my feet refused to move forward in the line. Sweat erupted on my brow and everywhere else, dripping down my body and the backs of my legs. I thought I might faint.

The young man waiting to receive my passport sounded concerned. 'Is there something wrong, Miss?'

'I . . . I don't know.'

'Step up and lean on the counter,' he offered, as though he was quite accustomed to managing fainting spells.

I did as I was told, but didn't feel any better. My head was swimming and a faint humming vibrated through my ears as though I had two large shells glued to them. I couldn't hear anything at all.

The young man reached for my passport, but I held it to my chest as if to still my heart. 'I can't go.'

He didn't hear me correctly. He was looking at the computer screen, one hand still open and waiting. The passengers who'd already cleared were taking anxious little steps towards the open door and the plane that awaited us. 'There's a bathroom on the plane, Miss.'

I staggered backwards onto the shoes of the person standing behind me. 'I can't go,' I said again and collapsed into the nearest chair. How could I forget how Alicia had looked when she first became a woman and fell in love? I reached inside my bag for the candle. She had lit countless candles over the years to keep hope alive when her world was crumbling around her. And now she wanted me to stay and see to Lucinda's freedom myself. I knew that as surely as I knew Jeremy wanted me to go back to him and our wonderful life in California.

I took a deep breath and tried to get a grip on myself and focus on the fact that I had to get on that plane. Perhaps Beba was getting to me, with her Santeria and rituals. But all I could think of was my vow to Alicia that I wouldn't abandon her child. I had promised her as she'd died in my arms.

I managed to stand and make my way to the window, smeared with sweaty palmprints and the remnants of squashed mosquitoes, to watch the plane bake in the heat as the mechanics milled around checking this and that. I had plenty of time to change my mind if I wanted to, and the passport still in my hand reminded me of this. Sweat accumulating on my fingers caused it to slip and fall to the floor. I didn't bother to pick it up until the plane had rumbled down the runway and lifted off Cuban soil.

Lucinda hugged me and laughed with joy. 'Tía Nora, you came back so soon! I didn't think you'd come back this soon, but I'm so glad you did.' Her hands fluttered over my face.

Beba wasn't at all surprised to see me standing there in my last good dress, an orange linen shift with matching sandals. She leaned in the doorway with her arms crossed, chuckling and shaking her head. She promptly busied herself preparing coffee and produced two chipped cups. As we drank our coffee, I explained what had happened the night before and showed her the candle I'd found.

Lucinda took it from me and pressed it against her cheek, already convinced that her mother had left it. But Beba, munching on a cracker with her one front tooth like a chipmunk, appeared unmoved. I was waiting for a supernatural explanation that would set me straight, anything that might help me justify my decision not to go back to Jeremy as I had promised I would.

'It doesn't matter what you saw last night, whether it was a ghost from heaven or hell or just your wild imagination,' Beba said finally. 'What matters is that you did what you thought was right.'

This was not what I wanted to hear. I needed something more substantial; assurances that I'd done the right thing. I pressed her about Jeremy and how she thought he'd take the fact that I wouldn't be on the plane. I pressed her like I'd done when I was a girl, insisting that she tell me yet another story before turning out the light.

'For God's sake, child, I can't give you what I don't have to give. All I can tell you is that time and happenings will let you know if you did right.'

Time and happenings, as Beba said, spoke to me soon enough. I spent the night at Beba's apartment and the next morning we were woken very early by a knocking at the door. By the solid sound of it, it was clear that whoever was on the other side was using some sort of object. And it wasn't just one person, because we could hear conversation. Beba, who always slept fully dressed, complete with handkerchief on her head, slipped on her sandals and headed towards the door while shooting a look in my direction that said, 'I'll handle this; just keep quiet.'

I pulled the sheet over both my and Lucinda's heads. From where we slept on the floor, the person at the door would have to pass Beba and enter the room to see she wasn't alone. I didn't have to tell Lucinda to keep quiet. We held each other tightly and hardly breathed.

Beba coughed and opened the door. I could easily imagine her sizing up the intruders. She had a stare capable of turning the blood running through anyone's veins to ice. I had been victim to it and had benefited from its protection on many occasions in my life. At that moment, I'd never felt more grateful to have Beba in my corner.

'We're looking for a child,' the man said, and I recognized the voice as that of the bespectacled man from the Federal Office of Education. 'Her name is Lucinda Rodriguez, and we were informed she's living here now.'

'What do you want with her?'

Another voice spoke up – a woman's voice, strained and high pitched, as though she had her vocal cords tied in a very tight knot. 'Are you a relative?'

'Yes, I am,' Beba replied without hesitation.

'That's funny, we were informed the child had no living relatives.'

'You got your facts wrong.'

Silence followed. They were staring each other down now, I was sure of it. They'd be no match for Beba. Their bones were probably already turning to jelly. I had to fight the bizarre temptation to giggle, and I held onto Lucinda more tightly.

'Your name, please,' the man asked.

'Beba.'

'And your last name?'

'It's just Beba.'

Silence again and the shuffling of feet. Not Beba's feet. 'Your lack of cooperation won't help you or the child, let me assure you,' the woman said in a superior tone. 'Unless you have documents indicating you have legal custody of the child, she'll be placed in the federal orphanage for her own protection. Is that clear?'

'Oh, very clear. You put your words together real good.'

It was the man who spoke this time. 'We'll be back . . . Beba.'

Beba closed the door behind them and went to the kitchen window. Once satisfied that they'd left, she lifted the sheet from over us and stood with hands on hips and a funny smile on her face. I knew she was afraid, but she didn't want Lucinda to notice; it was too hard for a woman as honest as Beba to look one way and sound another.

'I think now's a good time,' Beba said to Lucinda and me as she fixed our breakfast. 'Now's a good time to take that money and find a way out of here.'

'You mean not wait for the visa?'

'With the money you have, you don't have to wait for anyone or anything.'

It was an option I'd never considered. I'd always imagined we'd leave legally with my American passport and Lucinda's visa in order, and hadn't thought of the possibility of escape. I remembered what Alicia had written about securing passage on a banana boat a few years back. Perhaps we could find something similar now? Suddenly, I wanted to run to the nearest phone and call Jeremy, to tell him that all was well and not to give up on me. I'd be home soon.

Lucinda informed us that it was Pepe, the neighbour, who was known for helping in these matters, so I told her and Beba that I would go and see him. I found him a few hours later sitting on his front step unravelling a fist-sized ball of string. He explained that his wife had paid pennies for it because it was all knotted up, and it was very difficult to find string. He didn't seem particularly excited about having it, but he appreciated having something to do that didn't cause him too much anxiety.

When I told him what Lucinda and I needed, his long brown fingers stopped moving like spider's legs and he looked straight in front of him. With lips barely parted he asked, 'How much have you got?'

When I told him, his fingers started moving again and he nodded soberly. 'I can find you something with that. In a couple of weeks there's a shipment coming in and—'

'I don't have that kind of time. I need something for tomorrow or the next day at the latest.'

His brow furrowed. 'Ships come and go every day,

but the people coming in a couple of weeks, I know them. I know they'll be fair. I can't be sure about anyone else.'

'I'll have to take my chances. The authorities will come back any day and if they find Lucinda, I'll never see her again.'

Pepe nodded his agreement. I pulled the envelope of cash out of my bag and handed it to him, but he refused it, saying he only needed fifty dollars or so to secure an agreement. The balance I could pay myself. We agreed to meet later that same evening.

I told Lucinda and Beba that Pepe might find a way for us to leave the next day, and that we'd know by that evening.

'How should we spend our last day in Cuba?' I asked Lucinda.

She was sitting on the couch reading, where she'd been most of the morning. 'I don't think we should go out, Tía Nora, in case they see me. I think we should stay here and wait,' she said after a pause.

'You want to stay here all day?'

She nodded and her fingers returned to her reading.

Beba sat with me by the window, her arms crossed over her chest. The thought occurred to me that we might have enough money for Beba to leave with us too. Maybe there was enough time to inform Pepe? I mentioned this possibility to Beba, who grinned at the prospect.

'Could you see Beba in such a big fancy place?'

'I could easily see you there, Beba.'

She shook her head and pressed her lips together as if she'd tasted a sour lemon. 'It's too late for me, Norita. Maybe ten or fifteen years ago I would've gone, but not now. I'm going to die here in my country where I belong.'

'Don't you want to live in freedom again?'

'Maybe I don't think of freedom the way you do.

There's a freedom I've found over the years. It comes from discovering I don't need much to be happy. It comes from living past misery and fear and finding hope in your own tears.' Beba laughed that deep golden laugh that filled the room. 'I feel freedom standing in line all day with my ration book, only to learn they've run out of bread before it's my turn. I feel freedom when I pray at the water's edge and ask the good Lord to feed me with the wind and the sun and the sky.' Beba readjusted her handkerchief and tucked stray curls of hair underneath it. 'That's my freedom, Norita, and I don't have to escape anywhere to get it.'

There was no one at Pepe's house when I arrived in the evening, so I sat in his usual spot on the stoop. The breeze swept down the narrow street, and when I leaned over a little to my left I could see a portion of a plaza, where children played in an old fountain long since dried up. I remembered this plaza from when we drove to church on Sundays before the revolution. It was bordered by white and yellow roses and the fountain always flowed with the melody of soft water. Children were allowed to throw in pennies for a wish or two. And, at least in my case, this was usually followed by a treat of coconut ice cream. No wonder Pepe loved this spot. For a moment it was possible to dream of the days when Cuba was young and carefree.

He approached with his loping side-to-side gait. It was impossible to guess by studying his face whether or not he'd been successful in his quest. Pepe always looked the same. He barely nodded his head when he saw me, and when I stood up to greet him he handed me a folded piece of white paper.

'It leaves tomorrow at seven in the morning. You have to go meet the man tonight and pay him in advance.'

'How much?'

'Two thousand. And the rest when you get there.

The ship's going to Jamaica first. That's where you get off. It's easy to get a flight from Kingston to Miami.'

I couldn't help myself. I grabbed hold of Pepe and gave him a hug. He endured my affection without a word, although his stoical expression was rippled by a curious half-smile.

'I need to pay you for your help, Pepe, please.' I reached into my pocket for the wad of cash, which had felt thick and sticky against my thigh all day.

Pepe raised his hands slowly to stop me. For him this was the equivalent of an emotional hurricane and I froze. 'Don't pay me yet, Cousin Butterfly. If it all works out, you can send me some cash from home or a box of American cigarettes. I know you won't forget.'

34

LUCINDA AND I PACKED OUR FEW BELONGINGS IN THE MESH
bag we used for our picnic lunches when we went to
the beach. We took just the few T-shirts I'd bought
weeks earlier and a couple of pairs of shorts. The
rest of the bag was filled with crackers and fresh
fruit.

Beba brought out another bag of fruit and placed it
next to our bulging sack. 'Really, Beba, we'll be in
Jamaica before lunchtime. How many bananas can you
eat in three hours?'

Beba placed her hands on her hips and wagged her
head knowingly. 'You may not eat them, but a ship full
of men will make quick work of that. Better they keep
their minds on mangoes and bananas. You'll need all
the distractions you can handle.' She flicked her head
towards Lucinda, who was napping on the couch. Her
golden curls caught the light of the setting sun and
her heavy lashes barely fluttered against her rose-
tinted cheeks. Her long limbs were beginning to
assume the curvaceousness of womanhood and she
was looking as Alicia had when she was at her most
beautiful, except that Lucinda would be taller and her
face, although equally sweet in expression, was more
exotic in form and colour. There could be no doubt
that she was destined to be a beautiful woman. I put

the thought of potential trouble out of my mind. I had other things to worry about.

It was just as Pepe had described. A tall thin bearded man with a red shirt was fishing at the end of pier seventeen in the warehouse district. I was to hand him my plastic grocery bag, filled with any food items I wanted so long as amongst it was a coffee can stuffed with half the money. The other half would be delivered when we arrived in Jamaica.

I walked up to the man and held the bag out to him, but with a furtive nod of his head he indicated that I set it down at his feet. I did so and worried for a moment that the bag might tumble into the sea, but I steadied it well away from the edge before stepping back.

'Stay and talk for a bit,' he said without looking at me. 'It looks strange if you just walk away without a word.'

Looks strange to whom? Was somebody watching us? 'Of course,' I muttered.

'I understand there's a blind girl travelling with you?'

'My niece.'

'Getting out of the dinghy and onto the ship could be tricky. Do you think she can handle it?'

'I'll make sure she can.'

He studied the water and pulled on the line. 'Almost had it.' He reeled the line in a bit and turned halfway to face me, still avoiding my eyes. 'I expect you here tomorrow morning at five and not a minute later, or we'll miss the connection. We have two hours to paddle out to the ship and I can't be sure how rough the waters will be.'

Until that moment, this had never occurred to me. It was what I had to do to get home and keep Lucinda from becoming a ward of the state. It was what I had to do to see Jeremy again as soon as possible and save my marriage. 'Will it be dangerous?'

341

'Only if we get caught and they don't believe our story.'

'Our story?'

'We've gone out for a day of fishing. You're my wife and the girl is our daughter. It's her birthday and we wanted to catch some fish for a party and she's never been fishing before. If any boat comes towards us you immediately throw whatever you have in the ocean. And put something in the bag so it doesn't float.'

I studied the man's long European nose and glossy brown hair. His skin was darkened by the sun, but it was obvious he didn't have a drop of African blood in him.

'I'm afraid my niece would never pass as your daughter or mine, and especially not yours and mine together. Her father was mulatto and she looks a lot like him. We'll have to come up with another story.'

'OK. We'll go over it tomorrow at five sharp.'

'May I know your name?'

The man choked on a smile in spite of his efforts to remain serious and to the point. He looked directly into my eyes for the first time. 'My name is . . . José Gomez. What's yours?'

It took me a moment to understand. 'Maria Gomez, of course,' I replied.

He nodded approvingly and returned to his fishing without another word.

Lucinda wanted to know every detail of my conversation with the man at the dock who'd help us escape, and I told her what I knew, which wasn't very much. She listened as though we were planning a day's excursion. She hadn't been so animated since before her mother's death.

'I've never been on a boat,' she said, while holding onto the edge of her chair for the sheer joy of it. 'Mami never let me because I can't swim very well. But now I have to, don't I, Tía? Now I have no choice.'

The question caught me off guard. Of course she had a choice. She could stay here and go to the state school. She certainly wasn't the only blind child on the island. Maybe the school wasn't as bad as Alicia said. Would she have wanted me to risk Lucinda's life in this way rather than let her go to a state school for the blind? Because I was risking her life, wasn't I?

Beba listened calmly to our conversation, her face devoid of expression as she picked something out from under her nails. I wanted to talk to her without Lucinda present. She'd been short on answers lately, but this time I wouldn't let her get away so easily. Why was she suddenly so careful about giving her opinions on things? In the old days she always shot them out at whoever was nearby without worrying about the impact they might have.

Telling her that I needed her to help me select more food for the sailors, we left Lucinda resting in bed. I led Beba by the arm down the street towards the sweet breeze of the ocean. The malecón was still several blocks away, but its whispering mist seemed particularly lovely, if only because it would help disguise our voices.

'What do you think, Beba? Am I making a terrible mistake? Is this risk worth it?'

I'd bombarded her with questions before we were even halfway down the street. I whispered them in her ear, and felt I was having trouble breathing and walking at the same time.

Beba didn't answer me, but sat me down on the fountain in the plaza with a firm hand on my shoulder. Together we looked out upon the maze of streets, at this labyrinth of crumbling buildings with rusted gates and laundry dripping from the balconies. Children ran in and out of the open doors, barefoot and happy to be children. They took no notice of the grim faces of their parents, too tired to be amused by their play and too consumed by their hunger to notice that some of the

343

babies were getting close to the stairs or ambling out into the street.

Teenage girls strolled together, swinging their stretchy hips this way and that, walking so their young breasts bounced under tube tops and threadbare T-shirts. Young and old men alike called casually after them, making vulgar comments about the particular body parts they found most alluring, as if the breasts of one girl and the behind of another might jump off their respective torsos and find their way to them.

One particular drama played out before us. A girl, no more than fifteen, had been persuaded to exchange more than glances with a significantly older man. A few seconds later they walked off, the girl trailing behind like a puppy straggling on a short leash.

Beba turned to me. 'She's probably been whoring since about twelve, maybe younger.' She waved a hand at the group of girls left behind. 'They're just the same and I happen to know they all finished high school. The government saw to that all right.'

'Are you saying they could be Lucinda some day?'

'I'm saying that hunger makes you do things you thought only the devil could do. Lord in heaven, I never thought an ugly face and a big belly would be such a blessing.'

'So you think I'm taking a necessary risk with Lucinda? Is that what you mean, Beba?'

Beba looked a bit exasperated to be put on the spot again. Then, taking my hand in hers, she spoke to me as clearly as she ever had in all my life. 'The decision you make is not as important as the heart that's behind it. Stand by your decision and it will stand by you.'

Lucinda was dressed and ready when I opened my eyes in the faint haze of morning. Beba was already preparing our coffee and toast: our last meal in Cuba. We hardly spoke as we ate and I glanced frequently at the noisy plastic clock on Beba's TV.

'We have to go in a few minutes,' I said.

'Do you want me to walk with you?' Beba asked.

'I don't think it's a good idea, because the man is expecting only Lucinda and me. I don't know if it makes any difference . . .'

Beba put up her hand to let me know she understood. She took the breakfast dishes back to the little sink, but she didn't rinse them immediately as she usually did. She came back to be with us for every minute she could. We got up from the table and Lucinda reached out for Beba; when she found her, she buried her head into her bosom and wept openly.

'I wish you were coming with us,' she said as Beba stroked her hair and patted her back.

'Now, don't you worry about me. I'm going to be right here like I always been. One day we'll see each other again. That man can't live for ever.'

At the door, I hugged Beba long and hard. 'You'll keep trying to call Jeremy for me, won't you?'

'I'll be at that phone so often, people will think I'm a spy. And when I get a hold of him I plan to tell him a few things I got on my mind.'

I kissed her on the cheek. 'I think you should.'

After twenty minutes of brisk walking, we were halfway down the malecón. Lucinda stumbled a few times, but I didn't slow my pace. We couldn't risk being late and I'd long since given away my watch. Lucinda didn't complain. In fact, she didn't speak at all. She knew we had to concentrate on not appearing suspicious. Perhaps we already looked suspicious, because we were walking so urgently. Better slow down a bit and point towards the ships on the ocean, like sightseers. But what would sightseers be doing out at dawn? Of course we looked like we were trying to escape. What else would a woman and her child be doing out at this time of morning? The only people out at this hour were vagrants sitting on kerbs and young prostitutes dragging home with tired faces and high heels dangling from their fingers.

I pointed to the ships and told Lucinda that our ship was out there somewhere. So eager was I to appear the unlikely tourist, I forgot that Lucinda couldn't possibly see where I was pointing.

'Tía Nora?' Lucinda was slightly out of breath. 'I feel so sad inside. I never felt like this before, not even when Mami died.'

I slowed my pace slightly and struggled to push my mind away from the nervousness I felt. I remembered the first time I had said goodbye to my country so many years ago. Although I wasn't sure exactly what she meant, Beba's words had made all the difference to me then, and I knew they'd help Lucinda now.

'The sadness of leaving home is like nothing else you'll ever know,' I said slowly. 'And it comes in strong waves that can knock you off your feet when you think you're standing on solid ground. Everything can be just fine and then you'll hear the chords of a song or smell onions frying in olive oil and your heart will break into a million pieces all over again, just like that. You'll want to sell your soul to be home again or just to belong somewhere ... anywhere. That's when you have to hold on most to who you are. And don't ever give your true heart away, as broken and bleeding as it may be, because when you do, you've lost something you may never find again. Better to give away your ghost heart, and then you'll always know who you are.'

'What's my ghost heart, Tía Nora?'

'It's the heart inside you that can never be hurt by broken promises or the pain of too much longing. It goes right on beating, no matter what happens, because your ghost heart has many lives. But your real heart has only one precious life and you must always keep that one for yourself.'

The mild glow of dawn had begun to intensify on the horizon, causing both my hearts to beat erratically. There was no time to waste and I picked up my pace again. 'We'll talk more about this, but for now you must remember everything I told you.'

'I won't forget,' Lucinda said, running to keep up with me. 'Mami said I had the best memory of anyone she ever knew and that I'm rich because of it, because memories are like jewels that can never be stolen.'

We arrived at the dock flushed and slightly out of breath, but the man in the red shirt was nowhere to be found. I was certain this was the right place and I turned around several times in confusion and panic. My God, where was he?

'I hear something in the water,' Lucinda whispered.

I looked over the side of the dock to see José Gomez sitting in a small, battered-looking dingy that bobbed up and down in the receding tide. He watched us anxiously as he motioned for us to get in quickly. We carefully climbed down the steps and Lucinda dropped into the boat without any fuss. José didn't wait for introductions. He hurriedly untied the boat from the mooring and started to row away from the pier with strong thrusts of his arms and legs. Lucinda and I huddled together on the other side of the boat, with our small bag of provisions between us.

The sun had begun its glowing ascent in the sky, turning the water into pink and grey ribbons of light. All was still except for the rhythmic splash of the oars in the water. It was amazing how quickly José moved.

Satisfied that we were far enough out, he rested the oars on his thighs and began to instruct us between gasps of air. 'We're husband and wife, José and María Gomez. This is our niece and we're taking her fishing to celebrate her birthday.'

'My birthday isn't until July. And what about Tío Heremi?'

'No, honey, this is what we say if somebody stops to question us.'

José nudged the fishing rod resting at his feet towards me and resumed rowing. 'Better start fishing.'

I'd never been fishing in my life, but I knew better than to ask for instructions. I took hold of the rod, untied the line from its tip and dropped it into the water. I looked back towards the shore and gazed at the malecón. It too was pink and wavering in the morning light. The skyline cut a clear edge along the sky and the windows blinked with the reflection of the pale light. A few early risers were walking near the shore. Some were also launching boats closer to shore, with their fishing rods cast.

It was then that I saw her standing at the very end of the pier. She held one hand up to shield her eyes from the morning sun that peeked over the horizon. The light caught the brilliant white of her turban. It was Beba; she was waving to us frantically. Perhaps she had changed her mind and wanted to come with us after all.

'You have to turn back,' I said to José, standing up and rocking the boat. Lucinda gasped.

'What are you doing? Sit down before we tip over.'

'It's Beba. You have to turn back.'

'Is Beba here?' Lucinda asked.

'Who the hell is Beba? What are you talking about?' José stopped his frantic rowing and looked towards the pier. 'It'll take me almost an hour to get back there against the current and we'll miss the ship.'

The waves had grown taller and we could see Beba only at the top of the swells. She was still waving. Then she wasn't waving any more. And then she was gone.

José was drenched in sweat and his T-shirt clung to him. He observed Lucinda for a moment with curiosity. She was holding onto the side of the boat, keeping her eyes lifted towards the sky. He reached under the seat and threw a tattered life jacket to me. 'I brought this for the girl.'

I put the jacket on Lucinda quickly and fastened the buckles tight.

'What is this, Tía?'

'It's a special jacket that floats on the water, so if we fall in you'll float just like the best swimmer in the world.'

Lucinda smiled as she passed her hands along the coarse orange plastic ties. Then her eyes grew sombre. 'How about you and Mr Gomez?'

'We're good swimmers, honey. You don't have to worry about us.'

José began to row again, looking over his shoulder from time to time to see how far we'd gone. He told us that we needed to reach the far ship with the red stripe along the side. It was docked out further because of its immense size. The waves continued to roll higher and splash over the sides of the boat. Although José rowed harder than ever, it seemed that we were moving more slowly, and sometimes not at all.

'The current is crazy here,' José shouted over the roar of the wind and the ocean. 'It was working for us closer in, but now it's pulling us back.' He was exhausted from rowing and he grimaced with the pain of his effort.

'Can I help?' I shouted, but he didn't hear me. He just kept rowing with all his strength. At one point the swell got so high that one of the oars came completely out of the water and José almost lost it for lack of resistance. Lucinda held on to me tight. I could only imagine how frightening it must feel for her. All she could hear was a noise like thunder. Water splashed over the sides of the boat so that soon we were all drenched. Lucinda's feet slipped in her plastic sandals as she braced herself against the lurching movement of our small craft. The only comfort was the sight of the huge white ship with the red stripe along the side. Once we got on we'd be safe and easily hidden. Pepe had assured me that those ships were never searched, because government agents were bribed to look the other way. 'A lot of money for passage goes towards the bribe,' he'd said.

'Our ship is very close, honey,' I said to Lucinda, who nodded her head against my chest.

After another rolling wave had completely obscured our sight of the white ship, José instructed us to lean against the waves. We followed his directions and the boat stabilized significantly, and José rowed with renewed energy. I looked behind us. The malecón was still visible in the morning sun, which had fully revealed itself in a cloudless sky. We were too far away to see people on the shore and it was impossible to know if Beba was still watching us. I felt safer believing that she was, and I told Lucinda that Beba was there praying for us and making sure we were safe.

We'd been on the water for well over an hour, and the ship was close enough for me to make out the small portholes just above the painted red line. Perhaps one of those portholes would be our quarters for the five-hour trip to Jamaica. We'd be stashed in there with a load of bananas or raw sugar. It suddenly occurred to me that I didn't know whether or not José was escaping as well. Last night I figured he was taking a cut of the money in exchange for getting us to the ship, but he seemed to be interested in more than money. He was like a man possessed.

'Are you coming with us?' I asked during a brief instant when he rested his arms.

'Of course,' he replied. 'No matter what happens, I'm getting out.'

I didn't bother to ask what he meant, because he was pumping his arms and legs with amazing concentration and we were making significant progress again. I was glad to know he'd be joining us. We could continue to present ourselves as husband and wife, which would keep any inappropriate attention from the crew at bay. I'd mention this to José before we boarded the ship. The waves had calmed down now and he was rowing with greater ease, but I certainly couldn't bother him with questions, even though one loomed large and heavy in my mind: how were we going to board the ship?

As we approached, its enormity was more apparent than ever; our little boat was barely visible next to it. There was certainly no door or hatch so far below through which we might enter, and the portholes were several storeys above water level. The only way would be to pull us up by some sort of rope. I shivered at the thought of it – not for me, but for Lucinda, who was already shaken enough.

'There should be someone watching out for us on this side,' José said, looking up at the giant towering above us.

'Do you think they can see us?' I asked.

My question was answered when a thin rope was flung over the side of the ship. Far too thin, it seemed, to support even the weight of a small dog. But when it got closer to us we could see that the rope was actually quite sturdy. The problem was how to grab hold of it without hitting the side of the ship. The waves, although calmer now, still had the strength to slam us against it if we weren't careful, and it was obvious that our weathered dingy couldn't take much abuse. If the waters had been calmer it would have been an easy matter to swim out for the rope and bring it to the dingy, but I'd never swum in such water and I didn't want José to leave us alone in the dingy.

Although we hadn't spoken since the appearance of the rope, I was sure José's hesitation stemmed from the same concern. He held the dripping oars still over the water as we bobbed and rolled closer and then further from the ship with every passing wave.

'I can hear waves hitting the metal ship, Tía. It is very close.'

'It's right next to us, sweetheart. They'll pull us up as soon as they can.'

José rowed us in closer still. We were only a yard or so from reaching the rope, and every time the waves threatened to push us in too far, José held an oar out to keep us at a comfortable, if not stable, distance. He motioned for me to take hold of the rope while he held out the oar. Lucinda would be first. I tied the rope securely around her waist and instructed her to hold onto it as tight as she could. She nodded and blinked the water spraying up from the waves out of her eyes.

'They'll pull you up a very long way, but I'll be right below you.'

Lucinda took hold of the rope with both hands and waited. José pulled on the rope hard two times and it started to pull up, slowly at first, until Lucinda's feet were dangling off the ground. Her plastic shoes fell off, one falling into the boat and the other into the ocean, floating off on the waves before I had a chance to make a grab for it. I was afraid this might disorientate Lucinda and that she'd fidget and the rope would loosen, but she didn't move. Her hands gripped the rope and her little face pressed against it. She swayed to and fro over our heads as she inched higher and higher still, three storeys up, almost to the portholes. We were craning our heads as she went, but José was vigilant with the oar, although from time to time I thought he might get thrown off the dingy because of the force he had to withstand.

Lucinda was up to the portholes now, too far away to hear my voice. I could only imagine the fear she felt, and I began to shiver and pray.

'They've stopped,' José said.

Lucinda was still dangling, but not moving up or down. Then she started to move slowly down, and then up again, before she jerked to a stop. The rope shifted up her waist so that it was hidden by the life jacket. Suddenly she started to move down very rapidly. The rope was like a wild, vibrating snake and I realized she was freefalling. Paralysed, I watched her feet swinging wildly as she screamed, then disappeared into the waves about fifty yards from the boat.

I dived into the water and began to swim towards where I'd seen Lucinda fall. The waves rolled over me and I was barely able to gasp for air, such was the force of the water pushing me down and then up again. I caught sight of Lucinda's head bobbing beyond the crest of the next wave, her eyes closed and her chin resting on her life jacket, but I was unable to find the rhythm that would propel me to her. That familiar heaviness that I knew was brought on by my own fear was creeping into my limbs, making it almost impossible for me to stay above water, let alone swim. 'Fear doesn't float,' Abuelo always told us during our lessons. 'It sinks straight to the bottom every time. But courage,' he said, his eyes shining, 'not only floats, it flies.'

Suddenly, Abuelo was swimming alongside me, urging me on. 'I'm proud of you, Norita,' he said. 'You jumped in without thinking about it and now you will know what I have always known.' I felt his strength surging through my muscles and I became as sleek as a dolphin, my legs pumping like pistons and my lungs filled with pure oxygen. I swam for my Lucinda more surely than I had ever done anything in my life, and when I reached her I pulled her towards me by the strap of her jacket. She was breathing, thank God she was breathing, and I held her to me while José brought the boat close enough for us to get in. He pulled Lucinda in first, and then I followed, collapsing in a heap onto the floor of the boat.

Exhaustion took hold of me and everything became as dark and silent as a dreamless sleep, but not before I heard Abuelo whispering, 'You are an excellent swimmer, Norita.'

35

JOSÉ WAS FISHING AGAINST THE BACKDROP OF A PERFECT
blue sky. A pair of small bare feet were just below him,
the toes wiggling like little crabs peeking out of their
shells. I turned with a start and my head exploded
with pain. I settled back on my elbow and turned more
slowly.

Lucinda lay next to me and she was breathing. I saw
her little chest rise and fall, and it wasn't the movement of the boat because the boat was hardly moving.
It was very still. We were both completely dry and
Lucinda's corkscrew curls shot out from her lovely
face like fireworks.

I placed my hand lightly on her cheek. Her eyes
fluttered and rolled as if in a dream, and then she
smiled. 'I can see the light, Tía Nora, and it's so
beautiful.'

José heard us talking and turned only halfway
around to look at us, but said nothing. He caught two
fish one right after the other and threw them onto the
small deck between us. They flapped for a short while
as their lives quickly evaporated in the hot sun.
Apparently convinced that he wouldn't catch any
more, he gutted and skinned the fish and promptly
handed us each roughly cut strips of raw fish flesh. He
cut the rest into even thin strips and laid them out on

the narrow wooden seat to dry. He did this all without speaking or looking at us.

I encouraged Lucinda to take the warm white flesh into her mouth and chew it quickly before swallowing. It was a tasteless mass of hard jelly going down my throat, and I realized then how thirsty I was and that my shoulders ached when I sat up higher on my elbows to see over the side of the dinghy. I don't know exactly what I was expecting to find. Perhaps the Havana skyline sitting up on the Caribbean like a rusty crown, a few other fishing boats, Beba waiting for us on the pier with her hands on her hips because she had other business to get to and had been waiting long enough. It was a shock to see the vast blue ocean spreading out in all directions. I turned to where I thought Cuba should be, ignoring the ripping pain that shot through my shoulders, but there was nothing but the thin line of the horizon, unwavering and distant, circling us like an enormous ghostly ring.

'Where are we?' The air was so humid and thick that it was almost possible to drink from it.

José was chewing on fish as he carefully rewound the fishing line. 'On our way to freedom . . . Maria.' He smiled, revealing small, even teeth, teeth that had been well cared for. 'My mother's name was Maria. Who's wasn't?' He chuckled.

'Freedom,' Lucinda murmured as she obediently chewed and swallowed her fish.

José informed us that there must have been government agents aboard the ship. After Lucinda was dropped into the water, the rope had been quickly cut. He was keeping an eye on the two of us in the water while watching out for another rope, but it never came.

'If I hadn't been so tired from rowing earlier, I would've reached you sooner,' he said before stuffing his mouth with more raw fish. 'You were both so tired, I just let you sleep.'

'Why didn't you row to shore?' I asked.

'I told you I was getting out no matter what. Today was my last day on that island.'

'What about water and provisions?'

'I brought water and citrus fruits. With what you brought, I figure we have enough for two or three days if we're careful.'

I felt a terrible jolt of fear as I remembered hearing about Cubans who'd spent many more days than that in the channel because of shifting currents and storms. Many had drowned or died of dehydration before reaching freedom. I said this to José, who cast a wary eye towards Lucinda. 'That won't happen to us. I haven't come this far to lose it all now.'

José passed me a Styrofoam cup one third full of water. This was to be mine and Lucinda's ration of water for the morning. We'd have another at midday and another in the evening. I noticed that José poured his ration out exactly as he had ours.

'Stay under the shade,' he instructed, and I became aware of the makeshift cover over our heads, made out of an old blanket strung over half the boat and held up with the oars.

'Don't we need those for steering or something?'

'The current will take us where we need to go. Now get some rest.'

'How about you?'

José leaned back on the seat and stretched out his legs between Lucinda and me. He pushed his wide-brimmed straw hat over his face and crossed his arms. He muttered something under his hat, then fell asleep.

'I won,' Alicia says.

There's a contest to see who can find the most perfect shell. Abuelo always makes up games like these when he wants to take a nap or relax and not deal with our continual demands that he play with us in the water. Alicia holds up her palm-sized prize,

356

which swirls with delicate pinks and yellows from base to tip. It is indeed perfect.

I consider my own growing pile of shells. There are some interesting ones – even a blue oyster shell that I've never seen before, but it's chipped in several places. It'll be hard to find one that compares to Alicia's. She's standing over me now and I see her pink toes wriggling in the sand, digging in against the gentle current that scoots her along the edge. She holds the shell down to my face so I can get a closer look. It is truly spectacular. What looks like yellow from a distance is really fine threads of gold, and the surface is polished and smooth like the china cups for show in Mami's dining room. This is no mere shell, but a work of art.

'I want you to have it,' she says and drops it down on the sand before I have a chance to break its fall. I hold my breath and pick it up. Thankfully, it hasn't been damaged.

'This is the most beautiful shell in the world. You should keep it for yourself.'

'I want you to have it, Nora. I want you to sleep with it under your pillow every night and think of me.'

'It'll break if I do that.'

'It won't break, silly.' She snatches it out of my hand and dances along the shore, tossing it in the air, turning and catching it at once. I chase after her and try to catch the shell while it's still in the air, but it eludes me. Alicia is much quicker and she's able to jump much higher, and every time she catches the shell she laughs like a wind chime. Sometimes she catches it with just one finger and this delights her even more. Skipping in the water, she tosses it higher every time, so high that it pricks the sun with its swirling tip and returns to earth glowing even more than before.

I'm very upset now. She's jumped and played with my shell long enough, and I know that it's only a matter of time before she breaks it. I try my hardest, and jump with all my might, catching the shell mid-air with both hands. I hold it to my heart, but when I'm back on the sand I realize that I've crushed it. I watch the pieces, tiny bits of gold and rose-coloured loveliness, float out to sea. I look up to apologize to my cousin, but she is gone, and not even her footprints remain on the sand.

I awoke this time to an amazing panorama of stars, a dome of blinking lights against a midnight-blue sky, and a familiar sound against the stillness of the night. José was rowing differently this time, easing into each stroke with the gentle eloquence of a dancer. His refined features caught the fragile light of the stars, making him appear as though he were outlined by a fine dusting of iridescent powder. Lucinda was already awake and sitting up next to me. Her hand was on my arm and probably had been for hours, because I didn't notice it until I sat up myself and felt the cold emptiness where it had been. She reached for me and I took her hand quickly into my own.

Without a word, she passed me an orange, and I saw the broken pieces of orange peel in a neat pile next to her. I was thirsty and hungry, and the warm, sweet juice exploded in my mouth like little pricks of acid pain. I watched José as I ate. He appeared relaxed and quite satisfied with the progress we were making.

'We couldn't ask for better weather,' he confirmed. 'And it's better to row at night. I don't perspire as much. Anyway, I only need to row until we get back in the current that takes us towards the straights. Many cargo ships pass that way and one is bound to find us.'

José explained that he'd been studying the tides for months, just in case he needed to leave the island on his own. If we stayed with the proper current we'd keep on track towards freedom with very little difficulty. If we strayed too far, we could drift indefinitely and not be found for weeks, if ever. What was left of us, anyway. Of course, this didn't bother José at all. He spoke of the possibility of perishing without so much as a blink or a shrug. It was a possibility he considered with the same cold analysis he'd applied to his study of the tides.

He pulled the oars into the boat and I felt the pull of the tide moving us along like an invisible hand beneath the sea. The water was slick as glass and even reflected the stars, making it appear that our little boat was afloat in a vast universe of stars above and below us.

'Tía Nora?'

'Yes, Lucinda?'

'Mr Gomez knew my Papi in jail.'

José nodded. 'She looked familiar to me the moment I saw her on the pier. Her eyes are just like her father's. But I didn't put it together until she mentioned her mother's name. For almost three years, all Tony ever talked about was Alicia. I asked myself if any woman could be so many things ... so beautiful and clever and strong. I think I fell in love with her myself.'

'She was all those things,' I said, sitting up in amazement at the coincidence. 'And you're in good company. We all loved her.'

I was eager to hear his story, and, as he rowed, José told me what he'd begun to tell Lucinda. He was trained as a journalist, had travelled extensively in Europe and South America, and had been a loyal revolutionary, writing fervent articles supporting Castro's position as a socialist in the world. These articles had propelled him into the upper echelons of the government. His final and most prestigious assignment was as a television reporter who had the honour of regularly interviewing Castro on television. He knew what questions to ask so that his leader appeared well informed and balanced, and yet he asked them with the pointed indifference of a ruthless reporter in search of the truth.

'The closer I got to the inner circle, the more aware I became of the glaring disparities between their way of life and that of ordinary citizens. After a tiring day of endless speeches about the need to make sacrifices for one's country and about the honour of an empty belly, the powerful elite would retire to a life of royalty. Their homes are sumptuous and they dine on imported foods and wines of every kind. They laze over long elaborate meals as they discuss domestic and international concerns, while their mistresses serve them.

'Of course, I ate these beautiful meals myself and laughed along and offered my sage and objective opinion when I could. For a while, I fooled even myself into thinking I was beyond the desperation that motivates men and women to sell their bodies on our streets. It's the same for everyone. Some people sell their bodies and others sell their souls.

'Soon I came to see that my place in the inner circle was no different than the place of every Cuban who sits down to a meagre bowl of rice and beans, with a bit of meat if they're lucky. The promise of a sandwich is enough to entice them to wave flags as if their lives depend on it. My mother attends communist rallies whenever she can, not because she believes the government is doing right or wrong any more, but because she's tired of rice and beans and wouldn't mind tasting a little meat and fresh bread for a change. It wasn't a sandwich I was selling my mind and spirit for, but a seven-course meal complete with cigars at the end.'

José folded his thick forearms and shook his head slowly. 'I began to hate myself. Every time I smiled and agreed, it felt as though I was swallowing my own bile. I turned down dinner invitations and came to know other writers who weren't afraid of the truth. They were using their writings to educate people and to light a fire under those shackled by the day-to-day challenge of survival. We felt we'd become like Castro's poorly kept pets, chained to the fence out back and fed on the crumbs from the master's table.

'Together we wanted to urinate and defecate all over the polished floors and fine carpets of Castro's new hotels, which were popping up along the beaches. We wanted to bark and howl like wolves when he insulted the people with his droning, meaningless spectacles of absolute and thoughtless power. We did this by writing articles, brief and to the point. Just as I'd misled the people with my writings before, now I intended to tell them the truth.

'They took some of us from our houses at night, and others boldly by daylight. Tony was in the cell next to mine. He was a man of amazing strength, a natural leader, and because of that I knew they'd never let him out. He talked to me when I decided to take my own life before Castro took it from me. But Tony spoke of God, and of what we'd do when we got out of prison and how we had to keep ourselves strong. I used to tease him when he talked like this and ask him what kind of a revolutionary believes in God. Tony always said that even in the early days he was only a revolutionary from the neck up. From the neck down he'd always been a good Catholic boy.' José shuddered in the warm air and looked out at the open sea all around. 'I owe him my life.'

Lucinda's small voice came from the far corner of the boat. 'Did Papi miss us, Mr Gomez?'

'Every day he told me how much he missed you and your mother. He'd been planning to escape since the day he was imprisoned. Nobody knew it except for me, and he persuaded me to join him. Our plan was to wait until we were assigned to work near an area of dense vegetation where we could slip away and get lost in the jungle. The guards were disorganized and lazy, and we had a good chance if they didn't notice our absence for an hour or more. It was almost a year before the perfect opportunity came. We were to repair a road up in Matanzas, and Tony said he knew the area well. The group of men assigned was large, there were well over a hundred of us, and the road bordered the jungle.

'We didn't have time to think about it too much. When they removed the chains so we could climb down from the back of the truck without falling over each other, I took my place in line and Tony motioned I should go first. I stepped back into a ditch in the road. The guard assigned to our detail was the laziest of all. I was sure I'd be able to make it into the trees before he noticed I was gone, but I wasn't so lucky. He saw me and was raising his gun to shoot when Tony was on top of him in an instant. I ran as fast as I could into the jungle. I ran for hours. I hid inside the hollow of a tree for three days and prayed like I'd never prayed before. Then I hitched a ride into Havana and found some friends who took me in. For two years I've been hiding.'

'What happened to Papi?'

'Any aggression towards a guard is punishable by swift execution.' José paused and considered his audience before speaking more gently. 'I have no doubt your Papi met his death with honour and that his last thoughts were of you and your Mami.'

Lucinda nodded, and her sweet child's voice spoke with a depth of knowing appropriate to a much older and wiser person. 'Mami always said Papi would find a way to take care of us. And now you're here to take care of Tía Nora and me, because Papi can't be.'

'You better believe I'll take care of you. And you'll live in freedom just like your Papi wanted you to,' José said, clearly moved.

As if to toast his resolution, José poured out an even ration of water for the three of us. I sipped mine tentatively as if it were the finest champagne. I felt euphoric. Was it the expanse of stars over our heads?

Was it the sugar in the orange still dancing on my tongue? I had no doubt we'd make it to freedom with little difficulty. We were miles from the Cuban shore by now. Beba would have called Jeremy and he would be expecting us home. He'd be wondering why I hadn't called, but within a day or two I'd be phoning from somewhere in Miami to tell him that we were safe and that we loved him so very much.

Lucinda was dozing, her head resting on her arm. It was slightly chilly, and I pulled the blanket that had shielded us from the sun in the day up over her shoulders. Would Jeremy have remembered to prepare her room? How wonderful it would be to lie safe in his arms, knowing that Lucinda was safe and sound with us in her own little room. It would be a yellow room, the colour of the sun. I'd find her a good school right away and the family would fall in love with her instantly, as everybody always did. Of course, we'd have to adopt her as soon as possible.

José wasn't sleepy and his eyes shone as they searched the waters around us. He was watching out for huge ships and tankers, which could move silently and at speed through the water. The same ships that could rescue us in the day might destroy us by night.

'What's your real name?' I asked him after a long silence.

'Manuel Alarcon. And you?'

'Nora Garcia-McLaughlin.'

'Ah, married to an American, are you?'

I nodded and smiled at the thought of Jeremy – Tío Heremi, as Lucinda called him. 'He's a good man. I love him very much.'

'He'll be waiting for you, then.'

'Yes.' I thought of Jeremy's easy smile and kind hazel eyes. Even after we'd been married all these years, I couldn't think about him too long without feeling a hot blush spread all over me.

Manuel asked no further questions. He was a

practical and focused man, and he scanned the ocean with a disciplined eye as he wound and unwound the fishing line around his finger.

'Are you married?' I asked.

'No,' he answered, without removing his eyes from the sea.

'Why not?'

He pressed his lips, the first sign of anxiety I'd seen cross his face. 'Perhaps one day I'll have the time and the energy to find a wife.'

'Do you want her to be Cuban?'

'I hadn't thought about it.' And it didn't seem that he wanted to think of it now. 'I always imagined she would be, but right now I'd settle for an American wife.'

We talked for some time; at least, I did most of the talking. I told him of Alicia – how we'd grown up together and the promise I'd made to her before she died. We watched the stars rotate slowly through the night and I told him about how difficult it was to leave Cuba, and of my early struggles in the United States and with the American way of life. He agreed with me that the romance of Cuba was hard to resist, but that it had died for all Cubans, even those who had remained in their homeland. Now all we had were memories and stories to keep the romance alive, and that would have to be enough.

We talked, with long pauses in between, until the faint and delicate light of morning began to glow upon the horizon. 'This is the direction we must go,' Manuel said. 'Towards the rising sun. We're doing well.'

He repositioned the oars with the blanket draped over them, as I dozed with Lucinda next to me in the rising sun. How could I feel so relaxed and positive about my life when we were out in the middle of the ocean with only a couple of days' worth of water and just a little more food? Was I going crazy? And then I realized that it was probably the relief of having escaped, and knowing that no matter what happened now, nobody was chasing us or trying to take Lucinda away. Perhaps death was just as close as the creaking boards beneath us, but we were free and it was a beautiful feeling.

I told Manuel this, and he stopped his work for an instant and stood up carefully in the dinghy so as not to rock it. Cupping his hands around his mouth, he yelled into the fresh morning air: 'One day Cuba will be free and returned to the people who love her most, and Castro's lies will choke him like a noose around his neck!'

I stood up next to him: 'And when they bury him in the ground, we'll dance on his grave!'

Lucinda awoke and yelled above us both, catching us unawares: 'He's a son of a bitch!'

We laughed so hard that the boat rocked and we almost lost the oars. Then we observed the silent, undulating sea, unperturbed by our declarations.

'I guess you're right,' Manuel said. 'No matter what happens now, we're free.'

36

MANUEL MANAGED TO CATCH SEVERAL MORE FISH DURING
the next two days and the flesh dried quickly in the
hot sun, so we had plenty of food; but we were down
to three oranges and our fresh water was running low.
We decided to reduce the ration to only a quarter of a
cup three times a day. If another day passed without
spotting a ship, we'd drink only twice a day. It wasn't
that we hadn't seen any ships, because we had; but
they were too far away to see our little dinghy, which,
with the glare of sun on the water, probably looked
just like another piece of driftwood. If they'd been
looking for us it might have been different, but they
weren't, and we grew hoarse from yelling at these
metal giants and weary from waving our arms when
they passed.

We made a flag from the blanket and one of the oars
when the last ship came into view, but as we began to
wave it the blanket came loose and fell into the sea.
We spent most of the time the ship was in view fishing
it back out of the water. This wasn't just our flag, but
our cover at night and our sunshade in the day. It was
hard to imagine surviving without it. But Manuel
was not discouraged. He was certain that before long
another ship would pass by and this time we'd secure
our flag to avoid a similar accident.

On the third day, not even one ship was sighted and an ominous wave of desperation hit us all. Manuel didn't say it, but I knew he feared that we'd missed the channel where most of the ships passed. We began to worry that we were off course and drifting aimlessly. Every horrible outcome took shape in our minds, and we hardly spoke to each other for the next day and a half. The only things that were exchanged between us were pieces of dried fish and meagre cups of water. Manuel had further reduced the rations, so we were barely able to moisten our lips. I noticed that he refused to take any water during the last round, and he'd suffered severe sunburn on his arms and neck because there wasn't room for him under the blanket.

Without thinking about it, I stripped off my shirt so he could wrap it around his neck and face. I was past any self-consciousness I would normally have felt. I was past worrying about anything but survival.

The only thing that hadn't turned on us was the weather. The sea remained mild by day and night. Occasional swells gradually lifted our little boat before bringing us down, like a mother gently placing her babe in its crib to sleep. One day, when the sea was the stillest it had ever been and the only thing moving was the sweat rolling down my torso, I took off my shorts and slipped into the water. The ocean was cool and still and marvellous. I was smiling and refreshed when Manuel helped me back into the boat, but he was angry, afraid even.

'You shouldn't have gone in. There are sharks all over these waters.'

'I didn't see any sharks.'

'They see you.'

I filled an empty bottle and rinsed Lucinda's hair and the rest of her with the cool water. She closed her eyes and smiled. She'd stopped asking about the United States and Tío Heremi, but now she asked if it was true that everyone in the United States had hot water for a bath. I assured her everyone did, and that most people took showers every day, and sometimes more if they felt like it.

Manuel had stopped rowing by day or night and we drifted with the tides. Most of the time he didn't answer if we asked him a question, unless it required only a one-word response.

'Would you like a piece of fish?'

'No.'

'Do you think we're still in the right current?'

'Yes.'

'Do you want me to pour some water over you to cool you off?'

'No.'

'Do your shoulders hurt?'

'No.'

'Will it be long now?'

'No.'

I started to whisper to Lucinda without realizing it, because I had the impression that speaking in a normal tone of voice was beginning to irritate Manuel. Sometimes he grimaced in pain while he slept. At other times he laughed out loud. He continued to refuse water and said that he was no longer thirsty. There was no arguing with him.

That night I put two rations (the two that he had refused) in the cup that was already brown and stained. He slept with his mouth open and snored as loudly as a bear. Ever so slowly, I poured a thin stream of water in a little at a time, so that he couldn't possibly choke. His mouth was hot and dry and absorbed the water immediately. Then I took the last orange and split it between Lucinda and myself, giving most of it to Lucinda, who ate it without a word. Except for one dried fish, she knew as well as I did that this was the last food we had. We both knew Manuel would probably not fish again. In the last two days, he'd changed radically from a sober, self-assured man into a petulant, moody little boy. And there was a dryness creeping into his eyes, causing him to look rather like a lizard; I suspected I looked very much the same. Nevertheless, I wished I'd paid better attention to how he'd fished on that first day. What had he used for bait? How did he prepare the hook? He wouldn't answer these questions in his present mood.

I took the fishing rod that lay next to his sleeping form and inspected it closely. The only thing we had for bait was our last remaining food source. Would a piece of dry fish attract anything? I consulted with Lucinda in hushed whispers and she agreed that it was worth a try. I took a fairly large piece of dried fish from the bag behind the seat and pierced it with the hook. Slowly and carefully, I lowered it into the water as I'd seen Manuel do that first day. I waited with my back against the opposite side of the boat.

Manuel woke up an hour or so into my fishing. He stared at me with glassy eyes, as though he couldn't be sure if he was dreaming. It seemed that the water I'd poured into his mouth had revived him a bit. That and the cool night air. Lucinda could hear that he was awake; I knew by the way she repositioned her body slightly to face him.

His voice was hoarse. 'What did you use for bait?'

'A piece of dry fish. That's all that's left.'

'I'm sorry. I have no strength to help you.' He lay back down, his eyes gaping open at the darkening sky. 'I believe I may have failed you, Nora. You and Lucinda.'

I moved the rod back and forth and up and down, as I'd seen him do before. The bait was supposed to look lively. Our dried piece of fish should be looking spry and happy to be alive in the tropical sea if another bigger fish was ever going to go for it.

'I know Tony would forgive me because he was that kind of man,' he went on with a droning voice. I realized that he didn't care if anyone answered him or

369

not, he just needed to hear himself talk, but I didn't want Lucinda to hear his fatalism. She had buried her head in her knees for most of the day and had hardly spoken a word. Her head was up now and she was listening intently, just when I would've wanted her to be asleep.

'Don't talk like that, Manuel. It's not over yet,' I said.

'Tony always said the same thing. He'd always talk me out of these hopeless moments. There was something about the way he talked that always made me listen. I used to tell him that he'd make an excellent preacher when he got out.'

'Tony would want you to be strong and not lose hope. If you can't do it for yourself, do it for his daughter. She needs you, Manuel, we both do.'

'I know, but it should've been Tony here, not me. I can take fair knowledge of that to my grave.'

I jerked hard on the rod. 'Lucinda can hear you.'

'She might as well know the truth,' he droned on. 'I've always heard that before a person dies, there's a certain premonition, a sense that it's coming. If that's true, then—'

'Shut up! Do you understand me?' I hit the rod hard against the side of the boat, making a sharp flat noise that would go nowhere in the thick humid air. We might as well have been in a padded cell. Manuel was silent and turned over slowly onto his side. I was worried that I had made him angry, and I didn't know what he was capable of in a rage. What if he went insane? Would I have the strength and the will to push him overboard if he threatened Lucinda's and my safety?

He crossed his ankles and rolled up into a foetal position under the seat. I saw him watching us in the moonlight and caught the glint of one eyeball. It closed when I looked and opened when I turned back to my fishing. I could pretend I hadn't noticed he was staring at me and hope he'd stop, but I couldn't resist the temptation of turning to look, because he reminded me of a rat waiting underneath a cupboard for the right moment to make his move, whatever that move might be.

'There's something in the water, Tía.' Lucinda's voice caused me to jump and almost lose the fishing rod. 'I hear it, it's swimming all around us.'

I pulled in the rod and sat up straight to look about. The water was still calm and rolling in gentle swirls, but I saw nothing, only a sliver of moonlight, and the cloud cover almost obliterated that.

Lucinda sat up straight as well, her expression electrified, almost twitching with concentration. 'There it is again.'

'I don't hear anything, honey. Maybe it's your imagination.' But just as I said this I heard a soft rap on the bottom of the boat, quickly followed by another.

'They're everywhere,' Lucinda said, turning her head from side to side as if she were equipped with some kind of radar. I stared into the ocean once again, and this time I saw them. There were shapes in the water that rose and fell in the shadows. They could be anything I wanted them to be: the Miami skyline, a huge aircraft carrier, or a little pleasure craft close enough to touch with my fishing rod.

Manuel inched out from under the seat and sat in the middle of the boat. 'They're sharks,' he said drily.

Suddenly I could see the dark silhouettes of razor-sharp fins rising and falling in the sea, circling us, gliding beneath us in strange and fantastic formations. I could see them perfectly now. If I peered more closely I'd be able to look into their black and barren eyes, searching for food in the night. There were several more sharp blows under the boat. The sharks were powerful and focused.

'Why are there so many?'

Manuel was sitting up now and holding onto his knees, as Lucinda had done for most of the day. 'They must be feeding.' More knocks came rapidly this time. It sounded as though a very large man was punching the bottom of our boat with his bare fists. The boat would not handle much more of such abuse.

'Why do they keep hitting the boat, Tía?'

'I don't know. I'm sure they'll stop soon.'

'Because they think we're food and they won't stop until they're convinced we're not – or until we are,' Manuel said.

'We have to do something, Manuel, please,' I pleaded.

At that moment, one of the larger sharks rammed the side of the boat, propelling it towards a gathering of fins several feet ahead of us. They had their strategy for the kill, and their bodies near the surface of the water were like sleek submarines parked all around us. I wondered if these sharks had already acquired a taste for human flesh. How many rafts had been overturned by sharks such as these?

Manuel looked about with simple curiosity. 'There's nothing we can do except hope that something more appetizing comes along. But I don't think that's likely.'

I grabbed the oars, which had lain dormant for almost three days. I'd never handled them and I wasn't sure what to do now, but I assumed the rowing position Manuel had done before and directed Lucinda to sit away from me. The oars were heavy and awkward, but slowly I began to row. The blows continued on both sides of the boat. Manuel was stoical and unflinching, even when one of the blows was strong enough to cause the frame to splinter. Lucinda screamed and I would have done too if all my energy had not been concentrated on rowing. The oars hit the sharks' backs on several occasions, backs as solid as steel. They were trying to bite at them, hoping that someone had been foolish enough to dangle arms and legs over the sides.

'Forget it, you can't row fast enough,' Manuel said.

'They aren't feeding on anything else. They want us.'

The boat would splinter into nothing. I knew it was just a matter of time. I pulled in the oars and stood up to look around. Lucinda held onto my legs and sobbed, crying out for her mother. The blows came more rapidly and evenly now. It was as if the sharks were lining up to demolish the boat like a well-trained regiment of soldiers. I took one of the oars and began to whack the sharks when I saw their fins approaching the boat. I remembered reading somewhere that sharks were particularly sensitive on their noses, so these were what I aimed for. With what strength I had left, I brought the oar down on their backs over and over again as I screamed at the top of my lungs for God and the saints to help us. I hurled blood-curdling screams into the night to give me strength to scare away the enemy, the evil spirits and death itself. Death by drowning or dehydration I could imagine if I had to, but please God, not to be eaten alive by sharks, anything but that. As I shouted, I whacked them on their tails and their backs and their noses. I slapped the water on both sides with a surging rhythm as though possessed by the spirit of the jungle, the black spirit that conquers all.

It was then that the sea rose up in all directions, and we became covered in blood and water and the saliva of hungry sharks. Suddenly, there was complete and utter silence. Only the slipping sound of the sea and the soft murmuring of the breeze. I scanned the ocean with my oar still raised, then brought it down slowly. All the sharks had gone. Not a fin could be seen anywhere.

I looked about the boat. Lucinda was still crouching down, holding onto my legs. Manuel was back under the seat. I wasted no time and took up the oars once again, rowing until fire was burning through my back and arms, until the agony in my muscles overcame my fear of a repulsive and horrible death.

I collapsed onto the floor of the boat and turned to see if Manuel was still watching me like a little rat. I wanted him to be, so I could gloat and say I told you so, and why didn't you help me save our lives? He wasn't there. I turned my head the other way, but Manuel was nowhere in the boat. Manuel was gone.

I took hold of Lucinda by the shoulders and shook her. 'Where is Manuel, Lucinda? My God, where is he?'

In my frenzy to get away, I hadn't noticed that Lucinda was crying and pulling at her corkscrew curls so hard that there were chunks of hair in her fists.

'He whispered in my ear that freedom is for the living,' she said between sobs. 'Then he left and everything was still.'

37

I BEGAN TO UNDERSTAND HOW TIME IS MEASURED differently in different situations. In the normal world, Manuel's sacrifice would've ground into our psyches for weeks and months before we could have focused normally on the matter of living. On the boat, we were making our next plan for survival in less than an hour.

By the time the sun had risen, it was as if Manuel's death had occurred a couple of years ago and not a few hours before. One hour of survival was worth months in real time, and we had to make every second count or we would be lost. We had no water or food, and by midday our mouths were sticky as we huddled under the blanket, no longer bothering to tent it over the oars.

In the delirium of heat, my mind turned constantly to Jeremy. He was drinking American coffee at the kitchen table. Or was it dinnertime? He didn't cook much. Maybe Mami had made him his favourite chicken stew and packed it for him in layers of plastic, because she didn't trust the Tupperware alone. He's sleeping in our bed and reaching for me in his sleep. He could be sleeping with somebody else by now, because he doesn't think I'm ever coming back. He thinks my Cuban life swallowed me up whole.

Nobody knows we're out here. We could be drifting in the Atlantic. But the Atlantic waters would be dark and rough, whereas these waters remain a royal blue at their deepest and sometimes fade into swirls of turquoise.

Lucinda, your eyes are the colour of the sea. When you open them and turn to me, it's as if your eyes are giant round windows to the sea. I should be telling you this, but I can't open my mouth, it is so dry. Did I tell you that Jeremy brings me coffee in the morning? He knows I like it with a little sugar and cream, and he knows I have a favourite cup. He'll probably bring you coffee in the morning, too. Would you like that? You don't answer me, but that's because you're conserving your energy, just like I am.

Isn't if funny how we don't sleep or wake? We're asleep and awake at the same time. But I know when I'm more asleep than awake, because for an instant I'm not thirsty any more. I'm dreaming of swimming in drinking water. I'm pouring soft drinks over ice cubes that crack and swish in the glass like maracas. There is a strong gush of water pouring out of my mouth. It's so powerful I can't stop it. It pushes out my teeth and hurts my throat if I try to swallow against it. This is worse than the constant thirst I can understand and fight against with my mind. I cannot take this any more. I hope you don't feel this, I hope to God you don't.

Dark clouds gather as the sun sets. Another day has passed like a universe of time forgotten. The waves deepen and peak in their shadows, and a greyish gloom surrounds us when we come out from under the blanket. I feel a raindrop on my nose and then another. Tiny droplets perch on Lucinda's thick eyelashes, causing her to blink curiously. The torrent of rain comes all at once. I scoop the water up with Manuel's shoes and direct Lucinda to drink from the bottom of the boat. I do the same. Thank God we haven't lost our empty water bottles – I am able to fill one halfway before the rain stops, before Lucinda vomits the water she'd gulped in a frenzy. I vomit too. We'd been drinking water thick with almost a week's filth from our bodies. We've lost all the water we drank and maybe more, but it has absorbed into our skin and washed off the hazy salt film. Our blanket is wet and so are we, but we sleep deeper than a trance that night. We sip sweet water from the bottle a little at a time and watch the stars circle above us.

Lucinda, did I tell you about the time your mother and I ran away from home? She wanted to rescue me from becoming a nun. That's the last time I remember seeing stars this beautiful. We were certain we'd have much more fun as showgirls. The showgirl idea was your mother's. In fact, most of the ideas were hers, but she was always looking out for me. She was very brave and I always wished I could be more like her. She was the most beautiful and smartest girl I ever knew. When she walked down the street, every eye was on her, every word of praise, every second glance. She walked with eyes forward, back straight, neither proud nor ashamed, just happy to be who she was and where she was.

Lucinda, listen to me. If Jeremy doesn't want me any more, will you be happy living just with me? There's a chance, a big chance, that he won't, you see. Yes, he loves me, he just doesn't understand that I had to go back. I couldn't leave you and now we may both die here together. I'm not afraid to die, Lucinda. Your Mami died so easily in my arms that afternoon on the beach. She took a deep breath that quivered just a little and then she just died as beautifully as she'd lived. I miss her so much.

Take my hand, Lucinda. I want you to hold this. It's the candle your Mami left for me. I brought it in the bag with the oranges. I have matches, and if they're not wet I can light it when it's night. I knew you'd want to see it too. I can put it right here on the bench so we can both look at it when we lie down. Isn't it so beautiful?

I knew you'd like it. Now we can sleep here and feel safe. The light will protect us from all harm.

Somebody's pushing on my face and rubbing at my eyes and stretching me backwards and forwards. I reach for Lucinda, but she's no longer next to me. I try to sit up and many hands hold me down against a rough surface like sandpaper that smells of plastic and bleach. Men are speaking around me, soft muffled words that drift in and out. I must find Lucinda. She may have fallen in the water and she's blind and she can't swim. Don't you understand what I'm telling you? I have to find Lucinda!

'Lucinda is fine. She's very dehydrated, but she's sleeping peacefully below deck.' I can hardly open my eyes, but I know Jeremy's voice and those are his hazel eyes gazing down on me. 'And you're fine too, my love. Thank God.'

I want to speak to you, I want to speak to you, Jeremy, but I can't make the words.

He runs trembling fingers across my forehead and I look more closely into eyes swollen and tired from weeping and lack of sleep. Mine want to close, but I'm afraid that when they open again he'll be gone.

He whispers in my ear. 'Beba called me the morning you left. She said you weren't able to make it onto the ship and that I should search for you at sea. We've been searching all week and we found you both this morning, right before the sun came up. We were turning back when we saw the smoke. The boat was burning right underneath you. We would never have found you if not for the smoke.'

Jeremy cradles me in his arms as he weeps and kisses my face again and again. 'All that matters is that we're going home, my love. You and me and Lucinda, we're going home.'

38

IT IS AS IT HAS ALWAYS BEEN, THE SEA A TURQUOISE BLUE fading into a sky bluer still. Alicia and I wonder whether we should disturb the calm waters with a swim or whether we should stay right where we are, sitting on the sand side by side, our eyes half closed to the sun. One of us will soon break the silence with a thought about this or that. Usually it is Alicia, so I wait for her to draw in her breath and speak to me, and all the while it is the whispering sea I hear, and the wind calling my name . . .

'She opened her eyes. I'm sure she did.' Mami's voice reverberated in my head with such clarity that even if I hadn't opened them before, they flew open to look at her now. She was almost falling over the rail at the side of the bed, peering at me with swollen eyes, a handkerchief clutched between her fingers. Papi was next to her, calming her as best he could, but his voice was a bit shaky as well; neither of them looked quite as I remembered them. My eyes focused through a mild haze of pain: they'd both lost weight and their faces were drawn from lack of sleep. I could only imagine how I must look to them.

The fear in their eyes flared anew when I attempted to move my mouth to speak. I felt an enormous boulder pressing down on my diaphragm, squeezing the air out of my lungs, but I managed to squeak out a question just the same.

'Where's Jeremy?'

Mami released herself from Papi's arms and lunged across the bed before he could stop her. 'He's here, Nora. Oh my God, my baby, my sweet Nora!' She collapsed in a chair and began to sob, as she had no doubt been doing for days.

Papi leaned forward, trying to contain his emotion for my sake, but his hand trembled on my arm and he squeezed down in a way that betrayed his own quiet desperation. 'Jeremy's fine, Lucinda's fine and so are you.'

I tried to reach for Papi's hand, but felt the discomfort of a foreign object in my nose. I went to remove it, but Papi gently stopped me. 'The tubes are there to help you breath, but they'll take them out soon enough, you'll see.'

I nodded and allowed him to guide my hand back down to my side. 'Where am I?'

Mami had regained her composure and pulled her chair forward so she was almost at eye level with me. She slipped her hand through the bed rail and squeezed my shoulder. 'We're in the hospital in Miami. Lucinda is here too, in the paediatric ward. Jeremy's with her now, but I'm sure he'll be back down soon. He hasn't left your side for two days.'

'As soon as we heard you were found,' Papi continued, 'we took the first plane we could get. We arrived yesterday and we'll stay as long as you need us, Norita.'

Tears slipped down my cheeks. I felt like a child again, as frail and vulnerable as one who'd been caught in a terrible lie. But I had to ask the question and be rid of the burning anxiety I'd felt ever since I'd gone against their wishes and left for Cuba. 'Are you still angry with me?'

Mami was the first to speak, as I knew she would be,

and the strain in her voice was palpable and thick on her tongue. 'What you did was a foolish thing, Nora. For a child who was never prone to foolishness it was beyond understanding, and I can only say . . .' Her eyes began to stream, and Papi placed a soothing hand on her back as if reminding her of something they'd spoken about earlier.

'Nora's not a child any more,' he said gently.

Mami sniffed, and cooled considerably. 'No, she's not a child any more.' She released her anger with a sigh and looked at me with such hope and love that I could only smile back at her, my face stiff with what felt like the first smile I'd been able to manage in weeks.

In the evening, when we were alone, Jeremy climbed into bed with me, careful not to disturb the various tubes and lines attached to my arm and face. He rested his head on my shoulder and settled himself in as best he could.

I closed my eyes and tried to imagine that the humming of the equipment all around us was the whispering surf or the wind in the palms, but I was unable to conjure up a vision that might calm me. And the dread I'd felt before we were rescued came back to me in waves, as though we were still at sea fighting for our lives.

'I have exciting news,' Jeremy said softly in my ear. 'The doctors believe there may be hope for Lucinda, that she could regain some of her vision. It's not certain and I haven't said anything to her yet, but they're already making inquiries at UCLA.'

My heart beat furiously upon hearing this and I longed to rip out all the wires and go to her. 'When can I see her? I have to see her, Jeremy.'

'Tomorrow. I promise that first thing in the morning I'll look into it. She's doing well, my love. She's an amazingly strong child, and when she sees you it'll make her all the stronger.'

His breathing grew deep and relaxed, and I thought he'd fallen asleep until he spoke again. 'Don't leave me again, Nora. Don't you ever leave me again.'

Back in California, Mami arrived daily with Cuban casseroles and desserts of all kinds to help us recover from our ordeal. Lucinda would have heard her car down the street before Jeremy and I heard her in the drive. She'd open the front door before Mami had rung the doorbell and follow her into the kitchen, full of delight and awe at the feasts that revealed themselves out of brown paper bags and layer upon layer of aluminium foil and clingfilm. Even through packing that would put the NASA space programme to shame, Lucinda was able to detect clearly the delectable aromas of ropa vieja, carne con papas and arroz con pollo.

Mami served her meals to us on TV trays in bed, because I was too tired to sit at the table. She stood back and waited eagerly with arms crossed until we took our first bites.

'This is delicious, Abuela Regina,' Lucinda declared, and Mami beamed with satisfaction, both at the compliment and at Lucinda calling her Abuela.

I remembered how distant Mami had been with Lucinda at first in Miami. I had expected as much. Mami had always been stubbornly loyal to her traditional values, and in matters of the heart and the family she did not easily accept defeat. She'd been openly critical of Alicia's marriage to Tony for too long to accept Lucinda right away, especially with every-body looking on. I think she blamed her, too, for putting me at risk. In fact, for those first few days, Lucinda seemed to Mami to be the embodiment of all that had been wrong with Cuba since the revolution.

The day before Lucinda and I were scheduled to be

discharged, the family was gathered together in my room. Lucinda sat near me, as she preferred to do, listening to the chatter of new voices intermingled with familiar ones. Mami was particularly animated as she considered the prospect of going back to California. Papi even spoke of throwing a party to celebrate my homecoming. The thought prompted tears of joy, which began to flow down Mami's cheeks for the third or fourth time that day.

Only a foot or so away, Lucinda reached out and gently touched Mami's cheek with the tip of her finger. 'You're crying again, Señora Regina.'

Mami nodded, but said nothing.

Lucinda thought for a moment. Her eyes were shining as she turned fully to face her new relative. 'Mami always said it was good to cry as much as you want, as long as your tears fall on someone you love.'

Mami's face writhed with agony as she attempted to swallow her distress and battle with that reflex for blatant rejection she'd honed over the years. She might just as easily have told Lucinda to keep her thoughts to herself. Instead, she swept her up in her arms and wept openly, moistening the top of her curly head with a cloudburst of tears. She did not let her go for a very long time and, ever since, insisted that Lucinda call her Abuela Regina. Now she wouldn't tolerate any degree of criticism directed towards her precious Lucinda from anyone. When Papi commented on how naïve Lucinda was for her age, Mami thrust out her chin and her finger and let him have it.

'José, how you could raise two girls and know nothing about children is beyond me. That child is advanced in every way, and I won't be surprised if they discover her to be some sort of genius when she gets to a proper school. You mark my words.'

Mami glowered over me, watching me with growing concern as I moved the food she'd so carefully prepared around on my plate. She and I and everyone else knew I hadn't eaten for weeks. The truth was I had no appetite whatever, and Cuban food tasted particularly unpleasant. The richness of the spices, sauces, onions and peppers I had once loved so much now caused my stomach to turn with revulsion. I slept for most of the time, and complained about a heaviness about my chest and stomach that hadn't left me since my stay in the hospital.

Mami spoke to Jeremy in hushed tones when he returned from work late one afternoon, and Jeremy came and sat next to me as I lay on the couch. I'd hardly moved since lunch, interested only in the way the sun filtered through the trees, creating a wild and lacy pattern on the wall opposite me. I'd been staring at it for what seemed like hours.

'You're not going to get well again if you don't eat, Nora.'

'I know.'

'You haven't put on any weight like the doctor said you should. In fact, you've lost it and—'

'I said I know!' I rarely raised my voice to Jeremy, and the hurt and confusion in his eyes startled me for a moment. But when he left the room, I didn't have the energy to do or say anything about it. I was transfixed once again by the shadows of the encroaching darkness and the lovely pattern playing in the corners of the room.

A psychiatrist friend of Jeremy's from the university came to see me some time after that. He was a nice man with a double chin and thick-framed glasses, who insisted I call him Peter instead of Dr Mills. This was one of the privileges of being an academic's wife, I thought, and I answered his questions as best I could. Yes, I had very little energy, and there were few things I could think of doing that made me want to get out of bed and get dressed. No, I had no trouble sleeping; in fact, I preferred sleep to anything else, because only then was I released from the bitter nothingness that ate at me like a hideous worm. No, I had no appetite, and the sight and smell of food, especially Cuban food, was nauseating to me. No, I hadn't thought of killing myself, but I had thought about death a lot lately and how peaceful it seemed.

Peter had been listening to me, nodding his head, seeming to understand it all. With a pudgy finger he nudged his glasses back up his nose so his eyes were clearly focused on mine. 'What do you think is causing your depression?' he asked plainly.

Should I tell him? Could I tell him? I gazed at his kind bespectacled face. He was a psychiatrist, after all, and had heard things from his patients more bizarre than anything I could ever say.

'It's my heart,' I ventured.

'Your heart? What's wrong with it?' he asked, quite curious.

'It feels like I gave it away or lost it and that now I'm trying to live with a . . .' I glanced at him to see if he was still following me, and was encouraged to see that his expression was as intent and kind as before. '. . . I'm living with a ghost heart instead of a real heart.' Tears slipped down my face in quiet streams.

'I see. A ghost heart,' he repeated, still nodding.

'Beba would know what to do, but she's very far away in Cuba and I can't even write her a letter because she doesn't read.'

'Beba?'

'She was our maid in Cuba and she knows so many things, things that ordinary people don't know.'

'I see,' he said, and thought for a moment. 'This ghost heart you mentioned, tell me more about it.'

'I'm not sure how to describe it. It's the part of your-self you can give away without losing who you are, but somehow I did it wrong and gave away the part that's real and that's why I don't feel anything any more, not even hungry, and I care nothing about getting better. I don't even care about Jeremy or Lucinda any more.' I covered my face, ashamed by such a horrible disclosure, which I hadn't dared admit even to myself until that moment.

He gave me time to compose myself. 'I can see how upsetting this is for you, Nora. I think for now it's best that you rest as much as you can. Can you do that?'

I nodded obediently, and Peter left with assurances that he wouldn't say anything to Jeremy or my mother about how I felt. I knew this would only cause them to worry more. But he said he'd have to talk with Jeremy about his recommendation that I get a good rest.

Peter hadn't been gone for five minutes before Jeremy came in the room to sit with me. Lately, he'd been sitting with me for long periods without saying anything if he thought I didn't feel like talking, but I knew he was the one who needed to talk this time. The little lines around his eyes had deepened and his mouth was tight with worry. He could hardly contain his agitation.

'Peter thinks you should go to the hospital for a while.'

'The hospital? Do you mean a mental hospital?'

'He thinks you've been through a lot – much more than most people can take – and that getting some special care might help you.'

'Do you think I should go too?'

Jeremy lowered his head and tears fell on his hands, thick drops of pain. 'I don't know what to think, Nora.' He looked up at me with eyes that had always been so confident and serene, my perpetual sanctuary. Now they were helpless and pleading. 'I don't want to lose you.' He choked down a sob. 'I thought I had lost you once, and then—' He took hold of my hands. 'I just want you well again. I want my Nora back.'

'Give me until after Christmas,' I begged. 'If I'm not

better then, I'll go to whatever hospital you and Peter want me to. I promise.'

Christmas was less than a month away.

The dream I'd been waiting for arrived during one of those rare nights in southern California when the temperature dips down below thirty degrees. I was a child again. Alicia and I are holding hands by the water's edge and watching the tide dance upon the shore. We laugh as our feet scoot along the soft sand and we feel the writhing ribbons between our toes. Alicia is urging me forward into the surf, laughing and teasing all the while in her playful way that means no harm. Her fingers lock like a vice onto mine and I am unable to break free as she pulls me into deeper water, until we're floating loose like jellyfish, breathing memories through our gills. I look into the ocean depths and see Tony's mild green eyes glistening with the vision of his beloved, Manuel's burnt shoulders hunched over the boat as he fishes, Tío Carlos playing his guitar on the porch, Tía Panchita's curious smile flashing through a haze of cigar smoke, and Abuelo, standing at the water's edge after a long swim.

Alicia's fingers loosen and the surf lifts me back to shore as I watch them disappear back into the sea, receding into an oblivion of peace.

I woke up on the morning of Christmas Eve to an unusual and noisy commotion. The plan was for Mami and Papi to arrive early and help Jeremy prepare the meal for later that evening. Marta and Eddie and the kids weren't due to arrive until five or so. I was dreading the feast of roast pork and plantains, black beans, rice and yucca that lay ahead of me, and my stomach churned as I imagined the contents of the grocery bags I heard rustling in the kitchen. The conversation between Jeremy and my parents sounded nothing like the usual good-natured banter. It was agitated and strained. Voices were being raised and I could hear Mami's distinctly above the rest. 'The doctor said not to upset her. That much I know.'

The argument continued and I wondered if at the hospital there might be some peace. I'd made little improvement, and I hadn't forgotten my promise to Jeremy. Surely that's what the argument was about: when and how to get me to the mental hospital. I tried to garner the strength necessary to get out of bed and begin packing, and wondered what to say to Lucinda about my absence. Jeremy had managed to find a school for her, and had juggled his schedule around her appointments at UCLA. She'd be starting classes after the Christmas break. She knew I wasn't able to help Jeremy with this because I wasn't well, but she attributed my illness to what we'd been through and seemed to understand that talking about it was not in my best interest.

They were just outside the bedroom now and they were trying to be quiet, but the fear in their voices caused me to shudder. Then they burst through the door, their faces flushed.

'Jeremy, don't do this,' Mami said, puffed from her agitation.

'We should talk about this a bit more,' Papi added firmly.

Jeremy shook his head. 'I've never kept anything from Nora before, and I don't intend to start now.'

'But she's not the Nora we knew,' Mami implored. 'Don't you realize that? Nora is sick and if she reads this she could get worse.'

'What's wrong with Tía Nora?' Lucinda's small voice from the doorway forced everyone to pause.

'Nothing, sweetheart.' Mami led her into the room with a protective arm. 'Your Tía Nora is a little weak now, but she'll be fine.'

Jeremy held out an envelope to me. 'This came for you yesterday. It was postmarked a few days before

Alicia died. Perhaps it was lost in the mail, or got re-routed or something.' He glanced back at Mami and Papi, who were tight with fear as they held onto Lucinda. 'Your parents are upset because they believe Alicia's letters did you more harm than good. They say you're too vulnerable to read another one right now.' The letter dangled in his fingers between us. 'What do you think?'

With a deep breath I took the envelope from him and turned it over in my hand. The three postmarks printed near the Havana address confirmed Jeremy's suspicion that the letter had been lost, and I recognized Alicia's delicate script on the outside of the envelope. I stared at it for several long seconds as I imagined Alicia during her last days on the couch.

'I think I'd like to read this by myself,' I said without looking up. They all turned to leave and I held my hand out to Lucinda. 'Stay with me, Lucinda. Your Mami would've wanted you here.'

Lucinda made her way to the bed and nestled in next to me. I felt her head settle on my shoulder as I tore open the envelope and slowly unfolded the pages of the letter.

Dear Nora,

When you read this I want you to imagine you're relaxing under our palms at Varadero and looking up at the sky, because that's where I imagine myself at this moment. You're next to me, listening and smiling as you always do, so my worries float away on the breeze. Although I'm tempted, I won't write of my worries right now. I'll write instead about something you always wanted to know, ever since we were girls playing on the beach. Even now I can hear your voice asking me as we stare up at the sun through the trees, 'Did you see God? What did you ask for?' I guess it's OK to tell you now that I asked Him for a guardian angel to watch over me always. For years I didn't

389

think He was listening, because the angel didn't appear as I expected, over my bed with soft feathery wings and a silk gown like I saw in the paintings at church. But I know now that you, dear cousin, have been my guardian angel and comfort during the worst moments of my life. Even now, I wait for death with peace in my heart, knowing you will look after Lucinda with all that you are, and for that I will gladly give my life and more.

In truth, you have not only been my guardian angel but my confessor as well, and I'm afraid I have yet another confession to make. For almost two years I took the American dollars you so carefully folded inside your letters and set them ablaze by the flame of my candle one by one. I didn't want to admit how much I ached for your American life, your nice house, your hot running water and twenty-four-hour supermarkets and ranting reporters who hate all politicians and aren't afraid to insult them on television. I resented your personal telephone ringing off the hook and six brands of toothpaste, and sleeping in a clean bed after a full meal and waking to a strong cup of coffee in the morning, and so many things.

I tried to escape my jealousy by convincing myself that you and everyone like you had betrayed Cuba and that I betrayed her too with my envy. I ask your forgiveness. But I don't feel guilty any more and I don't think you should either, because we did not betray our country, Nora. Our country betrayed us. You and all who left are orphans, just like Lucinda will be. And just as she'll embrace you as her new mother after I'm gone, so must you embrace your American life with all your heart and soul, even if the tears of grief and parting are still moist in your eyes. Because if you wait for your tears to dry, you'll be waiting for ever.

But never forget, Nora, never forget the Cuba we knew, and tell it to Lucinda and your children before

they're old enough to understand, so it becomes a
part of them as it has become a part of us. Tell them
how we swam in the blue-green waters of the
Caribbean and how we ate sweet mangoes as the juice
dripped down our faces. Tell them about the
chaperoned dances and white linen suits and how
the musicians played their music to coax even the
moon from its quiet place in the sky.

And always remember the dream that was . . . the
sounds of enchantment . . . the breezes that caress the
soul . . . our palm trees in the sky.

All my love,
Alicia

Jeremy knocked softly, and, not hearing a response,
peeked in to find Lucinda and me embracing and
weeping after having read Alicia's letter three times
over. He wasn't sure whether or not he should enter,
but I held my hand out to him, and he crossed the
room swiftly and took us both in his arms.

'I love you, Jeremy,' I whispered, feeling my strength
returning as our tears flowed. 'Please forgive me.'

Epilogue

ALMOST A YEAR LATER ALICIA GARCIA-MCLAUGHLIN WAS born. When I brought her home from the hospital, Lucinda gazed at her through triple-thick glasses that made her eyes appear like giant emeralds.

'She smiled at me, Tía Nora. I saw her smile at me.' Lucinda was bursting with delight.

Later that evening, Lucinda laid her head on my lap as I rocked Alicia in my arms. In a few minutes, when he finished grading mid-terms, I expected Jeremy to poke his head into the nursery and remind Lucinda that it was time for her eye drops, and that she needed to brush her teeth before bed and it didn't matter if she'd already brushed them once that day. Lucinda would complain she wasn't tired and try to squeeze a few more minutes from him. These he almost always obliged her, knowing, as did I, that it was wonderful to see her behaving as a girl her age should.

'Tell me the story again, Tía Nora,' she said with a little squeeze to my knee.

'Again?'

'Yes, but this time start at the part I like – right at the beginning.'

I cleared my throat and stretched my legs out slowly so as not to wake my little girl, but I gazed into her sleeping face as I spoke, knowing she heard me through her dreams.

'What I most love about Cuba is the warmth. The way it spreads out to my fingers and toes so it feels like I'm part of the sun, like it's growing inside me . . .'

'Tía Nora?'

'Yes, Lucinda?'

'Will we ever see Cuba again? Will we ever go home?'

I was tempted to answer her with the same variations of 'maybe' that I'd received from my parents after leaving Cuba for the first time all those years ago. 'Perhaps if things change,' they would say, or 'We can't know for sure what will happen.' These hopeful crumbs did little to satisfy my soul's longing for home.

I tugged lightly on one of Lucinda's springy curls and the silhouette of her cheek plumped up with a smile. But I realized she was anxious for my reply, and I knew I'd have to answer her honestly as I did everything else.

I inhaled my own fear, and forced myself to exhale with a heart more resilient than resolved. 'Yes, Lucinda,' I told her. 'I'm sure one day we will see Cuba again. But until then, and perhaps afterwards too, this is our home.'

THE END

Author's Note

WHEN I LEFT CUBA FORTY YEARS AGO, I WASN'T ABLE TO TAKE any memories with me because I was only nine months old. I was, however, blessed with some wonderful storytellers. My parents and grandparents, aunts and uncles all shared with me their stories of life in Cuba before and after the revolution. Their memories became my memories, and for a long while they satisfied my yearning for home and family history. But it wasn't enough.

In writing *Ghost Heart*, I've been able to explore questions that have haunted me since I realized I wasn't born in the country I called home. Questions such as, 'What if I'd never left Cuba?' and 'Who might I have become in that life?' Sometimes, when I felt a need to escape my daily routine, I idealized my homeland and imagined myself living carefree in the tropics. At other times, I was simply grateful to be an American and to have been spared the suffering that so many Cubans endured, and continue to endure. Always, I felt a hovering between two worlds, grieving what might have been while embracing what I wasn't sure was mine to begin with.

My search for understanding has, in part, led me to my work as a psychotherapist with immigrants in Los Angeles. I've listened to countless stories from my courageous clients, and have learned that my struggle is shared by many, regardless of their countries of origin or motivations for leaving. My hope is that, apart from entertaining readers, *Ghost Heart* will offer some insights into that tender balance between grief and hope that shapes the immigrant heart.

I could not, in good conscience, put my name to this work without acknowledging some of the people who've made sharing it possible. People such as my agent, Moses Cardona of John Hawkins & Associates Inc., whose knowledge, good humour and tenacity have sustained me throughout this sometimes arduous process; Selina Walker, my editor at Transworld Publishers, who, with remarkable skill and grace, has transformed these words into the novel they were meant to be. I could say much more, but suffice to say that their names should be printed along with mine on the front cover of this book, and in my heart they are and always will be.

This work has also benefited from the talent and hard work of other literary professionals such as Frederike Leffelaar of De Boekerij Publishers, Kate Samano of Transworld Publishers, Sarah Menguc, Monique Oosterhof, and all the staff from the aforementioned publishing houses. I am ever grateful for their varied contributions and support.

I would not have found the courage to attempt this project without the understanding and patience of my family: my husband Steven Myles, stepchildren Jack and Lucy, and all the Myles family; my parents, José and Tania Samartin; my sisters, and brothers-in-law, Susana, Andy, Virginia and Jeff, and all the cousins, aunts and uncles and dear friends who've encouraged me along the way. I thank God for blessing me with the love and talents of the people mentioned above, and of others too numerous to list, but no less appreciated.

BRICK LANE
Monica Ali

'WRITTEN WITH A WISDOM AND SKILL THAT FEW AUTHORS
ATTAIN IN A LIFETIME'
Sunday Times

Still in her teenage years, Nazneen finds herself in an arranged
marriage with a man twenty years her elder. Away from the mud
and heat of her Bangladeshi village, home is now a cramped flat
in a high-rise block in London's East End. Not knowing a word of
English, Nazneen must rely on her husband. But unlike him she
is practical and wise, and befriends a fellow Asian Girl Razia,
who helps her understand the strange ways of her adopted new
British home.

Confined to her flat by tradition and family duty, Nazneen fills
her days by sewing for a living – until the radical Karim steps
unexpectedly into her life. Against a background of racial conflict
and tension, they embark on a love affair that finally forces
Nazneen to take control of her fate . . .

'*BRICK LANE* HAS EVERYTHING: RICHLY COMPLEX
CHARACTERS, A GRIPPING STORY AND IT'S FUNNY TOO . . .
THIS HIGHLY EVOLVED, ACCOMPLISHED BOOK IS A REMINDER
OF HOW EXHILARATING NOVELS CAN BE: IT OPENED UP A
WORLD WHOSE CONTOURS I COULD RECOGNISE, BUT
WHICH I NEEDED MONICA ALI TO MAKE ME UNDERSTAND'
Observer

'THE JOY OF THIS BOOK IS ITS MARRIAGE OF A
WONDERFUL WRITER WITH A FRESH, RICH AND HIDDEN
WORLD. HER ACHIEVEMENT IS HUGE. THIS IS A BOOK
WRITTEN WITH LOVE AND COMPASSION FOR EVERY
STRUGGLING CHARACTER IN ITS PAGES. NO WONDER I
FINISHED IT WITH SUCH A SENSE OF GRATITUDE'
Evening Standard

'THE KIND OF NOVEL THAT SURPRISES ONE WITH ITS
DEPTH AND DASH; IT IS A NOVEL THAT WILL LAST'
Guardian

0 552 77115 5

BLACK SWAN

EAT, DRINK AND BE MARRIED
Eve Makis

Anna's head reels with plans to escape life behind the counter of the family chip shop on a run-down Nottingham council estate. Her mother Tina wants nothing but the best for her daughter: a lavish wedding and a fully furnished four-bedroom house with a BMW parked in the driveway. She thinks Anna should forget the silly notion of going to college and focus on finding a suitable husband. Mother and daughter are at loggerheads and neither will give way.

Anna's ally and mentor is her Grandmother Yiayia Annoulla. She tells Anna stories about the family's turbulent past in Cyprus, the island home they were forced to abandon. Yiayia practises kitchen magic, predicts the future from coffee grains and fills the house with an abundance of Greek-Cypriot delicacies.

Anna longs for the freedom enjoyed by her brother Andy but spends time appeasing her parents, dodging insults from drunken customers or going on ill-fated forays with her petulant cousin – the beautiful Athena. It is only when family fortunes begin to sour that Anna starts to take control of her own destiny . . .

'HEART-WARMING, FUNNY, TRAGIC AND UPLIFTING . . . THE STORY HAS A FEELGOOD FACTOR TO EQUAL *MY BIG FAT GREEK WEDDING*'
Narinder Dhami

0 552 77216X

BLACK SWAN

SISTER OF MY HEART
Chitra Banerjee Divakaruni

'CHITRA BANERJEE DIVAKARUNI IS A TRUE STORYTELLER.
LIKE DICKENS, SHE HAS CONSTRUCTED LAYER UPON LAYER
OF TRAGEDY, SECRETS AND BETRAYALS, OF THWARTED
LOVE . . . [A] GLORIOUS, COLOURFUL TRAGEDY'
Daily Telegraph

Born in the big old Calcutta house on the same tragic night that both
their fathers were mysteriously lost, Sudha and Anju are cousins.
Closer even than sisters, they share clothes, worries, dreams in the
matriarchal Chatterrjee household. But when Sudha discovers a
terrible secret about the past, their mutual loyalty is sorely tested.

A family crisis forces their mothers to start the serious business of
arranging the girls' marriages, and the pair is torn apart. Sudha
moves to her new family's home in rural Bengal, while Anju joins
her immigrant husband in California. Although they have both been
trained to be perfect wives, nothing has prepared them for the
pain, as well as the joy, that each will have to face in her new life.

Steeped in the mysticism of ancient tales, this jewel-like novel
shines its light on the bonds of family, on love and loss, against
the realities of traditional marriage in modern times.

'DIVAKARUNI STRIKES A DELICATE BALANCE BETWEEN
REALISM AND FANTASY . . . A TOUCHING CELEBRATION OF
ENDURING LOVE'
Sunday Times

'A PLEASURE TO READ . . . A NOVEL FRAGRANT IN RHYTHM
AND LANGUAGE'
San Francisco Chronicle

'DIVAKARUNI'S BOOKS POSSESS A POWER THAT IS BOTH
TRANSPORTING AND HEALING . . . SERIOUS AND
ENTRANCING'
Booklist

'MAGICALLY AFFECTING...HER INTRICATE TAPESTRY OF
OLD AND NEW WORLDS SHINES WITH A RARE LUMINOSITY'
San Diego Union Tribune

0 552 99767 6

BLACK SWAN

A SELECTED LIST OF FINE WRITING
AVAILABLE FROM BLACK SWAN

77115 5	BRICK LANE	Monica Ali	£7.99
99313 1	OF LOVE AND SHADOWS	Isabel Allende	£7.99
77105 8	NOT THE END OF THE WORLD	Kate Atkinson	£6.99
99860 5	IDIOGLOSSIA	Eleanor Bailey	£6.99
99686 6	BEACH MUSIC	Pat Conroy	£8.99
99767 6	SISTER OF MY HEART	Chitra Banerjee Divakaruni	£6.99
99836 2	A HEART OF STONE	Renate Dorrestein	£6.99
99935 0	PEACE LIKE A RIVER	Leif Enger	£6.99
99954 7	SWIFT AS DESIRE	Laura Esquivel	£6.99
77078 7	THE VILLAGE OF WIDOWS	Ravi Shankar Etteth	£6.99
99721 8	BEFORE WOMEN HAD WINGS	Connie May Fowler	£6.99
99978 4	KISSING THE VIRGIN'S MOUTH	Donna Gershten	£6.99
99656 4	THE TEN O'CLOCK HORSES	Laurie Graham	£5.99
77178 3	SLEEP, PALE SISTER	Joanne Harris	£6.99
77109 0	THE FOURTH HAND	John Irving	£6.99
99871 0	PEOPLE LIKE OURSELVES	Pamela Jooste	£6.99
77153 8	THINGS TO DO INDOORS JACKSON	Sheena Joughin	£6.99
99807 9	MONTENEGRO	Starling Lawrence	£6.99
77104 X	BY BREAD ALONE	Sarah-Kate Lynch	£6.99
77216 X	EAT, DRINK AND BE MARRIED	Eve Makis	£6.99
77088 4	NECTAR	Lily Prior	£6.99
77093 0	THE DARK BRIDE	Laura Restrepo	£6.99
99810 9	THE JUKEBOX QUEEN OF MALTA	Nicholas Rinaldi	£6.99
77166 X	A TIME OF ANGELS	Patricia Schonstein	£6.99
99952 0	LIFE ISN'T ALL HA HA HEE HEE	Meera Syal	£6.99
99864 8	A DESERT IN BOHEMIA	Jill Paton Walsh	£6.99